LIBERATION
STREET

—.—

A PHILIP YE NOVEL

LAURENCE WESTWOOD

1st Edition, January 2023

Published by Shikra Press

An Imprint of Shikra Press Limited

Shipston on Stour

United Kingdom

www.shikrapress.com

E-Book ISBN: 978-1-9164569-6-9

Paperback ISBN: 978-1-9164569-7-6

Cover design by www.samwall.com

Cover photography copyright © Philippe Lejeanvre

For more information about the author: www.laurencewestwood.com

LIBERATION STREET

INTRODUCTION

THE CRIMINAL JUSTICE SYSTEM OF THE PEOPLE'S RE-PUBLIC OF CHINA

The Criminal Procedure Law of 1979 (extensively revised in 1996 and again in 2012) installed an inquisitorial model of legal process in China similar to the civil law tradition of continental Europe.

England and Wales and the United States, for example, use an adversarial model where the prosecution and defence argue their respective positions before a neutral judge or jury, where the judge or jury have no prior knowledge of the case.

Under the inquisitorial model, however, facts are discovered through a coordinated process led by officers of the state – police, prosecutors and judges – all of whom are involved in a theoretically impartial effort to get to the truth.

In China, the majority of criminal investigations are conducted by the People's Police – the Public Security Bureaus (PSBs). The police have powers to gather evidence and detain suspects, though the formal arrest of a suspect is subject to the approval of the People's Procuratorate. If the police deem a case serious enough to be dealt with by a court, it is forwarded to the People's Procuratorate. The police also have the power to impose administrative punishments for various, usually minor, offences. Except for special units, or in special circumstances, the police usually conduct their work unarmed, though because of increasing violence in Chinese society this is beginning to change.

The People's Procuratorate handles the prosecution of a case. Procuratorates have the power to interview suspects, witnesses and victims. They may also order further investigation work to be done by the police. It is the responsibility of procuratorates to draw up a Bill of Prosecution detailing the charges laid against a defendant and to present the case in the People's Courts. Procuratorates have the power to investigate those cases considered too sensitive or too complicated for the police to handle. They also supervise the work of the police and the courts to prevent errors in the administration of justice.

There are four levels of criminal People's Court: Basic Court, Intermediate Court, Higher Level Court and the Supreme People's Court. Less serious cases will be heard in the Basic Court; those, such as murder, for example, heard in the Intermediate Court. Cases are heard in public unless matters of state security or private affairs relating to individuals are to be discussed. Any death sentence pronounced by a court must be approved by the Supreme People's Court.

It should be noted that the police, procuratorates and courts can each investigate criminal offences, interrogate suspects and collect evidence. It is possible for a trial judge to preside over a case in which he was the lead investigator.

Political and Legal Committees supervise the work of the police, the procuratorates and the courts at all levels. If a Political and Legal Committee 'recommends' a certain trial outcome then that outcome is generally accepted by the court.

The People's Armed Police Force (PAP) is a paramilitary organisation under the joint command of the Central Committee of the Communist Party of China and the Central Military Commission. The CAPF's main duties are border and forest protection, fire-fighting, road construction and specialized transportation, the guarding of vital installations and VIPs, and the provision of anti-terrorist SWAT teams. The PAP often works alongside the People's Police and would be deployed to counter instances of mass social unrest. Unlike the blue of the uniforms of the People's Police, the PAP wear pine-green uniforms and have a similar rank structure to the army. They therefore often get mistaken for army personnel.

The Ministry of State Security (MSS) is responsible for foreign intelligence, counter-intelligence and domestic security. It has the same powers of detention and arrest as the police. It is also subject to supervision by the procuratorates and the courts.

The Central Committee for Discipline Inspection (CCDI) is the Chinese Communist Party's top anti-corruption body. It is tasked with the investigation of graft committed by government officials – these would most often be Party members – and acts usually on petitions or information received from informants. In theory it does not have the power to prosecute offenders, its cases handed over to the People's Courts once the investigations are complete. However, the CCDI has wide-ranging powers of detention. Officials under investigation by the CCDI can be held for many months undergoing interrogation before ever seeing the inside of a courtroom. And once an official has been under investigation by the CCDI, even if released without prosecution, he or she will discover their government career is almost certainly at an end.

Medical Provision in the People's Republic of China

Note that there is no system of family doctors in China. If someone requires medical assistance then this is usually sought at a pharmacist or at a hospital. Therefore Doctor He's situation on Liberation Street should be considered very unusual!

Ranks of the People's Police

COMMISSIONER-GENERAL

DEPUTY COMMISSIONER-GENERAL

COMMISSIONER (1st Class, 2nd Class, 3rd Class)

SUPERVISOR (1st Class, 2nd Class, 3rd Class)

SUPERINTENDENT (1st Class, 2nd Class, 3rd Class)

CONSTABLE (1st Class, 2nd Class)

A Short Note on the People's Liberation Army (PLA)

The People's Liberation Army is essentially the armed wing of the Chinese Communist Party (CCP) and was founded on the 1st August 1927. At its outset it was primarily a ground force, hence the use of 'army' in its title.

As of 2022, there are five branches to the PLA: the army or Ground Force (PLAGF), the Air Force (PLAAF), the Navy (PLAN), the Rocket Force (PLARF), and the Strategic Support Force (PLASSF).

Since 2016, the PLA has been divided into 5 theatre commands, one of which, the Western Theatre Command, is actually headquartered in Chengdu.

Prior to 2016, there were 7 military regions, one of which was the Chengdu Military Region, headquartered in Chengdu. As the story takes place in the summer of 2014, it is the Chengdu Military Region that will be referred to throughout the novel.

The 14th Group Army as described in this novel, that fought at the Battle of Lao Cai during the Sino-Vietnamese War, was deactivated in April 2017.

As stated in this novel, the highest award that could be given to a member of the PLA is the Heroic Exemplar Medal. This was true up until 2017 when Xi Jinping reinstated the August 1 Medal (Order of Bayi). The August 1 Medal was originally that highest award given to veterans of the Chinese Civil War.

Ranks of the PLA Ground Force in 2014

GENERAL
LIEUTENANT-GENERAL
MAJOR-GENERAL
SENIOR COLONEL
COLONEL
LIEUTENANT-COLONEL
MAJOR
CAPTAIN
1ST LIEUTENANT
2ND LIEUTENANT
OFFICER CADET
MASTER SERGEANT 1St CLASS
MASTER SERGEANT 2ND CLASS
MASTER SERGEANT 3RD CLASS
MASTER SERGEANT 4TH CLASS
SENIOR SERGEANT
SERGEANT
JUNIOR SERGEANT
PRIVATE FIRST CLASS
PRIVATE

PRINCIPAL CHARACTERS

In the People's Republic of China, a person's given name normally follows their family name. When a woman marries she usually keeps her father's family name rather than take her husband's family name. Any children from the marriage take their father's family name.

THE FAMILY YE

Philip Ye – Superintendent, Homicide Section, Chengdu PSB
Ye Zihao – Philip's father, former mayor of Chengdu
Ye Lan – Philip Ye's half-sister, restaurateur
Qu Fang – Ye Lan's husband, restauranteur
Qu Peng – Ye Lan's elder son
Qu Gang – Ye Lan's younger son
Day Na – Bodyguard to Ye Zihao
Night Na – Bodyguard to Ye Zihao
Kui Yang – Ye family doctor
Zhou Jin Jing – Zihao's former wife, deceased
Philippa Wilson – Philip Ye's mother, lives in the U.K.
Ye Yong – Philip Ye's half-brother (deceased)
Ye Jian – Philip Ye's paternal grandfather (deceased)
Ye Yiwei – Philip Ye's paternal uncle, in aerospace
Ye Peng – Philip Ye's paternal uncle, in pharmaceuticals

CHENGDU POLITICAL LEADERSHIP

Cang Jin – Mayor of Chengdu, *Shanghai Clique*
Li Zi – Chengdu Party Chief, *Shanghai Clique*
Wu Jing Zi – Secretary, Chair of Chengdu Political and Legal Committee

CHENGDU PEOPLE'S PROCURATORATE

Gong Wei – Chief Prosecutor
Xu Ya – Prosecutor, Legal and Discipline Procuracy Section

Deng Shiru (Fatty) – Investigator, Legal and Disciplinary Procuracy
Section
Hong Jia (Mouse) – Legal Clerk

CHENGDU PUBLIC SECURITY BUREAU
Criminal Investigation Department

Di Qi – Chief of Police
Miao Qing – Chief Di's secretary
Ma Meili – Constable (2nd Class), Homicide
Maggie Loh – Commissioner (3rd Class), Head of Robbery Section
Ji Dan – Commissioner (2nd Class), Head of Internal Discipline
Section, *Shanghai Clique*
Zuo Lu – Superintendent (1st Class), Homicide Section
Wei Rong – Commissioner (2nd Class), Homicide Section, *Shanghai
Clique*
Li Cheng – Superintendent (1st Class), Armoury
Dr Kong Ai – Pathologist
Wang Chao (Big-Mouth) – Constable (1st Class)
Zhi Fang – Constable (1st Class)
Zan Hong – Constable (1st Class)
Yang Da – Commissioner (2nd Class), Head of Building Security
Section
Si Ying – Superintendent (1st Class), Building Security Section
Zhu Shouqing – Commissioner (2nd Class), SWAT Commander

PEOPLE'S ARMED POLICE FORCE

Wang Yan Zhang – General, C-in-C
Wang Jian – Captain, son of General Wang
FATTY DENG'S APARTMENT BUILDING
Deng Mei – Fatty Deng's mother
Aunty Ho – neighbour
Uncle Ho - neighbour

THE FAMILY FU

Fu Bi – wealthy businessman, Chairman of FUBI International Industries
Fu Lu (Lucy) – businesswoman, daughter of Fu Bi

FUBI INTERNATIONAL INDUSTRIES

Xi Huan - lawyer

TRANQUIL MOUNTAIN PAVILIONS

Ni Peng – night concierge
Gan Yong – day concierge

PLUM TREE PAGODAS

Han Bai – night concierge

THE FAMILY GONG

Primo Gong – CEO of Ambrogetti Global Software
Alessandro Gong – Primo Gong's father
Gong Dawei – Primo Gong's paternal grandfather (deceased)
Li Ju – Primo Gong's paternal grandmother (deceased)
Alessandro Ambrogetti – Primo Gong's step-grandfather (deceased)

AMBROGETTI GLOBAL SOFTWARE

Wen Jiao – PA to Primo Gong
Zhou Rong – young programmer

THE HISTORIANS & RELATIONS

Bo Qi – Senior Colonel (retired), PLA
Hua Delun – Major (retired), PLA
Yao Yao – Lieutenant-Colonel (retired), PLA
Lan Liu – Major-General (retired), PLA
Zhang Yi – Major (retired), PLA
Mu Xin – Colonel (retired), PLA
Jin Huiliang – Lieutenant-General (retired), PLA
Jin Jing – Jin Huiliang's daughter
Fei Shi – Major (retired), PLA
Fei Song – General (retired), PLA, father of Fei Shi
Fei Qin – Fei Shi's wife

PEOPLE'S LIBERATION ARMY

Zi Hong – Major-General, 14th Group Army, Kunming
Si Yu – Captain, 14th Group Army, Kunming
Lin Heng – Master Sgt. Class 1, 14th Group Army, Kunming
Meng Hai – Master Sgt. Class 1, 14th Group Army, Kunming

CHENGDU CYMBIDIUM BANK

Min Feng - CEO

THE FAMILY DU

Du Luli – prostitute
Du Yue – Du Luli's daughter
Du Dong – Du Luli's father (deceased)

LIBERATION STREET TRADERS ASSOCIATION

Sun Mei – proprietor, Lucky Dragon Tobacco Emporium
Sun Yong – Sun Mei's father
Wu He – proprietor, Mister Wu's Cycle Sales and Repair Shop
Yu Ai – proprietor, Sweet and Lovely Cake Shop
Di Li – proprietor, Honest Mister Di's Second-hand Shop
Han Fu – proprietor, Bright Diamond Mini-Supermarket
Wei Ju – proprietor, Liberation Street Pharmacy
He Bo – local doctor

MISCELLANEOUS

Xu Da – Xu Ya's father
Yu Xiaoli – Xu Ya's mother
Qin Qiang (Beloved Mister Qin) – Xu Ya's former law tutor
(deceased)
Brother Wang – former criminal associate of Freddie Yun
Wang Jiyu – Secretary Wu's wife
Sarangerel – Mayor Cang's mistress
Yu Jianguo – Xu Ya's husband (deceased)
Wang Zizi – Superintedent Zuo Lu's wife
Lin Lin – senior Waitress, The Silver Tree
Yoyo – Ma Meili's pet cat
Stacey Corrigan – American business journalist
Li Du – lawyer, bound for the Black House
Ding Jie – Jin Huiliang's maid
Lu Shu – Jin Huiliang's typist
Li Dong – proprietor, Laughing Panda Hotel
Bing Ting – Li Dong's wife, Laughing Panda Hotel
Song Xue – proprietor, Magical Wilderness Adventures
Tang Hao – psychiatrist
Song Bo – Training Supervisor (retired), Chengdu PSB
The Brothers Ming – specialist contractors
The Sisters Ping – exotic dancers
Min Yan – Min Feng's daughter
Little Xiulan – not very well girl
Hong – naughty boy

CHENGDU
SICHUAN PROVINCE
PEOPLE'S REPUBLIC OF CHINA

SUMMER 2014

PROLOGUE

There was talk of flooding. Mister Wu, of Mister Wu's Cycle Sales and Repair Shop, had called an extraordinary meeting of the Liberation Street Traders Association to discuss the coming rainstorms and the state of the local drains. The drains were not good. They always overflowed after heavy rain. And yet, as far back as Sun Mei could remember, Liberation Street had always escaped the worst of the flooding in the city.

Sun Mei had mentioned this to Mister Wu in the forlorn hope he would see the meeting for the waste of time that it was. But Mister Wu occupied the Chair of the Traders Association. He also liked calling meetings – especially extraordinary meetings. And the drains had been worrying him for years, so much so that at least once a month he complained to both the Municipal Urban Planning & Management Bureau *and* the Municipal Environmental Protection Bureau for something to be done.

Making the mistake of reminding Mister Wu that no one could ever remember a time when a business had ever been inundated in Liberation Street, or, indeed, anyone ever being swept away by a flood, Mister Wu had replied to her, "Sun Mei, history is certainly an important consideration in regard to drainage. But we shouldn't let it influence our thinking too much. If we are all drowned this night and all our stock is ruined, what is the point in saying that this has never happened before?"

How could she argue with that?

So, with the meeting set, Sun Mei agreed, albeit reluctantly, for it to be convened in her very own shop, the Lucky Dragon Tobacco Emporium. Much as she did not enjoy the shop being full to almost bursting with people, there were definite advantages to holding the meeting there. Unlike most of the other traders, she had no family she could rely on to keep the shop open while she attended a meeting. And, even if customers could not squeeze into the shop because the meeting was in session, their money could still be passed, person to person, to reach her behind the counter. In return she could send them, by the same method, their cigarettes. Also, her father rather enjoyed these meetings – pointless or otherwise. It made him feel part of the local community. Lacking the use of his legs, it was difficult for him to attend meetings elsewhere. He hated to be seen out in his wheelchair and he trusted very few of the men of the street to carry him any distance in safety.

Even so, Sun Mei could have done without the meeting. She did not feel well. Nightmares had been plaguing her recently. And the constant heat and humidity of the past few days had leeched the very life out of her. So, it came as no surprise that her eyes quickly began to close soon after the meeting commenced. With Mister Wu droning on, speaking in the minutest detail of his latest fruitless interactions with the local government offices, she tried desperately to fight the sleep that threatened to overwhelm her. She bit her lip. She stood on one foot. None of it did any good. She felt herself falling and suddenly found herself in the midst of a dark and threatening landscape, hopelessly lost, not knowing what to do. Then she woke with a start, just in time to recover her balance. She glanced quickly out of the window, convinced momentarily that a fat man in a garish shirt was staring at her from across the street – a nightmarish figure about to upend her life forever. But she saw no one there, the fat man nothing more than the remnants of a disturbing dream.

"Sun Mei, are you alright?" asked Mister Wu, who, like all the others, had noticed her sudden discomfort.

Unable to conceal her anxiety, she replied, "I think we should all take very special care this night."

This wisdom, such as it was, was very well received by all present. Mister Wu praised her thoughtfulness, and Mister Han of the Bright Diamond Mini-Supermarket, taking the minutes as always, made a special note.

Fortunately, the meeting did not last much longer. Mister Wu made the decision – unanimously upheld – that he should immediately complain again to both the Municipal Urban Planning & Management Bureau and the Municipal Environmental Protection Bureau. As Mister Wu said, "At least our complaint will be doubly on file even if we are all drowned tonight." Mister Wu then asked if there was any other business, got no replies, and called the meeting to a close.

Sun Mei was assisted by two of the other attendees – Mister Yu of the Sweet and Lovely Cake Shop and Mister Di of Honest Mister Di's Second-hand Shop – to get her father back to his room. They even fiddled with his air-conditioning unit, the only one she and her father could afford, and somehow managed to get it working properly again. Sun Mei was then able to run up to the bathroom, splash some much-needed cold water on her face, and stare at her image in the mirror. There was an unhealthy pallor about her skin. Her eyes were dull and lifeless, and her hair was not as glossy as it should be. She was supposed to be in the prime of her life, and yet the young woman that returned her stare seemed to be little better than a corpse.

After lunch, she changed her clothes, put on the thinnest blouse and skirt she could find because of the heat, and returned to the shop counter to serve customers all through the afternoon. About six, she prepared a light supper for her and her father, eating hers mostly on the go as she took the opportunity to restock the shelves. She then set up the small blackboard in the back room, arranged the desks so all would be able to see the blackboard properly and put paper and pencils out for every child. Using pieces of coloured chalk, she wrote out the mathematical problems she had devised for the evening, there being different problems for their different ages, the youngest of her pupils being seven and the oldest thirteen. Of course, mathematics was not all she taught. Invariably, she would help each of her pupils with their respective homework regardless of subject. But, as to her general teaching, it was mathematics she had chosen to focus on for the next few weeks. Many of her regular pupils had been suffering recently from poor mathematics teaching at school and she did not want them to fall far behind.

Just after seven the children began to arrive. The expected rain had not yet begun to fall but all of the parents were carrying umbrellas. Most said they would come early for their sons or daughters if the heavens opened wide. Sun Mei sat the children at their desks, gave them each a cup of water to drink, checked that they all had had something to eat that evening – lamentably, not always the case – and set each of them to working with much encouragement.

"Problems do not solve themselves," she told them all, making them laugh.

That done, she prepared fresh tea for herself and her father, made sure he was comfortable and had selected the right TV channel for his favourite evening programmes – sometimes he got confused – and quickly returned to the shop counter to serve two local customers who had been waiting patiently in the knowledge of all that she had to contend with each evening. Then, after a quick check on the children and a quick glance at her watch – ten minutes before eight – she confronted the most hateful part of her day.

"It's just a cost of doing business," her father had said.

Maybe so, but that did not mean she had to like it.

She took four packets of cigarettes down from the shelves: two packs of Septwolves Blue, and one each of Double Happiness and Golden Bridge. None of the packets were very expensive but they still represented a loss to the business. As always, she gift-wrapped the cigarettes so it could not be ignored that they had been given for free; a useless gesture, she knew, but one that gave her a modicum of satisfaction. Then, at eight exactly, the door to her shop was thrown open and one of the four came in. This time it was the youngest and meanest, the one who a few months earlier had reached across the counter and slapped her face when she had refused to go out on a date with him. She hated him so much she could not bear to look him in the eye. She bowed her head and held the gift-wrapped cigarettes out before her. He snatched the package off her and left the shop without saying a word.

The police were as bad as criminals, thought Sun Mei – sometimes even worse.

With the cigarettes collected, Sun Mei breathed a sigh of relief. She swallowed her bitterness, put a smile on her face, and returned to her teaching of the children. Not until nine did she release them from their studies. She gave them all a little sweet each, told them they were all doing marvellously – even if this was not quite the case – and ushered them out of the shop one by one back into the care of their parents. The parents' umbrellas were up now. A light rain had begun to fall. Sun Mei was glad. Floods or no floods, the rain might at last bring some blessed relief from the incessant heat.

No money changed hands for the lessons. That was her choice, the teaching of the children her gift to the world. It was also true that, without the children, with only her father and the shop to manage, Sun Mei thought she would lose her mind.

At eleven, she finally shut up the shop. She threw the bolts across the door and pulled down the blinds. She helped her father undress and get into bed, but left the TV on for him. He would switch it off later when he was tired. She made herself a light snack, ate it quickly in the kitchen while leafing through a fashion magazine, staring at clothes she could not afford. And then, hoping this night she might get some sleep, she went up to her bedroom, changed into shorts and a singlet, cooled her face again in the bathroom with a splash of water, brushed her teeth and climbed into bed.

It was not long before the first flash of lightning lit up the room and the crash of thunder almost tumbled her out of bed. Sun Mei cursed. There would not be much sleep this night either. She tried to relax, tried not to worry about the rainstorm and the rapidly-filling drains down on the street, and especially tried not to worry about the fat man with the awful shirt she had imagined to be staring at her from across the road during the Association meeting.

She must have slept for a while. When she opened her eyes the drumming of the rain on the roof had ceased. The storm was now moving off to the east. Then she heard three sharp reports, one after the other, almost like muffled firecrackers exploding overhead. She sat up, hardly daring to breathe. That was not thunder. She checked her phone: one-thirty a.m. exactly.

She dared not part the blinds to look out of the window. Whatever had happened was no concern of hers. Instead, she ran downstairs to check on her father. He was sitting up in bed, awake, the TV off, listening intently.

"Daughter, did you hear?" he whispered. "Three rifle shots right over our shop. Help me to the window so I can see what's going on."

She took his hand with a view to reassuring him and herself. "No, father, it is nothing to do with us. If trouble comes to our door, then that is our *karma*. There is nothing to be done about that. But we shouldn't go out of our way to invite trouble into our lives."

"But, Daughter, we must—"

"No, Father – and if Mother were still alive she would agree with me."

He nodded, forced to concede the point. Sun Mei sat with him for some time, the two of them sitting on his bed holding hands, hearing nothing more than their own breathing and the rumble of thunder in the distance.

SATURDAY

ONE

— . —

*P*rosecutor Xu

We must meet. We must talk. A reservation has been made for us at eight on Monday evening at The Golden Persimmon. I cannot wait to hear the intimate details of your husband's most unfortunate and untimely demise.

Sarangerel

Xu Ya had discovered this note on her desk on arriving for work on Friday morning. How it had got there was a complete mystery. Due to the sensitive nature of her work – Xu Ya was a special prosecutor attached to the Legal and Disciplinary Section of Chengdu People's Procuratorate – she had developed the habit of locking her office door whenever she was not present. She had received other notes, of course, but these had been slipped under the door, and they had been offensive rather than threatening.

'Prosecutor Xu, you are a stuck-up bitch!'

'Prosecutor Xu, you are not wanted here so why don't you fuck off back to Chongqing.'

And so on.

But Sarangerel's note, unlike those printed others, had been written by hand, on the best quality writing paper. The note had been signed with a flourish, the paper then neatly folded and sealed with wax. And polite invitation though it seemed, it had terrified Xu Ya. Not one of the other notes had mentioned the passing of her husband, which had occurred a year ago almost to the very day. Moreover, not one of those other notes had alluded to the possibility that there might be something more to learn about her husband's death on top of the official story: how he had been suffering ill health for a number of months, how one unfortunate night last summer he had died suddenly, if not unexpectedly, in his sleep.

Xu Ya had thought of little else other than Sarangerel's note all Friday. She held it in her hands still, at almost three on Saturday morning, sitting up in bed, listening to the thunderstorms roll in and over Chengdu.

She wanted to cry, but could not.

She wanted to do something, but did not know what.

Most of all she wanted to speak to Philip Ye, to confess all, to unburden her heart to him.

But she had not heard from Philip Ye for almost three months, not since the investigation into The Willow Woman cult. And, if she were to be realistic, to not lose herself in one of her highly fraught and highly complex romantic fantasies, he being a homicide detective and as strait-laced as they come, would more likely sling her into a cell than protect her from Sarangerel.

I was a fool for believing I could escape my past, she thought, bitterly.

For in China, was it not a fact that the past was never truly past, that nothing was ever truly forgotten, and that the unhappy ghosts of the wrongfully dead – figuratively speaking, that is – never ceased to walk this ancient land?

Maybe it was time to flee.

Maybe it was time to leave China for good, seek out foreign shores, lose herself in some alien culture, and forget the person she was, is, and always wanted to be.

It was all her own fault. She had only herself to blame for attracting all the hateful notes, and now the attention of Sarangerel – the Witch-Queen of Chengdu.

A few weeks before, she had appeared on local primetime TV in what had become the smash-hit of the season: the trial of Commissioner Ho Feng, the former head of the Robbery Section of Chengdu

PSB – a corrupt, drunken, and thoroughly useless man. She had been given the honour of being lead prosecutor. And though the trial had been quick – over in a few days, the evidence against Commissioner Ho quite overwhelming – Xu Ya had made the most of her time in the limelight, wanting to make the best impression for all the right reasons, wanting the people to understand that the Procuratorate would not stand for such criminal behaviour – even if committed by a powerful policeman – and wanting to lecture the people via the medium of television on the necessity for the Rule of Law.

For those few days of the trial she had been a star, more famous even than some young singing sensation from Hangzhou – or so her friend Hong Jia said, otherwise known as Mouse, who worked in the archive at the Procuratorate, and who knew more about modern popular culture than Xu Ya ever would.

But fame had a price.

Other prosecutors at the Procuratorate had become envious. After the trial the hateful notes had begun to be slipped under her door. And, on one troubling day, a small cardboard box containing a severed cat's head had been delivered to her home address – thankfully intercepted, opened, and disposed of by the day concierge Mister Gan before she could see it (though she had later lectured Mister Gan that in future, should another similar delivery be made, such evidence had to be preserved).

Now she had attracted the attention of Sarangerel.

Was Sarangerel envious too?

Xu Ya doubted this, Sarangerel being the long-limbed beauty from Mongolia who always graced Mayor Cang's arm, often showing off far too much flesh at Chengdu's most prestigious functions, partying with the city's rich and well-connected, and who, so it was said, was more familiar with the corridors of power than even Party Chief Li. Sarangerel was rightfully feared, even if one was not taken in by the very tall stories of her being a shamaness from the northern steppe, a drinker of blood, a devourer of human flesh, and a wielder of the blackest sorcery.

Her mouth dry, giving up on sleep, Xu Ya rose from her bed. She put a silk robe about herself, and walked through the dark apartment to the kitchen to pour herself a glass of mineral water. She took her drink to the study and stood for a while looking out of the window at the blue-white streaks of lightning criss-crossing the sky. It was not good to live one's life in fear, she mused. Her father had told her not to worry, had promised her, that the ghost of her husband would not, could not, follow her from Chongqing. How wrong he had been! Sarangerel had caught a scent of something, heard a whisper from someone.

To distract herself from her fear, Xu Ya switched on her desk lamp and sat down to continue work on the draft of her proposal to install procuratorate staff in all the police stations across Chengdu. The intention was to finally, properly, supervise the work of the police, to deal immediately with any violations of the law or incidents of procedural malpractice by the police as they arose. Two months ago, her idea of conducting spot audits on police stations had stalled and then died an awful death in a meeting of the Political and Legal Committee. Secretary Wu and a majority of the other committee members had let themselves be swayed by a furious Chief of Police Di, who saw the proposed audits as an 'attack' on the PSB rather than a sincere offer of help to an overworked and underpaid police force struggling to stem the tide of criminality sweeping the city. Originally supportive, Chief Prosecutor Gong had sat on the fence at the meeting. And then, when the decision had been made not to move forward with the proposal, he had returned to the Procuratorate and lambasted Xu Ya for embarrassing him before the Committee. So now she had come up with a new plan to bring the PSB to heel, a plan that would have the support of the Supreme People's Procuratorate in Beijing who were conducting pilot studies of their own. It was a great pity that her plan was not original. But, in the draft she was preparing, she was determined to propose improvements to the pilot studies already in operation in Ningxia and Xi'an, to make Chengdu a flagship for the whole of China, and naturally a name for herself as well.

Hardly had she begun to write, to continue from where she had left off earlier in the day, when there was a most unexpected knock at the door. She almost tipped over her glass of water in shock. Who would come calling at three in the morning? She was friendly with very few people in Chengdu. Furthermore, in the three months she had been living in her apartment in Tranquil Mountain Pavilions, she had yet to introduce herself to any of her fellow tenants.

As she hurried to the door, conscious she was barefoot and only wearing a flimsy robe, she imagined for one insane moment that it was Philip Ye standing on the other side of the door, dressed in one of his fine suits, having just worked up the courage to ask her out to dinner – an invite she should surely, would surely, decline. But when she looked through the door peephole she was both relieved and a little disappointed to see that it was only Mister Ni, the night concierge. She opened the door ever so slightly so that she could speak to him and yet not reveal too much of her lack of apparel.

"Is something wrong, Mister Ni?"

"Forgive this dreadful intrusion, Prosecutor. There is a bad situation, not here but at Plum Tree Pagodas."

"I do not think I know that place."

"It is an apartment complex in the Wuhou District also owned by the family Fu. It is not far from the Ye family mansion."

"Ah."

"Your presence is required immediately, Prosecutor. I am to drive you. Mister Gan is rushing in as we speak to cover the front desk here."

"You have no more information?"

"I am sorry, no, Prosecutor."

"This is most unusual, Mister Ni."

"I agree."

"I will be ready in fifteen minutes."

The family Fu were reputedly the richest in all of Sichuan Province. The family business, FUBI International, had interests not just across China but in every corner of the world. Xu Ya owed her own luxury apartment to the fact her father was well-acquainted with Fu Bi, the patriarch of the family – her apartment being leased to her at extremely preferential rates. And even then she needed financial help from her parents. On a prosecutor's woeful salary she doubted she would have been able to rent a closet, let alone an apartment in Tranquil Mountain Pavilions. Therefore, if the family Fu had a problem, if they felt the need to summon her in the middle of a stormy night, Xu Ya had no choice but to respond. With Sarangerel's note lying on her bed there had been little chance of sleep anyway.

She dressed quickly – cream blouse, black jeans, ankle boots because of the rain – ran a brush through her long hair before tying it back in a pony-tail, quickly applied a minimum of make-up, pulled on a light leather jacket anticipating that the thunderstorms had brought some cooling of the air, and finally grabbed a pen, a notebook, and her phone. A last check in the long mirror in her bedroom – not bad for the middle of the night, she thought – and she was out of the door.

Mister Ni parked the limousine on the street right outside Plum Tree Pagodas. He did not want to use the underground car park, he said, the potential for bumping into residents, even at this hour, far too high. Even at night and in the torrential rain, Xu Ya could see it was a far grander building than hers. Plum Tree Pagodas probably had its own shops, cinema, gymnasium, and swimming-pool. Following Mister Ni's lead, Xu Ya jumped out of the limousine and ran for the lobby entrance, doing her best to avoid the deep puddles on the way. They were met by the night concierge who had been looking out through the glass doors for them.

"Have you any further information for us, Mister Han?" asked Mister Ni.

"Forgive me, no – but Prosecutor Xu is to go straight up to the fifth floor."

Mister Ni grew concerned. "Am I not to accompany her?"

"No, Mister Ni," replied Mister Han, grimly.

Warmed by Mister Ni's gallantry but quite used to working alone, Xu Ya headed over to the lift that was already awaiting her with its doors open. She pressed the button for the fifth floor. But, as the doors closed before her, she saw Mister Ni and Mister Han with their heads together, in urgent, whispered conversation. The warm feeling within her died. Secrets were being kept from her. Both Mister Ni and Mister Han knew far more than they were prepared to say.

When the lift doors opened again, Xu Ya stepped out onto the plush crimson carpet of the fifth-floor corridor. None of the doors to the various apartments off the corridor were open, but after fifteen metres or so, the corridor made a sharp dogleg and she could just hear people in muted conversation. She set off at a march, humming a nameless tune to herself, the apartment complex smelling like a brand-new construction. She wondered how many of the apartments were occupied and how much a lease would cost. She had no complaints about her own accommodation, though. And who would want to live only a few minutes' drive from the Ye family mansion?

Around the dogleg, a short distance in front of her, stood a trio of very important people, who abruptly broke off their conversation as soon as they saw her: Party Chief Li, the most senior Party official in all of Chengdu; Secretary Wu, the Chair of the very influential Legal and Political Committee, who, only a few months ago, had rescued her from obscurity in Chongqing and taken the risk of giving her a job at the Procuratorate in Chengdu; and, last but not least, Lucy Fu, daughter of Fu Bi, heir to the vast fortune of the family Fu, and a very successful and well-respected businesswoman in her own right. And it was Lucy Fu, her eyes glistening like ice, who was first to greet her. "Where have you been, Prosecutor Xu? We had almost given up waiting for you."

Xu Ya had first met Lucy Fu at a formal dinner in Chongqing back in the spring where they had agreed to be friends – or at least Xu Ya had remained mute when the offer had been made. But there was no friendliness in Lucy Fu's manner now. Of an age to Xu Ya – in her early thirties – Lucy Fu looked as wide awake as if it were midday, dressed in a pearl-white business suit with not a crease or blemish to be seen, hair cut incredibly short with not one out of place, fabulous diamond studs in her ears, and make-up as if she had spent the last three hours in some ridiculously expensive salon. Next to her Xu Ya felt frankly dishevelled.

"I came as quickly as I could," said Xu Ya, offering no apology.

"Of course," said Secretary Wu. "It is good to see you again, Ms. Xu."

"Yes! Yes! Enough of the pleasantries!" exclaimed Party Chief Li, impatiently. "We need to make progress."

Both men were dressed in dark suits but, unlike Lucy Fu, both appeared exhausted and more than a little worried. Party Chief Li actually looked ill, his skin pale and waxy, his bloodshot eyes almost the same colour as the corridor carpet. Xu Ya took her notebook and pen from her jacket pocket, thinking that it would be one or the other who would explain what all this was about, glad she had at least not been summoned to do the family Fu some kind of surreptitious favour. But, in fact, it was Lucy Fu who spoke again.

"Prosecutor, there shall be no mistakes in this investigation, nor shall there be any careless leaks to the media. I want this intruder – this murderer! – hunted down. I would have preferred someone else, someone more mature, someone more emotionally stable. But Party Chief Li and Secretary Wu are adamant that it has to be you. So be it. I just hope I don't regret my giving way to them."

This vindictive little speech done, Lucy Fu nodded to the two men, brushed past Xu Ya, and marched off down the corridor to vanish around the dogleg. No one spoke again until they had heard the chime of the lift doors as they closed after Lucy Fu.

Good riddance, thought Xu Ya.

Lucy Fu had once dated Philip Ye. Now Xu Ya had another reason to hate her.

"There must indeed be no leaks to the media," said Party Chief Li. "No police either...definitely no police. That rabble, even the officers I brought with me from Shanghai, not a single one is to be trusted. If it was up to me, I would sack the lot and begin recruiting all over again."

"Yes, Ms. Xu, this is to be a Procuratorate-only investigation," confirmed Secretary Wu. "In fact, we would prefer you to begin your enquiries on your own, without the assistance of any of the other prosecutors. You must not even contact the pathologist."

"Doctor Kong and her horde of white-suited monkeys must have no part of this," agreed Party Chief Li. "The morgue leaks like a sieve. Don't worry about the body, Ms. Xu. Once you are done with your examination, I will send some men to remove it."

Xu Ya wanted to protest. Without forensic support, without DNA, or fingerprint, or hair analysis, and without a proper examination of the crime scene then—

"You must just do as you are told," continued Party Chief Li, pre-empting any argument as he took a cigarette from a packet, placed it in the end of an ivory holder, lit it, and then blew smoke all over her. "No one is to know anything, at least not until Monday morning, not until I – others too – have been able to divest myself of my shares. Anyway, we already know who is responsible for this crime."

"Nothing is known for certain," said Secretary Wu.

Party Chief Li's temper flared. "Of course, we know! Who else has the reach to send someone in here, bypass all the security, and commit a murder in cold blood? Who else would know where all my money is invested? Who else has vowed to destroy me?"

Xu Ya was not following. "Sir, who has vowed to destroy you?"

Party Chief Li turned the full force of his temper upon her. "Ye Zihao, of course! Follow the evidence, Ms. Xu. Follow it all the way to the gates of that outlandish mansion of his. I know you can do it, Ms. Xu. You were a revelation on TV. This time he has made a terrible mistake. This time he has gone too far. When we have all the evidence we need, whether we have Beijing's blessing or not, I'll send in the army to smoke that bastard out. Forget about Lucy Fu and her stupid intruder, Ms. Xu – it's Ye Zihao that I want."

"Of course, sir," she replied, numb with shock. Ye Zihao was the disgraced former mayor of Chengdu, now under continuous house-arrest. He was also Philip Ye's father.

Secretary Wu touched Party Chief Li's arm. "Come, let Ms. Xu get to work. I am sure she will meet with us in a few hours to give us her initial thoughts. Then, together, we can map out the first steps in this investigation."

"Yes, that's it," agreed Party Chief Li, much happier. "The three of us will get that scheming bastard together."

"Ms. Xu, how is Investigator Deng?" asked Secretary Wu.

"Good sir, I think – still convalescing."

"When is he due back at work?"

"Two weeks on Monday."

Party Chief Li was already on his way down the corridor, but Secretary Wu paused for a moment as if considering her reply deeply, then he winked at her, confusing her, and turned away to follow in Party Chief Li's footsteps. Soon enough both had vanished around the dogleg. Xu Ya heard again the chime of the lift and then she was alone.

She listened intently. Not a sound except for the faint rumble of thunder in the distance. No one stirred on the fifth floor. For all she knew every apartment was empty. She made a mental note. She would need a full occupancy list for Plum Tree Pagodas and the names and addresses of all the staff. If the security was as good as Party Chief Li had suggested, then the intruder – the murderer – might have had inside help.

It suddenly dawned on her then that no one had told her who was dead – or, for that matter, where she might find the body. She looked around and noticed, for the first time, that the door to apartment 5014, a few metres further down the corridor, was slightly ajar. A light burned inside. She approached the door but then hesitated, her pulse pounding in her temples. What would she find inside? The body of a man? A woman? Heaven forbid, she hoped it would not be that of a child!

She was about to push the door open with the toe of her boot – forensics or no forensics, she was not about to leave her own fingerprints at the scene – when she recalled Secretary Wu's odd and unexpected question regarding Investigator Deng's recovery. She had met Secretary Wu a number of times in the last few months but not once had he inquired after Investigator Deng. It struck her that he had perhaps been making a suggestion, that despite Party Chief Li's insistence she work alone, a little bit of help might be in order.

Xu Ya checked her watch. 3:55 a.m. Investigator Deng was not going to thank her for this. The last time they had spoken he had been short with her, tired of her visits, of her pathetic attempts to make things right between them.

She took her phone out of her jacket, stared at it for a while, and then stuffed it back inside her pocket. She put her hand to her forehead, wishing she was a better person, wishing she knew how to easily get along with people. Then, cursing herself, she again took the phone from her pocket and dialled. Whether Investigator Deng hated her or not, she would not be able to take Ye Zihao down without him.

TWO

— · —

The holiday in England had been ill-starred from the outset, probably because it had been taken for the wrong reasons. Wanting to escape the summer heat of Chengdu and Constable Ma's increasingly oppressive moods, Philip Ye had arranged to spend a couple of weeks in Oxford with his mother. It had been his intention to sit in the quiet of his mother's garden, enjoy the relative cool of an English summer, and to think very deeply about what he was going to do – if anything – about Prosecutor Xu. For the last three months, apart from meditating bleakly from time to time on Constable Ma's many shortcomings as a homicide detective, he had thought of little else than Prosecutor Xu – even to the detriment of the cases he was working. But, hardly had he stepped over the threshold of his mother's house when the arguments with his mother had begun, both he and she quick to resurrect ancient history.

His mother had raised the subject of Isobel again, how his long-dead fiancée had distracted him from his studies at university, how he had then gone on to waste his physics degree by his subsequent decision to return to China, attend law school at Wuhan, and then throw away his life for a career in the police. For his part, resentful as ever, Philip Ye had reminded his mother of her complete absence in his life during his childhood, her refusal to ever visit him once in Chengdu, the lack of concern for him bordering on callousness after Isobel had died, her conspiring with his father to undermine his application to join the police, and – this never failed to induce a violent reaction in her – the ease with which she had given him up after his birth to the total, and highly dubious, care of his father. These old grievances aired, his mother began ranting about her latest concern: the failure of his romantic life, the 'brainless bimbos' he had wasted years on, and how it was high time he settled down and got married.

"I wish to be a grandmother before I am too old to enjoy it," she said, caustically.

To which he had replied, "Well, you could not be any worse a grandmother than you were a mother."

Doors were slammed, meals taken in frosty silences, his mother finding more work to do at the university than she had expected, and him spending hours aimlessly walking the streets of Oxford, his mother's garden no longer as inviting as he had imagined it to be back in Chengdu. By the end of just one week, Philip Ye had had enough. And deep down he knew that the answer to the problem of Prosecutor Xu lay thousands of miles away back in China, in Chongqing, where her husband had met his mysterious death. He was achieving nothing sitting in England just twiddling his thumbs and arguing with his mother.

On telling her that he needed to cut his holiday short, that the police urgently needed him back in Chengdu, his mother actually managed to squeeze tears from her eyes. She pressed presents upon him for his father and for the brothers Na – for whom she had developed an odd fascination – and told him, in spite of the mess he had made of his life, that she still loved him, and that all she wanted for him was to be happy.

"You look so tired, Philip," she said. "You must get more rest...not worry so much...smile a bit more...and find a nice girl to settle down with before it's too late."

To make their parting as easy as possible, Philip Ye promised he would do as she asked, and said he would return before Christmas if he could. They each then made a poor attempt at a hug, before she shut the door on him and he caught a taxi to the train station.

In London, the black cloud he had been travelling under since leaving Chengdu continued to follow him. The direct flight he had been hoping to catch was cancelled due to mechanical failure. Not wanting to spend any more time in England – painful memories of Isobel had begun to resurface and he had a strange, nagging feeling he needed to return home as soon as possible – he hopped on a shuttle to Paris and, after a couple of tedious hours in an airport bar, caught a direct flight to Chengdu. Roughly ten hours later, he found himself belted tightly in his seat, circling over the city at four o'clock in the morning, the aircraft being buffeted by incredibly turbulent air as the pilot searched for a way down through a band of thunderstorms and torrential rain.

"This pilot is crazy," said a French businessman sitting next to him speaking passable Mandarin. "The weather is too bad. We should be diverting."

Philip Ye thought so too. The prevailing advice to pilots, no matter how big the aircraft, was to keep well away from thunderstorms if at all possible, especially during take offs and landings. The odd lightning strike or two an aircraft could cope with, but a thunderstorm's updrafts and downdrafts – and that most violent combination of the two, wind shear – could easily propel an aircraft catastrophically into the ground.

But maybe the pilot had never heard of this advice, or maybe he or she was made of stronger stuff than the majority of the terrified passengers. For suddenly the aircraft was descending through the flashes of lightning and wall of rain, and before anyone could again question the pilot's sanity – or lack thereof – the aircraft slammed down on the runway and the pilot cheerily welcomed them all to Chengdu's Shuangliu Airport.

There was no need for a taxi. Philip Ye had phoned home from Paris giving an approximate time for arrival. He collected his luggage and stood out by the taxi rank with his umbrella up against the rain, glad that the thunderstorms had served to freshen the air somewhat, making his first breaths of the humid Chengdu air not so uncomfortable, and relieved to be still alive after such an eventful landing.

"Hello."

Philip Ye turned to whoever had spoken, and was mystified to see a slim and attractive Chinese woman with long, wavy hair and deep, sensual eyes, no older than forty, standing next to him, smiling warmly at him as if she knew him. He had no idea how she had got so close without him sensing her presence. Was his head so full of the problem of Prosecutor Xu that he had lost all awareness of what was going on around him?

"Hello," he replied, liking her, as well as the light floral scent that surrounded her – a perfume that evoked a garden full of rare orchids, orange blossom, and jasmine. Nothing about her unsettled him. She seemed unusually calm, quite at ease with herself, content even – a contentedness that was infectious, that immediately eased his troubled mind.

"I came to thank you," she said.

Puzzled, Philip Ye asked, "For what?"

Before she could reply, Philip Ye was distracted by the honk of a car horn as the Mercedes driven by Night Na skidded to a halt before him. When Philip Ye turned to face the woman again, she was nowhere to be seen. He remembered then that she had carried no umbrella and yet not a single drop of rain had touched her face.

THREE

— · —

The phone call woke him from the recurring nightmare: he was lying on his back in bed in hospital, in pain, tubes coming out of him, wired up to machines he did not understand, unable to move, speak, or even cry out.

He picked up his phone off the bedside cabinet. "Yes?"

"Investigator Deng, are you awake?"

"I am now, Prosecutor."

"How are you?"

"I feel better – much better."

"I know you are still on sick leave...that it's not right for me to call you...but something has happened."

"What?"

"A murder."

"Prosecutor, where are you?"

"Plum Tree Pagodas – in the Wuhou District."

"I know it."

"I am sorry to ask."

"I will be with you as soon as I can."

He dropped the phone on the bed and reached for his packet of cigarettes. He was worried. Prosecutor Xu had sounded nervous, not quite herself. He lit his first cigarette of the day, coughing painfully, clutching the lower left side of his chest where a knife had pierced his lung. His surgeon, cigarette dangling from his own lips, had advised him to give up smoking for good.

"I only smoke five cigarettes a day," Fatty Deng had told him – which was more or less the truth.

"I suppose that's not really smoking at all," said the surgeon, disappointed, after a moment's consideration.

Fatty Deng checked his watch. 4.01 a.m. A couple of hours left until dawn. He got out of bed and stared out of the window. There was not much to see – it was very dark, a couple of street lights were out – but he expected there would be flooding in various parts of the city. The thunderstorms had been intense, with more rain on the way, or so it was said. He was concerned for his mother. She was somewhere out on the Yangzi. The Procuratorate had given him an award of money for the part he had played in the investigation into The Willow Woman cult – an investigation that had almost cost him his life. The money had bought him a couple of good suits, a few conservative ties and shirts, as well as a raincoat similar in style to that worn by Philip Ye. The money that had been left over he had given to his mother. Tired of her fretting over him all the hours of the day and night, and listening to her fears of what might befall him once he returned to work, he had persuaded her to take a trip of a lifetime. She had always dreamed of a river cruise. Their good neighbours, Uncle Ho and Aunty Ho, had gone with her to keep her company. But Fatty Deng now worried for the three of them. This was not the sort of weather to be out upon the Yangzi. This was the sort of weather in which a poorly maintained, or poorly captained, boat capsized.

He dressed quickly. He chose one of his new suits to impress Prosecutor Xu. The holstered pistol tucked just behind his right hip felt odd, uncomfortable – in all his years with the police he had never once carried a firearm on duty. But, without consulting him, Prosecutor Xu had sought and gained permission for him to carry a pistol, citing the dangers of the special work he was expected to do, and not wanting a repeat of what had happened to him at the hands of The Willow Woman cultists. She had been deaf to his protests that the cultists had caught him off guard, that a pistol would have done nothing to save him from violent assault. She had also been deaf to his concerns that he might come to rely on the pistol too much, forget the skills he had learned in the police, the ability to be able to read and react to a volatile situation accordingly, to use his wits (or indeed his fists) without the need for lethal force.

"I'm not even a good shot," he had told her.

"Then practise!" she had shouted at him, losing her temper, the matter, as far as she was concerned, closed.

Over his suit he put on his new, grey raincoat. Looking at himself briefly in the mirror, he was unsure of the result. He had lost a little weight in hospital but not so much that anyone would notice. And though the raincoat was of a similar style to that worn by Philip Ye, no matter how Fatty Deng posed in front of the mirror, he was no match for Philip Ye's natural elegance.

On the way out of his apartment building he had paused to look up and down the rain-swept street, straining his eyes against the darkness, cursing the broken street lights, looking for anything out of place, anything that might constitute a threat. Prosecutor Xu had noticed this supposedly *new* behaviour of his a week ago, when she had come to take him to a local teahouse for a chat. Hypervigilance, she had called it – a result of trauma, of all that he had suffered at the hands of the cultists. No, he had protested, not hypervigilance, just plain common sense. Crime was on the up in Chengdu. One could not be too careful these days. Their little teahouse chat had then descended into argument, she telling him that he was no longer right in the head, and he telling her that his head had never felt better, that it was the one part of his body the cultists had not stabbed. She had tried to push a business card on to him, that of a Procuratorate-approved psychiatrist, a Doctor Tang Hao. He had thrown the card back at her, telling her that he had no memory of the attack, just of his long stay in hospital, and of her telling him again and again how sorry she was, how guilty she felt about what had happened to him. She had then made it clear that if he did not consult Doctor Tang she would not approve his return to work. To which he had replied, that if he did not return to work he would probably live a lot longer. His tough, smart, and fearless boss, the glamorous prosecutor off the TV, the Flower of the Procuratorate as the media had named her, had then, in front of everyone in the teahouse, begun to cry. He had been forced to quickly apologise and tell her that the medicines he was still taking did not make him think so straight. Of course, he would consult Doctor Tang. Of course, it would be good to talk to a real professional about all he had gone through. Prosecutor Xu's eyes had dried so quickly then that Fatty Deng had wondered if it had all been a show. But he had decided to give her the benefit of the doubt. He liked her. He really did. Beneath all of Prosecutor Xu's craziness there was a kind and generous heart. It was just a pity she was so much bloody hard work.

His journey across the city to Plum Tree Pagodas would have been quicker if his old Toyota had started first time. It had been playing up recently, especially when the engine was hot. But this time the rain was obviously affecting it. The award of money might have been better spent on a new ride rather than on sending his mother to a watery grave, he thought, as he tried again and again to get the engine to turn over. But once it finally started – and kept going – he found the streets not as bad as he had feared, only having to take a couple of detours around flooded intersections and in one instance backing out of an alley when confronted with a sinkhole of unknown depth.

Just after five, he parked across the street from Plum Tree Pagodas. The apartment block was one of those new constructions – completed only at the end of the previous year – that Chengdu natives either loved or hated. It was emblematic of all the new money pouring into the city. As he got out of the car, and stared up through the rain that was now falling heavily again, he decided, quite unexpectedly, that he quite liked it. He hurried across the road, not forgetting to look both ways, pushed open the glass door and entered the lobby, brushing the rainwater from his hair. He showed his badge and ID to the concierge behind the desk.

"Prosecutor Xu is on the fifth floor," he was told. "Apartment 5014."

Fatty Deng asked no questions. The concierge – a tough-looking man, probably ex-army – didn't look happy and did his best to avert his eyes. No answers would be forthcoming there. With no stairs in sight, and not feeling physically up to a long climb anyway, Fatty Deng faced down his fear of enclosed spaces and took the lift. Ascending to the fifth floor he began to wonder where all the uniformed police were. But, before he could mull over the strangeness of this, he noticed on the lift's steel handrail a couple of dark smudges, fingerprints possibly, left in blood. He took a quick photograph using his phone and made a note in his notebook. This was not going to be a gentle return to work, he decided.

When the lift doors opened, he found himself staring down a silent and empty corridor.

Why was there not more disturbance?

Why weren't the tenants out in the corridor, gossiping, trying to find out what was going on?

And where were the police?

He walked down the corridor, counting off the apartment numbers as he went, looking for more traces of blood. The deep-pile crimson carpet was a waste of time. Forensics would need their chemicals and their special lights to find any blood on that. So, he kept his eyes on the walls, and was rewarded when the corridor turned in a sharp dogleg, seeing a large smudge low down on the wall just above the carpet in the shape of a handprint, so small he thought it must have been made by a woman or a child. As he studied the mark, an image came to mind of a woman running for the lift, stumbling and falling to the floor, putting her hand against the wall to preserve a little forward momentum. He saw panic in the handprint, someone in terror for their life. He took another photograph using his phone, made another note in his notebook. He found no other traces of blood on the way to apartment 5014.

The door was slightly ajar, a light shining within. He listened but heard nothing except for the nervous rasping of his own breathing. The absence of police, the absence of anyone at all, was unnerving. Instinctively he pulled his pistol from its holster, dismayed at how weak-minded he had become, how easily he had resorted to its use. In his police days he would have confidently bounded into the apartment unarmed and uncaring.

He levelled the pistol in front of him. What he had told Prosecutor Xu was true: he wasn't much of a shot. His firearms instructor back at Police College – funny guy that he was – had told him not to bother ever applying for SWAT. He wondered if the Procuratorate had a practice range and an instructor gifted in the patience department.

He pushed open the door with the side of his shoe. The hinges were so well oiled the door did not make a sound. He was looking at a narrow entrance hall, a large mirror mounted on the wall to his left, and a painting – an ugly thing, some sort of weird modern art, daubs of colour upon a white canvas, in the approximate form of a naked woman – on the wall to his right. Beneath the painting was a low mahogany table. There was a shallow porcelain dish on the table containing a set of Porsche car keys. That was no surprise. Anyone who could afford an apartment in Plum Tree Pagodas had money – lots of money.

He glanced down at the carpet, a much more durable lower pile than the corridor, and in fawn. He saw stains that might, or might not, be blood. And, low down on the wall again, just beyond the mahogany table, another handprint on the wall. He listened intently and, as before, could hear nothing except his own breathing.

A few steps forward, pistol out in front of him, and the hall opened out into a cavernous lounge, so big the whole of the apartment he shared with his mother could easily have been dropped into it. In one corner of the room, sat on a comfy chair, her boots off, her legs tucked underneath her as if she was in her own home, oblivious to his presence, her concentration fully on her phone, was Prosecutor Xu. Fatty Deng sighed, and put away his pistol, unable to believe her stupidity, her carelessness. He could have been someone out to do her harm.

"Prosecutor," he said, softly.

She almost jumped out of her skin, dropping her phone to the floor. "Oh, Investigator Deng, you frightened me! I didn't hear you come in. I wasn't even sure you would come."

Fatty Deng was offended by her words. How could he not come? And she annoyed him further by running over in her socks, and putting her hand out to him in formal greeting. He felt like slapping her hand away. It wasn't like they had just been introduced. But she had been acting so very oddly since he had been in hospital, blaming herself for everything, that he took her hand anyway, trying not to hurt her with his big paw.

"I am so glad you are here," she said.

"It is no trouble," he replied, embarrassed by the emotion in her eyes, turning quickly away from her to stare about the room, amazed at its opulence, the quality of the furniture, the many expensive ornaments, and all the paintings – more bizarre modern art – on the walls. There was no sign of any disturbance, no signs of violence.

"How is your mother?" she asked.

"Enjoying herself on a cruise down the Yangzi with Uncle and Aunty Ho."

Prosecutor Xu was aghast. "In this weather?"

Ignoring the implied criticism of him for allowing his mother to take such a risky holiday, he asked, "What's going on here? Someone has left bloody handprints down the corridor and in the lift."

She grew thoughtful. "Ah, that makes a lot of sense...a lot of sense indeed. I wish I had been more observant on my way in."

"Prosecutor, over the phone you said murder."

"Yes, that is true."

"Then where are the police?"

"It's complicated. There is much to explain. First you must come with me to see the master bedroom."

He waited patiently while she pulled her boots back on and pocketed her phone. Then he followed her to the far end of the lounge, down a narrow hall, off which he saw a couple of bedrooms and a beautifully-fitted bathroom. The door at the end of the corridor opened into the master bedroom, the like of which he had never seen in his life except in magazines. It was massive, like a luxury hotel room. A window shrouded by blinds ran from floor to ceiling opposite the foot of the king-size bed. The blinds shifted slightly in the breeze. Again, there were no signs of a struggle, no upturned furniture, and no debris strewn over the floor. But, on the bed, flat on his back, his arms splayed out wide, his eyes staring up at the ceiling, was a dead man. He was dressed in a dinner-suit as if he had just returned from a formal engagement, polished shoes on his feet. There was a bloody wound in the centre of his chest. It seemed to Fatty Deng that the man had sat down on the end of the bed, perhaps to take off his shoes, when he had been struck, thrown backwards and died. There were a couple of bloody handprints on his white shirt around the wound. Someone had tried to staunch the flow of blood. Someone had tried to save his life.

"Stabbed?" he asked.

"No, gunshot," replied Prosecutor Xu.

He looked at her quizzically. There was no smell of gunpowder residue in the air. But he said nothing. He could sense her excitement. She had a story she was desperate to tell. "Who is he?" he asked.

"Don't you recognise him?"

Fatty Deng walked closer to the bed and leaned over the body. The man was older than he, maybe forty, maybe a couple of years more. He was Chinese – or at least of Chinese extraction – with fine features and very good skin. The face stirred no memories. "I don't know him."

"I didn't recognise him at first either. Isn't it funny how in death a person's features change?"

"Prosecutor, who is he?"

"Primo Gong, of course."

"Who?"

Exasperated, she put her hands on her slim hips. "The American businessman!"

"Prosecutor, does it look like I read the business papers?"

"But he is famous."

"Obviously not famous enough."

She shook her head at his ignorance. "Well, I had heard of him even when I was living back in Chongqing. He came to Chengdu a couple of years ago, moved his whole business, Ambrogetti Global Software, all the way from the United States. Chengdu has been offering some very attractive financial incentives for overseas companies to relocate here. Ambrogetti Global Software's stock is now listed on the Shanghai Exchange."

Fatty Deng shrugged. No one had offered him any financial incentives when he had been thrown out of the police five years before – and he had lived in Chengdu all his life. He glanced down at the body again. "I guess he must be regretting the move to Chengdu now."

She glared at him. "Have some respect!"

"Prosecutor, he's dead – he's not listening."

"That's not the point."

"What sort of name is 'Primo' anyway?"

"Italian – it means 'firstborn'," she replied. "There's a lot of research we must do. That's what I had begun on my phone when you walked in. Did you know his family were originally from Chengdu, going back before the revolution? He told everyone he had come to rediscover his roots, and also because China is the future."

Fatty Deng could not help laughing. "That remains to be seen."

Ignoring his scepticism, she continued, "A few months after he arrived in Chengdu, Primo Gong renounced his American citizenship and tore up his passport, much to the delight of the Party. He made headlines all around the world. He quickly became a friend to Party Chief Li and the rest of the Shanghai Clique. They held him up as a shining exemplar for all that Chengdu now stands for: a city of international commerce, populated by talented entrepreneurs constructing a bright future for us all. His wife, who is Caucasian – an American but of Scandinavian descent – saw Chengdu differently, though. After a few months here, about two years ago, she took the children back to the United States and hasn't been seen in Chengdu since. It seems she chose not to tear up her American passport."

Smart woman, thought Fatty Deng, choosing to keep this thought to himself.

"Prosecutor, this is all very interesting, but where are the police? Where is Doctor Kong? We're contaminating this scene just by walking around."

"They're not coming."

Fatty Deng couldn't hide his astonishment. "What do you mean?"

Prosecutor Xu's temper flared. "Don't look at me like that! It wasn't my decision. Don't you think I know how hard it is going to be to solve a murder without any forensic support? But I have to follow orders – as do you. When I arrived, Party Chief Li, Secretary Wu, and Lucy Fu were already here."

"In this room?"

"No, out in the corridor. You should have heard how Lucy Fu spoke to me."

"Prosecutor, you must tell me everything."

Which she did, her memory so good she could relay all that was said to her verbatim, about the intruder, how there was to be no involvement by the police or Doctor Kong, no leaks to the media, how she had but a short time to examine the body before it was to be removed by persons unknown, and, most important of all, who the prime suspect was.

Fatty Deng could hardly believe his ears. "Ye Zihao?"

"Party Chief Li said I had to follow the trail of evidence all the way to the Ye family mansion. However, Secretary Wu was much more circumspect. I believe he has serious doubts about Party Chief Li's theory, maybe even thinks him slightly paranoid. But what do you think, Investigator Deng?"

"About Ye Zihao?"

"Yes – is he capable of arranging a murder?"

"If you believe all the old stories."

"Stories?"

"Rumours more like – people crossing swords with Ye Zihao on his rise to prominence, people who just happened to disappear. Trouble is, in Chengdu, it is often hard to prove whether people have disappeared through their own doing or someone else's. There are even some who disappear only to reappear a few years later as if nothing has happened. All I do know is that if we are going to accuse Ye Zihao of murder, even though he is no longer mayor, even though he is under house-arrest, and even though he has been thrown out of the Party, we had better have the evidence to back up our accusation. Ye Zihao still has friends in this city – many friends – and in Beijing too."

"Regardless, we shouldn't be frightened of him," said Prosecutor Xu.

"Respectfully, I must disagree."

Prosecutor Xu scowled. "Anyway," she said, not wanting to argue the point, "Secretary Wu has his doubts about Ye Zihao's involvement in this crime and I am inclined to follow his lead. I don't think Party Chief Li is thinking straight. All his money is invested in Ambrogetti Global Software. It is likely the company will founder without the charismatic leadership of Primo Gong. Which is why Party Chief Li wants to offload all his shares before news leaks out that Primo Gong is dead. We can only hope that, when Party Chief Li has sold his stake in the company, he will no longer be so worried about potential leaks. He may then authorise some forensic assistance for us. In the meantime, we must do what we can on our own."

"So, what are we looking at, Prosecutor? Surely not an intruder? I don't buy Lucy Fu's story. This building is locked down pretty tight. I noticed CCTV looking up and down the street and inside in the lobby, as well as the tough-guy behind the front desk. I bet there's secure electronic access to the underground car park and more CCTV there too. Those bloody handprints I've seen are small, probably from a woman. This crime scene looks more like a lover's tiff gone wrong. But if it was a lover's tiff gone wrong, and this mystery woman shot him dead, it begs the question how she got hold of a firearm. Not easily done in Chengdu. Not easily done at all." He glanced around the bedroom and thought back to what he had seen in the lounge and in the hallway. "Do we have any other evidence a woman was here? This apartment is remarkably clean."

Prosecutor Xu got down on her knees, beckoning him to join her down on the carpet. Reluctantly he did so, worried about soiling the trousers of his new suit. She pointed toward an easy chair set in the corner of the bedroom. Underneath the chair was a pair of red court shoes, very stylish, very expensive-looking, with low heels, placed neatly together and tucked out of the way.

"I take it those don't fit Primo Gong?" he asked.

"No, I checked," replied Prosecutor Xu, with only a hint of a smile. "It took me ages to understand this crime scene. It would have saved me a lot of trouble if, like you, I had noticed those bloody handprints from the start – though, to be honest, I thought I had just been summoned here to solve a tricky little legal problem for the family Fu. I wasn't on the look-out for anything untoward."

"So, what have you figured out, Prosecutor?" he asked, getting up off the floor and giving her a helping hand to do the same.

"That not only did Lucy Fu attempt to misdirect me with her story about an intruder but she has also deliberately interfered with a crime scene. Let me give you some background. You probably know that Plum Tree Pagodas was constructed by the family Fu. But what I expect you don't know is that Lucy Fu is in the habit of moving around her family's buildings, keeping an apartment in each, staying only for a few days at a time."

"Like an imperial princess, moving from palace to palace."

"Indeed – and we should also expect for Lucy Fu to have been friends with Primo Gong. One does not apply to live in a family Fu apartment block; one is invited. And before you ask, I was myself invited to live at Tranquil Mountain Pavilions. My father is acquainted with Fu Bi. Anyway, earlier, using my phone, I checked some of the social media forums and found a few mentions of Lucy Fu and Primo Gong being seen out on the town together – no photographs though, which is a pity. There are also some rumours that they were more than just friends. What I know for sure is that when I got here Lucy Fu didn't look as if she had just been dragged out of bed and given the awful news about her friend. I think she has been staying here the last few nights. Her chosen apartment may well have been the apartment next door to this."

"You think she witnessed the murder?"

"No, she would not have misunderstood the crime scene if she had. Let me tell you what I think happened. Last evening, Lucy Fu, Primo Gong, and our mystery woman were out at some select social function. Or maybe Lucy Fu and Primo Gong were at the function together and then they met up with the mystery woman back here in this apartment."

"Prosecutor, couldn't Lucy Fu be our mystery woman?"

"No, those red shoes don't belong to Lucy Fu. They're not her style. They're also too small for her. Lucy Fu has big feet for a woman."

Fatty Deng was surprised. "She does?"

"It's the sort of thing another woman notices."

"Ah."

"Anyway, let us say the three of them – Lucy Fu, Primo Gong, and the lady with the red shoes – stay up drinking and talking a while. I know there are no glasses out, no bottles on show, but let me finish. Sometime later Lucy Fu goes to bed in her own apartment. And our couple, Primo Gong and the mystery woman, retire here to the master bedroom. The mystery woman sits in the easy chair to take off her shoes. Primo Gong is walking around by the foot of the bed. They are both talking quite happily. Then Primo Gong is suddenly shot in the chest."

"By who?"

"Investigator Deng, you must have patience," said Prosecutor Xu, feigning annoyance. "Our mystery woman jumps up from her chair and throws herself on Primo Gong in an effort to staunch the blood from his chest, desperate to save her lover's life. Then another shot rings out, narrowly missing her. Realising that Primo Gong is dead, that her own life is in mortal danger, she flees the apartment, runs to the lift, descends to the lobby or the underground carpark, and vanishes into the night."

"Leaving her shoes behind?"

"That's right. She was terrified, remember? Now this is most important: Lucy Fu, asleep next door, hears the commotion and comes running. She finds the door to the apartment open, comes inside, and finds Primo Gong dead on the bed with our mystery woman gone. Not having the investigative skills that you and I possess, and rushing to judgment, she assumes that it is our mystery woman who has murdered Primo Gong. What Lucy Fu does next is not only unforgivable, it's highly illegal. Lucy Fu decides she needs to remove all traces of herself from this apartment, as well as all traces of the mystery woman. So, I presume together with the concierge – who is acting under orders – Lucy Fu cleans this whole apartment, removing glasses, wine bottles, as well as all the mystery woman's clothes and possessions. She also searches Primo Gong's body, taking his phone and wallet, and whatever electronics he has left lying around, his laptop and tablet, for example – anything, I suspect, that can connect her to Primo Gong and the mystery woman, or possibly *identify* the mystery woman. Then, when all this is done, she finally phones Party Chief Li and Secretary Wu and tells them a tall story about an intruder. They arrive, probably only take a quick peek in here, and wrongly assume Lucy Fu is telling the truth, not realising that her story makes no sense. I bet she also suggested they assign a particularly stupid prosecutor at the Procuratorate – and there are many – to investigate the murder. It must have turned her stomach when Party Chief Li and Secretary Wu told her it had to be me. I think she is hoping that the mystery woman is never found, that this crime is never solved at all."

Confused, Fatty Deng asked, "I can understand that Lucy Fu would not want to be associated with any murder, and would want to hide her presence here, but, if she believes the mystery woman to be the murderer, why did she not name her?"

"Because I believe this mystery woman to be some kind of paid companion."

"A prostitute?"

"Yes – but in this instance let us call her an escort as her duties probably extended beyond the bedroom. It is likely she was paid for by the family Fu, maybe even employed by the family Fu on a long-term basis, and given as a gift for a night, or a week, or a month, or even longer, to make Primo Gong happy. Remember his wife left him, took the children back to the United States. And being a very busy businessman, he did not have time to waste looking for a date. A gift of a woman is a very old way of ingratiating oneself with a powerful man such as Primo Gong. It is the sort of thing the family

Fu would do even though they are powerful and wealthy in their own right."

"But couldn't Lucy Fu just be covering for a close friend?"

Prosecutor Xu snorted with derision. "Lucy Fu doesn't have close friends."

"Then how do we track this mystery woman down?"

"Difficult without forensic support. All we have of her are the red shoes under the chair, the bloody fingerprints you found, and a single, very long, wavy hair I discovered in the shower in the en suite bathroom. Lucy Fu did a real job on this apartment. But we will find her. Someone will know her. Then I will show the world what kind of woman Lucy Fu really is."

"Prosecutor, if there was no intruder, if the mystery woman didn't kill Primo Gong, and if Lucy Fu didn't kill him either, then who did kill him?"

"Ah, the first question you should be asking is: '*How* was Primo Gong killed?'" replied Prosecutor Xu, with a self-satisfied smirk.

"But you said gunshot."

"Do you smell gunpowder residue?"

"No, but I am now assuming it is many hours since Primo Gong was shot."

"That is a good point, Investigator Deng. We will have to establish a timeline for Primo Gong's last movements. However, I want you to look closely at the body. Apart from searching Primo Gong's pockets, wasting my time looking for his phone, I haven't touched him. I think we will see something very interesting when we turn him over."

Unsure of what she was up to, and surprised by how comfortable Prosecutor Xu was with the dead – his mother would not be caught alone in the same room as a dead body due to her fear of hungry ghosts – Fatty Deng did as he was instructed, wishing he had had the foresight to keep a stock of latex forensic gloves with him. Trying not to clamber all over the bed, with a little bit of effort they clumsily turned Primo Gong, who was heavier than he looked, over onto his left side. What Fatty Deng saw amazed him, as did Prosecutor Xu's sharp cry of satisfaction. The bullet that had entered Primo Gong in the dead centre of his chest had travelled right through him, leaving a massive exit wound in his back, a wound so big that Fatty Deng reckoned he could lose his fist in it. Blood had poured from the wound, soaking the coverlet. Fatty Deng saw bits of skin and flecks of white cartilage in the pooled blood. No small calibre weapon had done this much damage.

Fatty Deng cast his eyes more carefully now over the bed and saw blood spatter he had not noticed before, some even on the back wall behind the bed. Just below a more traditional painting, a landscape, he saw a couple of holes in the wall.

Prosecutor Xu had been following his gaze. "I tried to get the bullets out but they were too deeply embedded. But there is something else you should see."

She led him to the en suite bathroom. He thought she was to show him some more evidence there but she merely washed her hands. Thinking that to be a good idea, he did the same. Then she took him back across the bedroom, to the window directly facing the end of the bed and the body of Primo Gong. Fatty Deng saw the blinds moving gently again in the slight breeze and could hear the torrential rain falling outside. Below the blinds, on the carpet, he noticed shards of glass and realised what an idiot he had been. The window had not been opened at all. Prosecutor Xu pressed a button on the wall and the blinds began to rise, soon to reveal the large irregular hole that had been punched in the tough, tempered glass.

"Lucy Fu must have lowered the blinds after the murder, not realising that the shots had come from the outside," said Prosecutor Xu. "She had already decided that the mystery woman was the culprit, that a stray bullet had taken out the window."

Fuck, thought Fatty Deng, staring at the massive hole in the window. How could Lucy Fu imagine the shots came from anywhere other than outside? He considered for a moment that Lucy Fu might somehow be complicit in the murder, that only a fool or someone with a guilty conscience would have lowered the blinds and covered the hole. And Lucy Fu, by all accounts, had never been a fool. But he quickly dismissed the thought – for now at least. Prosecutor Xu had been first on the scene, had actually spoken to Lucy Fu. He would let himself be guided by her initial gut-feeling about what was what.

"I don't know how many shots in total," continued Prosecutor Xu.

"A police SWAT team will usually shoot out a window before attempting a kill shot...to avoid nasty deflections," said Fatty Deng.

"Unless, that is, the target was standing right up to the window looking out."

Fatty Deng glanced back at Primo Gong's body, imagining the window blinds to have been fully raised, perhaps so Primo Gong and his companion could look out at the storm. The businessman would have been standing near to the foot of the bed, maybe talking with the mystery woman who was sitting in the chair. The first shot punches a hole in the window. Then, before Primo Gong can react, a second shot takes him in the centre of his chest, ripping through his heart, the impact throwing him back on the bed. Then the mystery woman jumps out of her chair to go to her lover's aid, trying to stop the blood pulsing from his chest, unaware of the massive wound in his back, not realising that he had probably been dead before he had hit the bed, that there was nothing to be done. Another shot comes in. Maybe she moves her head at the last moment. The shot grazes her or goes wide. Her only thought then is to escape the apartment. Down on her hands and knees to avoid further bullets, forgetting her shoes, she crawls through the apartment, and out of the door. Then she is up on her bare feet, running down the corridor, stumbling at the dogleg, gets up again, and finally makes it into the lift.

The poor woman!

She must have been terrified!

As Fatty Deng stared out of the window through the hole made by the bullets, looking out into the night, he felt his own fear, imagining the sniper lining up on his own chest. He steeled himself, not wanting to embarrass himself in front of Prosecutor Xu, telling himself that the sniper was long gone.

"I stood here for ages trying to figure out which building the bullets had come from," said Prosecutor Xu. "There is only one place that looks directly into this apartment, one place that could have provided the shooter with the correct, flat trajectory. Even so, it was a hell of a shot."

She pointed to an office building directly opposite Plum Tree Pagodas, maybe a hundred or so metres away, hardly visible through the pouring rain, especially with the light on in Primo Gong's apartment. Fatty Deng squinted out into the darkness. He could just make out the top floor of the building, which appeared to be level with the fifth floor of Plum Tree Pagodas. Only a single light burned in the building and that was on the fourth floor. There were no other signs of life.

"Well, aren't you impressed with my analysis?" she asked, very proud of herself.

Fatty Deng was, but before he replied, to give her the praise she thought she was due, he kept staring out of the window, trying to get his bearings around Plum Tree Pagodas, to see for himself if there were any other possible firing points for the shooter. There were none. Prosecutor Xu was right. The top floor of the building opposite was the only place that had a direct line of sight into Primo Gong's apartment.

"I wonder who owns that building?" asked Prosecutor Xu.

Fatty Deng leaned closer to the hole in the window and looked down to the ground. A high wall separated Plum Tree Pagodas and its gardens from the narrow alley beyond, and on the other side of the alley were the backyards of a line of two-storey shops. Looking over the roofs of the shops was a street that seemed familiar to him, and on the other side of the street from the shops loomed the office building. He shook his head. He should recognise where he was. He knew this part of the city quite well. It was just that he had not seen it from this vantage point before. He stared down again at the line of shops and he suddenly realised he was looking down on Liberation Street, that the rooftop of the shop directly in front of him was that of the famous cigarette shop, the Lucky Dragon Tobacco Emporium, which meant the office building across the street from it, from where the shooter had fired, must be—

Fatty Deng suddenly grabbed Prosecutor Xu in a bear hug, lifting her up off the floor, making her squeal, and carried her as fast as he could out of the bedroom and into the short corridor beyond, only pausing briefly to punch off the bedroom light, and only putting her down when they were out of sight of whoever might have been watching them from the top floor of the office building.

"Forgive me, Prosecutor," he gasped, in pain, clutching at his side again, thinking he might have done himself some damage, hoping he had not re-opened any of his old wounds.

She was furious. "What has got into you? The shooter is long gone. I told you I spent a good ten minutes staring out of that window before I lowered the blinds again and nothing happened to me. You are not right in the head. You have to go see Doctor Tang."

"You don't understand, Prosecutor," he said, still struggling to get his breath, to get over his shock.

"What don't I understand?"

"I know that building."

"You recognise it?"

"It's police."

She laughed out loud at him. "It's not police. I have memorised the location of every police station in the city."

"I did not say it's a police station."

"Then what is it?"

"An old Black House."

She put a hand to her mouth. "A Black House?"

"It hasn't been used to make prisoners disappear for years. As far as I know it's now used for confidential file storage – or at least it was up until a few years ago when I was still police. I promise you, Prosecutor, no one can get access to that building without knowing the security codes to get in."

"Investigator Deng, let me understand you correctly: are you saying our shooter is police?"

Fatty Deng's mouth was dry. "Without a doubt."

FOUR

A s they headed away from the airport, Night Na asked, "How was your mother?"

"Full of her best advice as ever," Philip Ye replied, more bitterly than he had intended, made downcast by the appearance of the woman with the unusually long, wavy hair, who had confounded him by her expression of gratitude, and who had certainly just passed into the afterlife.

"It is right that we honour our parents," said Night Na. "But sometimes it is best that we honour them from a distance."

Night Na drove Philip Ye into the city, back to the Ye family mansion situated in the heart of the Wuhou District, and modelled on a Victorian English country manor house complete with extensive gardens. The city was awash, the rain showing no signs of abating. Philip Ye wondered if he should have remained in England, taken himself off to Yorkshire, alone, to remind himself of happier times with Isobel, who had been dead these last fifteen years and more. But then the woman with the long, wavy hair again intruded on his thoughts. It was right that he had come back to Chengdu. There was work to do.

"Your father has been up to no good while you have been away," said Night Na.

"Why am I not surprised?"

"A new plot to undermine the Shanghai Clique, we suspect."

By 'we', Night Na meant he and his twin brother, Day Na, once employed to enforce Ye Zihao's house-arrest, but who had since, by some sort of weird and inexplicable osmosis, moved into the Ye family mansion and who now worked in many varied and mysterious ways to serve the interests of the family Ye.

"I wish he would give up this pointless war," said Philip Ye.

"The problem is that your father has convinced himself he can defeat the Shanghai Clique," said Night Na.

The Shanghai Clique.

After the Wenchuan Earthquake had devastated much of Sichuan Province – miraculously Chengdu had been relatively untouched – and whether due to the perceived lack of compassion from the Mayor's Office, or due to the mounting rumours of corruption and abuse of power, Ye Zihao had been summarily dismissed from his joint post as mayor and Chengdu party chief. Unceremoniously ejected from the Party, he had been placed under house-arrest to await formal charges – which, to the surprise of many, had still not come.

To fill the power vacuum in Chengdu, the Party had 'parachuted' in a new mayor *and* a new party chief, as well as numerous executives, functionaries, and administrators, hailing, in the main, from Shanghai, with orders not only to take over the management of the city but also to defang Ye Zihao's loyal local following. Ye Zihao had cleverly named this 'foreign invasion force' the Shanghai Clique – a pejorative that had since entered into the common lexicon of the city.

The Shanghai Clique had worked quickly to cleanse all the local government departments and all the local Party committees of suspected Ye Zihao supporters. They had even dismissed a large number of police officers from Chengdu PSB, regardless of rank and experience, to make way for police officers imported from Shanghai and elsewhere – an event still referred to by many in the PSB as 'The Purge'. But, if one listened to Ye Zihao for any length of time, one would get the impression that the conquest of Chengdu by the Shanghai Clique was not as total as they might wish, and that their inability to formally bring charges against him for his supposed crimes was proof that he still had many friends left in the city, as well as in Beijing. Sooner or later, Ye Zihao believed, the Party would see the error of its ways, the Shanghai Clique would be sent packing, and he would occupy the Mayor's Office once more. It was only a matter of time. And if he could cause a little trouble here and there for the Shanghai Clique in the meantime, then so much the better.

It was a foolish dream, thought Philip Ye.

A dangerous dream.

"My father will yet bring destruction upon us all with his constant plotting," remarked Philip Ye.

"That is a fact," replied Night Na, smiling, seemingly untroubled by the possibility.

"So, what has he been up to?"

"It is hard to say," replied Night Na. "He has a new woman in his life. A journalist. American. And, for a *laowai*, quite good-looking."

Laowai – foreigner (informal, sometimes impolite).

"Is she older than me?" asked Philip Ye.

"I think so."

"That, at least, is something."

"Ah, but Boss, this seems all business. She doesn't stay the night. She comes for dinner in the evening. And then all they do is whisper and giggle together like children. They only speak English so we can't understand a word. We've checked up on her, though. She's freelance, focusing on international business. She does the rounds: Singapore, Manila, Tokyo, Bangkok, Hanoi, Hong Kong, Macao and Beijing."

"Reputation?"

"The best."

"Is she watched?"

"She has a PSB tail – but no one has tried to stop her coming to the house and meeting with your father."

"What's her name?"

"Stacey Corrigan," replied Night Na, having some difficulty with the pronunciation. "She seems quite smitten with your father."

"They always are until they find out what he's really like."

Nothing more was said until the iron gates leading to the house automatically swung open and Night Na steered the Mercedes slowly up the drive. Philip Ye was surprised to see his father in the doorway of the house, smoking his pipe, waiting for them.

"I told you he's up to something," said Night Na.

Ye Zihao walked out into the rain to help Philip Ye with his luggage. When they were all back in the house, with the door closed against the weather, Ye Zihao asked, "How was your mother?"

"She has suddenly got it in her head that I should be married."

"What utter foolishness!" exclaimed Ye Zihao.

"Then Father, would you please call her and tell her so."

"I will, Philip...do not worry."

"It would be nice to have a woman about the house," said Night Na.

"I hear Prosecutor Xu is available," said his brother Day Na, walking down the stairs, having just got out of bed, grinning, dressed only in slippers and a silk robe.

Night Na laughed out loud. But he was the only one. All Day Na received from both Ye Zihao and Philip Ye was a hard stare.

In the kitchen the mood lightened when they all gathered about Philip Ye to see what gifts his mother had sent from England. Philip Ye presented his father a boxed Dunhill pipe and a broad selection of pipe tobaccos in tins. And he gave the brothers Na each a box of twenty-five large Cuban cigars – Hoyo de Monterey Epicure No. 2 – much to their great pleasure.

"Your mother has spent too much money this time," said Ye Zihao, delighted with his pipe, examining it from every angle before testing it between his teeth.

Philip Ye had to agree, more than a thousand British pounds. And it wasn't as if Ye Zihao, or the brothers Na for that matter, could not place a phone call and get the same products delivered to the door the very next day if they so wished. But, like children, they all loved receiving gifts, and Philip Ye's mother was not short of money. She had her own inherited wealth, her salary from the university, some profitable consultancies, and the money that Ye Zihao sent her every year – Philip Ye did not know how much – for the advice she gave him on which European or American tech companies he should invest Ye family money in.

None of them asked Philip Ye what his mother had given him. They already knew the answer: nothing. Philip Ye had received not one gift from his mother, not even on his birthday, ever since he had made the momentous decision, over ten years before, to enlist in the police.

"I hear you have a new friend," said Philip Ye to his father.

"Oh, Philip, you will adore her," replied Ye Zihao. "She is a fine lady: intelligent, cultured, and very, very well-informed. She is coming to dinner again tonight. You must join us."

"She's an American."

"Philip, don't be so prejudiced," cautioned Ye Zihao. "Old enmities must be forgiven if China is to embrace the world."

"The way you have forgiven the Shanghai Clique?"

"That enmity is not past – and you know it!" exclaimed Ye Zihao, angrily. Then his mood softened again. "You will join us for dinner, won't you?"

"I would love to, Father."

Very pleased, Ye Zihao gathered up his tins of tobacco and retreated to his study. Leaving the brothers Na to gossip and examine their boxes of cigars, Philip Ye prepared himself some green tea and took the steaming cup into the garden. He sat for a while under the awning, watching the rain fall upon the lake. He checked his watch. Superintendent Zuo Lu, his friend and colleague, should still be at his desk at PSB HQ, working the night shift as always. Philip Ye took his phone from his pocket and dialed.

"What?" was the weak reply, not sounding like Zuo at all.

"Are you alright, old man?"

"Ah, Philip, it is you. You have returned home. No, I am not alright. I have been poisoned. I have been in bed for days. I am there still."

"Then who is looking after Ma Meili?"

"It is me you should be worrying about. I have been so sick, throwing up day and night. The doctor said that if I had been a few years older, and not so naturally fit, I would have died. The poisoning was quite deliberate...quite deliberate."

"Someone tried to kill you?"

"Zizi."

Philip Ye laughed. "Your adoring wife?"

"She waited until the day you went away. That evening she served me a shellfish dinner. I should have realised I was in trouble when she chose not to partake, saying she had eaten at work. I did not spot the cold glint in her eye. How can she work as a nurse and yet not have one ounce of compassion in her body? You must come and visit me, Philip. You must question her. You must discover why she hates me so much."

"I will, I promise – but in the meantime I need to know if there has been any fresh trade, particularly a woman with long, wavy hair, who—"

"Philip, has the flight made you deaf? I have no idea what is going on at work. I have been throwing up day and night this last week while Zizi just stands and laughs at me. You must come and arrest her. If you don't come visit soon, she will poison me again and all that will be left of me will be a stinking corpse."

"I will come – I promise. Now go back to sleep, old man, while I phone the PSB and discover what's what."

Philip Ye immediately contacted PSB Dispatch. "This is Superintendent Ye, Homicide. Have there been any suspicious deaths or murders reported across the city in the last week?"

"Ah, one moment, Superintendent," replied the young woman, who, after a brief pause, said, "No murders, no suspicious deaths, two suicides only: a depressed student living in the Jinsha Residential District; the other an old woman who threw herself from a roof in the Caojia Alley Residential District. It was so sad. Her son refused to visit her."

"You are sure?"

"About the son, Superintendent?"

"No, that there have been no other suspicious deaths in the last week."

"Oh, yes, Superintendent."

Philip Ye put his phone down on the bench next to him, relaxed and sipped his tea. The body of the glamorous ghost with the wavy hair was yet to be found. So much the better. He needed to be in on the investigation from the start.

He checked his watch again.

5.30 a.m.

Not long until dawn.

He had time to close his eyes for a few minutes before he called Ma Meili to discover what she had been up to. Without Superintendent Zuo to supervise her, he dreaded to think how she had been spending her time.

The pounding of the rain upon the lake soon lulled him into a deep sleep. Then he was dreaming, watching Prosecutor Xu walking up and down the courtroom in her high heels, flirting with the panel of judges, smiling for the cameras, and pointing a beautifully manicured finger at some hapless defendant. He was fascinated by her performance, disturbed he could not take his eyes off her. When he woke from the dream it was fully light, the rain still pouring from a leaden sky.

He checked his watch.

11.05 a.m.

His heart skipped a beat.

He phoned Ma Meili.

"Yes, Superintendent," she said. "Have you returned from your holiday so soon?"

"Do we have fresh trade?" he asked.

"Oh yes, Superintendent, but you need not worry. I have an important clue. A Russian called Trotsky was also killed by the same murderer."

Understanding none of this, he asked, "Where are you?"

"The morgue – it is most exciting."

"I'm on my way," he told her, wishing he had never gone on holiday at all.

FIVE

—◦—

Xu Ya had not enjoyed being manhandled by Investigator Deng out of Primo Gong's bedroom. But, as she got her breath, and rubbed the small of her back, sore from when Investigator Deng had lifted her off the ground, she saw real fear in his eyes. He'd not been himself since the knife attack that had nearly ended his life three months before. He was very nervy these days, more short-tempered. He had also been robbed of that police officer 'swagger', that natural self-confidence she had seen in him when she had first recruited him. Thankfully, there was nothing wrong with his memory. She had originally selected him not just for his familiarity with the police and their working methods – being a prosecutor assigned to the Legal and Disciplinary Procuracy Section, much of her work revolved around police oversight – but *also* for his intimate knowledge of the city. And so, if Investigator Deng said that the office building across the way was an old police Black House then she was content to take that as a fact. The sniper might well have gone. But, all this time, anyone could have been watching her through binoculars, wanting to see who had been called in to investigate Primo Gong's death. Since the trial of Commissioner Ho a few weeks before, where she had had a starring role as senior prosecutor, there would not be a single police officer in the city who would not know her face. The very thought made her shiver.

"It is rumoured that Ye Zihao still has a lot of friends within the PSB," she said.

"That is true," replied Investigator Deng.

"However, I cannot believe, regardless of how ruthless he is, of how much he hates the Shanghai Clique, that Ye Zihao would arrange the killing of an innocent man just to undermine Party Chief Li's personal finances."

"I agree."

"However, we cannot yet rule Ye Zihao out of this enquiry."

"No, Prosecutor."

"It would be wise to check if Primo Gong has had any business dealings with the Ye family business empire. It is possible Primo Gong might have crossed swords with Ye Zihao without ever meeting him in person. But, as Primo Gong was friends with Party Chief Li and Mayor Cang and Lucy Fu, I am sure they would have steered him well away from any of the Ye commercial interests."

"That is a fair assumption."

"So, it is Chengdu PSB that has to be our prime focus."

"Yes, Prosecutor."

"Then it is fortunate that Party Chief Li decided from the outset that the police were not to be involved in this investigation, even if he did make that decision for personal reasons."

"Very fortunate."

Xu Ya stared up at Investigator Deng and smiled. He looked glum, depressed probably by the thought that his old colleagues in the police were up to their necks in this murder. He also looked pale, sickly, and not a little weary. But she was relieved he was standing next to her now, that he had come when she had called. She needed him. She would not be able to do this on her own.

"We must tread carefully, Investigator Deng."

"I agree," he replied.

"I am thinking we should conceal much of what we have discovered here from Party Chief Li and Secretary Wu for the time being. Learning about the Black House and Lucy Fu's interference with the crime scene might cause Party Chief Li to lose his temper and overreact. We don't want police fighting police on the streets of Chengdu."

"That is sensible, Prosecutor."

"When we are done here, we will go and listen to what Party Chief Li and Secretary Wu have to say. And then we will go about our work quietly, methodically, and scientifically, and not announce our conclusions until we are certain."

"That is a good plan, Prosecutor."

"I am sorry for bringing you back to work before you are fully recovered."

"I was getting bored at home."

"This will be a difficult investigation."

"It is what we get paid the big money for."

His attempt at levity made her laugh. He was strong. He was capable. Together they made a good team. Together they would find justice for Primo Gong.

"Investigator Deng, when we are interviewing witnesses, trying to establish a timeline for Primo Gong's movements, trying to discover when and why and how he crossed paths with the police, we must have a cover story in place to hide the truth about his death. We will have to say that we are working on a major corruption case, that Primo Gong, although wholly innocent, is presently helping the Procuratorate with our enquiries."

"We are to lie?"

She sighed. "What other choice do we have? We have been placed in an unhappy situation. I know that this is not correct legal process but there is precedent. If the police are involved, as seems likely, then this will be a highly sensitive investigation with important political ramifications. And we also have Party Chief Li's personal wealth to protect."

"At the expense of others?"

"I don't like it anymore that you do. But, as my old law tutor, Beloved Mister Qin, used to say, 'The law as written is not always as it is done.'"

"Beloved?"

"He was very kind to me, Investigator Deng."

"Ah."

She thumped Investigator Deng on the chest, forgetting about his injuries. "Not in that way, you idiot!"

"Prosecutor, I didn't think that—"

"Yes, you did – I saw it in your eyes. Believe it or not there are some good men left in China. And Beloved Mister Qin is in the afterlife now, if you believe in such things – which I don't – so be respectful. Now let us concentrate and get down to work. We will lower the blinds in the bedroom, leave all as it was. But, before we leave, we will search the whole apartment again for anything I might have missed. We will need the occupancy list for the whole building and a copy of the concierge's logbook – though we shouldn't expect much cooperation from the family Fu. Before this case is done, I promise you, I will deal with Lucy Fu. We also need to get inside the Black House."

Investigator Deng shook his head. "That will be impossible, Prosecutor. Even to try, to pretend it's an inspection, will tip the police off to our investigation if they don't already know. There may be people I can speak to...people who may help. But one false move on our part and we might start a landslide that cannot be stopped."

She thought this wise. "Yes, you must utilise your old contacts. Now let's get down to work."

With the blinds lowered and the light switched back on, they searched the whole apartment again. Apart from another long, wavy hair found on the back of one of the chairs in the lounge, and a fashion magazine left casually on top of a tall bookcase that seemed not to be Primo Gong's usual reading material, they found nothing else of interest. Investigator Deng carefully rolled the magazine up in the hope that once the forensic embargo was lifted they might be able to find some latent prints. They went up and down the corridor on the fifth floor knocking on doors but got no replies. Then, with nothing more to do, Xu Ya put the pair of red shoes under her arm, closed the door to apartment 5014, and together they descended to the lobby. The concierge was still sitting behind his desk, pretending to be making a note in his logbook.

"Mister Han, we are done for now," she told him.

"Very good, Prosecutor."

"However, I will need a current occupancy list for Plum Tree Pagodas, the names and addresses of all staff who have access to the building, whether they were on shift last night or not, a copy of your logbook going back six months, copies of your CCTV for the last week – here in the lobby and in the underground car park – as well as a copy of the electronic record from the car park of all the comings and goings. That should do for a start."

Mister Han looked at her, sadly. "Prosecutor, forgive me, I cannot let you have those things." He produced a business card from his pocket and passed it to her. "All requests must be put to Mister Xi."

Xu Ya examined the business card and read:

Xi Huan
Senior Legal Counsel
FUBI International Industries

Unsurprised, this did not prevent Xu Ya saying, "This is a disgrace, Mister Han."

He lowered his head in shame. "I am also required to tell you that our CCTV has been broken these last two weeks and the secure entry system to the car park has not worked properly since the building was completed last year."

She levelled a finger at him. "When I am ready, Mister Han, you will be summoned for formal interview at the Procuratorate. Lie to me again and I promise it will not go well for you."

He nodded without looking up at her.

She placed the red shoes on his desk, reached over and pulled his logbook toward her, spinning it around so she could read the last few entries.

2.10 a.m. – report of disturbance in Apt. 5014
2.15 a.m. – access gained to Apt. 5014
2.20 a. m. – contacted Mister Xi to report the suspicious death of a tenant

There were two further entries: the time she had arrived and the time Investigator Deng had arrived. But there was no mention of Lucy Fu, Party Chief Li, or Secretary Wu. It was as if they had never visited Plum Tree Pagodas at all.

Xu Ya slid the logbook back toward Mister Han in disgust, wasting no more words on him. She believed nothing of what she had just read. She considered the logbook as untrustworthy as him. It was time to leave Plum Tree Pagodas behind. She picked up the red shoes and turned her back on Mister Han. She pushed open the glass door of the lobby and stepped outside, glad to be away from the stench of blood and death and deceit, even if the rain was still falling. It was fully light. They had missed the dawn while searching Primo Gong's apartment. And now a day of hard work lay ahead.

"My car is just across the street," said Investigator Deng.

Xu Ya nodded, lingering for a moment, wondering which way the mystery woman had fled, what had become of her, whether she still lived, whether it had been intended that she be murdered alongside Primo Gong in Apartment 5014, whether the murderer was somewhere out in the city hunting her still. Then Xu Ya hurried through the rain to catch up with Investigator Deng.

SIX

— · —

T he maid was sitting on the damp concrete stairs outside of the apartment, rocking back and forth, wailing noisily. At first sight, Constable Ma Meili, of the Homicide Section of the Criminal Investigation Department of Chengdu PSB, wanted to slap her. Instead, reluctantly sticking to protocol, Ma Meili merely flashed her badge and ID.

"Where have you been?" asked the maid, wiping her eyes. "It is not respectful. I phoned almost two hours ago. The General has been sitting all night unattended to."

"Stop snivelling," replied Ma Meili. "I have no time for people who snivel."

"But—"

"No, you listen! I am police – when I talk, you shut your mouth."

The maid did as she was told, taken aback by the rudeness of this plainclothes policewoman, the largest woman she had ever seen – a real bruiser to be sure.

"That's better," said Ma Meili, who believed whole-heartedly that the authority of the police should always be respected.

To be fair, however, the maid did have a point. She had phoned the emergency number 110 just after six, saying that there had been a murder in an apartment block in the Xiaojia River Residential District. A uniform had then been tasked from Xiaojia River Police Station to have a look. On arrival, he had confirmed to the dispatcher that the death did indeed look suspicious and that Homicide should be notified immediately, and then had, quite inexplicably, gone off to find some breakfast without sealing off the scene or asking for additional uniformed presence. Meanwhile, the dispatcher had phoned around looking for any available homicide detective to attend. Unfortunately, it was early Saturday morning, not the best time to find homicide detectives sitting at their desks. There was also a well-documented dearth of trained homicide detectives in the city. The dispatcher had been forced to cast a wider and wider net, phoning police stations all over Chengdu, until, after having a flash of inspiration, she had phoned the Homicide office in PSB HQ to speak to Ma Meili.

"Constable Ma, I know that Xiaojia River Residential District is outside your assigned patch. And I know Superintendent Zuo is off sick and that Superintendent Ye is on holiday in England visiting his mother. But you must help me. There has been a suspicious death and there is no one else in the city either able or willing to respond."

Under orders not to do anything without supervision, the dispatcher had put Ma Meili in an impossible position. No one had expected Superintendent Zuo to fall sick just as Superintendent Ye had flown out of the country. Left in the office on her own, with no direction from anybody, and thinking it necessary to cover both day and night shifts herself, Ma Meili had taken to sleeping at her desk, hoping that her cat Yoyo was not missing her – he was being well-looked after by Superintendent Ye's nephews – and petrified, as had now happened, that the phone might ring.

"If I do as you ask, Superintendent Ye will lose his temper with me when he returns from holiday," Ma Meili told the dispatcher.

"Please, Sister, I am begging you. The only other homicide detective on duty is Supervisor Lin from Chunxi Road Station. And the last death he investigated he concluded was a suicide even though the victim had been stabbed twenty times in the chest!"

The dispatcher was funny. She made Ma Meili laugh telling such a silly made-up story. Or, at least, Ma Meili hoped it was made-up.

"I will attend," said Ma Meili, believing she had no choice, that, as police, regardless of what Superintendent Ye might say, she was duty-bound to respond to any call for help.

"Oh, thank you, Sister," said the dispatcher. "You are such a good person. My name is Yanmei. I will owe you. And if Superintendent Ye gets mad when he comes back from holiday, you tell him to call me. *He* can lose his temper with me any day."

Days later, Yanmei would phone Ma Meili to apologise, to say that if only she had spoken to one of her fellow dispatchers, she would have learned that not only had Superintendent Ye returned early from his holiday, but that he had already been in touch inquiring if there had been any recent suspicious deaths.

So, unaware of this, Ma Meili had got up from her desk, put on her lightweight summer coat against the rain, picked up her waterproof shoulder bag which contained the homicide kit she had assembled for herself – notebook, camera, pens, pencils, sketching-pad, latex gloves, a full forensic body suit complete with shoe covers, exhibit tags and bags, police tape, a street atlas of Chengdu, and much more besides – ran down the stairs and out of the headquarters building, and was waiting for a bus to take her most of the way in the right direction when she was lucky enough to catch a ride with a boisterous SWAT team on their way to a narcotics raid in the south of the city. Though she was thrown about a bit in the back of the SWAT truck – the driver was eating, smoking and talking on the radio all at the same time – it was still a lot of fun.

"Ma Meili, you must come and join us," the SWAT team implored her. "SWAT is the best. We are one big happy family. Homicide is far too boring and depressing for an action-woman such as you."

And, to be sure, Ma Meili was seriously tempted. Homicide had turned out to be nothing liked she had expected. Although Superintendent Zuo had been helpful and always the perfect gentleman, Superintendent Ye had proved himself to be anything but. If Ma Meili had been a Buddhist and a believer in karma, she would have assumed she had done something truly awful in a past life to have ended up under Superintendent Ye's direct authority.

With Superintendent Zuo off sick and Superintendent Ye out of the country, the head of SWAT, Commissioner Zhu Shouqing, had popped into the office a few days before, knowing the coast was clear. "Constable Ma, you are wasted in Homicide," he had told her. "And everyone has been talking about how badly Superintendent Ye is treating you. Come and join us in SWAT. We can use a woman with your strength and skills. Homicide is not for you. Homicide is for tired and gloomy old men more interested in death than life."

Ma Meili had promised Commissioner Zhu that she would seriously consider his offer.

With much laughter and a few jeers and whistles, and cries of, "Don't forget the SWAT party on Sunday evening!" the SWAT team dropped her off a short walk away from the Xiaojia River Residential District. By the time she found the correct apartment block she still had a smile on her face despite the torrential rain, much cheered by the encounter with the SWAT team. That smile had faded, however, when she had discovered the wailing maid on the stairs.

"What is your name?" asked Ma Meili.

"Ding Jie," replied the maid.

"Where is the body?"

Madame Ding nodded toward the nearby apartment door that had been left ajar. "The door was closed when I got here but it was unlocked. I told the General again and again that he should lock his door. I told him that Chengdu had changed, that gangsters, robbers, and drug addicts were now everywhere. But he wouldn't listen to me. He was always so absorbed in his writing and—"

"That's enough! I must think and I must work," said Ma Meili.

Madame Ding clamped her mouth shut, terrified. Ma Meili dropped her shoulder bag to the floor, pulled her pistol, and pushed open the apartment door.

"The murderer is long gone," said Madame Ding, uncomprehending.

Ma Meili ignored her. Only a few weeks before, Superintendent Li Cheng who oversaw the PSB HQ armoury – a very kind man – had given Ma Meili a stern talking to, lecturing her on how she could never be too careful if attending a crime scene alone.

"Constable Ma," he had told her, "I am sure you will have already noticed how both Superintendent Ye and Superintendent Zuo are careless of their own safety. Do not emulate them. They have charmed lives. The rest of us do not. Even if it means contaminating the scene, always make sure it is secure before you do anything else."

Compared to the relative cool of the stairwell, the small apartment was hot and stuffy. It also stank of stale cigarette smoke and death. Ma Meili moved from room to room, sweat beading on her forehead, her senses alert to every possibility, her pistol held before her, the pistol moving with the track of her eyes. But, as Madame Ding had already told her, the murderer was long gone. She found the victim sat at a writing desk in a tiny study filled with books, magazines, and papers. The man was bent over, face down on the surface of the desk, a strange implement buried in the back of his head, congealed blood coating his short silver-white hair, a pool of blood covering the papers strewn across the desk. Flies already troubled the body. No expert on these things, Ma Meili thought it likely the victim had never even seen his attacker and that this crime was hours old at least. She put her pistol away and returned to the stairwell.

"Who is he?"

"General Jin Huiliang," replied Madame Ding, wiping away more tears from her cheeks.

"You worked for him?"

"Yes, most mornings, a bit of cooking, some cleaning, and I also shopped for him twice a week. In the evenings I have a second job cleaning at a local primary school."

"I thought soldiers lived in barracks."

"The General has been retired for years. All he does is write these days. I cannot understand who would hurt him, who would creep into his home and do such a thing. There was no finer man living under Heaven."

Ma Meili took her phone from her pocket and dialled. Her call was answered after a couple of rings.

"Constable Ma, what a pleasant surprise," said Doctor Kong. "Are you well?"

"Quite well, Doctor, thank you."

"I hope you are not out in all this rain."

"I was but now I am not. I am sorry to disturb you, Doctor, but I have a body needing examination in an apartment block in the Xiaojia River Residential District. To my untrained and inexperienced eyes it is murder."

"That is not your usual working area, Constable Ma."

"No one else would attend."

"Well, good for you, Constable! The more you see, the more you learn. I wish there were more police like you. Give me the full address and I will be along presently."

Ma Meili did as she was asked, pleased that Doctor Kong Ai, the city pathologist, seemed to work seven days a week and that she would be along soon, accompanied by her enviable confidence and impressive learning, as well as her team of white-suited young men and women who would scour the apartment for evidence and clues.

"Have you moved anything in the apartment?" Ma Meili asked the maid.

"I am no thief!"

"That's not what I asked you. I need to know if all is as it was when you found him."

Slightly mollified, Madame Ding said, "I touched nothing. I arrived just before six to do some cleaning and cook him his breakfast when—"

"You have a key?"

"Yes, he gave me a key. But, as I told you, the General was always careless about his safety. The door was closed but unlocked so I didn't need to use the key. When I went in I just knew something terrible had happened. And then, when I found him at his desk like that...oh, I have seen nothing worse in my life. I ran back outside and phoned the police. And except for that idiot who came to have a look around who would not even talk to me, you are the first police to arrive. It is a disgrace. You police have no compassion. It is like you don't even care."

"Did Jin Huiliang have any enemies?"

Madame Ding was incensed by the question. "Enemies? How ridiculous! There was no nicer man. To meet the General was to love him. Anyway, it was a madman who did this. Chengdu is not what it used to be. Now crazy people wander the streets and no one does anything. You police are all useless."

Madame Ding blew her nose and then started wiping tears from her eyes again.

Ma Meili pulled her camera from her shoulder bag as well as a pair of latex gloves and her protective bodysuit. "Don't move," she told Madame Ding. "I will need to take a note of your address in case I need to question you further. And when the forensic team arrive they will need to take your fingerprints and a DNA swab. You do not look like a murderer, but who is to say that you are not? Just know this, that if you run while I am working in the apartment I will hunt you down without mercy."

Madame Ding, trembling with fear, began to sob again. Ma Meili left her to it, and after pulling on her full bodysuit over her clothes re-entered the apartment. Superintendent Ye had given Ma Meili a number of books about crime scene analysis. The books had bored her silly even though some of the photographs of various people murdered in different ways were interesting. But it was Doctor Kong who had brought crime scenes to life for Ma Meili. Doctor Kong was so clever, so learned, and such a good teacher. The same could not be said for Superintendent Ye, who hardly explained anything he was doing (let alone what he was thinking), who got irritated by the most straightforward and – in Ma Meili's opinion – the most sensible of questions, and who, when he did occasionally deign to speak to her, often forgot himself and spoke in English – a language Ma Meili had no knowledge of – and who most of the time made it very clear that he did not want her around.

Ma Meili moved from room to room in Jin Huiliang's apartment, taking photographs using the digital camera she had bought herself just for this very purpose. She photographed everything, even though, when the forensic team arrived, they would do the same. But Ma Meili had learned that taking her own photographs helped her focus, helped her understand the crime scene better. As Doctor Kong had instructed her, the smallest detail could make all the difference. She photographed the kitchen where a cup of tea, cold, lay untouched, perhaps forgotten by Jin Huiliang as soon as he had made it. She photographed the couch in the lounge with a pillow placed at one end. Did Jin Huiliang prefer sleeping there rather than in his own bed? She photographed the large, framed black and white photograph of a group of young soldiers standing together on some desolate hillside that was hanging pride of place on the lounge wall, the soldiers all looking filthy and exhausted, yet smiling nevertheless for the camera. There was no title to the photograph, no clue as to where it had been taken, but it intrigued Ma Meili nevertheless. She photographed the bedroom and the narrow single-bed that did not look as if it had been slept in. She photographed the bathroom, which, she noted approvingly, sparkled as if it had only just been cleaned by the maid. And finally, in the study, she photographed Jin Huiliang's body from every angle she could, taking close-ups of the strange implement sticking out of his skull, the blood-soaked papers on his desk, the half-open desk-drawer full of pens, paperclips, and a business card carelessly tossed inside. She also took a close-up of the ashtray on the desk, filled to the brim with cigarette butts, and a close-up of the pack of Baisha Blue cigarettes still clutched in Jin Huiliang's left hand as if he was about to take out another cigarette at the very moment he was killed.

Ma Meili then heard a commotion from outside the apartment. She went quickly to investigate. She found to her great pleasure – ignoring the still weeping Madame Ding – Doctor Kong and her forensic team had already arrived and were lugging all their equipment up the stairs.

"Constable Ma, it is good to see you again," said Doctor Kong.

"And you, Doctor," Ma Meili replied, flushing, always slightly unnerved by Doctor Kong's genuine affection for her.

"Where is the miserable Superintendent Ye?"

"On holiday in England."

"Such a pity he doesn't stay there," said Doctor Kong. "He treats you so badly, Constable Ma. No one learns by being shouted at."

"I don't mind," said Ma Meili, untruthfully, but thinking it was her duty to defend her boss.

"Well, I do mind," said Doctor Kong. "I have already complained about his behaviour to Chief of Police Di. Anyway, what do you have for me?"

Ma Meili took Doctor Kong through the apartment and straight into the study. Doctor Kong bent over the body, staring intently at the strange implement lodged in Jin Huiliang's skull.

"What is it?" asked Ma Meili.

"An ice-axe," replied Doctor Kong. "How unusual. You should be aware, Constable Ma, that Trotsky was killed in much the same way."

"Trotsky?"

"A Russian – you should look the case up. I suspect your victim was killed sometime last evening by the look of him but I will know more when I have completed my tests. Constable Ma, would you like to come back with me to the morgue and attend the autopsy? I think the experience will prove very educational for you. I have no other work this morning so we can commence almost immediately."

Speechless at the opportunity being offered to her, Ma Meili could only nod her agreement. This was turning out to be a most auspicious day.

SEVEN

— · —

Any investigation that began with such a catalogue of deception was not going to end well.

So thought Fatty Deng.

Firstly, Lucy Fu had interfered with a crime scene and wilfully misdirected Party Chief Li, Secretary Wu, and Prosecutor Xu. Secondly, Party Chief Li had ordered the concealment of Primo Gong's murder, giving him time to offload his shares in Ambrogetti Global Software first thing Monday morning when the Shanghai Stock Exchange opened for business. Thirdly, Prosecutor Xu had decided to portray Primo Gong's sudden disappearance from society as a simple matter of him helping the Procuratorate with some of its enquiries – a story that surely was also destined not to fill the Shanghai Stock Exchange with confidence, though that could not be helped. Fourthly, Prosecutor Xu had decided, for the good of the city, that it might be best to refrain from mentioning to Party Chief Li and Secretary Wu that not only had Lucy Fu misdirected everyone, but also that Primo Gong had been shot by a sniper from a police Black House. And then, to cap it all, sometime today, over the phone, Fatty Deng was sure to tell his mother – presently having the time of her life on a cruise out on the Yangzi – that he was resting up at home watching TV rather than being back at work and already up to his neck in a case that made his head spin and his skin crawl. Surely, there was going to be a reckoning for so much deception. Surely, he, and everyone else involved, were going straight to hell.

Not that Prosecutor Xu seemed unduly concerned. In the car, as he drove them both to the offices of the Chengdu People's Government to meet with Party Chief Li, she appeared quite buoyant, as if she was actually relishing the challenge that lay ahead. In particular, she was making it very clear that she had it in for Lucy Fu. Fatty Deng was not sure why. There seemed more to her dislike of Lucy Fu than the simple meddling with a crime scene and the telling of a few lies.

"Prosecutor, Lucy Fu is just a distraction," he cautioned her, carefully watching the road ahead, worried that some of the puddles might be deeper than they seemed.

"She has tried to deceive me!"

"Maybe so, but—"

"It is no wonder that Philip Ye dumped her."

"I heard that it was she who dumped him."

Prosecutor Xu turned to him, surprised. "Is that true?"

"According to my mother – and she probably knows more about the family Ye than anybody. My mother says that Lucy Fu quickly realised the drawbacks of dating a man much more beautiful than her."

Prosecutor Xu laughed. "How ridiculous!"

"Is it, Prosecutor? Can you imagine dating Philip Ye, with all the cameras on him rather than on you, with all the other women staring at him, giving you the cold shoulder, trying to figure out how to get him away from you? I'm not saying I have any sympathy for Lucy Fu. It's just that any woman who thinks dating Philip Ye is going to be like living in some marvellous dream is in for quite a shock."

Prosecutor Xu became silent, thoughtful. Then, in a whisper, she said, "That never occurred to me."

"It's why I think Philip Ye has given up dating."

"He has?"

"That's what my mother says. Anyway, I think people like Philip Ye and Lucy Fu are tragic figures."

Prosecutor Xu was amazed. "You do?"

"Absolutely – to have so much and yet be so unhappy."

"I never took you to be a philosopher, Investigator Deng."

"I have thoughts occasionally."

"There is indeed wisdom in what you have just said."

"Thank you, Prosecutor."

"But Lucy Fu is still a liar."

"And still a distraction," said Fatty Deng, laughing.

"Yes, agreed – a distraction."

Fatty Deng had hoped to stay out of the meeting with Party Chief Li and Secretary Wu. He had no experience of dealing with senior Party officials and had no intention of gaining such experience now. But, when he tried to take a seat in the corridor outside of Party Chief Li's office, Prosecutor Xu gave him a 'look', and so he obediently followed her into the office, sweating more in the air-conditioned building than he had in the humid air outside.

Party Chief Li was sitting behind his desk, shouting at someone down the phone, something about a report from the Chengdu Bureau of Statistics that had gone missing. From all the stories Fatty Deng had heard, Party Chief Li was meant to resemble a reptile in almost every way: aloof, disinterested, and wholly lacking in human warmth. But, to Fatty Deng, he looked like a mad dog: red-faced, bulging eyes, and foaming at the mouth. The murder of his friend, Primo Gong, must have really rattled him.

However, it was the other man who occupied the office, sitting in an easy chair, who troubled Fatty Deng more. Dressed in an expensive dark blue suit, placidly watching Fatty Deng take a seat in front of Party Chief Li's desk next to Prosecutor Xu, saying not a word, was Secretary Wu, Chair of Chengdu's Political and Legal Committee – a very powerful man in his own right. He had the aura of someone fully in control of himself, even though Fatty Deng could sense he was extremely tired. Fatty Deng had never met him before but recognised him from photographs he had seen. Not knowing whether to bow, nod, or smile, Fatty Deng followed Prosecutor Xu's lead and ignored him for the time being, sitting patiently and keeping his eyes down on the floor.

"Well?" asked Party Chief Li, slamming the phone down. "Have you made any progress, Ms. Xu? Are you on the trail of that murdering bastard Ye Zihao?"

The question was absurd, of course. How, under Heaven, could they have made any progress in only a couple of hours without any forensic support? A pair of red shoes in the boot of his car did not, in Fatty Deng's opinion, a case make. But, to his great surprise, and to his great pride, Prosecutor Xu, unflustered, answered Party Chief Li with a question of her own.

"Sir," she asked, "why is it that Ye Zihao has never seen the inside of a courtroom?"

If the question astonished Fatty Deng, it left Party Chief Li speechless. He sought help from Secretary Wu.

"It is a fair question," said Secretary Wu. "A very fair question."

Party Chief Li nodded. He was pensive for a few moments and then, at last, Fatty Deng saw the reptile emerge from within. A subtle smile crossed Party Chief Li's face. His skin grew paler, cooler, and his eyes moved this way and that as he stuck a cigarette in the end of an ivory holder and carefully lit it with a silver lighter. He was in no hurry to speak. Fatty Deng guessed that Party Chief Li was the sort of reptile that could wait for hours in a tree before leaping out at its prey – a much scarier prospect to Fatty Deng than the mad dog he had just seen barking down the phone. Fatty Deng felt the need to reach for a cigarette himself. It was a pity no one felt the need to give him permission.

"You do pose a fair question, Ms. Xu," said Party Chief Li, blowing smoke around the office, "but it is not an easy question to answer. In many ways I am just as baffled. I suppose you know the history. After the earthquake, the Party ordered Ye Zihao from office and I was sent here – against my better judgment, I should add – to get to grips with the mess he had made. I was given assurances, Ms. Xu. I had the full confidence of Beijing...or so I was told. But, when I arrived, I discovered to my horror that the situation was more complex than I had been led to believe. Naturally, I had been allowed to bring my own support staff. And naturally the Party had supplied me with a list of those Party members in Chengdu – people like Secretary Wu here – who I could rely upon. However, it soon became obvious to me, after many heated phone calls with Beijing, that the Party was content to see Ye Zihao removed from office but reluctant to garner any undue publicity through a bruising trial. It was, to put it mildly, most peculiar. In the past, bigger fish than Ye Zihao had been dragged in chains to Beijing and held up to account before the people. I blame that half-breed son of his. I blame Philip Ye. After all these years there are some in Beijing still worried about what the imperialists might think. So what if Philip Ye has an English mother? So what if there is a big fuss about Ye Zihao in the international news? Anyway, soon enough, the Central Committee for Discipline Inspection refused to take any more of my calls – about Ye Zihao, that is.

"All my protests to the upper echelons of the Party fell on deaf ears. It was then that I realised I was on my own and also that I had a real job to do: to make Chengdu an international business hub for the whole of the south-west. I couldn't fritter all of my energy away trying to make Ye Zihao stand trial for his many crimes. I chose to put the matter of Ye Zihao to one side. Oh, I know what you are thinking, Ms. Xu, that only a foolish man would ever believe that Ye Zihao would stop scheming within that monstrosity of a mansion of his to regain all that he has lost. But, Ms. Xu, I assure you I have never lost sight of the problem of Ye Zihao. I have never lost the hope that Ye Zihao will one day face justice. Unfortunately, as the years have gone by, even those in Beijing who pride themselves on their knowledge of history, have somehow forgotten Ye Zihao's many crimes. Only the other day I was speaking to some young investigator from the Central Commission for Discipline Inspection who didn't even recognise Ye Zihao's name. Admittedly, he was a moron, and originally from some fly-infested village in the middle of nowhere in Shaanxi Province, but that should be no excuse! How am I to attract as much international investment as I can to Chengdu if I cannot demonstrate that there is Rule of Law in this city? How can I hold my head high when I am entertaining the most successful businessmen and businesswomen in the world, if I cannot prove to them that the corrupt and unsavoury will always get what's coming to them, that Chengdu is a safe place for them to do business? So, I have not forgotten Ye Zihao, Ms. Xu. And now, with the killing of my good friend Primo Gong, I am hoping that Ye Zihao has made the greatest mistake of his life. Prove that Ye Zihao conspired to kill Primo Gong to undermine me and my authority, Ms. Xu, and Beijing will not be able to ignore me this time. Do this for me, Ms. Xu, and you will earn my gratitude forever. Is that clear enough for you?"

"Perfectly, sir," said Prosecutor Xu. "But I am concerned about collateral damage."

"How so?"

"Primo Gong was murdered in a building owned by the family Fu. The family Fu may not be entirely blameless. Already my questions are being deflected and I have been told I must contact a Mister Xi, senior legal counsel to FUBI International, before I am to be provided with the information I need."

"I see," said Party Chief Li, unhappy, once more looking to Secretary Wu for guidance.

"Ms. Xu, please tread very lightly," said Secretary Wu. "The family Fu is important to the future of Chengdu, whereas Ye Zihao is not."

"Exactly," said Party Chief Li, very pleased. "Tread very lightly in regard to the family Fu. And always keep your eye on the prize – on Ye Zihao!"

If Prosecutor Xu was dismayed by this response, she did not show it. "I will also need to speak to the staff at Ambrogetti Global Software," she said.

"Is that necessary?" asked Party Chief Li.

"To understand how and when Primo Gong was targeted by his assassin, I need to learn more of his movements. I need access to his work files, his work diary. I intend to utilise a cover story when dealing with his work colleagues, that Primo Gong is helping the Procuratorate with some very important enquiries."

"Ah, yes, of course – very sensible, Ms. Xu," said Party Chief Li. "I will make a phone call on your behalf. You must speak to Primo Gong's personal assistant, Ms. Wen – a most efficient young woman. I will ensure she is expecting you."

"Thank you, sir."

Party Chief Li then stared at Fatty Deng as if noticing him for the very first time. "Who is this?"

"Investigator Deng, sir," replied Prosecutor Xu.

Party Chief Li reacted with horror. "Isn't he formerly police?"

Before Prosecutor Xu could reply, and before Fatty Deng could obey his first instinct and flee the office, Secretary Wu said, "Investigator Deng was police some years ago but he has never attended a party at the Ye family mansion and has never been a known supporter of Ye Zihao. He is proving a very useful addition to the Procuratorate – a very determined individual. He was instrumental in the crushing of The Willow Woman cult."

"Ah," said Party Chief Li, slightly mollified, but still staring at Fatty Deng suspiciously.

Thinking something very special was required of him here, sweating profusely, his pulse erratic, and desperate to keep his job, Fatty Deng said to Party Chief Li, "Sir, if you so order it, I will personally demolish the Ye family mansion brick by brick and drag Ye Zihao out by his hair."

Bemused, once more Party Chief Li looked to Secretary Wu for guidance.

"It is a big house, so let us hope that proves unnecessary," said Secretary Wu, with a smile.

EIGHT

— : —

P hilip Ye knew he only had himself to blame. He owed Constable Ma Meili his life for protecting him from some knife-wielding cultists. He thought he had been doing her a kindness by persuading the powers that be to let her transfer out of Robbery and be placed directly under his supervision in Homicide. Other options had been open to her. The People's Armed Police had wanted her. But, like always, he had thought he had known best. Chengdu was woefully short of homicide detectives and surely, under his guidance and tutelage, Constable Ma would soon prove competent. He could not have been more wrong.

Constable Ma was possessed of inexplicable mood swings, quickly boring of the slightest repetitive tasks, wary of books and book-learning, and seemingly unable to learn that the truth was not necessarily arrived at by picking up the nearest witness and shaking them until they talked. Her lack of aptitude for the job had almost brought Philip Ye and his colleague Superintendent Zuo to blows.

A month before, at Superintendent Zuo's apartment, at what was supposed to be a convivial dinner, tired of Philip Ye's continual criticism of Constable Ma, Superintendent Zuo had raised his voice, saying, "Listen, Philip, you are rich, she is poor; you grew up in the city, she on a remote farm; you see this world in shades of grey, she in black and white; she believes everything the Party tells her, you believe in nothing at all. If you are to teach her anything, if you want her to respond to you, you must meet her halfway. She is a simple soul, of the soil, courageous, and loyal to a fault – qualities you shouldn't be so quick to dismiss."

"Then you take her on," said Philip Ye.

To which Superintendent Zuo had replied, "A pet can only have one master."

Philip Ye had laughed derisively. "What sort of homespun bullshit is that?"

"The best there is!" shouted Superintendent Zuo, standing up, making it clear, as far as he was concerned, that both the dinner and the evening were over.

Philip Ye had also stood, making it clear that he was fine with that.

It was Zizi, Superintendent Zuo's wife, who had finished the argument for them. "Both of you are wrong! Husband, Constable Ma is not a pet. She is a grown woman. And Philip, if you can't learn to be kind to Constable Ma, if you can't tolerate someone who isn't as clever as you, then you will no longer be welcome in my home. Now both of you sit down and eat the dinner I have prepared, or it will be me losing *my* temper."

Philip Ye picked Constable Ma up from outside the morgue. She had been standing like an imbecile out in the weather without an umbrella. When she clambered in, the car rocking with her added weight, he could not only smell the rain in her long, lank hair but also the disinfectant from the morgue. She settled her massive frame into the passenger seat, her head almost touching the roof of the car, looking pleased with herself.

"Well?" he asked.

"Well what, Superintendent?"

This was how their conversations usually started. She never seemed to know what was expected of her, and he would lose his patience from the off.

"What is her name?" he asked, trying to conceal his frustration.

More confusion, the atmosphere in the car growing tense, Constable Ma's breathing becoming laboured. "Who are we talking about, Superintendent?"

"The victim!"

"Oh."

"Let me describe her to you, Constable Ma: she is very good-looking, mid to late thirties, with long, wavy hair."

Constable Ma pulled out her notebook and began to review her notes.

Infuriated, Philip Ye struggled to slow his breathing down, to keep his temper, to remember – as Zizi had instructed him – to be kind. "Constable, if you don't yet know the victim's name that is fine. Just tell me what you do know. Let us start with where the body was found."

"Ah, in an apartment block just off Xiaojiahe Street, in the Xiaojia River Residential District. I am sorry, Superintendent. I know that is not our patch and I attended a crime scene against your standing orders but there was no one else and—"

"Constable Ma, I don't care. Just tell me how she was killed and how long she has been dead."

Constable Ma studied her notebook again, frowning, saying nothing. Philip Ye snatched the notebook from her, snapped it shut, and tossed it behind him onto the backseat of the car.

"Constable Ma, please...just tell me what you found!"

"It was a man."

"Who was a man?"

"The victim."

Philip Ye could hardly believe his ears. He picked up his phone and contacted Dispatch again and was told what he had been told earlier, about the two suicides, but also that, as of this morning, a body of a man had been discovered in the Xiaojia River Residential District – the investigating officer being Constable Ma Meili.

"It's only in stupid films that the murder victim is always a beautiful woman," he heard Constable Ma mutter, her face turned away from him, as he put down the phone.

He closed his eyes and made a supreme effort this time to control his breathing, to recover the balance of his mind. Inhale for eight heartbeats, hold for four, exhale for eight. *In breath, there is life; in breath, there is serenity; in breath, there is clarity.*

When he opened his eyes he found Constable Ma's big eyes upon him, a look of consternation on her face.

"Are you ill, Superintendent?"

"No," he replied, as irritated by her as ever. "Tell me about this suspicious death you are supposedly investigating."

She reached to the back seat for her notebook. He did not stop her. All the resistance had gone out of him.

Where was the woman with the long, wavy hair?

When was her body going to be discovered?

"It was definitely murder, Superintendent. My victim was a retired soldier, a Lieutenant-General Jin Huiliang. Just like a man called Trotsky, he had an ice-axe in his head. Doctor Kong said so. Doctor Kong knows so much. Jin Huiliang was a heavy smoker. Doctor Kong showed me his lungs. They were disgusting. They were black. It is a good job you do not smoke, Superintendent. I would not wish you to have black lungs. Anyway, Doctor Kong could not be exact. The best she said she could do was to put the time of death sometime between ten and midnight last evening."

"What are your thoughts?"

"I spoke to the victim's maid, a Madame Ding. She told me that Jin Huiliang was so careless about his personal security he often did not lock the door to his apartment. However, I recovered his wallet and it was still stuffed with money. And nothing obvious had been stolen from the apartment or even disturbed. I also think to plunge an ice-axe into the back of someone's head...well, that cannot be a robbery gone wrong. That is about real hate. Whoever did this was Jin Huiliang's worst enemy."

"Maybe – suspects?"

"Since this Russian called Trotsky was also killed by an ice-axe, and since using an ice-axe is an unusual method of murder, I think it would be best if we discover which detective is investigating Trotsky's murder. Then maybe, with your permission, I could go speak to that detective and compare notes."

"That would prove a waste of time."

Constable Ma blinked, not understanding.

"Did Doctor Kong tell you when Trotsky was killed?" he asked.

She shook her head.

"Did you think to ask?"

She shook her head again.

"Then, Constable Ma, let me educate you. Leon Trotsky was a leading Russian revolutionary, who, some years after the October 1917 revolution, after the death of Lenin, and after he had fallen out with the new leader Stalin, was forced, in fear for his life, to go into exile. He moved from country to country until he finally ended up in Mexico. However, just because he was far away from the Soviet Union, did not mean that Stalin stopped thinking about him. In

1940, on Stalin's orders, a soviet agent, a Spanish national named Ramón Mercader, was dispatched with orders to assassinate Trotsky. Ramón Mercader was a clever and resourceful man. He managed to wheedle his way into Trotsky's entourage in Mexico. One day, he was able to get to meet with Trotsky alone in Trotsky's study, whereupon, even though he was also armed with a knife and a pistol, he set about Trotsky with an ice-axe he had kept hidden beneath a raincoat. But all did not go to plan. Trotsky was a very strong man. Though Mercader struck him a blow on the head, Trotsky managed to fight him off and Mercader was captured by Trotsky's security detail. Even so, the blow Trotsky had been given was mortal, and he died sometime later in hospital. Mercader spent the next twenty years in a Mexican prison and then made his way to the Soviet Union where he was given a very fine medal. He died in the late 1970s, in Cuba if my memory serves me correctly. So, Constable Ma, I think that it is safe to say that Ramón Mercader is not the man we are seeking in connection with Jin Huiliang's murder – unless, that is, he has come back as a ghost."

"There is no such thing as ghosts!" said Constable Ma, snapping at him, the atmosphere in the car again suddenly oppressive, and all because he had just made her look as uneducated as she really was.

Philip Ye rubbed his tired eyes. He felt like throwing Constable Ma out of the car, driving home and going to bed. Maybe by the time he awoke the body of the woman with the long, wavy hair would have been found.

"Show me the photographs you have taken," he said.

Muttering something incomprehensible under her breath, Constable Ma reached down into her shoulder bag and took out her camera. She passed it to Philip Ye. The viewing screen was small. But, as Philip Ye flicked through the images one by one, he was able to get a good sense of Jin Huiliang's apartment, of the solitary, almost hermitical life he had been leading, and of how someone could easily have entered into that apartment, crept up on him while he was writing at his desk, and attacked him.

Philip Ye glanced up from the camera. "Just one blow?"

"Yes, Superintendent – Doctor Kong believes the killer to be left-handed and fairly strong."

"She is certain?"

"I believe so, Superintendent."

Philip Ye had no liking for Doctor Kong. She had made it very clear from the day she had taken up the job of being the city's new pathologist that she thought Chengdu was nothing but a backwater compared to Beijing, and that the Chengdu police were nothing but an uneducated rabble. But, though he could not warm to her, her competence and skill had so far been beyond question.

He continued flicking through the photographs Constable Ma had taken. She might never make a good detective but the photographs were very good. This was no random break-in. And stranger killings, not just in Chengdu but across the whole of China, were relatively rare. Constable Ma was right. This murder was highly personal, the murderer highly motivated.

But why an ice-axe?

Philip Ye had never seen the like before in Chengdu.

Was the killer a mountaineer? Had the ice-axe been the first implement that had come to hand?

Or had Doctor Kong been right to invoke the memory of Trotsky? Was this method of killing meant to be symbolic, to send some kind of message? But, if so, to whom, and why not choose some method of murder, some message, that more Chinese people would understand? Who, apart from Doctor Kong, who was obviously very well read on the subject of death, and he himself who had an interest in history, would have picked up the connection with Trotsky? Not more than a handful in Chengdu PSB, that was for sure. Unless the message was meant for—

"Was Trotsky a good man?" asked Constable Ma.

"What?"

"Trotsky – was he a good man, Superintendent? Jin Huiliang was a good man. The maid said so."

Philip Ye passed the camera back to Constable Ma. "History has been kinder to Trotsky than it should. He was a brilliant man, a passionate speaker and writer. But, like most revolutionaries, he was very happy to tell people what to do but would never accept being told what to do himself. And, like most other revolutionaries, he believed the end always justified the means, even if that meant terrorising people into submission just so his concept of a socialist utopia could be realised. Now tell me about the maid."

"A snivelling wretch named Madame Ding Jie," said Constable Ma. "She always arrives early morning to cook, clean, and shop for Jin Huiliang. It was she who discovered the body about six. She has another job cleaning in a school in the evenings. I do not see her as a killer but I have no proof of her innocence."

"Did Jin Huiliang have any family?"

"The maid knows of an estranged daughter who lives somewhere in the city but she does not have the address."

"Estranged?"

"The maid could not say what the difficulty was between the daughter and Jin Huiliang."

"What did Jin Huiliang write about?"

"I didn't think to ask, Superintendent."

Philip Ye closed his eyes to ponder the case. If he had any sense, he should be working his phone, trying to track down a detective actually responsible for the area of the Xiaojia River Residential District, even if it meant dragging them out of bed. Didn't Superintendent Tu usually work that patch? Or had it been Superintendent Tu who had gone on long term leave due to depression a few months ago back in the spring? There had to be someone else, someone with a modicum of sense who could—

"Superintendent, do we continue investigating or not?"

"Be quiet, I am thinking."

"I suppose we could wait for a beautiful woman with long, wavy hair to die instead."

Philip Ye ignored Constable Ma's poor attempt at sarcasm. Still, the murder of Jin Huiliang was intriguing. A simple domestic dispute would not have interested him. A knife-attack would have bored him. But an ice-axe was something different. And Jin Huiliang was a writer....

"The killer could have escaped to Timbuktu by now," said Constable Ma, impatient to be doing something, using a phrase she had overheard Philip Ye use in the past.

"Do you know where Timbuktu is?"

"No, Superintendent."

"Then shut up and let us go and visit the crime scene. I want to see everything for myself."

NINE

—◦—

The meeting with Party Chief Li and Secretary Wu had not exactly filled Xu Ya with confidence. Not only did she feel she had not been told the full story in regard to the failure to bring Ye Zihao to justice – someone very senior in Beijing, maybe as high as the Politburo itself, must be protecting him – but also no direction had been given her on how to proceed with the investigation into the murder of Primo Gong. Furthermore, she had been ordered to be very circumspect in her dealings with the family Fu (and this after dropping the biggest hint imaginable that Lucy Fu's hands were far from clean!), and the legitimate request she had made, as the meeting had been drawing to a close, to have the full resources of the Procuratorate put at her disposal had been turned down flat. Chief Prosecutor Gong was presently on an extended holiday in Africa hunting animals and Party Chief Li stated that he did not want it to be seen that he was usurping Chief Prosecutor Gong's authority by effectively putting Xu Ya in command of the Procuratorate while Chief Prosecutor Gong was away. This was not quite what Xu Ya had meant. She had only been thinking about leading a properly managed and properly supported task force. Moreover, Chief Prosecutor Gong was used to having his authority usurped all the time, by almost everybody, so surely would not care. But Xu Ya did not press the point. Evidently, the threat of leaks to the media reigned supreme in Party Chief Li's mind: the fewer who knew about the murder of Primo Gong, the better. All further requests of any sort, she was told, were to put directly to Secretary Wu for consideration. So she and Investigator Deng were on their own. It made Xu Ya wonder, despite all the vitriol levelled at Ye Zihao, whether Party Chief Li and Secretary Wu were as committed to putting Ye Zihao before a People's Court as they maintained. Not that Xu Ya mentioned this concern to Investigator Deng. He was upset enough as it was with his performance during the meeting, where he had stated that he would demolish the Ye family mansion brick by brick, if so ordered.

It had been highly amusing.

Xu Ya had nearly laughed out loud.

So, to cheer him up, and to plot their next moves, Xu Ya had treated Investigator Deng to a late breakfast at the nearest Starbucks, ordering coffee for them both and a plate each of American-style pancakes dripping in maple syrup. Investigator Deng had stared at both the coffee and the pancakes with a fair degree of suspicion – all he had asked for was a cup of green tea – but soon, to Xu Ya's great satisfaction, the pancakes were gone and he was relishing the coffee as if he had been drinking it all his life.

"I don't know what came over me, Prosecutor," he said. "I don't hate the family Ye. They've never done anything bad to me."

"You were just nervous," she reassured him, already bored, needing the substance of their conversation to move on.

"But, if only I had—"

"Tell me about Sarangerel."

"Pardon?"

Reluctant to reveal that she had just received an invitation to dinner from Sarangerel, that she was petrified Sarangerel might somehow know more than anyone should about the night her husband had died, Xu Ya said, "Now I live in Chengdu, is it not wise for me to learn more about the history of the city?"

"Prosecutor," said Investigator Deng, gravely, "no one speaks about Sarangerel. It is considered bad luck by some just to mention her name. You are aware she is Mayor Cang's mistress?"

"Of course."

"And that she is also known as the Witch-Queen of Chengdu?"

"I had heard that."

"Then there is nothing more to learn."

"I would like to know where she came from."

"Prosecutor, we have an investigation to be getting on with."

"Don't be silly. We are just having a little rest and a chat. In ten minutes' time Primo Gong will be just as dead as he is now. Please

indulge me, Investigator Deng. Tell me the story of Sarangerel –
unless, that is, you're frightened of getting struck by lightning just
for speaking of her."

Xu Ya had hoped to appeal to his sense of masculinity, but Investigator Deng seemed genuinely afraid, and for a few moments she
thought he might not speak at all. But then he took a deep breath and
she travelled with him into the past, to when Ye Zihao was still mayor
of Chengdu, and when both she and Philip Ye shared a classroom in
the School of Law at the University of Wuhan – not that Philip Ye
had ever noted her existence then.

"Ye Zihao flew up to Mongolia on some sort of business trip,"
began Investigator Deng. "No one knows what he was really up to.
Officially, it was to take a tour of some factory on the edge of the Gobi
Desert. His plane landed safely in Ulan Bator, but as a car was taking
him in the direction of the factory a dust storm blew up, blinding the
driver, and sending them completely the wrong way. When the dust
storm had blown itself out, Ye Zihao found himself in the middle of
nowhere, in a filthy little coal-mining town without even a proper
name. As the driver was asking some of the locals for directions, Ye
Zihao spotted this tall, copper-hued beauty walking down the street
towards them."

"I thought Mongolians were generally pale-skinned."

"I don't know, Prosecutor – maybe they tan easily. I'm sure I've
seen photographs of dark-skinned Mongolian shepherds. Anyway, so
it is said, Ye Zihao fell down on his knees in front of Sarangerel and
pleaded with her to become his mistress. I doubt she was more than
seventeen at the time."

"And Ye Zihao was well into his forties."

"That is true, Prosecutor. But, as it turned out, Sarangerel – which
means 'moonlight' – was very happy to become his mistress. She is
supposedly from a long line of shamanesses. Some say she had used
her skill in making spells to lure Ye Zihao to Mongolia and then had
made more spells to create the dust storm that brought him to her
very feet."

"Wouldn't it have been easier for her to hop on a plane to Chengdu
and knock on the door of the Ye family mansion?"

"Maybe – but that is not what happened. Ye Zihao, smitten with Sarangerel, quickly forgot about the visit to the factory and flew straight back with her to Chengdu."

"Many middle-aged men make fools of themselves with young women."

"That is true, Prosecutor."

"What did her parents have to say about that?"

"I don't know. Maybe she was an orphan. Maybe she hated her parents. Maybe she just wanted to escape from Mongolia. Anyway, Ye Zihao took her into the Ye family mansion, more like a wife than a mistress. Remember, Philip Ye was away at university at the time. This is a very important fact. Now, Sarangerel wanted more than just to cling to Ye Zihao's arm at parties and city functions. It was real power she wanted – and it was real power that she got. People who got close to Ye Zihao were certain he was stuck in some kind of weird trance. This was when Sarangerel first became known as the Witch-Queen of Chengdu. Many of the household staff at the Ye family mansion ran for their lives. Sarangerel would attend local government meetings with Ye Zihao, and, if she spoke, Ye Zihao made it clear that she spoke with his authority. Sometimes she would turn up at meetings without Ye Zihao – even Party meetings. Those who spoke up against her presence quickly found themselves transferred to some bureaucratic backwater, their careers curtailed for good. I had just joined the police then, Prosecutor. I remember that time well. It seemed like the whole of Chengdu was covered with a blanket of fear. At night, terrible screams were heard from the Ye family mansion. Sometimes, strange yellow mists descended upon the mansion and its grounds, obscuring it from all who would see. People began to meet the ghosts of long dead relatives walking the nearby streets. There was talk that Sarangerel was trying to raise the dead, to gain even more occult power for herself. A lone raven was often seen flying high over the city. In the Mayor's Office, Ye Zihao began to look pale and drawn, a very ill man – a mere shadow of his former self. If Sarangerel ever left his side, Ye Zihao would lose his temper for no reason and afterward weep uncontrollably. The police at Sanwayao Station took complaints from the parents of two young maids employed at the Ye family mansion. The girls were missing. Rumours of human sacrifices began to circulate."

"Oh, how ridiculous, Investigator Deng. Mongolian shamans don't perform human sacrifices."

"Prosecutor, I am just telling you the story I know. Though the parents of those maids wept and tore out their hair, the police at Sanwayao Station were too frightened to investigate. Those girls were never seen again. But it was the disappearance of those girls that changed everything. The family Ye realised they could no longer stand by and do nothing. Philip Ye's half-sister, Ye Lan, who owns The Silver Tree restaurant, tried at first to rescue her father. But it is said she was turned back from the Ye family mansion by an invisible force. Then her husband, you remember the maître d' of The Silver Tree, Mister Qu...?"

She nodded, having liked the courteous and calm Mister Qu very much.

"...well, he took it upon himself to travel by train to Wuhan."

"To visit Philip Ye?"

"To bring Philip Ye back to Chengdu with him."

Xu Ya searched her almost perfect memory and stumbled upon a pain buried deep within, those three days in the spring term of her second year at Wuhan, the three days when Philip Ye had gone missing and no one could tell her where he had gone, when she had cried herself to sleep like a baby thinking he had quit the university and she would never see him again, and when, after those three days were up, he had suddenly reappeared as if nothing had happened, except that he had had a vivid scratch down the one cheek of his face, much as if an unseen bramble had caught his face.

"Prosecutor, what is it?" Investigator Deng asked of her, seeing the sudden memory in her eyes.

"Nothing, please continue."

"Now this is where many of the stories from that time diverge. I will tell you the most common story, the story my mother believes. It is said that Philip Ye waited until after midnight so he could clamber over the iron gates to the Ye family mansion unseen. Ghosts of the dead raised by Sarangerel assaulted him but he brushed them aside. The invisible force tried to turn him away but Philip Ye laughed at it. The front door was locked but he broke it down with his bare fists. He found the household staff, those that remained, cowering in their rooms, and freed them, sending them back to their families.

Then he found his father lying naked on the floor in front of an open fire, all manner of occult symbols daubed upon his body in blood, and Sarangerel naked also, dancing about the room, shouting out invocations to her Mongolian gods, doing her utmost to conjure up demons to do her bidding. At first Sarangerel tried to bewitch Philip Ye with her intoxicating beauty, showing off her naked body to him. But, as my mother always says, what woman alive is more beautiful than Philip Ye? Sarangerel made no impression on him. Then Sarangerel tried to cast her most powerful spell against him. But that too had no effect. Some say Philip Ye's green eyes made him invulnerable to her powers. And then, when she saw that none of her spells worked on him, she threw herself upon him like a tigress, trying to claw his eyes out. Philip Ye is strong, though – stronger than he looks. He picked her up and, as she screeched and cursed, he threw her bodily out of the house. Ye Zihao then awoke and told Philip Ye the last memory he had was of boarding the flight to Ulan Bator."

"What happened to Sarangerel?"

"Ah, now that, Prosecutor, is possibly the strangest story of all. She disappeared for years. She must have had help escaping the city for there were many who would have been out for her blood. In the police, we suspected Chief Di. His movements at the time were very mysterious. And even though he had been friends with Ye Zihao for many years, after Ye Zihao returned to his senses he would never exchange another civil word with Chief Di again. I heard a rumour that Chief Di was hiding Sarangerel in a lodge up in the mountains. I also heard a rumour that when Sarangerel fled she issued an ancient and powerful curse against the family Ye. For some, that curse came true after the earthquake when Ye Zihao was removed from office and put under house-arrest by the Shanghai Clique and Philip Ye never received another promotion, destined to be a superintendent first class forever."

"How did Sarangerel come to be at Mayor Cang's side?"

Investigator Deng shrugged. "That is another mystery. Mayor Cang came to Chengdu with the rest of the Shanghai Clique, with his wife and son in tow. Two weeks later, the wife and son vanished, and Sarangerel was at his side. Once again, Sarangerel was the Witch-Queen of Chengdu. By all accounts, Chief Di was a broken man. Some say the only reason Chief Di kept his job was because

Sarangerel put in a good word for him, as final payment for keeping her safe in the mountains."

Prosecutor Xu could not help laughing. "Investigator Deng, if all you have said is true, if all you have said is real history, then why isn't Mayor Cang walking around in a trance, and why isn't Chengdu under a blanket of fear again?"

"Ah, that is quite simple, Prosecutor. Not only do the people believe that Philip Ye stripped Sarangerel of most of her powers when he confronted her, it is also believed, that as long as Philip Ye is resident in Chengdu, as long as he is police and protecting the people, they will have nothing much to fear from her. But my advice to you, Prosecutor, if you ever see her walking toward you, is to run the other way."

"Investigator Deng, all you have told me is but a simple ghost story."

"Ghost stories are sometimes true."

"Ghost stories are never true!"

"Prosecutor, when I was a boy I would have agreed with you. But after I joined the police, when I was working the late shift one night down by the river—"

Xu Ya put her hands over her ears. "Investigator Deng, I don't want you to fill my head with nonsense!"

"But—"

"No, it is time we got back to work. I think Ambrogetti Global Software should be our first stop."

He finished his coffee, looking sad that she had not allowed him to tell his only ghost story. Then he said, "Prosecutor, you must go to Ambrogetti Global Software, of course. But I know nothing about computers or business. I would be useless to you. Let me go to Liberation Street, have a walk around, get the lie of the land. It has been some years since I have been in that part of the city. I can have a look about, chat to a few people, see what I can dig up about the Black House."

"What about lunch?" asked Xu Ya. At the end of the meeting with Party Chief Li, Secretary Wu had invited the pair of them to lunch at his house. "Don't you want to go?"

"I would only make a fool of myself again. I'd be so nervous I'd drop food all down me. Can you make an excuse for me?"

She smiled at the plaintive expression on his face. She would miss him at the dinner. She realised she always felt safer having him around. He was like the brother she had never had. "Of course, but you must keep in touch with me by phone."

"I promise, Prosecutor."

"And don't do anything dangerous. I don't want to have to sit by your hospital bedside again with your mother wondering if you are ever going to recover."

She watched him leave the restaurant then, making his way down the street, umbrella up against the rain, that new suit and raincoat of his not quite him. She would take a taxi back home, pick up her car, and then go find out more about Primo Gong's life at Ambrogetti Global Software. But before she did so, she ordered herself another coffee and considered the bizarre story Investigator Deng had just told her about Sarangerel. She would have dismissed it all as hearsay and nonsense if not for her memory of Philip Ye returning to university all those years ago with a fresh scratch down the side of his face. That was a fact, and in law, and otherwise, facts should never be ignored. It was a pity that she had no option but to attend that dinner on Monday evening with Sarangerel. Xu Ya would have preferred to not have her husband raised from the dead by Sarangerel, even if it was just in conversation. Xu Ya wanted her husband left right where he was: deep underground.

TEN

For Ma Meili, the gloss and excitement of working for Superintendent Philip Ye had quickly faded. At first, she had idolised him, quite unable to believe her good fortune in his not only arranging for her transfer from Robbery to Homicide, but also his choosing to ignore the fiction of her past. Before she had come to Chengdu she had never had any police training, never been to Police College, had never actually been police at all. But, since those first few days in Homicide, when everything had seemed so new, and every morning had begun with such promise, Superintendent Ye had proved himself to be a man of very bad character, always impatient and short-tempered with her, always secretive, never telling her what he was thinking or, most importantly, what she was supposed to think, and possessed of many little eccentricities, all of which she had grown to hate. His occasional fiddling with that stupid gold pocket-watch and chain of his, for example, really grated on her nerves.

He was fiddling with the pocket-watch at this very moment. As soon as they had entered Jin Huiliang's apartment, Superintendent Ye had taken the watch from his waistcoat pocket and had then, quite unconsciously, begun to open and close the watch case, again and again, as he looked about the apartment, ignoring Doctor Kong's white-suited technicians as they quietly went about their work. And, as his attention was grabbed by the black and white photograph of the group of dirty and dishevelled soldiers that hung pride of place on the lounge wall, the rate at which he opened and closed the watch case actually increased. It was more than Ma Meili could bear.

"The time is 11.45," she announced, so loudly that everyone in the room stopped what they were doing and turned to look at her.

Everyone except Superintendent Ye, that is. He continued to study the photograph, opening and closing the watch case as he did so, as if he had not heard her, totally lost within himself. Despite having a profound respect for her superiors, Ma Meili felt like snatching the pocket-watch off him and grinding it to dust underneath her boot.

Late one evening, some weeks before, after Superintendent Ye had gone home, Ma Meili had found her courage and mentioned the pocket-watch to Superintendent Zuo.

"Leave him be," said Superintendent Zuo. "He only plays with that watch when something is weighing heavily on his mind. The watch is a memento, a final gift from his English fiancée, dead many years now. The watch brings him comfort. Say nothing of this to him. He doesn't know that I know."

Ma Meili had indeed said nothing. But that Superintendent Ye had kept such a memento, that he would always play with it when his mind became full of worries, struck her as macabre. Surely it would have been better to bury the watch with his fiancée's body and get on with his life. The dead were dead and the past was gone; it wasn't as if his fiancée was ever coming back.

Superintendent Ye suddenly turned away from the photograph toward her. "Did the maid say anything was missing from the apartment?"

"She thought not, Superintendent. She said Jin Huiliang lived a simple life. Except his wallet, which I found untouched and still with cash within it, there was not much to take. He did not even own a TV. But when I took the maid from room to room, she thought his black leather journal was missing from his desk. She said he would often write notes in the journal, whatever thoughts came into his mind, and that he always kept this journal close to hand. But then she also said that sometimes she had seen him stick the journal into the wall safe."

"There's a wall safe? I did not see that on any of your photographs, Constable Ma."

"Forgive me, Superintendent, it is in the study, behind another framed picture. One of the technicians found it after I had finished with my camera. The maid doesn't know the combination. I asked the technicians to examine it for fingerprints."

The look he gave her was not pleasant. Feeling like the lowest of the low, Ma Meili dutifully followed him into the study. The wall safe was now in clear view, the picture – a dull and uninteresting black and white view of a village, perhaps Jin Huiliang's home village – resting on the floor. Ma Meili looked toward the technician working in the cramped study. He gave her the thumbs up, meaning he had completed his examination of the safe.

"Do we yet have any idea as to the combination?" Ma Meili asked the technician.

"No, Constable," he replied. "But we have summoned a locksmith. He should be here within the hour."

Superintendent Ye stepped forward and turned the handle of the safe. The door swung open with ease. He didn't say anything. He didn't have to. But there was a barely perceptible shake of his head. Ma Meili could have kicked herself. She should have known that if jin Huiliang had been so careless about his security that he hardly ever locked his apartment door, he might also close his safe without setting the combination.

"I am sorry, Sister," the technician silently mouthed to her.

She smiled and nodded at him, making it known that she did not consider it his fault. Who would have thought the safe would be unlocked except for Superintendent Ye?

There was no black leather journal in the safe. But Superintendent Ye pulled out a thick sheaf of papers bound together with a red silk ribbon. He stared at the top sheet. Looking over his shoulder, Ma Meili could read the title, set in the middle of an otherwise blank piece of paper, printed in a very large font:

AS EASY AS BREAKING BAMBOO!

Ma Meili did not know what to make of this. But Superintendent Ye smiled to himself and said, "It seems the General's speciality was military history – the Song Dynasty in particular."

How Superintendent Ye understood all this from a few cryptic words written on an otherwise blank page was a mystery to Ma Meili. But she did not make the same mistake she had made in the past at other crime scenes by asking him how he had come to his conclusion. He would only have stared at her in that condescending manner of his, making her out to be the most uneducated peasant under Heaven, and say, "Isn't it obvious, Constable Ma?"

She had had nightmares consisting only of Superintendent Ye saying this to her over and over again.

Isn't it obvious, Constable Ma?
Isn't it obvious, Constable Ma?
Isn't it obvious, Constable Ma?

She had woken from these terrible dreams dripping with sweat, never realising she could hate someone so much as Superintendent Ye.

To remedy her lack of knowledge and her lack of understanding of the direction in which an investigation might be going, she had taken to staying late in the office long after Superintendent Ye had gone home and reading his case notes – which sometimes helped, and sometimes didn't.

"Why can't he just tell me what he is thinking?" she had protested to Superintendent Zuo.

To which Superintendent Zuo had no answer.

Superintendent Ye reached into the safe again and this time took out a small, brown envelope. Ma Meili wanted to tell Superintendent Ye to put on some latex gloves, that he should not be handling evidence in this way. But she bit her tongue as he opened the envelope and took out a photograph. This photograph was in colour, a portrait, of a very beautiful woman, young, maybe not even twenty years old, with long, wavy hair.

"Ah, so there you are," said Superintendent Ye, smiling to himself.

Ma Meili was amazed, remembering he had mentioned a woman with long, wavy hair back in the car. "Do you know her, Superintendent?"

"No," he replied, simply, before sliding the photograph back in the envelope and then tucking the envelope inside his raincoat pocket even as the technician was helpfully offering up an evidence bag to him. It was enough to make Ma Meili weep.

"Move out of the way," Superintendent Ye said to the technician, who was now blocking his progress to the desk.

The technician mumbled an apology, bowed slightly, and scampered out of the room, but not before making Ma Meili smile by rolling his eyes in exasperation as he did so. She couldn't understand how Superintendent Ye could be so warm and charming one moment and so cold and rude another. At least he had now put away his stupid pocket-watch; whatever had been playing on his mind was no longer troubling him.

"What is this?" asked Superintendent Ye, leaning over the desk.

Ma Meili began to panic, wondering what she could have missed. All the blood-soaked papers that had covered the desk had been removed by the technicians in the hope it could be discovered what Jin Huiliang had been writing about at the time of his murder. Apart from a couple of books, and a few bottles of ink, there was little else there except for the ashtray and the packet of cigarettes she had personally taken from Jin Huiliang's cold, stiff hand.

Superintendent Ye pointed at the ashtray and repeated himself, more sharply this time. "What is this?"

Resisting the conflicting urges of either wanting to run from the apartment or to thump him, Ma Meili put her face as close as she could to the ashtray, hating the smell of the cigarette butts piled up within it. She had taken a close-up with her camera hours before and seen nothing untoward. But now, for the first time, she noticed that the butt at the top of the pile was very different to all the others, and, even worse, seemed to have a slight smear of lipstick around it.

Aiya!

A woman had been here!

Not Madame Ding, not the maid. She did not smoke. Another woman had been here.

Ma Meili realised she was in for it now.

"I am sorry, Superintendent," she said, lowering her eyes.

"I am not interested if you are sorry," he said, brusquely. "I am only interested in you using your eyes. I am only interested in you doing your job. Do not be lazy, Constable Ma! Do not rely on Doctor Kong's people to do your job for you! Now concentrate. We know that Jin Huiliang's preferred brand of cigarette is Baisha Blue – not only a popular brand with soldiers but also relatively cheap. But this odd cigarette butt is a Good Cat. If this belonged to our murderer then she has expensive tastes. Let us hope we can get DNA from the butt. I also want the manufacturer of this shade of lipstick identified as soon as possible."

"Yes, Superintendent."

"We cannot dismiss the possibility that a man came to this apartment disguised as a woman, or that a man who enjoys dressing up as a woman was invited here by Jin Huiliang. We know next to nothing about his private life. But my feeling is that we are indeed dealing with a woman, a woman known to Jin Huiliang, a woman familiar with the layout of this apartment, a woman who knew that Jin Huiliang was lax with his personal security, a woman who was motivated enough, and callous enough, to creep up on him, deliver him a mortal blow with an ice-axe, and then calmly smoke a cigarette as she watched him die."

"For a woman to commit this sort of crime...."

"It is indeed unusual," admitted Superintendent Ye.

Ma Meili remained unconvinced. "Could not a woman have visited him – his daughter, say – smoked a cigarette, and then left before the murderer arrived?"

Superintendent Ye nodded, giving Ma Meili some rare satisfaction by at least contemplating what she had to say. "Yes, that is possible. But I feel it is unlikely. We know Jin Huiliang was a heavy smoker. Left on his own, for any amount of time, he would have covered up the Good Cat butt with his own cigarette ends. I am sure the Good Cat was the last cigarette smoked in this room. However, you are right to point out to me that all we have at this moment is conjecture."

"What do we do next, Superintendent?"

Staring at the sheaf of papers, the manuscript with the strange title, in his hands, he replied, "I am going home to lunch. I want to have a good read of this manuscript and have a think. In the meantime, I want you to check the local shops to see if any have sold an ice-axe in the last day or two. Then go back to PSB HQ and get me an address for Jin Huiliang's estranged daughter. She shouldn't be too hard to find. And, when that is done, I want you to contact the People's Liberation Army. I want to know as much as possible about Jin Huiliang. Get me a copy of his service record – today, if possible."

Then, with the manuscript tucked safely under his arm, and without saying another word to Ma Meili or to any of the technicians – not even to thank them for the work they were doing – Superintendent Ye walked out of the apartment. Evidently, once she had finished trawling the local shops looking for whoever had sold an ice-axe, Ma Meili was expected to catch the bus back to PSB HQ.

She did not know what expression she wore on her face as she returned to the lounge, but, as she heard Superintendent Ye's footfalls fade away on the concrete steps outside of the apartment, all the technicians burst out laughing.

"You should know," she told them, liking them all, only feigning anger, "that this morning I was yet again invited to join SWAT."

"Take the job, Sister," they all replied, almost in chorus. "Before Superintendent Ye drives you to suicide."

ELEVEN

— · —

P hilip Ye turned the photograph over in his hands. There was nothing written on the back, no name, no date, nothing to help him identify the woman with the wavy hair. All he knew of her, whoever she was, was that she was no longer in the land of the living. At least he had a renewed faith in his visions of the departed, alongside an unsettling feeling that it was Constable Ma's failure to obey his standing order not to wander off their allotted patch in terms of accepting new homicide cases that had led directly to the discovery of the photograph. Almost certainly, if he had been in the office this morning, he would have refused to attend a body of a man in the Xiaojia River Residential District.

Was this then evidence of some supernatural influence directing his investigations? Did those in the afterlife sometimes have the power to influence events in the physical realm?

He did not know.

But at least he could now settle into this investigation in the knowledge he was where he should be, and doing what he was required to do.

He slid the photograph back into the envelope and returned it to his pocket when he saw his target walking toward him. She was laden down with groceries. It was still raining heavily. Though she carried no umbrella, he thought more tears than rain ran down her face. After knocking on her door only to find her out, he was glad that he had decided to wait in the likelihood she had not gone far. He was also glad Constable Ma had had the good sense not only to note down the maid's address in her notebook – an address he had memorised with but one glance – but also to take a photograph of her so he would now know her likeness. He stepped out of the car. "Madame Ding, may I assist you?"

She stopped suddenly, wary of him, not recognising him. "Who are you?"

He flashed his badge and ID. "Superintendent Ye."

She stared up at his face. "But—"

"My mother is English."

"Ah, then you favour her, Superintendent."

"Some say I do."

"I have told the little I know to that giant policewoman."

"I want to learn more about Jin Huiliang."

"The giant policewoman frightened me."

"There are times she frightens me."

Madame Ding let him take her heavy bags from her. While glancing again at his face, apparently still unsure about him, she led him through the door of her apartment block – a run-down building a few streets away from where Jin Huiliang had lived – and up the stairs to the second floor. She walked slowly even though she was of no great age. Philip Ye judged her to be no more than fifty, but could not be more definitive than that. She appeared to have had a hard life – a life lived mainly in the countryside by the texture of her skin and the manner of speech. This would also account for why his face was unknown to her. A Chengdu native of her age would have recognised him immediately.

He waited patiently as she struggled with her keys to open up her apartment. When she succeeded, she led him into a tiny, airless, box of a room, hot and suffocating on this summer's day but almost certainly frigid during the winter, with a kitchenette in one corner. He saw no bathroom. There had to be a shared bathroom for all the apartments on her floor. She set her groceries on the only table and went to the small stove to put some water on to boil.

"You are not from the city," he said.

"I am from a little village in Lushan County, just north of Ya'an. You would not have heard of it. Do you need to see my documentation?"

"No – how did you fare during the earthquake?"

"I was most fortunate. A landslide destroyed my house but my good neighbour, Mister Xie, dug me out with his bare hands. It was also my good fortune that my husband had recently got a job in a factory in Shenzhen, my son had just been accepted by the army – he is very fit and strong – and my daughter had been away visiting relatives in Ya'an, so none of them got hurt. I stayed for a few years after, did what I could to rebuild the house. But the village was not the same. Too many people were dead. And when my daughter left home after a distant cousin got her a job in an office in Chongqing – my daughter is very good with numbers – my husband told me to come join him in Shenzhen. But when I looked at the map it seemed too far. I felt like a coward and a bad wife, but my husband told me not to be silly and to look for work instead in Chengdu. He thought I would be happy here. So, I came to the city and got a job as a cleaner in a local school at evenings. But the pay was not enough to live on. But then I had the most marvellous good fortune. The General had just come out of a shop after buying his cigarettes. He was in a dream as always, thinking about his writing, and I was not looking where I was going. We collided in the street. Like a gentleman, he apologised, even though I was more in the wrong. He asked me who I was and where I had come from. When I replied, he told me he had also grown up in Lushan County. I could never have guessed from the way he spoke. I did not know then he had been away from Lushan County for many, many years and—"

"He asked you to work for him?"

"As a maid, yes, Superintendent. I don't know how he knew I was looking for work, or how he knew he could trust me. He told me he needed someone to cook, clean, and shop for him as he often forgot to do those things when he was writing. I accepted the job even though I did not know then that he was a very famous man."

"Famous?"

Madame Ding checked her tongue, pausing to think, and to first pour them each a cup of tea. "Please understand he did not tell me he was famous, Superintendent. I have never met a more humble man. For the first few weeks I did not even know he was a retired general. Oh, I guessed he had been in the People's Liberation Army. There was that big photograph on the wall of all those soldiers, and he had that military way about him. Apart from the papers on his desk, he was a most orderly man. But one day I picked up a letter off the floor that had just arrived for him and saw it was addressed to a 'Lieutenant-General Jin'."

Philip Ye accepted the cup of tea from her. "How did you learn he was famous?"

"My son is a good boy and calls his mother whenever he can. The army keeps him very busy. He is to be sent to Africa soon as a peacekeeper. He is very excited. Anyway, I told him I was now working for a Lieutenant-General Jin Huiliang. He was amazed. He said to me, 'Mother, he is famous – you are working for the Hero of Lao Cai.' My son was very proud of me. He told all of his army friends."

"Lao Cai?"

"My son says it is a town in Vietnam."

"Jin Huiliang was a veteran of the border war?"

"Yes, that is what my son said. He said there had been a terrible battle, that the General, though a young man at the time, had been the bravest of the brave."

"Was the photograph hanging in the lounge taken in Vietnam?"

Madame Ding shook her head. "I cannot say, Superintendent. One day I asked the General about it. He told me that most of those smiling men were now dead. He could not say anymore as he was suddenly overcome with terrible emotion. He returned to his study and his writing. He was not a great talker. And I try not to be a nosy person. When we did speak it was usually about the weather or about how Lushan County used to be. He would also politely enquire about my family, and was especially interested in how my son was doing in the army. Mainly he stayed at his desk writing. I told him he should get out of the apartment more. But he would not. I think he preferred living in his head than being out in the world."

"I understand he has a daughter."

"Yes, Jin Jing – but I don't know her address. I believe she lives close by, though."

"There was a difficulty between them."

"Yes, that is true but I don't know what it was."

"Did you ever meet her?"

"Once, Superintendent, about a year ago. One morning I was returning with the shopping and she was just leaving his apartment. I did not know who she was. She pushed past me and ran down the stairs. She was crying...most distraught. I found the General standing in his kitchen looking out of the window. I asked if that had been his daughter. He said it had and that he had always been a better soldier than a father. He did not say any more and it was not my place to enquire further. The next day he told me his daughter had bought him a phone for his birthday. She had visited him to give him the phone in person. But he did not want it. He did not like phones. He said he had no need for them. He gave the phone to me. It is sad when families go wrong, Superintendent. Sometimes there is nothing to be done. It is just the way life is. I am very fortunate. Though I only get to see my son, daughter, and husband perhaps once a year, and though we are usually separated by many, many miles, there has never been any difficulty between us. When we meet it is like we have never been apart."

"You are indeed fortunate."

"But now I cannot stop crying. The General was such a wonderful man. I will never meet his like again. And I wonder where I will find work again. In having such a nice family, in surviving the earthquake, in meeting a man such as the General, I feel I have used up all of my good fortune for this lifetime."

Madame Ding invited Philip Ye to sit, to drink his tea in more comfort. Philip Ye accepted her offer. Her tears had dried now, her telling of Jin Huiliang, and of her concerns for the future, having done her some good.

Philip Ye took the envelope from his pocket, withdrew the photograph and showed it to her. "Is this Jin Jing?"

Madame Ding leaned forward for a better view. "Oh, what a good-looking woman! And what wonderful hair! But that is not Jin Jing. She is much older...a plain sort of girl really."

"This photograph is old."

"It is still not Jin Jing."

"You are sure, Madame Ding?"

"Quite sure, Superintendent."

"Could this be Jin Huiliang's wife then? I found this photograph in his safe."

"That is possible. But the General divorced many years ago, so he told me one day, and that his wife was now dead, maybe ten years or more. He never showed me a photograph of her. I do not think it had been a happy marriage."

"Did he have a lover?"

Madame Ding smiled for the first time. "He lived only for his writing, Superintendent. He was more monk than man. As far as I know he only went out on a Wednesday afternoon, and then that was just to meet up with some old army friends of his."

"Do know where?"

"A local teahouse."

"Which one?"

"I do not know, Superintendent."

Philip Ye paused, to collect his thoughts, then said, "Jin Huiliang had a leather-bound journal."

Madame Ding shook her fist. "The giant policewoman had the nerve to accuse me of stealing it!"

"That was wrong of her."

"I did not take it, but why would the murderer take it, Superintendent? It had no value to anyone other than the General."

"Do you have any idea what he wrote in it?"

Madame Ding shook her head. She blew her nose in a tissue and wiped fresh tears from her eyes. "I think he had so many thoughts he liked to write them down before he forgot them. He was always thinking. He was like a scholar of old. A great man...a very great man. I shall never meet his like again. I should go and try and find Jin Jing and tell her what has happened to her father."

"Leave that to me, Madame Ding."

"When will the funeral be?"

"I cannot say."

"Do you believe in the afterlife, Superintendent?"

"I do."

"Do you think all those young men in the photograph, the men who died all those years ago in Vietnam, were waiting in the afterlife to greet the General when he arrived?"

"I do not see why not."

"If so, that would be a comfort to me."

"Then let it be so, Madame Ding."

TWELVE

— • —

M a Meili was well-used to being abandoned by Superintendent Ye. He had a habit of leaving her in the office and not telling her where he was going. He had also left her behind at crime scenes before, only to express surprise and to ask her where she had been when she turned up later after having had to catch the bus back to PSB HQ. But this time she was furious with him. This time he had gone too far. Finding an address for Jin Huiliang's daughter should prove no trouble. But how was she, a mere constable, going to convince the People's Liberation Army to give her Jin Huiliang's service record? And how was she supposed to find the shop that had sold the ice-axe out of so many shops in the local area? It made no sense. She could be walking the streets for hours. She was also of the firm opinion that such an unusual implement could only be sourced from a specialist supplier and that, in all likelihood, the murderer purchased it online. Superintendent Ye had sent her on a fool's errand. Superintendent Ye had just wanted her out of his way.

As she stomped around the streets, the response she got from the local shopkeepers was much as she expected. Most had never even heard of an ice-axe, or, if they had, thought it was used for chopping up ice for drinks or to cool people's homes.

"It is used for climbing mountains," she would tell them.

"Mountains? Here in Chengdu?" they would reply, puzzled.

One shopkeeper, a Mister Wang, more friendly than the others, made her a cup of tea and gave her a wholesale catalogue to flick through to see if she could spot the ice-axe. After a wasted ten minutes she had found no ice-axe. But she had seen a lot of stuff that she wanted to buy herself, particularly a sparkly collar for Yoyo.

Depressed, she handed the catalogue back to Mister Wang. It was then that Mister Wang had a bright idea. He told her that not more than five minutes' walk away there was an outdoor pursuits shop that sold some lovely winter coats. Mister Wang was saving up to buy such a coat for his wife who really suffered in the cold. He did not know whether they also sold ice-axes but surely it was worth a try.

Encouraged, Ma Meili had followed his directions and, staring through the window of *Magical Wilderness Adventures*, she did see some very fine winter coats. But it was the poster in the window that really grabbed her attention. A handsome man, smiling at the camera, was perched on the snow-capped summit of a mountain somewhere, surrounded by nothing but dazzling blue sky, and holding in his hand an ice-axe identical to that which had been plunged into Jin Huiliang's skull.

Inside the shop, two pretty young things converged on Ma Meili, only to stop short when she showed her police badge and ID.

"I want to know about ice-axes," she told them.

The pretty young things ran to get the proprietor, a Madame Song Xue, who turned out to be a very nice but very emotional lady. In her office, when Ma Meili showed her a photograph of the bloodied ice-axe laid out on a table in the morgue, Madame Song became very tearful. And when Ma Meili told her that the ice-axe had been used in a particularly brutal murder, Madame Song had to shout to one of the pretty young things to bring her some revitalising tea.

"This is all so terrible," said Madame Song.

"Is it one of your ice-axes?" asked Ma Meili.

"We do stock that brand. But there are other outdoor pursuits shops in Chengdu. And I am sure that ice-axe can be easily sourced all over China. It is a growing industry, Constable Ma. Everyone wants to get out into nature these days. Let me check if we have sold one recently."

Madame Song accessed her computer. Soon she was sighing heavily, her face in her hands.

"What is it?" asked Ma Meili.

"We sold one of those ice-axes only two weeks ago. But I have no record of who bought it. It was a cash sale and the customer declined to leave their address."

Ma Meili considered the problem. "Do you have CCTV?"

"Yes – but on a 48-hour cycle only. However, Ju might remember the man who bought the ice-axe. It was she who made the sale."

Ju, one of the pretty young things, came running into Madame Song's office as soon as she was summoned. She was so scared she would not look at Ma Meili. Madame Song interrogated her quickly. Ju shook her head emphatically. Madame Song was quite mistaken. The purchaser of the ice-axe had been a woman, not a man.

"How unusual," said Madame Song, perplexed.

Ma Meili took over the questioning. "Can you describe her?"

Ju could not. "She was very old, I think – definitely over twenty-five."

"Did she smoke?"

"Smoking is not allowed in the shop," replied Ju.

"We do pride ourselves on promoting a healthy lifestyle," added Madame Song.

"Did this woman say why she wanted the ice-axe?" asked Ma Meili.

"I cannot remember," replied Ju. "We usually do strike up a conversation with our customers in the hope of persuading them to spend more money. As Madame Song always says, 'the wilderness adventurer can never have enough equipment.'"

"I do say that," confirmed Madame Song.

"But I did compliment her on her beautiful handbag," said Ju, her memory suddenly come alive. "It was expensive, dark green, made of real crocodile skin. It is sometimes hard to tell. Good quality leather is often passed off as crocodile skin. But one look at that handbag and I knew...."

Ma Meili lost interest in learning how to tell the difference between crocodile skin and leather. Instead, she recalled what Superintendent Ye had told her about the odd cigarette butt in Jin Huiliang's ash tray, the Good Cat with the lipstick around it, and Good Cat being such a very expensive brand. Were not crocodile skin handbags expensive too?

Ma Meili raised a hand to stop Ju from blathering on further about handbags. "Would you recognise this woman again?"

"No," said Ju. "But that bag I would recognise anywhere. It is worth at least 20,000 *yuan*. I would murder for such a bag."

"Ju!" exclaimed Madame Song, quite shocked.

Ju apologised, but with her fear of Ma Meili now gone, happy to be talking about handbags, she pulled her phone out of her pocket, played with it for a few seconds, and then showed Ma Meili a picture of the very same handbag on a shopping website.

"You are certain?" asked Ma Meili, unable to comprehend how anyone could spend so much money on a simple handbag.

"Oh, yes – I have dreamed about that handbag many times in the last couple of weeks. One day I will marry well and my husband will buy me such a handbag. Oh, and jewellery as well. I do like jewellery."

Madame Song dismissed Ju. "I am sorry she was not more help, Constable. My customers are mainly rich men who like being fussed over by pretty girls – even if the girls' heads are full of empty space."

"Her information is still useful," said Ma Meili, making a few notes in her notebook, thinking about this rich woman with the green crocodile skin handbag, who had purchased an ice-axe two weeks ago, and who had spent – in Ma Meili's mind at least – the whole of those two weeks coldly planning a murder. That the woman with the handbag might well be innocent did not occur to her. As far as Ma Meili was concerned, she now had her target. And she knew that she was hunting a very dangerous woman indeed.

Ma Meili left her card with Madame Song in case Ju remembered anything else, or if the dangerous woman in question returned.

Before Ma Meili could make her escape, Madame Song asked, "Have you ever done any modelling, Constable?"

"Pardon?"

"Don't take this the wrong way, Constable, but you look as if you could climb Zhumulangma Feng[1] without oxygen. I am about to have a new catalogue printed, some posters too. If you wished to earn some extra money, I could do with a woman of your physique to model my new clothing range."

Ma Meili didn't know what to say. From her massive frame to her overlarge moon-face, she had never considered herself attractive, let alone imagined she could be a model.

"Please think about it, Constable," said Madame Song. "You look every inch the wilderness adventurer: big, strong, and fearless – able to wrestle bears if you have to."

---

1. Mount Everest

Standing at the bus stop, Ma Meili was still pondering this unexpected offer when the SWAT truck miraculously came by again and stopped to pick her up. She noted that many of the team had cuts and bruises on their faces.

"Ah, Sister, we could have done with your help this morning."

"The drug dealers cut up rough."

"The Narcotics detectives would not let us shoot them."

"It turned into a big punch-up!"

As it turned out, however, the fist-fight had made SWAT's day. That and when Ma Meili told them all about her morning, about the murder of Jin Huiliang, about the ice-axe in his head, and, naturally, about the exciting autopsy she had attended, conducted by Doctor Kong. All talk by SWAT of Homicide being only for depressed old men was forgotten for the time being. When they dropped Ma Meili off at PSB HQ, they pleaded with her to keep them apprised of developments, and to tell them more at the party on Sunday evening. They also reminded her that, if she ever needed back-up, they – and all their guns, crossbows, and flash bangs – were only a phone call away.

Before heading up to the Homicide office, Ma Meili first dropped in on the Household Registration Department. In exchange for a few tasty titbits about Jin Huiliang's murder – it seemed that everyone now wanted to know about the 'ice-axe murder' – they easily tracked down his daughter for her. Then, back in the office, after giving herself a stern talking to, and reminding herself that as a police officer she always had to be strong, she opened up the police directory she kept on her desk, found the number she needed, and telephoned the People's Liberation Army.

"Headquarters, Chengdu Military Region, which department?"

"Ah, yes, this is Constable Ma, and—"

"Which department?"

"I'm not sure, perhaps if you—"

The line went dead.

Hoping that the phone had been put down on her by mistake, Ma Meili dialled again.

"Headquarters, Chengdu Military Region, which department?"

"Yes, this is Constable Ma again, and I—"

"Constable Ma, we are very busy here. Please prepare your enquiry properly before contacting us again."

The line went dead again.

Disheartened, certain Superintendent Ye would be furious with her for not getting hold of Jin Huiliang's service record, Ma Meili wandered down to the canteen to grab some lunch and think some very bad thoughts about the PLA. She sat alone as she ate a bowl of hotpot, which was not very good, and wondered when, or if, Superintendent Ye would return to the office. He had such a bad character that some days he would promise to return just after lunch but she would not see him again until the following morning.

"Constable Ma, are you alright?"

Ma Meili glanced up and quickly stood to attention. Like most others in Chengdu PSB, she had no idea how Ms. Miao fitted into the command structure. As Chief of Police Di's personal assistant, Ms. Miao wore no uniform and had no official rank. Though she was relatively young – no more than thirty, of an age to Ma Meili herself – she carried herself around PSB HQ with a distinct air of authority. Very little was known about her. As Ma Meili understood it, Ms. Miao had arrived in Chengdu with the rest of the Shanghai Clique but appeared to have loyalty to no other than Chief Di. It was said Chief Di found her indispensable. Most of the men in PSB HQ found her extremely attractive – the air of mystery about her may have helped – but none would dare approach her or ask her out on a date. Despite her beauty, Ms. Miao had a most forbidding countenance and always gave the impression she did not suffer fools lightly.

"I am quite well, Ms. Miao," said Ma Meili.

"That is not what I asked you. I hear that Superintendent Ye has returned early from holiday."

"Yes, Ms. Miao."

"And that you are working on a most unusual murder."

"Yes, Ms. Miao."

"How is Superintendent Ye treating you?"

The question flummoxed Ma Meili. How did Ms. Miao know about her troubles? It was surely wrong to complain about Superintendent Ye, so instead she just hung her head.

"What has he done now?" asked Ms. Miao.

"Nothing," muttered Ma Meili.

"I will not ask you again, Constable Ma."

"He has ordered me to contact the PLA, Ms. Miao."

"For what purpose?"

"The victim killed by the ice-axe was a retired general. I am supposed to get his service record. But when I phoned—"

"They put the phone down on you?"

"Yes, Ms. Miao."

Ms. Miao put her hands on her hips and little patches of red appeared on her otherwise pale cheeks. "Superintendent Ye knew this would happen. He is deliberately tormenting you, Constable Ma. Even if you had got through to the right department, they would never have accepted such a request from a lowly constable – and never without the proper accompanying paperwork. But do not worry. I will have a sharp word with Superintendent Ye. This nonsense has got to stop. In the meantime, let me have your victim's details. I have very good contacts within the PLA. I will get a copy of the service record by the end of the day."

Ma Meili did not know what she had done to deserve such kindness. "Thank you, Ms. Miao."

"Do not mention it. But there is something else I have been meaning to speak to you about. Chengdu prides itself on being an international city – a city doing its best to attract international investment as well as tourism. There is a requirement for more police to learn English and to be schooled in Western culture. You are at the top of my list, Constable Ma. The course begins on Tuesday and will take up three of your evenings a week. May I sign you up?"

Ma Meili was terrified and thought it best to air her limitations. "I was no good at school, Ms. Miao."

Ms. Miao said nothing. She continued to stand with her hands upon her hips, looking as severe as any woman Ma Meili had ever known.

"However, I am always ready to improve myself," added Ma Meili, belatedly realising what was expected of her.

"That's the spirit," said Ms. Miao.

Then Ms. Miao was gone, marching across the shiny canteen floor, her back straight, her figure perfect, fully in charge of herself – a most impressive woman. Ma Meili pushed the poor hotpot to one side, her appetite gone. She tried to be optimistic. She knew that never in a million years would she ever be able to emulate such a stylish and confident woman as Ms. Miao. But maybe, just maybe, with a little bit of English, and with a little knowledge of Western culture, Superintendent Ye might treat her a little better.

THIRTEEN

— · —

The new development in the southern area of the Chengdu Hi-Tech Industrial Development Zone of the city known as the Tianfu Software Park had attracted software companies from all around the world. It was no surprise to Xu Ya, therefore, that Ambrogetti Global Software also had its offices there. Before stepping through the doors, hoping Party Chief Li had made the phone call as promised and that she would be expected, Xu Ya had sat in her car for a while doing what research she could on her phone, trying to flesh out the little she had already learned about Primo Gong.

Something serious had happened in San Diego in the United States within the family Gong. It was hard to discover what exactly. Primo Gong had been destined to take over the family business, Ambrogetti Global Electronics, from his father, Alessandro Gong. For some reason Primo Gong had turned his back on his family, brought his wife and children to Chengdu, and announced to the world that he had come 'home'. However acrimonious the family dispute had been back in San Diego, the family had not objected to Primo Gong setting up his own company and naming it Ambrogetti Global Software and then moving it to Chengdu – with the help of some very attractive incentives and subsidies provided by the Chengdu local government. Primo Gong had then gone on to renounce his American citizenship in favour of the passport of the People's Republic of China, his commitment to his new life in the country of his ancestry seemingly total.

Primo Gong and the launch of Ambrogetti Global Software in the city was an incredible coup for Chengdu and the Shanghai Clique, the reverberations from Primo Gong's 'defection' from the United States, and the internationally famous Ambrogetti Global Electronics, echoing around the business world. Educated, determined, eloquent, and always charismatic, there was no doubt in anyone's mind that Primo Gong would make Ambrogetti Global Software a roaring success.

"We are creating the future...right here...in Chengdu!" Primo Gong had announced to the world's business press on the day Ambrogetti Global Software had opened its doors.

The photograph she had found of that event had been instructive for Xu Ya. As he gave his very first interview from the lobby of Ambrogetti Global Software, Primo Gong had been flanked by both Party Chief Li and Mayor Cang. With the Party fully behind them, the company already had a list of potential clients queuing up at the door. Ambrogetti Global Software was not going to fail. Ambrogetti Global Software was *not* going to be allowed to fail. And, a couple of years later, that had been proved to one and all. Ambrogetti Global Software was, in terms of employee numbers, still a relatively small concern. But it employed the best and the brightest in the city, and its shares were hot property on the Shanghai Exchange. It specialised in the development of investment and trading software for the financial services industry. Its very first client, announced during that very first press conference, was the prestigious Chengdu Cymbidium Bank, so famous it was usually referred to as 'The CCB' – a bank heavily associated with the Party, with the Shanghai Clique, and with shadowy figures behind the scenes far away in Beijing.

With Primo Gong now murdered and with Party Chief Li and his friends due to sell off their stakes in the company as soon as the Shanghai Exchange opened on Monday morning, Xu Ya wondered what was going to become of the company. Nothing good, she assumed. With its charismatic leader gone, the company – as Party Chief Li well knew – was sure to founder.

Xu Ya decided this was no time to feel sad for all the employees. They would all find positions elsewhere. She had a job to do and the secret of Primo Gong's murder to keep. She had to discover how and when Primo Gong had crossed paths with the police. And why, because of that fateful encounter, someone in the police had chosen to murder such a close friend of the Party – that is, if, as she thought highly unlikely, Ye Zihao had not issued the kill order himself.

Xu Ya was met in the lobby of Ambrogetti Global Software by a young, fireball of a woman, Ms. Wen Jiao. She introduced herself as personal aide to Primo Gong. She led Xu Ya quickly through a state-of-the-art suite of offices – so different to the Procuratorate! Xu Ya was surprised, given it was a Saturday, to see so many, all of them young people, at their desks and computer screens. Some of them glanced fearfully in Xu Ya's direction, probably recognising her from the trial of the criminal Commissioner Ho that had been shown night after night on TV only a few weeks before. But Ms. Wen was made of sterner stuff. When she closed the door behind them so they could talk privately in a conference room, she made it clear what was on her mind.

"Prosecutor, this is not good timing for us. We have a very important deadline to make with the CCB. It is essential that Primo is here to lead us at this critical time."

Primo.

In her research on the company, Xu Ya had been fascinated to learn that Primo Gong had insisted his staff refer to him by his given name.

Strange.

So very modern, so very American, Primo Gong's sinification not as complete as some would like to believe.

"Without Primo we are rudderless," added Ms. Wen, pouting.

Xu Ya felt like giving her a slap. But those words proved to be the extent of Ms. Wen's courage. After Xu Ya took the seat offered her at the long, stylish table fashioned out of a single large slab of black glass, and after Ms. Wen took a seat next to her, their knees almost touching, Xu Ya saw that Ms. Wen was trembling from head to toe. Xu Ya began to feel more kindly disposed toward her.

"I am afraid there is no good time for Procuratorate investigations," began Xu Ya, continuing the lie that Party Chief Li would have told Ms. Wen over the phone. "But I am sure, as Mister Gong is being especially helpful, we will finish speaking with him in the next day or so."

Ms. Wen nodded sombrely. A large photograph caught Xu Ya's eye on the wall, Primo Gong at some business function in the city, laughing with Mayor Cang, while a tall woman clung on to Mayor Cang's arm, a woman displaying far too much of her tanned skin, a woman whose smile was as beguiling as it was intimidating.

Sarangerel.

Xu Ya felt a shiver go through her.

So the Witch-Queen of Chengdu and Primo Gong knew each other.

Interesting.

Or maybe not.

Primo Gong would have known many people in Chengdu.

"Are you cold, Prosecutor," asked Ms. Wen. "Is the air-conditioning up too high? It has been so hot of late and—"

"No, thank you, Ms. Wen – I am fine. I just need some information. I hope Party Chief Li made it clear to you that Mister Gong is not the subject of our enquiries and that you are to assist me in any way you can."

"Yes, Prosecutor."

"It is very possible that Mister Gong, quite innocently, met with people who are of interest to the Procuratorate. I need a full list of your employees together with their addresses, your current and prospective client list, and a copy of Mister Gong's diary for the last six months in electronic and paper form."

"Of course, Prosecutor."

"I will also need access to Mister Gong's electronics."

"He always has his phone with him. It never leaves his side. There is a laptop here in his office and he uses another laptop in his apartment as well as a tablet."

"At Plum Tree Pagodas?"

"Yes, Prosecutor."

Xu Ya felt the cold satisfaction of now having proof that Lucy Fu had taken Primo Gong's electronics from his apartment. The mystery woman could not have done so, not in a panic, not while running for her life. The phone, tablet, and laptop were all probably destroyed now, Lucy Fu choosing to erase all connections between her and the mystery woman, incorrectly believing the mystery woman to be a murderess after misinterpreting the crime scene, not wanting the family Fu to be implicated in any way.

What had been stored on Primo Gong's electronics? Photographs of the three of them out together socialising, perhaps? Or had Primo Gong been keeping a detailed diary?

Xu Ya thought it a great pity that she would now never get to know. Not unless....

"Do you have access to Mister Gong's electronic files?" Xu Ya asked, abruptly. "Are they stored centrally?"

"We have access here to the majority of his work files," replied Ms. Wen. "But not to his personal files. I am sure he will give you any passwords you need, Prosecutor."

Disappointed, Xu Ya said, "He is indeed being most helpful."

"Is it possible to speak with him?"

"Not at the moment."

"We were so worried, Prosecutor."

"You were looking for him?"

"There was a problem during the night. The head of our CCB development team tried to get hold of him."

"When was this?"

"About two – but Primo's phone appeared to be switched off. This is most unusual, Prosecutor. I was woken at home in the hope that I could find him. I was so worried I phoned Plum Tree Pagodas directly but was told by the concierge that Primo had left orders that he was not to be disturbed."

The pained expression on Ms. Wen's face told Xu Ya that this situation was highly irregular. "What did you do?"

"I did not know what to do. I thought about going down to Plum Tree Pagodas in a taxi and banging on Primo's door. I was very afraid. This was not like him. I had a feeling in the pit of my stomach that something terrible had happened. Nothing has been going right these last few months. It has been an awful time. Primo has not been himself. I don't think he has been well. I tried to get him to see a doctor but he wouldn't go. He said I worried too much, that I fussed over him like an over-protective mother. But I knew something was troubling him, something more than just the problems with the CCB contract. And now you are here...and now Party Chief Li has explained everything to me...I am so very relieved. I suspected he had fallen into some bad company. He had grown so unlike himself, so secretive. Please help him, Prosecutor."

"Do you not manage his diary?"

"I do – but sometimes he would insist I leave gaps in his day without telling me why. There have been some mornings or afternoons I had no idea at all where he was, though he would always answer his phone if I called him."

"Where was he last evening?"

"Oh, that at least is a simple question to answer. Every Friday evening, he attends a dinner with the senior executives from the CCB. The bank is our most important client and Primo really enjoys their company."

"Where was the dinner?"

"It's always at the Old Chengdu Restaurant."

"Who else attended?"

"You want the list of CCB executives at the dinner? It varies from week to week. I would have to contact Director Min at the bank to find out who attended last evening."

"I was actually asking if Mister Gong took along a date."

"Ah, I wouldn't know, Prosecutor," replied Ms. Wen, unable to conceal her misery.

Xu Ya realised that Ms. Wen's concern for Primo Gong was more than that of an employee worried for an adored boss. She was in love with Primo Gong. Xu Ya felt sad for her. Xu Ya also felt a sharp pang of conscience for telling the lie that Primo Gong still lived. She put her regret to the back of her mind. She could hate herself for all she was being forced to do this day in the weeks and months to come.

"You know of no romantic liaisons?" asked Xu Ya.

"No, Prosecutor – since his wife left him and took the children back to the United States with her, which was a most terrible thing, Primo has been dedicated to making a success of Ambrogetti Global Software. He had no time for socialising...apart from that which he has to do to build up his network of contacts in Chengdu and around the country. He never rests...never takes a holiday. But then..." Ms. Wen looked away, out of the window at the failing rain, more miserable than ever.

"But what, Ms. Wen?"

"Oh, nothing, Prosecutor."

Xu Ya noted the poor effort at concealment. "Ms. Wen, I wish to return Mister Gong to you as soon as possible. If you are withholding information then all that will do is serve to slow down my enquiries. You are not helping Mister Gong by not speaking to me. Don't you see that?"

"Oh, Prosecutor, I am glad you are a woman. I could never speak openly to a man. I have been so afraid these last few months when Primo has been insisting on my leaving those odd gaps in his diary. I suspected a woman from the start. But I did not understand how and when he could have met such a woman. Except for work functions, he didn't like socialising. And I was always kept abreast of whatever went on at those work functions. I always made sure someone was there keeping an eye on him. No matter what he might think, no matter that his ancestors were originally from Chengdu, Primo is not, and never will be, fully Chinese. I tried to warn him...as any friend would. I tried to explain to him how women were in China, how without his wife and children he would be easy prey to any money-hungry floozy. But he would only laugh at me, tell me that he had no time for romance of any kind, that his every waking hour was dedicated to the company. But I knew how much the departure of his wife and children had hurt him. I knew how vulnerable he was, how lonely he was. I think a competitor has sent a woman to destroy him, to destroy the whole company. I had no proof, Prosecutor. Not until the other evening. One of our young programmers, Zhou Rong, was out on the town with some of his friends. Primo had told me he would be working from home. But Zhou Rong saw Primo with a woman, walking down the other side of the street, probably on their way to a secluded restaurant. Zhou Rong was so surprised he did not have the good sense to run over and introduce himself and find out who she was. Zhou Rong is very shy. But he took a quick picture with his phone and he sent it to me. He knew how concerned I had been. These last few days I have been trying to decide how to confront Primo with the photograph, with the truth that this woman is most definitely up to no good. I am sure he will try to conceal her name from you, thinking that he is being gallant. He does not understand women in China. He does not understand them at all."

Xu Ya tried to control her excitement. "Do you still have the picture?"

Ms. Wen, hardly able to hold back her tears now, found the photograph on her phone and then passed her phone to Xu Ya. The photograph had been taken in low light, and from some distance. But, by expanding the photograph, Xu Ya could just make out Primo

Gong's face and that of the woman arm-in-arm with him – a mature, but very glamorous woman with long, wavy hair.

Ah, now I have you, thought Xu Ya, exultant.

"Do you think it could be so, Prosecutor...that a competitor has sent this woman to seduce him, to ruin him, to destroy all that he has been trying to build?"

"I do," replied Xu Ya, not wanting to disabuse Ms. Wen of her fantastical notion, not wanting to tell her that the woman with the long, wavy hair was, in all likelihood, a prostitute in the pay of the family Fu, and possibly now dead.

"If you speak to Primo, he will listen to you, Prosecutor. He admires you so much. All he would talk about for days, after seeing you on TV during the trial of that monster Commissioner Ho, is of how proud he was that there were people such as you in Chengdu, people always ready to make a stand against the corrupt and the wicked. He really believes in the Rule of Law, Prosecutor. I don't think I ever really cared about anything except for myself and my own pointless little life until I began working for him. But he has taught me to care not just about the business and the way we do business but about society as well. Everything we do has to be done for the good of the people and not just the good of the company, he always says. He is the best man I know, Prosecutor – the very best man."

Xu Ya passed the phone back to Ms. Wen, who began to stare despondently at the photograph, unconsciously tugging at her shoulder-length hair, a fruitless attempt, perhaps, to make it longer and wavy.

"I will need a copy of that photograph," said Xu Ya.

"Of course."

"One final question, Ms. Wen?"

"Anything, Prosecutor."

"Did Mister Gong ever have any run-ins with the police?"

Ms. Wen's face was a blank slate. "I don't think so."

"Are you certain?"

"I am not certain of anything anymore, Prosecutor. Wait...there was one time he had to pay a speeding fine. But that was well over a year ago and he drives much more carefully now."

"Nothing else comes to mind?"

"No, Prosecutor."

"Then, if you can go and get me all the information I need – Mister Gong's diary, all the details of your employees, and your client list – I will leave you in peace."

"And Primo will then be returned to us soon?"

"I expect so."

Ms. Wen stood to do as asked, but, as she put her hand on the handle of the door to leave the conference room, she turned to Xu Ya and said, "That woman...."

"I will speak to her as soon as I can find her."

Ms. Wen nodded, smiling weakly, satisfied by the first truth Xu Ya had spoken to her.

FOURTEEN

— : —

Something was not adding up. Fatty Deng sheltered from the rain in the doorway of Mister Wu's Cycle Sales and Repair Shop, right next door to the Black House on Liberation Street. He wiped the sweat and rainwater from his face with a handkerchief and lit a cigarette, struggling to get to grips with what was troubling his mind. For the last half-hour he had been walking the streets around Plum Tree Pagodas, trying to get the lie of the land, familiarising himself with all the local landmarks, and in the process confirming to himself that the shot that had killed Primo Gong could have only originated from the Black House. Only the top floor of the Black House provided the perfect vantage point to shoot flat and level into Primo Gong's fifth floor apartment. But, as Fatty Deng stared across the street at the Lucky Dragon Tobacco Emporium, and then at Plum Tree Pagodas that rose up behind it almost into the low clouds, Fatty Deng had reluctantly come to the conclusion that all was not as it seemed. Only the police had access to the Black House, or so he had told Prosecutor Xu. Only a police officer could have murdered Primo Gong. Now, however, he was not so sure.

As with every other city in China, in Chengdu there was the Golden Rule: *you don't fuck with the police*. If someone was so foolish as to do so, then there would be retribution. Forgiveness was not part of the police mentality. It had to be that way otherwise the police would lose face and would, in their minds at least, rapidly lose control of the streets.

That retribution usually followed one of two standard forms: either the offending person was lifted off the street and bundled into the back of a car, driven to some isolated patch of waste ground, and given the beating of their lives; or, if the sin was considered serious enough, the person might find themselves, without ever seeing the inside of a People's Court, without ever necessarily breaking the law, transported to some bleak labour camp for a year, or two, or three. Though occasionally people died from their beatings or from overwork and bad diet at a labour camp, the police never usually went out of their way to actually murder someone. Fatty Deng had never heard of a time when anyone had got so far on the wrong side of the police that it was decided they needed dispatching with a sniper's rifle.

And he should know; he had been police for ten years. And police did not keep secrets from one another. Police always talked, sometimes out loud, sometimes in whispers, sometimes at home, sometimes in bars – but they always talked.

It was the way of things.

It was police culture.

If a police officer had murdered Primo Gong with a sniper's rifle, by the end of the day half the PSB would know about it. And, by the following morning, the remaining half would know too. The details might not necessarily be clear, who had ordered what and why, maybe not even who had actually pulled the trigger, but there would be a common understanding that it had been a police job and that little was required in the way of investigation.

Sure, there were always those old stories of those police in the pay of gangsters acting as hitmen, but contract killings were more the stuff of films than reality. Gangsters paid police to look the other way. Fatty Deng had never heard of gangsters paying police to do their dirty work for them – not in Chengdu. Gangsters wouldn't trust the police to do the job right.

Fatty Deng threw away his cigarette and lit another. His maximum of five for the day was no longer feasible. He had too much thinking to do, too big a problem to solve.

Only police had access to the Black House.

Only police could have pulled the trigger on Primo Gong.

And yet....

The rain had held off for a time and so, stupidly, he had left his umbrella in the car. Not only hot and bothered and very troubled, he was also soaked to the skin. He had been hoping to find some

CCTV he might access, to have a look at the comings and goings at the Black House. But, as he stared up and down Liberation Street, all he could see were the usual police cameras. Unwilling to tip the police off to the Procuratorate investigation, the police cameras were useless to him. As for the lack of private CCTV, it was possible there was some local ordinance that prohibited its use so close to the Black House. Or else there was so little crime in this part of the city there was no need for such added security. Either way, it was a pity.

He glanced across the road at the Lucky Dragon Tobacco Emporium, wishing he could better make out the features of the attractive young woman who served behind the counter. He then looked up above the shop at Plum Tree Pagodas again. The hole that had been punched through Primo Gong's fifth floor apartment window was just visible through the rain and the haze.

In the daylight he could better judge the distance.

120 metres, he thought.

The bullet that had killed Primo Gong had had to travel from the Black House, across Liberation Street, over the roof of the Lucky Dragon Tobacco Emporium, over the yard and the narrow alley to the back of the shop, over the high perimeter wall that formed the boundary of the Plum Tree Pagoda luxury complex, over gardens and an ornamental fish pool, to smash through the window, smack into Primo Gong's chest, rip through his heart and then, taking bits of his spine with it, bury itself in the bedroom back wall.

120 metres.

Quite a shot, at night, and in bad weather – for an amateur.

So, no amateurs here.

120 metres with the bullet leaving the rifle at, say, 800 metres per second. A fraction of a second between trigger pull and Primo Gong being thrown back on his bed and breathing his last.

Fuck.

What had Primo Gong done to deserve such a sudden and violent death?

Who had he pissed off?

Despite what former mayor Ye Zihao might wish to believe, in Chengdu the Shanghai Clique was synonymous these days with the Party. And, as Primo Gong was close to Party Chief Li – and, by extension, to all of the Shanghai Clique – the assassin was either unaware of local politics or so arrogant as to be uncaring. There were certainly elements within the police, those who openly attended the monthly parties at the Ye family mansion, who were still loyal to Ye Zihao, and who had a particular loathing of the Shanghai Clique. These were the older officers in the main. But, since The Purge, when many officers – including himself – had lost their jobs to make way for a fresh influx of police from Shanghai and other faraway places, it was safe to assume that if a police officer had been the assassin, word would soon reach Party Chief Li. The police might grumble and moan, might air their grievances from time to time, but they would never make so blatant an attack on the Party. Even if Primo Gong had really pissed the police off somehow, he would never even have been lifted off the street and given a beating in some deserted alley in the middle of the night. Some other form of retribution would have been found for an elite like him, maybe the arrest for no reason of a favoured employee of his, a brick through his office window, or a quiet word in the ear of some senior Party flunkey in a smoke-filled bar saying that it was time for Primo Gong to cease and desist whatever wrong he had been committing. No, the more Fatty Deng pondered the problem, the killing of Primo Gong seemed to be nothing to do with the police at all.

But only the police had access to the Black House. Only a police officer could have pulled the trigger....

Now that the Black House had become nothing more than a repository for ancient and dusty confidential PSB files, the only police in and out of it would be the day and night shifts sent to guard it by the PSB Building Security Section – in Fatty Deng's opinion, not real police at all. It was true that they held rank, had usually attended Police College, and that the Building Security Section was a valued component of the overall PSB organisational structure. But inspecting window locks, walking the corridors every hour or so to check all was as it should be, and spending the rest of the time eating, drinking, and playing cards or *majiang* was not exactly proper policing. Fatty Deng considered the guard details hardly better than the private security to be found at shopping malls. It was highly likely that the Black House guard details didn't even wear uniforms, not wanting to give away the nature of the building they were tasked with guarding, even though everyone who lived and worked on Liberation

Street, from the oldest retiree to the youngest child, would have known well enough to keep away. Even as nothing more than a file repository, the Black House remained a grim and forbidding edifice.

Fatty Deng pondered the Black House building security detail. They might not do proper police work, but again, police culture being what it was, if they had been up to no good, sooner or later the whole of the PSB would have caught a whisper. Unless, that is, the security detail had, en masse, accepted a bribe and vacated the Black House for a few hours, neither knowing nor wanting to know who was going to use the Black House, or what it was to be used for, in the hours that they were absent.

Fatty Deng smiled to himself, liking the theory, liking it a lot. However, the theory told him nothing about the identity of the assassin. He put all consideration of the building security team aside for the time being and tried to zero in on just who had the capability to pull off such a murder.

He quickly dismissed all thoughts of a specialist assassin, an independent contractor. There were easier ways to kill a man than by somehow gaining access to a police Black House and waiting a couple of hours with a sniper rifle, easier ways of getting to someone like Primo Gong. Poison in a served cup of tea, for example, or a prick from a tiny needle while brushing past him in the street.

Who did that leave?

SWAT had the sophisticated weaponry and the skills. But, though they were generally acknowledged to be crazy, they weren't stupid. Also, more than most in the police, they couldn't keep a secret, always happy to boast about everything and anything they had done.

The CAPF – the People's Armed Police?

No, not those swaggering bastards either. Like SWAT they had the skills and the sniper rifles, but many CAPF officers were actually embedded with SWAT, and there was always lots of chatter going back and forth between the CAPF and the PSB (most of it derogatory). Few secrets between the CAPF and the PSB then. Moreover, like the city police, the CAPF's preferred method of dealing with problem people was to lift them off the street and throw them in the back of an unmarked car.

Then there was the MSS, the Ministry of State Security. They were sneaky fuckers, always turning up when least expected, often piggy-backing on police operations, never offering up their real names, never properly explaining whatever it was they were up to. But the MSS were smart enough not to over-complicate operations. If they had had a problem with Primo Gong, they would have invited him somewhere quiet for a cup of tea and a chat – an offer he would have been unable to refuse – or, if they had really wanted him out of the way, they would have sent one of those hot girls they surely had on their local roster to stick a stiletto between his ribs in his bedroom.

That just left the military: the People's Liberation Army.

But in Chengdu?

That would be insane.

But the thought began to take root in Fatty Deng's mind: a sniper team – two guys, in the dead of night, in the middle of a thunderstorm, one shooting, one spotting – would be just the PLA's style: over the fucking top. It was an insane thought – but was it that insane?

Fatty Deng lit his third cigarette in a row, the tobacco doing its job. He was close now to where he mentally needed to be.

Not for the PLA a simple snatch and grab off the street. The PLA wouldn't want to risk any of their guys being caught on police CCTV. And it would be just the PLA's style to opt for lethal force when maybe a simple conversation with Primo Gong might have done the trick, regardless of how he might have offended them. Furthermore, the PLA would either be unaware or uncaring of local Chengdu politics. If Primo Gong was a friend of Party Chief Li, then so what? Who was Party Chief Li to the PLA? The sniper team would have moved into Chengdu Friday evening and would have been gone well before the dawn – nothing for the police to whisper about there. All that remained to be solved, in terms of the mechanics of the assassination, was how a PLA sniper team got the security detail to vacate the Black House for a few hours and leave the door open.

There was another disturbing issue: Primo Gong occupying an apartment in Plum Tree Pagodas, perfectly opposite the Black House. Most of those apartments were very similar in design and outfitting. Had Primo Gong specifically asked for that apartment, or had someone in FUBI International, someone like his supposed friend Lucy Fu, offered just that one apartment to him? If so, could it be that Lucy Fu was guilty of much more than interfering with a crime scene?

Could it be that Lucy Fu had actually facilitated the assassination of Primo Gong? The thought gave Fatty Deng a headache – and he wouldn't be mentioning this notion anytime soon to Prosecutor Xu. Still, it was something to ponder.

Fatty Deng was mulling over this, and over the many police in Chengdu PSB who had joined the force after a first career in the military, when he was shouted at from behind.

"Are you going to stand in my doorway all day? You're frightening away my customers!"

Fatty Deng turned to see a small, bald-headed man whom he assumed to be the proprietor of Mister Wu's Cycle Sales and Repair Shop – Mister Wu himself.

"Maybe I'm here to buy a bike," replied Fatty Deng, cursing himself for staying in one place for too long, for being noticed.

Mister Wu looked Fatty Deng up and down. "You don't look the sort that takes much exercise."

Now it was Fatty Deng's turned to react badly. "Don't be so fucking rude!"

"Who are you anyway – police?"

"Look at my fine suit," replied Fatty Deng. "Do I look like police?"

"Absolutely," said Mister Wu.

"Well, I'm not. I'm actually a businessman, checking out the area for some office space to rent."

Mister Wu laughed in his face. "You? A businessman?"

Fatty Deng thought quickly, of Primo Gong. "I'm in computers...software...that sort of stuff."

"You look like police."

"I am *not* police."

"What interests you about the Lucky Dragon Tobacco Emporium?"

"Nothing."

"We're very protective about Sun Mei around here."

"Who?"

"The pretty young woman behind the counter of the Lucky Dragon Tobacco Emporium."

"I wasn't staring at her."

"If you are thinking of putting any moves on her, forget it!"

Exasperated, Fatty Deng said, "I am just looking for office space."

"Well, there isn't any office space around here. Now listen, Sun Mei has had a hard life. She doesn't need a fat policeman like you trying to romance her. Her father's a cripple. He used to be a para-trooper, but he landed badly one day and busted his back. His legs don't work anymore. It was Sun Mei's mother who opened the shop. Now that was one fine lady. She managed the shop, took care of her crippled husband, and raised Sun Mei properly all by herself. And Sun Mei is smart – very smart. She was heading to teacher training college. Any of the best schools in Chengdu would have snapped her up. Sun Mei would have been a headmistress one day. But then her mother died. It was so sad. I think I cried for three days straight. It was a tragedy that affected the whole street. Sun Mei could no longer go to teacher training college. Someone had to look after the shop, bring some money in."

"That's a tragic story," said Fatty Deng.

"Sun Mei had a boyfriend at the time," continued Mister Wu. "Everyone liked him – a real charmer. Handsome too, not like you or me. But, when Sun Mei could no longer go to teacher training college, he just dumped her. He couldn't see himself married to a simple shopkeeper, I guess. He turned out to be a real snake. You must understand that all of Sun Mei's dreams were shattered at once."

"Bad things happen to people all the time," said Fatty Deng.

"Isn't that the truth! But, Mister Policeman, Sun Mei is made of strong stuff. Like her father, she doesn't bemoan her life. She has built the Lucky Dragon Tobacco Emporium to be the best cigarette shop in Chengdu, maybe in all of Sichuan, better than her mother ever dreamed. She has customers contact her from all over China. She also has a way of dealing with the trade reps...flirting with them, getting all the speciality cigarettes she needs. Just harmless flirting, but it works. Anyway, they know she will always sell their products."

"That's fascinating."

"But, here's the thing, Mister Policeman. Sun Mei didn't give up on her dream of teaching. There are some kids who are a bit slow, or a bit too sensitive, not doing too well in normal school. And there are a few migrants from the country here and about who can't get a Chengdu hukou registration and so can't get their kids into school. Every evening, even while Sun Mei keeps the shop open, she teaches the local children in her sitting-room for free. For free, Mister

Policeman! So, you will understand when I tell you that Sun Mei is adored on Liberation Street. She is a heroine. It is why we are all so protective of her."

It was time to go. Fatty Deng had had enough of this. It was his own fault for standing still for so long, for drawing attention to himself.

"If there isn't any office space around here, I'd better be moving on," he said.

"That's it, Mister Policeman, you move along, and don't you be making eyes at Sun Mei again," said Mister Wu. "She doesn't need trouble like you in her life."

Fatty Deng turned his collar up against the rain and headed back toward where he had parked his car. He felt unsettled, and not only because of his coming to the conclusion – admittedly unsubstantiated – that the PLA was responsible for the murder of Primo Gong. Mister Wu had pegged him far too easily for law enforcement. And, as he was walking away, Sun Mei, the pretty young woman behind the counter of the Lucky Dragon Tobacco Emporium, had stared after him as if she had just seen a ghost.

Anxiety was a constant in Sun Mei's life. It had been so since the day her mother had died. She worried for her father, for the Lucky Dragon Tobacco Emporium, and especially for the children who came to her needing extra tutoring. But terror, real terror – that was something new.

The day before, during the extraordinary meeting of the Liberation Street Traders Association, convened to discuss the state of the drains, she had fallen asleep while standing up behind the counter, and had had a nightmare, a fat man in a garish shirt staring at her from across the street, about to upend her life forever. Now her nightmare had come true – well, almost. The fat man who had appeared in the doorway of Mister Wu's Cycle Sales and Repair Shop was not so fat, and was wearing a suit and raincoat rather than a colourful shirt.

But such minor details mattered not. One moment her life was as it should be, Mister Wu phoning her on the hour every hour to talk about the drains, how the drains had barely coped during the night, how they were barely coping now, and how, as more heavy rain was forecast for later that day, they were surely going to fail. And then, as she was serving Mister Peng his usual two packets of Hongmei White, and as Mister Peng was updating her on how his daughter was faring at her new job in the city, Sun Mei had happened to glance across the street to see the fat man standing in Mister Wu's doorway, staring in her direction. Such terror had welled up in Sun Mei that she had nearly fainted. Luckily, Mister Peng was half-blind and had not noticed her discomfort. As soon as he was out of the door she had run for the toilet and lost her breakfast.

She phoned Mister Wu. "There's a strange man in your doorway."

"I'm watching him, Sun Mei."

"I am frightened."

"He's just sheltering from the rain."

"Mister Wu, I know him. I recognise his face. I cannot remember from where...from long ago, I think. He's police."

"Are you sure?"

"Yes, Mister Wu – very sure."

"Do not worry, Sun Mei, I'll go deal with him."

"Forgive me for troubling you, Mister Wu."

"It is no trouble, Sun Mei – no trouble at all."

Mister Wu was true to his word. Sun Mei watched, amazed by Mister Wu's courage, as he confronted the fat man. A few sharp words, a few muttered replies, and the fat man was off, walking down the street, but not before giving Sun Mei yet another hard, terrifying stare.

She saw Mister Wu laugh, wave at her, and then shake his head once more at the drains. Sun Mei wondered whether she should cancel all the tutoring she was to do that evening, and not just because of the weather. If the fat man reappeared he would frighten the children.

Who was he?

What did he want with her?

And where had she seen him before?

Not only had he been staring at her but he had also been looking upwards, at the roof of the Lucky Dragon Tobacco Emporium. Too frightened to go out onto the street, instead she put on her transparent plastic raincoat and floppy hat and ventured out into the backyard. As far as she could see nothing seemed amiss with the roof. She turned around on the spot, wondering, perhaps, whether the fat man had actually been looking over her roof. She faced toward the ugly new apartment complex that was Plum Tree Pagodas, the construction of which had been the blight of everyone's lives on Liberation Street for well over a year. There was nothing much to see there either except a broken window on the fifth floor.

Back behind the shop counter, she served Mister Zha a packet of Pride cigarettes, the same cigarettes the fat man had been smoking. She had noticed the colour of the packet in his hands.

"Did you hear the thunderstorms last night?" asked Mister Zha.

"I did," replied Sun Mei.

"Did you know the last time Liberation Street was struck by lightning was 1927?"

"I did not."

"Of course, it was not called Liberation Street then. It was called The Street of Swooping Swallows. It was a pity they changed the name," said Mister Zha, sadly. "It was so poetic." But he quickly recovered himself and brightened and said, "Sun Mei, did you know that Chengdu was the last city in China to be liberated by the People's Liberation Army? My very first memory as a child is of the communist soldiers marching into the city."

"Is that so," said Sun Mei, happy to indulge Mister Zha, who fancied himself as the local historian but was otherwise quite harmless. He was a gentle and self-effacing man whose wife had died the year before. All he did now was read.

"The winter of 1949 was such an exciting time," said Mister Zha. "Exciting for a child; frightening for my parents."

"I can imagine," said Sun Mei.

Mister Zha pondered his own words for a time and then bade her goodbye. Sun Mei was left alone to think about the thunderstorms during the night, as well as the rifle shots that she and her father had plainly heard. No one else had mentioned the rifle shots, not even Mister Wu who had told her earlier that he had been up half the night worrying about the drains. Maybe no one else had heard them. Or maybe no one else had recognised them for what they were. She herself would never have understood the significance of the sharp reports unless her father, who had served in the army for many years, had not told her.

She remembered the broken window on the fifth floor of Plum Tree Pagodas.

Could it be the fat man was investigating the shooting?

Did the police believe that someone on Liberation Street so hated Plum Tree Pagodas that they been taking pot shots at the monstrosity in the middle of the night?

Sun Mei knew of no one on Liberation Street who owned a rifle. However, the police would soon learn her father had once served in the army and had the requisite skill with a rifle to put a hole in a distant window.

Was that why the fat man had been staring at her?

Was the fat man planning to take her father away for questioning?

Was that how the fat man was going to upend her life?

She ran for the toilet again but there was nothing else to come out of her stomach. She washed the beads of sweat off her face and then drank a glass of warm water, hoping that would settle her digestion. Back behind the counter she struggled to remember where she had seen the fat man before. Without realising what she was doing or in fact what she was looking for, her eyes began to scan the shelves full of stacked cigarette packets around her, moving upwards until her gaze settled on the top shelf, where she always kept a couple of packets of French Gauloises Blondes – not a popular brand with her regular customers. Then the past suddenly rose up before her as clear as crystal, and she remembered where she had seen the fat man before as well as the stupid face she had pulled at him. Sun Mei ran for the toilet yet again.

In the police, Fatty Deng had many times seen fear in the faces of the people. After the Shanghai Clique decided the police no longer needed his services, when he had worked for a short time for Brother Wang collecting debts for the gangster Freddie Yun, he had seen fear in the faces of the people many times then too. But he had never gone out of his way to create fear in people and certainly, unlike some, had never enjoyed the look of fear in anyone's eyes. He had joined the police because he had wanted to protect the people from those who would do them harm, the truly evil, those without conscience. He had collected debts for Brother Wang because then it had been the only job he could find and he had needed to make a living. He had never, ever, wanted to threaten, intimidate, or bully anyone. It was not in his essential nature; and yet, unfortunately, life had not turned out that way. As police, sometimes, through no fault of his own, from wrong information being given him, he had smacked around an innocent person. And while working for Brother Wang, well, intimidation and threats had been the name of the game....

"I am not a bad person," he had often told himself out loud.

Such utterances, however, were a waste of breath. He knew, from his very first day on the job, from the very first day after leaving Police College, his conscience had been irrevocably stained. It was the life. If one wallowed in the dirt of humanity, if one mixed every day with the criminal and the wicked, it had to be expected that some of that dirt would rub off. He was no longer a child. He was no longer wholly good. And, if he engendered fear in people, even now as an investigator for the Procuratorate, then so much the better, for at least that fear would help him get his job done. But the fear he had seen in the face of the young woman managing the Lucky Dragon Tobacco Emporium had shaken him, had made him depressed and introspective. He had once dreamed of marrying such a woman: attractive, hard-working, and good with people. Sun Mei was her name, according to that loud-mouth Mister Wu.

He lit another cigarette, cursing his weakness for tobacco, and closed his eyes, content to be out of the rain and alone for a while in the car, and content, for once, to allow a distant memory to rise up in him, and to wonder where all the years had gone.

As a young constable not long out of Police College, he had been tasked with transporting a criminal from Wangjiang Road Police

Station to the Black House on Liberation Street. The Black House was still in use then as a place to make people disappear for a time, not the graveyard it had now become for old PSB files. The criminal in question had been a lawyer, a nice man as it turned out, who had made the mistake of assisting some poor people in protesting the construction of a chemical factory just to the north of Chengdu. As a rule, the police had no time for lawyers of any stripe. A lawyer was a trouble-maker, simple as that. But when he, Constable Deng (second class) as he had been then, and no more than twenty years old, had pushed the lawyer into the back of the police car and set off for Liberation Street, he had begun chatting with him. Fatty Deng had found the lawyer to be both funny and charming and not at all bitter about the beating he had received back at the police station.

"You're all just doing your job," had said the lawyer, a Mister Li.

Fatty Deng had not been so sure about that. He fully agreed with the general police consensus that, if a lawyer earned a living defending criminals, then they were not much better than criminals themselves. But he had heard all about the construction of the chemical plant and the fears the local people had in regard to the release of dangerous pollutants. He would not want such a chemical plant being built next to the apartment block where he lived with his mother. If such a plant had been planned in his neighbourhood, he surely would have been protesting its construction too. However, someone high up in the PSB chain of command had decided it was for the good of all in Chengdu that Mister Li Du 'disappear' for a month or two.

"Don't worry, Constable Deng, I've been in the Black House before," said Mister Li. "It's not so bad."

Maybe so, but Fatty Deng had not envied him.

Thinking it would be a kindness, and that no one would ever know, Fatty Deng had allowed Mister Li to use his police phone and call home and tell his distraught wife he was okay and that he was only 'going on holiday' for a short time. Then, before delivering Mister Li to his temporary new home, Fatty Deng had decided it would be a good time for them both to visit the famous Lucky Dragon Tobacco Emporium across the street from the Black House and to purchase a packet of smokes that they would have had difficulty finding anywhere else in Chengdu. So, with Mister Li in handcuffs, Fatty Deng had taken him inside the tobacco shop, and both of them had stared about them in wonder at the incredible array of cigarettes and tobaccos, not just from China but from all around the world.

"To think such a heavenly shop is just across the road from a secret prison," said Mister Li, in awe.

Fatty Deng could not agree more.

Many of the brands of cigarettes were well out of Fatty Deng's price range. Mister Li said he had once spent a very enjoyable couple of months in Paris and pointed to a lonely blue packet of Gauloises Blondes high up on one of the shelves. It was more money than Fatty Deng had wanted to spend. Fatty Deng had had his heart set on a packet of Camel, an American brand that had fascinated him for years. The Lucky Dragon Tobacco Emporium stocked both the yellow and the blue packets. But, feeling sad for Mister Li, who was going to be apart from his family for some time, Fatty Deng pointed up at the Gauloises Blondes. The sweet woman behind the counter nodded and said it was an excellent choice. But it was a skinny but pretty girl in a cute school uniform and with pink ribbons in her hair – her daughter? – who ran up the wooden ladder like a squirrel and picked the Gauloises Blondes off the high shelf and then presented the cigarettes with a smile to Mister Li.

"You are a good man, Constable Deng," said Mister Li, as Fatty Deng handed over the best portion of a week's salary to the woman behind the counter.

Then, for a time, they had both sat in the car outside the Lucky Dragon Tobacco Emporium, smoking the tangy, strong-tasting cigarettes, with Mister Li speaking about his time in France and a number of other countries he had visited along the way. He really was a very interesting man. And Fatty Deng had been more impressed with the Gauloises Blondes that he had expected, not as over-refined as some of the American cigarettes he had tasted, and lacking the chemical flavour that those American cigarettes often left on the tongue.

Fatty Deng had wanted Mister Li to keep the remainder of the cigarettes but Mister Li refused, saying the packet would only be taken from him in the Black House. So, Fatty Deng had put the cigarettes in his shirt breast-pocket, taken Mister Li across the road, and put him in the care of the police in the Black House, making sure to get a signed receipt as he did so. Mister Li had smiled and nodded as he was led away, and Fatty Deng had returned to the car, smoking yet another of the French cigarettes, feeling quite downcast. But the pretty young schoolgirl with the pink ribbons in her hair had smiled and waved to him through the window of the Lucky Dragon Tobacco Emporium and pulled a funny face at him, cheering him slightly, and he had waved back, pulling a funny face at her, and then he was on his way back to Wangjiang Road Police Station. In the hours to come, he would be tasked with attending the aftermath of a 'robbery at knife-point', and a stupid domestic dispute that had got so out of hand that a young wife had drunk the best part of a pint of weed-killer, which would prove to be the last thing she ever did. He soon forgot all about the lawyer Mister Li.

Until now, that is.

Fatty Deng wondered what had happened to him.

Had he left the Black House still hale in body and mind?

And, if so, what was he doing now?

Fatty Deng hoped Mister Li had found a way to have a good life, and had learned to keep his head down, to not cause so much trouble that he had gotten himself beaten and locked up again.

Then Fatty Deng's thoughts drifted back to Sun Mei. She had to be the skinny little schoolgirl with the pink ribbons who had fetched the packet of Gauloises Blondes for Mister Li, all grown up now, her mother dead far too soon, now running the family business, taking care of her crippled father, and incredibly finding time to give free tutoring to those local children who needed a bit of extra help.

A heroine, Mister Wu had called her.

She is certainly that, thought Fatty Deng.

And all he had done, by standing in the doorway of Mister Wu's Cycle Sales and Repair Shop, was put fear in her life. She must have remembered him from all those years ago. She must have remembered he had once been police, and thought him still police, still delivering decent men to Black Houses to be disappeared.

He cursed.

What did it matter?

He cracked open a window and threw the butt of his cigarette out of the car. He needed to forget the past, forget Mister Li, forget the attractive Sun Mei, forget the fear he sometimes brought into people's lives, and get his head back in the game.

Primo Gong was dead, murdered.

Ye Zihao hadn't had him killed.

Nor had the police.

It was the fucking PLA.

Now all he had to do was convince Prosecutor Xu of his theory and figure out why.

FIFTEEN

— · —

O n arriving home, Philip Ye could hear his father entertaining
a guest in the kitchen with one of his outlandish stories. He
recognised Mouse's squeals of laughter. His father doted on Mouse
– whose real name was Hong Jia – as did the brothers Na. Philip
Ye regretted bringing Mouse home that one evening during the
investigation into The Willow Woman cult, though he had meant
well by it, wanting to keep her safe. He had not expected his father
to take to her so. Working deep in the archive in the Procuratorate,
Mouse could certainly prove useful to his father's endless war with the
Shanghai Clique. But that did not fully explain his father's affection
for her, or, indeed, hers for him. It was an oddly platonic relationship,
full of wit and good humour, and, on the occasional evening, a raft
of gin and tonics.

"She is good for your father," had said Day Na.

"Her mind is unsullied by ambition," Night Na had added. "She
wants nothing from your father except good conversation."

Maybe so, but Philip Ye did not want an innocent like Mouse
dragged into one of his father's dangerous schemes. In China, in
Chengdu, the wind could veer suddenly, and Mouse was more vulnerable than most.

Avoiding the kitchen, neither hungry nor in the mood for socialising, Philip Ye hid himself away in his private suite of rooms. He
laid the manuscript he had taken from Jin Huiliang's wall-safe down
on his desk, took off his raincoat, and settled down to read. Soon
enough he had forgotten the week of rancour spent with his mother,
the ongoing problems with Constable Ma, and his inability to decide
how to deal with Prosecutor Xu and the mysterious death of her

husband. The manuscript swiftly transported him almost a thousand years into the past. Jin Huiliang had had a rare gift. In the writing of the manuscript, he had managed to bring a long-forgotten military offensive to life, the ill-fated Lingzhou campaign of 1081, complete with the heat, dust, and biting insects of the summer, and the cold, dry, and equally biting winds whistling down off the steppe in the winter.

There were tears in Philip Ye's eyes when he put the manuscript aside. Jin Huiliang's writing was so evocative, so emotional, it was as if he had been walking alongside the desperate retreating armies, had witnessed for himself the carnage, the heartbreak, the extinguishing of so many lives.But there was so much more to Jin Huiliang's manuscript than a simple and powerful telling of a military disaster. It was a work of true scholarship, an analysis not just of the geopolitics of the time but also of what it meant to serve as a simple soldier in the armies of the Northern Song Dynasty. And though the manuscript was sadly incomplete – the typing ended mid-sentence and there were many handwritten notes and corrections in the margins – Philip Ye was delighted to find a whole section on the occult practices of individual Song regiments.

Impressed by what he had read, Philip Ye sat back in his chair and pondered the manuscript. He had been hoping to find some clue in Jin Huiliang's writing as to why he had been so brutally murdered, some pointed allusion to the China of today perhaps, maybe even to the current posture – domestic and international – of the People's Liberation Army, which might, if the manuscript were to be published, embarrass someone in a position of power. But nothing had jumped off the page to Philip Ye, nothing that would upset the most pedantic of government censors.

Which, in a way, was a pity.

Troublesome books had brought punishment down on the heads of numerous scholars during China's long and turbulent history. He would have relished investigating such a case, following the trail of evidence up and into the shadowy halls of power, to find and identify the faceless grey-suited individual who had issued orders for an example to made of Jin Huiliang – in the manner of the example made of Leon Trotsky by Josef Stalin.

It was nothing but a pleasing fantasy. If such a thing had happened, if the Party had decided it was in its best interests to do away with Jin Huiliang in such a violent and outlandish manner, then a lowly policeman from Chengdu, such as he was, would make little headway in discovering who had given the kill order. Perhaps it was for the best then, Philip Ye thought, that Jin Huiliang's manuscript was seemingly not the reason he had been killed. He had to fall back on the usual, more prosaic reasons for murder: a love-affair gone wrong; an argument over money; or an old family grievance that had recently, for some reason, come bubbling up to the surface. If only Jin Huiliang's journal had not been stolen. Surely the solution to the case had to lie within its pages....

A light tap on the door.

Philip Ye glanced up. He had left the door to his private suite slightly ajar. In the doorway stood a small, smiling figure, dressed for the worst of weathers, in heavy boots, a raincoat that fell down to her ankles, and a wide-brimmed hat tied on her head with a piece of string.

"Travelling somewhere?"

"I'm camping this afternoon in the hills."

Philip Ye was incredulous. "In this weather?"

Mouse took her hat off, the picture having been painted, and took a seat next to Philip Ye. "It was not my idea. My boyfriend thinks floods and landslides are exciting."

"Captain Wang *is* a man of action."

"I think he is going to propose to me."

"So soon?"

"As you say, he is a man of action."

"Will you accept?"

Mouse shrugged. "I know we are meant to be together. He is a very fine man. But I do not know which Captain Wang Jian of the CAPF I will be marrying. Some days he is kind and attentive, on others he is cold and remote, troubled by bad thoughts and bad dreams."

"It is likely he has seen much during his postings in Tibet and the Middle East."

"When he doesn't speak to me I feel useless."

"Not up to being a good wife?"

"Yes."

"Would you rather have a less complicated man?"

Mouse laughed. "No – I would not. Forgive me for being so maudlin, Superintendent. I am the luckiest of women. I really thought my time had passed me by. And it was you who introduced me to him!"

"The family Ye does a good deed at least once every hundred years."

Mouse fell silent, thinking deeply, and then she reached into her raincoat pocket and pulled out a folded piece of paper. "Forgive me, Superintendent, another good deed is needed from the family Ye."

"What is it?"

"Please read," said Mouse, passing the piece of paper to him.

So Philip Ye did.

Prosecutor Xu

We must meet. We must talk. A reservation has been made for us at eight on Monday evening at The Golden Persimmon. I cannot wait to hear the intimate details of your husband's most unfortunate and untimely demise.

Sarangerel

"Where did you get this?" asked Philip Ye.

"I called on Prosecutor Xu in her office on Friday afternoon. She was not there. She was in a meeting. But, unusually for her, she had left her door unlocked and I found this note lying on her desk. She has been getting a lot of nasty notes recently, mostly from hateful, envious people at the Procuratorate, ever since she became a TV star during Commissioner Ho's trial. I try to intercept as many as I can and destroy them before she reads them. She is a very sensitive person even though she pretends that she isn't. Somehow this note got past me. I don't know which of Sarangerel's minions delivered it. I made this photocopy, leaving the original on her desk, thinking I should show it to you."

Philip Ye made no move to hand the note back to Mouse. "And what do you expect me to do?"

"Help Prosecutor Xu."

"Why should I do that?"

"Because, Superintendent, you are a good person, and because Prosecutor Xu is my friend, and because Sarangerel is nothing but an evil, bloodthirsty witch!"

"What if I am in agreement with Sarangerel, that I too would like to hear the intimate details of Prosecutor Xu's husband's unfortunate and untimely demise?"

"Don't be cruel!"

"Mouse, I'm being perfectly serious."

"Prosecutor Xu is not a criminal!"

"I do not know that for sure."

"Then why did you drive all the way to Chongqing to rescue her from the clutches of The Willow Woman cult? And why have you ordered the brothers Na to keep a watch on her, to keep her safe, while she is out and about?"

"How do you know about that?"

"The Na brothers told me."

"Then they have big mouths."

"Please, Superintendent, don't let Sarangerel take advantage of Prosecutor Xu. You are the only person in Chengdu who Sarangerel is frightened of."

"And who told you that?"

Mouse rolled her eyes, exasperated. "It is a well-known fact."

"Tell me what you know about the night Prosecutor Xu's husband died and I promise I will help."

"I am sworn to secrecy."

"I am a police officer – you must tell me."

"I cannot because I promised Prosecutor Xu that I wouldn't open my mouth to anyone. And anyway, the little I know doesn't mean very much. Prosecutor Xu's husband was a bad man. He beat her and kept her prisoner for five years. I am glad he is dead."

"That is not the way the law works."

Mouse stood her ground, refusing to be intimidated by Philip Ye, doing what she had to do for a friend. Philip Ye was both amused by and proud of Mouse – so much strength in such a small person. She had also told him something he had not known: Prosecutor Xu had been kept a prisoner by her husband for five years – and beaten.

"Leave the note with me," Philip Ye finally said. "And tell the complicated Captain Wang that if he doesn't bring you back safe and sound from the hills then he will have to answer to me."

Mouse threw her arms about Philip Ye's neck and kissed him on the cheek. "You are the best, Superintendent!"

"I think you are a better friend to Prosecutor Xu than she deserves."

Mouse shook her head. "Her parents did not love her as much as she needed and her husband was a monster. I understand her better than she understands herself. Sometimes she is so wrapped up in her troubles and her law books she forgets I exist. But, when she does remember, there is no kinder heart."

"No kinder heart – really?"

"Yes, it is true. Don't you dare try and infect me with your awful cynicism, Superintendent," said Mouse, laughing. "China is full of good people. Being police, you just don't meet them. Oh, and don't forget that you are having dinner with your father this evening. He wants to show off his new best friend, the American journalist."

Then Mouse, with a brief wave and a smile, was out the door and gone.

Philip Ye was glad she had reminded him. He had indeed forgotten all about the dinner, about Stacey Corrigan, and that his father was almost certainly up to his neck in another madcap scheme to defeat the Shanghai Clique.

He read Sarangerel's note to Prosecutor Xu again. It was definitely Sarangerel's handwriting. He would recognise it anywhere. He dropped the note on his desk and rubbed his aching temples. He had much to think about. And he could do without having to cross swords with the Mongolian witch again.

Sixteen

S itting in her car in the car park outside of Ambrogetti Global Software, Xu Ya checked in by phone with Investigator Deng. She was excited by the progress she had made, the revelations that not only was there a problem with the fulfilment of the contract between Ambrogetti Global Software and their foremost customer, the CCB, but also that Primo Gong had been distracted from his work these last few months, not been his usual self. And she now had a photograph of the possible reason for that distraction: Primo Gong out on the town with a woman with long, wavy hair, who, in all likelihood, had to be the same woman who had fled his apartment after his murder last night.

"It's a pity we don't yet know her name," said Xu Ya, after sending a copy of the photograph to Investigator Deng's phone. "It's also a pity we cannot utilise the PSB's new facial recognition system. The photograph might be too poor in quality, the face of our mystery woman too distant for it to work, but I would like to see the system in operation."

"They seem in love," said Investigator Deng.

"Don't be fooled. I still think her a prostitute," said Xu Ya. "Some women are very good at masking their true feelings. And don't forget, the family Fu would only ever employ the best."

"I suppose."

Xu Ya sensed he was unconvinced. And she had to admit, from the photograph, the couple did look very much in love. She also had to admit that the mystery woman being a prostitute remained very much speculation. Only when they found her would they learn the truth. Only when they found her would they have enough leverage to confront Lucy Fu.

Xu Ya asked Investigator Deng how he was getting on, whether he had learned anything as he had walked the area around Plum Tree Pagodas. There was a brief silence at first, as if he was building up the courage to speak, and then she listened in utter disbelief as one by one he dismissed the involvement of Ye Zihao, the police, the CAPF, and the MSS in the murder of Primo Gong. She paid no heed to his mentioning the CAPF and the MSS as they had never before been up for discussion. And as for Ye Zihao, that seemed as unlikely to her now as ever. But to dismiss the police, that made no sense – no sense at all.

"Investigator Deng, you told me yourself that only the police have access to the Black House."

"Yes, Prosecutor."

"Well?"

"It is hard to explain."

"Try."

"Police culture."

"Well, that's an oxymoron!"

He fell silent and she realised she had either confused him or hurt him. He had once been police. He still had friends within the police. She also reminded herself that she should not be so quick to dismiss anything he said. Investigator Deng had proved to be anything but a fool.

"If not police, who?" she asked.

"The People's Liberation Army."

She struggled not to laugh. "How ridiculous!"

"I have some more thinking to do, Prosecutor."

"I am sure you do."

"And some more people to speak to."

"Of course."

"But my gut tells me that the PLA is behind the murder of Primo Gong."

"Investigator Deng, Ambrogetti Global Software develops software for the financial services industry. Its flagship contract is with the CCB. It has no connections to the military. I have just got hold of the client list."

"I'll wager Ambrogetti Global Software has no connections with the police either."

"No, but—"

"Prosecutor, I will call you later. Enjoy your lunch with Secretary Wu," he said, and quickly terminated the call.

Xu Ya dropped her phone on the passenger seat, furious with him. She took the printout of Ambrogetti Global Software's client list from her bag and ran her eyes down it again. Despite the ongoing effort by the government to force the PLA to divest itself of its many business interests, the PLA still had its sticky little fingers in many commercial sectors. But nothing stood out from the client list, no company from the defence industry, nothing overtly military. However, to be sure, she would need deep background on all the companies on the list. And that deep background would take time. She would also need Mouse's help in developing that deep background. And Mouse was not available this weekend, having mentioned something about going out into the country with that new boyfriend of hers.

Xu Ya felt a sharp pang of jealousy but then glanced up at the sky. The rain was easing but the sky was extraordinarily dark for the time of day. If the weather reports were to be believed, there were many more rainstorms to come this weekend. Xu Ya had never been camping and was not quite sure, even in the best of weather, if she would enjoy such a closeness to nature – and, most importantly, such a lack of basic amenities. But an isolated and luxurious mountain lodge? Now that would be something – with a hot spa, a talented chef, and scenic walks. She wondered if a man would ever invite her to such a place. She wondered if she would ever have a boyfriend again.

She thought of Philip Ye.

Then she grew angry and stuck her tongue at herself in the rear-view mirror.

She checked her watch. It was time to go. She was already late for lunch with Secretary Wu. She said a quick prayer for Mouse so that her little friend would be safe – not that Xu Ya really believed in the efficacy of prayer – started the engine and sped out of the carpark, pushing her way into the midday Saturday traffic, oblivious to the many curses and car horns directed at her, her mind far away from her driving.

The PLA?

What was Investigator Deng thinking?

A young maid admitted Xu Ya to the house. Having been a regular visitor these last few months, she was allowed to make her own way to the dining-room. She found Secretary Wu and his wife, Wang Jiyu, already seated, in the midst of an intense, but whispered, discussion. This discussion cut short by her appearance, they both rose to greet her with genuine warmth.

Xu Ya had had high hopes for a deep and lasting friendship with Wang Jiyu. They had had lunch in the city and had gone on shopping trips together. Though Xu Ya did enjoy the older woman's company – she was both highly intelligent and very well-educated – the emotion Wang Jiyu displayed at times simply overwhelmed Xu Ya: a tidal wave of memory, bitterness, and regret, all centred on the person of Philip Ye. Wang Jiyu had also asked for an impossible favour.

After Ye Zihao had returned from England with the baby Philip Ye, his birth-mother preferring an academic career to motherhood, Wang Jiyu had often stepped in as a surrogate, helping out while Ye Zihao was working, neither of them quite trusting maids and paid nannies, Wang Jiyu doting on Philip Ye as if he were a son of her own. Secretary Wu had been close friends with Ye Zihao then. With Secretary Wu and Wang Jiyu unable to have children, and – for reasons Xu Ya did not fully understand – unwilling to adopt, those years helping raise Philip Ye alongside Ye Lan, Philip Ye's elder half-sister, were, in Wang Jiyu's own words, the most fulfilling of her life.

But then the earthquake had struck. Ye Zihao had been removed from office and the Shanghai Clique had arrived in the city to take charge. A grown man then and already a homicide detective, Philip

Ye had gone to Secretary Wu and Wang Jiyu to plead with them to intervene on his father's behalf, to speak up in Ye Zihao's defence. For reasons of self-preservation, or perhaps because they were themselves sick of Ye Zihao's corrupt leadership, Secretary Wu and Wang Jiyu had opted to do nothing. Philip Ye had apparently never forgiven them and had refused every entreaty since to meet from Wang Jiyu – to her enduring distress. Xu Ya still had nightmares about the day, at a restaurant, when Wang Jiyu had taken her hand, to ask a great favour of her, imploring her to intercede on her behalf with Philip Ye.

"I am the last person Philip Ye would ever listen to," Xu Ya had told Wang Jiyu.

"But you could try," said Wang Jiyu.

"Please, Elder Sister, do not ask this of me," said Xu Ya, getting upset. "I am not very good with people. If I should speak to Philip Ye, all that would happen is we would argue and I would make matters worse."

Wang Jiyu had seen her mistake and withdrawn her hand. That dinner at the restaurant had taken place over a month before. Wang Jiyu had not asked Xu Ya to go shopping together since, much to Xu Ya's great relief. It was impossible for Xu Ya to explain to Wang Jiyu how much she feared any confrontation with Philip Ye, how, if they argued, her tongue might betray her, she confessing all about the night her husband had died; or how he, being a homicide detective, might stare deeply into her eyes, and see things he must never see.

A soon as Xu Ya was seated, a light lunch – cold diced rabbit with chillies and peanuts – was served. Xu Ya had learned that Secretary Wu was content to discuss work-related matters, regardless of their political sensitivity, in the presence of Wang Jiyu. Today was to be no exception.

"Is Investigator Deng on his way?" asked Secretary Wu.

"Unfortunately not," replied Xu Ya. "He is pursuing an important lead."

"Ah," said Secretary Wu, apparently disappointed.

"It is far too soon for him to return to work," said Wang Jiyu.

This surprised Xu Ya. She had hardly ever mentioned Investigator Deng in this house and found it odd that Wang Jiyu would even care about the wellbeing of a lowly procuratorate investigator she had never met.

"Have you made progress then, Ms. Xu?" asked Secretary Wu.

"Much is not what it seems," replied Xu Ya.

"You will find Ye Zihao guilty, won't you?" said Wang Jiyu.

There was no one in Chengdu, not even Party Chief Li, who hated Ye Zihao more than Wang Jiyu. Why this should be, Xu Ya did not know. But Wang Jiyu's hatred had very deep roots, going back well before the earthquake, well before the disappearance of Philip Ye from her life.

"I cannot answer for what Ye Zihao may have done in the past but as yet there is nothing to link him with the murder of Primo Gong," said Xu Ya.

"Show her!" Wang Jiyu insisted to her husband.

Secretary Wu picked up a slim manilla folder that was on a seat next to him, previously unseen by Xu Ya. He passed it to her. Xu Ya opened the folder and saw inside a Record of Surveillance, made by the PSB, in regard to an American journalist, Stacey Corrigan. Xu Ya quickly scanned down the notes, learning that Stacey Corrigan had visited the Ye family mansion every evening this last week. There was no further information, no speculation from the police as to why. There was an attached photograph. Xu Ya stared at the attractive auburn-haired woman, who was in her mid-forties with steely, blue eyes.

"This Record of Surveillance only crossed my desk this morning," said Secretary Wu.

"Useless police!" exclaimed Wang Jiyu.

"What sort of journalist is she?" asked Xu Ya.

"Freelance, international business, specialising in East Asia," replied Secretary Wu. "She is very fair, very insightful. There has never been any concern about her work. We understand she is here to write a story on the high-tech industry in Chengdu, a piece we would normally encourage."

"The connection to Primo Gong is obvious," said Wang Jiyu.

"Her visits to Ye Zihao may be coincidence," said Secretary Wu.

"Husband, with Ye Zihao there is no such thing as coincidence, and you know it," said Wang Jiyu. "If she is to write about the success of the high-tech industry in Chengdu, what better than to focus on Ambrogetti Global Software?"

"Wife, I am yet to be convinced of Ye Zihao's involvement in the murder of Primo Gong," said Secretary Wu, sharply.

"You were always blind to the evil in that man," replied Wang Jiyu, her tone just as sharp. "You were always too willing to forgive—"

"Lucy Fu lied to us this morning," interrupted Xu Ya, suddenly, not wanting to witness a full-blown argument between husband and wife – theirs being a rare good marriage. She could not have stunned the couple more if she had leaned across the table and slapped them both.

"How did she lie?" asked Secretary Wu.

"Investigator Deng and I believe there was no intruder in Plum Tree Pagodas last night. That was a story Lucy Fu concocted for her own ends. But there was a woman with Primo Gong – a woman Lucy Fu does not want us to identify."

Xu Ya used her phone to show them the photograph of Primo Gong out on the town with the woman with long, wavy hair.

"Who is she?" asked Wang Jiyu.

"As yet, we don't know," said Xu Ya. "But I suspect her to be an escort, a gift if you will, given to Primo Gong by the family Fu. This would explain Lucy Fu's need to mislead us. Lucy Fu almost certainly believes the escort murdered Primo Gong."

"And don't you?" asked Secretary Wu.

Xu Ya tried to hide how pleased she was with her morning's work. "Actually, no – we think she fled Plum Tree Pagodas immediately after the murder, that she played no part in the crime, that she is possibly another victim, her body yet to be found. Primo Gong was killed by a gunshot originating from outside of the building."

Secretary Wu's brow furrowed. "But Primo Gong's apartment is on the fifth floor."

"Sir, there is no doubt. The shot came directly through the window. Not that Lucy Fu understood this. She was so intent on clearing away all trace of her socialising with Primo Gong and the mystery woman, stealing Primo Gong's phone, laptop, and tablet, that she took no time to understand the crime scene."

"Ms. Xu, surely you joke!" exclaimed Secretary Wu.

"I do not, sir," said Xu Ya. "Lucy Fu has a lot to answer for."

"I always disliked that young woman," said Wang Jiyu. "Cold eyes! Cold hands! Cold heart! And to think Ye Zihao was so intent on marrying her off to Philip."

"I just assumed Lucy Fu was just another of his short-lived love-affairs," said Xu Ya, stunned by this revelation.

"Oh no, it was to be a marriage and it was all Ye Zihao's doing," said Wang Jiyu. "All he saw were the financial benefits of joining the family Ye to the family Fu. Lucy Fu was always a spiteful little thing. I knew her when she was no more than a girl. Fu Bi used to love showing her off at his famous parties. Fu Bi has taught her she can have anything she wishes in life if she is willing to work hard and compromise every moral under Heaven. One would have to search the four corners of the Earth to find a woman more unsuitable for Philip. As usual, Philip did his best to please his father but thankfully Ms. Fu was not minded to settle down."

"Tell me about the gunshot that killed Primo Gong, Ms. Xu," said Secretary Wu, uninterested in Lucy Fu.

"A single shot, large-calibre, killing him instantly," said Xu Ya. "A sniper's rifle, we presume, the bullet fired from a building some distance away."

"Which building?"

"The Black House on Liberation Street."

A hiss of air escaped between Wang Jiyu's clenched teeth. Secretary Wu put down his chopsticks. Xu Ya noticed a slight tremor in his hand.

"Are you certain?" he asked.

"There is no doubt," replied Xu Ya.

"The police were always in Ye Zihao's pocket," said Wang Jiyu.

"I did not speak up earlier," said Xu Ya, "as I did not want Party Chief Li to know – not just yet. I was concerned...am still concerned...he might do something rash. We have yet to find any connection between the police and Primo Gong."

"Only police can gain access to that Black House," said Secretary Wu, resting his chin in his hands, his elbows on the table, looking miserable – and old too.

"Investigator Deng tells me the Black House is now nothing more than a file repository," said Xu Ya.

"That is true," said Secretary Wu.

"A house of secrets," muttered Wang Jiyu.

"What are you going to do next?" asked Secretary Wu.

"We need more on Primo Gong's movements last night and what actually happened, and when it happened, at Plum Tree Pagodas," replied Xu Ya. "The concierge was not particularly helpful this morning. It seems all communications with the family Fu are to go through FUBI International's senior counsel, Xi Huan."

"I have met him," said Wang Jiyu.

"You have?" said Secretary Wu, turning to his wife, surprised.

"At one of Mayor Cang's receptions, a year or two ago. He did not know who I was. I forget where you were that day. He mistook me for an easy conquest. Play on his vanity," said Wang Jiyu to Xu Ya. "He is quite in love with himself. Like Lucy Fu, he will try to deceive you. But flatter him and he will reveal more than he should."

"I appreciate the advice," said Xu Ya.

"And Investigator Deng?" asked Secretary Wu.

"He is presently researching the Black House," said Xu Ya.

"He must tread carefully," said Wang Jiyu.

"Only police can access that Black House," said Secretary Wu, looking pensive, repeating himself.

Whether it was to cheer Secretary Wu slightly, or whether she just could not help herself, Xu Ya said, "Investigator Deng is not so convinced the police murdered Primo Gong. He has developed an odd theory."

"Which is?" asked Secretary Wu.

Wishing she had not opened her mouth, she shrugged and said, "It's ridiculous, really. He suspects the PLA."

Wang Jiyu laughed out loud.

However, Secretary Wu said, "That is most interesting," his mood lightening a touch, picking up his chopsticks, commencing to eat again.

"What is it, Husband?" asked Wang Jiyu.

"I had thought it unimportant. There was another murder last night...a very strange murder...in the Xiaojia River Residential District," said Secretary Wu. "I read the brief police dispatch report, saw the incident was far from Plum Tree Pagodas, and dismissed it as unrelated. A retired general officer, a Jin Huiliang, was killed by a single blow to the head with an ice-axe. It is the talk of the PSB today."

"Trotsky," said Wang Jiyu.

"Indeed," said Secretary Wu, with a smile, their friendship renewed.

"Who is investigating?" asked Xu Ya.

"Philip Ye," replied Secretary Wu, for some reason amused.

SEVENTEEN

— • —

Big-Mouth Wang was depressed. "I looked up to Maggie Loh. I really worshipped her."

Fatty Deng had given his old mate from Wangjiang Road Police Station a call. Working nights at the moment, but glad of an excuse to escape the madhouse at home – some distant relatives had come to stay – Big-Mouth Wang, more properly known as Constable Wang Chao, had been happy to meet Fatty Deng for lunch, especially as Fatty Deng had offered to pay. It was also a chance for him to sink a few beers and get a lot off his chest.

"About the time you got knifed to death and miraculously came back to life," continued Big-Mouth Wang, "that drunken bastard Commissioner Ho got himself arrested by Internal Security for employing some of the pretty recruits to be his own private bodyguards. Even the Shanghai Clique couldn't overlook that. Maybe you caught the trial on TV while you were in hospital. Your boss, the Flower of the Procuratorate, was the star. My wife wouldn't let me watch. My wife thought it was indecent. She said Prosecutor Xu spent more time playing up to the camera and showing off her figure than she did laying out the evidence against Commissioner Ho. Anyway, with Commissioner Ho gone there was a sudden vacancy at the head of Robbery. Before we could place wagers as to who was going to get the job, Maggie Loh was bumped up to commissioner 3rd class and put in charge. This is not to say we all weren't happy for her. She made this big speech back at the station, saying how proud she had been to work with all of us, that she was determined to clear all the rats and deadwood out of Robbery, and to give her a call if any of us wanted a change of scene. I was so excited I went home and told the wife. I was up for a change, Fatty. I could see myself cruising around the city in plain-clothes, looking for trouble. So, I put my transfer request in, left a message with Maggie Loh's new secretary, and settled down to wait. Guess what happened next?"

"Nothing?" offered Fatty Deng.

"You got it, Fatty – fuck all!" Big-Mouth Wang almost spat his beer out. "I tried calling Maggie Loh directly but suddenly she wasn't taking calls from Wangjiang Road. Then I phoned Personnel and some little administrator – not even a police officer – told me I didn't have the aptitude for Robbery. Aptitude! What the fuck did she mean by that?"

Fatty Deng shook his head in sympathy. "Did anyone from Wangjiang Road get in?"

"No one."

"You're too honest for Robbery anyway."

"Fatty, when I told my wife that I hadn't got in, she went and told her mother. Then they both started cursing me to my face like I was nothing but a piece of garbage. Her mother starts saying that I had never been any good for her daughter, that she had never wanted a policeman in the family. I felt like strangling the pair of them. I told them because I was police I could murder both of them and get away with it. Not that that shut them up. It's no kind of life, Fatty. You don't know how lucky you are not to be married. A wife is supposed to support her husband, isn't she – not nag him to death? Anyway, with Commissioner Wei of Homicide now on his last legs in hospital, the rumour is that Robbery and Homicide are going to be merged into one big section – with Maggie Loh in charge of it all. Crazy Maggie Loh! Can you believe it, Fatty?"

Fatty Deng was sad for his friend. "I'm sorry."

"It's not your fault, Fatty. You're better off out of it. You're Procuratorate now...a big man...a fucking hero, or so everyone says. They even gave you a medal."

"No medal, just a useless certificate and a bit of cash that helped me pay off a few debts. I don't know if it was worth it, though. My body is covered in scars, it hurts when I smoke, and every time I leave home I imagine someone is waiting in the shadows ready to jump me. Sometimes, mostly in the middle of the night, I think I was meant to die that day."

"Fatty, there are some in the police – the young kids mainly – who are saying that you are a hero reborn from ancient times, a man who cannot be killed. It's fucking hilarious the shit people believe. But I'm famous because I'm your old mate. I bet you could get any girl you want these days. Hey, why don't you ask a couple out? You and I can live it up. My wife and her mother can go to hell."

Fatty Deng laughed and dropped some of his noodles down his chin. Dabbing his chin with his napkin, he knew it was time to get down to work. "Big-Mouth, I need a bit of information."

Big-Mouth Wang drained his beer and eyed Fatty Deng suspiciously. "I'm no snitch."

Fatty Deng shook his head. "I'm not after police – just fat-cat government types."

"Those greedy bastards!"

"Big-Mouth, I can't say much, but I am looking at someone who has business interests in Liberation Street, in the Wuhou District, where the old Black House used to be."

"It's still there."

"Really?"

"Full of rotting old files now, some going back sixty years or more. Don't know why they keep them. Most of the people in those files are long dead."

"Is it guarded?"

Big-Mouth Wang spooned some of his noodles into his mouth and spoke with his mouth full. "Yeah, by Superintendent Si Ying's mob."

"Who?"

"Oh, that's right, you wouldn't know the sour-faced bitch. She only joined a couple of years ago. She doesn't seem to realise that Building Security are not real police. Commissioner Yang Da runs that section now. You wouldn't know him either. He's also a new arrival. Don't know much about him. He's not Shanghai Clique. He's former army. Spends most of his time in his office reading books, from what I understand. Fancies himself as a bit of a scholar. He comes from money, though – and is a favourite of Chief Di. The rumour is, he bought his way into the police. Why, I don't know. If I had family money I wouldn't be working for a living."

"Tell me about Superintendent Si Ying."

"I actually met her once, Fatty – a real arrogant cow. One of her security team had gone sick. They guard the Black House in shifts: two guys during the day, four through the night. Don't ask me why. Anyway, as I said, one of Superintendent Si Ying's guys had gone sick. For some reason she walks into Wangjiang Road Police Station looking for a replacement for the night. This was six months ago, maybe more. You remember Dopey Yan, don't you?"

"Sure."

"She just points at him and says, 'You'll do.' None of us could believe our eyes. Dopey Yan had been on the job ten years to her two and—"

"How did she become a superintendent after only two years?"

"I'll come back to that, Fatty. Let me tell you about Dopey Yan. This Superintendent Si Ying takes him by the arm and starts dragging him out of the station like he's some kind of dumb animal. But then Maggie Loh appeared. Those were the good old days when Maggie Loh was working her homicide cases from upstairs. Maggie Loh tells Superintendent Si Ying to leave Dopey Yan alone and get her replacement elsewhere. You wouldn't believe what happened next. Did I tell you that Superintendent Si Ying is a real hard case, all muscle and no brain, about a head taller than Maggie Loh? She gets right up in Maggie Loh's face. It was like she didn't care that Maggie Loh outranked her...like she thought herself untouchable. But Maggie Loh isn't called crazy for nothing. A wicked little knife suddenly appears in Maggie Loh's hand and then she has Superintendent Si Ying by the neck in some kind of death grip with the knife in her face. I swear, Maggie Loh just frogmarched Superintendent Si Ying out of the station. We've never seen Superintendent Si Ying since. It was fucking beautiful, Fatty. But that was it for Dopey Yan. His nerves were shot. He's now earning good money working construction."

"Did Maggie Loh have Superintendent Si Ying disciplined?"

"That's what I was trying to tell you, Fatty. It wasn't worth the trouble. This is all about Commissioner Yang Da. He's a favourite of Chief Di and he's ex-army."

"I don't understand."

"Fatty, don't you remember how it works in the police? Cliques within cliques! Commissioner Yang Da and Superintendent Si Ying are connected. They're both ex-army."

"There's lots of ex-army in the police."

"Sure, sure...but Commissioner Yang Da and Superintendent Si Ying are *really* connected. A few years ago, Commissioner Yang Da buys himself into the police. He had been a senior officer in the army, a colonel or something. Chief Di immediately put him in charge of Building Security, which isn't real policing so no one raised an eyebrow. And, by all accounts, he's a decent guy. But then, so the story goes, Si Ying turns up in Commissioner Yang Da's office, dressed in her army uniform – she was a senior NCO, nothing fancy – and carrying a baby in her arms. No one knows what happened between her and Commissioner Yang Da. Maybe the baby is his, maybe it isn't. Either way, Si Ying is suddenly in the police, put in charge of the security detail at the Black House and is then made a superintendent within two months even though she's never even been to Police College. Fatty, I've been busting a gut on the streets for fifteen fucking years and I am still only a constable first class. It's outrageous. Superintendent Si Ying has even got herself a sweet little apartment barely ten minutes away from the Black House in that fancy new complex on Peaceful Street. I would love to know who's paying for that – and who pays for the maid to take care of the baby when she's working. I tell you, Fatty, I'm sick of it all! A cousin of mine is now working security for some rich fucker down in Meishan. He says there's a job waiting for me anytime I want. I told my wife and she told her mother but they both got to moaning at me again and...."

Fatty Deng had to listen to another hour of this, sinking a couple of beers of his own as he did so. It was sad that Big-Mouth Wang had fallen out of love with the job. But that was life. And Fatty Deng had got what he needed: a couple of names, a couple of pieces of the puzzle, and confirmation – if his gut really needed it – that, somehow, the murder of Primo Gong was all about the PLA, about old army loyalties. This was nothing to do with the police. All he had to figure out was how Primo Gong had upset the PLA.

Which was not going to be easy.

Not easy at all.

EIGHTEEN

— · —

Xu Ya had taken no great satisfaction in the lunch with Secretary Wu. Though she owed him everything, her life-transforming move from Chongqing to Chengdu, the resurrection of her procuratorial career, the man was – to her at least – a sphinx, impossible to read, his reasoning, as well as his motives, always unclear. His initial shock at being told Lucy Fu had lied to him, that she had wilfully altered a crime scene and thereby had impeded the investigation into the murder of Primo Gong, had not been translated into any orders regarding her disposition. Bitterly disappointed, Xu Ya could only suppose that, because of who she was, because of her usefulness to the Party, Lucy Fu was, for the time being at least, beyond reproach – and, in effect, above the Rule of Law.

Which was a pity.

The people of Chengdu deserved better.

Primo Gong deserved better.

However, Lucy Fu was, as Investigator Deng continued to insist, nothing more than a distraction.

More baffling than Secretary Wu's lack of reaction on learning of Lucy Fu's meddling was his fascination with Investigator Deng's theory of PLA involvement in the murder of Primo Gong. It was almost as if he had been relieved to hear any theory, no matter how ridiculous, that pointed in any direction other than the police or Ye Zihao being responsible for the murder of Primo Gong.

This made no sense to Xu Ya.

The shot that had killed Primo Gong had been fired from a police Black House.

Only police could gain access to the Black House.

Therefore, only police could have murdered Primo Gong.

Those were the indisputable facts.

The PLA were not saints. Years ago, before her disastrous marriage to a former PLA officer, during a corruption investigation she had been conducting when she had been a prosecutor for Chongqing People's Procuratorate, she had met a disillusioned former officer from the 27th Group Army. He had done his duty and followed orders during the Tiananmen Incident in Beijing and had received a wristwatch – now broken and discarded – as a memento for his troubles. Though she had only been interested in the information he had had for her regarding her investigation, he had taken the opportunity to ease his conscience and tell her all he had seen, and heard, and done, early in the morning of the 4th June back in 1989. She had made no notes. And, considering his mental state, she had quickly decided against using him as a witness as she had originally intended. But the story he had told had affected her deeply, giving her many sleepless nights, and continued to serve as a useful reminder to her of the price to be paid for failures of leadership in times of crisis. The former officer's story had also extinguished any romantic notions she may have held about the PLA. But, in general, it still had to be said that, compared to the police, the PLA was a paragon of virtue. Regardless of Investigator Deng's instinctive need to develop a theory that would exonerate his former colleagues, and regardless of Secretary Wu's fascination with that theory, she was convinced the evidential trail would soon lead her directly to PSB HQ.

As for the murder of the retired general officer being investigated by Philip Ye, that had to be a coincidence. Relatively rare as murders were in Chengdu, the different methods of murder in these two cases – ice-axe as opposed to sniper's bullet – had led Xu Ya to swiftly conclude that the murders had to be unconnected, their perpetrators very different men.

"Primo Gong was killed at a distance," Xu Ya had told Secretary Wu. "This retired general, killed close up. That speaks to a very different homicidal mind-set. One very personal, inflamed by violent passions, the other not at all."

"Agreed," had said Secretary Wu, albeit reluctantly.

Secretary Wu had also been forced to accept that Plum Tree Pagodas and the Xiaojia River Residential District were not exactly next door to each other. And that, whereas he had been acquainted with, or at least knew the names of, all of Primo Gong's professional circle, Secretary Wu had never once heard the name Jin Huiliang mentioned before this day. There was no link between the murders and that was that.

"But I would still like to be kept apprised of Superintendent Ye's progress," she had requested of Secretary Wu, unable to resist hearing about what Philip Ye was up to, and also because of a nagging feeling at the back of her mind that the murder of Jin Huiliang ought to be proved as a coincidence rather than just assumed, and that her argument in regard to the different modes of murder did not exactly hold water if professional assassins were involved.

Wang Jiyu had further muddied the waters by harping on about the American journalist who had been seen visiting the Ye family mansion every evening this last week. That Stacey Corrigan was a business journalist interested in the high-tech industry – which would, of course, include Ambrogetti Global Software – was evidence, according to Wang Jiyu, of Ye Zihao's guilt, that he must have ordered, or at least colluded in, Primo Gong's murder.

Xu Ya had kept her own counsel on this, as had Secretary Wu, not wanting to shoot Wang Jiyu down in flames, neither of them wanting to upset her. In regard to the family Ye, her powerful emotions overruled all good sense in Wang Jiyu. If anything, that Ye Zihao had been socialising with the American journalist spoke more to Xu Ya of his innocence rather than his guilt. Not only would no professional American journalist involve herself in a murder conspiracy in China, Ye Zihao would have been well aware that all of her movements would be subject to surveillance by the police. There was also no proof that Stacey Corrigan had ever met Primo Gong, or was even going to make more than a passing reference to Ambrogetti Global Software in her article. Ambrogetti Global Software was certainly a Chengdu success story, but Chengdu was home to so many others.

No, as with Lucy Fu, Stacey Corrigan and her socialising with Ye Zihao – interesting though it may be – was nothing more than a distraction. Xu Ya knew she had to follow the evidence. To begin with, she needed to know the truth, or at least try to get to the truth, of what had happened in the hours that preceded Primo Gong's death. And for that she needed the help of Mister Xi Huan, senior counsel for FUBI International. There was always the chance, if she put him on the spot, he might reveal something Lucy Fu might wish he had not.

So, back in her car, she took his business card from her handbag and placed a call direct to his office. And, to her pleasant surprise, she did not reach his messaging service as expected, but actually managed to speak to the man himself.

"Prosecutor Xu, I have been awaiting your call," he said, his voice light, seductive, almost caressing her ear.

"I am on my way into the city."

"Prosecutor, do you know the FUBI International building?"

"I do."

"Then I shall see you soon."

The rather grand offices of FUBI International Industries were situated in the heart of the central business district. Within, there was none of the atmosphere of anxiety and frantic work on display at Ambrogetti Global Software. On walking through the shining doors into the plush lobby, Xu Ya had the distinct impression that FUBI International was a company that knew exactly what it was about: calmly, methodically and confidently making money in every part of the globe. Hardly had the immaculately dressed receptionist provided her with a visitor's pass then Xi Huan appeared at her side, taking her hand, telling her how privileged he felt to meet her.

"Oh, Prosecutor, I saw you on TV. You were wonderful – magnificent even!"

Not quite forty, very handsome, and wearing a suit expensive enough to rival those worn by Philip Ye, Xu Ya was initially very impressed with Xi Huan, believing Wang Jiyu, in saying he was a man only in love with himself, to have been unnecessarily cruel and inaccurate in her observations. Xi Huan was most attentive to her as he escorted her to the lift, asking her how she was finding life in Chengdu, and how she was settling into the Procuratorate. It was only in the lift, when they were ascending to the tenth floor, when she caught him examining himself in the mirrored steel of the lift frame hardly listening to her answers, that she understood what Wang Jiyu had meant.

He offered her a seat in his office and shut the door so they could speak in private; though, as far as Xu Ya could see, they had the whole of the tenth floor to themselves. Being a Saturday, it was likely he had only travelled into work on the orders of Lucy Fu to await Xu Ya's call. He poured her tea from a beautiful ornate teapot decorated with flowers, birds, and butterflies – definitely an antique but Xu Ya had not the expertise to properly assign a date or value – before he took his seat behind his desk.

"I have been instructed to give you every assistance, Prosecutor," he said. "It is dreadful news about Primo Gong – quite dreadful. I am most upset. I am, of course, sworn to secrecy in the matter. He was a most inspirational man, wholly committed to the future of Chengdu."

Xu Ya glanced around the office and saw the requisite diplomas on the wall. As expected, Xi Huan had graduated from an elite law school: Renmin University, one of the best and possibly the oldest, situated in a suburb of Beijing. Its motto was proudly displayed on the diploma: '*Seeking truth from facts*'. She tried not to laugh.

Xi Huan noticed her focus. "You were top of your class at Wuhan, weren't you?"

"That was a long time ago," she sighed.

"Ah, not so long, Prosecutor" he said, smoothly. "You then passed the bar examination in record time, were head-hunted by Chongqing People's Procuratorate, and immediately became a prosecutor in their Criminal Procuracy Section, the usual probationary training period being waived."

"Again, a very long time ago, Mister Xi."

"You are a rare talent, Prosecutor."

"There are many who would disagree."

"My condolences on the death of your husband."

"Thank you."

"And may I say that Chongqing's loss is Chengdu's gain. I know for a fact that Director Fu is very relieved you are in charge of the investigation into the murder of Primo Gong."

Ah, the first lie.

"I am relieved that she is relieved," said Xu Ya, bristling inwardly, but determined to play the game.

"What is it you need from me, Prosecutor?"

"I require the full occupancy list for Plum Tree Pagodas, together with who was home and who was not last night. I also need a list of all the FUBI International employees who work in the building, together with their home addresses – contractors too, if you use them. I noted that the concierges maintain a log book. I need a copy of all the log book entries for the last three months. I appreciate that your tenants have an expectation of privacy, but the needs of my investigation outweigh this expectation."

"Naturally," said Xi Huan, making notes, his handwriting very neat, very controlled, and very precise.

"I have been told all the CCTV in the building is non-functional."

"That is also my understanding," replied Xi Huan, sadly. "Let me assure you, heads will roll."

"And the electronic entry system to the car park has never operated properly?"

"Also true – a most regrettable situation."

"A great pity."

"I agree."

"I wish to formally interview the night concierge, Mister Han."

Xi Huan nodded, as if expecting this. "I am instructed to accompany Mister Han to any interview. I am aware there is no obligation in law for you to allow this but—"

"I have no objection."

Very satisfied, Xi Huan said, "Thank you, Prosecutor."

"The interview is to take place at the Procuratorate at ten tomorrow morning."

Xi Huan suddenly stopped taking notes. "But tomorrow is Sunday."

"That is true."

"I had a prior obligation that—"

"How is that my concern?"

It pleased Xu Ya to see the realisation creep over Xi Huan that none of his fine words, none of his charm, none of the powerful reputation of the family Fu, had had any effect on her.

Xu Ya knew her limitations. Though Wang Jiyu had advised flattery, Xu Ya was well aware she herself had no genuine skill in the art. She had no natural ability to manipulate or seduce men. She just didn't know how. But she could provoke, and she could undermine, and she could shock – sometimes unwittingly. She had learned, often to her cost, that she was very good at that.

He made a play of opening his desk diary and stared at the entries within. "Don't worry, Prosecutor – I think I can make myself available."

"I was not concerned."

Showing the first signs of nerves, Xi Huan ran his hand through his hair. "I am just not sure how much help Mister Han will prove to be. I have already questioned him. He didn't see the intruder."

"What intruder?"

Taken aback, Xi Huan said, "The intruder who murdered Primo Gong."

"So far there is no evidence of any intruder."

"But—"

"You have stated that the CCTV and the secure electronic entry system into the car park at Plum Tree Pagodas are not functioning. And, as you say, Mister Han saw nothing."

"Yes, but surely you must agree, Prosecutor, it is impossible Primo Gong was killed by another tenant or one of our employees."

"How so?"

"All our employees are fully vetted and all our tenants are beyond reproach."

"And visitors to the building?"

"Are all recorded in the concierge's log book. But there were no such visitors last night, Prosecutor."

"Is that so?"

Xu Ya saw it in his eyes then, a slight flicker of trepidation, the knowledge that perhaps she was wise to him, to all that Lucy Fu had instructed him to do.

"It seems to me, Mister Xi," she said, "that much of what happened last night in Plum Tree Pagodas remains somewhat uncertain." Then, to taunt him, she pointed at his diploma and added, "But I will continue seeking truth from facts. I am quite sure I will get there in the end."

Xi Huan found no humour in her words. "I will have the occupancy list, the employee and contractor list, and copies of the concierge's log ready for you in a few hours," he said, making further notes.

"I am glad."

"I could pass them on to you this evening by hand."

"By hand?"

"Over dinner – if you are free."

It was Xu Ya's turn to be put off her stride. But she recovered quickly. "Mister Xi, I am flattered. However, I am in the middle of a criminal investigation."

"Forgive me, Prosecutor, perhaps I didn't make myself clear. Though your beauty does indeed dazzle, I do not lack for girlfriends. There is a business matter I wish to discuss with you."

"What kind of business matter?"

"FUBI International is creating a new legal team at its offices in London. We are looking to recruit someone to head that team. Your name was proposed to me a week or so ago and I think you would be perfect for the role. We at FUBI International are well aware of your proficiency in a number of foreign languages, your year studying comparative law at Harvard, your easy familiarity with English Common Law and European Continental Civil Law. We need someone trustworthy in London, someone who can build a legal team for us. Your salary requirements, within reason, will be accommodated. Prosecutor, please join me for dinner this evening to discuss this incredible opportunity. Name a restaurant of your choice. Your talents are wasted in Chengdu."

London.

She would be safe there.

She could escape her past there.

Sarangerel could not hurt her there.

"Any restaurant you wish," added Xi Huan. "Let us just chat, mull the opportunity over together. We will not push you for an immediate decision and I admit, with regard to the tragic loss of Primo Gong, the timing is not ideal. But a journey of a thousand miles begins with a single step, does it not?"

She smiled at the quote from the *Dao De Jing*, as he had expected her to. She thought of the Old Chengdu Restaurant, the last place Primo Gong had supposedly dined before losing his life. She needed to visit the restaurant, to determine if Primo Gong had indeed been there last evening with the CCB executives. But what came out of her mouth was a quite different location.

"The Silver Tree."

"Ah, yes, a most excellent choice, Prosecutor – not too formal, food and service said to be of excellent quality. I will make the booking immediately."

"They are always very busy on a Saturday night," said Xu Ya, dreamily, her mind already far away in London.

"No restaurant would ever be so foolish as to refuse a booking from FUBI International," said Xi Huan, gravely.

NINETEEN

— · —

P hilip Ye picked up Constable Ma from outside of PSB HQ. She had been standing in the rain without an umbrella like an idiot again. "Well?"

She made him wait. She made a show of getting herself comfortable in her seat, putting her seatbelt on, and then taking her notebook out of her shoulder bag. She opened the notebook at the correct page and then read from it. This was a trick he had seen his friend and colleague Superintendent Zuo use when confronted by senior officers. Not only could he hide his eyes – and therefore his true thoughts – but, when faced with the written word, senior officers would generally accept them as fact and not argue.

"There is only one shop I could find near to Jin Huiliang's apartment that sells ice-axes," Constable Ma began. "This is an outdoor pursuits shop – Magical Wilderness Adventures – owned by a Madame Song Xue. The shop has sold only one ice-axe in the last month, a cash sale, two weeks ago, to a woman who just walked in off the street. No record of her name was made and the CCTV is only on a 48-hour cycle. All that is remembered of her is that she owned a very expensive, genuine, green crocodile-skin handbag."

"Is that it?"

"Superintendent, the shop assistants are young, pretty, and very stupid. I understand that this is what men prefer."

Philip Ye could not tell whether this was a general comment or aimed specifically at him. "What are your thoughts?"

"The woman with the crocodile-skin handbag is our target."

"If so, Constable Ma, then we have to accept that either this murder was two weeks in the planning, or else it took this unknown woman all that time to build up her courage. Is that consistent with our crime scene? We know from his maid that Jin Huiliang's life hardly varied from day to day, except that he went out on Wednesday afternoons to a teahouse to meet with his old army friends. Therefore, what kind of planning was needed for this murder? Secondly, from the cigarette butt left in the ashtray, we have made the assumption that our murderer calmly smoked a cigarette after committing the murder. This speaks to considerable self-possession and callousness, not a trait one would associate with someone who needed two weeks to build up the courage to kill? Is it not more likely that this woman with the crocodile-skin handbag was just making a spur-of-the-moment purchase to surprise a husband or son who was thinking of taking up mountaineering as a hobby?

"It is her," said Constable Ma, her expression set hard.

"Why?"

"I have a feeling."

Philip Ye was amused. "A feeling?"

Superintendent Zuo told me I must trust my feelings."

"Is that so?"

"It is more than you have taught me these last few months."

Philip Ye ignored this last comment. "Have you managed to obtain Jin Huiliang's service record?"

"It will be on my desk by the end of the day, Superintendent."

That was an impossibility. Philip Ye knew from past experience that the PLA only responded to police requests for information when backed up by a letter from Chief Di, and countersigned by another member of the Political and Legal Committee – and even then the PLA took their time. He had only intended this task to be a lesson for her in dealing with organisations that were very protective of their people and their information – organisations that would do all they could to shield themselves from proper scrutiny. It she had found a way to get service records from the PLA without any obstruction or stalling then that would be unprecedented. He looked for the lie in her overlarge moon-eyes but saw nothing except the desire for him to challenge her. He held his tongue.

"Is anything the matter, Superintendent?"

"No, I was just thinking. Did you manage to get an address for Jin Huiliang's daughter?"

"Jin Jing – yes, Superintendent. She also lives in the Xiaojia River Residential District, within easy walking distance of Jin Huiliang's apartment."

"Are you prepared to deliver the bad news?"

"Yes, Superintendent – and to see if she owns a crocodile-skin handbag."

There is no correct reaction to the news of the death of a close relative: unstoppable tears, rage, dumb-founded silence – Philip Ye had seen it all. After nervously welcoming him and Constable Ma into their apartment, the husband politely enquiring after the health of 'Mayor Ye', Jin Jing and her husband sat in silence, holding hands, as Philip Ye gently told them that Jin Huiliang had been discovered murdered earlier that morning. Jin Jing reacted by asking the same question over and over again. "Are you sure?"

"I am," replied Philip Ye, patiently.

"And he was definitely murdered?" asked the husband.

"He was," said Philip Ye.

"But are you sure it is my father?" asked Jin Jing.

"There is no doubt," said Philip Ye.

He was very aware of Constable Ma scanning the room, searching for the crocodile-skin handbag. But he could have told her she was wasting her time. No murderer lived in this apartment. Neither Jin Jing nor her husband smoked and, though he did not yet know their occupations, by the look of the apartment all their spare money was spent on their only child, a teenage son, who had been confined to his bedroom to play his computer games for the duration of this little talk. They were not the kind of family who had the money to waste on expensive cigarettes or luxuries like crocodile-skin handbags.

There was also Jin Jing herself. Philip Ye sensed a long-standing sadness about her, tiredness too, but no malice, no capacity for extreme passion – for good or ill. She seemed a rather shy, rather modest person, as did the husband. At first glance Philip Ye would not have taken her for a famous general's daughter. Maybe, like he himself, she favoured the mother rather than the father.

"Was he robbed on the street?" asked the husband. "He had money. He was always very generous with us. He paid for our wedding."

"No, he was attacked in his study."

"He was always writing," said the husband.

"Always writing," echoed Jin Jing.

"He was a war hero," said the husband. "He showed me his medals once. But the war damaged his mind. He did not sleep well."

"The border war against the Vietnamese?"

"Yes," said the husband.

"I was a very young girl at the time," said Jin Jing, abruptly. "My father was not the same man when he came home. He beat my mother. I remember my mother screaming, my father slapping her. It was terrible."

"Where is your mother now?" asked Philip Ye.

"Dead, some years now...stomach cancer," replied Jin Jing. "Now my father is dead perhaps he will do what is right and go find my mother in the afterlife and apologise to her. My mother was a good person. Before the war we were a good family. I do not know what we did to deserve such suffering."

"Superintendent, you must not think of the general as a bad man," said the husband. "He was not. But, until he started his writing, he had awful rages he could not control. In his apartment, on the wall, there is a photograph from the war. Those boys were his friends. Most of them were killed only a few hours after the photograph was taken. He could never forget. Only his writing brought him any peace."

"When did you last have contact with him?" asked Philip Ye.

"I don't remember," said Jin Jing.

"Yes, you do...it was only last month, the day after your birthday," said the husband. "You went to shout at him."

Jin Jing nodded, sadly, now lost in the memory.

"Why were you angry at him?" asked Philip Ye, conscious of Constable Ma's impatience with his questions. She was poised to rip the apartment apart looking for that stupid handbag.

"He would not stop," said Jin Jing, putting her hands to her eyes.

"Stop what?" asked Philip Ye

It was the husband who explained. "He felt such guilt over being a bad father, that when he left the army...maybe ten years ago now...he moved down from Beijing to Chengdu to be near us. I think he intended to make amends. This was also when he began writing. He was not the easiest of men. He didn't know how to make small-talk. I think he struggled to know what to do, besides giving us a gift of money every now and then. So, on my wife's birthday, every year, he would visit us...well, not visit exactly. Whatever the weather, he would stand on the street outside our apartment, looking up for a moment at our window, and then get down on his knees and put his head to the ground. It was his way of asking for forgiveness for being a bad father."

"He would not stop," said Jin Jing, beginning to cry now. "All the neighbours would see him...this crazy old man, kneeling in the rain. They would point their fingers at me. They think I am a bad daughter for making my father do this. So last month I went to see him. I told him never to do this again, that it embarrasses me...that it upsets me. But all he did was hang his head. I told him off about the phone as well. He does not like phones. He would not have one in his apartment. I gave him a phone, wanting him to learn how to use it, to carry it about with him for emergencies. But then I learned that he had just given it to his maid. I was so angry with him. I did not see him again after that."

"Was there a woman in his life?" asked Philip Ye.

"No," said the husband.

"Are you sure?"

"Superintendent, I think he was tired of this world," said the husband. "I don't think he thought much about people anymore. He just lived for his writing."

"I understand he met up with old army friends every Wednesday afternoon," said Philip Ye.

"Yes," said the husband, "at the Cry of the Crane Teahouse. It is not far. But we never met them."

"Do you have contact details for any of them?"

The husband stood and rummaged around in the apartment's only bookcase, which was full of papers and magazines rather than books. He came away with a small white envelope. He passed it to Philip

Ye. Inside was a piece of paper on which was written a name and a Chengdu address.

"Senior Colonel Bo Qi?"

"His best friend in the army," said the husband. "The General told us that if anything happened to him to tell Senior Colonel Bo Qi."

"Was he worried for his safety then?" asked Philip Ye.

"He smoked too much and coughed too much," said Jin Jing, wiping the tears from her eyes. "He told me he did not expect to live much longer. He would not have eaten if his maid had not cooked for him. I had forgotten all about that envelope. My husband has a better memory than I."

"May I keep the envelope?" asked Philip Ye. "I will contact Bo Qi for you."

Jin Jing nodded and said, "This is like a terrible dream."

"When can we arrange the funeral?" asked the husband.

"It is too early to say when the body will be released," replied Philip Ye. "I will need one of you to make a formal identification in the next day or so."

"Luli mustn't get any of his money!" Jin Jing exclaimed, suddenly.

The husband took Jin Jing's hand again, trying to calm her. "Luli is long gone. The General told me himself that he hadn't heard from her for twenty years. Don't you remember?"

But Jin Jing was having none of this. She pulled her hand from her husband's and threw herself down on her knees, much as her father had been wont to do on her birthdays out on the street, and pleaded with Philip Ye. "Please, Superintendent, I beg you...don't let Luli get his money. She stole my father from me before. Do not let her steal from us again."

"Who is Luli?" asked Philip Ye.

"A whore!" cried Jin Jing, holding her head in her hands.

Philip Ye was forced to re-evaluate Jin Jing, not in terms of her being a potential suspect, but in the depth of the reservoir of emotion that lay trapped inside her. He looked to the husband for an explanation.

"Superintendent, forgive my wife – some old hurts will never heal. It is why the General and her mother fought so much when he returned home from the war. A friend of his had died. We don't know his name or why he had no wife. But there was a daughter –

Luli. On the battlefield, the General had made a promise to take care of Luli if this friend was killed – a solemn oath, I think, a blood-oath. The friend was indeed killed. But, when the General returned home, his wife did not want to take another daughter into the family. This was why they argued, this was why the General beat his wife, this was why the General finally walked out on his family, and this is why my wife could not properly forgive him no matter how many times he prostrated himself in the street. My wife loved him but could not forgive him – it is the way of families sometimes."

Philip Ye looked down at Jin Jing, still on her knees, her hands covering her eyes, sobbing. He caught sight of Constable Ma out of the corner of his eye, shaking her head, unimpressed. Constable Ma was not one for emotion – not other people's emotion, that is.

"So did Jin Huiliang raise this Luli as his daughter?" Philip Ye asked the husband.

"We think for a few years at least, Superintendent. Ten years ago, when the General first came to Chengdu to live, my wife would not see him at first. It was up to me to make the peace. I visited him, to thank him for the money he had sent for our wedding. We drank tea together. I smoked a cigarette with him though I do not like them. It made me cough and my eyes water. I told him straight that my wife wouldn't see him if he was still in touch with Luli. He told me not to worry, that he had not seen Luli for many years, that, despite his best efforts, she had fallen into dissolution."

"Dissolution?"

"He would not say it, Superintendent, but I think Luli ran away from him to become a prostitute. I don't know why she did this. He said to me, 'I was a good soldier but a poor father. I have so much to atone for, I do not know where to start.'"

Philip Ye took the photograph of the woman with the long, wavy hair he had discovered in Jin Huiliang's wall safe from his pocket and showed it to the husband. "Is this Luli?"

"I would not know, Superintendent. I never met her. But this woman is very pretty and I understand Luli was very pretty too."

Jin Jing made a grab for the picture. "Let me see!"

Philip Ye did not allow Jin Jing to touch the photograph for fear she might try to destroy it, but he held it up for her to see. A whole gamut of emotions raced back and forth across Jin Jing's face but there was no recognition in her eyes.

"Did you never meet Luli?" he asked of her.

She shook her head unable to take her eyes from the photograph. "All I know is that my father loved Luli more than me."

"Wife, that cannot be true," protested the husband.

"It is true!" insisted Jin Jing.

"Are you sure you do not know Luli's family name?" asked Philip Ye.

"No," said the husband.

"No," echoed Jin Jing.

"You might find her in Beijing," said the husband. "That was where the General said he had last heard from her. Please forgive my wife for speaking about money, Superintendent. We have enough to survive. If the law says that Luli should have some of the General's money then that is how it should be. The arguments of the past should be forgotten. I asked the General once what the war with Vietnam was all about. He laughed – the only time I ever saw him laugh. He said it was what arguments are always about: everything and nothing. He had his pain, Superintendent, but he was the wisest man I knew."

"Luli was a whore who ruined our family," said Jin Jing, still unable to take her eyes off the photograph."

"Wife, for the good of your health, for the sake of our son, you must let the past go," said the husband.

"I cannot," replied Jin Jing. But she allowed her husband to take hold of her, to lift her off the floor and set her down on the couch next to him.

Philip Ye put the photograph back in his pocket. He was glad, despite her blighted childhood, Jin Jing had at least married well. However, he was disappointed he had not yet managed to properly identify the woman in the photograph and discover where she lived. He was certain it was Luli, that Luli was indeed the woman whose ghost he had encountered back at the airport. Had Luli, unbeknown to Jin Huiliang, followed him all the way from Beijing to Chengdu? And was it possible that Luli had got herself into some kind of trouble, had gone searching for Jin Huiliang for help, and inadvertently brought that same trouble to his door? Philip Ye thought it likely –

highly likely. But, if he was going to prove this theory, he needed to know who she was and where her body had been dumped. Maybe it was time to pass the photograph to the new facial recognition team. They had been screaming at Homicide for weeks for a real photograph from a real case to test out their software. He was, though, loath to do so. Not only did he suspect it would be a waste of time – if Luli had been living in Beijing she would not necessarily appear in their local databases – but also, to pass the photograph to someone else, for another team to examine, would feel like he was giving Luli up, would feel like he was somehow betraying her, infringing on her privacy even in death. A nonsensical feeling, he knew, but it twisted his insides nevertheless.

TWENTY

— • —

S tarbucks was crowded. Fatty Deng wished they had decided to meet somewhere else – Prosecutor Xu's nearby apartment, for instance. The more he reflected on the strange murder of Primo Gong the more worried he became regarding its implications. He did not want to take the chance on someone overhearing their conversation. But Prosecutor Xu was deaf to his concerns. She had something important to tell him, she said. She wanted to meet him at their favourite Starbucks, she said. He had sensed her excitement bubbling over on the phone. However, she had given him no clue as to what she had discovered, what vital information the lawyer Xi Huan might have let slip in her meeting with him.

As Fatty Deng pushed his way into the packed restaurant, four giggling teenage girls stood up from their table by the window. Taking his chance to secure the choice table for himself, he muscled a couple of skinny youths out of the way and sat down. The youths, out to impress their girlfriends with how tough they were, protested.

"Hey, fat man – we were here first!"

"Yeah, fat man, you can't take up a whole table on your own!"

Not in the mood for a confrontation and gripped with an unsettling foreboding that the meeting with Prosecutor Xu was not going to go well, Fatty Deng flashed his badge and told the youths to go fuck themselves.

The youths slunk away to another part of the restaurant, taking their pouting girlfriends with them.

Prosecutor Xu arrived late, complaining about the heat, the rain, and the traffic. Not that she was really angry. Fatty Deng noted a lightness of spirit about her. She was almost like a teenage girl herself, her eyes shining, her skin glowing, as if all her concerns had been suddenly taken away from her. As she dropped herself into the seat opposite him, she fished a mirror from her handbag and began to dab the rainwater and sweat from her face with a tissue, talking, as she did so, about how grand the offices of FUBI International had been and how pleasant the lawyer Xi Huan had been to speak with.

"FUBI International was quite a revelation," she said.

Not caring one way or the other about FUBI International, Fatty Deng excused himself for a moment to order them a pot of green tea each. As he paid the cashier, he glanced back over his shoulder, watching Prosecutor Xu now touch up her make-up, smiling to herself in the mirror. He marvelled at how beautiful she was, how oblivious she was to the stares from all the men in the restaurant – even those with wives and girlfriends in tow. But this new, gay, almost carefree mood of hers both charmed and dismayed him. Something was up with her. She was hiding something from him.

When he placed the tray of tea down on the table and slumped back down in his seat, Prosecutor Xu continued to talk about FUBI International, the many countries they had interests in, how quietly successful they were, and how even though Xi Huan had read law at Renmin University and she at Wuhan, the two of them had still managed to find common legal ground. They had shared concerns about the need for more rigorous enforcement of intellectual property law – that is, if China was to continue to prosper well into the 21st century, to attract further investment and more creative industries to its shores.

"It's common sense, don't you see, Investigator Deng? If our courts do not have the power to enforce—"

She almost jumped out of her skin as Fatty Deng reached forward and touched her hand.

"Prosecutor, we have a murder to solve," he said.

"I am aware of that," she replied, pulling her hand away from him, her eyes darkening, losing most of their luminescence.

"What did you discover from Xi Huan?"

"No, you tell me about your findings first," she said.

So he did.

Not mentioning his informant – Big-Mouth Wang – by name, he described to her the shift patterns at the Black House on Liberation

Street, how the security details were led by a Superintendent Si Ying, a hard case, a former army NCO, who had been promoted by the head of PSB Building Security, Commissioner Yang Da – a former army man himself – much faster than anyone in the police had any right to expect.

"This means nothing, Investigator Deng. For many in the PLA, a career in the police is a natural progression," said Prosecutor Xu.

"That is true."

"And yet you still suspect the PLA are behind the murder of Primo Gong?"

"I do, Prosecutor."

"Do you not see that because you were once police, you are blind to the wickedness of the police? You told me yourself that only police could gain access to the Black House. Have you uncovered any evidence at all that the security detail at the Black House last night admitted an army sniper team to murder Primo Gong?"

"No, Prosecutor."

"Or developed a theory as to why the security detail might do such a crazy thing?"

"No, Prosecutor."

Seeing how cold and dismissive she had become, he did not waste his breath explaining to her about old army loyalties, how some ex-army men in the police would speak with more warmth about their old army comrades than they would about their own families, or how those old army loyalties could prove useful in times of trouble, or how those old loyalties could possibly be exploited by those with evil on their minds. He also did not bother mentioning Superintendent Si Ying's baby. As he had gotten to know her better, he had noted in Prosecutor Xu a prudish streak, a disapproval of anything that might be described as tittle-tattle. She would consider the possible fathering of Superintendent Si Ying's baby by Commissioner Yang Da as something far below her consideration – meaningless gossip, nothing more. For someone involved in law enforcement, in pursuing the very worst of humanity, Fatty Deng thought this a strange idiosyncrasy, as well as an investigative weakness – a weakness he was determined to correct one day. But that day was not today.

"What do you intend to do next?" she asked.

He again wondered what was up with her.

Were they no longer a team?

Should not the next steps be decided together, after she had told him what she had found out from the lawyer Xi Huan?

He told her what was on his mind anyway. "I want to return to the Black House this evening...observe the shift-change for myself...familiarise myself with a few faces. There are a number of shops on Liberation Street, a famous cigarette shop in particular. The security detail might buy their cigarettes there. It's possible I might learn who was on duty last night. I would also like to find some way of getting hold of Commissioner Yang Da's and Superintendent Si Ying's PSB personnel files."

"We cannot tip the police off to our investigation," said Prosecutor Xu.

"I am well aware, Prosecutor," said Fatty Deng, irritated by her stating the obvious. "Maybe Secretary Wu could get them for us?"

Prosecutor Xu nodded. "He might – but I prefer we wait until Monday, until Mouse returns from her stupid camping trip. She has a knack of getting files quietly, without making waves. For now, I have a little job for you. I was going to visit the Old Chengdu Restaurant this evening, to have a little chat with the staff there, to find out if Primo Gong had attended his usual Friday night dinner with the executives from the CCB. According to his diary he was meant to be there. It would be useful to know if he took along a date – I'm thinking of our mystery woman with the long, wavy hair – what time he left the restaurant, and what time he might have returned to Plum Tree Pagodas. We need that timeline of all of his movements leading up to his death. Unfortunately, I cannot make the restaurant myself this evening. I have to be somewhere else."

"Where, Prosecutor?"

"I'm having dinner with Xi Huan."

As his mind was a blank, Fatty Deng assumed his face would be blank as well. But Prosecutor Xu immediately became angry and snapped at him.

"Don't look so shocked! It's not what you think, Investigator Deng. It is not a romantic dinner. We will not be eating by candle-light. Xi Huan is a handsome man. I cannot deny it. But he already has enough girlfriends."

"I am very pleased for him," Fatty Deng managed to utter.

"He just needs all this afternoon to gather the information that we need," continued Prosecutor Xu, "the occupancy list, the employee list and the concierges' log book – for all the good they will do. They are sure to have been doctored on the orders of Lucy Fu. But we must have them, nevertheless, and it would not hurt for him to hand them to me over a fine dinner."

She averted her eyes from him. She stared out of the window at the crowds of shoppers braving the rain, smiling briefly to herself as she saw a stressed mother holding shopping bags in one hand and dragging along a screaming child with the other.

"Prosecutor, this is not right," said Fatty Deng.

She returned her gaze to him. "What is not right?"

"Having dinner with Xi Huan. I understand we are meant to tread carefully with the family Fu, but if Xi Huan is hiding evidence from us on the orders of Lucy Fu, then—"

"Investigator Deng, have you ever attended a course on legal ethics?" she asked.

"You know I have not."

"Then don't lecture me!"

"Prosecutor, having dinner with Xi Huan is asking for trouble."

"We will not be discussing the case."

"Then what *will* you be discussing, Prosecutor?"

She averted her eyes from him again, this time looking down into her teacup. "He has offered me a job."

So that was it.

So that was what was up with her.

So that was what she had been hiding.

Fatty Deng heard the roaring of blood in his ears. He reached for his packet of cigarettes, only stopping himself just in time, remembering no smoking was allowed in the restaurant, that Prosecutor Xu also detested the habit.

She glanced up at him, her face slightly flushed, her lips pale and taut. "It's not a bribe, you understand – not some tactic dreamed up by Lucy Fu to put me off my stride. It seems my name has been in the mix for some time. FUBI International is setting up a legal team in London. They need someone to lead the team – namely me. It is a sensible decision. A good business decision. I am more than qualified. You should be happy for me."

Not one happy thought crossed Fatty Deng's mind.

"It is an incredible opportunity," she continued. "And a corporate legal team is sure to need a corporate investigator. You could come with me. You would enjoy working in London. It is like the whole world wrapped up in one city."

"Prosecutor, I cannot speak English. And who would look after my mother?"

She carried on speaking as if she had not heard him, lost in a world of her own. "I have found Chengdu to be too much like Chongqing: full of the same kind of idiotic people, the same kind of stultifying bureaucracy...impossible to get anything done. I am wasting my life here. I cannot make a difference. I need a new beginning...in another country. Xi Huan says it is the opportunity of a lifetime. And he is right. I cannot turn him down. To be honest, I am so excited I can hardly breathe. Anyway, time is pressing and I must rush. I need to read through all the paperwork given me by Ambrogetti Global Software – Primo Gong's diary, the client list, the employee list – to see if there is anything worthy of further investigation. And then I have to get dressed for dinner. I have no clue what I am going to wear. Did I tell you that we are going to eat at The Silver Tree? It's going to be such fun."

Then she got up from the table, flashed him a brief smile, and was gone.

Twenty-One

By the time Ma Meili had climbed back into Superintendent Ye's car after leaving Jin Jing's apartment she was burning with rage. As far as she could see, as police, they had not done their job. They should have turned Jin Jing's apartment upside down looking for the crocodile-skin handbag and packets of the expensive Good Cat cigarettes. So what if the family *appeared* poor? Ma Meili had had an uncle who had lived in the worst, most run-down house in her home village, and yet it had been well-known that he had had more money than most. Jin Huiliang surely had had the means. Jin Huiliang could have given Jin Jing the money for the crocodile-skin handbag as a gift. Jin Jing had also admitted being angry at her father as well as making it plain that his money was at the forefront of her mind. Ma Meili had said as much to Superintendent Ye as soon as the husband had waved them goodbye and closed the door on them. But Superintendent Ye had ignored her. Now, in the car, all he could do was continue staring at the old photograph of the woman with the long, wavy hair.

"Superintendent, I am going to lodge a formal complaint," said Ma Meili.

"What about?" he asked.

"About you."

"Is that so?"

"We should have arrested Jin Jing."

"Because she spoke about money?"

"Superintendent, it is a motive!"

"Money is a motive, very often – but in this case I think not. Jin Huiliang does not seem the type to have taken advantage of his seniority in the PLA to line his pockets. I am beginning to like Jin Huiliang a great deal. I think he was a man of honour, a warrior-monk, dedicated first to the art of war and the welfare of his fellow soldiers and then, latterly, to his writing."

"Jin Jing could not forgive him."

"So?"

"She couldn't forgive him even though he got down on his hands and knees on her birthday. If my father had been a war hero then—"

"But your father was not, Constable Ma. Your father was an illiterate pig-farmer who beat you every time you did something he did not like. Difficult as your life has been, do not imagine anyone else's life has been easier until you have walked a while in their shoes. Jin Huiliang returned from Vietnam a very troubled man. Moreover, in Jin Jing's eyes, he had also transferred his affection to someone else's daughter – Luli. Such a betrayal can neither be easily forgiven nor forgotten."

"Jin Jing did murder him then!"

"I think not."

"Then who?"

"*That* we are yet to determine."

"Maybe it was Luli."

Superintendent Ye tapped the photograph. "If this is Luli – and I suspect it is – then she is no murderer."

Ma Meili thought her head was going to explode. "But how do you know?"

He refused to look at her. It was then that her rage began to die away, to be replaced with a seething hatred, as she suddenly realised that he was hiding something from her. He had done this before, on other cases. Even Superintendent Zuo had told her in confidence that Superintendent Ye was, like the rest of the family Ye, a man who enjoyed his secrets. Well, enough was enough. Come Monday morning, she was putting in for a transfer. Come Monday morning, whether he liked it or not, she was going to SWAT.

Superintendent Ye drove them to the south of the city. Ma Meili sat
in silence as he showed his badge and ID to a private security guard
at the entrance to a luxury gated community. The guard opened the
barrier to admit them, but not before saluting Superintendent Ye like
a moron and asking that his good wishes be passed along to Mayor
Ye Zihao. Constable Ma shook her head in disgust. Superintendent
Ye drove for a few minutes more until he found the house he was
looking for, all modern architecture, fabricated out of glass, concrete,
and steel. He parked up on the road nearby. Ma Meili was impressed.
The house looked like a palace of the future. She had visited the Ye
family mansion a couple of times, though not out of choice. She
thought a facsimile of an English country manor house smack in the
middle of a Chinese city not only ugly but incredibly stupid. She did
not hesitate to make the comparison.

"This house is far better than yours, Superintendent."

"Keep your wits about you when we are inside," he said, refusing
to be drawn.

He had not told her whose house it was, but she guessed it had to
belong to Bo Qi, whose name and address had been passed to them
by Jin Jing's husband. Why she had to keep her wits about her, Ma
Meili did not know. Bo Qi had not only been Jin Huiliang's best
friend but he was also a man; whereas Jin Huiliang's killer – probably
Jin Jing – had been a woman.

To gain access to the house they needed to pass through a large steel
gate. Superintendent Ye pressed the button on the intercom and held
up his badge and ID to what Ma Meili had to assume was a micro
security camera.

"Police – for Bo Qi," he said.

This was not exactly polite, thought Ma Meili. But the steel gate
swung open automatically nevertheless and she followed in Superintendent Ye's footsteps up the drive, past a parked limousine – a
Rolls-Royce Ghost according to Superintendent Ye, as if this should
mean something to her – to knock on the large front door. A young
man opened the door to them and ushered them inside out of the
rain. He asked to see their credentials, introduced himself as Bo Qi's
private secretary, and told them Bo Qi could only spare them a few
minutes as he was between conference calls in regard to his many and
varied business interests. The private secretary then led them into an

open-plan lounge. Ma Meili's eyes were drawn to a large painting hanging on the wall, a pair of finches perched on bamboo. The scene was so beautiful that Ma Meili could not stop the tears that suddenly clouded her eyes.

Noticing her fascination as well as her emotion, the private secretary said, "Only a copy, I am afraid, of Emperor Huizong's original painting. The original is held by the Metropolitan Museum of Art in New York. However, look at this." He pointed to a small statue of a horse made out of stone or terracotta – she could not tell which– in a glass case and standing on a wooden pedestal in the corner of the room. "It is Tang Dynasty – quite valuable." The private secretary then vanished to go find Bo Qi.

Ma Meili would have liked to discuss the artwork with Superintendent Ye and comment on how unusual she thought it was that there were no military photographs on show as in Jin Huiliang's apartment, no military paraphernalia of any sort, nothing to remind Bo Qi, or indeed visitors to the house, of his time in the army. But she saw Superintendent Ye had gone within himself, closing his eyes while standing up, doing his stupid breathing exercises again. He would do this at the most unexpected times. She did not know why.

Soon enough, however, Bo Qi arrived, a stocky man in his late middle years, of average height, his hair dyed jet-black, dressed in a business suit, a pale old scar visible on his forehead. But it was the eyes that transfixed Ma Meili – strong, warm, confident, and welcoming. She knew instinctively that Bo Qi was a great man, that she was in the presence of yet another war hero. She lowered her head in respect.

"Bo Qi?" asked Superintendent Ye.

"Yes," was the simple reply, Bo Qi staring intently at Superintendent Ye's face.

"Your friend, Jin Huiliang, has been brutally murdered."

Ma Meili could not believe her ears. In the three months she had been working with Superintendent Ye, he had never once spoken to the bereaved – even those he considered suspects – with anything less than gentleness and civility. It was his one saving grace. Why would he now be so rude to Bo Qi?

However, if Bo Qi was devastated by the terrible news he had just so rudely received, he did not show it. Instead, he grew angry and pointed a finger at Superintendent Ye's face.

"I know you," he snarled. "You are the son of Ye Zihao, the former mayor – a man in disgrace, under house-arrest, guilty of perhaps a thousand crimes. Leave my home this instant. I will have no conversation with the son of such a man!"

Ma Meili might never have heard Superintendent Ye speak so badly to the bereaved before, but she had also never heard anyone dare speak to him so, not other police, not the common people out on the street, not even those wicked people they had had cause to arrest. In fact, most had wanted to be remembered to Ye Zihao!

As each man stared each other down, Ma Meili felt her hand reach under her smock to rest on the butt of her pistol. She did not know what to expect next. There had been no spoken threat from Bo Qi. But it was difficult to read him, to see what lay behind his strong and level gaze. Homicide detectives did not ordinarily go about their work armed. But, on surrendering her old pistol to the armoury, after transferring from Robbery to Homicide, the senior armoury officer, Superintendent Li Cheng, had, to her great surprise, issued her with a brand-new pistol – a QSZ-92, as used by SWAT.

"Recently," Superintendent Li Cheng, had told her, "Superintendent Ye has got himself into a couple of scrapes. It wouldn't go well for any of us if he was to get hurt. His father is very famous. Do you understand, Constable Ma?"

She did.

Or at least she thought she did.

It was her duty to look after the welfare of her immediate superior, whether she liked him or not.

On the verge of pulling her pistol from its holster, knowing Bo Qi to be a former military man, and, though now of an age, probably still capable of extreme violence, Ma Meili was relieved to hear Superintendent Ye speak with courtesy again.

"If I leave your house, Mister Bo, will you at least speak with my colleague, Constable Ma?"

"Of course," replied Bo Qi, his eyes never leaving Superintendent Ye's face.

Without another word, without offering Ma Meili a scrap of advice or guidance, Superintendent Ye turned on his heels and walked out of the house. Ma Meili watched him through the window as he walked slowly down the drive through the rain and climbed back into his car.

She felt terribly abandoned. She had never been left alone with the bereaved before.

She turned back to Bo Qi who was carefully appraising her.

"Tea?"

Ma Meili nodded, accepting the offer, not knowing what else to do.

TWENTY-TWO

— · —

When they were both seated, when the private secretary had brought in a tray of tea, Bo Qi began to speak.

"Were you in the army, Constable Ma? You look the type."

"No, sir – I worked on my parents' pig-farm in Pujiang County and then joined the police."

"Pujiang County? Jin Huiliang was raised in Lushan County – on a poor farm similar to yours, I expect. In the army, when I first met him, he was always shy of speaking about his roots, his closeness to the land. He wanted us to know first that he was an intellectual, a real thinking man – which he was. But unlike those of us who grew up in the cities, he had a real understanding of terrain – an understanding that would serve him well in our time of war. When he retired, I assumed he would return to the country. He surprised us all by settling in Chengdu, wanting to be close to his daughter."

"We have just come from her apartment," said Ma Meili.

"There were difficulties between them."

"She has told us."

"Is she distraught?"

"It is hard to say," replied Ma Meili, in her mind at least Jin Jing still a suspect.

"Jin Huiliang meant well, wanting to repair what had been broken with his daughter. Family is family, is it not? But I often think it is a mistake to revisit the past, to try to correct the wrongs that have been done there. Sometimes, all that is achieved is the opening of old wounds. Time moves forward, not backward. It is foolish to think otherwise, is it not, Constable Ma?"

"I suppose," said Ma Meili, realising that she was seated not just near to a war hero but a philosopher too, and that it would be ridiculous for her, an uneducated farm girl, to enter into any debate with him. All she could add was, "I am just very sorry that your good friend is dead."

"Why was he murdered? I suppose it was robbery. It has to have been robbery. Society is not what it used to be. He was oddly lax about his personal security. Many of us who came through the war can hardly walk down the street without worrying about what is waiting for us around the next corner. Jin Huiliang was different. The war had changed him. But I think he had merely ceased to care whether he lived or died."

Ma Meili saw the emotion in Bo Qi's eyes and was deeply moved. She promised herself then that she would not rest until she had found Jin Huiliang's murderer. She would put in her transfer to SWAT as intended on Monday, but she would delay that transfer – if the SWAT commander was in agreement – until an arrest had been made.

"It was not a robbery," she said.

Surprised, Bo Qi asked, "Are you sure?"

"The apartment was undisturbed. I also found cash in his wallet. Only his journal seems to be missing."

Bo Qi dabbed at his eyes with a silk handkerchief. "He was always making notes in journals, even in the army. I believe it was his way of arranging his thoughts."

"Why would the murderer steal it?"

"I assume it was Madame Ding, his house-keeper, who told you what was missing and what was not. She wouldn't understand the way he worked. His journals were not like diaries. Once a journal was full, he would discard it and purchase another. His journals were of no value to anyone but himself. No, I suspect the journal has either been mislaid or he had just discarded it and was about to go out and get another. This must be a failed robbery. The intruder murdered him, then panicked and fled. With all the corruption scandals in the news recently, someone must have thought – a neighbour possibly – that Jin Huiliang had mountains of cash lying about his apartment. They wouldn't have known that he was unbothered by money, that he was a man without vice."

Ma Meili was unsure about that. "Jin Jing told us that when he came home from the war he beat her mother."

Bo Qi frowned and reached for a packet of cigarettes off the low table before them: Baisha Blue, the same as smoked by Jin Huiliang.

"When I speak of vice, Constable Ma, I am referring to a corruption of the soul – a natural propensity for evil. Like all of us, he made mistakes, did things he would later regret. He had a temper, I assure you. But of all of us, in the army then, and in our little grouping of writers now, he was the best."

Ma Meili jotted all of this down in her notebook. "So, sir, do you write also?"

"Did his house-keeper not tell you?"

"She told me nothing useful," replied Ma Meili. "All she did was cry."

"Of course, of course – it was foolish for me to imagine a simple house-keeper would have known what we are all about. We call ourselves The Historians; a rather grandiose title, but there it is, and Jin Huiliang was our leader. We had all joined the army together, all full of patriotic fervour. Then came the war with Vietnam. I will save you the gory details, Constable. But, suffice to say, those of us who did survive returned as very different men. I stayed in the army as long as I could. But I was not happy. I wasn't sleeping well. And sometimes, sitting at my desk in my office at the barracks, I would have waking dreams, images of the dead and maimed appearing before my eyes, so much horror that my heart would race and rivulets of sweat would run down my face. I finally resigned from the army. If I hadn't had a family to support, I think I might have hidden myself away in a remote monastery somewhere, and taken up the study of the Buddhist sutras. Fortunately, I had an area of expertise – communications – and I found I had a natural flair for making money.

He gestured to the house around him. "As you can see, I did well for myself. I now own many businesses all over Sichuan. And for most of that time I was living in Chongqing, the city of my birth. But even as I made money, within I remained tormented, prone to nightmares both day and night. I got so desperate I thought I might go see my old friend, Jin Huiliang. Being a knowledgeable and thinking man, I hoped he might know of some remedy, something that would bring peace to my disordered mind. Little did I know then that he had been suffering as I had, that he had struggled to find a remedy for himself. I had heard he had retired from the army, that he had abandoned his home in Beijing and gone south, here to Chengdu, to be near to his estranged daughter. I visited him in his apartment, poured all my troubles out to him. When I was done, he told me, 'I have suffered as you suffer. For a while I sought the help of a psychiatrist but he could do little to help. But then I began to write, and the writing did much to keep the ghosts from knocking at my door.'

"It was then that I learned, to my great surprise, that other old comrades of mine had also come to Chengdu seeking his help. He had advised them to write, and they had followed his advice, all writing military history as he did, all moving to Chengdu to be near him. I returned to Chongqing to speak to my wife. My wife didn't want to leave Chongqing – that is where she is at the moment, visiting relatives – but she also wanted me to find peace of mind. To cut a long story short, my wife gave her approval and I bought this house. And, though I have no special skills as a writer, I began to research and write about a period of history that interested me: the failed 1951 Spring Offensive during the Korean War. And I joined Jin Huiliang's group of veterans, The Historians, meeting up every Wednesday afternoon at the Cry of the Crane Teahouse in the Xiaojia River Residential District, where we speak, not of old times, not of the war, but of our various projects. I am happier now than I have been for many years – or at least I was until you brought me this most awful news."

"So, are you now cured, sir?"

"No, Constable – I don't think there is a cure for the trauma of war. Not in this life anyway. But the writing, the mental focus, has mitigated my symptoms, made me a better person to be around...or so my wife says. I have Jin Huiliang to thank for this. I suppose your boss, the *laowai*, will need to know the names of all The Historians – to eliminate them from his investigation?"

"Yes, sir."

"Well, I can do better than that, Constable. Tomorrow morning, you must come to the Cry of the Crane Teahouse, about ten, say. I will assemble The Historians. It will be best if I inform them first about Jin Huiling's tragic passing. Then when you speak to them –

only you, though, like me they will not speak to the *laowai* – they will each give you their recollections of Jin Huiliang, how he helped each and every one of them. Is that fair, Constable?"

Ma Meili nodded, thinking it very fair.

"But just you," insisted Bo Qi. "It saddens me that the spoiled son of a corrupt mayor is tasked with investigating the murder of a true hero. Such are the contradictions of our great and complicated country. Now that is all I have to say today, Constable. Please leave me to my grief. I must mourn the passing of my friend – the Hero of Lao Cai."

"Lao Cai?"

"A town in Vietnam where Jin Huiliang proved he was the best of us."

When Ma Meili clambered back into Superintendent Ye's car, she felt drained by the meeting with Bo Qi, more tired than she had been in ages. Now she dreaded the meeting with The Historians to come, having forgotten to ask Bo Qi how many of them there would be, fully aware of how difficult it would be for her to sit with such important men, to listen to their stories, and think of anything useful or relevant to ask them.

"Well?" asked an unsmiling Superintendent Ye.

Unable to speak, not even from the notes she had made in her notebook, Ma Meili handed it to him, hoping he would not criticise the neatness of her writing as he had done on numerous previous occasions. However, he flipped over each page in turn, reading in silence, and then handed the notebook back to her without comment.

"What did you make of Bo Qi?" he asked.

"A very good man, made very sad by his friend's death."

"Why did he insist the murder of Jin Huiliang had to be a robbery gone wrong?"

"I don't know."

"Did he ask you how Jin Huiliang had been killed?"

"No, Superintendent."

"Did he ask what time Jin Huiliang had been killed?"

"No, Superintendent."

"Did he ask to see any pictures from the crime scene?"

"No, Superintendent."

"Did he ask what progress we were making in identifying any suspects?"

"No, Superintendent."

"Then I suggest, when you are lying awake in bed tonight, you think on all these questions and on any others that Bo Qi did not ask, and come to some understanding as to why."

Ma Meili did not know what Superintendent Ye meant by this. He said nothing more until he dropped her off at PSB HQ. He told her that they were done for the day. He told her he had to go home and prepare for a dinner engagement. He would pick her up at nine sharp in the morning from outside The Silver Tree. He made no mention of her attending the meeting with The Historians alone. She was too afraid of his temper to remind him that he was not supposed to come.

On her desk in the Homicide office, Ma Meili found a copy of Jin Huiliang's service record waiting for her, with an attached note from Ms. Miao.

Constable, some sections have been redacted – I assume for reasons of state security – but I hope this document will prove useful to you.

Ma Meili did not know what redacted meant, but she stuffed the document into her shoulder bag to read when she got home. Ms. Miao had left another note on her desk confirming the course on English and Western culture was due to commence this Tuesday evening. Ma Meili's heart sank. She had hated school. She was certain she would hate this course also.

Ma Meili caught the bus home, the rain worsening all the time. Some of the side-streets would soon be impassable. Expecting Yoyo to be waiting for her in her little apartment, very vocal as always when he saw her, Ma Meili belatedly remembered she had left him in the care of Ye Lan's sons for the week. His absence made her feel sad. It was not nice coming home to an empty apartment. She prepared a light snack for herself before settling down in her chair to read Jin

Huiliang's service record. It was mostly dry and factual information, where he had served, which units he had been attached to, comments from senior officers – all very favourable – on his performance. At the end of the document, she found a section on his medal citations, with brief descriptions as to how and why he had received the awards. It made for disturbing reading, the things he had done.

Under intense enemy fire, Platoon Commander Jin, single-hand-edly, and with no concern for his personal safety did....

With all senior commanders killed, Platoon Commander Jin gath-ered the surviving troops together and held the line until....

With ammunition almost depleted, and with no chance of addi-tional artillery support, Company Commander Jin, suffering badly from wounds received, inspired his men to counter-attack yet again and....

The citations went on and on. Lao Cai was mentioned repeatedly. Ma Meil soon understood what Bo Qi had been telling her, how Jin Huiliang had been the best of them. Jin Huiliang had been awarded the Heroic Exemplar Medal. Even she, who knew nothing much about anything, understood that that was the highest military decoration there was. Ma Meili found her throat tightening with emotion and repeated her earlier vow to herself to track down his killer before she transferred to SWAT.

She put the service record aside. It had been a long, exhausting and emotionally trying day. It was time to take a shower. It was time to drop the case from her mind. It was Saturday evening, her favourite evening. She was about to go out visiting. This was the evening she helped out at The Silver Tree.

TWENTY-THREE

— · —

F atty Deng picked up some take-out food on the way home: a
supposedly healthy salad, brown rice, and a couple of side-dishes
of stir-fried mixed vegetables. He ate while watching the TV. The
food wasn't great and the TV even worse. Some academic from a
university in Beijing was mouthing off about the 'pivot to the East' by
the United States, the United States doing its level best, so he said, to
prevent China from exercising its ancient rights to most of the South
China Sea.

"How can the Americans be so stupid?" asked the professor. "Do
they want to provoke a war?"

The interviewer tried to calm the professor's fiery rhetoric but
Fatty Deng had already had enough – of the TV and of the food.
He put the food aside and switched the TV off. More likely than
a coming war with the United States was him losing his job at the
Procuratorate – that is, if Prosecutor Xu took up a corporate position
in London. The Procuratorate may well have given him a certificate
for bravery, but, with Prosecutor Xu thousands of miles away, and
with all the enmities and jealousies she had provoked these last few
months, none of the other prosecutors would be queuing up to give
him a job.

Fatty Deng recalled the sad story told him by Mister Wu of Mister
Wu's Cycle Sales and Repair Shop concerning Sun Mei, the young
woman now managing the Lucky Dragon Tobacco Emporium. With
the death of her mother, all her dreams had turned to dust. Unable
to go to teacher-training college, her rat-bastard boyfriend dumping
her, Sun Mei now had to stay home to manage the shop and care for
her crippled father. But she was as strong and compassionate as she

was pretty. She had not given up on her dream. Now, in the evenings, she tutored those local children in the most need, for free, at the back of her shop.

Fatty Deng decided he had to take a leaf out of her book and actually do something constructive. It was no time to give up now, to succumb to depression and lethargy. He had to dismiss all his body's aches and pains, the lingering exhaustion from his extended convalescence, the stomach-clenching fears that gripped him from time to time when he was out on the street. He couldn't sit idly by and watch his future go up in smoke. If Prosecutor Xu was intent on running away to London, he had to take care of himself. To continue his career at the Procuratorate he needed to get results quickly. It was time to impress Secretary Wu. It was time to bite the bullet and go visit an old friend.

He hung up his suit and showered. Wrapping a towel around himself, he paced the apartment, smoking a cigarette, going over and over in his mind the insane idea that had come to him as he had been driving home.

He wished his mother was around. He could have done with her counsel. He gave her a call. She said she was having a fantastic time out on the Yangzi despite the weather, sightseeing whenever the boat moored up, playing *majiang* when they sailed from one destination to another, and eating far too much.

He lied to her.

He told her he had been resting up all day. He told her that he had not heard from Prosecutor Xu, that work was the farthest thing from his mind.

Relieved she was safe and enjoying herself – the excursion had been money well spent – Fatty Deng dropped the phone on his bed and stared at himself in the mirror, not liking himself for being overweight in spite of spending weeks in hospital, hating the ugly scars that now covered his body, despairing of what a pretty girl like Sun Mei would think of him, and distraught by the anxiety he had seen on her face when he had walked off down Liberation Street away from her and Mister Wu.

Both of them had made him for police.

How had they done that?

Okay, so he was not police, but he was close enough.

Was it something about his face, or how he carried himself out on the street, or how he took notice of everything and everyone around him?

Or was Sun Mei's memory so good that she recalled the time, almost fifteen years before, that as a child she had run up the ladder at the Lucky Dragon Tobacco Emporium to fetch a packet of Gauloises Blondes for him and the lawyer Mister Li? He had been proudly wearing his new police uniform then.

Whatever the truth he could not take the chance of being made for law enforcement again this evening.

It was time to ditch the suit.

It was time to put on clothing no respectable law enforcement officer would be seen dead in.

Out of the cupboard he picked one of the genuine Hawaiian shirts Prosecutor Xu had bought him when she had been feeling guilty about him being laid up in hospital. It was the most lurid shirt he could find, in black and grey and various shades of red, all exploding volcanoes and terrified exotic creatures fleeing for their lives. He liked colourful Hawaiian shirts, but he had to wonder, in respect of this particular shirt, for a woman as stylish as Prosecutor Xu, what had she been thinking?

He pulled on some casual trousers, a pair of comfy shoes, and let the outrageous shirt fall loosely over the top of his trousers. Almost a size too big, the shirt easily concealed the pistol holstered on his hip. He then picked out an old cream jacket and threw that on top. But, staring at himself in the mirror, he thought the jacket a step to far. The Hawaiian shirt would do. It was going to be a very warm evening anyway. He picked up his umbrella, opened the door of the apartment, checked no one was waiting in the shadows for him before stepping out into the corridor, and did the same again before stepping out of the apartment block onto the street. Opening the umbrella, he set off at a brisk pace, choosing to leave his car behind for the moment. His first stop was close-by, down one of the narrow back alleys of Wukuaishi.

On the way he passed a number of his favourite watering-holes, one of them a bar often frequented by police from Wukuaishi Station. As he glanced in the window, he caught sight of Boxer Tan and young Baby Wu, both with fresh beers in their hands, laughing and joking about something. He would have loved to have joined them. But he had a job to do, and a career to preserve. It would do him no good to get drunk and to spend a few hours cursing Prosecutor Xu. He kept walking until he arrived at the entrance to a badly-lit alley. He turned into it and knocked on the first unmarked door. A few low denomination notes to the doorman and he was inside the Singing Monkey KTV club – a real dive, even for Wukuaishi.

Two scantily-clad but grubby looking waitresses, who appeared to have just got off the bus from the country, tried to grab his hands and escort him to one of the karaoke booths. But he told them to leave him be and instead took a seat at the bar next to a man in a black suit and tie. Badly distorted music was blaring out from nearby speakers, but not so loud the barman could not hear his order for a single beer in a glass. When the beer was placed in front of him Fatty Deng lit a cigarette – he had lost count how many that now was for the day – and then grimaced as he tasted the watery beer.

"How've you been?" asked Fatty Deng.

"Fuck off!" replied the man in the black suit, not bothering to look at him.

"Ah, don't be like that."

"Fatty, just leave me alone."

"But we were mates."

Brother Wang then turned to him, his face flushed with anger. "Fatty, when I saw your name in the newspaper...when I read you had been attacked by crazy cultists...I prayed...I mean I really fucking prayed...that you would die."

"I'm guessing you got into trouble with Freddie Yun."

"What the fuck do you think? Like everyone else, Freddie Yun assumed you must have been undercover for the Procuratorate while we were collecting debts for him. When his guys dragged me into his office, I thought they were going to cut my throat there and then. I was crying like a baby, Fatty – pleading for my miserable life. I tried to tell him that you were a stand-up guy, that you had only taken the job with the Procuratorate *after* you had stopped working for me. I honestly shit myself while he phoned one of his contacts at the Procuratorate to confirm what I had said was true. Even then he told me, 'Brother Wang, you are a fucking imbecile.' I thought my time had come, Fatty – I really did."

"I'm sorry – truly."

"Freddie Yun chucked me out of the gang for six months to teach me a lesson. No one wants to speak to me now. It's like I've got the fucking plague."

"Do you want me to have a word with Freddie Yun?"

"No, I fucking don't! Haven't you done enough? I thought you and I were mates, partners in crime, blood-brothers for ever. I really liked you, Fatty. And now I'm sitting in this fucking shit-hole, drinking my beer and smoking my cigarettes alone, wondering how I'm going to pay the rent this month and whether the missus is going to walk out on me. She also thinks I'm a fucking imbecile, by the way."

"I've a proposition for you."

Brother Wang glared at him. "I'm not a snitch!"

"It's a one-off job for the Procuratorate...off the books...no one is to know. I need someone lifted off the street – a simple snatch and grab."

"Not interested."

"Name your price."

Brother Wang eyes widened. "Twenty thousand."

"I said name your price, not the biggest number you could think of."

"Ten thousand then!"

Fatty Deng shook his head. "Six thousand for you – that's enough to impress the missus and pay the rent for a few months – and a thousand each for the four operators you are going to find me. They need to be young, fit, and strong – smart too."

"I've four cousins."

"I said smart."

"Funny guy," said Brother Wang, accepting the offered cigarette. "Who's the target?"

"I'll explain everything once you secure the four operators."

"But—"

"I'll check in with you later," said Fatty Deng, getting off his stool, leaving the majority of his beer.

Outside in the rain he opened up his umbrella again and lit another cigarette. He hoped he was doing the right thing. He was taking an awful risk. If Prosecutor Xu ever found out she would throw a fit. But she was off to London soon, so what did it matter? If he was going to remain at the Procuratorate he had to start doing things his way – the old Chengdu way. If things got a little rough, so what? Things were set to get a lot rougher in Chengdu if he did not get results quickly – and not just for him. If Party Chief Li remained convinced that Ye Zihao was the guiding hand behind the murder of Primo Gong, then outright warfare on Chengdu's streets was just around the corner. No one, not even the gangster Freddie Yun, would want that.

TWENTY-FOUR

— ◆ —

L ondon.

Corporate law.

Easy work and long lunches.

At least ten times her present salary.

Over five thousand miles away from her judgmental parents.

Out from under Sarangerel's prying eyes.

And a final escape from Philip Ye.

Xu Ya knew she should be excited. This was her chance, maybe her one and only chance, to begin a new life, to forget that the past had ever existed, to be wholly reborn. In London, she could live free from guilt, free from fear of discovery, free from the person she had once been. She had hoped the move to Chengdu would have achieved all of these things. But now she understood she had not travelled far enough, that in finding Philip Ye again she had only come full circle – *revisiting* the past rather than leaving it behind. A different life's trajectory was needed, one that took her far, far away from China.

However, back in her apartment, the first thing she did – after turning down her air-conditioning as the air felt so chill – was to collapse in her chair and burst into tears. The look of betrayal that Investigator Deng had given her when she had told him of her good fortune had cut right into her soul. Maybe it had been far too much to expect him to be happy for her. Before the job offer, before the frightening note from Sarangerel, she too had been looking for their professional partnership to grow and develop, for them to become the best of friends. It grieved her deeply that she could not explain to him the real reason she had to leave, how terrified she was that the truth about the evening her husband had died would come to light. She would put a good word in for Investigator Deng at the Procuratorate. He would be fine. Secretary Wu would be sure to keep an eye on him.

She dried her eyes and jumped out of the chair to fiddle with the air-conditioning again. Outside it was sweltering, inside her apartment was like a fridge. She shivered, the fine hairs on her wrists and on the back of her neck standing tall. Perhaps she was coming down with a bout of summer flu. She went into the kitchen and opened up a bottle of red wine, a Shiraz from Australia. She poured herself a small glass – not too much as she wanted to be clear-headed when she negotiated the London deal with Xi Huan. She then sat at her desk in her study, to stare out at the skyline of the city, the rain on the windows blurring her view, the city drowning under the weight of all that water.

It was a pity.

She liked Chengdu.

But she had to leave.

It was time to run.

Xu Ya turned suddenly in her chair, feeling a cold breeze on the back of her neck. For a brief moment she thought someone had been standing behind her, staring down at her. Frightened, she got up from her chair and checked she had shut the door to her apartment properly. She walked from room to room, making sure she was quite alone. But the apartment was just as she had left it when she had got up well before dawn to attend the summons to Plum Tree Pagodas. No one had forced their way in. The apartment was as disorderly as ever, clothes and books strewn everywhere, not unlike the time that Philip Ye had had the nerve to search her apartment during the investigation into The Willow Woman cult, hoping to discover where she had vanished to, finding little of use to him but pausing long enough nevertheless to tidy the clothes off her bedroom floor and return her breakfast fruit juice to the fridge. Why he had done this she did not know. Had he purposely been trying to infuriate her? Had he been trying to make her feel guilty at being unable to keep a tidy home?

She returned to her desk and laid out the documentation given her by Ms. Wen at Ambrogetti Global Software, intent on reading it all thoroughly, hoping she might spot some clue or discrepancy that would either lead her to the identity of the mystery woman with the long, wavy hair, or indeed provide a reason as to why Primo Gong had been killed.

But she found it difficult to focus.

Her eyes kept clouding over with tears.

She picked up her phone, intent on calling Investigator Deng. She wanted to tell him that everything would turn out alright. She wanted him to like her again, for them to remain friends. Her offer to take him to London with her had been sincere – ill-considered though it may have been. But, before she could dial his number, she remembered once more the look of betrayal on his face, and she placed the phone back down on her desk. What words did she have that could console him? Three months before she had almost gotten him killed and now she was abandoning him. What must he think of her? Probably no worse than she thought of herself.

She considered phoning Philip Ye, to inquire about how his investigation into the murder of that retired PLA general was progressing. Not that she was really interested – she expected no connection to the murder of Primo Gong – but it would be a useful pretext to tell him about her impending move to London, not only to ask him to look out for Investigator Deng but also to gauge his reaction to her most important news. Her stupidly romantic heart hoped he would be devastated. She imagined him pleading with her not to go, telling her that he wouldn't be able to live without her, that he would follow her to the four corners of the world if he had to in the hope of one day bringing her back home.

The cold breeze touched her neck again. She turned once more in her chair, the fantasy quickly fading. The breeze seemed to be coming through the doorway from the lounge. She got up from her chair, checked the apartment door again, and then every window in her apartment. None had been left open. It was quite mystifying. Most likely the air-conditioning had malfunctioned. She made a mental note to make a complaint to the day concierge, Mister Gan, before she left for the restaurant that evening.

She returned to her study, glad at least the mysterious breeze had stopped her doing something as stupid as phoning Philip Ye. Being the man he was, he would have been more interested in why she was inquiring about his investigation rather than getting upset over her leaving Chengdu. In the last three months he had not contacted her once. Did that not say everything about him? Was she not free to leave for London without any emotional encumbrances at all?

Philip Ye could go to hell.

All of Chengdu could go to hell.

The cold breeze again touched her neck. Exasperated, she leapt out of her chair and ran into the lounge. But the world about her had already changed. She was in blackness, except for the twinkling of distant stars. She was falling, disorientated, her head spinning. She landed in a large open courtyard, thick snow lying all around. In front of her was a *yamen* – a government building from dynastic times, the official residence from where a magistrate would govern a district on behalf of the emperor, supervising the collection of taxes and enforcing the law. It was night. Outside the entrance to the *yamen* flaming torches fluttered in the icy breeze. She wrapped her arms about her, the breeze slicing through her flimsy summer blouse. She ran into the *yamen* to get out of the cold. It appeared empty, deserted, not a soul in sight. But, as she walked from room to room, the flickering oil-lamps bringing a little light and warmth to her new surroundings, she heard the sound of a man's voice, speaking, reciting, as if reading from a text.

She knew this all to be a dream. But, nevertheless, she was frightened when she entered the magistrate's private room and found him sitting at his desk, dressed in his full magistrate's regalia, writing, and then reading aloud to himself all that he had just written. No image of him existed to her knowledge, but she knew it to be her hero, Huang Liu-Hong, as a young man, eventual author of the seventeenth-century instruction manual for magistrates, *A Complete Book Concerning Happiness and Benevolence*. She recognised him from a previous dream, experienced while her husband had still been alive. Could she really be seeing Huang Liu-Hong at his desk during his first posting as a magistrate to impoverished and earthquake-ravaged Tancheng County in Shandong Province? Was this the terrible winter of 1671 when it would not stop snowing and it was said that the drifts of snow lay ten foot high?

She listened as Huang Liu-Hong, quite unaware of her presence, once more spoke out aloud.

"In consideration of the case now before me, it should be noted that if a suspect is found guilty of premeditated homicide then he shall be put to death by beheading. If he has accessories, and the accessories assisted in the formulation of his murderous plan, then, even if they did not assist in the perpetration of the homicide itself, they shall be treated as principals and also put to death by beheading. However, those accessories who knew of the plan but did nothing to prevent it, even though they did not assist in formulating it or even assist in the perpetration of the actual homicide, shall have their punishment reduced by one degree and shall instead suffer death by strangulation."

Xu Ya knew the relevant statute of the *Da Qing Lü Li* – The Great Qing Legal Code – to which Huang Liu-Hong was referring. But what was he trying to tell her? What was she supposed to learn from this dream?

Mulling over this, she was startled when Huang Liu-Hong suddenly looked up and stared into the darkened corner of the room where she stood shivering. She saw the surprise – no, the shock! – on his face.

He pointed an accusing finger at her. "I am my desk doing my duty; why, may I ask, are you not at your desk doing yours?"

She tried to back away but found herself toppling over backward and falling through space again. She woke sitting in her chair at her desk, her face and hands numb with the cold. She picked up her glass and downed the red wine in one.

TWENTY-FIVE

—·—

Though he himself had been far from blameless for the alter-
cation, while dressing for dinner Philip Ye pondered Bo Qi's
emotional reaction to him, his refusal to be interviewed by a scion of
the family Ye, his clumsy attempt to conceal the grief he surely already
felt at the passing of his great friend – the feigned anger inadvertently
bringing even more suspicion down upon him.

On being invited into the house by the private secretary, Philip Ye
had felt as if he was walking through treacle, the atmosphere within
thick with hopelessness and despair. And, if truth be told, Philip Ye
thought he had caught a tantalising and all-too-brief glimpse of Jin
Huiliang's ghost standing in the far corner of the large sitting-room,
the vision disturbing him so much that he had resorted to his rhythmic breathing, and causing him to be blunter with Bo Qi than first
intended. But that bluntness had done the trick, the unchanging
nature of Bo Qi's haunted eyes when informed of Jin Huiliang's
death had confirmed what Philip Ye had already sensed about the
house: Bo Qi had knowledge – possibly even foreknowledge – of Jin
Huiliang's murder.

But knowledge of a murder, and the presence of the victim's ghost,
did not necessarily constitute a crime. The problem was what to do
next, specifically how the encounter with Bo Qi and the rest of The
Historians should be handled at the teahouse in the morning. Philip
Ye wanted to be there, to look into the eyes of each and every one
of them. However, in the presence of Constable Ma they might all
prove a touch more talkative, not so much on their guard. Constable
Ma might have understood little from her interview with Bo Qi, but
she had done very well, eliciting more information than Philip Ye had

expected – useful information, at that – and she might just do the same at the teahouse. But, was Constable Ma his only strategy?

Philip Ye adjusted his tie in the mirror, mulling over his options.

"Boss?"

Philip Ye turned to see Night Na in the doorway. "What is it?"

"The American has arrived."

"I'll be right down."

With a nod, Night Na vanished.

Philip Ye slipped on the jacket of his casual powder blue suit. Earlier he had carried out some rushed research on Stacey Corrigan, read a couple of her business reports, stared at her photograph for a few minutes to get a sense of her. He had been impressed. The brothers Na had been right to be concerned about her. Apart from Mouse – who did not count – his father did not have a track record of courting the attention of very intelligent women. He had learned his lesson with Philip Ye's mother. The only conclusion Philip Ye could reach in regard to Stacey Corrigan was that his father was up to no good – but what?

Philip Ye descended the stairs, saw his father hard at work in the kitchen and found Stacey Corrigan in the dining-room, a glass of wine already in her hands, dressed in a long emerald green *qipao* that set off her pale skin and auburn hair. Philip Ye appreciated the gesture of the dress, as would his father. She was standing with her back to him, staring out of the window, the gardens lit by the white lanterns the brothers Na had put up for the occasion. She turned as she sensed his presence.

"Welcome to my father's home," Philip Ye said, extending a hand to her.

Stacey Corrigan took the offered hand and attempted a reply, struggling with the dialect. He repeated the welcome in English, and asked her if she would be more comfortable conversing in her native language.

She laughed with relief, flirtatiously smoothing back her hair. According to his research she was forty-three years old. He would have guessed ten years younger despite the toughness – gained from much experience, he guessed – about her brown eyes.

"My Japanese is good," she said, "but I have always struggled with the tonal languages. If you think my Sichuanese is bad, you ought to hear my Thai."

"I am sure you would get by wherever you are," he said. "What brings you to Chengdu? It can't be just my father's cooking."

"That would have been reason enough. Your father has fed me very well this week. It is a wonder I can fit into this dress. But I am really here to work. I am writing a piece on the rise of the high-tech industry in Chengdu. Your father has been most helpful to me, providing me with the historical context – a lot of detail from the years he was in office."

"In his mind, his achievements were very great."

She laughed again. "He warned me about you, Superintendent Ye. He told me your humour was more English than Chinese."

"Philip, please."

"Then Philip it is – now tell me, a homicide detective, is your father proud or appalled?"

"It depends on the day."

"Your life must be interesting."

"It has its moments."

"And complicated...your father being under house-arrest?"

"Whose life is not complicated?"

"But I think the Chinese do complicated especially well."

"Thank you, Ms. Corrigan."

"Stacey, please!" she exclaimed, making him smile.

Ye Zihao appeared, apron around his waist, unlit pipe sticking from his mouth, holding up a miniature gong which he proceeded to sound. "Dinner is served!" he announced, in English, before disappearing back into the kitchen.

"It's been like this all week," said Stacey Corrigan, allowing Philip Ye to seat her at the table, the Na brothers fussing about them, pouring more wine for her, a mineral water for him. "I expected to meet a brooding, embittered man, but I cannot remember ever being so royally entertained."

Philip Ye kept his own counsel. If Stacey Corrigan hung around long enough, she would meet – as Mouse would eventually meet also – the other Ye Zihao, the man who could neither forget nor forgive what had been done to him, the man who would stop at nothing to regain his old life. There would also come a time when Stacey Corrigan would receive no more invitations to dine, when her phone calls would go unreturned, when she proved no longer useful in that regard.

There was small talk around the table as they ate, Ye Zihao leaving the table briefly between each course to quickly prepare the next, the Na brothers helping clear the dishes, shovelling uneaten food into their own mouths when they thought they were out of Stacey Corrigan's field of view. Stacey Corrigan was happy to talk, about her work, her travels around the world, the many important people – not only those in business but politicians and entertainers too – she had met, those she had liked and those she had not. She was irrepressible. She was fun. Philip Ye quickly warmed to her. As each new course was served, she found as much joy in the food as had any who had visited the house in the past few years, making Ye Zihao very content. Philip Ye could see that she was no stranger to making people feel good, that she was ruthless in her own way, prepared to do whatever was needed to get the story she was after. Though, in regard to the food, he was certain she was sincere. His father had excelled himself, creating a seven-course banquet, starting with an appetizer of spicy crayfish. This was one of Philip Ye's favourite dishes, and he began to wonder whether it was he who was the important guest at the table, the person to be 'softened up' so to speak and not Stacey Corrigan – a suspicion confirmed by the mouth-watering courses to follow. After dinner, the three of them retired to Ye Zihao's personal sitting-room, cognac for both him and Stacey Corrigan, and a jasmine tea for Philip Ye brought in by Day Na. Ye Zihao lit his pipe, blowing clouds of aromatic smoke around the room. As was his way, he did not think to ask permission of Stacey Corrigan for his smoking, but Philip Ye could see she did not mind.

"Philip, your help is needed," said Ye Zihao, the serious matter of the evening now to begin.

Assuming it was Stacey Corrigan who needed his help even if she was acting as an unknowing pawn in his father's great game, Philip Ye replied, "Father, you are quite aware I know very little about the business world."

"Yes, but you do like mysteries," said Ye Zihao.

"It's not much of a mystery, I'm afraid," said Stacey Corrigan. "And if you cannot help, I will perfectly understand."

"He will help," growled Ye Zihao, chomping down in his pipe. "Let us speak of Ambrogetti Global Software."

"That is Primo Gong's company," said Philip Ye.

Ye Zihao laughed out loud, pointing the stem of his pipe in Stacey Corrigan's direction.

She explained. "Your father made me a little wager. He told me you would pretend ignorance of the business world but then know immediately who we were talking about."

"In my defence," said Philip Ye, "Primo Gong is famous – or infamous – depending on your point of view."

"My son considers Primo Gong an idiot or a phoney for giving up his American passport," said Ye Zihao to Stacey Corrigan. "Being police, he is suspicious of everyone...including me."

Stacey Corrigan almost choked on her cognac. "Oh, I cannot believe that to be true."

Philip Ye saw his father's brows knit and his eyes narrow. This was exactly what his father believed – and rightly so. Philip Ye distrusted his father as much as any other man alive.

"When your father first suggested Ambrogetti Global Software," continued Stacey Corrigan, "I have to admit I was very sceptical. That story had been done to death a couple of years ago, at the time Primo Gong burned his United States passport. Everyone assumed Primo Gong was going to succeed in his new venture. It wasn't in his nature to fail. But then, at the pressing of your father this week, I did a little digging, phoned a few local sources, and discovered to my astonishment that all is not as well with Ambrogetti Global Software as it appears."

It was no great secret that Primo Gong was a creature of the Shanghai Clique. Philip Ye glanced at his father, wondering what it was he was up to. Ye Zihao was studying the bowl of his pipe, pretending to be lost in his own thoughts. Philip Ye turned his attention back to Stacey Corrigan. "What did you discover?"

"Rumours that Primo Gong's mind has been elsewhere these last few months, that he has gone missing for hours at a time from his company with nobody being able to contact him. There is also a problem with Ambrogetti Global Software's flagship contract with the Chengdu Cymbidium Bank."

"What sort of problem?"

"Not only is the rollout of the software being developed for the bank running well behind schedule, but – if my sources are to be believed – even when Primo Gong has been at his desk, both his capacity for inspired decision-making and his natural leadership qualities seem to have abandoned him."

"Have you tried to interview him?"

"I have, for most of this week – but no joy," replied Stacey Corrigan. "This hiding away is meaningful in itself, Philip. Primo Gong has never before been shy of the media. I even camped out at the Old Chengdu Restaurant last evening to try to impose myself on his usual dinner with the CCB executives but he didn't show. Then, at your father's suggestion, I later went round to Plum Tree Pagodas where Primo Gong leases an apartment. But I couldn't get past the concierge. I sat outside Ambrogetti Global Software this morning in the rain, waiting for him to show. He never did."

"But someone else showed up instead," said Ye Zihao, some dark pleasure in his eyes.

"Who?" asked Philip Ye, genuinely curious.

"A woman," replied Stacey Corrigan. "Beautiful, slim – very professional-looking in spite of her casual clothes."

"That could describe many women in Chengdu," said Philip Ye, a sinking feeling in his gut, dreading what was to come, already instinctively aware of who it was that had arrived at Ambrogetti Global Software this morning.

"It was Prosecutor Xu," said Ye Zihao, exultant.

"Are you sure?" asked Philip Ye.

"My source within the company told me her name," said Stacey Corrigan. "It seems she is quite famous. She has been on your TV recently. Most of the staff at the company are terrified. It is common knowledge that Primo Gong has been detained."

"By the Procuratorate," added Ye Zihao, needlessly.

"You are certain?" asked Philip Ye.

Stacey Corrigan looked to Ye Zihao. Ye Zihao relit his pipe and shrugged. "Not certain, no," he said. "It is just as possible that Primo Gong has vanished...run for the hills...and that Prosecutor Xu has been tasked by that snake Party Chief Li to find him and bring him back to face the music."

"But what has Primo Gong done wrong?" asked Philip Ye.

"That is the mystery," replied Ye Zihao.

"I don't want you to get into any trouble, Philip," said Stacey Corrigan. "But if you could confirm that Primo Gong has either been arrested or has absconded, say, with all of Ambrogetti Global Software's cash, then that would be the story of the year. Your father told me that you are acquainted with Prosecutor Xu."

"Pah!" exclaimed Ye Zihao. "She owes my son her life!"

Which, thought Philip Ye, though true – indirectly at least – did not mean Prosecutor Xu would prove forthcoming. He also did not want to be, like Stacey Corrigan, yet another pawn in one of his father's chess games with the Shanghai Clique. He could see his father's strategy now. His father had heard somewhere on the Chengdu grapevine that there were serious problems at Ambrogetti Global Software and so had cultivated a willing journalist – a respected Western journalist at that – to investigate the story, to write a damning piece on Primo Gong, to be syndicated in all the business journals around the world, which, because Primo Gong was their creature, would also heap as much embarrassment onto the Shanghai Clique as was humanly possible. The reverberations would reach as far away as Beijing. Party Chief Li might come in for severe criticism, might even be relieved of his post – as well as possibly lose a fortune. Party Chief Li was rumoured to have invested heavily in Ambrogetti Global Software.

Ye Zihao's plan was as beautiful as it was simple. Even Philip Ye had to admit it was a master-stroke. But, before Philip Ye could give his answer, seeing no way out of the corner into which he had been forced without making his father lose face in front of Stacey Corrigan, Night Na put his head around the door, his eyes wide, his face as white as a sheet.

"Forgive this abominable intrusion," Night Na said. "Boss, you are needed."

This was directed at Philip Ye.

Philip Ye was glad of the interruption, wanting more time to think. He had not spoken to Prosecutor Xu in three months. There was no telling she would welcome his call. He apologised and told his father and Stacey Corrigan he would return in a few minutes and then joined the brothers Na in the kitchen. They both had big cigars on the go and stank of alcohol from, Philip Ye suspected, raiding his father's drinks cabinet. Neither man looked well. If fact, for tough men, they both seemed scared out of their wits.

"What is it?" asked Philip Ye.

"The Witch-Queen is at the gates," whispered Night Na.

"Sarangerel," whispered Day Na.

"You must protect us, Boss."

"You must send her away."

"Unlike us, you are immune to her evil spells."

"Absolutely – quite immune."

Callers at the gates, at any hour day or night, were not unusual. Sometimes people stopped by just to shout their good wishes to the family Ye. Others tied petitions to the gates with red ribbons in the hope that Ye Zihao would take pity on them, and intercede between them and whatever difficulty was afflicting them. Most of these petitions ended up in the bin. But Philip Ye knew for a fact that his father did indeed help out one or two, enough to perhaps cynically spread the word that, though he was under house-arrest, he remained a man of influence and compassion, ready to take up his post as mayor to serve the people again at a moment's notice. Other kinds of notes were sometimes tied to the gates, from young women in the main, professing their love for Philip Ye – these notes often left on his desk in his private rooms while he was out at work by the brothers Na to their great amusement. Occasionally – at least once every few months – a young woman (or an older woman who should know better) would actually tie herself to the gates so she could profess her love in person, only to be set free by the brothers Na as soon as she was picked up on the security cameras, and given a severe talking to before being sent roughly on her way. But never had Sarangerel turned up at the gates – not in many years at least. She had not dared.

Philip Ye took the umbrella offered him by Day Na, left the brothers puffing nervously on their cigars, opened the front door and stepped out into the rain. He was beginning to wonder if he had been better off arguing with his mother back in England. He trudged down the long gravel drive, annoyed as his newly-shined shoes were getting wet, the evening so warm and humid his fresh shirt soon sticking to his skin. However, before he had walked more than twenty or so paces, his mind was no longer concerned with the weather but with the sudden weakening of the veil about him – the veil that separated the land of the living from that of the dead. A thousand or more spirits gathered about him, all desperately vying for his attention, their voices a cacophony of noise, far from the usual isolated communications he usually received from the afterlife, and not experienced since the last time he had encountered Sarangerel.

He put his hands to his ears, a futile exercise as the voices continued inside his head. He began to breathe – in for eight heartbeats, holding for four, and out for eight – to calm his fears, to return control to his mind, and silently, firmly, ordered the spirits to leave him be.

Slowly, the voices in his head diminished until they constituted nothing more than an annoying background hum. He felt the veil about him strengthen, his natural sense of balance and order return. Relieved he picked up his umbrella, not having realised he had dropped it, and stood up straight to stretch his back, the burden of the afterlife – or at least the myriad concerns of those spirits closest to the veil – no longer weighing him down.

He cursed Sarangerel, her reckless delving beyond the veil, her search, no matter the cost, for the perfect invocation to raise the spirits before her, to discover how to make them do her bidding – a crime in the making, if there ever was one. When was that woman going to learn to leave well enough alone?

Determined to give her a piece of his mind for continuing to meddle in things that were beyond her understanding, and to remind her that she had sworn an oath never again to set foot on Ye family property, he continued on down the drive, gritting his teeth against the constant low-level hum inside his head. And yet when he walked around the last bend in the drive, the high trees on either side of the drive no longer blocking his line of sight, he saw it was not Sarangerel waiting for him at the gates, but a teenage girl, no more that fourteen or fifteen years of age, wearing nothing but a summer blouse and jeans, tall and lanky, all skinny legs and arms, the spitting image of Sarangerel except that she was half her age and her skin was as pale as alabaster as opposed to Sarangerel's usual copper hue. The girl was soaked to the skin, the rainwater running down her face and dripping from her long black hair. She was holding a small suitcase in one hand

and had been dragging another on its wheels behind her. She was a picture of abject misery. But, even with her head bowed and her eyes hidden from him, Philip Ye could not fail to sense her power, the shimmering of the air about her, the weakness of the veil that surrounded her. The brothers Na had mistaken her for Sarangerel due to the poor image received from the security cameras trained on the gates. But they were right to stay away. Some kind of sorcery was at work here – and not just emanating from the girl. Philip Ye had a profound feeling, not of déjà vu, not of simple synchronicity, but that this encounter had been long in the making.

"I am Philip Ye," he said through the bars of the iron gates.

She raised her face to him, astonishing him with her likeness to Sarangerel, but enabling him to see the subtle differences too, the lack of arrogance, the anxiety, the fragility of her teenage persona, as well as the obvious intelligence that lay behind her eyes; not that Sarangerel lacked for intelligence, rather her intelligence was of a different order, more preternatural cunning than cleverness, more an expert hunter's instinct for seeing the weaknesses in her prey.

"I am Yue," said the girl, her voice hardly perceptible above the sound of the falling rain.

"Yue, you must quieten the spirits about you."

"Forgive me, when I get frightened...."

Yue brushed the rainwater from her face, closed her eyes, and began to murmur to herself. A few moments later Philip Ye was relieved to find the constant hum gone from his head.

"I do not know how it happens," Yue said. "When I get frightened it is like everyone steps forward to help me, everyone trying to give me advice."

"You have a rare gift."

"I have never met anyone else who can hear what I hear."

"What can I do for you, Yue?"

"I ask for sanctuary."

"Sanctuary?"

"I am being pursued."

"By whom?"

"I do not know."

"Then how—?"

"Please, Isobel sent me to you."

TWENTY-SIX

— • —

S un Mei couldn't remember a day like it – a day of unremitting terror. Hour after hour she had spent staring out of the window, dreading the return of the fat man, or again and again running out into the backyard to stare up through the rain at Plum Tree Pagodas, at the broken window on the fifth floor, wondering if indeed the fat man was investigating the shooting on Friday night, and whether the broken window had anything to do with that. She had been unable to keep anything in her stomach. She was convinced the fat man would make it so that her life was never the same again. Only the steady stream of customers looking to stock up on cigarettes in case the floods really did come and trap them in their apartments kept Sun Mei from going crazy. For the most part her customers were good people, living normal lives, keeping themselves to themselves – as she herself wanted to do. Was it too much to ask for a simple life, a life without further pain and tragedy, a life without the fat man haunting her every step?

She had told her father nothing about the fat man. But he had noticed the fear in her eyes. Thinking it was to do with the expected floods, thinking his daughter had been infected by Mister Wu's acute concerns for the efficiency of the drains, he had tried to comfort her, to tell her that the rains, bad as they were, were not enough to submerge Liberation Street. Unfortunately, the potential flooding of Liberation Street was now the least of Sun Mei's worries.

By the time the children began to trickle in for their lessons that evening, Sun Mei was feeling slightly better, more her usual self. It was probably because her fear was no longer just for herself and her father but for Little Xiulan – her favourite – whose mother had rung to say that the child was too ill to attend. Bright as a button but over-sensitive, Little Xiulan had been bullied at school and her studies had suffered accordingly. After only a few months under Sun Mei's care, Little Xiulan had blossomed into a different girl: quick to laugh and even quicker at her studies. Sun Mei had herself gone to the school, berated the useless teachers, found the little culprits, banged a few heads together and publicly shamed their parents, all in a couple of hours while Mister Wu had looked after the Lucky Dragon Tobacco Emporium.

"What is wrong with Little Xiulan?" asked Sun Mei.

"A fever, Teacher Sun," replied the mother. "You know how she doesn't like the heat. And the thunderstorms kept her awake much of the night. She has been listless and anxious all day."

Sun Mei knew how Little Xiulan felt. "Have you taken her to a doctor?"

"I did not know what to do."

"I will visit later this evening."

"You are so kind, Teacher Sun."

Sun Mei shook her head as she put the phone down. How bright Little Xiulan could have been born to such dopey parents she did not know. She got the other children settled down in their chairs and put a cup of water on each of their desks. Thankfully, all of them told her they had eaten that evening. But she went to each child in turn and put the back of her hand on their foreheads to check if any others had come down with a fever. Satisfied all was well, she told them to get straight down to work. Hardly had she done this when the phone rang again. She took the call at the shop counter.

"The fat man is back," said Mister Wu.

Sun Mei glanced up and out of the window. It was now dark, the rain still pouring down, the few street lights doing little against the gloom. She could not see him. She could not see a thing. Her heart in her mouth, she asked, "Where is he?"

"On your side of the road, in the shadows, standing in the doorway of the pharmacy."

Madame Wei Ju, who owned the pharmacy next door, always shut up shop early on a Saturday evening so she could go and visit her sister in the north of the city. Her doorway was the perfect place for the fat man to conceal himself.

"What is he doing?" asked Sun Mei, desperately trying not to cry, not wanting to embarrass herself or frighten the children.

"It is hard to say," replied Mister Wu. "I noticed him first when he walked past my shop before crossing to your side of the road. He is holding a big umbrella and doing his best to conceal his face. But I recognised him immediately. He is wearing the most ridiculous shirt. I cannot even begin to describe it. If you want me to guess what he is up to, I think he has been watching the shift change at the Black House."

The Black House!

With all that had been going on, her fears about the fat man, her worry for sick Little Xiulan, she had forgotten to prepare the package of free cigarettes for the police at the Black House.

She hung up on Mister Wu quickly, thanking him for his concern for her, telling him she had to get back to the children. She hastily gift-wrapped the cigarettes, reciting the order as she went so as not to make a mistake.

Two packets of Septwolves Blue.

One of Double Happiness.

One of Golden Bridge.

No sooner was the package ready when the door opened. She held the package out before her, about to lower her gaze, hoping it would not be the youngest and meanest again, when she saw it wasn't any of the police from the Black House at all.

The fat man!

Oh, and that shirt!

She had never seen anything like it: a riot of colour, black and various shades of red and grey, erupting volcanoes and assorted wildlife running for their lives. In wondering where he had come by such a shirt, and where he found the nerve to wear it, she momentarily forgot her fear.

"Good evening," he said.

Her eyes wandered slowly up from his shirt. His face was not as she had expected. Though she had a vivid memory of him from all those years before, when she had been but a girl, try as she might, she had been unable to recall the detail of his face. Her fear being what it had been through the day, her imagination had created a face for him, adding layers of fat, wrinkles, and a number of blotches for the intervening years, the result being the face of the ugliest pig imaginable with beady, staring eyes.

His face, in reality, was not that of a pig. He was far more handsome than she had expected. And, though a large man, not as fat either. There were no wrinkles or blotches on his face. But he did not look well. And there was a weariness emanating from him not unlike that of an old man. It was his eyes, though, that fascinated her most: dark shining stones, sad, but full of kindness too. She suddenly wondered how she must look to him – her unhealthy complexion, her dull eyes, her useless hair – how the heat, the fear, and the nausea she had suffered all day must have left her looking quite a fright.

"Good evening," he repeated.

Before she could respond, the door flew open and in walked the sour-faced woman, the most senior of the police from the Black House. As usual, she was not in uniform but kept a shiny police badge on the belt of her jeans as Sun Mei had seen some police do in the films her father watched on the TV. Unusually, she was not alone. With her was a man Sun Mei had never seen before, about thirty years of age, short-hair, attractive in an arrogant kind of way, bristling with self-confidence. He was not wearing a uniform or indeed sporting a badge on his trouser belt but Sun Mei assumed he had to be police also.

The policewoman at first ignored the fat man. She snatched the package from Sun Mei's hands and pointed to the man with her. "This is my cousin. He needs some smokes as well."

Sun Mei nodded.

What else could she do?

She looked to the cousin to take his order, but he ignored her. He pushed past the fat man, moved behind the counter so he was almost standing next to Sun Mei, and helped himself to three packets of Marlboro, manufactured in China but still not cheap. The cousin stuffed the cigarettes into his pocket, blowing Sun Mei a kiss as he did so. She calculated the loss, money she was never going to see again. And that loss on top of the free cigarettes she was already forced to give to the police at the Black House every evening.

But the cousin was not yet done. When he returned to the front of the counter, he pointed to the fat man's shirt and said, "You must have been on fucking drugs when you bought that."

The theft of cigarettes was no problem to the policewoman but it appeared that incivility was. "Get out of here!" she shouted at her cousin.

Laughing, the cousin ran out of the shop and vanished into the gloom. Sun Mei hoped never to see him again.

"My apologies," said the policewoman to the fat man. "My cousin is on leave from the army. He is already slightly drunk. He's now off to meet his friends at some local club."

"No offence taken," replied the fat man, smiling. "This shirt was bought for me by my boss."

The policewoman laughed. "So, you have to wear it!"

"Unfortunately, yes."

She stared at the fat man. "Don't take this the wrong way...but it actually suits you."

"Really?"

"That's a compliment, I assure you. You're new around here, aren't you? I've never seen you before."

The fat man nodded. "My boss has me checking out the local area. We're looking for new office space."

"What's your line of business?"

"Computers...stuff like that."

"Maybe you could fix me up with a cheap laptop."

"Maybe."

"But I think you're better off looking for office-space elsewhere. The glory days for Liberation Street, if ever there were any, have long gone. It's an aging population around here. Most of the people wouldn't know a computer if it fell on their heads. Though there are a few perfumed old ladies around the corner that spend most of their time dancing in the street if that sort of thing takes your fancy."

"It just might," said the fat man, still smiling.

"Maybe I'll see you again," she said.

"You won't miss me in this shirt," replied the fat man.

"Apologies again for my cousin."

"No problem."

Sun Mei studied the fat man as he in turn watched the policewoman leave the shop, walk across the road, splashing through the puddles as she went, punch in the code on the door to the Black House and then disappear inside. She watched the smile drop from the fat man's face and his shoulders relax. She also saw his hand drop from behind him, from underneath his shirt, and caught a brief glimpse of the butt of pistol. She put her hand to her mouth to stop herself gasping.

Why would the fat man fear the sour-faced woman?

Why would the fat man pretend not to be police?

Why would police fear other police?

She remembered from earlier in the day that the fat man now smoked cheap Pride cigarettes rather than the expensive pack of Gauloises Blondes he had bought all those years ago. She quickly reached up to the shelves behind her – what a day for giving away stock! – and put down two packets of Pride on the counter in front of him. He made no move to pick them up.

"Who was that woman?" he asked, instead.

Sun Mei had heard her name spoken of by a couple of the other police at the Black House. But it was not her place to speak, to get involved in a war between police. Only an idiot would do that.

"Is it Superintendent Si Ying?" he asked.

She felt faint but held her tongue. He stared at her, more curious than angry, she thought. She pushed the two packets of Pride on the counter closer toward him. He ignored the cigarettes. A badge and ID appeared in his hand. It was not a police badge. Sun Mei recognised the insignia of the Chengdu People's Procuratorate.

"You must answer my questions, Ms. Sun," he said.

Her tongue woke from its deep sleep. "Please...I see nothing...I hear nothing...I know nothing. I am quite insignificant...quite stupid really. Please take the cigarettes. They are a gift for you."

The fat man pointed out of the window to the Black House. "Do they ever pay for their cigarettes?"

Was that a trick question?

Did he think her a moron?

Whatever answer she gave him – truth or lie – would surely come back to bite her. She clamped her mouth shut. Let him beat her if he wanted, but she would say nothing.

"Are you teaching again this evening, Ms. Sun?"

Aiya!

He knew about the children.

The fat man knew all about the children!

A terrible dread gripped her heart that he would order the children away from her, that the Procuratorate would make it so she would not be allowed to teach again in the future.

"Please," she said, her voice nothing more than a whimper.

She tried to block his way but he firmly eased her aside, not hurting her but so as she would know she could not compete with his strength. With tears of desperation in her eyes, she followed him into the backroom.

"Good evening, children," he said.

The children, all thankfully still at their desks, replied in chorus, "Good evening," before they put their hands over their mouths to stifle their giggles at his shirt. Except for one naughty little boy – Hong, of course! – who couldn't resist pointing at the fat man's shirt as if all the other children were blind. Sun Mei thought it would be a blessing if a hole opened up beneath her feet and swallowed her.

The fat man did not stop with the children. He pushed through the maze of desks crammed into the room and headed through the next doorway as if he knew where he was going. Sun Mei paused to calm the children.

"Please keep working," she said, trying to conceal her fear from them.

"But, Teacher Sun, his shirt is so funny," said Hong.

Sun Mei felt like picking Hong up and shaking some sense into him. Why was it that children couldn't sense danger? Why was it that they couldn't tell good people from bad?

Sun Mei clapped her hands together to give them all a big shock. "Children, you must concentrate! It is no business of yours what shirt my guest likes to wear. And, Hong, it is very rude to point. If you do not concentrate, you will not learn. And if you do not learn, you will not amount to very much. Your parents expect greatness from you. *I expect greatness from you.* Now, get down to work!"

Reminded of the stakes, and surprised by the unusual sharpness of her tongue, the children – including Hong – began scratching their pencils once more across their paper. Relieved, Sun Mei hurried after the fat man, and almost groaned out loud when she found him in conversation with her father.

"No, you are quite wrong, Investigator Deng," her father was saying. "It was not two-thirty but one-thirty exactly. Three rifle shots...quite unmistakable...one after the other. It was not a dream, I assure you. My daughter heard them too."

Sun Mei felt the fat man's sad but kind eyes upon her again. She did not know what to do. She just stood in the doorway to her father's room like a fool, unable to speak, unable to retreat, wishing her father would shut his fat, stupid mouth.

"Your daughter chooses not to speak to me," said Investigator Deng.

"She doesn't trust easily," replied her father. "Now me, I'll speak to anyone."

Isn't that the truth, thought Sun Mei, convinced her father was going to ruin both of their lives.

"Was it one rifle or two?" asked Investigator Deng.

"Ah, now that I cannot say."

"You were in the army?"

"Not exactly, Investigator Deng, the PLA Air Force – but that was many years ago. I was a paratrooper, one of the elite, the 15th Airborne Corps – The Sword of the Blue Sky. I landed badly on my back one day. All my own fault entirely. I was invalided out. That is why I am now either in my bed or my wheelchair."

A pity you didn't land on your head, thought Sun Mei.

"I am sorry," said Investigator Deng, sounding sincere.

"It was *karma*," said her father.

"Mister Sun, I do need your daughter to answer a few questions for me," said Investigator Deng.

"She will answer this time, I assure you."

Sun Mei felt the nausea return, wishing she had any other father but this one.

"Ms. Sun, is the name of the woman I just met in the shop Superintendent Si Ying?"

Sun Mei kept her mouth shut.

"Daughter, you must answer!" exclaimed her father, angrily. "Investigator Deng is investigating a murder – a very terrible murder! It is our civic duty to assist him."

Civic duty!

Sun Mei had never heard the like from her father's mouth.

Investigator Deng spoke again. "Well, Ms. Sun?"

"Yes, I think Superintendent Si Ying is her name," said Sun Mei, hating her father, hating herself.

"And what is the name of her cousin?"

"I have never seen him before."

"What is Superintendent Si Ying's brand of cigarettes?"

"Golden Bridge," replied Sun Mei, feeling empty now, certain both she and her father were doomed, that her father's recklessness had condemned them both to some terrible fate.

"Is she the only one at the Black House who smokes Golden Bridge?"

"Yes."

"And how often do you include Golden Bridge in the package you hand over at the commencement of the night-shift at the Black House?"

"Four nights."

"Which nights?"

"Thursday, Friday, Saturday, and Sunday."

"Are you saying that the cigarette order is different on the other days?"

"Yes, on the nights she works, the order is two Septwolves Blue, one Double Happiness, and one Golden Bridge; the other nights, two Septwolves Blue, one Cocopalm Red, and Red Golden Dragon."

"My daughter has an excellent memory," said her father, very proud.

Investigator Deng wrote all this down in his notebook. Sun Mei could not help but notice his excellent writing, so neat she was astonished. A stupid thought occurred to her that she should invite him to teach the children sometime.

"How about the day-shift?" he asked.

"I have never seen them," she replied. "Maybe they do not smoke."

He made a note of this as well before turning back to her father and saying, "Thank you for your cooperation, Mister Sun. I have what I need. I will trouble you and your daughter no longer."

But her father was not done. "Investigator Deng...before you leave...some months ago I read in the newspaper about an Investigator Deng of the Procuratorate who had been nearly killed rounding up some crazy cultists."

Sun Mei had not heard this story. She had little interest in life beyond Liberation Street. She saw the smile leave Investigator Deng's face, his eyes sadder than ever.

"That was my own fault entirely," he said, using the same words her father had used about his accident.

"It is said you are a hero...that the Procuratorate gave you a medal," said her father.

"Goodbye, Mister Sun...Ms. Sun," said Investigator Deng, choosing not to comment, easing past her again, but this time taking her breath away, though she did not know why.

A hero.

What did that mean?

Sun Mei advanced on her father, shaking her fist in his face. "What is wrong with you? Why is your mouth so big? Anyone would think you broke your brains not your back!"

"I like him," said her father by way of explanation.

"Fool!"

He waved her complaint away and turned up the volume on his TV to drown out anything else she might have to say. She shook her fist at him again, determined to give him another piece of her mind later that evening when the children were gone.

The children!

She ran after Investigator Deng but found the children all safe at their desks, working on the problems she had set them; except for Hong, that is, who was drawing a picture of the fat man and his ridiculous shirt. As Sun Mei passed by, she gently smacked Hong's head. As with her father, she was going to have to have a stern word with that boy.

She got back to the shop counter just in time to see the door close and Investigator Deng, umbrella up against the rain, walking off down the street.

"Good riddance!" she shouted after him.

Then she saw that the two packs of Pride were gone from the counter and felt more sadness than anger. Hero he might be, but he was just like all the others – no better than a criminal.

Her phone rang.

"What did he want?" asked Mister Wu.

"Just some cigarettes," she replied, unable to speak about everything else that had happened, all the questions he had asked, the stupidity of her father.

"Who is he?"

"Procuratorate – his name is Deng. My father says he is famous...that he is a hero."

"He did not say what he wanted?"

"No, Mister Wu."

"Be careful, Sun Mei."

"I will, Mister Wu."

"Bandits and heroes are two sides of the same coin: the common people always suffer in their wake."

"I understand, Mister Wu."

She put the phone down, feeling awful. She felt a tug at her skirt. She looked down. It was Hong, holding up to her a fist full of money.

"What is this?"

"He said it is for you."

"Who said?"

"The man with the shirt."

Sun Mei took the money from Hong. It was too much, far too much. Investigator Deng had left behind not only the money for his two packets of Pride, but enough to cover the three packets of Marlboro taken by Superintendent Si Ying's horrible cousin also.

"Don't cry, Teacher Sun," said Hong, throwing his little arms about her.

TWENTY-SEVEN

"I sobel sent me."

That was what the girl had said, in perfect English, the girl who, except for her pale skin, looked the very image of the witch Sarangerel, the girl who smelt of witchcraft herself, the girl who up to only a few moments before had been surrounded by a host of whispering voices.

It had been fifteen years since Isobel had passed into the afterlife. Since that time Philip Ye had not had one vision of her, not one word, not even a fleeting whiff of her perfume to give him hope that her spirit lived on, that, wherever she was, she was happy. But now, supposedly, Isobel had spoken to Yue, to this strange girl, and had brought her to him.

He took hold of the iron gates to steady himself, the ground unstable beneath his feet. "Did Isobel say anything else?"

Bedraggled and forlorn, looking like the loneliest girl in the world, Yue said, "That you would keep me safe."

Philip Ye did not hesitate. He opened the gates manually, already imagining the protests from the brothers Na to come. Yue was not Sarangerel, but only a blind person would fail to see the strangeness of her, and only a fool would fail to wonder just what sort of girl he was about to welcome into his father's house.

He took the heaviest suitcase from her, the suitcase she had been dragging behind her on its wheels. Once she was through the gates, he glanced up and down the street for whoever might be in pursuit of her. He saw very few out and about, and all hurrying to their destinations because of the rain. He sensed no eyes on him, no immediate threat from anyone. Though there was no doubting Yue's fear and that she herself was convinced she was being pursued. She was soaked to the skin but, nevertheless, he covered her with his umbrella and walked her slowly up the drive to the house. Inside, the brothers Na, glaring balefully at Yue and still puffing nervously on their cigars, handed them each a towel to dry their hands and faces. Philip Ye then took her up to a guest suite next to his own private rooms. He told her to take off her sodden clothes, to shower, and to put something dry on. He promised to bring her tea in a few minutes, to sit with her, to talk. He expected no protest from her and got none. Back down at the bottom of the stairs the brothers Na were waiting for him.

"Boss, you have doomed us all," said Day Na.

"You have basically cut our throats," said Night Na.

"That girl is a witch."

"Make no mistake."

"Weird."

"Very weird."

"This is not going to end well."

"Not well at all."

He ignored them, though he felt the same foreboding. He went directly through to his father's sitting-room where he found his father deep in conversation with Stacey Corrigan, the subject now the real estate market in Japan. His father noticed immediately something was amiss.

"Philip, what is wrong?"

"Nothing, Father – just an urgent police matter I have to attend to. I have taken a young guest into the house this evening for her own safety. I will explain more later." Then to Stacey Corrigan, he said, "I will inquire after Primo Gong for you. But I make no promises. I'm not sure how much I can discover. At least I should be able to confirm whether he is being held by the Procuratorate or not. That should be enough for you to file your story."

"Thank you, Philip," said Stacey Corrigan, giving him her warmest smile.

"I told you he would help," said Ye Zihao, very proud.

Philip Ye left them to their conversation, putting aside his concerns for the moment about whatever it was his father was up to in regard to Primo Gong. One day his father would push the Shanghai Clique too far and they would take their revenge. His father too often forgot how precarious his situation was, how swiftly formal charges could be laid against him, if the Shanghai Clique – or whoever was taking an interest in Beijing – saw the political opportunity to do so. One false step would be all it took for his father to bring his unusual legal and political stasis – probably better defined as a dangerously unstable equilibrium – to an end.

Philip Ye prepared fresh tea in the kitchen with the brothers Na dogging his every step.

"Boss, that girl has got to go," said Day Na.

"She's a freak of nature," said Night Na.

"You know it's for the best."

"Absolutely, for the best."

Philip Ye continued to ignore them. Isobel had brought Yue to him. That was enough for him. That had to be enough for him.

He left the complaining brothers behind and ascended the stairs with the tray of tea. He laid the tray on the small table in his sitting-room and relaxed back into his favourite leather armchair. He closed his eyes to meditate but quickly became conscious of the stabbing pain in his heart; Isobel, as a spirit, had found the wherewithal to communicate with Yue and not with him. There had been such a profound silence that he had long begun to wonder whether she was being prevented from speaking to him by persons or agencies unknown, or whether she had passed into a realm – were there many realms in the afterlife? – where communication with the living was not possible. Up until this encounter with Yue, it was as if Isobel had disappeared forever, leaving him with nothing more than fading memories, making him no better off – if not worse – than those people with no belief in the afterlife at all.

He opened his eyes and saw Yue standing in the doorway. She was wrapped in a heavy cotton towelling bathrobe she had found in the guest suite with white cotton socks upon her feet. Her long, wet hair fell loose down her back. Only young she might be but Philip Ye could see she would blossom into a real beauty in the years to come. Tightly gripped in her hands was a book he presumed had some importance to her. He ignored the book for now.

"Please, come and sit with me," he said, indicating the leather chair on the other side of the low table from him.

She obeyed without question, sitting herself down, her feet placed flat on the floor, her knees together, her back straight, and with her hands clasped together on top of the book on her lap. Whoever had taught her to sit had taught her exceptionally well.

"Earlier you spoke to me in English," he said.

"I did not realise that."

"You are fluent?"

"I have been attending a school in England since I was seven."

"A private school?"

"Yes, St. Lucy's, just outside of Abingdon in Oxfordshire – do you know of it?"

He shook his head. So, she came from money. "How old are you?"

"Fourteen."

"And where are your parents?"

"I have never known my father. My mother has never told me his name. As for my mother, you know her already."

"I do?"

"You have her picture," said Yue, pointing toward his desk positioned against the window in the corner of the room.

Puzzled, Philip Ye glanced over at the desk. On top he had laid Jin Huiliang's incomplete manuscript, and upon that he had placed the photograph of the woman with the long, wavy hair. He was so stunned he was momentarily at a loss for words.

"I know you are police," said Yue. "Uncle told me on the airplane from England. And I know my mother is dead. When I flew to England for the summer term I had a bad feeling I would never see her again."

"Who is your uncle?"

"He is my friend, not my real uncle," replied Yue, holding up her book to him to see. It was a biography of Qin Jiushao, the famous 13th Century mathematician.

Stunned, all Philip Ye could think to say was, "In life he was not a nice man."

Yue was not disturbed by this information. "Uncle tells me that his character is very much reformed. But sometimes he is very rude about my teachers back in England."

"Is he with you all the time?"

"No, only occasionally."

"Tell me what he said to you on the airplane from England."

"The summer term had just finished and it was time for me to come home to Chengdu. My direct flight from London was cancelled so Uncle told me to catch a flight to Paris. I saw you there, at the airport, but you did not see me. You did not look happy. On the flight from Paris to Chengdu I was sitting a few rows behind you. When we were about to land the thunderstorms frightened me. Uncle spoke to me and told me that everything would be okay. He also told me then that you were police, that, like me, you were caught twice between two worlds: between the East and the West, and between the physical and the afterlife. He said nothing more. After we landed, and I went to collect my luggage, I lost sight of you."

It troubled Philip Ye that his mind had been so preoccupied with his resentments about his own mother as well as his indecision about what to do with Prosecutor Xu that he had not sensed Yue in the airport or on the airplane. "What did you do?"

"I waited for my mother to collect me."

"I thought you believed you would not see her again."

"That was my feeling but, as no one had spoken to me of my mother, I still hoped she would come and collect me. She had left me a message on my phone the day before saying she would. I waited for an hour at the airport but she did not come. Nor did she answer her phone. I caught a taxi and went home by myself."

"Where is home?"

"Not far – an apartment in the Caotang Residential District."

"Go on."

"When I got home I found the apartment empty. There was no sign of my mother. Then I knew for certain that I would never see her again...that she was dead."

"Did Uncle speak to you again?"

Yue shook her head. "I haven't heard his voice since the airplane. I cannot predict when he will speak to me. Sometimes a month goes by without me hearing his voice. He doesn't come when I call him. Sometimes, when I listen intently, I hear ten thousand voices all speaking at once; at other times, silence is all there is. I cannot explain it. I do not yet understand the mathematics."

"The mathematics?"

"It is to be my life's work...was to be my life's work. Now there is no hope. Now, with my mother dead, and my father unknown, I will be sent to an orphanage and I will learn nothing. I am so afraid for my future I cannot think properly. I want to discover the mathematics that describes the veil that separates the physical world from the afterlife, and also the mathematics that govern all communications across this veil. You must believe me when I say I sense the mathematics there, just waiting to be discovered. I know that if I work hard, have the best tutoring, one day I can reveal this mathematics to the world."

"I believe you, Yue," said Philip Ye, fascinated by this first real expression of intense emotion from her – in regard to mathematics, rather than the disappearance of her mother.

He pondered what she had told him for a while, certain without needing proof that she was a mathematical prodigy. Why else would Qin Jiushao come speak to her? Why else would he choose to be her – admittedly intermittent – guide?

He felt relief also, relief in the knowledge that the spirits did not always speak to Yue, that, talented clairaudient though she might be, they did not come at her bidding. At least he was not alone in this. At least this made him feel not so useless.

He forced himself to focus, to forget the afterlife for a moment, to think like a policeman again. "Yue, after you had arrived at your apartment and found your mother not to be there, what did you do next?"

"I waited."

"For what?"

"I don't know."

"Did you not think of going to the police?"

"I would not have known what to say. And I do not know where the nearest police station is. I do not like Chengdu. It is a crazy place. I am more English than Chinese now."

"You waited at the apartment?"

"Yes."

"All day?"

"Yes – I slept a bit, read my book, and cooked myself a meal."

"Then what?"

"Nothing – until an hour or so ago."

"What happened?"

"Isobel spoke to me."

"Just her voice?"

"Just her voice in my ear."

"Has she spoken to you before?"

"Once."

"When was that?"

"When I was seven, on my first flight to England. I was on my own and very frightened. My mother did not see the need to accompany me. Isobel spoke to me, though I did not know her name then. She said, 'Be brave, Jenny Du.'"

"Jenny?"

"The English name I chose for myself."

"Then this evening was the first time Isobel has spoken to you since you were seven?"

"Yes – I never forget a voice."

"Yue, tell me exactly what she said to you this evening."

Yue closed her eyes to assist her memory. "She said, 'Run, Jenny Du, run! There is no time to lose. You must go find Philip. He will keep you safe. It's not far. I will guide you. Tell him that it is me, Isobel, who has sent you.'"

"She said all that?"

"Yes."

"And you walked all the way here in the rain?"

"It was not far and Isobel made me run most of the way, saying 'turn left' or 'turn right' as I did not know where I was going. When I reached the gates, she left me."

"Why did you think you were being pursued? Did Isobel tell you?"

"No, I just felt a woman was hunting for me."

"A woman?"

"Yes, I think so."

"Out to do you harm?"

Yue shrugged. "Maybe."

Trying not to let his frustration show, Philip Ye got up from his chair and went over to his desk. He picked up the photograph of the woman with the long, wavy hair. "Are you certain this is your mother?"

"Yes – but when she was much younger. That very same photograph is on the wall of our apartment."

"Your family name is Du?"

"Yes."

Philip Ye took a deep breath. Now for the most important question. "Is your mother's given name Luli?"

"Yes."

Philip Ye was almost overcome with both sadness and relief. He retook his seat, keeping hold of the photograph in his hands. The pieces of the puzzle were beginning to fall into place – but not without a little help from Isobel who had brought this strange girl to him. He now had a name for the woman who had appeared to him as a ghost back at the airport. He now had a name for Jin Huiliang's charge from long ago, the daughter of a dead comrade he had sacrificed his own family to care for, the girl who had eventually betrayed him – if that was the correct word – by choosing a life of dissolution. He also had confirmation that Du Luli had followed Jin Huiliang on his retirement from the PLA – with or without his knowledge – from Beijing to Chengdu.

"What has happened to my mother?" asked Du Yue.

"As yet, I do not know."

"But she is dead?"

"Yes – her ghost appeared to me back at the airport."

"I have never seen a ghost."

"Have you not?"

"Sometimes, out of the corner of my eye, I see shadows about me. But when I turn to stare at them they vanish."

"Is the name Jin Huiliang known to you?"

"No."

"How long have you lived in Chengdu?"

"I was born in Beijing but came here as a young girl."

"What did your mother do for a living?"

"She entertained men."

Du Yue's face was expressionless. Philip Ye decided it was no time to beat around the bush. "What do you mean by that?"

"My mother was a prostitute. She never told me but I figured it out. She never brought men to the apartment. I do not know where she went when she was working. But she often went out in the evening and did not return until the next day. I did not mind. I had my books. I was not lonely. And we always had money – lots of money. That was how she was able to send me to school in England. She said I could be anything I wanted to be. But now I will be sent to an orphanage and a bad school in Chengdu where no one will know much at all about mathematics."

"When was the last time you spoke to your mother?"

"It was here, in Chengdu, when I was home for the holidays. We had dinner together at a restaurant on my last evening. She was very happy. I had never seen her so happy. She said there would be changes when I got back. She said we were going to move to a new, bigger apartment. She said she was in love but that she couldn't tell me his name...not yet anyway...because he was rich and famous. I did not speak to her again. She never called when I was at school in England."

No name for the man.

A great pity.

But not unexpected.

Philip Ye had the sense that Du Luli not only had inhabited a world of secrets but had been well-versed in keeping those secrets – even from her daughter.

It was time to move.

Further questions could wait.

"Du Yue, I need the keys to your apartment. I have to continue my investigation into whatever happened to your mother. In the meantime, you will stay here at this house. You will be quite safe."

"This house is haunted."

"I know."

"Unquiet and unhappy spirits."

"Have they spoken directly to you?"

"No, but I can hear them muttering."

"Then let them mutter, Du Yue – they cannot hurt you."

There was no need to contact Constable Ma. It was Saturday evening. She would be at The Silver Tree. She had formed an unlikely friendship with his half-sister, Ye Lan. Philip Ye took Du Yue down to the kitchen, happy for her to remain in her bathrobe and for her to bring her book with her. He sat her down at the table. He gave her permission to read as she ate. He hoped her book would distract her from her fears about the future. He felt sad for her. There would be no return to England for Du Yue. As for orphanages, and what could happen to teenage girls under their sometimes indifferent care, it did not bear thinking about. He took the brothers Na to one side to speak to them out of her earshot.

"Feed her and keep her safe. Is that clear? Don't let my father throw her out of the house."

He walked away from their vociferous protests, trusting that even when pushed to the very limit of their courage, the brothers Na would always do the right thing. Moments later he was out of the house and steering the Mercedes down the drive. Once through the gates, his wipers on double-speed, he looked up and down the street. He saw nothing out of place, nothing to disturb him. He drove off at speed into the city.

Back in the kitchen, the brothers Na cautiously laid some of the food left over from the banquet before Du Yue as well as a glass of water. The young witch, who looked for all the world like Sarangerel but who was not, looked up from her book.

"Thank you," she said.

"What are you reading, young lady?" asked Day Na, deciding the best tactic was to appear friendly.

"A teenage romance, I'll wager," said Night Na.

Du Yue stared directly at the brothers, her gaze so intense they each took a step backwards. "It is a biography."

Day Na found this hilarious. "A biography!"

"Must be really boring," said Night Na, just as amused as his brother.

"It is about the life of my best friend Qin Jiushao," said Du Yue.

"Who?" asked the brothers.

"Qin Jiushao – don't you know him?"

"Don't think so," said Day Na.

"Nope, never heard of him," said Night Na.

"Qin Jiushao is very famous for the complete proof of what is now known as the Chinese Remainder Theorem, which he published in his Mathematical Treatise in Nine Sections – the *Shushu Jiuzhang*."

"Oh, *that* Qin Jiushao," said the brothers, as clueless as before.

"Yes," said Du Yue. "Though he has been dead for over seven hundred and fifty years, I consider him my very best friend. He speaks to me all the time." Then Du Yue rolled her eyes into the back of her head and showed the brothers Na only the whites.

Horrified, the brothers Na fled the kitchen, Day Na beating Night Na by a fraction of a second to Ye Zihao's drinks cabinet in the main communal sitting-room.

TWENTY-EIGHT

S aturday afternoon, after a busy lunch-time service, Mister Qu was sitting in his little office, up to his neck in paperwork. He was feeling hot and bothered, fed up with the rain that was continuing to fall, trying to decide where exactly to open up the new restaurant. When the phone rang, he decided to take the call himself so as to distract himself from his thoughts rather than leave it to one of the waitresses.

"This is The Silver Tree, Mister Qu speaking."

"Ah, Mister Qu, my name is Xi. I am senior counsel at FUBI International. I wish to book a table for two this evening."

"Ah, my apologies, Mister Xi, but we do not have a free table."

"But I work for FUBI International!"

"Ah, Mister Xi, I am sorry to hear that. But I understand there are other restaurants in Chengdu."

Mister Qu tried not to laugh at his own joke. He would not normally be so rude. But he and Ye Lan had agreed never to take a booking from anyone who purported to work for FUBI International – a petty but necessary revenge for the misery Lucy Fu had inflicted on Philip Ye for the few weeks they had been dating.

"But I promised her," said Mister Xi.

"I am sure your lady-friend might enjoy some street-food instead," said Mister Qu, twisting the knife.

"I will leave an incredible tip."

"I am sure you are very generous, Mister Xi, but alas I cannot help you."

"Please, Mister Qu, you must rescue me from a difficult situation! I cannot tell Prosecutor Xu that I have failed to secure a table at your fine restaurant."

Mister Qu nearly fell through the floor. "Excuse me, Mister Xi, did you say Prosecutor Xu – *the* Prosecutor Xu of Chengdu People's Procuratorate?"

"Yes – yes, indeed!" replied Mister Xi, suddenly hopeful.

Mister Qu thought quickly, remembering what Lin had told him about Prosecutor Xu, that she had no great liking for the hustle and bustle of the main restaurant. "Mister Xi, it is true that we do not have a free table in the public area of the restaurant. However, we have recently decorated a small private room – quite tastefully, I might add – with a view to using it for select private functions. It was not meant to be open to patrons until next month. Would that, perchance, be of any interest to you?"

"Mister Qu, you have saved my life."

"It can be made ready for eight."

"That would be perfect!"

Mister Xi then rang off, almost crying with relief. Mister Qu sought out Lin and told her all that had transpired.

"Why so sad, Mister Qu?"

"But she is on a date with another man. I also did not like the sound of his voice – far too smooth – *and* he works for the family Fu. He is probably a creep."

"You must have faith, Mister Qu. I should say that the stars are moving into alignment quite well. Don't you feel the electricity in the air today?"

Lin ran off laughing. Now that she mentioned it, Mister Qu did feel there was something in the air this day, something hard to define. But this did not mean something wouldn't have to be done about the slick Mister Xi.

A persisting concern for Mister Qu was Philip Ye.

Mister Qu was a traditionalist at heart. He thought it important a man was married and settled by the time he was thirty. Philip Ye was now thirty-six, pushing thirty-seven, with no sign of marriage on the horizon.

It would not do.

It would not do at all.

Unfortunately, no one else in the family seemed to think this way. After the Lucy Fu debacle, Mayor Ye had washed his hands of his beloved son's personal affairs. As for Ye Lan, she held to the foolish romantic notion that a man can only ever have one true love in his life and, for her Handsome Boy, that one true love had been Isobel. Mister Qu was not stupid, though. He understood well enough that Ye Lan had an ulterior motive for not wanting Philip Ye to marry. She had come to the conclusion that there was no woman under Heaven good enough for her Handsome Boy. Which was a pity, for Mister Qu would have loved to have sat down with his wife to share his concerns and to come up with a plan. He thought himself quite alone in his thinking that it was high time Philip Ye was married. It took a most curious event for him to discover he was not as alone as he thought.

One busy Saturday evening three months before, an extraordinary meeting had taken place in the sitting-room above the restaurant, the room where Mister Qu's sons usually sat to do their homework at the table or to watch TV, the same room where Mister Qu and Ye Lan were at times supposed to sit back and relax but so rarely did. Mister Qu had at first no clue as to the reason for the meeting and only knew one of the attendees: Philip Ye. It was to Lin, his best girl, to whom he looked to supply the missing information.

Lin had come from a problem family. She had fallen in with a bad crowd. She had been thrown out of school. At the age of seventeen she had been arrested for petty theft and for fighting in the street. She was due to be sent away to a place where her character was to be reformed – a place of harsh punishments for the slightest of infractions. Philip Ye had come across Lin sitting handcuffed in a corridor in Jiangxi Street Police Street awaiting her transportation to that dread place of reform. For reasons never made quite clear to Mister Qu, Philip Ye had taken a different view of her future. He had spoken to the arresting officers, undone her handcuffs, put her in his car, and driven her directly to The Silver Tree.

"This restaurant is not a place of rehabilitation," Mister Qu had told Philip Ye, eyeing Lin with not a little trepidation. The girl had a wild look in her eyes.

"I am sure you will do your best, Mister Qu," was Philip Ye's reply.

Then Philip Ye leaned in close to Lin and whispered something in her ear. Mister Qu never learned what was said to her. But whatever it was, it did the trick. Mister Qu put Lin to work as a trainee waitress, keeping a very close eye on her, but he need not have worried. He supposed that in life miracles sometimes did happen. Lin appeared to thrive under the strict discipline he imposed on the waitresses. The wildness in her eyes faded away and by the end of her first year she was already a favourite with some of his most important patrons. Four years on and she had become his best girl, her sharp eyes missing nothing, in charge of all the other waitresses, always immaculately turned out, never a speck of dirt or a spot of food upon her clothes even after a full evening's service, more than popular with the patrons – especially the men – and destined, he was sure, for greatness. When Mister Qu had finally decided on the location for his new restaurant, Lin, though she did not know it yet, was to manage it.

"You have saved my life, Mister Qu," Lin had once said to him.

"No, it was Superintendent Ye who saved your life," he had replied. "I just offered you a place in which you could blossom."

Lin was smart enough to understand what he meant.

Lin knew she owed Philip Ye.

And how she intended to repay him became very clear to Mister Qu on the night of that extraordinary meeting, that gathering of heroes and heroines in his sitting-room.

Lin came to him to report. "Mister Qu, apart from Superintendent Ye, the other attendees are Constable Ma Meili of the PSB, Investigator Deng Shiru of the Procuratorate, and Prosecutor Xu Ya also of the Procuratorate. I believe them to be discussing a sensitive investigation. I recommend you taking a very close look at Prosecutor Xu."

"Why is that, Lin?"

"She is the one."

"Meaning?"

"She is a match for Superintendent Ye."

It took a few long moments for Mister Qu to realise quite what Lin was saying. "Are you sure?"

"I have no doubt."

It was not that Mister Qu didn't trust Lin's eyes or her good sense. But he had to see for himself. When the meeting broke up Mister Qu made sure he took a long hard look at Prosecutor Xu Ya of the Chengdu People's Procuratorate. It moved him greatly to see her personally thank the cooks on her way out of the restaurant.

"What did I tell you," said Lin, afterward.

"She is like an imperial princess reborn," replied Mister Qu.

This description did not quite do justice to all Mister Qu had seen in Prosecutor Xu. Later, in his journal he would jot down a few notes to try to organise exactly what he thought about her.

Magnificent
Beautiful
Complex
Challenging
Overly sensitive
Strong and yet fragile
Difficult
Hot-tempered
Superior, but not always condescending
Full of darkness but always struggling to do good

When the list was done, Mister Qu realised he may as well as been describing Philip Ye. Not that anyone before had ever said of Philip Ye that he was fragile – he was one of the mentally toughest men Mister Qu had ever known. But Mister Qu had always been careful around Philip Ye. He had always had the feeling that he was walking on eggshells, that the slightest misstep could result in a terrible scene. Mister Qu saw the same quality in Prosecutor Xu.

The next morning Mister Qu spoke to Lin. "I think them too similar...different sides of the same coin."

Lin pondered this. "I did not say it would be an easy match. But sometimes people are just made for each other."

Reflecting on his own experience with Ye Lan, Mister Qu thought that this might possibly be true. It also helped his thinking when he learned that Ye Lan had hated Prosecutor Xu on sight, his wife's protective instincts toward her Handsome Boy working all too well, seeing Prosecutor Xu for the threat that she was.

Much as he would have liked another look at Prosecutor Xu there was not to be another such meeting at The Silver Tree. Mister Qu had not seen Prosecutor Xu since.

Constable Ma Meili on the other hand had become a much-loved fixture at The Silver Tree. She visited every Saturday evening, always willing to help out, with Ye Lan taking her to her bosom as the sister she had never had. Constable Ma had saved her Handsome Boy's life – a fact confirmed by Philip Ye himself. And it helped that, belied by her great size and strength, Constable Ma was a sweet-natured girl. She was also a good talker when Philip Ye was not around, happy to tell everyone in the kitchen about the fascinating work they got up to in Homicide and, more to the point, what it was really like to work for Philip Ye. It had to be said that sometimes Constable Ma had arrived on a Saturday evening in tears and Ye Lan would pick up the phone to give her Handsome Boy a piece of her mind – not that it ever did any good. All the cooks and waitresses, as well as Mister Qu himself, were on tenterhooks, waiting for Constable Ma's decision: was she going to transfer to SWAT or not?

As for Prosecutor Xu, nothing was heard of her for weeks and weeks. Until that it is, Lin dragged Mister Qu into his small room where the waitresses changed for work and where he had placed a small TV for their entertainment when they were on their breaks. The room was crowded, all the waitresses and some of the cooks trying to get a look at the small screen. It was a serious breach of restaurant discipline. But Mister Qu forgave them all when he saw just who it was they were all staring at.

For the duration of the trial of the incredibly wicked Commissioner Ho, Mister Qu had another TV set up for the cooks in the kitchen so that no one would miss a moment of Prosecutor Xu enforcing the Rule of Law and bringing justice to the people. In watching her on TV, Mister Qu felt a thrill as he had not known since the day Ye Lan had agreed to marry him. Prosecutor Xu was, quite simply, mesmerising.

"She is a true heroine," said Lin.

"A heroine reborn," agreed Mister Qu.

For a while, the trial of Commissioner Ho was all the patrons wanted to talk about. Not a few times was Mister Qu summoned to a table of his most important and influential patrons and asked to tell the story of the secret meeting held upstairs at The Silver Tree, and how afterward Prosecutor Xu had personally thanked all the cooks in the kitchen.

"She is a real lady," Mister Qu would say. "Quite without flaw."

Many asked when she was due to eat at The Silver Tree again. Mister Qu would only smile and laugh – he had told all the waitresses to do the same – as if this was some great secret he was keeping close to his heart. None of the patrons were to know that it nagged at him, even kept him awake at night, wondering if he was ever to see Prosecutor Xu in the flesh again.

One day Mister Qu spoke to Lin, asking her if she thought it sensible to fabricate some kind of celebration – an anniversary for the restaurant, for instance – and to send invitations out to Philip Ye and Prosecutor Xu, with a view to bringing them together.

"That would be a mistake," said Lin.

"But why?"

In matters of the heart, timing is everything, Mister Qu – and that timing is governed by Heaven."

"It is?"

"Naturally," said Lin, as certain of this as of summer following spring, which of course it did.

Mister Qu had been born into an ordinary family and had wanted nothing more than an ordinary life. But, by mistake, he had married into the family Ye. How this had happened was a very long story – a story he would one day have to tell his sons when they were old enough to understand. Suffice to say, the love of his life, Ye Lan, had not been entirely open about whose daughter she actually was, so much so that Mister Qu had assumed Ye Lan to be an orphan. Only his few relatives had attended their modest wedding. It was only on their wedding night that Ye Lan, in tears, had confessed all.

"Forgive me, for I have cheated you out of a normal life," said Ye Lan, her hands covering her eyes.

His natural calmness reasserting itself, the spinning room coming to a stop, he gently took her hands in his and pulled them from her face so she could see the truth in his own eyes. "No, Wife, it was quite impossible for me to marry anyone else."

"A long time ago the family Ye came to Chengdu to gain as much power and to make as much money as it could; which we did, not caring how many laws we broke or how many other families we ruined along the way." Ye Lan spoke as one who plainly believed that the sins of the family were passed down from generation to generation. "I bear a heavy burden," she said.

And yet, it seemed to Mister Qu, that Ye Lan suffered most not because of any karmic family inheritance but more because of her difficult relationship with her father. Ye Lan both hated and worshipped her father in equal measure; an impossibility Mister Qu had thought for anybody until she had taken him to meet Ye Zihao. This had been when Ye Zihao's star had been at its zenith, when he had been both mayor of Chengdu and Party Chief, and while Philip Ye had been away at university in England.

The meeting took place at the breath-taking Ye family mansion. It was evening, but Mayor Ye was in his home office working through a pile of official papers, puffing furiously on his pipe, sending clouds of smoke everywhere, the great house a frenetic whirl of secretaries, maids, and servants. As Ye Lan dragged him in front of her father, Mister Qu was quaking in his boots.

"Father, this is my new husband," said Ye Lan.

Mister Qu thought it best to bow. Mayor Ye glanced up from his papers and gazed at him from under dark eyebrows, his gaze that of a predatory wild animal, wholly unforgiving and without mercy. Mister Qu thought he was going to be sick, feeling naked before Mayor Ye, as vulnerable as a child.

Mayor Ye said to Ye Lan, "Daughter, is this man truly the best you could find?"

It was not quite the auspicious beginning Mister Qu had been hoping for.

Philip Ye had not been invited to the wedding of Ye Lan and Mister Qu because, as Ye Lan later explained, he would have betrayed her real identity immediately. This was true. Mister Qu may not have known much about Chengdu history but at that time Philip Ye's photograph – in newspapers and magazines – was hard to miss. When he did return from England with his fiancée Isobel in tow – those same newspapers and magazines were reporting that Mayor Ye was furious about the engagement – the first thing he did was visit the newly married couple at The Silver Tree.

Once more, Mister Qu had been shaking in his boots. But the half-English son was nothing like the father. In those days, it could be said that Philip Ye was the happiest young man alive. And this was nothing to do with the great wealth he was sure to inherit or his movie-star looks which made all the young girls swoon. He was happy because he was soon to marry the love of his life. Philip Ye bounded into The Silver Tree dragging a giggling Isobel behind him, professed it to be the best restaurant he had ever seen, picked up Ye Lan in a bear hug – he always referred to her as Little Mother – and then took Mister Qu warmly by the hand.

Isobel embraced Ye Lan also and then, quite shockingly, kissed Mister Qu on the cheek in greeting. Apart from his mother when he had been a child, and apart from Ye Lan from the day they had been married, no other woman had ever kissed Mister Qu. Not that anyone ever forgot their first encounter with Isobel. It was no over-statement to say that every room she entered she filled with light.

Philip Ye made a wedding gift of a set of professional European cooking knives for Ye Lan. For Mister Qu, he took him to a tailor to be measured for a couple of handmade suits.

"This is too much," Mister Qu had protested.

"No, it is nowhere near enough, for you have made my sister very happy," replied Philip Ye.

A year later Isobel was dead.

On hearing the news, Ye Lan stayed up all night crying, tearing out some of her hair, shouting out loud that the family Ye was cursed, that none of the family could ever expect a contented life for all the bad that had been done in the past.

It was said in the newspapers that Mayor Ye was delighted. There was even a rumour that he had been responsible for her death. Though how the mayor of Chengdu could have caused a cancer in the bones of a young woman thousands of miles away was anyone's guess.

Mister Qu believed none of it.

Soon after, Philip Ye returned home a changed man. When Mister Qu met him and offered his heart-felt condolences, Philip Ye hardly responded, lost, it appeared, in a very dark place. He left Chengdu again, but this time for Wuhan, to study law. By all accounts both Mayor Ye and Philip Ye's English birth-mother were furious with his decision. Mister Qu was certainly astonished. Why would a son do something in such opposition to his parents' wishes?

"Handsome Boy has a mind of his own," explained Ye Lan. "My father will rage at him, even strike him from time to time, but my father will always adore him. It is a strange bond they have."

As for Mayor Ye's other son, Yong the Nomad, he received no attention from his father at all. Mister Qu pitied him. Yong the Nomad drifted in and out of Chengdu on a whim. Mister Qu had no idea how he earned a living. Ye Lan said that he was good with electrical items and could fix more or less anything. Sometimes they got letters and cards from him, posted from towns Mister Qu had never even heard of.

While Yong the Nomad was away travelling, and while Philip Ye was at university and still in mourning, Mayor Ye went north to Mongolia on business and brought home with him a young copper-skinned woman of enticing beauty – a woman soon to be known as the Witch-Queen of Chengdu.

Sarangerel.

The very thought of her struck chills into Mister Qu's heart and continued to do so to this very day. But, as fate would have it, it was Sarangerel who had inadvertently brought for Mister Qu the full acceptance of the family Ye.

It was no great secret that Mayor Ye preferred to dally from time to time with local actresses and models. Though these stories must have brought Ye Lan some distress, she never spoke of her father's romantic entanglements. She was happy that The Silver Tree was profitable enough for some cash to be diverted to the care of her mother, Zhou Jin Jing, whose health was sadly deteriorating year on year. But soon Mister Qu heard – and thought himself duty bound to repeat to his wife – that Sarangerel was quite unlike those actresses and models. She had somehow managed to take up residence in the Ye family mansion, and was slowly but surely taking over every aspect of Mayor Ye's life – including the attendance of local Party meetings.

The Party had no time for organised religion, less so for any talk of the supernatural or the occult. But one evening, a senior Party official out for dinner with his wife and children at The Silver Tree, asked to speak privately to Mister Qu.

"Mister Qu, you are much respected in Chengdu."

"I am?" said Mister Qu, quite surprised.

"For a man who had unknowingly married into the family that you have, you carry yourself with remarkable aplomb. Your help is needed."

"It is?"

"Something must be done."

"It does?"

"Mayor Ye is bewitched and no one is willing to take action – not even his great friends Chief of Police Di and Secretary Wu. They are too frightened of Sarangerel. It is up to you, Mister Qu. It is up to you to save Chengdu."

When the service was done for the night, Mister Qu told Ye Lan what the Party official had said to him.

"No, Husband," said Ye Lan, "you are family but it is not your place. Indeed, something must be done. But this is women's work. It is I who should go to my father's house."

Ye Lan picked up her best cleaver.

"I will go with you," said Mister Qu.

"No, Husband, you must stay to take care of our baby."

Their first son, Qu Peng, had not long been born.

Fearing for his wife, but seeing the wisdom of her decision, he watched Ye Lan go off into the night, intensely proud of her but also anxious for her life. Chengdu was a city in the grip of fear. There were wild rumours flying around of human sacrifices taking place at the Ye family mansion, about a raven flying high above the city during the day and apparitions walking the streets at night.

He waited up for hours.

Ye Lan returned just before dawn, drained of all energy and hope. Her failure was etched painfully across her face.

"Husband, I managed to climb over the gates but I was turned back by a wall of thick mist. I heard voices in the mist. They were taunting me, laughing at me. The witch is more powerful than I imagined. I was unable to save my father."

Mister Qu put Ye Lan to bed.

When the dawn had fully broken, he phoned one of his waitresses and asked her to come and look after the baby. There was something he needed to do. A few hours later he was on the train to Wuhan. It was quite an adventure. Mister Qu had never before been out of Chengdu.

He found his way to the university and then to Philip Ye's accommodation on the campus. He found the door open to Philip Ye's room, the young man still in mourning, staring out of the window, lost in a world of shadows.

"Your father has been bewitched," Mister Qu told him.

"Why should I care?" was Philip Ye's reply.

"He is your father."

"So?"

For the first and only time in his life Mister Qu lost his temper. What quite came over him, he did not know, but he struck Philip Ye across the face, and said, "There is nothing more important than family! Is this how Isobel would have you behave?"

For a moment Mister Qu feared for his life.

Like all of the family Ye – Ye Lan included – Philip Ye had a temper that seemed always to be barely under control. Violence flared in his intense green eyes. Mister Qu wanted to run but held his ground as he would with any difficult patron at the restaurant. But the violence in Philip Ye's eyes soon died. Soon enough they were on the train together heading back toward Chengdu.

It was dark when they reached the great iron gates that barred the way to the Ye family mansion. A heavy mist lay across the city. Mister Qu was scared to death.

"I will be fine from here," said Philip Ye.

Mister Qu thought this wrong. "But I am family."

"Do you see any other family here, Mister Qu? Do you see my father's brothers, my cousins? And where are all of my father's close friends? No, Mister Qu, you have done quite enough. Go home to my sister and the baby. I would not wish any harm to befall you."

A sensible man, Mister Qu knew, would indeed have run for home. But Mister Qu could not. He would not have been able to face Ye Lan. "I know I am not the husband Mayor Ye wished for his daughter. But, for good or ill, I am family. I will not let you confront the witch on your own."

Philip Ye smiled then – perhaps the first smile that had crossed his face since Isobel had breathed her last.

What happened next, after the two of them had clambered over the iron gates, was seared into Mister Qu's memory for all of time. He was unable to speak of it, even to Ye Lan. Never a nervous person, he was afterward left with a childish fear of the dark, with the knowledge that there was much more to old folk tales and traditional ghost stories than he could ever have imagined – and with a respect for Philip Ye that would never, ever, diminish.

A few days later, Mister Qu was summoned to the Ye family mansion. This time the sun was shining and the air was heavy only with the scent of spring flowers. He found Mayor Ye much recovered, Philip Ye still with him.

Mayor Ye opened a very expensive bottle of *Luzhou Laojiao*. "I am indebted to you, Mister Qu."

"I did very little, sir," Mister Qu replied.

Regardless, a glass was pushed into his hands and the three of them drank a toast.

"To family!"

No great drinker, Mister Qu drained his glass in one, to him the clear liquor, redolent of peach, tasting unusually sweet.

There had been challenges and tragedies to come: Ye Lan's un-expected second pregnancy; the sad, painful, and lingering demise of Ye Lan's mother; the mysterious death of Yong the Nomad and his young family in that blazing car wreck; and Mayor Ye's forcible removal from office and house-arrest – to name but a few. But the night Sarangerel had been thrown out of the Ye family mansion had been a fundamental turning point for Mister Qu. When he offered his thoughts on matters that concerned the family – always done reluctantly, and with trepidation – he was listened to by all, especially by Ye Zihao.

And it was soon time to offer his thoughts up again to the family. Even if Ye Lan chose to chase him around the kitchen with her sharpest cleaver, it was time to speak up about Philip Ye and Prosecutor Xu. But first something indeed had to be done about the slick Mister Xi.

TWENTY-NINE

—·—

I t was well after eight when the taxi finally pulled up in front of The Silver Tree. As Xu Ya passed the fare to the driver, he said, "Do you know who owns this place, Prosecutor?"

Not in the mood for yet another conversation about the family Ye and still shaken by her extraordinarily vivid dream of Huang Liu-Hong, she replied, "A criminal syndicate, I believe."

The driver, thinking this the best joke ever, roared with laughter. Then he tried to return the fare to her, saying it had been the honour of his life to drive her, that he and his family had watched her on TV, that his daughter, still at school, now harboured ambitions to be a prosecutor.

She refused to accept the money back from him. "As a prosecutor, I must be beyond reproach," she said, her words hollow to her ears, laughable even.

But the driver was moved to tears. "Prosecutor, the day you came to this city was like the sun coming up after the longest night. The people now have hope. The people really believe there is to be the Rule of Law."

Feeling like the lowest of the low, she thanked him for his kind words, took his business card from him, and wished his daughter all the best in her studies. She then stepped out into the deluge. In her hurry to leave the apartment she had forgotten her umbrella. But she need not have worried. An umbrella was immediately covering her, a smiling man at her side.

"Welcome back, Prosecutor," he said.

"Mister Qu, it is a pleasure to see you again," she said, glad she had done her research since the last time she had visited The Silver Tree.

She saw that the speaking of his name pleased him greatly. He pushed open the door of the restaurant and she was almost thrown backwards by the clamour, every table full of people having the best of times. She wondered if she had made a terrible mistake, whether she should have asked Xi Huan to take her to a more restrained establishment. But Mister Qu gently took her arm and guided her between the tables. And, as if he understood how self-conscious she was with so many eyes suddenly upon her, he spoke to her to keep her attention on him.

"Are you well, Prosecutor?"

"Quite well, Mister Qu."

"And your parents?"

"In good health also – or they were when I last spoke to them. I have been so busy, Mister Qu, that I have been unable to visit them recently in Chongqing. How are your two boys doing? I hope Qu Peng and Qu Gang are working hard at school."

Mister Qu's face lit up at the mention of their names. "They are both good boys. I have much to be grateful for. But I admit they are quite spoiled by their uncle."

Xu Ya's mind drew a blank. "Their uncle?"

"Superintendent Ye."

Xu Ya could not believe her own stupidity. "Forgive me, Mister Qu – it has been a long and trying day."

"Ah, don't be concerned, Prosecutor. You are not the only one to be surprised about how fond Superintendent Ye is of his nephews. People think because he is not yet married that he has no liking for children. And yet the opposite is true. It is one of the great regrets of his life that he is not yet married and a father."

"He has said this?"

"Prosecutor, it is well known within the family."

"I thought there was no shortage of candidates for marriage."

"None have yet to make the grade."

"Why am I not surprised?" replied Xu Ya, shaking her head, feigning amusement, remembering the painful years at university when Philip Ye had not looked once at her, and the three months since The Willow Woman investigation when she had heard not one word from him. Back at university she had not made the grade; now she had failed to do so again.

Mister Qu pushed open the double swing doors at the back of the restaurant. This was not the route she had been taken last time when she had been led directly into the kitchen and then upstairs to the living-quarters. These swing doors opened into a short corridor off which the toilets were located as well as a number of other rooms.

"Where are you taking me, Mister Qu?"

"Let me quickly explain, Prosecutor. When Mister Xi called to make the booking, I had no free tables. And I also remembered that the hubbub of the main restaurant was not quite to your liking. Instead, a cosy function room has been prepared where you and Mister Xi can converse in complete privacy." He pointed to an open door at the far end of the corridor.

Xu Ya was alarmed. "Mister Qu, this is not a date. Mister Xi and I are here to talk business only."

Mister Qu put his hand to his mouth. "Thank goodness! I am so relieved. Mister Xi is quite handsome, I admit, and I am sure he has plenty of money. But an important lady such as yourself, as beautiful as you are talented, can do so much better."

Before she could reply, a lively young waitress came running up to them, and dropped down into a quick curtsey.

"This is Lin, your waitress for the evening. I will leave you in her capable hands," said Mister Qu, vanishing into the kitchen which could be accessed at the opposite end of the corridor to the function room.

"Prosecutor, don't be concerned," said Lin. "It will appear like you are alone with Mister Xi but I will always have eyes upon you. You are quite safe."

"You think I need protecting?"

Lin tried not to laugh. "I think every woman in this restaurant needs protecting from Mister Xi."

Xu Ya was troubled. "He has been here before?"

"Oh no, Prosecutor, we cater more for families that for self-important men with an eye for the ladies. I heard you tell Mister Qu that your meeting with Mister Xi is all about business. Please do not think me rude or impertinent if I say that I am as relieved as Mister Qu. A much better man than Mister Xi awaits you, I am quite sure. But oh, your hair, Prosecutor! It is still a little wet from the rain. Let Mister Xi wait a few more minutes longer so I can fix you up."

Lin dragged Xu Ya into a small side-room explaining it was usually used as a changing room and rest area for the waitresses. Lin produced a hairdryer and brush as well as a small bag of good quality cosmetics. In no time at all, Lin had her looking better than she had in days.

"Lin, you are a marvel."

"Prosecutor, you look even good enough to meet Superintendent Ye."

"What do you mean?"

"Ah, forgive me, Prosecutor – it is just a stupid expression we waitresses have. I am afraid we judge all men in relation to Superintendent Ye."

"Physical attractiveness is a very superficial method of judgment. Character is far more important in a man."

"But I *was* speaking of character, Prosecutor – though, to be sure, him being the handsomest man in Chengdu, doesn't hurt. Superintendent Ye is a real gentleman and I know of no kinder man."

Xu Ya thought she was hearing things. "Kinder?"

"Indeed, Prosecutor, but I will not bore you now with my personal story. There are so many such wonderful stories about Superintendent Ye. I am far from the only lost soul he has taken pity upon."

"No, please tell me, Lin – what did Superintendent Ye do for you?"

"I am pledged to secrecy."

"I am very good with secrets," said Xu Ya.

"I was on my way to a labour camp when Superintendent Ye chose to see only the good in me. I will be grateful to him until the day I die. Now, that is enough gossip, Prosecutor. I have already said too much. Superintendent Ye is as modest as he is kind. He would not appreciate me speaking so of him. And Mister Xi will by now be growing fretful. He looks to me like the impatient and sulky sort...not used to having to wait for his dates."

Lin escorted her into the function room. Mister Xi, looking as sulky as Lin had suggested and not quite as handsome as Xu Ya remembered, got up from his seat and greeted her with a curt handshake. Xu Ya apologised, blaming her lateness on pressing Procuratorate business. She chose to cheer him up immediately.

"Mister Xi, I am almost ready to accept your offer."

His demeanour changed instantly. "That is marvellous news!"

"I just need to learn more of your plans for the London office, the salary and benefits package you can offer, and a few days to speak to my parents. I believe then I will be all too happy to accept. It is time for a new life. It is time I left Chengdu. But, before we get to all that, do you have the occupancy and employee lists for Plum Tree Pagodas for me, as well as a copy of the concierge's log?"

Xi Huan pointed to a package wrapped in brown paper lying on the corner of the table near to him. "As promised, Prosecutor."

"And there are no redactions, alterations, or exceptions?"

"None."

She thought him a liar but said, "I am pleased, Mister Xi. What about Mister Han?"

"I have informed the concierge he is to be interviewed by you in my presence tomorrow morning at the Procuratorate at ten. I am not sure what he can add to what has already been said but I assure you he will be there."

"You are most efficient, Mister Xi."

"You will find FUBI International the very model of corporate efficiency. Now let me tell you what we have in mind for the new legal office in London...."

The red wine Lin served to Xu Ya was like velvet on her tongue, the food as delicious as she remembered. But, as she listened to Mister Xi droning on about London, Xu Ya found her mind drifting away, first to Philip Ye, to ponder his supposed desire for marriage and for children, to the waitress Lin in whom Philip Ye had only seen good, and then to Investigator Deng, who still had left no message for her, who was somewhere out on the streets of Chengdu, putting his life on the line yet again, and who must surely hate her more than he had hated anyone.

Fearing tears were about to spring from her eyes, Xu Ya excused herself from the table and headed quickly into the Ladies. She stared at her own reflection in the mirror and reminded herself that Investigator Deng could never hate her more than she hated herself.

"Life has not been fair to me," she said out loud.

But was that really true?

Had she not been the real author of her own destruction?

No one had forced her to marry a monster.

If she had not been so desperate for love, to be loved, to escape the hold Philip Ye had had on her heart, would she not have seen her husband for the man he really was before it was far too late?

But now she was being offered a priceless opportunity.

She could put the past behind her.

She could begin her life anew.

She had to get back to Mister Xi. She had to convince him that he was not mistaken about her, that she was fully committed to working for FUBI International, that she was the only woman for the job.

She breathed deeply, got a grip on her turbulent emotions, and exited the Ladies in some haste. Unfortunately, she collided with a man walking past. He put out an arm to steady her as she mumbled her apologies. She found herself staring up into his intense green eyes and all her thoughts about herself, about FUBI International, about London, and about Investigator Deng, were suddenly taken from her – as was her capacity for speech.

He was not so hamstrung though. "Where is Primo Gong?" asked Philip Ye.

THIRTY

— : —

S o far it had been a splendid evening. The kitchen was working like a finely-tuned machine, none of the waitresses were off sick or had otherwise gone missing, and every table was full of happy, paying customers. Moreover, the date between Mister Xi and Prosecutor Xu had turned out to be nothing more than a business dinner. Mister Qu could not have been happier. And, to cap it all, both he and Lin – as previously arranged – had managed to plant (hopefully) fertile seeds in Prosecutor Xu's mind about Philip Ye's willingness to marry. But then the evening suddenly began to unravel.

Lin came running after him into the kitchen, troubled, no longer her usual effervescent self. "Mister Qu, I have the most terrible news. Mister Xi has just offered Prosecutor Xu a job in London."

Mister Qu could not believe his ears. "Has she accepted?"

"Mister Xi thinks so...but to me her words were not entirely clear."

"Then there is hope."

"Oh yes, Mister Qu – we must have hope."

"What should be done?"

"I have an idea, Mister Qu. Let me suggest to Prosecutor Xu that the family Ye is in the process of creating a list of suitable candidates for Superintendent Ye – by which I mean a marriage list – and that I have heard on the grapevine that she has been pencilled in at the very top."

Mister Qu liked the way Lin was thinking. But, before he could respond positively or negatively to Lin's audacious suggestion, his wife, Ye Lan, standing quite far away but her ears very attuned to all that went on in the kitchen, spoke up.

"What was that about Prosecutor Xu?"

Mister Qu cursed himself for not speaking to Lin within the confines of his office. He smiled at his wife to show her that no conspiracy was afoot. "Just that Prosecutor Xu is dining with us tonight."

Some of the young cooks, all men, paused what they were doing to whisper excitedly to one another, hoping they were going to get another glimpse of the Flower of the Procuratorate.

Ye Lan was not so pleased. "Husband, why did you accept her booking? She is nothing but trouble."

"A lot of trouble," added Constable Ma, speaking with her mouth full, in the midst of wolfing down a bowl of noodles.

"I was not to know," said Mister Qu, disingenuously. "It was a Mister Xi who made the booking. He is a lawyer who works for FUBI International."

"We don't need the family Fu's business either," said Ye Lan.

"Evil attracts evil," said Constable Ma.

Ye Lan nodded in approval. "Sister, that is so right. Prosecutor Xu and the family Fu are made for each other."

Mister Qu decided he had to stamp out this nonsense immediately. "Prosecutor Xu is not evil. She is a heroine. She upholds the Rule of Law. I will not have a bad word spoken about her under my roof."

Ye Lan laughed and said to Constable Ma, "My husband is just like all the other men...taken in by a pretty face!"

"Personally, I do not think Prosecutor Xu so pretty," said Constable Ma.

"Sister, you are quite right," agreed Ye Lan. "She is not that pretty at all. And I expect she has had work done on her face to improve the little she was born with."

Exasperated, and not a little tired of his wife's and Constable Ma's constant sniping about Prosecutor Xu – this had been going on for three whole months! – Mister Qu was about to drag Lin out of the kitchen so they could sit down and formulate a new approach in regard to Prosecutor Xu, when who should walk in through the door from the alley at the side of the restaurant but Philip Ye. He did not look happy. By all accounts, his holiday with his mother had not gone well. Mister Qu could not understand why he still insisted on visiting her at least once a year. Mister Qu believed whole-heartedly in the importance of family, but even he knew that there was a time to call it quits.

"Constable Ma, get your coat!" barked Philip Ye.

One of the youngest cooks – a rather sensitive boy – dropped a bowl on the floor in shock, only to get an earful from Ye Lan and ordered to clean up the mess. Mister Qu shook his head. That boy was going to have to toughen up if he was going to continue working at The Silver Tree.

Mister Qu saw Constable Ma scowl at Philip Ye. It was obvious their relationship was close to breaking-point. She made a point of finishing her bowl of noodles before obeying his order and disappearing upstairs to get her stuff together. Philip Ye, pretending not to notice her insolence, bent over Ye Lan to give her a kiss. But Ye Lan pushed him away and gave him a hard punch on the arm.

"You've been treating Ma Meili badly again, Handsome Boy," she said. "It has got to stop! You were not raised this way."

"She has to learn," said Philip Ye.

"People do not learn by being shouted at," said Ye Lan.

Mister Qu thought this a bit rich coming from Ye Lan. She shouted at her team of cooks all the time, and would kick them if she thought they were not reaching her high standards. It seemed to be the Ye family way.

"Do I advise you on how to manage your kitchen?" asked Philip Ye of Ye Lan.

"Ma Meili saved your life, Handsome Boy," she replied. "You owe her everything. Now teach her how to be a good detective rather than making her sad all the time."

"Little Mother, stay out of police business," said Philip Ye, his expression darkening.

Fearing an all-out argument, Mister Qu thought to distract them both, Philip Ye especially. "Prosecutor Xu is dining here this evening," he announced.

Philip Ye switched his furious gaze from Ye Lan to Mister Qu. "Where is she?"

"In the new private function room with—"

Philip Ye pushed past both Mister Qu and Lin before Mister Qu had a chance to say more, and out through the door into the short corridor beyond. Mister Qu and Lin ran after him, just in time to see him collide with Prosecutor Xu just emerging from the Ladies.

"Where is Primo Gong?" Philip Ye asked her, rather brusquely.

To Mister Qu, Prosecutor Xu appeared dumbfounded by the question. Her mouth dropped open and her cheeks coloured pink.

Philip Ye repeated the question, more insistent this time. "Where is Primo Gong?"

What happened next was as hard for Mister Qu to watch as it was to follow. It was as if the air about Philip Ye and Prosecutor Xu exploded into a fireball. It was well-known within the family Ye that if Philip Ye ever lost his temper he would switch from Mandarin to English and back again, sometimes mid-sentence. What Mister Qu had not expected was for Prosecutor Xu to hold her ground and do the same. It made for an awe-inspiring but highly incomprehensible spectacle.

"Primo Gong is not a police matter, Superintendent!"

"Tell me where he is!"

Unintelligible!

Unintelligible!

"So much for your precious Rule of Law!"

"I did not think you police had ever heard of the Rule of Law!"

Unintelligible!

Unintelligible!

"What about the ordinary investors in Ambrogetti Global Software?"

"As if the family Ye ever cared about the common people!"

Unintelligible!

Unintelligible!

"Just tell me why you arrested him!"

"Who says I have arrested him?"

Unintelligible!

Unintelligible!

Unintelligible!

Unintelligible!

"Like your father, Superintendent, you think you can do as you please in Chengdu. Get it into your thick skull that those times are long gone!"

"At least I don't have blood on my hands!"

This last retort, Philip Ye delivered with such venom that Prosecutor Xu tottered backwards on her high heels. Mister Qu saw the shock and hurt in her eyes. His heart went out to her. And maybe Philip Ye saw he had gone too far for suddenly he became still, silent, breathing hard.

Prosecutor Xu ran from Philip Ye and into the function room, only to reappear a few moments later clutching the brown paper package that Mister Xi had arrived with earlier. She glared at Philip Ye as she ran past him and then she was out through the double swing doors and into the restaurant proper. Lin did not need to be told. She was on Prosecutor Xu's heels in a flash.

Mister Xi then made the mistake of emerging from the function room. "What is going on?"

Philip Ye turned his temper on Mister Xi. "Who the fuck are you?"

Mister Qu was appalled. Never had he heard Philip Ye use such profanity before. Prosecutor Xu must have really got under his skin. Mister Qu could well imagine that bad language was most common in a police station, but in The Silver Tree it would not do.

"Mister Xi, please return to the function room," said Mister Qu. "I will attend to you presently and explain all."

Mister Xi, knowing full well who Philip Ye was, and thinking better of opening his mouth again, did just as he was asked.

Then Mister Qu said to Philip Ye, "Brother, you have no right to disturb the harmony of this place or so abuse my patrons. I am more than disappointed with you. And my wife is quite correct, you treat Constable Ma abominably."

His point made, not liking the way that Philip Ye was now glowering at *him*, Mister Qu made his way through the swing doors and into the restaurant proper, smiling as he did so, to reassure all the patrons at the nearby tables who might have overheard the disturbance. He manoeuvred his way through the many tables, ignored a couple of questions thrown at him about just who it was who had upset Prosecutor Xu, told others that Prosecutor Xu was not feeling so well – a summer cold, he thought, from overwork, from doing all that was humanly possible and more to uphold the Rule of Law in Chengdu – until he stepped out onto the street and saw Lin holding an umbrella over Prosecutor Xu's head while simultaneously hailing a taxi. Before Mister Qu could reach them and issue any sort of meaningful apology for Philip Ye's uncharacteristically boorish behaviour a taxi had screeched to a halt, Prosecutor Xu had jumped inside, and then was gone. Mister Qu was mortified.

Lin turned to face him, to cover them both with the umbrella, not looking as unhappy as he thought she should.

"Lin, please go and inform Mister Xi that Prosecutor Xu has been taken ill and has had to go home. Tell him there will be no charge for the meal this evening and that he is very welcome to return at any time."

"Of course, Mister Qu," she replied, passing control of the umbrella to him and skipping back inside the restaurant.

Mister Qu stayed standing on the street for some time. He was very upset. It had been three whole months since Prosecutor Xu had last visited The Silver Tree. It was now doubtful she would ever visit again. Not wanting to face all the patrons and their many questions just yet, he walked down the side-alley and entered the restaurant directly into the kitchen just as Philip Ye had done. Passing the umbrella to one of the cooks, he ignored the inquiring look from his wife and found Philip Ye in close conversation with Constable Ma in the short corridor, and was also just in time to see Lin leading Mister Xi out of harm's way through the swinging double doors. Constable Ma now had her coat on, her bag over her shoulder, and, Mister Qu noted with some consternation, her pistol back on her hip.

Philip Ye said, "Forgive me, Mister Qu, but there are things happening that—"

"No, Brother, that is not right!" interrupted Mister Qu. "Even if the world is coming to an end, even if Heaven and Earth are no longer in their proper places, I will not have such behaviour, such incivility, in The Silver Tree. Prosecutor Xu should never be spoken to in such a way. And that goes for you too, Constable Ma. Prosecutor Xu is a real lady...and I am very fond of her."

"I am very fond of her too," said Lin, returning from getting rid of Mister Xi.

"Did I ruin her date?" asked Philip Ye.

"What business is that of yours?" asked Mister Qu, still smarting.

Lin, however, took a very different tack. "Superintendent, it was no romantic dinner. Mister Xi Huan is a lawyer working for FUBI

International. He has just offered Prosecutor Xu a most prestigious job in London. I am sure, after being so badly treated this evening, she is bound to jump at the opportunity. I have never seen her so upset. Just before you arrived, Superintendent, she had been inquiring after your health, and said how sad she was to hear that your holiday in England had not gone as planned, how terrible it was that you and your mother could not bury your differences, how she wanted only happiness for you. Is that not true, Mister Qu?"

"It is," agreed Mister Qu, astounded by Lin's quick thinking, her ability to lie when required, her adapting their overall strategy to bring Philip Ye and Prosecutor Xu together, and enjoying very much the consternation he now saw on Philip Ye's face.

"What was in the package she was carrying?" he asked.

"How are we to know that?" said Mister Qu, shaking his head.

But once again Lin chose a different tack. "Oh, I actually do know, Superintendent. That package contained the occupancy and employee lists for Plum Tree Pagodas – a building I think owned by the family Fu – as well as a copy of the concierge's logbook. Prosecutor Xu was most insistent with Mister Xi that there be no redactions, alterations, or exceptions. She is most professional and he was most wary of her – if not a little frightened. Also, it seems, Prosecutor Xu is to interview a Mister Han, the concierge, at ten in the morning at the Procuratorate with Mister Xi present. I could tell that Mister Xi is not looking forward to the interview. I hope all this information is useful to you, Superintendent."

"Are you certain of all this?" asked Philip Ye.

"Of course, she is certain," said Mister Qu. "Lin is my best girl."

"This is true," said Lin. "I am his best girl."

Philip Ye stood for a few moments lost in thought. Then he said to Constable Ma, "Come, we have work to do."

They filed through the door into the kitchen and then on and out into the night. Mister Qu was not sorry to see them go. He loved Philip Ye dearly, and would always hold him in the highest esteem, but sometimes he was the scariest, most unpredictable man he had ever met – more so than even Ye Zihao. Mister Qu wandered into the function room and flopped down onto one of the seats, weary in mind and spirit. He did not protest when Lin opened a bottle of *baijiu* and poured a small glass for them both.

"A toast, Mister Qu!"

"To what, you silly girl?"

"To success, of course."

"Did you not witness the argument?"

"I did – and it was wonderful."

"But they hate each other."

"No, Mister Qu – quite the opposite is true. And did you not notice her dress was the exact same shade of blue as his suit?"

"I did not."

"It proves that there is already a deep and profound connection between them."

"Are you certain?"

"Oh yes, Mister Qu."

"But what about London?"

Lin laughed contemptuously. "If Prosecutor Xu accepts that job then I promise I will work for you without pay for a whole six months."

"You will starve."

"I will not, Mister Qu – but I admit that we do have to help things along a little. We should send Prosecutor Xu a gift of food. She didn't get a chance to eat much of her dinner. A bottle of wine also, I think. We will attach a note of apology purporting to come from Superintendent Ye pleading emotional turmoil and exhaustion having just returned from visiting with his mother. That is hardly stretching the truth."

Mister Qu knocked back the liquor served him by Lin, feeling it burn the back of his throat. It may have been the sudden rush of alcohol into his usually sober system but Lin's idea sounded very fine indeed.

"Mister Qu, who is Primo Gong?" asked Lin.

Mister Qu shook his head. "I have no idea."

THIRTY-ONE

A s Fatty Deng left the Old Chengdu Restaurant, Sun Mei and the Lucky Dragon Tobacco Emporium were very much on his mind. Her frantic plea to leave her and her father alone had left a sore ache in his heart. What she had meant by saying she seen nothing, heard nothing, and knew nothing, was quite simple: whatever had been going on at the Black House was nothing to do with her and her father and only risked bringing trouble to their door.

Fatty Deng doubted there would be any repercussions for the family Sun. All he had needed Sun Mei and her father to do was to confirm the exact time Primo Gong had been shot. The identification of Superintendent Si Ying had been a bonus, as well as the confirmation that she had been on duty last night. But Fatty Deng understood very well Sun Mei's fear, the fear of someone who had already lost so much. She could afford to lose no more. And it troubled him that he had had to push by her, disturbing the children at their lessons, just so he could get to her father, his instinct telling him her father would be much more talkative – as it so proved.

Fatty Deng had never wanted to instil fear in anyone, and certainly never to such a genuinely good person as Sun Mei. But bringing fear, applying pressure, was all part of the job. Sometimes it was necessary to commit a little wrong to correct a greater wrong. However, when he jumped into his car and tossed his dripping umbrella onto the backseat, he promised himself, when this investigation was over, whether the security detail at the Black House were innocent of murder or not, he would return to Liberation Street and crack a few heads together. Sun Mei would never have to give out 'free' cigarettes ever again.

He put the key in the ignition and tried to start the engine.

Nothing.

He cursed and tried again.

Again, nothing.

What was it about this car, especially hot starts?

He needed to get his cousin the mechanic to give the car a good look over. It was probably nothing, maybe a stupid dodgy sensor mistaking his engine for cold when actually it was hot, and causing too much fuel to be dumped into the mixture. He hoped that was the case. After giving all his spare money to his mother so she could take her holiday of a lifetime he didn't have anything left to fork out on another car. And he was certainly not going to take out a loan, not if Prosecutor Xu was soon to leave the country, thereby leaving him in the lurch.

He turned the key in the ignition again.

The engine coughed and spluttered but this time it caught. He laughed in triumph. Then his phone rang.

"Investigator Deng, I am quite unsettled," said Prosecutor Xu. "Philip Ye has been asking questions. Please come to my apartment."

Then she was gone.

Philip Ye asking questions.

Fatty Deng wondered what she meant by that. But he had heard the distress in her voice and he suspected that whatever had happened was not good. He could have told her that she was asking for trouble dining out at The Silver Tree.

Mister Ni, the night concierge at Tranquil Mountain Pavilions, had nothing to say for himself when Fatty Deng entered the lobby. Fatty Deng had been hoping Mister Ni might by now be more talkative. But, if the thought of opening his mouth ever did cross Mister Ni's mind, he ignored it, and instead wrote a short note in his logbook. Fatty Deng assumed the note to be his time of arrival.

That simple action by Mister Ni was enough to disturb Fatty Deng as the lift doors closed in front of him. He wished Prosecutor Xu had had the good sense to meet up in some anonymous smoky bar rather than her own apartment – which might be bugged. Surely the family Fu wouldn't be above listening in to their tenants' conversations if knowledge might be gained that would one day benefit them. Fatty Deng tried to tell himself not to worry, that he was suffering nothing more than a mild case of paranoia. Lucy Fu didn't seem the type to lower herself to eavesdropping. It would not hurt, though, to suggest to Prosecutor Xu that she get an electronics team out from the Procuratorate to sweep her apartment – the sooner the better.

At the tenth floor, relieved to be out of the claustrophobia-inducing lift that had done nothing for his nerves, he walked along the corridor. This was the first time he had been invited up to Prosecutor Xu's apartment. He was nervous, as well as more than envious of the luxury in which she dwelled. Though not quite as plush as Plum Tree Pagodas – Tranquil Mountain Pavilions was an older building and constructed on not quite as grand a scale – Fatty Deng would have loved to have been able to afford to live here with his mother. When he reached apartment 1021, he shook his head as he found the door ajar. It was almost a repeat of the morning's episode at Primo Gong's apartment when he had arrived to find Prosecutor Xu distracted and playing on her phone, wholly unaware of whoever might be creeping up on her. This time he could hear Prosecutor Xu singing – if it could be described as such – along to some dreadful modern romantic ballad.

He knocked on the door.

Prosecutor Xu kept up her awful, sad wailing.

He pushed the door open with his shoe. Prosecutor Xu was sitting with her back to him, cross-legged on a chair, with headphones connected to her phone over her ears, the music so loud Fatty Deng could hear it quite distinctly. There was going to be no easy way to do this. He closed the door, approached her, and not wanting to give her the shock of her life, walked into her line of sight. Unfortunately, her eyes were shut. Her mascara had run. She had been crying.

"Prosecutor!" he shouted.

No good, she wailed on and on.

Having no choice but to reach out and touch her arm, he felt her body go rigid. Her eyes sprang open. For a split-second he saw she didn't recognise him, her fear so great it had totally clouded her mind. But then she jumped up and threw her arms about him – the most unlikely show of affection he had ever received in his life.

He held her for a time, trying not to crush her slim body with his big arms, waiting for her to stop shaking, to gain control of her emotions. How many seconds or minutes went by he did not know, but eventually she disconnected herself from him, ripped her headphones from her ears, and without a word disappeared into the bathroom, and then to return, her face cleaned of mascara. smiling, back to her old self, impatient to get down to business as always.

"There has been a development," she said, inviting him to sit, which he was happy to do, glad to take the weight off his tired feet.

"Philip Ye?"

"I bumped into him at The Silver Tree. He asked after Primo Gong. I was so surprised that for a time I was rendered speechless."

"Speechless?"

"Don't laugh, Investigator Deng – this is serious."

"Primo Gong is a famous person," said Fatty Deng. "And you did spread the word that he was helping the Procuratorate with our enquiries."

"True – but what is Philip Ye's interest?"

"Didn't you ask him?"

"Oh, Investigator Deng, I am so embarrassed to admit I lost control of myself...by which I mean my temper. He was standing in front of me, closer to me than you are now, staring at me with those green eyes of his...so arrogant and entitled...as if he had the right to know everything that went on in Chengdu. I felt so cornered – trapped. I responded badly. I don't even know what I said to him. He said some terrible things to me – unforgivable things. I am sure I said terrible things back to him. I might have given away that Primo Gong is dead. I just don't remember. I am so sorry, Investigator Deng."

"Prosecutor, you needn't apologise to me. Mister Ye is a difficult man to withstand. And I am sure you have given away nothing of importance. Do you want me to have a word with him? He should treat you only with the utmost respect."

"No, that is kind of you to offer. It is done now and maybe...hopefully...I will never have to speak to him again. But I began to wonder, when I got back home, whether he has discovered something of interest to us. I didn't mention it before. I thought it had no bearing on our case. But Philip Ye has been investigating the murder of a retired PLA general last night in the Xiaojia River Residential District. I am a long way from being convinced of your theory of PLA involvement in Primo Gong's murder. We have as yet turned up no evidence of any connection between Primo Gong and the military. And yet I am now beginning to wonder—"

"When was this general murdered?" asked Investigator Deng, masking his annoyance, wishing she had told him about this other homicide a lot sooner. Weren't they supposed to be communicating more, trusting each other more?

"I don't know the full details. Secretary Wu promised to keep me fully apprised of the PSB investigation. But the murders were so far apart, geographically speaking, and the methods of murder so different – a sniper for Primo Gong, an ice-axe for the retired general – that I assumed no connection. But, after my confrontation with Philip Ye, I am beginning to doubt myself."

"And for two murders to occur on the same night in Chengdu—"

"—is a rarity, I know, Investigator Deng."

"An ice-axe – that's a bit brutal and unlikely."

"In the back of the head, reminiscent of Trotsky."

"Who, Prosecutor?"

"A Russian revolutionary who fell out with Stalin and was eventually assassinated on Stalin's orders in Mexico back in 1940. An ice-axe was used."

"Oh."

"It makes me wonder if the murderer was trying to send some kind of political message or whether the ice-axe was an implement that was just close to hand. A message seems unlikely in Chengdu. There are so few here who would understand the significance of an ice-axe or indeed know of Trotsky."

"But a political message cannot be ruled out?"

"No, it cannot. I suppose we will have to wait until we have a further briefing from Secretary Wu on any progress made by Superintendent Ye."

"You could phone Mister Ye."

Prosecutor Xu grimaced. "And say what? Don't forget we are not supposed to have anything to do with the police. Regardless of whether you believe the PLA are ultimately behind the murder of Primo Gong, the security detail in the Black House has to be complicit or at the very least criminally negligent. We cannot afford tipping the police off to our investigation."

Fatty Deng thought to change the subject briefly. "How did your meeting with Mister Xi go?"

"Badly," she said.

Hope blossomed in Fatty Deng's heart. "So, you're not going to London after all?"

"Oh no – I'm definitely going to London. I just meant the dinner was ruined by Philip Ye's intrusion. I did receive from Mister Xi the occupancy and employee lists for Plum Tree Pagodas and a copy of the concierge's log – for the little I think they are worth. How did you get on observing the shift change at the Black House?"

Desperately trying to hide his disappointment, Fatty Deng said, "First let me tell you about the Old Chengdu Restaurant. I spoke to the manager. As usual on Friday evening, there was a large party of executives from the CCB. The manager is very well acquainted with Primo Gong. He told me that Primo Gong often does attend the dinners but last evening he was not there."

"Interesting – so his diary entry was a mistake, or he changed his plans at the very last moment, or the entry was nothing but a distraction, a cover for what he was really up to."

"The manager had more to say, Prosecutor. I showed him the photograph of Primo Gong out on the town with our mystery woman. The manager recognised her...said she had been to the restaurant for a private dinner with Primo Gong just over a week ago. The manager knows her as 'Luli'."

"Her real name?"

"The manager wasn't sure. He didn't want to say too much. Primo Gong is a valued patron. I had to lean on him a bit. He did say that he had seen this Luli before, years ago, with other men."

"Was he trying to tell you she is a prostitute?"

"Possibly – in the past. But he mentioned that Primo Gong and Luli had seemed very much in love, that they made a great couple. Maybe she has given up the life, Prosecutor."

"We still need her family name to track her down. Let us throw the name Luli at Mister Han tomorrow. I bet we get a response. Now tell me about the Black House shift change."

"Prosecutor, let me just mention Mister Han's log. He made a note that there had been a report of a disturbance in Primo Gong's apartment at 2.10 a.m., didn't he?"

"That's correct."

"I have a witness who says otherwise."

Prosecutor Xu visibly brightened. "Who?"

"The shots from the Black House flew directly over the Lucky Dragon Tobacco Emporium on Liberation Street. The owners of the shop are a young woman, Sun Mei, and her father, Sun Yong. The father has no use of his legs, spends much of his time in bed or in his wheelchair and doesn't sleep so well at night. Most importantly he is a former airborne soldier who knows the difference between thunder and gunfire. He told me he heard three rifle shots, one after the other, at exactly 1.30 this morning – not 2.10."

Prosecutor Xu clapped her hands together. "Hah! Now we have Lucy Fu! Let's see if she can wheedle out of that discrepancy."

"As for the Black House shift change, it is as I was informed: at eight in the evening the two plain-clothes officers from the day shift leave and four plain-clothes officers come on for the night. I have also managed to identify the team leader as a Superintendent Si Ying."

"Well?"

"Tough, confident, definitely ex-army, but I wouldn't say she's the sharpest tool in the box."

"Was she working last night?"

"Yes, the night shift get free cigarettes from the Lucky Dragon Tobacco Emporium. Sun Mei has a perfect memory for who has what cigarettes on what night – it's like she has the security detail rota in her head. Superintendent Si Ying was definitely at the Black House last night."

"Free cigarettes?"

"Just the usual petty extortion."

"That's already grounds for arrest."

"Sun Mei and her father will say the cigarettes are gifts. They will be too frightened to say otherwise."

Prosecutor Xu pulled a face, not hiding her disgust.

"Not all police are like this," protested Fatty Deng. "Anyway, there's something else. While I was in the shop talking to Sun Mei, Superintendent Si Ying came in to pick up the free cigarettes. Thankfully she didn't recognise me for what I was. It could be this shirt you bought me – a perfect disguise."

Prosecutor Xu put her hand to her mouth to suppress her laughter. "It does suit you."

"Thank you, Prosecutor – it was a very kind gesture. Anyway, accompanying Superintendent Si Ying was a man she identified as her cousin. She didn't give me a name but she said he was army, on leave in Chengdu with some of his mates. There was something about him. He was nothing like Superintendent Si Ying. Sure, he was confident just like her, and tough, but he looked very smart – maybe an officer – and a killer too."

"Are you sure you are not letting your imagination run away with you?"

"Prosecutor, believe me, for some reason the PLA are behind the murder of Primo Gong. And I reckon the kill team are still here in Chengdu. Either they are relaxing, having a good time, thinking they are untouchable, or else their work is not yet done."

"I am not saying you are wrong but surely it is too early in the investigation to come to that—"

"Prosecutor, these are very dangerous people. We will need help. We cannot take on Superintendent Si Ying, her cousin, and whoever else might be at large in Chengdu on our own."

"When we have firm evidence, then we can request—"

"But—"

Their argument was nipped in the bud by a knock at the door. Fatty Deng looked to Prosecutor Xu. She shook her head indicating she was not expecting any other visitors this night. Fatty Deng put his finger to his lips, got out of his chair, pulled his pistol from its holster, and looked through the door's eyepiece. He relaxed when he saw Mister Ni out in the corridor. He opened the door and, without a word, Mister Ni passed him a large plastic bag full of what Fatty Deng took to be take-out food. The aromas arising out of the bag were incredible. He could also see the neck of a wine bottle sticking out from between the food cartons. Mister Ni retreated back down the corridor and Fatty Deng closed the door.

"Did you order food?" asked Prosecutor Xu.

"No – did you?"

Prosecutor Xu shook her head, getting out of her chair so she could examine the contents of the bag after Fatty Deng had laid it down on the table. She first raised her eyebrows when she examined the label on the bottle of wine. "Expensive," she said. Then from among the cartons of food she found a folded note. She opened it. "It's from Mister Qu of The Silver Tree." She read the note out loud.

Prosecutor Xu

Please accept my abject apologies.

Superintendent Ye sends his apologies too. He is quite distraught about ruining your dinner with Mister Xi. It is Superintendent Ye who suggested, and paid for, this gift of wine and food.

He has just returned from an emotionally draining trip to England. He admits to not being quite himself this evening. He is most ashamed of his behaviour.

Though he will not tell you this himself as he is a naturally shy man, he has always spoken of you in the warmest terms. And, like the rest of Chengdu, he was glued to the TV during Commissioner Ho's trial. Indeed, one evening he said to me, 'Mister Qu, never has the Rule of Law been so glamorous, never the sword of justice so bright.'

Always, your servant

Mister Qu

"What a lovely note," said Prosecutor Xu, her distress of earlier now wholly forgotten.

Fatty Deng thought the note might have been more credible if it had been actually written by Philip Ye. Those words attributed to him didn't sound quite right. Not that he thought it worth opening his mouth and upsetting Prosecutor Xu again.

"Are you hungry?" she asked of him.

He remembered he had eaten very poorly earlier. "I am."

"And could you manage a glass of red wine?"

"A large glass – if you have one, Prosecutor."

An hour and a half later, the day finally taking its toll, Fatty Deng watched Prosecutor Xu fall asleep in her chair. He stared at her for a time, marvelling at how in sleep all the tension swiftly drained from her face, how beautiful she was, how her dreams were taking her to a much happier place – maybe London.

He would miss her.

Crazy as she often was, and infuriating at times, he couldn't help but adore her. Underneath her spikiness, her natural over-sensitivity and defensiveness, she had a warm and moral heart. He had only known her a few months but her absence was going to leave a large hole in his life. Not that there was anything to be done about that.

He found a blanket in a cupboard and gently draped it over her. The air-conditioning in the apartment was a bit fierce. She stirred slightly in her sleep. He let himself out and made certain the door was properly shut. Rather than take the lift, he descended the stairs. In the lobby, Mister Ni avoided his gaze, making another note in his logbook.

Outside, the rain had finally stopped but the streets were still awash. Fatty Deng did not go home. Instead, he drove south, to an exclusive part of the city, and parked up outside a beautiful house. It was now quite late. He could see no lights burning within. He did not let that stop him. He could not turn away now. He knocked on the door. When a maid finally opened the door, he showed her his badge and ID.

"I don't have an appointment," he said.

She closed the door again, leaving him outside on the step. But he did not have to wait long before she returned, smiling this time, welcoming him into the house and escorting him into what Fatty

Deng took to be a study. A single desk-light illuminated a pile of official-looking papers on the desk. Fatty Deng thought it best not to glance at them. They were none of his business. He was more concerned by his garish shirt, how at odds he was with the classical décor of the room.

Wearing a shirt and tie even at this late hour but overlaid with a silk robe displaying a fancy crane motif, Secretary Wu walked into the study and extended a hand of welcome to Fatty Deng.

"Thank you for seeing me, sir."

"Not at all – how is Ms. Xu?"

"Sleeping, sir – exhausted from the day."

"I am sure."

"But we are making progress."

"Of course – now what can I do for you?"

"Sir, the key to this investigation is the team leader of the security detail for the Black House on Liberation Street. As yet we have no evidence of wrongdoing on her behalf. And if she is formally taken in for questioning then word will leak out immediately and the remainder of our prey will scatter."

"You think a conspiracy then?"

"I do, sir."

"And the PLA?"

Fatty Deng saw there was no turning back. "Sir, I have a theory that is not supported by Prosecutor Xu. The team leader of the security detail at the Black House is Superintendent Si Ying. She is former army. Her boss, Commissioner Yang Da, is also former army. Superintendent Si Ying has a cousin in the city at the present – name unknown – and some friends of his, also army. I don't know what Primo Gong's murder is about, but I sincerely doubt it has anything to do with the police."

Secretary Wu took a seat behind his desk and considered all he had been told. He sighed and said, "Ms. Xu does not hold the PLA in any great esteem, especially after the awful marriage she endured to a former soldier. But she does possess an intense antipathy toward the police which perhaps clouds her judgment. I don't know Superintendent Si Ying, so I cannot offer an opinion on her. Commissioner Yang Da I have met a few times. An odd fish, for the police...for the army too, I expect. He keeps himself to himself, spending most of his time reading in his office, from what I gather. Comes from a wealthy family here in Chengdu, so I am not sure why he even wants to work for the PSB. He has friends among the Political and Legal Committee. They actively promoted his appointment within the PSB. He is also a favourite of Chief Di. He is quite charming, humorous even. I chose not to block the appointment. He has administrative skill. In the time he has been in post he has done some good and little harm. Perhaps I should have taken a closer look at his past associations."

"Sir, time is of the essence. We need to catch the assassins before they leave the city and cover their tracks. We also need to prove that Ye Zihao had nothing to do with Primo Gong's murder so Party Chief Li is not inclined to...ah...."

"Take precipitate action?"

"Yes, sir."

"What do you have in mind?"

"Superintendent Si Ying is key. She has a baby and has much to lose. I want to lift her off the street. I need to put her in a position where she feels she has no option but to talk to me. I want to bring in independent contractors."

"Without Ms. Xu's knowledge?"

"She would not approve."

"Is there no other option?"

"Sir, if there is a rogue PLA unit operating on the streets of Chengdu then...."

"Yes, forgive my stupidity, Investigator Deng. How much do you need?"

"10,000 *yuan*, sir."

"So little?"

"Yes – just a simple snatch and grab."

Secretary Wu weighed what had just been said to him for a moment, unlocked a desk drawer, took out a small cashbox, opened it, counted out the money, and passed it over to Fatty Deng who quickly stashed the notes in his wallet.

"Is anything else troubling you?" asked Secretary Wu.

Fatty Deng thought of Prosecutor Xu's job offer, as well as the fear he had caused Sun Mei this evening, both troubling his heart, but he held his tongue. "No, sir."

Fatty Deng made to leave but Secretary Wu was not done with him.

"Investigator Deng, would you have a drink with me?"

"I would be honoured, sir."

Secretary Wu indicated Fatty Deng should sit and opened the drinks cabinet. He picked out a decanter containing a honey-coloured liquid. Not knowing what to expect, Fatty Deng was surprised when the intense aroma gathered about him while Secretary Wu was still pouring the two small glasses.

"You like Scotch whiskey, Investigator Deng?"

"I don't know, sir," replied Fatty Deng, accepting a glass. "I have never tried it before."

"Then you are in for a treat."

Fatty Deng took a sip. It was so smooth and yet so strong – almost like Heaven in a glass.

"Do you like it?"

"It is incredible, sir."

"It is a 25-year-old Macallan, matured in sherry casks – worth the cost, I assure you."

"Ah."

"Cigarette?"

"Yes, thank you."

Secretary Wu took a packet of Huanghelou 1916 gold-tipped cigarettes from the pocket of his robe. Fatty Deng accepted a cigarette, guessing that that one cigarette cost more than an entire packet of his usual Pride. He lit their cigarettes using his cheap lighter and breathed in the smoke. He felt no need to cough. He made himself laugh by thinking he could get used to drinking very expensive whiskey and smoking equally expensive cigarettes.

"How are you, Investigator Deng?"

"Fine, sir – thank you."

"Are you sure?"

Fatty Deng shrugged. "When I am out on the street I am scared out of my wits, imagining someone is always creeping up on me. But it is good to be back at work, to be doing something useful again. As every hour goes by, I feel more like myself. And I would never abandon Prosecutor Xu."

"She blames herself for what happened to you."

"It wasn't her fault."

"She takes the whole world upon her shoulders."

"I understand."

"But I worry about her a lot less when you are at her side."

"Thank you, sir."

"No need to thank me – it is just a simple fact."

THIRTY-TWO

M a Meili decided very quickly about whom she liked and disliked. Superintendent Ye was unusual in that she had initially thought there to be no better man in all of China, only to find, as she had begun working for him, that his character was seriously flawed. But Superintendent Ye was the exception to the rule. After that first telling impression Ma Meili rarely changed her mind about anyone. And this was certainly true about Prosecutor Xu. Ma Meili had hated her on sight, ever since she had stood by and refused to intervene when Chief Prosecutor Gong had been physically abusive during The Willow Woman investigation. Nothing that had happened since had influenced Ma Meili's opinion otherwise. Ma Meili was not one to forget. Ma Meili was not one to forgive. It therefore came as a pleasant surprise when a chance encounter this evening between Superintendent Ye and Prosecutor Xu had ended in a blazing row. Ma Meili had missed whatever had ignited the argument. But she had arrived in time to witness its conclusion, to see a totally defeated Prosecutor Xu flee The Silver Tree. Ma Meili could not have been prouder of Superintendent Ye. His character might well be irredeemably flawed. He might well be impossible to work for. But no one could say he didn't have a backbone. He had proved more than a match for a haughty prosecutor with delusions of grandeur.

Unfortunately, after the argument was done, Superintendent Ye had reverted to his usual brooding, uncommunicative self. Try as she might, Ma Meili could discover nothing about what had provoked the argument, its substance, or what Superintendent Ye had meant when he had ended it by saying that Prosecutor Xu had blood on her hands.

Ma Meili dearly wanted to know.

Ma Meili was certain Ye Lan would also want to know.

However, not only was Superintendent Ye not speaking about the argument during their short car ride to a very nice apartment block in the Caotang Residential District, it seemed he was not speaking at all.

"I'm glad you put Prosecutor Xu in her place."

No reply.

"There is not one bone in her body that isn't wicked."

Again, no reply.

"I don't know why men find her so attractive."

Finally, Superintendent Ye spoke, sounding tired and more subdued than usual. "Constable, let us concentrate on the job in hand."

The job in hand.

Ma Meili was not quite sure what that was.

All Superintendent Ye had told her was that they were on their way to search an apartment as a matter of urgency and that she needed to keep her wits about her. Ma Meili was used to being told very little about anything, but it irritated her to be instructed to keep her wits about her. As far as she was concerned, at no time in her life had she ever lost her wits. So, to punish him, if he wanted silence then that was what he was going to get. It saddened her that she was not now able to boast about getting hold of Jin Huiliang's service record, or even tell of what she had read within it, but she would wait for him to ask her – if, and when, he remembered that is.

After they parked up on a nearby street, the day's rain finally petering out, Superintendent Ye surprised Ma Meili by producing an electronic key card to access the apartment block. She followed him up the stairs to the third floor, her hand resting on the butt of her holstered pistol. He stopped outside of apartment number 32. Superintendent Ye listened at the door. Ma Meili could hear nothing. But she was very aware of a musky perfume lying heavy in the air. It reminded Ma Meili of leather, of tall grasses, and, strangely, of an old horse kept by a farmer back in Pujiang County. Ma Meili was not one for perfume. Most gave her a headache. But this perfume she found intriguing – not unpleasant at all.

Satisfied that all was as he expected within the apartment, Superintendent Ye used the same electronic key to open the door. Ma Meili would have preferred he step aside, let her go in first and check for threats. But she had to content herself with following him into the stylishly decorated apartment, all shades of pink and cream – very feminine – with a white plush carpet underneath her feet which Ma Meili imagined must be a devil to keep clean. The perfume from the corridor was present in every room as she checked the apartment was as empty as she sensed it to be. She then joined Superintendent Ye in the sitting-room where he was staring up at a large photograph mounted on the wall. Ma Meili felt like punching Superintendent Ye. Why did he have to keep so much secret? The photograph was an enlarged version of the photograph of the woman with the long, wavy hair found in the wall safe in Jin Huiliang's study. Ma Meili knew immediately that she was now standing in the woman's apartment, that somehow, as if by magic, Superintendent Ye had tracked her down.

"May I introduce Du Luli," said Superintendent Ye, "former charge of Jin Huiliang, a woman who despite his best efforts or indeed because of them, fell into a life of dissolution many years ago in Beijing – where this photograph was taken, I imagine. She dropped out of contact with Jin Huiliang, only to follow him to Chengdu years later for reasons so far unclear, to set up home here, to continue in the business of prostitution, to raise a child, a daughter – the father unknown – and to spend a fortune, the vast bulk of her earnings I expect, on sending that daughter to a private school in England to receive the best education possible."

So many questions filled Ma Meili's mind it was difficult to choose only one. "Superintendent, how did you find this apartment?"

No reply.

"Superintendent!"

"The daughter, Du Yue, has just arrived home from school in England. She found her mother missing. She decided to seek refuge at my father's house. Don't ask me why – serendipity, I guess."

Serendipity!

Ma Meili wasn't sure what this was but she knew Superintendent Ye to be a liar. He knew exactly why the daughter had sought refuge at the Ye family mansion. He just did not want to say. Ma Meili took her hand off the butt of her pistol before she was tempted to draw it and shoot him.

"Why did Du Luli keep a photograph of herself on the wall?" she asked.

"Some people do," replied Superintendent Ye, "to remind themselves of their youth, of when they were at their happiest; or, in Du Luli's case, I suspect, when she felt most attractive to men. She was certainly glorious when she was younger."

"If you like long, wavy hair," said Ma Meili.

"There is that."

"Do you think it was this Du Luli who murdered Jin Huiliang?"

"I do not."

"Then why has she run away?"

"I did not say she had run away. All her daughter has told me is that she has gone missing. I am certain, Constable Ma, that Du Luli was murdered at or about the same time as Jin Huiliang. Do not ask me how I know this. I just feel it in my bones. And don't ask me why, for as yet I do not know."

"Then why is it I can smell her perfume everywhere?" asked Ma Meili. "Not just in here but out in the corridor too. Du Luli has only just gone."

"That is not her perfume."

"But—"

"Constable, begin your search in the master bedroom. I will begin here in the sitting-room."

"What am I looking for?"

"Anything of interest."

This was the usual poor level of guidance she got from Superintendent Ye. She took her shoulder bag with her to the master bedroom, shut the door so he could not see what she was up to, and sat down on the bed to think and orientate herself. The master bedroom was as well appointed as every other room in the apartment, the bed large and luxurious, paintings on the walls instead of photographs. On the dresser Ma Meili spotted a collection of perfumes. Curious as to why Superintendent Ye thought the perfume in the air not Du Luli's, Ma Meili got up from the bed and sniffed each perfume in turn. Ma Meili recognised some of the labels from advertisements, all of the perfumes very expensive, but none of them proved to be the perfume hanging in the air.

The daughter's then?

Ma Meili doubted it. It wasn't a young girl's scent. Ma Meili had the distinct impression that Superintendent Ye knew full well whose perfume it was and who had been to this apartment only a very short time before them. Yet another fact about this case he was prepared to keep to himself. She had also to get to the bottom of how, from the moment he had picked her up from the morgue earlier that morning, he had been expecting a woman with long, wavy hair to be murdered.

Ma Meili went over the room as thoroughly as she could, checking in every cupboard, every drawer, even looking under the bed, searching for anything that would provide a clue as to the whereabouts of Du Luli – or to give proper weight to Superintendent Ye's conviction that she was dead. Ma Meili found nothing. But even that lack of evidence was useful to the investigation. There was nothing about the room that spoke to Ma Meili of violence or that Du Luli had left in a hurry. She even found Du Luli's passport in a drawer. There was a walk-in dressing room off the master bedroom, all the shoes, the handbags, the clothes kept in a supremely orderly fashion. There were gaps though. A pair of shoes was missing and a handbag. To Ma Meili it appeared as if Du Luli had gone out for the evening and had not come back. That would tie-in with Superintendent Ye's theory that Du Luli had been murdered about the same time as Jin Huiliang. Ma Meili placed the passport in an evidence bag but left everything else in situ.

On returning to the sitting-room, she found Superintendent Ye making his way slowly down a bookcase full of what appeared to be a series of romantic paperback novels with lurid covers. He was opening each book in turn to see if anything dropped from the pages. Ma Meili left him to it and turned her attention next to the bathroom. It was as pristine as every other room in the house: no signs of blood, no signs of violence. Ma Meili made a mental note to inquire with Superintendent Ye whether Du Luli had employed a maid as Jin Huiliang had done. She examined the bath and shower carefully. There were signs the shower had been used in the last day or so, droplets of water still beading the drainage area. From down the plughole Ma Meili recovered one of Du Luli's long, wavy hairs which she placed in an evidence bag. The medicine cabinet was full of vitamin supplements and a small bottle of what Ma Meili recognised to be anxiety medication. But the date on the prescription was from over a year ago and, curiously, only a few tablets had been consumed. Ma Meili wasn't sure what to make of that. Maybe the tablets had made Du Luli feel unwell and she had discontinued taking them. Ma Meili made a note in her notebook.

It could be something – but more likely nothing. Superintendent Zuo had told her to make a note of anything that seemed unusual or out of place.

She left the bathroom behind, saw Superintendent Ye was still at work in the sitting-room, and walked into the second bedroom, the daughter's room, shutting the door behind her again. There was no disguising the room belonged to a teenager. It was messier than the other rooms, posters of boy bands – some possibly English, some most definitely Chinese – on the walls, as well of photographs of smiling children, all girls, all in a very smart school uniform, only one of whom was Chinese.

Du Yue.

She looked nothing like the mother.

Ma Meili had no idea how Du Luli looked now, but even in her younger days Du Luli had not the high cheekbones possessed by her daughter, or the long *straight* hair, or the tall athleticism of her youthful body, or the almost gem-like quality of her eyes. The most recent photograph seemed to suggest Du Yue was about thirteen or fourteen years old. If all the men at the police thought Prosecutor Xu a beauty, Ma Meili wondered what they would think of Du Yue when she grew into her maturity: a model or a film star in the making, perhaps. Sad as she was that Du Yue had probably just lost her mother and had never known her father, Ma Meili couldn't help but feel envious, not only of Du Yue's looks but also of the education she was receiving in England. Surely, with those looks and that education, Du Yue was to live a life more charmed than most.

Du Yue's bedroom yielded nothing of significance. Ma Meili re-turned once more to the sitting-room – Superintendent Ye was now absently looking up at Du Luli's photograph again – and, lacking orders to the contrary, she decided to search the final bedroom. The room appeared to be used partly as a home office – there was a laptop sitting on a small desk – and a room to store more clothes. Ma Meili disconnected the laptop from its wires and placed it in an evidence bag without switching it on. The cyber forensics team back at PSB HQ would take a look at it when they could. At present there was a long queue. It might be a couple of weeks before they got around to it.

There was a large diary open on the desk. Ma Meili flicked through the pages. There were a few appointments written inside – doctors, dentists, and such-like – and the term times for her daughter's school in England. But it seemed Du Luli was not one for keeping a written record of her life, which was a pity – a great pity. Ma Meili put the diary in an evidence bag.

The majority of the clothes in the cupboards were wrapped in plastic covers, presumably for long-term storage. In the final cupboard to be searched, under a pile of winter sweaters, Ma Meili found an old scrapbook. Ma Meili had come to doubt Du Luli had any great feeling for her daughter, carrying on in the dubious profession that she did. So what if she did spend lots of money on her daughter's education? What was that compared to the shame the daughter might feel for the rest of her life for what her mother had chosen to do to earn that money? But the scrapbook gave a lie to that first impression. Ma Meili had never seen anything like it before. It seemed that almost every day of her daughter's growing up had been captured by Du Luli's camera – or by a camera belonging to someone else in England.

Ma Meili leafed through the pages, watching Du Yue grow page by page, already a striking girl at a very young age but improving year on year even if her poses became more self-conscious and her smile somewhat less fulsome. There were no photographs of Du Luli. Curiously, interspersed with the photographs of the daughter, were business cards – sometimes one card every two pages, sometimes two cards. None of the names and companies (or government departments) meant very much to Ma Meili. But as she kept turning the pages of the scrapbook, moving ever forward in time, the truth suddenly dawned on her. The business cards were a means of Du Luli injecting herself into the scrapbook, a shameless record of whichever man she was carousing with at that time; or possibly, if the company had not been at all pleasurable, a reminder to Du Luli of what had had to be endured to pay for her daughter's upbringing.

Ma Meili felt a shiver of excitement run through her. Inexperienced detective she might be, but she knew enough to realise she had struck real gold.

Ma Meili skipped forward to the final completed pages, Du Luli continuing to paste photographs into the scrapbook even though these days most people kept their photograph collections on their computers or on their phones. Like the other business cards, the name on the last card stuck in the scrapbook meant nothing to Ma Meili. The only difference with this final card was that she had seen it before. Her heart nearly leapt out of her chest. This was real treasure – not gold but the finest jade.

She took the scrapbook through to Superintendent Ye who was now slumped in one of the comfy seats in the sitting-room having given up searching completely. He looked utterly miserable. He was not even playing with his pocket-watch. If Ma Meili had been a mind-reader, she would have guessed he was reliving his argument with Prosecutor Xu.

"Superintendent, I have found something of significance," she announced, stirring him from his thoughts.

"What?"

"A scrapbook – photographs of Du Yue from when she was a baby."

"So?"

Ma Meili pushed the scrapbook under his nose. "In between the photographs, Du Luli has pasted in the occasional business card. I think these belonged to her male clients. They go back years and years. Now turn to the last page."

Superintendent Ye did so. He put his finger on the last business card and read out loud. "Primo Gong, Ambrogetti Global Software." Then he looked up at Ma Meili in wonder. "This is incredible, Constable Ma – absolutely incredible."

"You know him?"

"Of course – he is famous."

Ma Meili was disconcerted, not only by the fact she had never heard of Primo Gong but also by Superintendent Ye's enthusiastic reaction – before she had even got to the good bit. "Please wait a moment, Superintendent – there is more."

Ma Meili took her camera out of her shoulder bag. She flicked through the many photographs she had taken that day until she found the shot she was searching for, of Jin Huiliang slumped over his desk. But the focus of the photograph was on the desk drawer next to him which Ma Meili had opened to examine the contents. She expanded the picture for a better view.

"Look!" she said.

Superintendent Ye took the camera from her. Easily seen in the photograph, carelessly thrown on top of the other contents of the desk drawer – a collection of old pens, a stapler, odd bits of paper and rubber bands – lay a business card, an exact copy of the same final business card as stuck in Du Luli's scrapbook.

"Isn't that something?" said Ma Meili.

But Superintendent Ye's reaction was not as expected. She had hoped that Superintendent Ye would be overjoyed with the revelation that as Jin Huiliang knew Primo Gong, and Primo Gong knew Du Luli, and therefore it meant it was more than likely that Jin Huiliang and Du Luli were still very much in touch with each other. But the original enthusiasm Superintendent Ye had shown was now gone. His profound sadness had returned.

"Superintendent?"

He passed the camera back to her. "I felt something was wrong with Prosecutor Xu...that her reaction was more than her usual defensiveness, her dislike of being questioned. I understand now. I understand it all."

"Understand what, Superintendent?"

"Primo Gong is dead, probably murdered, and Prosecutor Xu and Fatty Deng – if he is back at work – are investigating the murder all on their own, a murder that has no doubt shaken the Shanghai Clique to their very core."

"But the Procuratorate does not investigate homicides."

"That is true, Constable – in normal circumstances. But Primo Gong was a close friend to Party Chief Li, who has never trusted the police in Chengdu. I assume Prosecutor Xu is under orders to keep her investigation secret. Which is regrettable...and not only because Prosecutor Xu has no experience of investigating homicides. She will not realise the death of Primo Gong is linked to two other homicides in the city last night."

"Should we call Fatty?"

"No, not yet – I need to think. But this is good work, Constable – exceptional work. I hadn't noticed Primo Gong's business card back at Jin Huiliang's apartment. You have opened a door in this investigation I did not even know to exist."

He smiled at her then and Ma Meili felt such happiness that all thoughts of his flawed character, of how much she had suffered working for him these last few months, and of her plan to transfer to SWAT as soon as this current investigation was over, just evaporated from her mind.

THIRTY-THREE

— · —

F atty Deng had never been to Brother Wang's apartment. When they had been collecting debts for the gangster Freddie Yun they had always met up at some local dive. Fatty Deng had not even known Brother Wang was married – or at least co-habiting – until a scowling woman, about thirty or so, cigarette hanging from her mouth, and mewling baby in her arms, answered the door.

"Are you Fatty?" she asked.

Before Fatty Deng could reply, Brother Wang appeared behind her and steered her out of the way. "Fatty, get in here – the troops have arrived."

And so they had.

Around the table in the sitting-room sat four young men, no more than twenty years old or so, more or less identical, all slim, strong, and fit. So much for the one-child policy.

"These are the brothers Ming," said Brother Wang, proudly. "They are my cousins from my mother's side of the family." He began to point to each in turn. "That's Number One, that's Number Two—"

"I get the picture," said Fatty Deng, impatiently, taking a seat, in desperate need of his bed, not planning for this to be a long meeting.

Fatty Deng tossed one of the packets of Pride cigarettes he had bought from Sun Mei onto the table, offering them all around. Each of the Ming brothers took a cigarette, mumbling their thanks, quiet curious eyes upon him, sizing him up. Which was fine by Fatty Deng. The brothers Ming looked like young men who took what they did very seriously. Brother Wang had done well.

Brother Wang returned from the kitchen with six mismatched glasses and a cheap bottle of *baijiu*. He poured each of them a generous measure. Fatty Deng sipped the fiery liquid and almost choked. Secretary Wu's 25-year-old Macallan whiskey had probably spoiled him forever. He put the glass to one side and lit one of the Pride cigarettes. Not as smooth as the expensive Huanghelou 1916 cigarette given him by Secretary Wu, but at least it didn't burn like Brother Wang's bad *baijiu*.

"What do you think?" asked Brother Wang, nodding towards the kitchen. Still holding the mewling baby, the scowling woman was somehow loading the dishwasher.

"She seems nice," Fatty Deng lied. "I didn't know you were a father."

"Nor did I until she turned up at my door six months ago as big as an elephant. Fatty, I swear I didn't even remember her. But she says the baby is mine so...."

"Don't you know for sure?"

Brother Wang shook his head. "I thought when the baby popped out it would be obvious. How was I to know that babies all look the fucking same?"

"No, I definitely see a similarity," said Fatty Deng, thinking another lie wouldn't hurt.

Brother Wang was pleased. He poured everyone another measure of his *baijiu*.

Fatty Deng knew he had to focus, to get on with the business at hand. There was no point in hesitating now. For good or ill, with Secretary Wu's backing, he was committed. He addressed the brothers Ming, none of whom had taken their eyes off him – or off his shirt for that matter.

"Listen guys," Fatty Deng began, "this is a simple job...just a couple of hours work, no more. I need a woman snatched off the street early tomorrow morning – fast and easy, no fuss, no bother. She is not to be hurt. She works nights and is due home at her apartment at about eight-fifteen. We need to be in position by eight. She lives just to the south of the city centre, in Wuhou, on the edge of the Xiaotianzhu Street Residential District." Out of his pocket he pulled a street map he had bought from a street-seller on the way over and laid it out on the table. He pointed to where Superintendent Si Ying lived and marked the route she would probably take home from the Black House on Liberation Street which was barely ten minutes away by car. "As soon as she is out of her car, we pick her up, and bring her back here to Wukuaishi. I need her stashed somewhere safe and out of the way where I can have a quiet chat with her. A word of warning: she's tough and may have fighting skills."

"We'll be okay," said Number One Ming.

"Good," said Fatty Deng, liking his confidence. "I need you to get hold of a van...something fairly old and unmemorable...something that can't be traced back to you...something that you can dispose of quickly. Get some masks for yourselves as well, though I doubt if you will need to use them. I've already scouted the area this evening. The only CCTV in the immediate vicinity is an old camera above a shop front about 50 metres from the entrance to the apartment block. I've already dealt with it. It's now pointing skywards. I'll be parked up in my own car down the street from where you will grab her. I've got some radios and earpieces for us all which I'll distribute tomorrow morning. I'll identify her and give the go ahead when I see her. But it will be Brother Wang who will be out on the street with you who will make the final decision on the snatch. When it's done, I'll pick up Brother Wang and follow on. Is that clear?"

The brothers Ming nodded as one.

"Any trouble," said Fatty Deng, "anything that doesn't look quite right to Brother Wang, we back off...try again another time...or come up with a wholly different plan. Whatever happens, you will all get paid for your time."

"Who is she?" asked Brother Wang.

Fatty Deng had been dreading this question. But he thought it fair to everyone around the table to know exactly what it was they were getting themselves into.

"Police," he said, simply.

The brothers Ming did not bat an eyelid. Brother Wang, though, jumped out of his chair, nearly knocking over the table, cursing loudly.

"Fuck me, Fatty – are you trying to get us all killed?"

"She won't be armed," replied Fatty Deng.

"That's not the point! It's bad enough that I've been temporarily chucked out of Freddie Yun's gang. I don't want to be hunted down like a dog by the whole of the fucking PSB!"

"Just calm down and listen," said Fatty Deng. "It's not what you think. Firstly, she's just a building guard. No one is going to miss her for a few hours. And second, this has been sanctioned at the very highest level. She's bad – rotten to the core. One way or another I am taking her in."

"What's she done?" asked Brother Wang, nervously lighting another cigarette.

"I can't tell you."

"Why not use the Procuratorate police?"

"I can't tell you that either," replied Fatty Deng, losing his patience, wanting to be in bed, for this day to be over. "Now do you want the job or not?"

The scowling woman still carrying the mewling baby came into the sitting-room from the kitchen. She pointed a finger at Brother Wang. "You do what Fatty wants. We need the money. You need to pay the rent and I need to feed the baby."

Brother Wang turned to face her. "Woman, if there is one rule that I live by, it's that I never fuck with the police."

"I don't care about your rules," replied the woman. She held the baby up for him to see. "If you don't take this job then I will strangle your baby right now. Better that than watch it get sick and die from starvation."

By the look on her face, Fatty Deng thought she might actually mean what she said. Brother Wang cursed again and sat back down at the table. The woman returned with the baby to the kitchen. Fatty Deng looked at each of the brothers Ming in turn.

"We're in," they said, in unison.

Brother Wang splashed some more *baijiu* around, his hand now trembling. "What time?"

"We meet here at six," said Fatty Deng. "Any questions?"

The brothers Ming shook their heads.

"A policewoman – I can't fucking believe it," muttered Brother Wang.

"It will be okay," said Fatty Deng.

"That's fine for you to say," said Brother Wang. "You have a Procuratorate badge and a gun hidden under that daft shirt of yours."

Fatty Deng got up from the table and, after nodding towards the brothers Ming, made his way to the door. Brother Wang followed him.

At the door, Brother Wang whispered to him, "Are you sure about this, Fatty? I've got a really bad feeling."

"It will be okay," repeated Fatty Deng. "Just think of the money. You're going to make five month's rent for a couple of hours of work."

He sighed and nodded. "I suppose I have no choice. I have a baby now...responsibilities."

"That's the spirit," said Fatty Deng.

After Brother Wang shut the door behind him, Fatty Deng took the stairs out of the apartment block. Out on the street, he looked both ways, seeking out any threats, or any sign of anything out of place. He saw nothing that worried him. The rain had stopped but the night had grown very warm, the humidity sapping the life out of him. He collapsed into his car – thankfully, home was five minutes away – lit another cigarette and turned the key in the ignition.

Nothing.

He tried again.

The engine struggled then died again. He waited a minute or so, tried again, and this time the engine caught.

He sat back for a while, smoking his cigarette, maybe his twentieth for the day, waiting for the engine to settle. He was very aware his mind should be on the next day's snatch and grab, but he couldn't drag himself away from the upset he felt about Prosecutor Xu leaving for London or the fright he had given Sun Mei. There was nothing he could do about Prosecutor Xu. However, he reaffirmed his promise to himself that, after all this was over, he would make things right with Sun Mei. He would make it so she would never have to give out free cigarettes again. He imagined her happiness at this turn of events and him then having the nerve to ask her out. But the fantasy – which was surely what it was – suddenly turned dark, with her politely thanking him for his interest in her, and telling him, in no uncertain terms, that not only did she find him physically unattractive, but she had no intention of getting herself involved in the violent and uncertain world of a procuratorate investigator.

Sensible girl, thought Fatty Deng, grimly. He stubbed out his cigarette. If he was Sun Mei, he would have nothing to do with him either. He put her out of his mind and drove home.

THIRTY-FOUR

— · —

After dropping Constable Ma back at The Silver Tree – she was to stay the night there – Philip Ye sat for a while in his car leafing through Du Luli's scrapbook. It was a curious collection of mementos, one part a visual record of Du Yue's growing up, the other a log of Du Luli's paid sexual encounters. Some of the business cards belonged to men he had heard of. And a few of those belonged to men who had visited his father at the house, and whom he had actually liked. But it was the last six business cards that were of particular interest to him, including the card of Primo Gong.

Though the ever-changing, ever-evolving networks of people – political, business, religious, and criminal – in Chengdu were often hard to follow, even for an experienced observer like himself, he was certain those last six business cards belonged to men who had very close ties to the family Fu. Indeed, rumours had reached his ears last year that Primo Gong was romantically involved with Lucy Fu – a rumour that, unfortunately, his colleagues in police intelligence had so far failed to confirm. What was known was that Primo Gong had a month or so ago been one of the select few to be given first choice of apartment within the newly-constructed Plum Tree Pagodas luxury complex and that he had been seen out on the town with Lucy Fu. Philip Ye wondered if any police intelligence operation had captured a photograph of Du Luli with Lucy Fu and Primo Gong. It would not be unheard of for a powerful family like the family Fu to hire high-class escorts like Du Luli for their special friends and clientele. Maybe it was time to have a word with Lucy Fu – or at least discover whether she was in the country or not.

He also had to make a decision about his own family. It had to be no coincidence that his father had been encouraging Stacey Corrigan to look closely at Ambrogetti Global Software. And, despite whatever protestations he might make, his father had the sources – often better than police intelligence sources – to be already aware Primo Gong was dead. For his father, all this intrigue might be a bit of fun at the Shanghai Clique's expense. What his father might not realise – or if he did, not quite see the danger – is that he himself might be the subject of Prosecutor Xu's enquiries, might indeed be the target of her homicide investigation. If Prosecutor Xu had caught the slightest scent that the former mayor of Chengdu had been looking to stir up a bit of trouble – using Stacey Corrigan as his proxy – that might prove more than enough for the serious legal and political operator that she was to overturn the current unstable equilibrium to put him away for good.

Too disturbed to go home, Philip Ye drove to the Sichuan Cancer Hospital. Leaving the scrapbook safely locked away in the secure compartment in his car, he stopped at a kiosk to purchase two bottles of Lucky Buddha beer and three packets of Zhonghua cigarettes and then went up to the wards to visit Commissioner Wei Rong, his boss, his mentor, and his friend. Though it was now late in the evening, with but a couple of nurses on duty at their station in the dimly-lit corridor outside, Philip Ye found Commissioner Wei awake and sitting up in bed in his room, reading a novel by the light of his bedside lamp.

"It's only when everyone else has gone to sleep I get any peace in this place," explained Commissioner Wei, extending his hand.

Philip Ye gripped that hand gently, finding it bony and cold. It had been a couple of weeks since he had last visited and it was now obvious to even him, the most sympathetic and optimistic of observers, that the life-force was quickly draining out of Commissioner Wei, that the awful cancer of the blood was soon to complete its work despite all the drugs the doctors were pumping into his system – not to mention the few thousand years of Traditional Chinese Medicine also being brought to bear.

Philip Ye placed the packets of cigarettes and the bottles of beer on the bedside cabinet and reached inside the cabinet for the bottle-opener Commissioner Wei kept hidden there.

"You spoil me, Philip," said Commissioner Wei, lighting one of the cigarettes.

It was against the rules and the nurses would confiscate any cigarettes they could find, but Philip Ye reckoned the cancer of the blood had rendered meaningless any lasting harm the cigarettes could possibly do. Philip Ye passed Commissioner Wei one of the open bottles of beer, keeping the other for himself. He took a seat next to the bed.

"What's bothering you, Philip?"

"Oh, just the usual stresses of life."

"You have returned from holiday early."

"After thirty-six years, my mother and I are yet to find common ground."

"I am sorry."

"It is but a trifling matter."

"I assumed it was the ice-axe in the back of a retired general's head that might be on your mind."

Philip Ye smiled. "Who told you?"

"Ms. Miao came by earlier this evening with some meaningless paperwork for me to sign. I am sure Chief Di has tasked her with finding out how many days I have left in me. They are tired of paying my salary and want me in my grave as soon as possible – to be quickly replaced and forgotten. I should be offended, but I do enjoy the company of the charming and enigmatic Ms. Miao. If I had been a younger man...."

"She is quite the puzzle, isn't she?"

"She is that, Philip – I put in a good word for you."

"Thank you."

"I told her, when she had run out of other options, she could always demean herself by dating a troubled homicide detective. She was most amused."

"I am sure."

"She informed me about your case. Odd, don't you think – echoes of Trotsky."

"It is more than a simple assassination. Do you wish to hear the details?"

Commissioner Wei took a swig of his beer and shook his head. "Forgive me, no, Philip. After Ms. Miao's visit I find I have no appetite for murder. It is very confusing to me, but, as a dying man, all I can do is dream of romance."

"You are not dying – and who would not be thinking of romance after a visit from Ms. Miao?"

Commissioner Wei held up the paperback he had been reading. "One of the young nurses lent it to me. It is about a doctor working in Africa, so dedicated to his work that it takes him the whole book to realise that the nurse by his side is as equally dedicated to him. I am finding it quite enthralling."

"Really?"

"Talk to me about Prosecutor Xu."

Philip Ye smelt a trap. "What about her?"

"She is on your mind."

"So?"

"Are you going to pursue her to the four corners of the Empire?"

"For murdering her husband?"

"No, Philip – for romance!"

"She is not my type."

"I beg to differ."

"You have never met her."

"I saw her on TV."

"That trial was a charade!"

"I couldn't keep my eyes off her."

"It was quite a performance, I grant you."

"I do not think she was acting, Philip – she really believes in the Rule of Law."

"Old man, I thought it was your blood that was diseased, not your brain."

"Listen, Philip, lying in this bed, staring out of the window and waiting for death, it has come to me that sometimes the past is best left where it is, best left forgotten. For a woman like that, I could forgive the shadows that lie in her past."

Philip Ye thought he was hearing things, this from a man who had always been relentless in his pursuit of murderers, who had refused to close case files no matter how cold the trail. "If Prosecutor Xu has killed, I could not forgive that."

"No?"

"How could I? How could I explain myself to the ghost of her husband?"

"Regardless of the circumstances?"

"Have you heard something I have not, old man?"

"No, Philip, I have heard nothing. But I have started to question the work you and I have done, the value and virtue of it, whether sometimes more harm than good is done from the uncovering of old wounds."

"We have brought justice to the bereaved and the dead."

"That is true."

"Without law, without justice, all that remains is chaos."

"That is also true."

"And if wounds are not uncovered, and if wounds are not properly cleansed, then they will fester – to the lasting corruption of us all."

"I just wonder if occasionally, just occasionally, we should not look away, put justice in the hands of Heaven instead of a panel of semi-literate judges."

"What are you saying, old man?"

"Philip, last night I had a dream. I was walking in a foreign land. The sky was the same as ours but it was not quite, if that makes any sense. A man approached me. I recognised him as a young fellow I arrested years ago in Shanghai, who had eventually been sent to the execution yard for the murder of an uncle. He bowed to me and said, "Good day to you, Commissioner Wei." Then he went on his way, smiling to himself, leaving me perplexed, wondering why he had not demonstrated any hate toward me. He had killed his uncle. But there had been extenuating circumstances, facts that had not made it to the final prosecution file due to my negligence and the negligence of others – his death sentence, in my view, a miscarriage of justice. The face of that young man has haunted me for years. When I awoke, I began to wonder whether the dream might have been real, whether I had been walking the streets of the afterlife, whether he had indeed forgiven me. I have always held to the tradition that in the afterlife there were panels of spirit-judges to hear the cases of those who escaped justice in this world, that I might be a policeman again in the afterlife and be charged with hunting down those in need of a spirit-trial. But now I have begun to wonder if there is any need for police in the afterlife, whether all is peace and harmony there, whether the lesson of death is that we are required to forgive all that has gone before. I do not want to be sent to a spirit-police station, to sit at a desk twiddling my thumbs, with an eternity of boredom to contend with."

"That sounds more like Beijing than the afterlife."

Commissioner Wei did not smile. "I am afraid."

"I know."

"Have you no words of comfort – no special insight into what awaits me when I die? Hunting murderers is all I know."

"I have no such insight, other than that life goes on."

"I am so tired, Philip."

"I will pray for you."

Commissioner Wei closed his eyes and smiled and relaxed back into his pillows. Philip Ye had wanted to talk some more, about Jin Huiliang, Du Luli, and Primo Gong, about whatever it was his father might be up to, and about the persistent rumours that Maggie Loh might soon be bumped up yet another grade and put in charge of a combined Robbery-Homicide Section. Instead, he watched his friend drift off into sleep. Philip Ye took the still smoking cigarette from Commissioner Wei's hand and stubbed it out. He hid the packets of cigarettes under the pillows out of sight of any passing nurses and poured the remaining beer in the sink, placing the bottles in the bin. He promised himself he would return in a day or two.

Exiting the room, he found the corridor darker than before, the overhead fluorescent lights off, just a desk light burning at the nurse's station that was unusually vacant. He had only walked a few paces toward the lifts when he felt the electric charge in the air, the weakening of the veil between the physical world and the afterlife – very much as he had felt when he had been on his way down the drive to meet Du Yue for the first time earlier that evening.

He smelt perfume about him, the same perfume that had been present in the air within and without Du Luli's apartment. He sighed. He was in no mood for this.

He turned around.

Not more than twenty paces from him, on bare feet, clothed in a raincoat identical to his – she had to tease, she had to have her fun – but belted at the waist, and wearing apparently little if anything underneath, stood the Witch-Queen of Chengdu.

"How is he?" asked Sarangerel.

"Do not pretend to care."

She glided toward him, tall, lean, and graceful, her copper-hued skin gleaming in the light from the nurse's station, her long waist-length hair flowing out freely behind her, her eyes as dark and intense as ever, her perfume fully enveloping him, intoxicating him, lulling him into insensibility. Of a height to him, tall for a woman, when she stopped before him she reached up and stroked his face, her long fingers light on his skin, her touch far from unpleasant. She smiled when he did not flinch. Years had gone by but he thought her lovelier than ever, more dangerous than ever.

"Commissioner Wei is correct," she said.

"About what?"

"The shikra – the little hawk with the blood on her feathers – would be a perfect match for you."

"And not you?"

"Ah, Philip, don't tease me – you have proved remarkably resilient against all of my devices. And you had your chance. Together we could have ruled Chengdu."

"What is it you want, Sarangerel?"

"You have something that belongs to me."

"I doubt that."

"The girl is mine."

Philip Ye thought of Du Yue, of her uncanny likeness to Sarangerel. "She is under my protection."

"But I dreamed it, Philip. I saw her mother tortured, murdered, her body dumped in some water-logged field, never to be found. I saw it all. Her mother is never coming back. The girl is to be mine – a gift to me from a host of grateful spirits. I am to be her mother now. It took me time, too much time, to find out where she lived. When I got there she was gone, already swallowed up by your father's mansion, a place you have forbidden me to go. I did not follow her, Philip. I did not betray the blood-oath that I made. But she is mine. I know it and you know it. You have seen her face. You have looked into her eyes. Fifteen years or more might separate us, but she and I are truly twin souls."

"Did you murder her mother?"

"Ah, Philip, you disappoint me."

"Innocence is not a quality I associate with you."

She put a finger to his lips. "That girl is meant for me. You know of what I speak. She has a great gift...the words of the dead flow through her and all about her. Let me raise her as my own. No harm will come to her, I promise. I will nurture her gift. Under my tutelage and care her talent would surely grow. She will want for nothing."

"No."

"Philip!"

"You will make her over in your own image."

"Is that so wrong?"

"I would wish a different future for her."

"A trade then?"

"What kind of trade?"

Sarangerel's eyes grew cold. "Give the girl to me and no harm will come to that little hawk of yours."

Philip Ye remembered the note passed to him by Mouse, the copy of the dinner invitation Sarangerel had sent to Prosecutor Xu, the veiled threat toward Prosecutor Xu within its words.

"Even the spirits are whispering about you and Prosecutor Xu," continued Sarangerel. "Think on it, Philip. What better trade could there be? Give me the girl and you need never fear the past catching up with the woman of your dreams."

"I do not dream of Prosecutor Xu."

Sarangerel laughed, mocking him. "Oh, Philip – I did not think I would live to see such a thing, you brought so low, made a liar by a mere woman. I am more excited than ever to meet Prosecutor Xu, to see for myself what it is about her that consumes you so. I am sure the TV did not do her justice. I will give you a day or so to think on my offer. You know my word is good. Give me the girl and I will let your little hawk fly free."

Sarangerel leaned forward and planted a kiss on his cheek. She turned and walked away, glancing back just the once before she turned a corner, smiling as she did so. Philip Ye breathed again. One of the overhead fluorescent lights flickered back on. A phone softly rang at the nurse's station. He heard the patter of feet behind him as a nurse ran to answer it.

He cursed.

Dark sorceress she might be, a woman without a conscience, but Sarangerel was right about his dreams. Prosecutor Xu had starred in them all too often.

THIRTY-FIVE

— · —

D ay Na and Night Na accosted Philip Ye as soon as he walked
through the door.

"Boss, that girl has got to go."

"She's a freak."

"Remainder theorems."

"Speaking to dead men."

"A witch!"

"Make no mistake!"

Philip Ye waved them and their complaints away. He walked
through to his father's study and found his father smoking his pipe,
lost in thought, Stacey Corrigan gone.

"Philip, what have you discovered?"

"Primo Gong is not being held by the Procuratorate." Philip Ye
slipped off his raincoat and took a seat opposite his father, studying
him carefully. "I believe him to be dead."

Ye Zihao had never been a placid man. Like every other member of
the family Ye, he had trouble governing his emotions. He was more
prone to rages, ecstasies, and depressions than any man Philip Ye had
ever known. And yet, unlike the rest of the family Ye, he was well
aware that his father's intense moods did not necessarily reflect what
was going on deep inside. As a child, he had seen his father rage at a
member of his staff, his anger so intense that the pulsing of his veins
at the side of his neck could be seen, only to laugh to himself, the veins
no longer standing proud, as soon as that staff member had scurried
out of sight. How his father could do this, Philip Ye did not know.
But very little of Ye Zihao was to be believed or taken at face value
– especially his emotions. Like a human *matryoshka* doll, find one

Ye Zihao and there was yet another hidden underneath. Now, after being told of Primo Gong's likely demise, Ye Zihao's expression was decidedly blank.

"You seem concerned," said Ye Zihao.

"Father, it will be common knowledge that you have been speaking with Ms. Corrigan. It will be common knowledge that she is preparing a story on Ambrogetti Global Software and has been trying to interview Primo Gong for days. You have made yourself vulnerable. If there is something I should know then you should tell me."

Ye Zihao took the pipe from his mouth. "Such as?"

"You could start by telling me that you had nothing to do with Primo Gong's disappearance."

Ye Zihao returned Philip Ye's stare. "In this house you are not police. I am your father and I need tell you nothing."

"Father!"

"If Primo Gong is dead then think of the fascinating story Ms. Corrigan will be able to write."

Philip Ye struggled to keep his own temper in check. "This isn't a game. Prosecutor Xu is no fool. And she is likely being assisted by Fatty Deng who should never be underestimated. If any trail leads back to this house then they will find it. I cannot think why you would push Ms. Corrigan to write her story. I cannot think why you continue to provoke the Shanghai Clique so. It's a miracle you have survived so long."

"I still have friends in Beijing."

"Who are old and dying off one by one."

"I am not afraid of Prosecutor Xu."

"You should be."

"Then why didn't you let her die at the hands of those crazy cultists in Chongqing? Why did you choose her over your father?"

"That was not the calculation I made."

"Was it not?" asked Ye Zihao, angrily pointing the stem of his pipe at Philip Ye. "It comes to something when a father is unsure of the full support of his son."

"Father, just tell me you had nothing to do with whatever has happened to Primo Gong. Convince me and I will do all I can to divert Prosecutor Xu's attention from you."

"Are you so sure she is looking at me?"

"I would be."

"Very well, Philip – as you wish. I admit to wanting to stir the pot a bit. I heard there was trouble at Ambrogetti Global Software. There have been rumours floating around the financial community for months. And then a little bird told me Ms. Corrigan had landed at Shuangliu International Airport looking for a story to write. That was all that was on my mind, I assure you. I have done many bad things in my life, Philip. When I was mayor, I always had to make tough decisions for the good of the city – decisions that sometimes caused much suffering in some quarters. But I am no murderer. I just wanted a bit of fun. I honestly do not know how Primo Gong's murder – if murder is what you are talking about – profits anyone."

"It profits someone."

"Then Philip, on your mother's life, I give you my word that I did not lift a finger against Primo Gong."

Philip Ye realised this was the best he was going to get. "Thank you."

"Tell me, is this anything to do with that curious child you have taken in under my roof?"

"I believe so."

"The brothers Na are terrified of her."

"They think her a witch."

Ye Zihao laughed, relighting his pipe, now full of good humour. "She does have a passing resemblance to Sarangerel."

"Sarangerel is hunting her."

Ye Zihao was amazed. "The Witch is mixed up in all of this?"

"It seems so."

"We should have strangled that copper-skinned demoness when we had the chance all those years ago."

"Maybe."

"Philip, will you protect me from Prosecutor Xu?"

"I will attempt to divert her to a more constructive line of inquiry."

"Make her understand that she owes this family her life."

"I will, Father, I promise – and promise me in return that you will breathe not a word of what I have told you to Ms. Corrigan. She will have her story, just not yet."

"Agreed."

———⊰≋⊱———

The brothers Na were now in the kitchen, puffing furiously on their big cigars. Philip Ye ignored their hard stares and went upstairs to shower and change, wanting to wash Sarangerel's scent off his skin. He put on a fresh suit, dark green, and picked out a sea-green paisley silk tie. Looking in the mirror, he thought the tie a touch striking and, unusually for him, wondered if he should ignore his first instinct and change. Hating himself for this self-doubt, he left all as it was, and went along to the guest suite and knocked on the door. It was very late and part of him hoped Du Yue was sleeping off her fear from earlier as well as the loss of her mother. He was pleased, though, when he heard a faint reply. He opened the door and found Du Yue sitting up in bed, her book open in her hands. His father had been wrong when he had said Du Yue had a passing resemblance to Sarangerel. After having just been in the presence of Sarangerel, his memory of the witch fully refreshed, he thought Du Yue the daughter or even the sister of Sarangerel in every respect but fact.

It was uncanny.

Was Sarangerel correct?

Had fate always intended Du Yue to be hers?

Philip Ye forcibly reminded himself that Isobel had thought differently, that she had gone as far as to communicate from wherever she now existed in the afterlife to make it so that Sarangerel did not come to possess Du Yue, to guide the girl into his safe-keeping. Somehow, he needed to honour Isobel's faith in him and keep Du Yue away from Sarangerel's dubious influence.

"Have you found my mother's body?" asked Du Yue.

It unsettled Philip Ye that Du Yue was so calm, that as yet she demonstrated no sign of real grief. "No, I have not."

"Will you keep looking?"

"I will – but for the moment, if you are not too tired, I wish you to meet a friend of mine."

"May I take my book with me?"

"Of course."

Philip Ye left her to get dressed. He waited for her at the foot of the stairs, the brothers Na not far away, looking on, filling the house with their choking cigar smoke. Fortunately, he did not have to wait long. Du Yue came down the stairs dressed as before in a pair of jeans and a summer blouse, her book clutched tightly in her hands. When she noticed the brothers Na, she rolled her eyes and stuck her tongue out at them. Philip Ye took Du Yue by the hand and led her out of the house.

"You should not torment them so," he said to Du Yue when she was settled next to him in the passenger seat of the car.

"They do not like me."

"They are wary of you – there's a difference."

"I told them I hear voices."

"That was a mistake."

"I will not mention the voices again."

"I think that is for the best."

"The friend we are going to see is a woman."

Philip Ye glanced at Du Yue as he steered the car down the drive. "What makes you say that?"

"You are dressed very well."

"I always dress well."

"You look both anxious and excited."

"That is my normal expression."

Du Yue laughed. "I do not think so."

"It might be politic, while you are living in my father's house, to keep any acute observations to yourself. Watch, listen closely, but whatever you do, do not speak your mind."

She nodded. "The Chinese way."

"If you like."

"I am more English than Chinese."

"So you have said."

"What about you?"

Philip Ye drove the car through the gates and out onto the road. "What about me?"

"You have an English mother and a Chinese father."

"You have been doing your research."

"When I was eating in the kitchen your father came in, sat down, and stared at me while smoking his pipe. He did not say a word.

Then, on the Oxford University website, I found a picture of your mother. She is very beautiful. You get your looks from her."

"Thank you."

"Is your soul English too?"

"I don't think souls take on the qualities of nations or races. Such notions are of the mind only. But to answer the question you are truly asking, what I feel to be when I look in the mirror, it really depends where I am. In England, I feel Chinese; in China, I feel English."

"China frightens me."

"How so?"

"In England, even when the streets are crowded, even if there is trouble, it feels as if order is always trying to assert itself. In China, even when all is peaceful, it feels as if chaos is never far away. I prefer order."

"As do I."

"Am I stuck in China forever now?"

"I have told you to leave the future where it is for now."

Du Yue fell silent for a while. There was nothing he could say to bring her lasting comfort. Without a mother, with an unknown father, she was destined for an orphanage even if there was money left in her mother's estate. Her future was in the hands of the State. There was little he could do about that.

THIRTY-SIX

— · —

X u Ya was woken by a knock at the door. Confused to find herself in a chair with a blanket draped over her rather than in her bed, she glanced at her watch. It was just after midnight. Who could be calling at this hour? It had to be Mister Ni again. Either he had found the courage to defy Lucy Fu and finally tell all he knew of what had happened in Plum Tree Pagodas during the hours preceding and following the death of Primo Gong, or else he had news of some other happening. He would not be delivering more food – not at this hour. Xu Ya threw the blanket to one side and got up from her chair. She was amused to see that, before he had left, Investigator Deng had tidied up the remnants of the meal they had shared together – except for those remnants, that is, that stained the front of her new dress, much to her displeasure. How was it she had learned so much at school and university and yet was unable to eat without throwing her food everywhere like a child? Not that she cared what Mister Ni thought of her. She padded over to the door and opened it without glancing through the security eyepiece – a decision she was quick to regret. Mister Ni was nowhere in sight.

"Forgive me calling at this late hour," said Philip Ye.

"Hello," said a tall, teenage girl, in English, standing next to him.

This was unbelievable.

This was unacceptable.

She was going to have Mister Ni's job for this.

No one was supposed to get past the concierge unless specifically invited. Or, at the very least, if someone just turned up at the door, the concierge was required to contact her by phone and ask whether she was receiving visitors. It appeared that the rules did not apply to Philip Ye.

"May we come in?" he asked.

Xu Ya had not forgotten how angry she was with Philip Ye, how much he had hurt her back at The Silver Tree by accusing her of having blood on her hands – either an uncalled for and ignorant reference in regard to her competence as a prosecutor, or a hint that, just like Sarangerel, he too might have heard a whisper from someone in Chongqing about the terrible night her husband died. Xu Ya was unsure which. She wanted to slam the door in his face. But the presence of the girl made such behaviour impossible. She suspected this had been Philip Ye's plan all along. He was wearing a different suit to earlier, a different shirt and tie also. He was also freshly shaved, smelt of some exquisite cologne, and, though she could sense his exhaustion – he had only just returned from England after all – his skin radiated cleanliness and health. By contrast, her eyes were clogged from her short sleep, she was wearing the same dress as before – now stained with food and crumpled from her sleep – and, as for her hair, she could not imagine how bad it looked. Furthermore, her head was fuzzy from the bottle of wine she had shared with Investigator Deng. She needed the floor to swallow her up.

"I will not discuss Primo Gong with you," she said.

"I have a story to tell," he replied.

It was not quite the commitment to stay away from forbidden territory she wanted, but Xu Ya stepped aside anyway, silently thanking Investigator Deng for making her apartment vaguely presentable after she had fallen asleep.

"May I introduce Du Yue," said Philip Ye, presenting the girl to Xu Ya after she had shut the door.

"Hello," said the girl, in English again.

Xu Ya was forced to shake Du Yue's offered hand, unnerved by how the girl towered over her and, despite her lack of years, by her almost fairy tale-like beauty. There was an ethereal quality about her, a sense that she was only half in this world. Not only did she appear to be listening to something only she could hear, but her eyes, even when staring at Xu Ya, remained slightly unfocused. The effect was quite unsettling.

"May I trouble you for some tea?" asked Philip Ye.

"Water for me, please," said Du Yue.

In a bind, not wanting to appear ill-mannered, Xu Ya stalked off to the kitchen in her bare feet and put on fresh water to boil. Conscious that Philip Ye had followed her and stood in the doorway watching her, Xu Ya said, "Do you find the preparation of tea that interesting?"

"No, I—"

"What is it about the family Ye? Why do you think that neither the law nor the rules of common courtesy apply to you?"

Pleased to see her question throw him off balance – he was struggling to construct a reply – she poured a glass of mineral water, pushed past him, and took the water to Du Yue in the sitting-room. Du Yue was now in the chair formerly occupied by Investigator Deng with the book she had brought with her open on her lap. It was most unusual behaviour – rude also. Du Yue accepted the glass of water with a 'thank you' – in English again – before losing herself in her book once more. Xu Ya had never been shy of correcting the bad behaviour of others. But in this instance she held her tongue, not knowing quite what to make of the girl. She was an oddity, make no mistake.

Xu Ya returned to the kitchen, pulling the door behind her. Philip Ye had made himself useful by finishing the preparation of the tea. He was arranging cups and the teapot on a tray, his movements careful, controlled and methodical, making a much better job of it than she would ever have done. She had never shown much interest in becoming the best of hosts.

"The girl—"

"I will explain all," he said, picking up the tray. "Perhaps it would be best if we spoke in your study."

Too tired to argue, Xu Ya led him out of the kitchen – Du Yue was still showing no interest in the proceedings – and into her study. Unfortunately, Investigator Deng had not been in here to tidy up. The room looked like a bomb had hit it. There were papers and books strewn across her desk, on the two chairs, and also over most parts of the floor.

"I have been busy," she explained.

"I see that," he said.

"I need a maid."

"That could be one solution."

She avoided his eyes, refusing to be judged by him, clearing a space on her desk for him to place down the tray of tea. He then lifted a pile of papers off a chair and stood still, like a dummy, undecided about where to put them. She snatched the papers away from him and let them drop to the floor in a heap.

"Sit!" she ordered.

He did as he was told. "About earlier, at The Silver Tree, I wanted to apologise—"

"Mister Qu has already seen fit to apologise on your behalf. He sent me a lovely note and a gift of food and wine, some of which I have spilt down my dress as you can see."

"I had not noticed."

"It is far too late to attempt to be gallant now."

"But—"

"Mister Qu, however, is the perfect gentleman."

"I agree."

"But he should have taken proper advice before marrying into the family Ye."

Philip Ye smiled at the barb. "Mister Qu did not fully comprehend my half-sister's genealogy when he married her. He is not at fault, I assure you."

Xu Ya was horrified. "He was tricked into marriage?"

"Let us just say he was not presented with all the available facts. And yet Mister Qu is quite content with his fate. He and Ye Lan are a love-match. And the family Ye is all the better for his quiet wisdom and calming influence."

"It is a pity you were not calmed by him earlier."

"No one is more perturbed by my loss of temper than I."

"You have just returned from a difficult trip to England?"

"I will not use my mother as an excuse for my behaviour."

"You ruined my dinner with Mister Xi."

"Ah."

"It was a business dinner."

"Of course, may I enquire as to—?"

"No, you may not. But you can explain to me what you are doing calling on me at this ungodly hour and the importance of that strange girl. Your story had better be interesting. I have already fallen asleep in front of Investigator Deng this evening."

"How is he?"

She tried hard to suppress the tears that came to her eyes. "He is not the same."

"It will take time."

"I know but—"

"He is strong."

Xu Ya took a quick sip of her tea, scalding her tongue. Her guilt about Investigator Deng, about London, about everything, threatened to overwhelm her again. To distract herself, and conscious of his green eyes continuing to bore into her, studying every detail of her face, and feeling very vulnerable because of it, she said, "Superintendent, I am waiting to hear your story."

He afforded her a disconcertingly attractive smile but then began to talk, about an unusual murder, about retired PLA Lieutenant-General Jin Huiliang, an apartment door left unlocked, an ice-axe, the butt of an expensive cigarette left in his ashtray bearing lipstick, a crying maid, an embittered daughter, a border conflict with Vietnam that most had all but forgotten, the daughter of a dead comrade Jin Huiliang had taken to be his ward, only for this ward to disappear into a life of dissolution, and finally The Historians, all former comrades of Jin Huiliang, all veterans of the border war, all come to Chengdu to be near Jin Huiuliang, to write military histories as he did, all hoping this writing would help heal their damaged minds.

"You suspect this Bo Qi?" she asked.

"I do," Philip Ye replied.

"Even though all the indications are that Jin Huiliang's murderer was a woman?"

"Yes."

"And the other Historians?"

"I will tell you after I meet with them tomorrow."

"You can tell guilt or innocence just by staring at people?" she asked, sceptically.

"More often than not," he replied, in all seriousness.

She avoided his gaze again, not wanting him to see too deeply into her. "The ice-axe – a curious weapon, don't you think? Have you discounted Ramón Mercader?"

Her question surprised him. When it eventually registered with him that she had actually made a joke, he began to smile, showing all of his perfect teeth.

"Did you just mistake me for one of these dim-witted actresses or models you usually spend time with?"

"No, it is just that—"

"You think far too much of yourself, Superintendent – and far too little of others."

"That is unfair."

"Was the ice-axe meant to send a message?"

"I don't know."

She nodded toward the sitting-room. "Speak to me about the girl."

"Du Yue is under my protection. Her mother is missing. I believe her mother to be dead...murdered...at or about the same time as Jin Huiliang. She is in fact the daughter of Jin Huiliang's former ward, Du Luli."

Luli.

Was that not the same name of the woman with the long, wavy hair; the name of Primo Gong's companion these last few months, bought and paid for by Lucy Fu; the name only just discovered this evening by Investigator Deng, told him by the manager of the Old Chengdu Restaurant.

"I see the name is familiar to you, Prosecutor."

Philip Ye reached inside his pocket and took out a photograph, holding it up for Xu Ya to see. It was an old portrait of the woman with the long, wavy hair, the same woman whose photograph Xu Ya now had on her own phone, but taken only a few days ago by the young software engineer from Ambrogetti Global Software, out on the town with Primo Gong.

"Aiya!" exclaimed Xu Ya, unable to help herself. She could hardly believe it. So Primo Gong's murder *was* connected to the PLA – or retired PLA officers at the very least. Investigator Deng had been right all along.

"I know Primo Gong is dead," said Philip Ye, slipping the photograph back in his pocket.

Xu Ya felt her face grow hot. "I cannot speak about that."

"I have recovered a scrapbook from Du Luli's apartment. She had the dangerous habit of collecting the business cards of those men she...ah...did business with. The last card in the scrapbook was Primo Gong's."

"Where is this scrapbook?"

"Safe."

"I want to see it."

"You will – in due course."

Xu Ya felt like slapping him. "What does the girl know?"

"Nothing – she has just returned home from school in England to find her mother missing."

"And how did you come by her?"

"That is not important."

"I will be the judge of what is and is not important. Who is her father?"

"Not even she knows."

"Can he be identified from the scrapbook?"

"No – the scrapbook was begun after Du Yue's birth."

"I will still need to question her."

"Not tonight."

"Have you contacted social services?"

"No."

"Why not?"

"For the time being she is staying with me at my father's house."

"Superintendent, that is inadvisable."

"I will take no risks with her life."

"Is she in danger?"

"Who can say?"

Xu Ya bit her lip. Philip Ye had not given her all of the known facts. There had been odd gaps in his story, his telling of the investigation so far into Jin Huiliang's murder cautious, his presentation of his findings selective.

This would not do.

"I brought Du Yue with me tonight," he continued, "so you could see her for yourself, so you could understand the need for us to work together, to pool our resources. Like it or not, for the duration of this investigation, you and I are bound to each other."

Bound to each other.

What an odd choice of words.

If she had not felt so tired, if she had not already decided she was to catch the soonest flight to London, if she had not given up hope that Philip Ye would ever look upon her as anything other than a prosecutor, or that she would be anything other than a means to an end for one of his investigations, she might have thought he was flirting with her.

As it was, she thought quite differently about their respective investigations. She was, after all, under orders. And, despite her and Investigator Deng's scepticism, Ye Zihao remained a prime suspect. There were not two connected investigations; there was but one investigation – hers.

"Superintendent, the girl will remain with me tonight. The Procuratorate will now take over your investigation into the murder of Jin Huiliang and the possible murder of Du Luli. Please make sure all your investigation notes are up-to-date and all the evidence you have recovered, including that photograph of Du Luli, has been logged appropriately. Forward everything to me at the Procuratorate tomorrow morning. You will breathe not a word of this investigation to anyone at the PSB. Do so, and you will find yourself on a charge. Is that understood?"

THIRTY-SEVEN

— · —

H e had talked his way past the concierge, Mister Ni making no great effort to restrain him. He had quickly gained access to Prosecutor Xu's apartment, aided not only by the intended distraction of Du Yue but also by a stroke of luck, Prosecutor Xu literally caught napping. And so, certain the gods were with him this night, Philip Ye had allowed himself to be lulled into a false sense of security. He had convinced himself that Prosecutor Xu would quickly come to the sensible conclusion that they should pool their resources and form a working partnership. He could not have been more wrong.

"Superintendent, do you understand what I am telling you?" she asked him. "The Procuratorate is now taking over your investigation. Your services are no longer required."

He had no trouble hearing her words. But it took some long moments for it to finally sink in that all he had achieved by this surprise late-night visit was to show her all the cards he held in his hand. "I do not answer to you, Prosecutor,"

"You must comply," she said, colour coming into her cheeks.

"I do not answer to you, Prosecutor," he repeated, more firmly this time, struggling to control his temper, well aware they were but seconds away from another full-blown argument.

Unfortunately, Prosecutor Xu had no great interest in controlling her temper. She slammed her cup of tea on the desk, spilling much of the contents across her scattered papers and jumped to her feet, levelling a finger at him. "I order you!"

Philip Ye also stood, expecting his height, his physical nearness to her in the confined space of her study, to intimidate her, to quieten her. He was wrong about that also. He had learned nothing from the confrontation in the narrow corridor back at The Silver Tree.

She jabbed her finger into his chest, hard and sharp, her behaviour as unexpected as it was extraordinary. "You will do as I say!"

It occurred to Philip Ye then that, if there had been a sharp knife lying nearby, Prosecutor Xu might well have used it instead of her finger. Had it been a situation much like this, an argument that had spiralled out of control, that had done for Prosecutor Xu's late husband? Philip Ye saw it in her eyes: her mind brilliant though it might be, was now lost to all reason.

He turned his back on her.

There was nothing else to be done.

"You will do as I say!" she yelled at him, punching him in the back.

Philip Ye ignored her and walked out of the study. He told Du Yue it was time to leave, took the girl by the hand, pulled her out of the chair, and guided her swiftly out of the apartment, slamming the door shut behind him, wishing he were deaf to the stream of abuse directed at him by Prosecutor Xu. It was only in the lift, after the doors had closed after them, that he realised how shallow and rapid his breathing had become, how his heart was racing, how shocked he had been by the sudden turn of events. The relationship between the PSB and the Procuratorate in Chengdu had never been great. Now it had sunk to an all-time low.

"I like her," said Du Yue.

"Forgive me – I had hoped the meeting would go better."

"She is very beautiful."

"More scary than beautiful, I think."

"Mister Qin is very amused."

Philip Ye turned to Du Yue in surprise. "Your friend has been in contact with you again?"

Du Yue shook her head. "Oh no – I do not mean Uncle Qin. He only turns up when it suits him. Beloved Mister Qin is someone else entirely."

"Beloved?"

"Her name for him."

"Prosecutor Xu is aware of him?"

"No, no...she knew him when he was alive. I do not know when or how. I did not get a chance to learn the details. But I think Beloved Mister Qin watches over her constantly – a guardian spirit."

"Ah."

"He likes you."

"Is that so?"

"He likes you a great deal."

"That's nice – but does he have any advice for dealing with Prosecutor Xu?"

"No, but I do: a gift of flowers, an invite to a lovely restaurant, and plenty of warning so she can put on her finest clothes and make herself up so she feels the best she can."

"I was trying to discuss murder with her, not romance her."

"Ah, my mistake."

"Did this Beloved Mister Qin have anything to say that is useful?"

Du Yue shook her head. Philip Ye stared at her, wondering if she was concealing something from him. She returned his stare, not intimidated by him either.

"Your eyes are very green," she said.

"Thank you."

"Do you know the mathematical probability of inheriting the green of your mother's eyes?"

The opening of the lift doors saved him from learning this fascinating fact. Mister Ni was at his desk, in the process of putting down the phone, looking very unhappy.

"Superintendent, I am to pass on a message to you from Prosecutor Xu," he said. "You are never to visit Tranquil Mountain Pavilions ever again."

"I understand."

"It also seems that my position here is also in doubt," said Mister Ni, sadly.

"She will calm down."

"Oh, I do hope so, Superintendent."

"She is volatile, not mean-spirited."

Mister Ni nodded, somewhat cheered. "I am sure that is right. Out of all the tenants in this building, she is my favourite. She never fails, even after a long day, to stop for a chat, always asking after my wife and family. One day last month, when my wife was sick and I had to work, she went to my apartment, stopping for groceries and medicines along the way, and then spent an hour helping my son with his homework."

"How old is your son?"

"Ah, fifteen, Superintendent. He had hoped to be an engineer – a career choice my wife and I encouraged. Alas, after the visit from Prosecutor Xu he is quite besotted. He is now considering a career in law and has a photograph of her on his wall. He is quite the talk of his school."

"Best keep her bad temper a secret for now so as not to confuse him."

"Of course."

"Good evening, Mister Ni."

"Superintendent, please, before you go...there is a little matter I would discuss with you."

"Yes?"

"A friend of mine, Mister Han, the night concierge at Plum Tree Pagodas, is in a spot of difficulty."

"I see."

"With Prosecutor Xu."

"Ah."

"She is to interview him tomorrow morning at the Procuratorate. He has committed no crime. Suffice to say something terrible happened last night at Plum Tree Pagodas that he has some knowledge of. If he tells Prosecutor Xu the truth, he is sure to lose his job; if he tells her a lie, she is sure to find him out."

"What do you have in mind, Mister Ni?"

"He would speak the truth to you."

"Why me?"

"Once his story is told, he believes – as do I – that you will have the wisdom to advise him accordingly. It is also a story that I think would benefit you to hear."

"Where and when?"

Mister Ni scratched his head and pondered. "Mister Han gets off shift at eight in the morning. Around the corner from Plum Tree Pagodas is Liberation Street. There's a famous cigarette shop there called—"

"The Lucky Dragon Tobacco Emporium."

"Ah, so you know it."

"Tell your friend I will be happy to meet him there just after eight."

"Thank you, Superintendent, he will be most relieved. He has been so worried—"Mister Ni's phone rang again. Disconsolately, he put his head in his hands.

"Good evening, Mister Ni," said Philip Ye.

"Good evening, Superintendent," replied Mister Ni, taking a deep breath and picking up the phone.

Philip Ye saw no need to endure Mister Ni's suffering with him. He took Du Yue by the hand again and led her from the building. Thankfully, the rain was still holding off. Inside the car, he couldn't help smiling. The all-too-short excursion to Tranquil Mountain Pavilions had not been a waste of time after all. He was excited to hear Mister Han's story.

"May I go with you to the Lucky Dragon Tobacco Emporium in the morning?" asked Due Yue.

"No."

"Why not?"

"It is police work."

"Will Mister Han have information about my mother?"

"It is possible."

"Are you in a lot of trouble with Prosecutor Xu?"

"In what sense?"

Du Yue paused a moment to properly frame her question, then said, "Does she have the authority to order you to stop investigating what happened to my mother?"

Philip Ye started the car's engine. "That is not so easy a question to answer as you might think. The PSB investigate most crimes, including murder. The Procuratorate usually restricts its own criminal investigations to local government officials suspected of corruption. However, in theory at least, the Procuratorate does have legal oversight over all PSB investigations. But we police are hard to order around. And I will not give up on finding out what happened to your mother."

"I did like Prosecutor Xu, though."

"So you said."

"She is a good match for you."

"I sincerely doubt that."

"Beloved Mister Qin agrees with me."

"Is he speaking to you now?"

"No."

"So, you just made that up?"

"Maybe – maybe not."

THIRTY-EIGHT

— • —

Xu Ya's fury was such that a couple of phone calls to Mister Ni just would not do. Mister Ni had to fully understand her mind, had to understand how much the betrayal of her trust had hurt her. She went down to the lobby to confront him.

"Mister Ni, I am so angry...so very disappointed in you. What were you thinking? You should not have let Superintendent Ye come up to my apartment without warning. This is my home. I am supposed to feel safe here."

Mister Ni hung his head.

"Look at me, Mister Ni!"

"I cannot, Prosecutor."

"What *were* you thinking?"

"That you should not be alone in what you are doing," mumbled Mister Ni.

"Alone? How ridiculous! I have Investigator Deng."

"I suppose."

She waited for Mister Ni to say more, to offer up a better argument as to why he had let Philip Ye and the girl Du Yue up to her apartment without issue. But Mister Ni said no more and continued to hang his head. Feeling awkward, aware that Philip Ye was – and should be – the real focus of her ire, Xu Ya began to calm down. She needed a clear mind. She had phone calls to make.

"I did not mean to threaten your job, Mister Ni," she said.

"But I was at fault, Prosecutor."

"That is true."

"I will not make the same mistake."

"I should hope not."

"But, in my defence, Prosecutor, I think there is no better man in all of Chengdu. Though I work for the family Fu, and am loyal to them, if ever I found myself in real trouble then I would take my wife and son to the gates of the Ye family mansion and beg the aid of Superintendent Ye."

Xu Ya was contemptuous. "You think he would just help you – a nobody?"

Unable to meet her eyes, Mister Ni said, "Yes, Prosecutor."

Exasperated by such foolishness, Xu Ya stormed off to the lift, her bare feet padding across the lobby carpet. But back in her apartment she regretted her intemperate words – as well as her condescension. She picked up the phone to apologise to Mister Ni but inexplicably dialled Investigator Deng's number instead.

"Prosecutor?"

"He has been here."

"Who has been where, Prosecutor?"

"Philip Ye, of course – in my apartment!"

Xu Ya launched into a telling of all that had happened, how Philip Ye had arrived unannounced at her door with the strange Du Yue, how unprepared she had been, how she had been sleeping, how she had had some of the remnants of their meal still staining her dress. "He had changed his suit, Investigator Deng...from only a few hours earlier!"

She then spoke of everything Philip Ye had told her about the investigation into the murder of Jin Huiliang, almost word for word, her memory perfect, giving emphasis to the holes in Philip Ye's story, such as how he had come across the girl Du Yue.

"It's incredible," said Investigator Deng.

"It is."

"Did he mention the Black House?"

"No."

"Or how Primo Gong died?"

"No."

"I am relieved, Prosecutor – we still have the advantage."

"What he said about the other retired PLA officers, The Historians, is interesting, isn't it? It lends credence to your theory about PLA involvement in the murder of Primo Gong."

"It does, Prosecutor, but the different methods of murder concern me as they do you. There is also the puzzle as to what a man such as Primo Gong would have in common with Jin Huiliang."

"Du Luli has to be the connection between them."

"True, Prosecutor, she must have decided for some reason to introduce Primo Gong to her old guardian...but why?"

"Philip Ye is convinced Du Luli is dead."

"Once she fled Plum Tree Pagodas, she would have been easy prey out on the street."

"I fear so."

"Then three murders, Prosecutor."

Xu Ya thought of her vivid dream of Huang Liu-Hong, sitting at his desk, speaking aloud his thoughts on the statute regarding conspiracy to commit murder. Her unconscious mind had been talking to her then, trying to persuade her of the truth well before Philip Ye had ever knocked on her door.

"Investigator Deng, may I ask if you think I did the right thing, ordering Philip Ye to hand over all his case notes and remove himself from the investigation?"

"You had no choice, Prosecutor."

"I confess I lost my temper when he refused."

"That is understandable. We are under the direct orders of Party Chief Li not to involve the police. What would happen if Party Chief Li discovers we are working with the son of the man he considers to be the prime suspect? Party Chief Li would have us both shot."

"I hit him."

"What did you say?"

"When Philip Ye refused to comply with my order to hand over his case notes, I actually hit him."

Investigator Deng laughed. "Prosecutor, I am in awe of you!"

"It was not my proudest moment."

"But I am proud of you. I know of no other in Chengdu who would have the nerve to raise a hand to Mister Ye – you are a true heroine!"

"Oh, don't be silly," said Xu Ya, wiping tears of laughter, and of sadness, from her eyes. She always felt so much better talking to Investigator Deng. By going to London, she was leaving the best friend she had ever had far behind.

"You should call Secretary Wu," advised Investigator Deng. "He would have the authority to get Mister Ye to step aside."

"Yes, I think I must."

"Call me back when you are done, Prosecutor."

She promised she would.

So, despite the late hour, feeling much more confident about herself after talking to Investigator Deng, she dialled Secretary Wu's number. He answered immediately.

"Yes, Ms. Xu?"

"I have just had a visit from Philip Ye."

"That is interesting."

"His investigation into the murder of the retired PLA officer is directly linked to the murder of Primo Gong."

"There is no doubt?"

"No, sir."

"Does Philip Ye know Primo Gong is dead?"

"He does."

"How?"

"I am not certain," she replied, choosing to conceal her argument with Philip Ye at The Silver Tree earlier that evening, that she might have revealed more than she had intended. "He is very astute."

"He has always been that."

"Sir, I need you to order him to remove himself from his investigation and to hand over all his case notes to me."

"Ms. Xu, I am very much relieved."

"Sir?"

"If Philip is choosing to approach you, then it will be because he sees no conflict of interest, nothing that points to his father being involved in Primo Gong's death."

Unconvinced, Xu Ya said, "I beg to differ, sir. A devious person will—"

"Philip has never been devious."

But Philip Ye had brought the girl Du Yue to assist him in gaining access to her apartment, thought Xu Ya. If that was not devious, what was?

"A good son will always protect his father," she said.

"Ms. Xu, do you believe Ye Zihao is guilty of these crimes?"

Xu Ya sighed. "I do not, sir. But, even so, Philip Ye must recuse himself from his investigation. This is not the time to test Party Chief Li's patience."

"I have an idea, Ms. Xu, to get Party Chief Li off both of our backs. Let us formally rule out any involvement by Ye Zihao. I want you to visit the Ye family mansion. I want you to put that wily old fox on the spot. Ask him any question you wish but concentrate on his relationship with that American journalist. Discover what that is all about. Ye Zihao is under house-arrest. He cannot refuse to be interrogated by you. This direct approach will do much to calm Party Chief Li's mind. He will be most impressed. He has never had the nerve to confront Ye Zihao himself. Once the interview is done, we will speak again and discuss Philip's future role in this investigation. How does that sit with you, Ms. Xu?"

Xu Ya felt faint, nauseous. "I'm not sure, I—"

"Visit Ye Zihao early tomorrow morning, say about eight. That is the best time to catch him off-guard. He was never a morning person. Don't worry about recording the interview. Just take notes. Those will suffice. Phone me immediately after you meet with him. I am interested in any observations you might have in regard to his health, his mental state, and his continued willingness to stir the pot in Chengdu. Good night, Ms. Xu."

Then Secretary Wu was gone.

Refusing to burst into tears, Xu Ya phoned Investigator Deng immediately and told him their new orders.

"Interview Ye Zihao!" exclaimed Investigator Deng, aghast.

"We have so little time to prepare."

"Prosecutor, I cannot be there...not right away."

"What do you mean?"

"I am meeting an informant about eight tomorrow."

"Then you will have to rearrange."

"I cannot," replied Investigator Deng. "It could be our only chance to find out what really happened in the Black House. But I promise you, Prosecutor, I will get to the Ye family mansion as soon as I can. I will not abandon you."

"Oh, how can this investigation get any worse?"

"Prosecutor, please do not despair. You will be quite safe in the Ye family mansion. And I am sure Ye Zihao would have seen you on TV. He will be petrified of you."

She tried to be brave. "You think so?"

"I do."

"Do you promise to come as soon as possible?"

"I promise, Prosecutor."

She let him go, let him get some sleep. She, however, would not be doing much sleeping tonight. She had questions to prepare. Interviewing Ye Zihao in the cells in an interrogation room in the bowels of the Procuratorate would be difficult enough but, in his own house...Aiya!

Where was she going to find the inner strength?

Where was she going to find the courage?

She thought of Investigator Deng, his words to her, his promise to not abandon her. But, by jetting off to London, she would soon be abandoning him. Perhaps she deserved to be sent into the dragon's den all alone. Perhaps she deserved everything she got.

THIRTY-NINE

— · —

D^u Yue was in bed, finally asleep, her book laid next to her pillow. Philip Ye closed the bedroom door gently after looking in on her. He was amazed by her resilience, the emotional distance she had placed between herself and the disappearance of her mother. In her place, even at his age and with the wall of bitterness separating them, if his own mother were to disappear, if his own mother were to be murdered, he would be distraught. Either Du Yue was so disconnected from the world, so conscious of the spirit-world around her, that normal human grief did not touch her, or else there would soon be a delayed reaction and he would have on his hands an inconsolable teenager – not an experience to look forward to.

He thought on The Historians, those veterans of the Sino-Vietnamese war, all come to gather around Jin Huiliang in Chengdu, all writing military history to ease the trauma of battle, how odd that was. Would it have not been better for them all to focus on the living – the study of nature, say – rather than continue their exploration of the arts of war? Then again, what did he know about the trauma of battle? The closest he had ever come, the closest he ever hoped to come, had been the shoot-out on the Zhimin East Road. That had been enough to haunt his dreams for many months. He should not be the one to judge the path to healing of any damaged mind. It was his place only to understand what had happened to disturb the harmony of The Historians, the close brotherhood forged in the cauldron of war, that had caused at least one of their number – if his instincts were to be relied upon – to turn on their erstwhile leader Jin Huiliang. It was his place to bring that person or persons to justice – and he would do this with or without the help of Prosecutor Xu.

He returned to his private rooms, took off his suit-jacket, donned a silk robe, and sat down in his favourite chair to ponder the case, feeling far too uneasy to sleep. Much as he tried to focus on the known facts of the case, trying to understand how and why Jin Huiliang, Du Luli, and Primo Gong had come together – hopefully some light might be shed on this by the concierge Mister Han in the morning – he kept being drawn back to Prosecutor Xu, her extreme reactions to him as well as his mystifying reactions to her.

Her husband was dead.

She had questions to answer.

And yet, not more than an hour before, he had suggested to her a partnership. It was right that there was but one investigation. But it troubled him that he had actually been excited at the prospect of working alongside Prosecutor Xu, to admire at close hand the workings of her clever and mercurial mind, and to feed off her passion for the Rule of Law – or at least the Chinese semblance of it.

But what about her husband?

How was one death any less important than any other?

His exercise in self-criticism was interrupted by a knock at the door. The brothers Na entered cautiously, almost sheepishly, thankfully no longer smoking their big cigars.

"Boss, about the girl..." said Day Na.

"The spooky girl..." said Night Na.

"There will be no further debate," said Philip Ye, to pre-empt any more stupidity. "Du Yue is to stay a few days at least. Her mother is dead...murdered, I think. As far as I am aware she has no other family. And you should both be aware Du Yue is being hunted by Sarangerel. She is not to leave this house."

The very mention of Sarangerel struck terror into the twins. Philip Ye thought for a moment they might cling to each other like children. It was remarkable how much fear one Mongolian shamaness could inspire in two otherwise very hard men.

"It is said," continued Philip Ye, "that if you wish to protect yourself from witchcraft it is best to employ a witch. If I were you, I would stick close to Du Yue and befriend her. In protecting her, she might in the future just save you from some terrible curse."

Day Na nodded. "Black magic to stop black magic."

"Sorcery to stop sorcery," agreed Night Na.

"That makes a lot of sense, Boss."

"A lot of sense."

Philip Ye thought it time to change the subject. "How goes the surveillance of Prosecutor Xu?"

The twins glanced at each other, instantly suspicious, wondering what lay behind the question.

"It goes well," said Day Na.

"Very well," said Night Na.

"When did she visit Plum Tree Pagodas?" asked Philip Ye. "She might have had Fatty Deng with her."

"Ah, we would not know," replied Day Na.

"We ordered an overwatch only," said Night Na.

"You did not ask for a proper log to be made, Boss."

"But we are told she likes to shop."

"Loves to shop."

"And she also—"

"Who are you using?" asked Philip Ye.

"Mister Wei," replied Day Na.

"He employs the best team of watchers in Chengdu," said Night Na.

The name meant nothing to Philip Ye. "I want no expense spared. Prosecutor Xu is now wading in some very murky waters. She is investigating a criminal conspiracy the extent of which I do not yet fully understand. Tell this Mister Wei that if he has to hire protection specialists, he should do so – and I now want a proper log of all her movements to be kept. Oh, and tell Mister Wei and his people to be especially careful from now on. Fatty Deng is back in the game. He has good eyes and a nose for people paying more interest than they should. Now leave me be. I have much to ponder. And remember what I said about Du Yue. Even in the house, be aware of where she is at all times."

The brothers Na grinned, bowed to him as if he were some noble lord, and then backed out of the room, happy to have a little fun at his expense.

Philip Ye got up from the chair and picked Jin Huiliang's manuscript up off the desk, thinking it might distract him from further disturbing thoughts about Prosecutor Xu. He still hoped to find within its pages some clue as to why three people had been murdered. Back in his chair, he began to read, soon becoming lost in Jin Huiliang's enthralling prose, the Lingzhou campaign of 1081, Chinese armies against the barbarian Xi Xia, almost as alive in his mind as it had been for those who had lived it.

He lost track of time.

Hours later, when he was done, all he could think of was the tragedy of war, the loss of so many lives – and for what? The manuscript ended abruptly, was sadly incomplete. But Philip Ye knew what had come after, how the campaign against the Xi Xia had been conducted at the apogee of Song military power, how, eventually, out of the complex and fluid mass of peoples and politics on the other side of the northern border to the Song, a new threat had emerged, the Jurchen, who would, barely half a century later in the year 1127, capture the Song capital of Bianjing – now known as Kaifeng – and go on to conquer most of northern China, and who in turn would be overthrown by an even greater threat, the Mongols, who would in 1271 declare a dynasty of their own, the Yuan, and who would ultimately conquer all of China by 1279.

Reading history had always been a reminder to Philip Ye that the world was in a state of constant flux, that nothing was ever truly stable, that nothing lasted forever – certainly not the ties that bound people together, not even those of the same family. He thought about Jin Huiliang, how he had abandoned his family to take care of his ward, Du Luli, how she in turn had abandoned him – only to reappear in Chengdu years later with a daughter of her own, about to enter his life once more but this time hand in hand with Primo Gong.

The question was, why?

Why had Du Luli sought out Jin Huiliang?

Had she wanted to show off Primo Gong to him?

Or had Primo Gong been in need of something? Had Du Luli, seeking to impress him or help him, decided to introduce him to Jin Huiliang in the knowledge that the retired general could provide that missing something?

But what would a man such as Primo Gong need from a man such as Jin Huiliang? Could Jin Huiliang have been working on something for Primo Gong, researching some forgotten history, for instance?

Philip Ye sighed, unable to progress further in this thinking until he had more facts. But the possibility that Jin Huiliang had some sort of side-project underway was intriguing and certainly a line of enquiry worth pursuing. Jin Huiliang, Primo Gong, and Du Luli had been up to something – and that something had gotten them all killed. Notes on this side-project, whatever it was, would have been made by Jin Huiliang in his journal. His killer had been clear-headed enough to take the journal with her.

Philip Ye glanced down at the manuscript again, intent now on reading the handwritten notes Jin Huiliang had made in the margins, the corrections to be done, the additions to be made, the reminders of further sources to be interrogated or familiar sources to be reread. It was then that it occurred to Philip Ye that he had seen no computer, no printer, nor even an old electronic typewriter in Jin Huiliang's apartment. And Constable Ma had made no mention that she had ever seized such an item. Furthermore, Philip Ye had seen no space on the desk or in any other part of his apartment where such an item would be sited.

Philip Ye studied the margin notes carefully, flicking through page after page. Initially, he had interpreted the notes as made by Jin Huiliang for his own benefit. But now he saw many of them in a different light, more as instructions to a professional typist. This would make sense. An old army man, unless filling a series of administrative positions, would never have learned to type. No, Jin Huiliang wrote in longhand and someone, someone who knew him well – his handwriting was often hard to decipher – would translate that handwriting onto the printed page. Which was interesting – and, potentially, very important.

The remaining Historians might well know the name of this typist. They all might even share the same typist. But, not wanting to tip off The Historians to the next step in the enquiry, after speaking to the concierge Mister Han, and after looking each and every Historian in the eye at the tea shop with Constable Ma, he and Constable Ma would pay the maid Madame Ding another visit. If anyone would know the name of this typist most likely it would be she. And if that typist could be found, then he or she might have information regarding a little side-project Jin Huiliang might have been working on for Primo Gong.

Philip Ye closed his eyes, satisfied at least that he had an investigative path to follow – and, of course, the meeting to come with the concierge, Mister Han. He drifted off to sleep, smiling to himself, thinking of Prosecutor Xu's temper, how she had actually punched him when she hadn't gotten her own way, how her apartment was always such a mess, how she had dropped food down her lovely summer dress, how....

SUNDAY

FORTY

—◦—

Philip Ye woke at dawn, Jin Huiliang's manuscript in his hands. Without thinking, he telephoned his friend Superintendent Zuo to see if there had been any further trade in the night, hoping Du Luli's body had turned up.

"How would I know?" responded Superintendent Zuo, tetchily. "I'm still stuck at home sick. How's the investigation going into my wife? She had both the motive and opportunity to poison me."

"Ah, cautiously – she has some important connections."

"You mean the women she plays *majiang* with?"

"One cannot be too careful."

"I heard about the body with the ice-axe in its head."

"Do you think your wife is involved with that case as well?"

"I wouldn't be surprised."

"The evidence from the scene does point toward a woman. But it's a complicated case – there was another murder Friday night, connected, a very serious individual whose death is being investigated in secret by the Procuratorate."

"Who?"

"Primo Gong."

"Never heard of him."

"American businessman...gave up his American citizenship for a Chinese passport...a real believer in the future of Chengdu...a favourite of the Shanghai Clique."

"Which dummy at the Procuratorate is investigating?"

"No dummy – Prosecutor Xu."

Superintendent Zuo whistled. "My wife adores her."

"I tried to speak to her, to suggest my investigation should be joined to hers. All she did was order me to hand over my investigation notes to her and to leave well enough alone."

"And did you?"

"What do you think?"

Superintendent Zuo laughed. "You are such a bad boy, Philip. Have you had a call yet from Chief Di?"

"Strangely, no."

"Maybe our glamorous little TV star has had a change of heart...realises she needs you after all."

"Unlikely."

"Then what are you thinking?"

"Not sure."

"Come visit me today, Philip. Let's discuss the case. I need some sensible conversation to help me recover."

"I'll do my best."

After showering and dressing, Philip Ye was down for breakfast just in time to witness a confrontation between his father and Du Yue, the brothers Na warily looking on.

"No books at the table, young lady," said Ye Zihao. "This is my home and that is the rule."

Du Yue refused to sit, clinging fiercely to her book. "Then I will not eat!"

"Then you will starve!" replied Ye Zihao.

It cheered Philip Ye to see such spirit from the girl. But he regretted allowing her to read at the table the evening before and was forced to intervene.

"Little Sister, while we eat let's put your book on the kitchen counter. It will be quite safe."

Staring daggers at Ye Zihao, Du Yue allowed Philip Ye to take the book from her and place it within sight on the counter. She then took a seat at the table but not before sticking her tongue out again at the brothers Na, much to their shock. Ye Zihao returned to the cooking of the breakfast, satisfied his authority – within the house, at least – was still absolute.

With Du Yue now sitting next to him, Philip Ye could sense the tension in her body as well as the combative nature of her spirit –

a quality he had somehow failed to notice the day before. She was going to be a handful.

When the food was served and Ye Zihao had sat down with them, Ye Zihao followed his usual pattern of quickly forgetting his temper, and set about questioning Du Yue on her life and schooling in England. Surprisingly, her show of temper also quickly forgotten, Du Yue was happy to oblige. She began to talk and talk, telling them all about the history of the school, about the teachers – some excellent, some not – her friends, how much she loved England, how she thought of herself now as more English than Chinese, how desperately she wanted to go back, how she was destined for a career in higher mathematics.

"I should have sent Philip to such a school," Ye Zihao said after Du Yue had stopped for breath, apparently approving of all she had said.

"A girls' school!" exclaimed the brothers Na, simultaneously, thinking themselves hilarious even if everyone else around the table thought not.

Not really hungry, and anxious to get on the road, Philip Ye left most of his breakfast uneaten, making his excuses, saying he would be hopefully home for lunch.

"What should I do?" asked Du Yue.

"Whatever my father tells you to do," replied Philip Ye.

Outside, the weather remained warm and humid but at least the sun was trying to poke out from behind the clouds. Unfortunately, more heavy rain was forecast for the afternoon. He got into the car in good humour, though. His depressing trip to England was behind him and he had a fascinating case to absorb him – as well as further battles to come, no doubt, with Prosecutor Xu. Philip Ye phoned Constable Ma, telling her to expect him slightly earlier than originally intended. By the time he pulled up outside of The Silver Tree she was already waiting for him out on the street. As he drove them to the rendezvous with the concierge from Plum Tree Pagodas, Philip Ye told Constable Ma of his difficult encounter with Prosecutor Xu the evening before.

"Can she steal the case from us?" asked Constable Ma.

"Certainly – if Party Chief Li and Secretary Wu agree to her request and they tell Chief Di to order us to desist. But I have yet to receive a phone call from anyone. I take that to mean, for the moment at least,

Prosecutor Xu's request has not been granted. Or else Prosecutor Xu has come to her senses. Three murders are a lot of ground for her and Fatty Deng to cover."

"Is Fatty Deng back at work then?" asked Constable Ma.

"I get the impression so."

"I like him."

"I do too."

Philip Ye knew the area around Liberation Street well. When he had first started working for the police, well before the family Fu had drawn up plans for the construction of Plum Tree Pagodas, he had been posted to Shuangnan Police Station, not a great distance away. At the time he had made the terrible mistake of purchasing some pipe tobacco for his father from the Lucky Dragon Tobacco Emporium, thinking it would make him happy, forgetting that his father preferred to import his tobacco directly from England. As his father had told him, losing his temper as he did so, pipe tobacco was so rare in China it was either old, of dubious quality, or contaminated. His father had thrown the gift in the bin. Philip Ye had never made the same mistake again.

It was Constable Ma who spotted him first. Philip Ye was concentrating on looking for a good place to park on Liberation Street when she pointed him out, a man loitering at the window of the Lucky Dragon Tobacco Emporium, not doing a very good job of blending in with all the other pedestrians out and about. It was already after eight and he was probably nervous they were not going to show. Philip Ye quickly parked the car and they approached him on foot.

"Mister Han?"

"I was frightened you might not come," said Mister Han, visibly relieved.

"Traffic was bad," replied Philip Ye.

"I am due at the Procuratorate at ten."

"So I understand."

"I am being forced to lie."

"By the family Fu?"

"Yes, Superintendent – what I know could cause great embarrass-ment. If I tell Prosecutor Xu the truth I will lose my job. If I do not, Prosecutor Xu is so clever that she will surely find me out."

Philip Ye was aware they were being stared at by the young woman behind the counter at the Lucky Dragon Tobacco Emporium. He did not recognise her. It was not she who has sold him the much-maligned tobacco for his father all those years ago. He wondered if the shop had changed hands since then. The displays in the window were now more colourful and the stock seemed more varied, more international, than before. Not wanting the young woman, or anyone else for that matter, to take undue interest in their little meeting, he took Mister Han by the arm so they could walk and talk.

"Ah, there is something I need to show you, Superintendent," said Mister Han, leading them around a corner and into an alley that ran down the side of the Lucky Dragon Tobacco Emporium.

Philip Ye and Constable Ma followed him a short distance, away from the bustle of Liberation Street, though they had to be careful not to step in puddles of black stagnant water and to avoid an old man on a bicycle coming the other way. Mister Han stopped about halfway down the alley. A stray dog came running up to them. Philip Ye's first thought was to shoo it away. But Constable Ma stepped between them, bent down to pet the dog, and, quite bizarrely, found some food in her shoulder bag to feed it – her preference for animals over humans, as always, on show.

"Look up there, Superintendent," said Mister Han, pointing up at Plum Tree Pagodas looming over them.

The sun, still doing its best to break through the clouds, reflected wanly off the windows. Philip Ye was not quite sure what he was supposed to be looking at.

"What are you showing me, Mister Han?" he asked.

"See the fifth floor...the broken window?"

Philip Ye noticed the window for the first time, the hole that had been punched through it. "What of it?"

"That is Mister Gong's apartment."

"Primo Gong?"

"Yes, Superintendent – it's a very great secret, no one is supposed to know, but Mister Gong is dead."

"I am aware."

Mister Han was shocked. "How is that possible, Superintendent? No police were to be—"

"Just tell me what you know, Mister Han."

"I tried to tell Ms. Fu but she wouldn't listen."

"Lucy Fu?"

"Yes – she was in a panic and refused to hear anything I had to say."

"She was in the building when Primo Gong was murdered?"

"Ms. Fu, Mister Gong, and—"

"Du Luli?"

Mister Han gripped Philip Ye's arm. "Oh, Superintendent, tell me that you have found her...that she is safe. I have been so worried. I have been searching the streets when I was off duty but found no trace of her or where she might be. I even went to her apartment building but could not get in."

Mister Han was a tough-looking man, early forties, with what Philip Ye took to be a sound, disciplined, and well-ordered mind. The family Fu chose their staff with care. He was probably former army and very, very dependable. Though he obviously had a sweet spot for Du Luli, the emotion in his voice very real.

"I am sorry, Mister Han," said Philip Ye.

"She is dead?"

"Her body is yet to be recovered but I believe so."

It was Philip Ye's turn to reach out to hold Mister Han, the shock of the news affecting his legs. Philip Ye helped him lean up against the nearby fence. Constable Ma kept on petting the stray dog but was missing nothing.

"It is all my fault, Superintendent," said Mister Han, tears in his eyes.

"How so?"

"I wasn't quick enough to stop her."

"Mister Han, you must tell me everything."

"She has a daughter who—"

"Du Yue is safe."

"Ah, at least that is something," said Mister Han. "Du Luli was so proud of her, always showing me photographs of the girl whenever she was working in Plum Tree Pagodas. I did not care what Du Luli did for a living. Unlike some, she was not crazy or high on drugs all the time. She was sensible, careful, and loved her daughter very much. She was a lovely woman, very discreet...."

"I know what she did for a living."

"But do you know she was employed by the family Fu – for six or seven years now? Ms. Fu met her at some party. I am not sure where. Ms. Fu always has had an eye for talent. She offered Du Luli a permanent contract – financial security, you understand – Du Luli to be offered, whenever the situation required it, to potential clients or friends of the family Fu. Ms. Fu trusted Du Luli implicitly. Du Luli was clever, perceptive, and remembered everything she was told."

"Both courtesan and spy."

"That is it, Superintendent – exactly. But she was getting older and, I think, tired of the life. Ms. Fu offered her one last job, to befriend Mister Gong, who worked very long hours, whose wife had left him and taken the children back to America, and who needed cheering up."

"Ms. Fu and Primo Gong were just friends?"

"I believe so, Superintendent. Anyway, what Ms. Fu didn't expect was for Mister Gong to fall in love with Du Luli. And why not? In his place, I might have done the same. Mister Gong cared little about Du Luli's past. He was a good man."

"This made Lucy Fu unhappy?"

"Oh, no, just the opposite. I know everyone believes Ms. Fu not to have a heart...and I am aware you have a bad history with her, Superintendent...but in my humble opinion she was genuinely happy for Mister Gong and Du Luli."

"So what happened Friday night?"

"The three of them had been out all evening...I don't know where, or even if they had been together. They were all in good spirits when they returned just before midnight, Ms. Fu arriving separately to Mister Gong and Du Luli. They continued to party in Mister Gong's apartment. Ms. Fu was to stay in the apartment next door. Anyway, it was just after half one in the morning. I had heard nothing, Superintendent. None of the security alarms had gone off.

Then the lift doors opened in the lobby and out came Du Luli. I could not believe my eyes. She was crazed with fear, blood on her hands, smears of blood on her face too. I don't think she even noticed me. She ran past me, barefoot, out through the doors and into the night. It all happened so fast, Superintendent. I am sure I will live those few seconds again and again for the rest of my life. I was so shocked I could not move. When I recovered, I ran out of the door after her. It was a terrible night. But at that moment there had been a break in the storms, the rain not so bad. I couldn't see any sign of her, though. Then I heard the screech of tyres. Du Luli was gone. I prayed she had jumped into a taxi...that she would be alright. I went back inside, armed myself, and went up to Mister Gong's apartment. Ms. Fu was already inside and was staring down at his body. He was on his back, lying on the bed, a hole in his chest, quite dead. Ms. Fu was in shock. She was shaking all over. She turned to me and said Du Luli had gone mad...had stabbed Mister Gong to death."

"But that wasn't true, was it?"

"No, Superintendent – but you must understand that Ms. Fu was not lying to me. She was not thinking straight. She would not listen to me. She would not use her eyes. I tried to point out the flaws in her argument but all she did was order me to clean the apartment, remove all traces that Du Luli had ever been there, destroy the phone she had left behind, and destroy Mister Gong's phone, tablet, and laptop in case they contained any evidence of Du Luli, any saved photographs of the three of them together. She wanted me to make it like an intruder had broken in and murdered Mister Gong. That was the story she was going to tell Party Chief Li. Then she said she was going to hunt down Du Luli herself."

"To hurt her?"

"I cannot say what was in Ms. Fu's mind."

"But you were worried enough for Du Luli's safety to go out looking for her yourself?"

"Yes – because I knew Du Luli had nothing to do with Mister Gong's death. I tried so hard to explain but Ms. Fu would not listen to me. She ordered me to keep my mouth shut, to alter the concierge's log. Then she made some phone calls. Party Chief Li and Secretary Wu came right away."

"Party Chief Li and Secretary Wu were here?" said Philip Ye, astonished.

"Yes, and that is when Ms. Fu started lying for real. She told them an intruder had got into the building. She told them that she had just returned late from some business engagement in Chongqing and found the door to Mister Gong's apartment open and then discovered him murdered in his bedroom. She persuaded them that there should be a secret investigation...that the good name of the family Fu was on the line. Party Chief Li and Secretary Wu didn't need much persuading, though. After they took a quick look at the body, Party Chief Li went crazy, shouting at the top of his voice, saying he knew who was responsible. He said it was your father, Superintendent, who had to be behind the murder. Ms. Fu said nothing. She refused to correct him. I think she was pleased with Party Chief Li's false assumption. Secretary Wu spent some time trying to calm Party Chief Li. Ms. Fu told them she wanted to bring in private investigators. But Secretary Wu stood up to her. He told her the Procuratorate would lead the investigation, that Prosecutor Xu would be put in charge. I could see this made Ms. Fu very unhappy."

"She was worried Prosecutor Xu would uncover her lies?"

"Oh yes, Superintendent. Ms. Fu is very frightened of Prosecutor Xu – as I am."

"Why no police?"

"I heard Party Chief Li say he didn't trust the police, that too many police were still loyal to your father, and that the police leaked like a sieve – his words, Superintendent."

"Of course."

"I do not like being party to such deceit, Superintendent."

"What do you think happened to Primo Gong?"

"I was in the army, Superintendent – I know a bullet hole when I see one. There were two that I saw: one in Mister Gong's chest, dead centre, the other in the back wall. Mister Gong would have died instantly. It could be the second bullet was aimed at Du Luli which is why she ran for her life. The bullets had not come from Du Luli or from anyone else inside the building."

Mister Han pointed up at the broken window on the fifth floor of Plum Tree Pagodas again.

"A sniper?"

"Yes, Superintendent – a professional kill."

Philip Ye almost laughed in Mister Han's face. There were no high-rise buildings next to Plum Tree Pagodas. But, seeing the seriousness of Mister Han's expression and understanding the risk he was taking in coming forward to tell his story, Philip Ye decided to make a show of taking seriously Mister Han's dubious theory by looking all about him. Philip Ye kept his eyes skywards and turned slowly on his heels until he was facing back up the alley toward Liberation Street. He stopped then, his eyes on the concrete monstrosity that was the old police Black House, now used, as far as he knew, as nothing but a confidential file repository. Then, with a sinking feeling in his heart, he glanced back toward Plum Tree Pagodas, noting that the top floor of the Black House was about level with Mister Gong's apartment window.

"Jesus Christ Almighty," he muttered under his breath, in English, a habit he had picked up long ago from Isobel.

"It's less than 120 metres, Superintendent – a easy shot for someone trained even at night and in the rain. I saw Mister Gong had been standing by the window. The impact had thrown him back on the bed."

"This cannot be," said Philip Ye, softly.

"Superintendent Ye, please listen to me," said Mister Han. "My friend Mister Ni, who is the concierge at Tranquil Mountain Pavilions, warned me that Prosecutor Xu was so clever she would easily see through Ms. Fu's lies. When they came down from examining the body – Prosecutor Xu and the fat man, that is – I could see it in their eyes. They knew the truth. They knew how Mister Gong had been killed. I was then forced to show them the concierge's log with the false entries. I felt so bad I wanted to scream out loud. Prosecutor Xu just stared at me, her eyes so cold I thought my soul might freeze. She had Du Luli's red shoes in her hand. Never have I been so frightened of such a beautiful woman. Now I have to go to the Procuratorate and be interviewed by her. Even with the lawyer, Mister Xi, I am doomed. I am going to end up in prison. My family will starve without me. I will not be able to cope with the shame. Please help me, Superintendent. Please intercede with Prosecutor Xu for me. If she will listen to anyone, it is you."

But Philip Ye was no longer listening to Mister Han. He continued to stare up the alley, across Liberation Street, and up at the Black House.

Jesus Christ Almighty.

Police are involved.

Only police have access to the Black House.

Fatty Deng would know this.

Fatty Deng would know all about the Black House.

It was no wonder Prosecutor Xu had ordered him to give up all his case notes and recuse himself from the investigation.

It was not pride.

It was not personal animosity.

It was pure common sense.

He, as police, was not to be trusted.

Jesus Christ Almighty.

Then terrible screams erupted from Liberation Street, but from out of sight, around the corner from the alley. Philip Ye turned to Constable Ma to give the order, but she was already off and running, shoulder bag abandoned, pistol in her hand, careless this time of the puddles, the stray dog following her, excitedly barking at her heels.

FORTY-ONE

— . —

On her arrival in Chengdu and her installation as a public prosecutor for the Chengdu People's Procuatorate, Xu Ya had quietly and methodically gone about researching Ye Zihao, specifically his many and varied business interests in China and around the world – some transparent, most not so – as well as the terms of his house-arrest. She had done this fully expecting, as a prosecutor, that she might have to bring him to trial one day – or at least assist others to do so. In her initial meeting with Secretary Wu, he had hinted she might be given special tasks, and there could be no more special task than prosecuting Ye Zihao. Researching the Ye family's business interests she quickly decided was probably going to be the work of a lifetime. But it was the little she had uncovered at the Procuratorate in terms of any ongoing investigation of Ye Zihao that had both concerned and appalled her.

There appeared to be no extant file (either paper or electronic) on Ye Zihao anywhere in the Procuratorate – a disturbing fact confirmed by Mouse who worked down in the basement archive. All that Mouse had been able to dig up was a faded paper copy of the order of house-arrest made by a judge (signature illegible) at the Chengdu Intermediate People's Court, presumably at the direction of the Chengdu Political and Legal Committee, chaired, then as now, by Secretary Wu. And that faded order of house-arrest left a lot to be desired. It was so vague, so badly worded, it might well have been drafted by a child. It stated only that Ye Zihao was to be confined to his place of residence pending further enquiries. But which place of residence? The family Ye had houses not just in Chengdu but in Hong Kong and Macao, and at least one other she was aware of far away in Geneva, Switzerland. And what were these further enquiries? And who had been charged with conducting them? As far as she could determine, no one, not even after the Shanghai Clique had become firmly embedded in the life, politics, and administration of Chengdu, had lifted a finger to actually get to the bottom of whatever criminality it was Ye Zihao had actually done during his term as mayor. It was a complete scandal. More mysterious still was an unsigned handwritten communique Mouse had managed to find in the archive (it had been referenced in the minutes of a Political and Legal Committee meeting convened a few weeks after Ye Zihao's removal from office) that detailed the recruitment – by whose order was not revealed – of two professional operators from the north-eastern port city of Dalian, to keep a watchful eye on Ye Zihao as Chengdu PSB could not be relied upon to do so.

"Is this all the paper-trail there is?" Xu Ya asked of Mouse.

"I think so," replied Mouse.

"There is nothing else?"

"Not that I can find."

"Would these two operators be the brothers Na?"

"I do not know, Prosecutor."

"They have northern accents."

"They do."

"But if they were recruited to keep a watch on Ye Zihao, what are they now doing living in the Ye family mansion and apparently working for the family Ye?"

"I cannot explain it, Prosecutor."

"Please find out who they are for me."

"I have already tried."

"You have?"

"I have contacts all over."

"And?"

"And nothing, Prosecutor – they may as well be ghosts. There is no record of them ever living in Dalian...or anywhere else for that matter. I have even spoken to my good friend Nüying at the Ministry of State Security. The brothers Na do not appear on their list of employees, contractors, or informers either – though, as you know, nothing is really certain with the MSS."

"This is most unsatisfactory."

"I agree, Prosecutor."

It was worse than that, thought Xu Ya.

It was a complete joke.

Since she had not yet been tasked with bringing Ye Zihao to justice, and not wanting to rock the boat or be seen to be presumptuous, Xu Ya had previously chosen not to raise the rather vague legal status of Ye Zihao with either Chief Prosecutor Gong or Secretary Wu. In fact, she had bided her time quite well, she thought. Until Primo Gong's murder that is, when she had decided to question Party Chief Li on just what was going on with Ye Zihao. Party Chief Li's admitted frustration with Beijing, the lack of support he had received from anyone in authority there, had been a revelation. More revealing still, despite all of Party Chief Li's rage and bluster, was Xu Ya's distinct impression that there was still no real commitment to bringing Ye Zihao to justice. Even if Ye Zihao was innocent of Primo Gong's murder – which he almost certainly was – the murder was all the political justification needed by Party Chief Li to set up a new taskforce at the Procuratorate – led by Xu Ya, of course – to finally put the matter of Ye Zihao to rest. Instead, she was now being sent into the dragon's den, the Ye family mansion, just to ask a few pointless questions of Ye Zihao, for no other reason than to placate a supposedly enraged Party Chief Li.

It was a fool's errand.

A complete waste of her time.

Especially as the real murderers were on the loose.

And she had been put at a serious disadvantage by not being given the requisite number of days to prepare all her questions and for being forced to conduct the interview – it could not be called an interrogation – in the comfort of Ye Zihao's magnificent home.

But there was no use crying about it.

And there was no use losing sleep over it.

She had her orders and that was that.

And yet she did cry, out of frustration. And she did lose sleep, tossing and turning all night, her dreams full of all manner of tense situations: Ye Zihao refusing to let her in the gates; Ye Zihao physically attacking her before she had asked her first question; Philip Ye sitting in on the whole of her interview with Ye Zihao, staring at her with those intense green eyes of his; and she and Philip Ye getting into yet another argument while Ye Zihao looked on, laughing at the pair of them.

It did no good to remember that Investigator Deng had promised to join her as soon as he could. Or that the brothers Na liked her, as she indeed liked them, and would ensure she came to no harm. Her nerves were shredded enough by Sarangerel's invitation to dinner, and the guilt she was wrestling with over accepting the lawyer Xi Huan's offer of a job in London. She did not need a face-to-face encounter with Ye Zihao.

At five in the morning, strung out and mentally exhausted, she gave up on sleep and decided to rise from her bed and imagine how she wanted the interview with Ye Zihao to unfold. Not having the luxury of interviewing him at the Procuratorate, she would be unable to suspend the interview any time she wished, consult her notes, have a think, and go at him again. She had just this one chance to find a chink in his armour. Ye Zihao's past, his time as mayor, was not a place she could go – at least not yet. This was not a fishing trip. All she had was the one tenuous link Ye Zihao had to Primo Gong: the American journalist, Stacey Corrigan, and the story she was supposedly writing on Ambrogetti Global Software. Ye Zihao may well have been using her to stir the pot, so to speak, in Chengdu, but she was also his weakness, the lever Xu Ya could use to get inside his mind. After all, it would be easy for her to imply that consorting with foreign journalists to write a damning story about Primo Gong and Ambrogetti Global Software could be interpreted as an attempt to subvert the socialist economic system and therefore endanger state security – an indictment that could potentially invoke the death penalty.

Her strategy in place, Xu Ya stayed a long time in the shower, languishing in the hot water, using it to ease her muscles and soothe her worried mind. After drying her long hair and pulling it back into a tidy ponytail, she treated herself to a luxurious breakfast of dumplings and fresh fruit, and then spent the longest time deciding on her wardrobe for the day. Not wanting to appear too severe in front of Ye Zihao and perhaps to play on her femininity a little – and ever conscious that Philip Ye might be lurking around – she picked herself out a long, white floral summer dress, black court shoes and a matching black handbag. Then she took a deep breath, reminded herself that Investigator Deng would join her soon enough, told herself she was the best and brightest prosecutor of her generation – which she supposed could be true – and walked out of the door.

As it was before eight, Mister Ni would still be on duty in the lobby. She avoided him by descending in the lift directly to the underground car park which thankfully had not been flooded by the incessant rain of the last few days. The weather forecast for the morning was fine. She spent an annoying length of time putting the roof of her little sports car down, found her sunglasses in her bag, admired herself for a few moments in the rear-view mirror, and then sped out onto the streets of Chengdu.

The roads were not fun. Isolated stretches of flooding, a few roads closed here and there, and the usual congestion even early on a Sunday morning made the going slow. But she managed to reach the impressive iron gates leading to the Ye family mansion at eight exactly. Expecting to have to get out of the car and speak into an intercom while holding up her procuratorate badge to a security camera, she was surprised as the gates opened automatically for her as if she had been expected. She drove slowly up the gravel drive. At first, the tall trees on either side of the drive obscured her view of the house and kept her in shadow. But, when she emerged from the trees and out into the sunlight, her breath was unexpectedly taken away by her first glimpse of the house, a copy of a massive Victorian country manor house, complete with manicured lawns and flower beds – an idyllic English oasis slap bang in the middle of a noisy and chaotic Chinese metropolis.

The photographs she had studied for years had not done the house justice. Great emotion welled up in Xu Ya. Her heart ached with wonder, admiration, and envy. The Ye family mansion was incredible, the largest private house in China she had ever seen. She could easily imagine what it would be like to live in such a house, how it would make her feel: like an empress, she suspected, like the Empress of Chengdu – a thought that made her smile.

After avoiding a wandering peacock, she parked her car outside the front of the house next to a black Mercedes she assumed must belong to Philip Ye. Hardly had she got out of the car when the brothers Na tumbled out of the front door to greet her.

"Prosecutor, it's been too long," said Day Na.

"Far too long," said Night Na.

"We saw you on TV."

"A stellar performance."

"Beautiful as ever."

"But more beautiful still in the flesh."

The twins bowed deeply toward her. All her fears suddenly departed. Xu Ya was so happy to see them again. She stepped forward and kissed each brother on the cheek, surprising them both, leaving a smudge of scarlet lipstick as she did so. It was no way to begin a formal interview but the brothers Na delighted her so. Then she had to scold them, telling them to stop squirming, as she used a tissue from her handbag to wipe her lipstick from their faces.

"The Boss is gone out," said Day Na.

"He's investigating dire goings-on in the city," said Night Na.

Xu Ya was both disappointed and relieved. "It is his father I have come to speak to."

She could not have amazed the brothers Na more.

"You're here to see Mayor Ye?"

"The Big Boss?"

"I am," she said, putting on her best smile, as if interviewing former mayors was something she did every day. "But first I have a little gift for each of you...for when you were kind to me...on that terrible night three months ago...when you brought me back from Chongqing."

From her handbag she took two small presentation boxes. She handed a box to each brother. The brothers Na opened their individual boxes to reveal identical gold rings featuring a face of a tiger fashioned out of jade. They were both rendered speechless. They first held the rings up to the hot sun to admire them and then slipped them onto their fingers. It seemed incredible to Xu Ya – she had assumed some resizing would need to be done – but the rings fit the brothers Na as if made for them.

"They are antique," she told them. "Qing Dynasty, maybe late 17th or early 18th century. I remembered you both to be a superstitious pair. The jade tigers will bring you luck, as well as protect you from evil spirits and sorcery."

She had said the last with a laugh, wanting to poke fun at the brothers. But they replied in all seriousness.

"We have no words, Prosecutor," said Day Na.

"No words at all," said Night Na.

"You may well have saved us...."

"....from a most terrible fate."

Their seriousness made this last ridiculous uttering difficult to mock. After a slightly uncomfortable silence, the brothers Na led her into the house.

"Mayor Ye is in an odd mood today," said Day Na.

"Very odd," said Night Na.

Not knowing whether this was meant to be a warning or just a meaningless observation, Xu Ya instead concentrated on the house, taking it all in. It may well have been very quintessentially English on the outside, but within it was all Chinese, its décor the most modern, the house full of light and air, painted screens, both traditional and contemporary artwork hanging on the walls, furniture and carpets fabricated in shades of brown and grey and cream, and little in the way of clutter or ornamentation – room after room an aesthetic marvel. It was a house of peace, a refuge – a home to die for. That Philip Ye returned to this veritable palace every evening was enough to make Xu Ya want to weep.

"This house is a marvel," she said.

"Haunted is what it is," muttered Day Na, darkly.

"Ghosts everywhere," added Night Na.

"And now we have a young witch living here."

"A very weird girl."

"Do you mean Du Yue?" asked Xu Ya.

Either the brothers Na did not properly hear her question or they chose not to answer. They led her to a closed door. Day Na was about to knock but Xu Ya shook her head, wanting her appearance to be a complete surprise. The brothers Na said they would prepare fresh tea and wandered off toward the kitchen, still staring in amazement at the rings she had bought them.

Her fear made a sudden return. Her stomach turning over, Xu Ya knocked on the door.

"Yes?" came the gruff reply.

Xu Ya opened the door and stepped into a large, airy, but smoke-filled study. Ye Zihao was seated behind a majestic mahogany desk, pipe in his mouth, his body twisted away from her. He was staring out of the window and across the vast artificial lake that had been constructed at the rear of the house. The water was so placid Xu Ya could see the reflection of the pale sun and hazy clouds on its surface. Within its waters, Xu Ya had read, there were tens, if not hundreds, of massive silver-scaled fish, mirror carp, imported at great expense from England.

"Mayor Ye?" she said, to get his attention, surprising herself by using a title he no longer owned or deserved.

He turned to her, grabbing his pipe before it fell from his mouth, his eyes widening in astonishment.

"I have some questions for you," she said.

He recovered his composure, his eyes narrowing, his bushy eyebrows knotting together. "I did not realise we had an appointment."

"I am a public prosecutor. You are under house-arrest. Why would I need to make an appointment?"

He began to smile, though his eyes remained hard. He stuck his pipe back into his mouth. He relit it, surrounding himself with a cloud of pungent smoke. She would need to send her summer dress for professional cleaning later, she thought.

"May I sit?" she asked.

He nodded, somewhat reluctantly, she sensed, indicating she should take the comfy seat in front of his desk. She did so, ignoring his glare as she took her time organising herself, taking her notebook and pen from her handbag, placing the bag then upon the floor, crossing her legs and adjusting her skirt so it fell just right, controlling her fear as best she could. She now was in the dragon's lair, make no mistake – though, to her, Ye Zihao resembled more a dangerously unpredictable bear.

"Have you eaten, Ms. Xu?" he asked.

"I have, thank you," she replied, annoyed at his refusal to use her proper title.

"What can I do for you?"

"As I said, I have a few questions."

"Concerning?"

"Stacey Corrigan, the American journalist."

She had hoped to unsettle him.

She did not succeed.

He continued to glare at her and then took his pipe from his mouth, rudely pointing the stem in her direction, saying, "Ms. Xu, why don't you ask me that which you really want to know?"

"And what might that be?"

"Whether I was responsible for the murder of Primo Gong."

Xu Ya knew she should have expected this. From all her research on the family Ye, she had learned Ye Zihao possessed an almost Western directness, having no patience for small-talk or circumlocution – just like his impossibly handsome son.

Xu Ya opted to respond in kind. "Well, *are* you responsible?"

His eyes brightened at the challenge. "Before I answer, Ms. Xu, may I ask a question of my own?"

She saw no harm in this. "If you so wish."

"How long have you had designs on my son?"

She blinked, unable to utter a word.

It made no sense.

She had never met Ye Zihao.

She had only ever visited this house before in her dreams.

She had never spoken to anyone of her feelings for Philip Ye – complicated and illogical as they may be – not even to Mouse.

And yet, with one simple question, Ye Zihao had been able to prise the sad truth from her, so slow she was to mask her face, to conceal the depth of her emotion. He had also succeeded in throwing her questioning of him into complete disarray.

"Well, well, well," he said, never taking his eyes from her.

"It matters not," she said, trying to be brave. "Your son has never, and will never, show any interest in a woman such as me. I am far too ordinary."

Ye Zihao laughed, cruelly. "Ordinary, no – but ruined, yes."

"You are speaking of my past?" said Xu Ya, a horrible lump forming in her throat.

"Your unfortunate marriage."

"A tragic lapse of judgment."

"You have been offered a job in London, I hear."

Astonished, she replied, "I have."

"You should accept."

"I have."

Ye Zihao nodded, satisfied, then twisted around in his seat to stare out of the window again. A small flock of geese flew in to land, sending ripples out across the lake.

"Mayor Ye?"

He turned back to her, his eyes now surprising her, indescribably sad. "What, Ms. Xu?"

"Primo Gong?"

"I had no part in his death, Ms. Xu – and that is the simple and honest truth. I have never met him. He was neither friend nor enemy. But, from all I had heard of him, even though he was the Shanghai Clique's creature, I respected him. It took courage to give up his American citizenship. It took courage to devote himself to the future of Chengdu. I shall mourn his passing."

"And Stacey Corrigan?"

"A lovely woman – what else is there to tell?"

"She has visited this house almost every evening this last week. It is understood she is working on a story about Ambrogetti Global Software."

Ye Zihao had no time to respond. Day Na came running into the study, no tray of tea in his hands, his eyes alight with excitement.

"Fortress! Fortress!" Day Na exclaimed. "Boss, you must get downstairs...you too, Prosecutor!"

"What is happening?" asked Ye Zihao. "My son...."

"We are in communication with him, Boss – please, there is no time to lose," replied Day Na, before disappearing back the way he had come.

Ye Zihao did not hesitate. His pipe still in his mouth, he came out from behind his desk, took Xu Ya by the hand, dragged her out of her seat, his strength impressive, impossible to resist, forcing her to leave her handbag behind her. He pulled her out of his study, made a sharp turn to the left, along a short corridor to a flight of narrow stairs leading downwards into darkness. He let go of her hand but she followed him down the steps nevertheless, almost losing a heel in the process, a light at the bottom flickering on automatically, revealing a large, metal door. Ye Zihao tapped a code into a keypad at the side of the door – Xu Ya memorised the numbers – and the door slid open, revealing a well-lit room measuring about four metres by four metres, devoid of any furniture except for a padded bench than ran around the walls. Xu Ya recognised it to be a panic room, having seen one before in a film. At the rear of the room was another door, but leading where she could not guess. Ye Zihao pulled her inside and was about to punch another code into a keypad within the room when Night Na appeared with a struggling teenage girl in his arms, Du Yue saying to herself, over and over again, "Be brave, Jenny Du! Be brave, Jenny Du!"

Night Na gently dropped the girl to her feet. Seeing what was needed, Xu Ya took Du Yue's hand and pulled her down to sit beside her onto the padded bench against the left side of the room, whispering urgently to her not to worry, that no harm was going to come to any of them even though Xu Ya had herself no clue as to who or what it was that threatened them. Ye Zihao then punched a code into the inner keypad and the door slid back in place, trapping them within, Xu Ya last view of the outside being a grim-looking Night Na, running back up the stairs, a pistol now in his hand.

Ye Zihao took a seat opposite them. Xu Ya put an arm about the shoulders of the whimpering Du Yue, no longer the enigmatic girl of the evening before, just a sensitive teenager scared out of her wits.

"Mayor Ye, what is happening?" Xu Ya asked.

Ye Zihao shook his head. "Truly, I do not know, Ms. Xu."

"You are afraid?"

"Only for my son – I do not know where he is or what he is about this morning."

"Afraid for Superintendent Ye?"

"Always, Ms. Xu, and I beg you never to tell him. Every morning I pray for his continued safety. When I took him away from England as a baby, when I separated him from his mother, all she asked of me is that I keep him safe. Heaven knows I have tried, Ms. Xu. But contrary to my wishes, contrary to all good sense, he chose to become police. He desired to look into the darkness, to contemplate the many ways of death, rather than the art of being alive. It has been difficult for me – so difficult."

It was then that Xu Ya had the revelation of her life. She could ignore Stacey Corrigan. The American journalist was nothing more than a blind alley. She had just seen what perhaps few others, if any, had seen. Ye Zihao's only weakness, the one true chink in his armour, was his son, Philip Ye. Now all she had to do was figure out what to do with such secret knowledge.

FORTY-TWO

F atty Deng woke just after five, sweating profusely, his bedroom a veritable furnace. Sometime in the night the air-conditioning unit, poor as it always had been, had stopped working. He ran the shower cold to wake himself up properly, turned on the TV to watch the news, to check no boat had gone down on the Yangzi during the continuing summer storms – none had done so, so he would call his mother later – and then dressed quickly, in no mood for breakfast. He opted for another Hawaiian shirt, more conservative this time – dark blue, with a simple display of coconut palms – which he let hang over his trouser belt to conceal his pistol. He lit a cigarette as he stepped out of the apartment block, not forgetting to check up and down the street for anything untoward, and then slid into his car, glad the weather forecast for the morning was fine, not wanting anything, including inclement weather, to mess up the snatch and grab. He drove the short distance to Brother Wang's apartment. He found the brothers Ming already there, sitting outside the apartment door on the bare concrete staircase, looking bored.

"Did you get the van?" he asked them.

They jumped to their feet, all nodding in unison.

"And did you find a safe place to stash our target?"

They all nodded again.

"Good – now why aren't you all inside with Brother Wang?"

"His woman said he was still in bed," said one of the brothers. "She wouldn't let us in. She said we would wake the baby."

Fatty Deng checked his watch. It was almost six. They had to get a move on if they were to cross the city and get into place.

He thumped the door.

No reply.

He thumped it harder.

Again, nothing.

He didn't have time for this.

He put his shoulder to the door. Wood splintered and the lock gave way. Brother Wang's woman came running out of the kitchen, wailing baby in her arms, screaming foul abuse. Fatty Deng ignored her, went into the bedroom and found Brother Wang lying naked face down on the bed, snoring loudly. Fatty Deng picked up one side of the mattress and rolled Brother Wang onto the floor.

"Fatty, what the fuck!"

"You've got five minutes to get ready or we're leaving you behind and you don't get paid."

Fatty Deng ignored Brother Wang's foul-mouthed woman and her wailing baby again and walked out of the apartment. He led the brothers Ming down the stairs. They would wait out on the street by the vehicles. The brothers Ming proudly showed off the beaten-up old Daihatsu van they had found somewhere. He smiled at the fake plates. He was beginning to like the brothers Ming. He offered cigarettes all round. Fortunately, they did not have long to wait. Brother Wang soon came shambling out of his apartment block, tucking his shirt into his trousers, wearing his trademark black suit and tie.

"Fatty, you broke my fucking door!" he said, when he reached them.

"You'll be able to buy a new one when we finish the job," replied Fatty Deng, not caring.

He handed out the radios and their respective earpieces. He then quickly laid out the only plan he had. He would park up on Peaceful Street some distance from Superintendent Si Ying's apartment block so he would not be spotted and recognised by her. He described her to them again and told them she would be driving a blue Toyota. He had spotted her park the Toyota near to the Black House the evening before. He told them her plate number. He doubted she would have changed cars for any reason during the night. However, he would only give the go-ahead for the operation when he spotted the blue Toyota approaching her apartment block and confirmed it was Superintendent Si Ying at the wheel and she was alone in the car.

Three of the brothers Ming would be out on the street, blending in with the environment, ready to converge on Superintendent Si Ying when she got out of her car and before she got inside the relative safety of her apartment block. The other brother Ming would be in the van, driving around and around the local area with Brother Wang, looking for anything untoward, ready to pull up parallel to the blue Toyota when Fatty Deng gave the go ahead. It would be up to Brother Wang to give the final confirmation that all was as it should be to make the snatch and grab. Once the van had come to a halt, Brother Wang would jump out to supervise and act as look out, the three brothers Ming would subdue Superintendent Si Ying as best they could – no broken bones but a few slaps would not be amiss – before she was bundled into the van, with the brothers Ming jumping in after her to head off back to Wukuaishi. Fatty Deng would then pick up Brother Wang and follow on.

"Any questions?" asked Fatty Deng.

There were none.

He asked them if they wanted to use masks.

"There's no working CCTV nearby and we won't ever be going back there again, so what's the fucking point?" said Brother Wang.

The brothers Ming nodded in agreement.

The plan set, the brothers Ming took off first in their van. Brother Wang elected to ride across the city with Fatty Deng. Fatty Deng's car, the engine now warm, again refused to catch first time.

"The brothers Ming could get you another cheap motor," said Brother Wang, shaking his head.

"I work for the Procuratorate."

"So?"

"I can't drive a stolen car."

"Are you earning so much you can be that fussy?"

"That's not the point."

"Suit yourself."

They could have done with a dress rehearsal. They could have done with following Superintendent Si Ying for a couple of days, weeks even, getting to know all her movements, getting a feel for the local area in which she lived, looking for anything and everything that could go wrong. They could also have done with another man sitting outside the Black House to radio ahead and tell them when her shift was done. They could have done with driving all the roads around her apartment block way ahead of time, mapping the various routes out of her housing estate so they could avoid any instances of local flooding and have alternative escape routes prepared in case of unexpected traffic jams or unforeseen hazards. They could also have done with a lot more background on her, specific intelligence on how good her fighting skills actually were, where her baby might be when she was at work, who was looking after it and so on. But time was pressing. Answers were needed from her and quickly. She was worth a risk or two.

By a quarter to eight they were all in position. Fatty Deng had found a convenient and unobtrusive spot about thirty metres or so from the entrance to Superintendent Si Ying's apartment block and Brother Wang had transferred over to the van to begin circuits of the local roads. Three of the Ming brothers were now on the street, split into one and a pair, the one standing on a nearby street corner pretending to have some in-depth discussion on his phone – or at least Fatty Deng assumed he was pretending – while the other two had visited a local shop, bought themselves a sports magazine and were now standing outside the shop arguing about its content, an argument so voluble as to attract a couple of local men out and about who were only too happy to join in. The brothers Ming were naturals, Fatty Deng had to admit. It was just another Sunday morning in Chengdu. If all went well, if he was still in a job after this investigation and after Prosecutor Xu had flown away to explore new horizons, he might just use them again.

He cracked open a window and lit another cigarette, trying to relax, trying to tell himself that everything would work out just fine. As he smoked, his thoughts drifted again to Sun Mei, what a good person she was, how much she would disapprove of what was about to go down, how much she would disapprove of the many other bad things he had done in his life, especially those dubious jobs he had been forced to take after being thrown out of the police just to earn a crust.

He grew angry.

He had never pretended to anyone that he was a saint.

He had never pretended to be anything at all.

If Sun Mei hated him and feared him, that was fair enough.

He had a job to do and that was that.

A kid on a bicycle passed him by, looking in on him, checking out the Hawaiian shirt. Fatty Deng ignored him, not wanting to draw any further attention to himself, catching sight of the van containing Brother Wang and the other brother Ming about to pass him, to make another circuit of the local roads.

Fatty Deng checked his watch.

Ten after eight.

Showtime soon.

Prosecutor Xu would be inside the Ye family mansion by now.

Sun Mei would be serving her first customers of the day.

The inquisitive kid on the bicycle returned, stopping next to Fatty Deng's car, staring in again at the shirt. Fatty Deng ignored him and tossed his cigarette butt out of the window. He looked around again and the kid was gone. He then spotted the blue Toyota turning into Peaceful Street.

She was a few minutes earlier than expected.

Better that than late though.

"Stand-by! Stand-by!" he said into his radio.

He glanced around, satisfied the kid on the bicycle was now nowhere to be seen. The lone Ming brother finished his conversation on his phone and began walking toward the entrance to the apartment block. The other two, laughing and joking now, separated themselves from the small group of local men who had gathered about them to argue sports and approached the entrance from the other side. Superintendent Si Ying, alone in her car – thank the gods! – parked up right outside the entrance.

She had a reserved space.

How the fuck had she managed that?

More corruption!

The brothers Ming were closing in on her, pretending to be just out for a stroll, enjoying the rare bit of sun. Fatty Deng twisted his neck around. Where was the van? Where the fuck was Brother Wang?

He was about to panic, about to call the whole operation off, when the van suddenly appeared in his side mirror speeding along the road. There was nothing he could do now. The operation was out of his hands. This was it.

Superintendent Si Ying jumped out of her car, unaware, lost in her thoughts, secure in her familiar surroundings.

Just because you're police doesn't mean you're untouchable, you murdering bitch, thought Fatty Deng.

He heard Brother Wang over the radio.

"Go! Go! Go!"

The van screeched to a halt parallel to the blue Toyota. Brother Wang opened the sliding door on the side of the van and jumped out. Superintendent Si Ying became aware of the threat far too late. The three brothers Ming were on her. To give Superintendent Si Ying her due she fought like a tigress. But the brothers Ming turned out to be quick and strong and mean, not that it didn't take an extra bit of muscle provided by Brother Wang to finally throw her into the van. Unfortunately, as the brothers Ming jumped in after her, Fatty Deng heard, even from within his car, Superintendent Si Ying utter an ear-piercing scream. Then Brother Wang slid the door shut and the van was on its way.

Fatty Deng could not believe it.

The plan had worked like a dream.

He was elated.

Brother Wang, standing in the middle of the street, having gathered up the handbag Superintendent Si Ying had dropped during the scuffle, turned to him and gave him the thumbs-up, grinning broadly, uncaring about the few local people out on the street who were trying to figure out what was going on. Fatty grinned back at him. Then Fatty Deng heard a sharp crack! He watched, stunned, as Brother Wang went down as if hit by a sledgehammer, clutching at his head, blood pouring through his fingers, to lie still in the middle of the road.

Fatty Deng glanced up at Superintendent Si Ying's apartment block. A half-dressed man was leaning out of a window on the fourth floor, a pistol in his hand. Fatty Deng recognised him. It was Superintendent Si Ying's army cousin, the arrogant bastard who had laughed at his shirt the evening before in the Lucky Dragon Tobacco Emporium. The man vanished back inside the apartment and Fatty Deng stared, unable to move, at Brother Wang's body lying in the road.

What had he done?

He had just got his friend killed.

FORTY-THREE

— · —

The money left in payment by Investigator Deng of the Cheng-du People's Procuratorate not only for his own cigarettes but also for those stolen by Superintendent Si Ying's army cousin had burned red-hot in Sun Mei's hand. She did not know why but she could not stop crying. Not only the boy Hong, but the other children as well, had gathered about her, all concerned, wanting to know what was wrong, whether she was taken ill like Little Xiulan. Unable to explain the vortex of emotions whirling around within her, not even able to understand them herself, she had told the children she did indeed feel under the weather, that it might be best for her to ring all their parents to come collect them early, which she did.

Naughty boy Hong was the last to go. "We all love you, Teacher Sun," he had told her, hugging her tight, before running out of the shop to join his waiting parents.

She went to the bathroom to wash her face and dry her eyes. She knew she had to pull herself together. She had promised to look in on Little Xiulan.

"I am going out for a short while," she told her idiot father.

"Daughter, I did what I thought was right."

"You have made informants of us both."

"I told Investigator Deng the truth."

"You have doomed us."

"If so, then at least I will be able to hold my head up high in the afterlife. I will be able to greet your mother as the proud and honourable man I used to be when I was a soldier."

Sun Mei shook her head, turned her back on him, and went to phone Mister Wu. He was only too willing to man the shop counter for her while she went out for half an hour or so. She put on a light jacket though the rain was tailing off and walked the short distance to Little Xiulan's home. The parents let her in, as deferential and as clueless as ever.

"We did not know what to do," they said.

Sun Mei knelt by Little Xiulan's bed and smiled at her reassuringly. Little Xiulan complained of a bad throat and how it was painful to talk. Sun Mei put her hand on the girl's forehead and found it far too hot. The girl was burning up with fever. Not a little frightened, and furious with the parents for doing nothing all day, Sun Mei immediately phoned Doctor He Bo.

Doctor He Bo had only last year opened up a practice at the far end of Liberation Street. Not much was known about him except that he had once worked very long hours in a hospital until he had cracked under the pressure and ended up in some mental institution. Somehow he had not lost his licence to practice medicine and somehow he had got his wits back together to open up a practice all by himself. Sun Mei had thought that Doctor He's nervous breakdown did not bode well for the future. But the overwhelming majority of the Liberation Street Traders Association voted to welcome him with open arms in the belief that a local doctor was such a rarity that a doctor with a damaged mind was better than no doctor at all. Since that time, Sun Mei had been overjoyed to have been proved wrong. Doctor He – a married man in his late forties with a lovely wife and a daughter already at Chengdu Medical College – had quickly shown himself to be both skilled and compassionate, happy to make house-calls even in the middle of the night, and displaying no obvious signs of mental disturbance or incapacity at all.

Within half an hour of her call, Doctor He was taking Little Xiulan's temperature and examining her throat. His diagnosis, to Sun Mei's great relief, was a simple throat infection brought on by the recent heat and humidity. A short course of antibiotics would sort it out. The equally relieved parents pushed the cash that Sun Mei had given them earlier – they promised to pay her back as soon as they could – into Doctor He's hands.

Back on the street, after offering to walk her back to the Lucky Dragon Tobacco Emporium – an offer she had politely declined – Doctor He asked Sun Mei if she was feeling alright.

"I am just tired," she said.

"You carry too much on your young shoulders, Ms. Sun."

"If not me, who?"

Doctor He smiled, nodded, and bade her good evening. When she got back to the shop, and saw all was well under Mister Wu's temporary management, Sun Mei could not help but burst into tears in front of him.

"Tell me the little girl is not dead?" said Mister Wu.

"Oh no, Mister Wu, forgive me – Little Xiulan has nothing more than a throat infection. I do not know what has come over me. I am not myself at the moment."

"Is the fat man playing on your nerves?"

"Yes, a little."

"Sun Mei, you must never forget that the Liberation Street Traders Association will always have your back."

She wiped her tears away. "That is good to know."

"You must also maintain some perspective. If you are to worry about anything at all, it should be the bad weather. If the drains fail, as surely one day soon they must, then Liberation Street will be flooded and we shall all be washed away. What use would it have been then to have spent all your time worrying about the fat man?"

"Of course, Mister Wu," she replied, warmed by his attempt to cheer her.

"You are the rarest flower, Sun Mei."

"You are too nice, Mister Wu."

Sun Mei locked up after Mister Wu had left, wishing she could have been braver, that she could have told him all that her father had done, about how her father had spoken to Investigator Deng about the three rifle shots, about how there was, in all likelihood, a war raging between the police and the Procuratorate, about how she and her father had become informants, and were, in all likelihood, doomed.

Before she closed the window blinds, she stared up at the Black House, cursing it under her breath. Lights burned in a few of its windows. She had always hated the building. It had cast a shadow, in more ways than one, over Liberation Street for far too many years. Not a single crack had appeared in its walls during the big earthquake a few years back, much to everyone's disappointment.

She checked on her father. He was watching TV. Unable to stomach anything herself, she prepared him a light snack, refused to enter into any conversation with him, and took herself off to bed.

She did not think she would sleep but she did. She dreamed she was standing behind the counter serving her customers as usual but dressed, quite incredibly, in the same ridiculous shirt Investigator Deng had worn. She awoke in the middle of the night, slick with sweat, puzzled by the dream.

She went to check on her father. The TV was still on but he was now fast asleep. She turned the TV off and cleared away the remains of his late-night snack. She then went into the bathroom to throw cold water on her face and towel herself down. After, she went from room to room, checking all was as it should be, before ending up at the shop door and peering out through the blinds at the Black House. Three in the morning and lights still burned within. She wondered what had happened in the Black House on Friday night, why someone had fired three shots at Plum Tree Pagodas – she had come to the conclusion that this must have been what had happened – and who, in Plum Tree Pagodas, had died as a result.

After checking the lock to the shop door, Sun Mei returned to her bed and began to think more about Investigator Deng.

Was he married?

There had been no ring on his finger.

Perhaps he had a girlfriend.

She wondered what it would be like to date a hero – if that, indeed, was what Investigator Deng was. Not much fun, she concluded. With his kind and sad eyes, Investigator Deng had been all business – not many laughs to be had there. Her old boyfriend, who had dumped her on the advice of his parents, had always made her laugh. Not only had he been slim, fit, and handsome, ten thousand jokes would roll of his tongue in the space of an hour. Sun Mei smiled at the memory, and then felt, for what had to be the millionth time, the pain of his eventual betrayal of her. According to Mister Wu, who knew more than most, her old boyfriend was now dating some fancy floozy who worked at an advertising agency while he, as had always been his ambition, was employed by some up-and-coming tech company and was now making a bundle of money.

Sun Mei sighed and tried to go back to sleep. But no further sleep would come. Well before dawn she got out of bed and busied herself cleaning the living-quarters and the shop from top to bottom. Then she stared at her reflection in the bathroom mirror. A few years before, she had thought herself very pretty. Now she looked older than her years and definitely unwell. For once she put on some make-up, wanting to put some colour into her face and take away the worst of the shadows from underneath her eyes. Then she woke her father, put on his TV, took him his breakfast – all without speaking to him – and then opened up the shop. She stepped out onto the street and looked up at the sky, seeing none of the overcast of the day before, but high wispy clouds – nothing more than a haze – covering the rising sun.

Back inside, her phone rang.

It was Mister Wu, enquiring after her emotional wellbeing. She apologised to him for her display of the evening before. Good man that he was, he made no comment, wanting to save her from further embarrassment. He reminded her about the storms forecast for the afternoon.

"It will be quite an onslaught," said Mister Wu.

"We must hope for the best," she told him, her mind far from the drains.

Sun Mei served customers for the next hour, ever on the look-out for the return of Investigator Deng. But there was no sign of him. Feeling slightly better, Sun Mei managed to keep some fruit and a cup of green tea in her stomach. She was almost back to her old self again until, just after eight, a strange man appeared at the window, frightening her out of her wits.

It was not his appearance. He looked a decent, ordinary man – not a criminal, or ruffian, or undercover policeman at all. It was that he was paying no heed to the cigarettes on display. More like he was using the shop window as a mirror to see what was going on up and down the street.

Sun Mei's stomach began to tighten.

Her breathing began to come in gasps.

Her legs would not move.

This was it.

She was sure.

Her doom was upon her.

She did not know how, or why, but it was surely here.

Soon the strange man was joined by the biggest woman Sun Mei had ever seen, taller than most men, stronger-looking too, her hands as big as shovels. And from just behind the big woman appeared the most handsome man who had ever lived in Chengdu, dressed in a beautiful three-piece suit that must have cost a small fortune and covered with a long, stylish raincoat despite the heat, a man she knew only too well, a man whose face had once appeared in a thousand magazines, a man her mother had once confessed to being in love with, a man about whom her mother had boasted of once selling pipe tobacco to, a man with eyes of the greenest jade.

Her phone rang.

She picked up the phone without looking. "Yes, Mister Wu."

"That is Philip Ye."

"I know, Mister Wu."

"He is standing right outside your shop."

"That is true, Mister Wu."

"Should I tell him about our bad drains?"

"It might not be the appropriate time."

"It could be an opportunity missed."

"It might," she agreed.

Thankfully, before Mister Wu could come to a decision and come running out of his shop, Philip Ye, the big woman, and the man who had been using her window as a mirror, all moved away as a group and turned the corner into the narrow alley that ran down the side of her shop.

"What do you think is going on?" asked Mister Wu.

"I do not know," she replied.

"I will keep watch," said Mister Wu.

"Thank you," said Sun Mei, scared out of her wits.

Philip Ye was police.

Investigator Deng was Procuratorate.

If there was a war between the police and the Procuratorate, if Investigator Deng returned this moment, then surely the two of them would come to blows, or, even worse, a shoot-out on Liberation Street might ensue.

Sun Mei felt faint.

She put her hands down on the counter to steady herself.

Terrified as she had been of him – and she still was – she would not want any harm to come to Investigator Deng.

Not to Philip Ye either.

But certainly not to Investigator Deng.

Though not humorous at all, and not as handsome as her old boyfriend, Investigator Deng had kind, sad eyes. And he had paid for his cigarettes, and for those cigarettes stolen by Superintendent Si Ying's horrible cousin.

Sun Mei closed her eyes.

She prayed for all she was worth.

Then her heart almost stopped as she heard the screech of tyres from out on the street and opened her eyes just in time to see an old wreck of a car mount the pavement outside the Lucky Dragon Tobacco Emporium and come to a grinding stop just before it smashed into the window.

"Aiya!" she cried, believing her end had come, that both she and her father were about to be dragged away, never to be seen again.

FORTY-FOUR

—.—

Time stood still for Fatty Deng.

He had killed his friend.

One simple miscalculation and Brother Wang was dead.

It was not as if he had ever forgotten about Superintendent Si Ying's army cousin, the man who had insulted him over his shirt, who had then stolen cigarettes from Sun Mei. In his mind he even had the cousin pegged as one of the rogue army team that had, for whatever reason, murdered Primo Gong. But it had never occurred to him that the cousin would have been staying with Superintendent Si Ying, that he would have returned to her apartment after going drinking with his army buddies. And it had never occurred to him that, upon hearing Superintendent Si Ying's scream for help, the cousin would be crazy enough to lean out of the window and start shooting.

What had he done?

What the fuck had he done?

If he had had his wits about him the evening before, instead of speaking with Sun Mei and her father, he should have tailed the cousin to wherever it was he was going to meet his army buddies and surreptitiously taken photographs of them. He should have stuck with them all evening instead of consoling Prosecutor Xu at her apartment after her argument with Philip Ye. After the soldiers were done with their drinking, he should have followed the cousin back to wherever he was lodging – Superintendent Si Ying's apartment.

That's what he should have done.

But he had let himself get side-tracked. He had been fascinated with Sun Mei, with the story she might have to tell, with gathering evidence enough to impress Prosecutor Xu, instead of listening to his gut.

And now Brother Wang was dead.

He turned the key in the ignition.

Nothing.

"No!" he raged at his car, thumping his fists against the steering wheel, furious with himself for turning the engine off when he knew damn well his car had a problem with hot starts.

He turned the key.

Nothing.

"For fuck's sake, start!"

He turned the key again and this time the engine caught. He released the handbrake, put his foot down, and the car shot forward, covering the thirty metres or so to Brother Wang's body in – for his car at least – record time. Fatty Deng jumped out, fearful that Superintendent Si Ying's cousin was almost certainly running down the stairs of the apartment block at that moment, pistol in hand, to discover just who it was he had shot. Fatty Deng knelt down beside Brother Wang's body. Fatty Deng rolled him over and – miracle of miracles – Brother Wang groaned, and pressed a hand tight against the side of his bloodied head.

"Fatty, they've killed me," he said.

So relieved Brother Wang was still alive, Fatty Deng could think of no sensible reply. It took all of his strength, and much cursing, to get Brother Wang off the ground and onto the back seat of his car. Just as he did so, Superintendent Si Ying's cousin burst out of the apartment block, pistol in hand.

They exchanged a brief glance, just long enough for the cousin's face to contort with anger and shock at the recognition of him, and Fatty Deng was back in the car, slamming the door, foot down to the floor, leaving a trail of rubber along the street as he accelerated away.

It was not fast enough, though.

More shots rang out.

Brother Wang screamed as the back windscreen shattered. Fatty Deng bent as low as he could over the steering wheel as another bullet whizzed past his head and out through the front windscreen, crazing the glass, blinding him. Fatty Deng put his fist through the windscreen so he could see, then yanked the steering wheel hard to the left to skid around the corner. His last view of the cousin was of him standing in the middle of the street, pistol down at his side, phone to his ear.

Relieved, Fatty Deng headed towards the city centre, reaching for a cigarette as he did so, his hands trembling. He wanted to be back in Wukuaishi as soon as he could to give Superintendent Si Ying the third degree. But first he had to figure out what to do with Brother Wang. As soon as he felt safe enough from foot pursuit, he pulled the car over, leaving the engine running this time, and twisted around in his seat to check on Brother Wang.

There was blood everywhere, down the whole right side of Brother Wang's face, streaking down his neck, staining crimson his white shirt under his black jacket. Fatty Deng needed to see the wound, though. Brother Wang screamed as Fatty Deng pulled his hand away from his head. Blood matted Brother Wang's hair but there was no pulsing of blood from the wound, no arterial flow. From what Fatty Deng could see, the bullet had merely creased the side of Brother Wang's skull and taken away most of his right ear. The wound was ugly, and surely very painful, but Brother Wang had to be one of the luckiest men alive.

"Fatty, I'm dying," said Brother Wang.

"No, you're not," replied Fatty Deng, sticking a lit cigarette in Brother Wang's mouth.

"Since when have you been a doctor?"

"You're going to live."

"But I've been shot through the fucking head."

"And the bullet has somehow missed your tiny brain. Now stop moaning. As soon as I get you back to Wukuaishi I'll find the cheapest doctor in the area to stick a bandage on you."

"Promise me, Fatty, you'll take care of the baby."

"I'm not even sure it's yours."

"Promise me, Fatty."

"I promise – but the baby only, not that crazy woman of yours."

Fatty Deng started the car moving again, but slowly, fearful that they might attract the attention of any watchful traffic police, and be forced to explain the shattered windscreens and the bleeding Brother Wang. He was just as concerned about Prosecutor Xu. He was supposed to be on his way to the Ye family mansion.

"It hurts, Fatty – all my brains are leaking out," moaned Brother Wang.

Fatty Deng ignored him, trying to concentrate on his driving, wondering how far ahead of him the Ming brothers were with his costly prize. His mind strayed back to the look of recognition he had exchanged with Superintendent Si Ying's cousin, wishing he had had the good sense to have asked to be properly introduced the evening before, to at least get his name and his PLA unit. He wondered who the cousin had been speaking to on the phone. Maybe his army buddies supposedly on leave with him, the rest of the rogue army team.

Fatty Deng slammed on the brakes, throwing a whimpering Brother Wang about on the back seat, and almost causing the car behind to rear-end him. He was blocking the road. It sounded like a hundred car horns were being sounded at him at once.

The cousin had recognised him.

The cousin would remember where they had met.

The cousin would assume he was a regular customer of the Lucky Dragon Tobacco Emporium. The cousin would suspect that Sun Mei might not only know his name but also where he lived. If he were the cousin, he would return to the Lucky Dragon Tobacco Emporium and rough Sun Mei up a little, or maybe rough her up a lot, and try to discover where the kidnapped Superintendent Si Ying might have been taken – or at least phone his army buddies and tell them to do it for him.

Oh no!

Sun Mei had pleaded with him. Sun Mei had wanted no trouble. Sun Mei hadn't wanted to get involved.

"I'm dying," groaned Brother Wang.

Sun Mei.

If anything happened to her, Fatty Deng knew he would never be able to forgive himself, not even if he lived for a million years.

He spun the car around, the tires screeching, waving his procuratorate badge out of the window at all the protesting drivers. He put his foot down again.

Ten minutes to Liberation Street.

Maybe less if his little old car could manage it.

Was it enough time?

It had to be.

FORTY-FIVE

— · —

The only thought to cross Sun Mei's mind when she saw Investigator Deng jump out of the old car that had nearly crashed through her shop window – apart from that his shirt today was of a far more conservative and therefore more attractive design than the shirt he wore the evening before – was to come running out from behind the counter and to lock the door and draw the blinds. It was only a thought though. Her feet would not budge.

"Ms. Sun, there is no time to waste," said Investigator Deng, breathlessly, after he burst through the door. "You and your father are in great danger. You must both come with me."

She saw real concern in his eyes. But it was the blood that stained his shirt, his hands too, that really grabbed her attention. She feared he had been hurt even if he did not seem to be in any pain. And if it wasn't his blood, whose was it?

"Ms. Sun, are you hearing me?"

"Please leave me alone," she said, meekly.

"Ms. Sun!"

"I cannot abandon my father. I cannot abandon my shop. And I could never abandon the children. The war between the police and the Procuratorate is nothing to do with me."

Investigator Deng stared at her for a moment as if she had gone mad. Then he leaned forward to try to grab her hands, to pull her out from behind the counter. At last, her feet came to life. She stepped backwards and away from his flailing grasp, while vigorously shaking her head, needing him to fully understand that she wanted nothing to do with him, that she had no time for heroes or for anyone else who would separate her from the little she had.

Investigator Deng mouthed something under his breath about difficult women and then he was gone, into the back of the shop, only to return a few moments later carrying her father in his arms.

"Daughter...follow us...we must run!" her father shouted at her as Investigator Deng carried him out through the shop and onto the street, to deposit him in the back of the old car.

Her phone rang.

That would be Mister Wu, wanting to know what was going on. She let it ring.

Investigator Deng returned, looking pale and exhausted from the effort of carrying her father. He held his bloodied hands out to her again, imploring her to go with him.

"I cannot," she said.

"Ms. Sun, you must."

"I am afraid."

"I will take you to a place of safety."

"There is no such place."

"Ms. Sun, I beg you."

"No!"

"Ms. Sun, if something happened to you I would never forgive myself."

Sun Mei thought then of her old boyfriend, how in such an emotionally charged situation he would have made some wisecrack, making her laugh, making her fear seem silly. But Investigator Deng did not do that. He slowly joined her behind the counter. There was no place for Sun Mei to go. She put her hands up to her face but he gently took her hands in his, making her look at him, smiling at her reassuringly, his eyes as she remembered them from the evening before, both kind and sad.

"I will not leave you behind," he said.

"You must," she whispered.

He said nothing more. Keeping hold of her hands, he walked backwards, and she found, to her consternation, that her feet kept pace with his, that somehow those eyes of his had hypnotised her, her body no longer her own. Then she was out from behind the counter and with his strong arm around her waist both guiding and supporting her – did he fear she might faint? – he walked her out of the shop.

She was vaguely aware of Mister Wu watching her from the doorway of his shop, of other people on the street also, who had stopped to stare, and of someone on the back seat of the old car sitting next to her father, holding his head in his hands. But mostly she was aware of Investigator Deng, the physical strength that emanated from him, the determination too – like no man she had ever met before, except perhaps her father, when she had been a very small child, when he had been home on leave from his unit, before the accident that had taken away his ability to walk.

Never feeling more useless or self-conscious in all her life, Sun Mei allowed Investigator Deng to walk her around the back of the car with the intention of placing her on the front passenger seat. She did not know what to make of the damage to the car, the shattered windscreens, back and front. Investigator Deng opened the passenger door for her and she was about to take a seat, her body wholly under his control, when a man wearing a plastic wolf mask to hide his face came from nowhere and slammed his body into Investigator Deng, tearing him away from her and knocking him to the ground. The stranger placed a knee hard onto Investigator Deng's chest, winding him, and stuck an evil-looking pistol into his face.

"Where is she? Where is she?" screamed the young, fit, and very strong-looking stranger at Investigator Deng.

Investigator Deng, fighting for breath, could only issue a hissed profanity.

The stranger took his pistol and brought the butt sharply across Investigator Deng's face. Sun Mei heard the crack of metal against bone, felt the pain Investigator Deng must have felt, and then did something extraordinary. Without thinking, she threw herself on the stranger's back, ripping the wolf mask off him, trying to drag him off Investigator Deng, screaming profanities herself that arose up from deep within her, from where she knew not.

It was a futile gesture, however.

She was not very strong and she was certainly no fighter. The stranger easily shrugged her off and then she had trouble of her own, for another stranger had appeared, breathing as if he had been running hard, just as young and strong as the other, also wearing a wolf mask. He picked her up from the ground by her neck and placed the business end of a pistol against her temple.

I am to die today, thought Sun Mei.

I am to join my mother in the afterlife today.

"Tell us where Si Ying is, or your girlfriend will die right this instant," raged the first stranger at Investigator Deng, still kneeling on his chest.

Sun Mei averted her eyes, struggling to breathe, the grip of the second stranger's hand tight around her neck. This was all her fault. If she had only run when Investigator Deng had first asked her. Feeling the pressure of the cold metal of the pistol against the side of her head, the imminence of her death upon her, Sun Mei looked up at the sky. The sun was burning quickly through the haze, no sign yet of the afternoon storms to come. It was going to be a hot day – a real furnace. She felt herself disconnect from her body. She floated high and above Liberation Street, a free spirit, able now to look impersonally down on the scene of violence below, the one stranger kneeling upon Investigator Deng, beating and shouting at him, the other holding her up by the neck like a ragdoll. Feeling nothing but a curious sense of peace, Sun Mei thought being a ghost was not so bad, the worries she had had about who was going to take care of the children, her father, and the shop, strangely distant. It meant little to her when she saw Mister Wu standing in the doorway of his shop with his head in his hands, or the screams of some of the passers-by, many of them known to her from when she was a little girl. And when she saw the big woman come running around the corner from the alley, pistol in hand, with Old Man Shao's yapping mutt of a dog at her heels, Sun Mei was more curious than disturbed.

And then Sun Mei was slammed painfully back into her body. She fell to her knees retching, her ears ringing from the sharp crack of a pistol fired far too close to her, the acrid smell of gunpowder filling her nostrils, her head spinning. She tried to push away Old Man Shao's flea-bitten dog as it began to lick her face. Then she changed her mind, holding the dog close, finding comfort in its unconditional affection.

Sun Mei opened her eyes and saw the big woman standing over Investigator Deng, smoking pistol in one massive hand, the other offered up to help him off the ground.

"You okay, Fatty?" the big woman asked.

"Sister, I owe you," he replied, getting to his feet.

On her knees still, Old Man Shao's dog now sitting by her side – she was going to have to give Old Man Shao a piece of his mind for letting his dog run free again – Sun Mei's attention was drawn to the two strangers, now both on their backs, their wolf masks at their sides, their eyes open and unseeing, pools of blood forming beneath them, blood that soon trickled over the kerb and toward the already full drains.

Sun Mei struggled to her feet, using the old car as a prop. She heard her father shouting from within, asking if she was alright. But she ignored him, not knowing whether she was alright or not. The impossibly handsome Philip Ye appeared, not at war with Investigator Deng but to speak rapidly to him as if they were friends, and then to speak just as rapidly into his phone. Lost in some kind of terrible dream, Sun Mei paid no attention to what was being said, her eyes being drawn back to the bodies of the two men, the two strangers that the big woman had ruthlessly shot down. They looked so young. For some reason Sun Mei felt guilty. She wondered what their names had been, where they were from – their accents had not been local – and what their families would say, how they would react, when they learned of their deaths.

Old Man Shao's dog suddenly ran off to play with the big woman. Sun Mei saw she was good with animals. The big woman showered the dog with plenty of love and attention but betrayed no obvious emotion from just having killed two men. Sun Mei could not understand this. How could someone be so violent one moment and yet so playful, so gentle, the next?

Investigator Deng appeared before Sun Mei, his face bloodied, bruised, and swollen, his right eye almost closed shut. She wanted to say how sorry she was, how her hesitation back in the shop had caused him this hurt. But he showed no anger toward her, only kindness, helping her into the passenger seat of the car and closing the door after her.

"Are you alright, Daughter?" asked her father.

"Yes," she said, not turning to face him, ashamed for being the cause of so much trouble. Nor did she want a closer look at the man in the black suit and tie sitting next to her father, busy moaning to himself. Even without the blood running down his face and neck, he looked a disreputable sort.

Investigator Deng got into the car. He helped her with her seat belt. He did not speak, which she was glad about. He started the engine after a couple of turns of the key in the ignition and a few curse words muttered under his breath. As the car moved off, the big woman with the dog at her side clearing a way for them through the crowd, the last sight Sun Mei had of Liberation Street was of Mister Wu sidling up to an unsuspecting Philip Ye.

Oh no, thought Sun Mei.

Surely this was not a good time.

Why couldn't Mister Wu just forget about the drains for once?

FORTY-SIX

A few days after, Philip Ye had the opportunity to sit down with the SWAT commander, Commissioner Zhu Shouqing, and review all the available footage of the Battle of Liberation Street as it was now being called. Commander Zhu was intent on renewing his pleas for the immediate transfer of Constable Ma to his team.

Too slow to catch up with Constable Ma – for a woman of her considerable size she was remarkably fleet of foot – Philip Ye had arrived on Liberation Street too late to witness the short exchange of gunfire. Instead, his heart had skipped a beat when he had seen the two young men with buzz-cut hairstyles lying bleeding out on the street, mistakenly assuming Constable Ma had stumbled into some kind of undercover police operation and shot dead two of their own. Only when he had witnessed Constable Ma offering a hand to help a badly-beaten Fatty Deng get to his feet did Philip Ye breathe a sigh of relief. Surely Fatty Deng had far too much good sense to put himself in the middle of a police operation.

"Constable Ma is a wonder," said Commissioner Zhu for the umpteenth time, playing the CCTV footage again and again for Philip Ye. "See how she comes running around the corner and...." Commissioner Zhu used his fingers to count off the seconds, one, two, three, four, five; all it had taken for Constable Ma to assess the situation, bring her pistol to bear, and, unruffled by the couple of hastily and badly aimed shots fired at her, put two bullets centre-mass into each of her opponents.

For Philip Ye, the CCTV made uncomfortable viewing. He took no joy in watching two men die. He was also grimly aware, that if he had been in Constable Ma's shoes, he himself would have died that day. In those few seconds afforded to Constable Ma to correctly assess the situation *and then to act accordingly*, he would have struggled to comprehend the nature of the threat and most likely would have fallen under a hail of bullets.

"She is indeed a wonder," Philip Ye had agreed, meaning it.

However, in the moments after the Battle of Liberation Street, Constable Ma's natural gift for unhesitating violence was furthest from Philip Ye's mind. Thanking all that was holy that no one appeared to be seriously hurt except the two dead men, Philip Ye had confronted a rather shaken Fatty Deng, demanding answers.

"It's all my fault," said Fatty Deng, unsteady on his feet, gingerly touching a fingertip to his right eye, almost swollen shut by the beating he had just received.

"What is this all about?"

"The murder of Primo Gong," replied Fatty Deng. He nodded to the young woman from the Lucky Dragon Tobacco Emporium, kneeling on the ground, her eyes glassy with shock, the stray dog from the alley licking her face. "That's Sun Mei. She and her father heard the shots on Friday night that killed Primo Gong. It was my mistake. I let myself get noticed speaking to Ms. Sun. I put her in danger. I had to come back, Mister Ye. I would not be able to live with myself if anything had happened to her."

Philip Ye recalled the story told him by Mister Han, the concierge – who appeared to have vanished into the crowd – how the shot that had killed the American-born businessman had to have originated from the Black House. Philip Ye's fear about the two dead men being police suddenly returned. "Fatty, please tell me these dead guys aren't Building Security from the Black House."

"No, Mister Ye – they're almost certainly army."

"Army?"

"Yes, Mister Ye."

"Are you telling me PLA personnel gained access to the Black House on Friday night solely with the intention of murdering Primo Gong?"

"Yes, I believe so."

"How?"

"It's a long story, Mister Ye. I will explain later when I've got my head back on straight. First, I must get Ms. Sun and her father to safety. There's at least one other bad guy loose in the city – maybe a few more. All you need to know about the Black House is that the nightshift is compromised."

Philip Ye then heard the sirens of approaching police cars only a few streets away. "What about local police?"

"Okay, as far as I know," replied Fatty Deng. "But best if you tell them the big girl just prevented an armed robbery until we can decide what to do next."

"Fatty, you must tell me what is going on."

"Mister Ye, please – I have to get Ms. Sun to safety. I owe her that much. It's all connected...the murder of Primo Gong...that dead general of yours with an ice-axe in the back of his head...the military historians you told Prosecutor Xu about...I just haven't quite figured it all out yet."

Philip Ye cursed, furious with Prosecutor Xu for telling him none of this the previous evening. Her silence could have gotten both him and Constable Ma killed. But it all made sense now. There was some sort of internecine conflict underway within the PLA, involving both present and retired personnel, precipitated by whatever Jin Huiliang and Primo Gong had been working on together.

"Mister Ye, you must let me go," pleaded Fatty Deng. "I have to take Ms. Sun to safety. And I have to report to Prosecutor Xu. She is going to have my head for all this."

Prosecutor Xu!

A powerful and irrational fear took hold of Philip Ye's mind then that Prosecutor Xu was in imminent danger, that men similar to those lying dead on the ground were at this moment stalking her just like they had been stalking Fatty Deng, intent on murdering her.

"Fatty, where is she?" asked Philip Ye, a slight tremor in his voice.

Fatty Deng, still dazed, merely shrugged. "I don't know...with your father, I think."

"My father?"

"She had orders to question him...rule him out of our enquiry...to placate Party Chief Li."

Philip Ye's head began to spin. "Fatty, get yourself and Ms. Sun over to my father's house. You will be safe there. I will phone ahead and instruct the brothers Na to let you in."

Fatty Deng nodded and stumbled off to help Sun Mei into his car. Philip Ye phoned home.

"Yes, Boss?" said Day Na.

"Is Prosecutor Xu there?"

"Oh yes – and looking lovelier than ever."

Still in the grip of his terrible, incomprehensible terror, Philip Ye shouted down the phone, "Fortress! Fortress!"

Philip Ye kept the phone to his ear, waiting to learn all were safe, hoping he was not too late.

Fortress.

A Ye family code word.

The brothers Na would get everyone – his father, Prosecutor Xu, Du Yue – to the panic room beneath the house. The brothers would arm themselves to repel any potential invasion of the house. Then they would also make a series of rapid phone calls to summon help, all of it unofficial, contacting men and women ready to drop all they were doing to appear at various points around the Ye family mansion and The Silver Tree, to keep watch, to protect, to form what Philip Ye hoped would be an impenetrable ring of steel.

Philip Ye tried unsuccessfully to regulate his breathing while waiting for Day Na to come back on the line, to reassure him Prosecutor Xu was safe. Philip Ye watched as Constable Ma waved her arms about and cleared a path through the crowd for Fatty Deng's car. Philip Ye was horrified by the state of it, the shattered windscreens back and front. The police sirens were closer now. He watched as Fatty Deng's car turned off Liberation Street heading in the direction of the Ye family mansion, and, as he did so, he felt a gentle tug at his sleeve. He turned to see a man in his middle years, of no great distinction other than he had the most intense gaze Philip Ye had ever seen other than that of a mentally deranged person he had once had to lock up years before.

"Yes?"

"Ah, forgive me, Superintendent Ye. My name is Wu. I am the proprietor of Mister Wu's Cycle Sales and Repair Shop just over the other side of the street. You should be aware that I am also the Chair of the Liberation Street Traders Association. As befits my position, let me be the first to welcome you to Liberation Street. I hope you will extend my good wishes to your father, the best mayor Chengdu has ever had. Now, if you have a few spare moments, I wish to speak to you about the parlous state of our local drains...."

FORTY-SEVEN

F ollowing on from her revelation that Ye Zihao's one true weakness was his son, Xu Ya had another revelation, much more personal this time: she could talk for a thousand years about morality and the importance of the Rule of Law, but there would always be a secret place in her heart, a very dark place in her heart, that was attracted not only to Philip Ye but to all that the family Ye had, so much so that sitting in the panic room beneath the Ye family mansion she felt very much at home. In London, if she ever made it there, she knew all her dreams would be of Philip Ye and this great house.

Made upset by this revelation, this disturbing insight into the workings of her psyche, as well as being angry and frustrated at being trapped in the panic room with no knowledge of what was going on outside, Xu Ya snapped at Ye Zihao. "Put that pipe out! What use is this panic room if, when the door is opened, we are all found choked to death?"

Ye Zihao surprised her by not responding in kind with his own infamous temper. Instead, he took the pipe from his mouth, tapped the contents against the sole of his shoe so the embers scattered over the wooden floor, and then leaned toward her, speaking softly in a low, conspiratorial tone.

"You do have alternatives, Ms. Xu. You need not take up the offer made to you by Mister Xi."

Xu Ya felt her mouth drop open. How was this possible? How could Ye Zihao know of the offer of a job made to her by the lawyer Xi Huan? She gripped Du Yue's hand all the tighter and tried to maintain her composure.

"Consider this, Ms. Xu," continued Ye Zihao. "Fu Bi is a most dull individual. You would not take to him at all. He made all his money by boring people to death. And as for his spiteful daughter, Lucy Fu, you would not be working for her long before there was blood spilt upon the carpet. She does not suffer competition well. Nor, I suspect, do you. Now it is true I wish you out of Chengdu...far away from my son...but I would not see you suffer or your considerable talents squandered. Come work for the family Ye, for my brothers and me. We have interests all around the world. It is true that some of those interests are rather complicated and by necessity opaque, but a woman such as you would be an invaluable asset to us. The work would involve a lot of travel. There would be much for you to oversee. But you would be very well-rewarded and you may base yourself anywhere you wish: London, if that is your preferred choice, but New York and Paris have their attractions – even Mombasa if you like the heat."

Xu Ya's head began to spin. She was falling under Ye Zihao's spell and she knew it. "Mayor Ye, I have come here to question you about a murder and you have the nerve to offer me a bribe?"

Ye Zihao did not blink. "A bribe? No, Ms. Xu – that was what that creep Xi Huan offered you, and you know it. Unlike Lucy Fu, I have nothing to hide. As I have already told you, I was neither friend nor foe to Primo Gong. I am merely offering you the opportunity of a lifetime. You would never want for anything ever again."

"I do not want for anything now."

"You have no allegiance."

"I have the law."

"Pah! What is that? It is family you need, not the law."

"I have family," she protested.

"Is this the same family that disowned you on the day of your marriage?"

Stunned by Ye Zihao's intimate knowledge of her parents' heart-breaking behaviour, Xu Ya was gripped by a sudden terror that this was not all he knew.

"Come work for me," said Ye Zihao. "Chengdu is nothing but a dead-end. The Procuratorate is but a place to grow stale, old, and die. Think about it, Ms. Xu: instead of spending all your time prosecuting petty corrupt officials and being at the beck and call of the famously intemperate Party Chief Li, I am offering you a life lived on your own terms – a life of travel, of limitless adventure. I am offering you nothing less than your freedom."

"My name would forever be associated with the family Ye."

Ye Zihao laughed. "Is that so bad?"

Xu Ya was forced to smile. "Some would say so."

"Promise me you will think on my offer."

"I will."

His pitch made, Ye Zihao sat back, crossed his arms, and closed his eyes, a bear now in hibernation – or, at least, seemingly so. Xu Ya tried to do likewise as Du Yue leaned her head on her shoulder, but she found it difficult to control the fluttering of her heart, her excitement at being offered the chance to take flight, to make the whole world her playground. She could have drinks at a fashionable bar in Cape Town. She could go shopping down the Champs-Élysées. She could lie on a beach in Rio de Janeiro. She could photograph the cherry blossom in Tokyo. She could ski the slopes of Val d'Isère. And she could live anywhere, maybe find herself a home in the English countryside to rival the magnificence of the one within which she now sat.

But could she really work for the family Ye?

In her need to escape Chengdu, to escape Sarangerel's malicious attentions, to escape the difficult truth of what had happened the night her husband had died, could she stoop so low?

She thought, maybe, yes.

Xu Ya soon began to lose track of time. Twenty minutes had passed by, or was it forty, or possibly an hour?

Unable to check her watch for fear of disturbing Du Yue who was now sleeping against her shoulder, Xu Ya tried to relax and close her own eyes, only to open them again soon after and find Ye Zihao studying her as a cat might study a mouse. She smiled at him to show she was not afraid even though she was. He returned the smile and nodded, perhaps a gesture of friendship, perhaps in appreciation of her courage. Then she heard the buzz of the intercom and the muffled voice of one of the brothers Na saying the emergency, whatever it was, was over. Ye Zihao was instantly out of his seat to punch in the code to open the door. The door slid open and Day Na was standing there, grinning from ear to ear, no weapons visible upon him.

"Report!" said Ye Zihao.

"Ah, it's all a bit complicated, Boss," replied Day Na. "Philip is fine but is in high-dudgeon as is usual when nothing is quite as he thinks it should be. There has been a shooting on Liberation Street outside the Lucky Dragon Tobacco Emporium. The Big Girl has shot two dead...plain-clothes army it seems...we think an element of a rogue unit loose in the city. We have increased security around the house and around The Silver Tree. Philip thought the Prosecutor may well be a target but on further reflection suspects this rogue army unit might not even be aware of her existence. There is much that is just speculation. You also now have a full kitchen. The Prosecutor's man, Fatty Deng, has arrived – a bit beaten-up though. And he's brought a friend of his, a Brother Wang, who is on temporary suspension from Freddie Yun's two-bit operation in Wukuaishi. Brother Wang has had an ear shot off. We'll fix him up with a doctor in a while. You have two other guests, a Ms. Sun and her father, proprietors of the Lucky Dragon Tobacco Emporium. I think fresh tea and some food might be in order."

Ye Zihao asked no questions and hurried past Day Na, forgetting the pipe he had put down on the seat next to him. Day Na entered the panic room to retrieve it as Xu Ya gently roused Du Yue.

"Prosecutor, how did you get the boss to put out his pipe?" asked Day Na.

"I just told him to," replied Xu Ya.

Day Na laughed, scowled at Du Yue who was rolling her eyes at him, and then vanished upstairs after Ye Zihao.

"I do not like them," said Du Yue.

"Who?"

"The brothers Na."

"I find them rather fun," said Xu Ya, insensitive to the girl's feelings, her mind now fully occupied processing the report given Ye Zihao by Day Na, not liking the sound of any of it, finding far too many gaps, and desperate to get upstairs and discover for herself what was going on.

When Xu Ya reached the kitchen, dragging a somewhat nervous and reluctant Du Yue after her, she found it resembled more an aid-station than a place for the preparation of food. Night Na was busy bandaging the head of a distressed man dressed in a black suit and tie, with Day Na looking on, laughing. Ye Zihao, his pipe back in his mouth, sending clouds of smoke everywhere, had an apron around his waist and was speaking animatedly to a man of similar years to himself perched on a kitchen stool, who, Xu Ya could sense by the way he sat, had lost the use of his legs. Philip Ye, dressed in yet another expensive suit Xu Ya had never seen before, was looking far from happy. He was speaking to Investigator Deng, whose face was bloody and swollen, and who was in the process of changing his shirt, revealing a body covered in angry scars as he did so. Xu Ya shuddered with guilt. But she saw she was not the only person fascinated with Investigator Deng's wounds from three months before. A pretty young woman sitting in a dark corner of the kitchen as if trying to hide herself away, was staring at Investigator Deng as if she had never seen a semi-naked man before, her hand over her mouth, shocked by all she saw. Xu Ya felt a moment's irritation with the young woman – Ms. Sun from the Lucky Dragon Tobacco Emporium, presumably? – feeling very proprietorial toward Investigator Deng. But then Xu Ya felt a very unfriendly gaze upon her. In the far doorway to the kitchen had appeared Constable Ma, who had to be the 'Big Girl' as referred to by Day Na. Xu Ya found no joy in seeing her again either.

By all rights, as a prosecutor, Xu Ya should have raised her voice and called the whole scene to order, demanding answers, making them all explain themselves in turn. But, not liking the aura of hatred emanating from Constable Ma, and furious with Investigator Deng for speaking to Philip Ye first rather than to her, and indeed feeling faint at the thought that her supposedly secret investigation into the murder of Primo Gong had somehow spiralled out of control, Xu Ya realised she could not trust herself to keep her emotions in check. Instead, she turned on her heels and walked out of the kitchen the way she had come, dragging an unprotesting Du Yue with her. More by luck than by any deep knowledge of the layout of the great house, Xu Ya quickly found an open door to the outside and soon she and

Du Yue were standing under a hot sun by the lake, looking down upon its calm, cool, clear waters.

Xu Ya felt her mind steady, her pulse slow, and the emotions recede that had only a few moments before threatened to explode out of her. It was hard for her to believe she was standing in such extensive gardens, surrounded by so much tranquillity, so much natural beauty, at the very heart of Chengdu. She marvelled at the tiny silver fish schooling near the water's edge. She was in paradise and she knew it.

"I could stay here forever," she said.

Du Yue, still holding her hand, said, "The man with the scars...."

"Investigator Deng?"

"He is a great hero reborn."

Xu Ya smiled. "Well, I think—"

"And there are bodies buried under this lake."

Xu Ya laughed at the dark and somewhat fantastical imaginings of teenage girls. She, too, at Du Yue's age, had read far too many ghost stories and supernatural romances.

"But I am not worried," added Du Yue.

"Are you not?" said Xu Ya, smiling, humouring her.

"No – the ghosts are angry with the family Ye, not me."

FORTY-EIGHT

— · —

Ripples upon the water. A slight cooling breeze moved across the lake. It caressed Xu Ya's face, making her smile. The breeze also spoke to her that this fine weather was not to last, that storms as yet unseen on the horizon were on their way. Still holding hands with Du Yue, she glanced upwards and saw, circling high above the city, a large black bird, crow or raven she could not tell. She knew very little about birds but recalled the story told to her by Investigator Deng, how when Sarangerel first came to live in Chengdu and took up residence in the Ye family mansion the people became paralysed by fear, many seeing at that time a lone raven flying high above the city – a harbinger of doom. She dismissed such superstition from her mind. But the bird did remind Xu Ya that Sarangerel was breathing down her neck, that it was time to leave, to leave Chengdu forever and never come back. She did not belong here, she never did.

"Thank you," said Du Yue.

"For what?"

"For giving me courage in the panic room."

Xu Ya smiled at Du Yue and squeezed her hand more tightly. "When I was your age, I was frightened of my own shadow...I still am at times."

"You ordered Mayor Ye to put his pipe out."

Xu Ya laughed. "I did."

"That was so funny. I would never have had the nerve. He frightens me a lot."

"And Philip Ye?"

"All my friends back at school in England would be in love with him, he is so handsome."

"But?"

Du Yue shook her head. "He is complicated."

Xu Ya was amused by Du Yue's use of such a grown-up word. "There are women who are attracted to complicated men."

"Are you?"

Xu Ya was startled by the directness of Du Yue's question. "I think, if given the choice, I would always opt for a quiet life, a glass of wine, a good book."

"Will you accept Mayor Ye's job offer?"

"I might."

"Oh, please come live in England. If I am ever able to return to school there, if my mother has put money aside for me, then we could be friends."

Before Xu Ya could answer, before she could reassure Du Yue that she would personally investigate her mother's financial affairs and do her utmost to secure a future for her, she heard footsteps approaching from behind. Xu Ya did not need to turn and look. In the peace that was the garden, her mind having become remarkably receptive and clear, she could easily sense his barely controlled temper, as well as the weary impatience with which he viewed the world.

"Yue, please go inside and help my father look after our guests," said Philip Ye.

Du Yue did not argue, nor did Xu Ya try to prevent her going. Du Yue's hand slipped from hers and then she was gone, back into the house. Xu Ya thought this was no way to speak to a young girl who was suffering the trauma of losing her mother – if Du Luli was truly dead. But then, as Philip Ye stood shoulder-to-shoulder with her to look out onto the lake, close enough so she could smell his expensive cologne, she began to wonder if his firmness, his certainty, was actually good for Du Yue, when her future – much like Xu Ya's own – was one great big unknown.

Philip Ye was still wearing his three-piece suit. How he did not seem to sweat in the heat of the sun she did not know. It was unnatural. He took his stupid –and pretentious! – pocket-watch from his waistcoat pocket to check the time. But then he proceeded to play with the watch, opening and closing the watchcase again and again. The peace of mind Xu Ya had gained from her short time in the garden soon faded away, as did the cooling breeze from across the lake. A few moments standing next to him and she was ready to do murder herself. And it appeared it was up to her to initiate the conversation.

"How is Investigator Deng?" she asked.

"He'll live."

"He was supposed to be only meeting an informant."

"His ambition was somewhat greater than that."

Philip Ye offered no more, revenge she suspected for the little she had told him the last evening. What kind of trouble had Investigator Deng got himself into now? But Philip Ye would be surely mistaken if he thought she was going to ask, going to plead with him, for an explanation of all that had gone on. And so, not inclined to return to the house to finish her questioning of Ye Zihao, she contented herself with standing next to Philip Ye, hoping to outlast him in this game of patience. But, as Philip Ye continued to play with his pocket-watch, opening the watchcase and closing it, again and again, she soon realised it was a game she was never going to win.

"Stop that!" she snapped.

"Stop what?"

"Stop playing with that ridiculous watch!"

He stared at her, his green eyes darkening, but the expected argument did not come. Instead, he looked away from her, took a few highly-exaggerated deep breaths, and returned the watch to his waistcoat pocket. Still he offered up nothing of the morning's happenings, still she continued to fume. She glanced down at her own watch. Soon she would have to leave if she was going to make her appointment at the Procuratorate. However, when she spoke again it was not about the planned interview with Mister Han.

"I have been offered two jobs in two days," she said.

"Is that so?"

To Xu Ya, his reply sounded maddeningly dull, even uninterested, but she continued nevertheless. "FUBI International has asked me to head up a new legal team for them in London."

"You would work for Lucy Fu?"

"You think that a mistake?"

"Blood would be spilt."

"Your father used those exact same words."

Philip Ye turned to her then, his mouth open in astonishment. "You sought advice from my father?"

"Oh no – but he was happy to offer it."

Philip Ye smiled then, the warmest smile she had ever received from him, a smile she could only return. It was a sweet moment, them almost communicating as human beings for once.

"He made you a better offer, didn't he?" said Philip Ye.

"He did."

"To work for the family Ye?"

"Indeed."

"Where?"

"Anywhere but Chengdu it seems."

She searched for some sadness in his eyes, something to tell her that he would actually miss her. But the smile had already faded, and the cool mask had returned, those green eyes of his impossible for her to read. She had never been good at reading people – especially men.

"Was your father's offer genuine?" she asked.

Without turning to her again, Philip Ye replied, "I would assume so. My father did not miss a moment of Commissioner Ho's trial on TV. You made a great impression on him."

"That trial was not much more than a bit of theatre, something for the people, something to make them believe, incorrectly, that we are winning the fight against corruption in this city."

"Then you played your part well."

She felt herself blush. "You watched also?"

"Only as much as I could stomach."

Hurt now, Xu Ya pretended to be distracted by the landing of more geese far out upon the lake. Did he not appreciate the serious-ness of Commissioner Ho's trial, the message that was being sent? Did he not realise all the work she had had to do to prepare for the trial? How, beforehand, she had had to personally walk the panel of three idiot judges through the mass of evidence? Did he not realise how much she had had to struggle with terrible anxiety every morning of the trial, well aware that she herself was about to be judged, not just by the people but also by the Party elite, and not just for her performance as a public prosecutor in front of the cameras, but also for the clothes she chose to wear, the make-up she applied to her face, the way she carried herself around the courtroom, the slightest expression that crossed her face.

And she had been judged.

In her mind, unfairly so.

Some commentators had accused her of flirting with the panel of three ridiculous old judges as well as vamping it up for the camera to secure for herself a new husband. Others had expressed sympathy for Commissioner Ho, saying he was not the worst of the corrupt tigers in the city, that her treatment of him bordered on the cruel and vindictive, that black venom filled her veins rather than blood, that her 'grotesque' performance actually *undermined* the Rule of Law rather than upheld it.

Remembering all these painful comments, Xu Ya said to Philip Ye, "It wouldn't hurt you to say something nice to me."

"About the trial?"

"What else?"

He shook his head, offering her nothing.

Angry, she said, "Well, am I wasting my time in this city as a prosecutor? Should I take up your father's offer and work for the family Ye?"

"The decision is yours, is it not?" replied Philip Ye, coldly. "I am sure you'll earn more in a year working abroad for my father than you would in a lifetime at the Procuratorate. The business affairs of the family Ye are complex and intricate and far beyond my simple mind to comprehend. But I expect you have both the wit and ambition to find your way. You will be required to take phone calls from my father day and night, stand up to him when he is in a particularly abusive mood, and reassure him when he is feeling lonely and hard done by. But I am sure a TV star, the Flower of the Procuratorate no less, will have no difficulty wrapping him around your little finger."

"I asked for advice, not sarcasm."

"I assumed you to be a woman who understood her own mind. Last night you didn't need any help with the investigation into the murder of Primo Gong."

"You are police – I couldn't ask for your help."

"You are just too proud."

"I am acting under orders."

"Under orders because Party Chief Li has deluded himself in believing my father is behind every crime in Chengdu? Because all Party Chief Li's cronies need to unload all their stock in Ambrogetti Global Software before Primo Gong's murder becomes common knowledge and the company goes belly-up? So much for the Rule of Law, Prosecutor. So much for all your fine words during the trial of Commissioner Ho."

Furious, Xu Ya forgot herself again and jabbed a finger into Philip Ye's chest. "Listen, you stupid man! The shot that killed Primo Gong was fired from the Black House on Liberation Street. That's why I cannot involve you. Some of your esteemed colleagues, some of your beloved police, are up to their necks in murder!"

"I know."

Surprised, Xu Ya said, "You do? Has Investigator Deng opened his big mouth again?"

"It was Mister Han."

"The concierge from Plum Tree Pagodas?"

"Yes."

"He has spoken to you – told you the truth?"

"He has, so you may as well cancel your planned interrogation of him. He is under orders to lie to you. If you manage to get him to tell the truth, which I suspect you will – he is a decent, honourable, and compassionate man – then all you will achieve is to lose him his job."

"I will have proof against Lucy Fu."

"She is nothing but a distraction."

"But—"

"No, now you listen to me, Prosecutor. Cancel that interview and forget Lucy Fu. We have no time to waste on personal enmities. Instead, phone Secretary Wu and tell him you have found my father to be innocent of Primo Gong's murder and that you formally request my help with the investigation."

"But you are police!"

"Do you think I haven't investigated police officers for murder before?"

Startled by his vehemence, she said, "When?"

"That need not concern you. It was a few years ago, in Chongqing. It was how I came to meet Wolf. You were already married then. You had already resigned from Chongqing People's Procuratorate. Now, back to the matter at hand. The nightshift at the Black House may well be compromised, but your man Fatty Deng has convinced me that the heart of this conspiracy against Primo Gong, Jin Huiliang, and the unfortunate Du Luli, originates within the PLA and not within the PSB. So, once you have phoned Secretary Wu, and once you have phoned that sleezy lawyer Xi Huan to cancel your interrogation of Mister Han, you and I are going to confront The Historians. They are hiding truths from me. They are expecting Constable Ma. Let us both go instead. Let us shock them. They may well think they can turn aside a lowly police superintendent, but I want to see their reaction to a real-life public prosecutor, a TV star – a celebrity, no less."

"I will make any and all decisions about *my* investigation."

"You are out of your depth, Prosecutor – especially as your mind now appears to be focused on how much fun you'll have in London, or wherever else you choose to go to further your career. And Fatty Deng knows this too. Why do you think he took it upon himself to make some real progress instead of wasting his time taking tea with my father or stewing about Lucy Fu?"

Anxious, Xu Ya asked, "What has he done?"

"He has picked up the team leader of the Black House nightshift."

Xu Ya put her hands to her face, horrified, thinking of all the potential repercussions, the Procuratorate taking action against the police without first getting permission from the Political and Legal Committee, before liaising with Commissioner Ji Dan of PSB Internal Security, before securing any real evidence. "Don't tell me he has arrested her."

"Not exactly."

"What does that mean?"

"It might be best if he explains."

"No, you tell me."

"Suffice to say he has stashed her somewhere safe and out of the way. Sometimes you must turn a blind eye, Prosecutor. In a land where the Rule of Law is often not all that it's dressed up to be, real justice sometimes has to take place outside of the courtroom. Unfortunately, Fatty Deng had a bit of bad luck. He was not to know that Superintendent Si Ying's cousin – who is PLA, by the way – was staying in her apartment. This cousin not only let off a couple of shots, wounding Fatty Deng's mate Brother Wang – he's the guy in the black suit missing an ear, a low-level gangster – but he also remembered where he had seen Fatty Deng before, speaking to the proprietors of the Lucky Dragon Tobacco Emporium. Being the good man that he is, Fatty Deng hightailed it back to Liberation Street to get Ms. Sun and her father to safety, just in time for another two PLA assassins to make an appearance. If I had not been meeting with the concierge Mister Han just around the corner, and for Constable Ma's natural talent with a pistol, I do not know what might have happened. Constable Ma has accounted for two of our conspirators – I searched the bodies and found no IDs, PLA or otherwise – but there is at least one other, Superintendent Si Ying's cousin, at large in the city, maybe a woman also, Jin Huiliang's assassin. I suspect we are dealing with a small PLA kill team, hopefully rogue, working as mercenaries, operating under the direction of a person or persons unknown. I swung by Superintendent Si Ying's apartment on the way back here and found the cousin long gone. I have covered our tracks for the moment, telling the local police that Constable Ma stopped an armed robbery in progress – an excellent suggestion from Fatty Deng, by the way. That should buy us a few hours with the PSB. But we need to move quickly before anyone else gets killed. So, you and I should confront The Historians. I am convinced Bo Qi is up to his neck in all this. And, if you agree, Fatty Deng and Constable Ma can commence the interrogation of Superintendent Si Ying. She may have all the answers we need. Please phone Secretary Wu and tell him we are now working together, that you and I have declared a truce."

"I am not at war with you, Superintendent."

"It certainly feels like it."

She poked him in the chest again. "If I was at war with you, you would know about it."

She turned her back on him and marched toward the house, to retrieve her phone from her handbag, left in Ye Zihao's office. First, she would call Xi Huan, cancel the interrogation of Mister Han, and then apologise, telling him that she was no longer in a position to accept a job with FUBI International. It *had been* a bribe, an inducement for her not to involve Lucy Fu in the investigation into

Primo Gong's murder. And both Ye Zihao and Philip Ye were right: blood would indeed be spilt if she had to work for any length of time for Lucy Fu. Then she would phone Secretary Wu. She had a sneaking suspicion Secretary Wu had wanted Philip Ye involved in the investigation all along. Not that she cared anymore. Once the investigation was done, and she had spoken to Ye Zihao again to negotiate the terms of their new arrangement, she would be on the next flight out of Chengdu – to work for the family Ye, to escape Sarangerel, to embrace freedom, to fly the world, never again to bear the exhausting burden of upholding the Rule of Law very much on her own.

FORTY-NINE

— · —

A leopard does not change its spots. Superintendent Ye had said this once about a criminal they had detained. Ma Meili had not understood what he had meant until Superintendent Zuo had explained the English saying to her. She now saw it applied to Superintendent Ye too. After the compliment she had received the evening before from Superintendent Ye for her finding of the business card, the only evidence so far definitively linking Primo Gong and Jin Huiliang, she had believed her relationship with him had turned a corner, that she would in the future be treated with much more kindness, patience, and respect. But Superintendent Ye had hardly said one word to her since she had shot the two men dead on Liberation Street. Had she done wrong? And now he had run off with the wicked Prosecutor Xu in her stupid little sports car to meet with The Historians – a meeting Ma Meili had herself arranged. Ma Meili could not conceive of a worse betrayal.

Ma Meili had gone in search of Fatty Deng for an explanation. She had found him sitting all by himself under an awning in the garden, sheltering from the hot sun, smoking a cigarette, looking as defeated and depressed as Ma Meili felt. But, when she sat down on the bench next to him, he laughed off the injuries to his face and had the patience to explain it all, what he and Prosecutor Xu had discovered so far in their investigation into the murder of Primo Gong, how Superintendent Ye now had a theory that Primo Gong and Jin Huiliang had been working on some kind of secret project together, and how that project – whatever it was – had, for some reason, inspired a murderous conspiracy among retired and serving PLA officers, as well as the night shift at the Black House on Liberation Street.

Ma Meili was appalled. Not only had she not known that the men she had shot dead were in all likelihood serving soldiers, she had actually liked Bo Qi – Superintendent Ye's supposed prime suspect – and had thought him a hero.

"Are you sure about all of this, Fatty?" she asked.

"I'm certain we are dealing with a rogue PLA unit that somehow gained access to the Black House – most likely with the help of Superintendent Si Ying. As for The Historians and a secret project worked on by Jin Huiliang and Primo Gong, that's Mister Ye's contention. It could be right. We'll just have to wait and see."

Ma Meili had believed that the two men she had killed on Liberation Street had been no more than common gangsters, out to hurt Fatty Deng for some reason, possibly more of the same mad cultists that had nearly done for him three months before. Only now, after Fatty Deng had explained all, did she think back and remember the speed with which the two men had reacted to her appearance on Liberation Street, how quickly they had brought their pistols to bear on her, and how close she had come to dying herself as one bullet had whistled past her ear and another had put a hole through her jacket before she had put the two of them down on the ground.

"You did a good thing today," said Fatty Deng.

"Are you sure they were soldiers?"

"They had the look."

"But soldiers are supposed to be loyal, honest, and decent."

"Who told you that?"

Ma Meili shook her head. She had not made this up. Everyone knew it was true.

"Sister, do not fret," said Fatty Deng. "The police are supposed to be good but sometimes they are not. The same is true for the PLA. People are people. Don't get fooled by a fancy uniform. Some people are good, some people are bad – but most of us are somewhere in between. Remember that PLA general from up north who was in the news not long ago for being caught sleeping on a bed made out of bank notes? The two men you shot might well be PLA but they were really bad people. I won't forget what you did for me, Sister. If ever you need a favour...."

Ma Meili nodded. She liked Fatty Deng. She was glad she had rescued him. Despite being a smoker, he was as nice a man as there ever was: brave, kind, and patient. He was also a kindred spirit, having to work for a boss as unlovable as her own.

"I don't need a favour, Fatty."

"You might."

"But I could use some advice."

"Sure, anything."

"I'm thinking of transferring to SWAT."

"Are you serious?"

"Fatty, I've been invited to join. They are such nice people, like one big happy family, always laughing and joking. They have parties every weekend. Life with them would never be dull."

Fatty Deng became very serious. "Sister, listen carefully to me: half of SWAT were dropped on their heads as babies, the other half should have been. I know it can't be easy working for Mister Ye. But you are a homicide detective. I would give my right arm to be back in the PSB, to be a proper detective like you. You must give it time. You've only been doing the job three months. I promise you, one morning you'll wake up and the job will suddenly make sense. There is no better job, no more rewarding job, no more challenging job, than finding justice for the dead."

"I suppose," said Ma Meili, unconvinced.

It was Fatty Deng who briefed Ma Meili on what the two of them were to do next: interrogate Superintendent Si Ying. The very thought filled Ma Meili with trepidation. How was she, a mere constable second class, meant to ask questions of a more senior officer? Fatty Deng seemed far from bothered, though. He seemed to be relishing the task ahead.

It was also Fatty Deng who told Ma Meili that Superintendent Ye had been in contact with Ms. Miao at PSB HQ to request Superintendent Si Ying's personnel file. It might prove useful for the interrogation. They were to stop off at PSB HQ to pick up the file on the way to Wukuaishi where Superintendent Si Ying had been stashed somewhere out of the way. Why, thought Ma Meili, if Superintendent Si Ying had been working with the bad soldiers, was she not presently languishing in a police cell? It was only later, in the car with Fatty Deng, that the penny dropped, that she realised what all the secrecy was about: her police colleagues were not to be trusted until it was known how far the rot had spread from the Black House on Liberation Street – if it had spread at all. This realisation brought a funny feeling to Ma Meili's stomach, the sense that working as a police officer in Chengdu was not as black and white as she had assumed it to be. When she mentioned this to Fatty Deng, he simply laughed, not maliciously, but hard enough to let her know she had a lot to learn.

Ma Meili and Fatty Deng left the Ye family mansion without saying goodbye to anyone. Ma Meili supposed that Fatty Deng would at least have wanted to check up on his friend, Brother Wang, whom Ma Meili did not like the look of. But Fatty Deng was adamant. Once he had finished his cigarette it was time to go. Ma Meili wondered if his reluctance to return to the kitchen had anything to do with the young woman from the Lucky Dragon Tobacco Emporium. But she kept her thoughts to herself. That Fatty Deng had seemed unable to look Sun Mei in the eye when he had been in the kitchen was no business of hers.

In the car, however, Fatty Deng was all smiles, his swollen face notwithstanding. Superintendent Ye had done him a great kindness. Before going off with Prosecutor Xu, after seeing how shot-up Fatty Deng's car had been, Superintendent Ye had thrown Fatty Deng his car keys. Not having any interest in cars, and hardly able to tell one car from another, Ma Meili found it amusing how, as soon as Fatty Deng slid into the driver's seat, he became a different person, an excitable child.

"It's just a car, Fatty," she told him.

"No, Sister, this is a Mercedes E63 AMG – a rocket-ship!"

Which he had then tried to prove after pushing the engine start button, by racing down the drive at speed and making the tyres squeal as he drove through the gates and out into the road before slowing down to what Ma Meili considered to be a more civilised speed. Not that she was overly concerned. Superintendent Ye would drive at high speed whenever and wherever he could, traffic police cheerily waving to him as he flew by. At least alongside Fatty Deng, Ma Meili didn't have to endure grim, unrelenting silences.

They arrived at PSB HQ in no time at all. As Fatty Deng preferred to stay in the car, Ma Meili went up to the Homicide office alone. She had hoped to find Superintendent Si Ying's personnel file waiting for her on her desk. But her desk was clear, just as she had left it the afternoon before. This left her in a quandary. As no one else in the PSB was to know about the interrogation of Superintendent Si Ying, Ma Meili doubted the file would be waiting for her down in Personnel. This meant then a trip up to the commanding officers' floor to seek out Ms. Miao – an experience Ma Meili had never enjoyed before. Though it was a Sunday and the top floor was not going to be fully staffed, staring at herself in the mirror in the lift, Ma Meili recognised she was not exactly dressed for the occasion in her summer jacket and shapeless jeans. Compared to some of the other policewoman walking around the building, with their dainty figures and done out in their starched blue uniforms, she looked like a big scruffy lump. But when she stepped out of the lift, the first person she bumped into was Commissioner Zhu Shouqing of SWAT, grinning from ear to ear, dressed head to toe in black – his operational clothes – more than pleased to see her.

"Constable Ma, are you hurt?"

"No, Commissioner."

"It is all over the radios – the Battle of Liberation Street."

"I did not know that."

"Did they get off any shots?"

Ma Meili showed him the bullet hole through her jacket.

"Bastards!" exclaimed Commissioner Zhu, shaking his head.

"They are dead," said Ma Meili, simply.

"I would expect nothing less of you. In a few days you and I are going to have a long talk. You are wasted where you are. Superintendent Ye and Superintendent Zuo are both good men, the very best, but they walk a strange beat, spending all their time communing with the bereaved and the dead. You are like me, Constable Ma, full of life – born for action!"

Ma Meili did not think there was a senior officer in the PSB more likeable than Commissioner Zhu. He was always laughing and joking, having time for everyone, including the cleaners who mopped the floor. And, as he led her down the corridor, happy to show her the way to Chief Di's office outside which Ms. Miao had her desk, Ma Meili began to resent what Fatty Deng had said about SWAT, about how half of them had been dropped on their heads as babies and the other half should have been so. Fatty Deng had been unfair. SWAT were good people. SWAT were like a family. And, being alone in the city, Ma Meili felt she could do with a family.

When they arrived at Ms. Miao's desk, Commissioner Zhu announced, his voice loud and booming, "Ms. Miao, I present to you a true heroine!"

"A true heroine indeed," replied Ms. Miao, her eyes twinkling, her smile broad.

When Commissioner Zhu left them to return to the SWAT command office – he told them he had a feeling in his bones there was going to be more trouble today – Ms. Miao said, "Constable Ma, I hope you didn't say too much to him. Commissioner Zhu is as in the dark as everyone else in the PSB as to what you and Superintendent Ye are investigating. He believes you prevented an armed robbery, nothing more."

"I did not speak of what I know," said Ma Meili.

"Good – I have Superintendent Si Ying's personnel file for you. You may find it interesting. I will be contacting Chengdu Military Region Headquarters for her service record and also that of Commissioner Yang Da who commands the Building Security Unit. I suspect important links will be found."

"Thank you, Ms. Miao."

"Before I can let you go, Chief Di would like a word."

Ma Meili would rather have faced more armed assailants. But what could she do – run? Ms. Miao knocked on Chief Di's office door and opened it without waiting for an answer. Ma Meili followed her in and stood to attention in front of Chief Di's desk.

Ma Meili did not know what to make of Chief Di. He was a very thin man, who smoked constantly – as he was doing now – his eyes always hidden behind small, tinted spectacles. Occasionally, he would visit the Homicide Office to either speak to Superintendent Ye or Superintendent Zuo, but he had never ever seen fit to acknowledge her existence. Ma Meili had the sense that he was a tired, sad, and rather lonely man. She would have thought him weak too, not a good leader at all, except for the stories she had heard from other police, how in the past, before the coming of the Shanghai Clique, he had been considered a hard man, a true inspiration to everyone at the PSB. He was, by all accounts, the most heavily decorated policeman ever in Chengdu. Certainly, Ma Meili had never heard a word of disrespect directed at Chief Di by either Superintendent Ye or Superintendent Zuo – neither of whom were shy of finding a sharp word or two for those in the PSB who fell below their exacting standards.

"How are you, Constable Ma?" asked Chief Di.

"Very well, sir."

"I know the truth, of course. Superintendent Ye has fully briefed me. And I have taken calls from both Party Chief Li and Secretary Wu this morning. This is a Procuratorate-led investigation, I have been told. I am to sit on my hands, I have been told. I have PLA assassins roaming the streets of my city and I am to do nothing, I have been told. Some of my own police may be involved, I have been told. And yet I am to sit at my desk like an idiot twiddling my thumbs. It is a disgrace. But what am I to do? I am just the Chief of Police and I must follow orders. I must wait for Prosecutor Xu, our seductive little TV star, to reach her conclusions. If Commissioner Ji Dan, our Head of Internal Security, wasn't away this weekend, he would have something to say, I can tell you. Prosecutor Xu is no investigator. She is a public prosecutor, a pen pusher, a paper sorter, a reader of law books, more at home in a trendy wine bar than out on the streets fighting crime. You've met her, haven't you, Constable Ma? What do you make of her? Tell the truth now."

The truth.

Ma Meili found her mouth had gone very dry.

"Speak up, Constable Ma – don't be shy," said Chief Di.

"Sir, I have to say...and it is only my naïve and uneducated opinion...but I think there is not one good bone in her body."

Chief Di stared at Ma Meili a long, hard moment. She thought she was going to lose her job. But then he violently stubbed out his cigarette in the ashtray, lit another, looked over at Ms. Miao and said, "Did I not tell you? Did I not say when Secretary Wu travelled all the way to Chongqing to recruit Prosecutor Xu that we in the PSB had all better watch our backs?"

"Superintendent Ye knows what he is doing, sir," said Ms. Miao.

"Does he? Does he, though? I am sure the prosecution of Commissioner Ho was just the beginning. Prosecutor Xu is coming for all of us – Philip included. Party Chief Li has always hated us police. Even after The Purge, even after he filled our ranks with his own people, he is still suspicious of us, and will stop at nothing to ridicule us, and weaken us, and finally, if he has his way, dismember us – and Prosecutor Xu is his perfect weapon."

"I am sure that is not so, sir," said Ms. Miao, her voice gentle, soothing.

Chief Di turned his attention back to Ma Meili. "Where are you from, Constable?"

"Pujiang County, sir."

"You were raised on a farm?"

"A pig-farm, sir."

"A pig-farm...how marvellous. I wish I were a farmer. Think of how simple, how peaceful, my life would be. And pigs are such charming, intelligent, and loyal creatures. Pigs will never turn on you, will never stick a knife in you. Still, *karma* is *karma*. I was born to be police so here I am. Constable Ma, promise me you will watch out for Philip...keep Prosecutor Xu, that clever seductress, from getting her claws into him. He is like a son to me. His father and I were once very close. Not now, alas, too much water has flowed under the bridge. He and I no longer speak. But I care deeply for Philip. He was an unusual boy, so sensitive and intelligent. I assumed he would grow up to be a scientist...a naturalist, possibly...he had such a love of animals. I never guessed he would be police and yet here he is. He never shirks in his duty even though he is well aware I am not allowed to promote him. Promise me you will watch out for him, Constable Ma."

Ma Meili wanted to say she was not long for Homicide, that she was soon to be taken into the happy family that was SWAT, but instead she replied, "I promise, sir."

Back outside Chief Di's office, the door now closed, Ms. Miao handed Ma Meili a sealed envelope as well as Superintendent Si Ying's personnel file.

"Keep in touch," said Ms. Miao.

In the lift, descending to the ground floor, Ma Meili saw the envelope was addressed to her. She broke the seal. Inside was a short note, written in pen, and signed with a flourish by Chief Di.

Constable Ma

For meritorious service this day.

*You are hereby promoted to the rank of constable first   class,
effective immediately.*

*Personnel will be advised, and your privileges and salary adjusted
accordingly.*

Chief of Police Di

Ma Meili blinked a few times, taking it all in, and then began to
smile.

FIFTY

— · —

In retrospect, Fatty Deng wondered if he would have taken the decision to snatch Superintendent Si Ying off the street if Prosecutor Xu hadn't told him she was seriously considering the offer from FUBI International to work on the other side of the world. Not that he was apportioning blame to Prosecutor Xu. He alone had made the decision to pick up Superintendent Si Ying and to involve Brother Wang and the brothers Ming. And yet, if he had not been worrying about the future – a future on his own at the Procuratorate – would he have been so rash as to push the investigation forward without doing the legwork on Superintendent Si Ying? Or, indeed, do his utmost to discover where her cousin was staying, who his buddies were, and where they were staying as well? His rash decision had cost Brother Wang his right ear and had seriously endangered the lives of Sun Mei and her father – unforeseen consequences he would surely have to live with for the rest of his life.

Philip Ye had tried to cheer him up.

"No one died today, Fatty – except those shot by Constable Ma. You just had a bit of bad luck. So what? You also had some good luck, with Constable Ma just around the corner. So put a smile on your face. And don't worry about Prosecutor Xu. She might shout and stamp her feet but she would be lost without you – and she knows it. Get your head together and get back in the game. There's work to be done."

Get back in the game.

Fatty Deng wasn't sure about that.

Homicide investigations were far from a game.

But Fatty Deng appreciated the effort Philip Ye had made in trying to cheer him up, to get his mind back in the right place. There was something else to be grateful for. Whether Prosecutor Xu liked it or not, Philip Ye was now part of the investigation. They were going to get the benefit of his experience and his wisdom – as well as the private resources of the family Ye, if needed. Philp Ye had already advanced the investigation by somehow getting the truth out of the concierge Mister Han.

Philip Ye had also lent him his car: the black Mercedes E63 AMG.

"What if I break it, Mister Ye?" Fatty Deng had asked.

Philip Ye had stared at him strangely for a moment before going off in search of Prosecutor Xu. It took a little while for Fatty Deng to realise the car, expensive as it was, meant very little to Philip Ye. With all the money the family Ye had, and with all the necessary contacts at their disposal, if Fatty Deng happened to drive the Mercedes off a cliff it was likely Philip Ye could have an identical car delivered to the Ye family mansion the very next morning if he so wished.

The spare shirt the brothers Na had lent him did not fit – too tight in every respect – so after Constable Ma had picked up Super-intendent Si Ying's personnel file from PSB HQ, they stopped off at Fatty Deng's apartment for him to change. He picked another of his Hawaiian shirts, depicting this time a fine sunset, in luxurious oranges and yellows. He frowned as he donned his new shirt, conscious of his pistol holstered at his waist, how it had never occurred to him while Brother Wang was being shot at by Superintendent Si Ying's cousin or when he was being pummelled by the cousin's army buddies to draw the weapon. No one had seen fit to mention this, not Philip Ye or Constable Ma or even the teasing brothers Na. He mentioned his failure to Constable Ma as he was buttoning up his fresh shirt.

"I don't know what I was thinking," he said.

Constable Ma had shrugged in response.

"What does that mean?"

Looking uncomfortable, Constable Ma replied, "Nothing."

"Tell me, Sister."

"Fatty, if you had drawn your pistol then you would have died this day."

The truth, as she saw it, stung him. It made him feel less of a man. But he could not fault her reasoning. Armed or not, he was no match for highly-trained PLA soldiers. He did not have Constable Ma's unerring eye, her nerves of steel, her uncanny ability to put a bullet wheresoever she desired. He was probably better off leaving the pistol at home and relying on his wits, as he had done the ten years he had spent in the police – not that his wits were working that well at the moment either.

From the fridge he got them both a small bottle of mineral water. He placed a quick call to his mother – she was still enjoying herself on the river – while Constable Ma had a quick read of Superintendent Si Ying's file.

"Anything useful?" asked Fatty Deng, when he got off the phone.

Constable Ma told him Superintendent Si Ying had indeed been in the army, a senior NCO, an aide to a Major-General Zi Hong of the 14th Group Army garrisoned in Kunming. No reason was given in the file for her leaving the army, no mention of her baby. And there was a glowing letter of recommendation from Major-General Zi Hong addressed personally to Commissioner Yang Da of PSB Building Security.

"Is that usual, Fatty – for a general to write a letter on behalf of an NCO?" asked Constable Ma.

"I don't know."

"Fatty, what if her baby is his – Major-General Zi Hong's, I mean? What if Major-General Zi Hong had an affair with Superintendent Si Ying when she was his aide and wanted her away from him so no one asked any questions, but close enough so he could visit the baby if he so wished? Kunming is only a short flight away."

Fatty Deng was surprised by Constable Ma's turn of mind. One moment she had trouble believing there were any bad apples in the PLA, the next she was accusing a senior officer of having an affair with a woman under his command. She was thinking like a true detective. And he told her so, making her blush and hide her face from him for a few moments. For all her prowess with a pistol, her great strength and size, she was really a sweet girl.

"Anything in the file about why Superintendent Si Ying was promoted so quickly after she joined the PSB?" he asked.

"A couple of performance reports from Commissioner Yang Da."

Fatty Deng took the file from Constable Ma and read the performance reports for himself. The reports were glowing, but superficial,

lacking substance, full of waffle. There was no logical reason for
Superintendent Si Ying to be made up to a superintendent within
a year. But, according to the file, the promotion had been properly
signed off by Chief of Police Di, the performance reports initialled
as read by him. It did not make sense. Fatty Deng hoped Chief Di
was not involved in this conspiracy, that he had only seen fit to trust
Commissioner Yang Da's recommendation that Superintendent Si
Ying was fully worthy of her new rank.

The basement decided upon by the brothers Ming for the interrogation of Superintendent Si Ying was only a short walk away, so Fatty
Deng chose to leave the Mercedes parked outside his apartment block.
Any passing gangster or ne'er-do-well would recognise the number
plate and leave it well enough alone. The basement was beneath a
disused warehouse, in the midst of a warren of narrow streets and
alleyways only those born and bred in the local area would have any
hope of navigating. The brothers Ming had chosen well. One of the
brothers was guarding the entrance to the warehouse, sitting on an
outside wall, reading a newspaper, cigarette hanging out of his mouth.
The cigarette fell out of his mouth and onto the ground when he
clasped eyes on Constable Ma, awed by the size of her, and then on
the state of Fatty Deng's swollen face.

"What happened to you?" he asked.

"It's a long story," replied Fatty Deng, not up for the telling.

"Where's Brother Wang?"

"That's a long story too."

The Ming brother – Fatty Deng could not tell if it was brother one,
two, three, or four – opened the door to the warehouse, revealing
a pile of rotting cardboard boxes and a disorderly heap of rusting
machine parts. He led them down a flight of dark, dank stairs to
the basement. Not only did the basement smell bad – machine oil,
industrial effluent? – it was also partially flooded from all the rain.
Fortunately, the concrete floor was not level. All the filthy water had

congregated down one corner, a shiny scum – illuminated by a dull ceiling-light – visible on the surface. The basement was a place to die, its only saving grace the respite it gave from the rising heat of the day.

The other three brothers Ming were sat on wooden stools with their backs against the wall watching Superintendent Si Ying, who had been hooded and tied to a chair and positioned directly below the ceiling-light. With a nod from Fatty Deng, the brothers gave up their stools and placed them before Superintendent Si Ying for Fatty Deng and Constable Ma to use, then retreated back upstairs but not before each of them had taken a long, hard look at Constable Ma. While all this was going on, Superintendent Si Ying moved her head slightly from side to side as if listening intently. But credit to her strength of mind, she did not speak or cry out. In her place, Fatty Deng knew he would have been frantic.

Fatty Deng had discussed strategy with Constable Ma on the short walk over. He had found her very nervous about interrogating a police officer – an officer more senior to herself. Fatty Deng had quickly come to the conclusion it might be advantageous if Superintendent Si Ying did not at first know whom she was dealing with, who was holding her and why. The more uncertain she was of her circumstances, and of her potential fate, the more talkative she might prove – or at least that was the plan.

As Constable Ma took her seat, happy to be nothing more than an observer, Fatty Deng pulled off Superintendent Si Ying's hood. Superintendent Si Ying blinked a few times to get accustomed to the light before first setting her eyes on Constable Ma, evaluating her, trying to estimate her chances against her, and then on Fatty Deng as he took his seat, her eyes widening in recognition. Then, still silent, she glanced around the basement, getting a better sense of her environment, her eyes lingering on the stairs, the only way out of there.

"Who's the muscle?" asked Superintendent Si Ying, speaking of Constable Ma.

"A friend," replied Fatty Deng.

"I thought your business was computers."

"I lied."

"You have made the mistake of your life."

"Is that so?"

"I am police."

"Really?"

"If you think I have money, then you are wasting your time. I am not worth holding for ransom. If you know what is good for you, you will untie me and let me go. Not only will the whole of Chengdu PSB be searching for me but my cousin also. You met him last evening, remember? Whatever gang you belong to, however well connected, my cousin will not be deterred. He will hunt you down like a dog and kill you."

"He did not seem that scary to me," said Fatty Deng, pleased she had so much to say for herself.

"My cousin is Captain Si Yu of the 14th Group Army, Special Operations Brigade – a born hunter, a killer. Realise your mistake, release me now, apologise, and all will be forgotten."

Fatty Deng could not believe his luck. Without asking a single question, she had volunteered what he had most wanted to know – the name, rank, and unit of her cousin.

"One man doesn't frighten me," said Fatty Deng.

Superintendent Si Ying laughed at him then, straining against her restraints, testing them, he guessed, not for the first time. He afforded himself a smile. The brothers Ming were no mugs. She wasn't going anywhere. But her confidence in her cousin did give him cause for concern. Who knew what resources Captain Si Yu might have to call upon in the city? It was time to bring this charade to an end and let Superintendent Si Ying know just where she stood.

He reached into the breast pocket of his shirt and took out his badge and ID, holding it up for Superintendent Si Ying to see. "My name is Deng. I am a special investigator for the Chengdu People's Procuratorate. And you are in a great deal of trouble."

Tough as she was, Superintendent Si Ying could not hide her shock. Nor could Constable Ma hide her emotions. Fatty Deng heard her chuckle to herself next to him with satisfaction. He wished he could turn to her and tell her that her satisfaction was premature, the battle with Superintendent Si Ying far from won.

"I have done nothing wrong," said Superintendent Si Ying, her tone more measured now, almost respectful.

"That remains to be seen," said Fatty Deng.

"This is not the Procuratorate," she said, making a show of glancing around the basement, wrinkling her nose in distaste at the smell."

"That is true."

"I have a baby."

"I have no interest in your baby. What does interest me is the shift you worked on Friday night."

"At the Black House?"

"Where else?"

"There is nothing to tell."

"I disagree."

"Mister Deng, if you would but contact my superior Commissioner Yang Da then—"

"I want you to tell me."

"There is nothing to tell," she repeated.

"Start with when you arrived at the Black House just before eight in the evening."

"It was just a normal night, Mister Deng. I have three officers working for me. We prepared tea, made the rounds of the Black House to ensure all was in order...and one of my men did a circuit outside of the Black House to look for any external threats. There were none. We then settled down for a quiet night. I wrote a few reports, worked on the rota for next month...two of my guys are taking annual leave soon...and made more rounds at regular intervals."

She offered nothing more. Fatty Deng chose to keep his own silence. He had done a lot of reading while in hospital, particularly of a book given him as a gift by Philip Ye, a text on interview techniques. While in the police he had questioned many lowlifes in the interrogation room at Wangjiang Road Station. But, back then, neither he nor any of his colleagues had ever considered the interviewing of suspects to be an art form. It was enough to curse, shout, threaten, and sometimes even hit a suspect to get the desired result. He hadn't realised, until he had started reading the book, about how little he knew of interview technique. Not only had he learned about managing the conversation, about being very brief and precise in the questions he posed, about the need to build up a *relationship of trust* with the interviewee, but also, most startlingly, he had learned about the power of silence.

Most people did not enjoy silence.

Most people spoke up to fill the void.

And Fatty Deng found Superintendent Si Ying to be no different than most, becoming unnerved when he posed her no further questions.

"At midnight I got a call," she said.

"From whom?"

"My superior, Commissioner Yang Da."

"So?"

"He ordered me to conduct an inspection at another site."

"Was that unusual?"

"I suppose."

"Which site was that?"

"It was another Black House."

"Where?"

"I am not allowed to say."

Fatty Deng smiled at the tactic used against him. Superintendent Si Ying was proving no fool. Only a few people in Chengdu, those at the very highest echelons of power, were privy to the full list of Black Sites in and about the city. He doubted anyone at the Procuratorate would have access to that list – not even Chief Prosecutor Gong. The PSB protected its secrets very well. He chose not to force the issue – not yet anyway.

"Did you carry out that inspection?" he asked.

"I did – I always follow orders."

"Alone?"

After the briefest hesitation, as if weighing up the lesser of two evils, she replied, "No, I took my whole team."

Fatty Deng feigned a look of horror. "You left the Black House on Liberation Street unguarded?"

"I was following orders," she said, defensively.

"Are you saying Commissioner Yang Da ordered you to take your whole team to this other site, to leave the Black House on Liberation Street unguarded?"

"Yes."

"Didn't you find that odd?"

For the first time there was a flicker of fear in her eyes. "Yes...yes, I suppose I do now. But it is not for me to question orders. I am but a lowly superintendent. Mister Deng, you must allow me at least to make a phone call. A neighbour cares for my baby when I am at work. I should be home by now. She will be worried sick."

"I have no interest in your baby. Tell me about your cousin."

"Mister Deng, it was wrong of me to threaten you with him. He is a good guy really. He was only teasing you last night about your shirt. He meant nothing by it. It's just his way. Soldiers are like that. They can be a bit rough in their humour."

"Where is he lodging?"

"He returned to barracks in Kunming this morning."

"His friends too?"

"Yes, Mister Deng."

"What are their names?"

"I did not think to ask...I did not meet them."

"Where were they lodging?"

"Somewhere in the city, I suppose."

"You don't know?"

"Again, Mister Deng, I did not think to ask. My cousin just gave me a call, told me he was in the city on leave for a day or two. I have a busy life, working fulltime, looking after the baby and—"

"I need a contact number for him."

"Why would—?"

"Quickly, Superintendent – I do not have all day."

"He is not allowed a phone when he is on duty. And I think he will be away on operations now for—"

"Just give me his number, Superintendent."

"I cannot remember it."

"Will it be on your phone?"

"I don't know...maybe...I think, possibly, yes."

If Captain Si Yu had called as she had stated, even if she did not have him in her phone's address book, there would be a record of the call made, and then he should not be hard to trace via his phone. Unfortunately, Fatty Deng did not have Superintendent Si's phone. Philip Ye had it. After the snatch and grab, after Brother Wang had picked up the phone just prior to having his ear shot off, and after Fatty Deng had finally got them all to the Ye family mansion, he had gone through Brother Wang's suit jacket pocket and found the phone. It had been smashed beyond repair – a bitter blow. Philip Ye had promised him the tech unit back at PSB HQ would need a couple of days or so to retrieve the data from the phone, and the phone log from the service provider would take as long as it took.

"Mister Deng, now I have answered all your questions, may I leave now. My baby will—"

He shook his head, stunning her, cutting her off in mid-sentence. She was not going anywhere. But, for now, the interrogation was over. He needed time to think, to consider her answers. She had put Commissioner Yang Da in the frame. And he would not be snatching Commissioner Yang Da off the street without the say so of Prosecutor Xu or Philip Ye – preferably both. He also wanted to think about Captain Si Yu's army friends, the men Constable Ma had shot dead. They had got to the Lucky Dragon Tobacco Emporium so quickly they had to have been lodging close to Liberation Street. He wanted to return to the area, trawl the local hotels and guest-houses, those most likely to welcome soldiers in the city on leave.

Fatty Deng stood to replace the hood over Superintendent Si Ying's head, not realising Constable Ma had one final question all of her own.

"Superintendent, do you own a green crocodile-skin handbag?"

Superintendent Si Ying's mouth dropped open, as dumbfounded by the question as Fatty Deng.

FIFTY-ONE

— · —

X u Ya's phone call to Secretary Wu had left her with the distinct impression she was no longer needed in Chengdu. Relieved as he had sounded to hear that Ye Zihao was, in her opinion, innocent of any involvement in Primo Gong's murder, Secretary Wu had been almost joyous on learning that she thought it useful if Philip Ye performed a more active role in *her* investigation. And as for Investigator Deng going crazy and detaining Superintendent Si Ying prematurely, and Constable Ma's shooting dead of two suspects who had almost certainly been up to their necks in the conspiracy – thereby, regrettably, rendering them unavailable for questioning – Secretary Wu seemed not at all concerned. Xu Ya nearly resigned over the phone there and then. That she didn't, she thought, was testament to her strength of character, to her determination to finish this final investigation, to achieve justice for Primo Gong. Then she could fly off to London, or wherever, and begin the next stage of her life as a legal trouble-shooter for the family Ye. No more working in her dull office at the Procuratorate. No more attending Procuratorate meetings and being forced to listen to all the idiots have their say – in whose ranks she included Chief Prosecutor Gong – before putting them all in their place and educating them on the letter of the law, on correct legal procedure, on the proper way to put a prosecution file together, and, just as importantly, on the proper way to comport themselves as public prosecutors. There would also be no more appearances on TV, thank goodness. She would not miss that kind of exposure – not at all!

In the car on the way to the Cry of the Crane Teahouse to meet with The Historians – Xu Ya was yet to be convinced of their involvement in any crime – Philip Ye, had, maddeningly, retreated deep within himself. If she was to guess his mood – and it would be a guess – it would be that he was sad. But about what? He had already made it quite clear that he wasn't going to lose any sleep over her leaving Chengdu.

Was he missing his dead fiancée again?

Or was he, by nature, an unhappy and unfulfilled person?

To initiate a conversation – they could not just drive in silence! – she settled upon neutral and common ground. "Investigator Deng is not the same since the attack by those cultists. I do not think he sleeps properly anymore and he continually glances about him when we are out together. It's what is called hypervigilance. I looked it up. I have arranged through the Procuratorate for him to see a psychiatrist. But he won't go. Maybe you could speak to him...man-to-man?"

"He's an adult – able to make his own choices."

"But he is not well."

"He is doing his job, which is all that matters."

"He blames me. If I had not gone off to Chongqing then—"

"Prosecutor, contrary to what you think, it isn't always about you. He blames himself for his lack of awareness, for putting himself in such a vulnerable position. Now, as I said, he's a grown man. He will work it out. He got by before you arrived in Chengdu, and, believe me, he will get by after you leave him to jet off around the world."

"That's not what I—"

"In fact, we will all get by after you have gone. Naturally there will be a hole in the TV schedules but I am sure we will find a way to cope."

"That's not fair!"

"Isn't it?" he replied, angry. "Do you actually care about anything other than yourself?"

Xu Ya shut her mouth and kept her eyes on the road ahead, willing away the tears that threatened to spring from her eyes. Like father, like son, she thought. Best not to prod a brooding bear – especially a bear who knew nothing, who could never understand her, and who, if he had any great insight into people, would have seen instantly that her problem was not that she did not care but that *she cared too much!*

She glanced out of the corner of her eye at him and saw he was doing that stupid deep breathing thing of his, his eyes closed. She felt like slamming on the brakes and pushing him out of the car. In the rear-view mirror she noticed, not for the first time, a black Mercedes identical to that usually driven by Philip Ye, not far behind them. Worried that they were being tailed by people out to do them harm, it was only when she was forced to come to a stop at traffic lights, the black Mercedes pulling up close behind, that she could see who was in the car, the brothers Na, flashing the rings she had bought them and smoking big cigars.

She knew immediately what they were about: providing protection. She had been wondering, if the threat was so great from the rogue PLA unit, why Philip Ye had chosen not to arm himself. She was pleased the brothers Na had personally taken it upon themselves to watch over her. Regardless of their obscure origins, the anonymity of their original employer, their inexplicable transfer of loyalty to Ye Zihao, their unusual authority to carry firearms – if indeed they had such authority – Xu Ya was comforted by their presence. Unlike the brooding, deep-breathing Philip Ye next to her, at least they appreciated her and had made it very clear, no matter what, they would always keep her safe.

There was an unmistakeable air of sadness hanging over the Cry of the Crane Teahouse when Xu Ya entered, Philip Ye following on behind her. The sadness struck Xu Ya like a wave, moving through and over her, swallowing her whole, deepening the depression that had already taken hold of her mind since she had received the note from Sarangerel. Never before had Xu Ya sensed such emotional pain emanating from a group of men – reason perhaps for why there were no other customers in the teahouse. They had pushed a couple of small tables together so they could huddle close and talk. Her first instinct was to turn around and leave them to their grief, not wanting to deal with such intense emotion; she was hardly able to deal properly with her own. But she also experienced a measure of self-satisfaction. Was this sadness not proof that none of these men could have had anything to do with the murder of their former comrade and friend Jin Huiliang? Was this not proof that Philip Ye's suspicions toward Bo Qi – he had to be one of those present – were unfounded, that Philip Ye's self-professed ability to tell the innocent from the guilty just by looking at them was nothing but baseless boasting? There were no guilty men here.

There were seven of them, all with short, military-style haircuts, their faces deeply lined by the gathering years and by lives spent outside in all weathers; and, she supposed, from living through periods of intense battle-stress. But, as she approached them – Philip Ye had, for some reason, agreed to let her lead the meeting – they all politely stood as one to greet her, all putting, as one would expect from old soldiers, a brave face on their loss.

"I am Prosecutor Xu," she said, extending a hand to each of them in turn. "I have come to personally offer my condolences and to assure you that I will stop at nothing to bring Jin Huiliang's murderer to justice."

As each of them shook her hand, staring at her in wonderment as they did so, they gave her their names as well as their ranks on retirement.

"Hua Delun, major, attached to the 14th Group Army – as all of us once were."

"Yao Yao, lieutenant-colonel."

"Lan Liu, major."

"Zhang Yi, major."

"Mu Xin, colonel."

"Fei Shi, major."

Only the last, who introduced himself as Senior Colonel Bo Qi, demonstrated any lack of pleasure in greeting her. But Xu Ya thought that his coolness was less about her than about Philip Ye who was standing somewhere behind her.

"We were expecting Constable Ma," said Bo Qi.

"I am afraid she was involved in a police shooting earlier this morning and is otherwise engaged," explained Xu Ya.

"Is she hurt?" asked Bo Qi, his concern, in Xu Ya's view, quite genuine.

"Quite unhurt, I assure you," said Xu Ya, accepting the seat that was offered to her so she could join the circle of mourning, and smiling her thanks at Lan Liu – who, for an old man, she thought very handsome – for waving toward the waitress to summon fresh tea and additional cups.

"We all saw you on TV, Prosecutor," said Hua Delun.

"You were most impressive," said Zhang Yi.

"A solitary rose growing in a garden of weeds," added Lan Liu, confirming Xu Ya's already good opinion of him.

It was a great pity Philip Ye could never find such charming words for her. Speaking of whom, Philip Ye had quite rudely not bothered to introduce himself to The Historians, and had, she saw, with a quick glance behind her, taken a seat at the back of the teahouse, almost as far away as he could get.

What was he up to?

If he was still sulking about her readiness to accept a job working for his father, did he really have to be so unprofessional as to bring his personal issues into the investigation?

So childish!

So petty!

"I am so very sorry for your loss," said Xu Ya to The Historians, needing them to know she was full of sympathy for them, and hoping they would focus on her rather than on the ignorant buffoon sitting behind her. She took a pen and her notebook from her handbag. "I only wish to learn a bit more about Jin Huiliang – and about each of you, if you are willing. Hopefully, the more I understand about Jin Huiliang's life, the better I might be able to understand how he came to cross paths with his killer."

"It had to be a heartless burglar," said Bo Qi.

"A drug-addict looking for money," said Zhang Yi.

"Yes, we have been talking and we are all in agreement, Prosecutor," said Hua Delun. "It was most likely a drug-addict. Society is not what it once was. Since the Reform Era, the criminal element has run out of control. There is nothing but greed, corruption, and licentiousness everywhere. That is why, Prosecutor, it was so refreshing to see you on TV. There are so few willing to enforce the Rule of Law. You are a beacon of hope in these troubled times."

"Commissioner Ho was a monster. There's nothing worse than corrupt police," said Bo Qi, taking a hard glance over her shoulder to where Philip Ye was seated.

Xu Ya thought it politic not to mention the many instances of corruption uncovered in the highest echelons of the PLA in recent years, not wishing to antagonise The Historians in any way and undermine her own purpose in meeting with them.

"I understand," she said, "that since his retirement from the army, Jin Huiliang had made himself into a writer of military histories – an expert in the conflicts of the Song Dynasty. And I also understand that you all came to Chengdu to be near him, also to write. It would be useful for me to learn all your fields of study."

Purposely, she had avoided all mention of their creative endeavours as a means to ameliorate battlefield trauma, to distract themselves from their memories of those nightmarish scenes they must have been witness to during the Sino-Vietnamese War, scenes that surely continued to haunt them to this very day. She made notes as they spoke.

"The failed Spring Offensive, Korea, 1951," said Bo Qi, again glowering in Philip Ye's direction.

"The An Lushan Rebellion, Tang Dynasty," said Hua Delun.

"Prosecutor, I have two projects on the go," said Yao Yao. "The Wang Lun uprising of 1774 and the Eight Trigrams uprising of 1813 – though researching just one of those campaigns is quite enough for my little brain."

Some muted laughter, some nodding of heads. Xu Ya smiled in acknowledgement. Yao Yao looked anything but stupid. There was a fine mind lurking behind his fine eyes, she saw.

"I am researching the War against Japanese Aggression, 1937-45," said Lan Liu. "Especially how the war affected the south. The work is proving fascinating, Prosecutor. I am mainly documenting the heroic resistance of the Nationalist armies against the Japanese, unearthing historical truths that have often made the Party uncomfortable. Thankfully, old attitudes are changing now; Communist or Nationalist, we were all Chinese, fighting a common enemy."

"The Taiping Rebellion for me," said Zhang Yi. "A people's history as well as a military history. With probably up to 30 million dead, the costliest civil war in human history. And to think the Americans still teach their children that their civil war – which happened at about the same time – was the bloodiest conflict of the 19th Century. Such ignorance, such blind stupidity! I am also working on a side-project: a short biography of the leader of the Qing forces during the rebellion, General Zeng Guofen. However, Prosecutor, I must confess I appear to have taken on thirty years of work when I have only about ten years remaining."

"Nonsense – you seem but a young man to me," said Xu Ya.

"Ah, the lady is as kind as she is beautiful," said Zhang Yi. "A most devastating combination."

There was laughter around the table, teacups raised in salute to her. Xu Ya found herself blushing under the admiring stares of the old soldiers. She wondered what Philip Ye was thinking.

"Zhang Yi, never forget that we all have faith in you," said Bo Qi. "Jin Huiliang believed in you...Jin Huiliang believed in us all."

The laughter around the table died out, the mood in the teahouse sombre again, reflective, each of The Historians lost in their own thoughts. Xu Ya felt great emotion well up in her. She wanted to speak meaningful words of comfort to these men who were hurting so deeply. But only empty platitudes came to mind.

"My work concerns the Sino-Japanese War of 1894-5," said Mu Xin, eventually, his voice barely more than a whisper. "I have no side-project."

Xu Ya thought him a shy man. He blinked constantly, a nervous tic, she assumed.

Fei Shi was the last to speak. Of all The Historians, it was he who seemed the most bereft, the most overcome with emotion. He brushed tears from his eyes as he spoke. "I am researching our own little war, the Sino-Vietnamese Border War, 1979-90, Deng Xiaoping's nasty little campaign. I did not want to write this history. I thought I was done with the war. I wanted to write about some other conflict instead. But Jin Huiliang pushed me to write our story. If I did not, he told me, the ghosts would continue to wander in and out of my house until the end of time. He encouraged me, Prosecutor...put steel in my spine...as he had done so all those years ago at Lao Cai, when my courage was as scarce as our food and water, when my resolve, my fighting spirit, was faltering by the hour."

Xu Ya feared Fei Shi would lose his composure then, would make her feel more awkward than she already did – an unwelcome intruder in their house of mourning. But Bo Qi spoke up, taking her attention away from Fei Shi.

"Fei Shi is being modest. He was as brave as any of us on the field of battle. He is also working on a side-project: a biography of his father General Fei Song, hero of the Revolutionary War, hero of the war in Korea against the Americans and their lackeys, and overall commander of the 14th Group Army during the opening stages of the war with Vietnam. Unfortunately, the biography must be completed with haste. General Fei Song is now a very old man. His few remaining memories are like precious diamonds. Prosecutor, you may not have heard of him, but to any soldier, retired or serving, General Fei Song is a legend. His biography is awaited with much excitement."

"I have heard of him," said Xu Ya.

It was not quite a lie. Caught up in the emotion of the moment, Xu Ya *imagined* she had heard of General Fei Song. Hours would pass before she would realise that she had fooled herself, that his name had meant nothing to her at all.

"I promise you all I will soon complete my father's biography," said Fei Shi, dabbing at his eyes with a handkerchief. "And here today, with Prosecutor Xu as my witness, I will make you all another promise, that when I am done writing of my father, I will write another biography...of my friend...of our friend...the very best of us...the greatest soldier of our generation...the hero of Lao Cai: Lieutenant-General Jin Huiliang."

They all raised their teacups into the air again, and this time Xu Ya followed suit – a toast to the departed spirit of Jin Huiliang. When the teacups had been lowered, she asked, "What did Jin Huilaing do at Lao Cai?"

"He did not falter when others faltered, Prosecutor," said Bo Qi. "That is all you need to know."

There were nods of agreement from all The Historians, but Xu Ya felt slightly miffed by Bo Qi's cool tone, the terseness of his answer. Out of all of them, Bo Qi was the least likeable – a trait that might have contributed to Philip Ye suspecting him of being a criminal. She had no such suspicions, though. She could only guess what each of these men, including Bo Qi, had gone through during the war. They had withstood the bullets and shells of the enemy; she could certainly withstand a little sharpness of tongue.

Before she could frame another question, quite unexpectedly, Philip Ye spoke up from behind her.

"What was Jin Huiliang's side-project?" he asked, his voice brusque, almost rude, full of his detective's authority, expecting a full and immediate answer.

"None," they all replied, almost as one.

Except for Fei Shi that is, who quickly looked away from Xu Ya's sympathetic gaze, covering his eyes with his hand, fully overcome with emotion.

Philip Ye asked nothing more, but the damage had been done. The atmosphere of the teahouse was not what it had been, the grief of The Historians – except for that of Fei Shi – replaced with a simmering hostility. Xu Ya cursed Philip Ye's bad timing.

Was he not an experienced detective?

Was he not supposed to be expert in the questioning of witnesses?

And yet now he had made her job that much harder. None of The Historians looked as if they wished to answer further questions. All had closed their minds to her. Nevertheless, she was unwilling to give up. She pressed on. She owed this much to Jin Huiliang.

She enquired about Jin Huiliang's love-life.

He had none.

Family disputes?

A difficult relationship with his daughter, but nothing out of the ordinary. His ex-wife was dead some years now, of cancer it was thought.

Did he have other friends in Chengdu?

Bo Qi spoke up for all of them. "Prosecutor, believe me when I tell you that you are wasting your time with all your questions. Jin Huiliang was a hermit, a man dedicated to his writing. He had not an enemy in the world. He had even corresponded with Vietnamese veterans of the battle of Lao Cai, happy to forgive and to accept forgiveness in return. Concentrate on the local thieves, the neighbourhood drug-addicts, who have no respect for anyone or anything – not even for themselves. It is with those scum you will find your answers...all the evidence you will need."

"It is like we fought for nothing!" exclaimed Fei Shi, suddenly uncovering his tear-filled eyes and shaking his fist in the air. "Society has gone to hell!"

She decided against pressing The Historians any further. It was pointless raising either Primo Gong or Du Luli with them. If they had had something more to offer her, those men, those honourable men, would have spoken up. Back on the street, after she had shaken their hands in parting, after they had wished her the very best with her investigation, after they had charmed her again by saying they hoped to see her on the TV again very soon, Xu Ya turned to Philip Ye to give him a piece of her mind. He had ruined the meeting with The Historians with that one, ill-timed question. But Philip Ye's eyes were on the sky. The breeze had picked up and she could see for herself a bank of threatening black cloud on the horizon to the south-west.

"Rain is on the way," he said.

Before she could reply to that unremarkable observation, her phone rang. It was Investigator Deng. She reminded herself to keep her temper. She would deal with Investigator Deng for detaining Superintendent Si Ying without her express permission some other time. She listened intently as he told her all he had learned from his first pass at Superintendent Si Ying, about how she had placed herself and her security detail *away* from the Black House at the time of Primo Gong's murder, how she had received a surprise order from Commissioner Yang Da. Investigator Deng then explained that he had decided to let Superintendent Si Ying sweat for a few hours and to return to Liberation Street with Constable Ma, intent on searching for the lodgings of the men shot by Constable Ma.

"Be careful," Xu Ya told him.

Philip Ye had not been listening in to her phone conversation. Instead, he had already climbed back into her car. Annoyed by his lack of interest, it was only when she got back into her car beside him that she realised he had taken a phone call all of his own.

"Constable Ma?" she guessed, as he slipped his phone back in his pocket.

"Yes."

So that was how it was going to be. "Interesting development about Commissioner Yang Da, don't you think?"

"Perhaps."

She started the engine, checking in the mirror that the brothers Na were ready for the off in their Mercedes. "Well, our meeting was a waste of time, wasn't it?"

"I think not," said Philip Ye.

"By that I take it you mean that the elimination of potential suspects might also be considered progress?"

"No – I mean that we now have our man."

Xu Ya thought her head was going to explode. "*What* are you talking about?"

He turned and stared at her with complete disdain. "Fei Shi is our man and the others, with Bo Qi as their new leader, are complicit."

Xu Ya laughed out loud.

"Laugh all you want, Prosecutor. I do not care. I know my trade. All I have to discover now is what Jin Huiliang and Primo Gong were working on, how their work connected back to Fei Shi, and why Fei Shi felt so threatened by this work as to have them both murdered – not to mention Du Luli. If you don't agree with me, that is fine. Just keep out of my way."

"This is my investigation!"

"Then grow up and see those men back in the teahouse for what they are rather than what you wish them to be."

"I saw only grieving men."

"Then you are blind."

Xu Ya threw a hand up at his face, not to strike him, just to frighten him. But real anger lay behind her movement and it was misjudged. And he, probably expecting her to bow to his greater knowledge and insight of the criminal mind, had expected no reaction from her except dutiful female submission. He flinched at the last moment and pulled away from her but still she caught him a glancing blow across his face.

"What is wrong with you?" he protested, raising his hands to ward off any further strikes.

"Oh, don't be a big baby!" she replied.

She steered the car out into traffic, happy to see the black Mercedes in hot pursuit. The brothers Na, who had been witness to the confrontation, were laughing so hard their Mercedes was veering from side to side.

FIFTY-TWO

— · —

The three months Philip Ye had spent trying to understand the essential nature of Prosecutor Xu seemed to him as so much wasted time. He was no closer to a conclusion as he had been the day she had arrived in Chengdu. He could not even profitably cast his mind back more than a decade to when they had spent four years together studying at the University of Wuhan. He vaguely remembered the university, the lectures, and even some of the teaching staff, but of his fellow students, of the young Xu Ya, he had no memory at all – no extra data upon which to call. She was a conundrum, impossible to fathom. Her bursts of temper – indeed, her flashes of violence – had become somewhat predictable even if he could not necessarily divine their cause. But as to her essential nature, as to whether she was a good person or bad, he had no clue.

Could she have murdered her husband?

He thought, yes.

But she was equally likely not to have done so.

He could honestly say he had never known – not counting his own father, of course – anyone so difficult to pin down.

However, comprehend her or not, Prosecutor Xu could still be used. And he had used her. He had flown her – as he had once wanted to fly his pet hawk, the shikra, at prey – at The Historians. Not to draw blood, but to flush them from the bushes, out of their hiding places, to make them panic, take flight, and reveal themselves for who they really were. Of all The Historians it had been Bo Qi who had first realised the nature of the threat posed by Prosecutor Xu, trying desperately to keep his star-struck comrades to the agreed plan, to blame the local hoodlums and drug-addicts for the death of their friend. But in the end The Historians had folded in the presence of Prosecutor Xu as he had guessed they would, old men awed by her beauty and not inconsiderable magnetic allure, to reveal themselves as the criminal conspirators they truly were. One of them, Fei Shi, had seemed to be so filled with guilt as to be on the verge of nervous collapse. He would have confessed all, Philip Ye was sure, if not given strength by his comrades. Whether he was merely the weakest link in the conspiracy or the actual instigator of the dreadful murders, Philip Ye did not know, but Fei Shi was his man. And Philip Ye would have him as soon as he understood what it was Jin Huiliang and Primo Gong had been working on.

Next stop, Madame Ding's apartment, to discover from her – with luck – the identity of Jin Huiliang's typist. And from the typist, Philip Ye hoped to learn the work Jin Huiliang must have been doing for Primo Gong. Back at the teahouse, Philip Ye had asked but one question: "What was Jin Huiliang's side-project?" So taken had The Historians been with Prosecutor Xu, the question had surprised them, the truth revealed in their eyes long before the denials that Jin Huiliang had ever engaged in a side-project had tumbled from their lips.

He was onto them and they knew it. The pace of the investigation was now a serious consideration. If he didn't act quickly evidence would be lost, witnesses and potential suspects would vanish, and phone calls might well be received by the highest echelons of the Party in Chengdu from someone within the Chengdu Military Region headquarters, complaining that a certain homicide detective was looking too closely at something he should not. Philip Ye doubted a lowly city Party chief such as Party Chief Li would want to lock horns with the PLA. He knew he had to quickly present a *fait accompli* to Chief of Police Di, and therefore to Party Chief Li – with or without Prosecutor Xu. Speed was the key. And so far, by virtue of her crazy driving, Prosecutor Xu was unwittingly doing her best to help. She was driving as a shikra could fly, darting this way and that, swerving around corners and from lane to lane, sometimes – as he was at pains to point out – on the wrong side of the road, her mystifying response: to stick her tongue out at him. Finally, dreading to think how the brothers Na were coping with the car-follow, Philip Ye was forced to close his eyes against the rapid nausea-inducing shifts of momentum.

He only opened his eyes again when she slammed on the brakes, throwing him painfully against his seatbelt, and announced, quite redundantly, "We're here!"

Outside of Madame Ding's apartment, Prosecutor Xu put her hands to her ears. "What is that awful noise?"

Philip Ye had already noticed her unusual sensitivity to sound, to disturbance of any kind – except that of the sound of her own voice. Back at the teahouse, when speaking to The Historians, he had seen her flinch when a waitress, some distance away, had dropped a teacup to the floor, breaking it. None of The Historians, all suffering from the trauma of battle, had moved a muscle.

"Madame Ding is singing," said Philip Ye.

"That is singing?"

"Traditional opera."

"I know what it is supposed to be, Superintendent...but she has no voice, no voice at all."

Philip Ye knocked on the door. The wailing – it could be described as nothing else – stopped. Madame Ding opened the door, hesitantly at first, revealing a face streaked with tears. Philip Ye assumed she was still grieving the loss of Jin Huiliang, as well as the loss of her main income stream.

"Oh, Superintendent, it is you," she said, forcing a smile – a smile that broadened considerably when her eyes lit upon Prosecutor Xu. "Prosecutor Xu! I cannot believe it! I saw you on TV. I told the General all about you. He had no TV, you understand – he lived only for his writing. But I told him how beautiful you are, how you have come to Chengdu to bring justice to the people, to uphold the Rule of Law. I am so relieved. I can sleep easily now. Prosecutor, you will catch the General's killer. I am quite sure of it." Madame Ding then threw her arms about Prosecutor Xu, squeezing her so tightly that Philip Ye thought he might have to intervene so that Prosecutor Xu could breathe. Philip Ye had never seen anything quite like it.

In a corner of the apartment, in Madame Ding's basic kitchenette, Philip Ye set about preparing tea for them all, while watching, with some curiosity, another facet of Prosecutor Xu emerge: the comforter, the woman of infinite compassion, the woman who knew all the right words to ease Madame Ding's distress.

When he took the tea through to them, it was as if they were sisters, holding hands as they were, both satisfied with each other's company, Madame Ding happy Jin Huiliang's investigation was now going to get attention it deserved – the police, evidently, no longer good enough – and Prosecutor Xu happy to bask in all the praise she was receiving, justified or not. The two women could not have been more different, though: the one raised in the country, both skin and personality roughened by a hard-scrabble life, separated from her husband and children by the harsh economic realities of having to earn a living; the other raised in comfort, and gifted by Heaven with both beauty and a quicksilver mind that could take her anywhere, if she so wished, in the world.

"Superintendent, you must feel so honoured to be assisting Prosecutor Xu today," said Madame Ding.

"You cannot imagine," replied Philip Ye, wearily.

"The Superintendent has some more questions for you," said Prosecutor Xu.

"Did you help him prepare the questions?" asked Madame Ding

"I did," replied Prosecutor Xu, with a little laugh.

Finding no humour in Prosecutor Xu's continued goading of him, Philip Ye asked Madame Ding, "Did Jin Huiliang have a computer of any sort?"

"Oh no, Superintendent – he was not one for new technology. I told you, he wouldn't even use a phone."

"Who did all his typing for him then?"

"Ms. Lu, of course."

"You did not speak of her yesterday."

"But you did not ask, Superintendent. Ms. Lu is a very nice lady. Like me, she is quite devoted to the General. Years ago, she was his secretary in the army. She is retired now. She just tends to her pot plants in her apartment. She has two cats as well. She spoils them rotten. She has no children, you understand."

"I do."

"I tried to tell her yesterday about the General," said Madame Ding, upsetting herself again, getting another hug for her trouble from Prosecutor Xu. "But she wouldn't answer her phone and wouldn't open the door to me when I went round to her apartment. It is possible she has gone away. The General told me she has family in Anhui Province, that she visits them from time to time."

Doing his best to keep the suspicion from his face that Ms. Lu might no longer be in the land of the living, Philip Ye asked, "May I have her address?"

"It's apartment number 14."

"Where exactly?"

"Oh, I don't know for sure. I forget the name of the street. But it's only a short bus ride away."

"You will show us the way?"

"Yes, Superintendent – I think it would be best if I am there anyway when Ms. Lu hears the awful news," said Madame Ding. "Constable Ma was quite cruel to me yesterday when I was so upset about the General. The police do not always understand that the people have feelings."

"That is so true," said Prosecutor Xu.

"Madame Ding," said Philip Ye, struggling to concentrate, "have you heard the name Primo Gong?"

"I don't think so."

"He's an American."

Madame Ding turned to speak to Prosecutor Xu directly. "Oh, now I come to think of it, the General did have a visitor. I did not like the look of him. It was a few months ago. He looked Chinese but his manners were so bad he could have been an American. It was late-morning. I was behind schedule. I had just done some shopping for the General. When I got back to the apartment block there was this fancy sports car parked in the road outside. When I entered the apartment the General was not at his desk. He was in the lounge, in conversation with this man I had never seen before, much younger than the General, about your age Superintendent, dressed very casually, though, like a lot of young people these days. I did not take to him. He seemed very brash to me, too sure of himself...not respectful enough toward the General."

"They were arguing?"

"Oh no – nothing like that," replied Madame Ding. "But the stranger thought too much of himself. He looked through me as if I was not there. I understood nothing of what they were speaking. It was like another language entirely."

"English?"

"I wouldn't know, Superintendent – but the General was a very clever man. He might have learned English in the army. Anyway, once I had put the shopping away I had to leave. The very next day I asked the General who his guest had been. He would not answer me. He was most evasive. He also didn't look happy and, now I come to think about it, it wasn't long afterward that he began having bouts of illness. That was how I came to meet Ms. Lu. The General, too ill to leave the apartment, asked me to drop some of his writings in to Ms. Lu to be typed. Ms. Lu made me tea and we did have a laugh. She told me lots of funny stories of her time in the army."

"Did you ever see this stranger again?"

"No, Superintendent – which is why I didn't mention him to you before. I had quite forgotten him."

"Is this the man?" asked Prosecutor Xu, showing Madame Ding a photograph of Primo Gong on her phone, the photograph retrieved from some business news website.

"Yes, that's him!" said Madame Ding, excited. "Is he the murderer? Did this Primo Gong kill the General?"

"No, Madame Ding," replied Philip Ye. But he knew in his heart, that even if Primo Gong had not actually wielded the ice-axe, that by his visit to Jin Huiliang's apartment all those months ago, he might as well have done.

FIFTY-THREE

M ister Wu, of Mister Wu's Cycle Sales and Repair Shop, stood in his doorway, cup of tea in hand, and stared suspiciously up at the sky. The prospects for the remainder of the day were not good. On the horizon, away to the south-west, lay a threatening band of black cloud. Furthermore, the weather announcer on his favourite local radio station – a Ms. Qu, whom he had come to trust implicitly – had, only a few moments ago, warned that torrential rain was due over the city in a matter of hours. Which was a pity, thought Mister Wu. For this very morning, acting in his capacity as Chair of the Liberation Street Traders Association, he had achieved a notable victory – a victory that would surely enable him to lay claim to be one of the most influential Chairs in Liberation Street history. It would be a terrible shame if now, before the fruits of his victory could be realised, a great flood would arise – the drains unable to cope – and reduce Liberation Street to so much rubble and its occupants to so many bloated corpses.

Mister Wu sighed and sipped his tea. The day had not begun well. Not long after he had opened up the shop for the day's trade, two armed gangsters had tried to rob the Lucky Dragon Tobacco Emporium. Or at least that was the story propagated by the local police who, though the bodies of the two gangsters had now been removed and the street returned to some measure of normality, continued to swarm the area.

Mister Wu did not believe the story. The fat man had been up to his neck in whatever it was that had happened, the fat man who, according to a particularly talkative young policewoman, was named Deng – confirming what Sun Mei had already told him – and who, quite incredibly, worked directly for Prosecutor Xu Ya, the very same glamorous public prosecutor who had so recently appeared on TV.

"Investigator Deng is quite the hero," said the evidently star-struck policewoman.

No, thought Mister Wu, the fat man is nothing more than a liar. All that stuff he had said about being in the business of computers, about looking up and down Liberation Street for more office space, had been nothing more than bullshit. The day before, Mister Wu had quickly made him for what he was – not police, admittedly, as Mister Wu had initially thought, but the Procuratorate was near enough. The fat man had been taking too close an interest in the Lucky Dragon Tobacco Emporium and Sun Mei – too close for Mister Wu's liking. And now, this morning, when the two gangsters had arrived on Liberation Street, they had seemed more interested in beating the fat man to a pulp rather than in stripping the shelves of the Lucky Dragon Tobacco Emporium of all its cigarettes or in taking the cash from the till. Mister Wu was no expert on armed robberies – there had been no such crime on Liberation Street in living memory – but to say he had his doubts about the whole incident this morning was an understatement.

And what had happened to Sun Mei and her father? None of the local police, not even the especially talkative young policewoman, would say. Either they were all under orders to keep quiet or else they didn't know. The person who would have known, Mister Wu had forgotten to ask. If anyone wanted to understand why he had forgotten to pose that most important question to Superintendent Ye, he would explain that the excitement had befuddled his brain, that the shock of witnessing the Battle of Liberation Street had undermined his usual deep concern for his friends and fellow shop-keepers. Unfortunately, the truth was far more prosaic. As his two ex-wives – he was very happily divorced from both of them – would surely testify, he had a simple, one-track mind.

It had been his one chance to do something about the drains.

He had had to act.

Was that not the way of men who made history, men who wouldn't let their natural compassion for their fellow human beings get in the way of making a notable achievement?

He had been brave.

He had faced down his fears.

He had walked right up to Philip Ye, who was not only a super-intendent in the PSB but was also, more importantly, the son of the former mayor of Chengdu.

Mister Wu had not known what to expect. Years ago, Philip Ye had been all over the local news and the society magazines, often photographed out on the town with the most important people and usually with a beautiful woman clinging to his arm. He had been a man to envy, make no mistake. But, with the coming of the Shanghai Clique, and the shocking placing of Mayor Ye under house-arrest, Philip Ye had all but dropped out of sight.

What sort of man had Philip Ye become in the intervening years? Had his time in the police corrupted his soul? Was he so bitter about the misfortune that had been visited upon his own family that he now wanted nothing to do with the concerns of the common people?

Happily, even after all the excitement of the Battle of Liberation Street, with all the frightened people and the local police milling around, Mister Wu had found Philip Ye to be the perfect gentleman: cool, poised, not a single hair out of place, and quite willing to listen to every word Mister Wu had had to say. Mister Wu had spoken about the parlous state of the drains, about the risks posed to the people and businesses of the street if the drains were not improved, and about the lack of any meaningful action from either the Municipal Urban Planning and Management Bureau or the Municipal Environmental Protection Bureau.

Philip Ye had not interrupted him.

When Mister Wu was done, Philip Ye had taken time to seriously consider the problem.

Then Philip Ye had said, "I will speak to my father."

Mister Wu had nearly fainted with delight.

He had not then outstayed his welcome. That would have been the height of rudeness. He had bowed deeply to Philip Ye, and quickly retreated to the confines of his shop to savour the victory, only realising some time later he had forgotten to ask Philip Ye what the Battle of Liberation Street had actually been about and, of course, what had happened to Sun Mei and her father.

"Mister Wu?"

Mister Wu nearly spilled his tea as he took his eye off the threatening sky to see who it was had addressed him. He was dismayed to see the fat man standing before him, the fat man's face now somewhat beaten out of shape, and standing next to him the big woman who had done the majority of the shooting during the battle.

Not forgetting the lies the fat man had told the day before, and feeling rather incautious in regard to authority after his little chat with Philip Ye, Mister Wu said, rather abruptly, "What do you want?"

"Information," replied the fat man.

"I don't trust you," said Mister Wu.

"I don't care," said the fat man.

"I want to know what you have done with Sun Mei and her father," said Mister Wu.

"That's none of your business," said the fat man.

Mister Wu took a deep breath. He was on shaky ground. If the fat man really worked for Prosecutor Xu, he didn't want to be dragged in chains before her and appear on TV charged with obstructing a Procuratorate investigation. Mister Wu made a choice, the only real choice he had.

"What is it that you wish to know?"

"Where the two men shot this morning were lodging," said the fat man.

The question confused Mister Wu. Was it some kind of honesty test? Was the fat man trying to discover whether he was a good citizen or not? Or did the Procuratorate and the local police simply not communicate with each other? From Mister Wu's extensive experience of local government bureaus and departments that could well be the case.

By now most people on Liberation Street not only knew the names of the two gangsters – a Mister Wang and a Mister Wang – but also that they had been lodging these last few nights around the corner on Red Hero Street, at Mister Li's place, the Laughing Panda Hotel. The local police had already found their way there, scaring Mister Li witless, emptying out the room the two gangsters had been staying in, discovering nothing of interest except a couple of packed valises stuffed with clothes. After the police search, Mister Li had come to speak to Mister Wu in person, almost in tears, apologising for his stupidity for welcoming gangsters into his hotel, for being the cause of so much trouble on Liberation Street.

"I don't know if I will ever be able to face Sun Mei again," had said Mister Li.

"She will bear you no ill will," Mister Wu had told him.

"But—"

"Mister Li, you know there is no better heart in all of Chengdu than that which beats in the chest of Sun Mei."

Which was true.

"Mister Wu, are you going to help me or not?" demanded the fat man, impatiently.

The big woman was also looking bored and restless, ready for action. Mister Wu was frightened of her. She was massive, built like a wrestler – a real killer, make no mistake.

"Around that corner," said Mister Wu, pointing down Liberation Street toward an intersection about fifty metres away, "is Red Hero Street. Halfway up the street, on the left, you will find the Laughing Panda Hotel. It's a decent place, cheap but clean, popular with travelling businessmen as well as with Western tourists with not a lot of money to spend. Mister Li Dong is the proprietor, a good man, a dear friend of mine. He is most upset. He is very fond of Sun Mei. He always buys his cigarettes from the Lucky Dragon Tobacco Emporium. Though, for obvious reasons, he is not a member of the Liberation Street Traders Association, I have offered him as much support as I can. He didn't realise Mister Wang and Mister Wang were gangsters. If he had worked in retail as long as I have he would have a much better understanding of the basic wickedness of human nature. Mister Li is a straight arrow, only a few years out of the army, and believes people to be as upright and honest as—"

Mister Wu stopped speaking as, quite rudely, both the fat man and the big woman turned their backs on him and walked off in the direction of Red Hero Street.

He felt a drop of rain touch his forehead. Mister Wu looked up at the sky and sighed.

FIFTY-FOUR

For Ma Meili there was no denying her world would never be the same again. In the space of a few days, during the course of an investigation that made her head ache, she had found both the police and the PLA not to be the paragons of virtue she had always thought them to be. That very morning she herself had shot dead bad soldiers. And, during Superintendent Si Ying's interrogation, Ma Meili had recognised her for the thoroughly bad person that she was. However, what disturbed Ma Meili the most was the ease with which Fatty Deng coped with all this, how he seemed to consider bad soldiers and bad police as part and parcel of normal life. She was also baffled by Fatty Deng's confidence, the instinct he had for what had to be done next. Ma Meili would have continued hammering away at Superintendent Si Ying until the lying cow had finally given up the truth. But Fatty Deng had been adamant. Before he questioned her again, he said he wanted to know more about what had happened on Friday night.

"Best we know more of the answers before we pose any more questions," Fatty Deng had said.

This made no sense to Ma Meili. If the answers are already known, why ask any more questions?

But, not wanting to appear stupid in front of Fatty Deng – she had been stupid too many times in front of Superintendent Ye as it was – Ma Meili had followed Fatty Deng out of the stinking warehouse basement, waited patiently as he had given the brothers Ming orders to keep Superintendent Si Ying fed and supplied with water but otherwise under wraps, and then allowed herself to be driven all the way back to Liberation Street. Despite his beating, despite the lack of progress with Superintendent Si Ying, Fatty Deng turned the radio on in the car, and as they drove across the city, the traffic as bad as usual, the pair of them did their best to sing along to the latest songs, often laughing as one or the other forgot the words or fell hopelessly out of tune. It was such a marked contrast to driving around the city with the ever moody and most usually silent Superintendent Ye.

Once back on Liberation Street though, Fatty Deng was all business. He waved to a couple of the local police he knew from years gone by, but otherwise didn't engage with them in conversation, presumably not wanting to explain in any detail just what it was they were up to. Ma Meili followed Fatty Deng straight over to Mister Wu's Cycle Sales and Repair Shop to speak to Mister Wu, to be told, much to Ma Meili's embarrassment, what the local police evidently already knew. But even that loss of face did not put Fatty Deng off his stride. He actually began whistling to himself as they walked the short distance to the Laughing Panda Hotel. Ma Meili wondered what could have made Fatty Deng so happy. It was only when they neared the hotel that the penny dropped, that Mister Wu had given them an important bit of information, a most tantalising clue: Mister Li, the proprietor of the Laughing Panda Hotel, was former army too!

A police car was parked outside of the hotel. Its two occupants were sleeping soundly. Fatty Deng laughed out loud but Ma Meili was furious, deciding to make an entry in her notebook of the time and the place, the car registration, and the names and serial numbers of the slumbering officers.

"They shouldn't be asleep on duty," she told Fatty Deng, who stood by shaking his head.

"Sister, sometimes policing is all about catching up on sleep whenever you can," he said.

The Laughing Panda Hotel was, as Mister Wu had described, a decent place, very clean and tidy, not like some of the rat-infested firetraps Superintendent Ye had taken her to during the course of some of their other investigations. As they walked into the lobby, Ma Meili could see a group of smartly-dressed businessmen talking over an early lunch in the dining-room. And, through windows that looked out onto a small but well-maintained garden, she could see a group of young *laowai*, Western backpackers, enjoying whatever remained of the short break in the wet weather before they headed off for some other great adventure. Ma Meili envied them. She thought back to her visit to Magical Wilderness Adventures, Madame Song's outdoor pursuits shop, how it would be good to return there and purchase some proper outdoor clothing, and then head off to the forests and the mountains herself, either on her own or with a group of like-minded people, just so she could breathe fresh air again and clear her mind.

"Mister Li is presently indisposed," said the young woman behind the desk in the lobby.

"Not to us," replied Fatty Deng, holding up his badge.

The young woman pulled a face, picked up the phone, and whispered into the receiver. Soon enough, a middle-aged woman appeared, who looked to Ma Meili as if she had been recently crying, who introduced herself as Bing Ting, Mister Li's wife, and who pleaded with them to return later, preferably in a day or two.

"My husband is very ill," she explained.

"Is he at the hospital then?" asked Fatty Deng, making Ma Meili smile. Fatty Deng was so funny.

"No," said Bing Ting. "But he is—"

"Take us to him before I detain you for obstruction and burn this place to the ground," said Fatty Deng.

A look of horror crossed Bing Ting's face. This time even Ma Meili could not tell whether Fatty Deng was joking or not. Bing Ting put her hand to her mouth, trying not to cry again, and led them to a small office at the rear of the hotel. Mister Li was sitting at his desk, apparently smoking cigarette after cigarette – a heavy fug hung in the air – the pallor of his face grey, sweat beading on his forehead, not that there was anything wrong with the air-conditioning in the hotel.

"Oh no, not again!" exclaimed Mister Li, as Fatty Deng flashed his badge and ID. "I have told you police everything. If I had known Mister Wang and Mister Wang were gangsters, if I had known they were going to try to rob the Lucky Dragon Tobacco Emporium and hurt my friends then—"

Mister Li's mouth froze in the open position as Fatty Deng slammed the door shut, drew his pistol, walked around the side of the desk until he was standing right over Mister Li, and pointed the pistol at Mister Li's head.

Ma Meili began to worry.

Had the beating he'd received finally affected Fatty Deng? Had his brain been slowly swelling inside his skull all this time?

"Mister Li," began Fatty Deng, "let me tell you a little story. Maybe a week ago, possibly two, you received a phone call from someone you used to serve with in the army. It was a reservation request. You were asked to provide a room for two very special guests. You were to give these special guests – let us call them by some fake names, Mister Wang and Mister Wang – anything that they needed, including a set of keys to the hotel so that they could come and go anytime they wished in the middle of the night, and to ask no questions of them no matter how strange or suspicious their activities might seem. How am I doing, Mister Li?"

His focus on the business end of Fatty Deng's pistol, now hovering right in front of his face, Mister Li ran a handkerchief over his forehead. "I have told the truth, Mister Deng. I have told of everything I know."

Fatty Deng touched Mister Li's forehead with the cold tip of the pistol. "No, Mister Li, you have lied to save your own skin. You are a black-hearted conspirator. You are up to your neck in bloody murder."

"No! No! I know nothing of murder!"

"Liar," said Fatty Deng, his voice low, menacing, frightening even Ma Meili. "I want to know what Mister Wang and Mister Wang did on Friday night. Tell me the truth or I will blow your fucking head off right here, right now!"

"Tell him, Husband!" wailed Bing Ting, her hands now fully covering her face.

"All I know is that they went out," said Mister Li.

"When?"

"Just after midnight. But a lot of my guests were out that night, enjoying the clubs and the late-night bars. There's nothing wrong—"

"They were dressed for a night out?"

"No, not exactly but—"

"And what about the bag they were carrying?"

Mister Li began to panic. "How did you know about—"

"What time did they return?"

"About two, Mister Deng...but on a Friday night it is not uncommon for guests to return at—"

"Tell me about the phone call!" demanded Fatty Deng.

"But—"

"I will just shoot you in the face here and now in front of your wife if you don't tell me."

"It was last Sa-Sa-Saturday," stammered Mister Li.

"Who was it?"

"I don't—"

"Tell him the truth, Husband!" screamed Bing Ting.

"It was a Mister Zi," said Mister Li.

"You mean Major-General Zi Hong?"

"Yes."

"Commander of the 14th Group Army, Kunming?"

"Yes – that is him."

"A friend of yours?"

"No, Mister Deng – nothing like that. I'd never spoken to him before in my life. I didn't think he even knew I existed."

"But you were in the 14th Group Army, weren't you?"

"Yes, Mister Deng – but I was a lowly captain, in logistics. I had only ever seen Major-General Zi from a distance. But he rang me up and spoke to me like we were old friends, comrades-in-arms. He knew all about me, the years I had served, as well as the men I had served with. It was like he had my service record in front of him. He said it had always been his honour to command men such as me."

"What favour did he want?"

"A couple of friends needed to visit Chengdu to do some business."

"This was to be a cash transaction...no records to be kept?"

"Yes, Mister Deng...it seemed like nothing at the time...no problem to help out my old commander. You know how it is. I would not be human if I—"

"Do you know a former Major Yang Da of the 14th Group Army? He is now a commissioner in the PSB."

Mister Li shook his head. "No, I don't think—"

"The truth, Mister Li!"

"I swear, Mister Deng, I do not know him."

"How about Si Ying, formerly a Master Sergeant Class 4 and aide to Major-General Zi Hong? She is currently police also."

"No, that name is not familiar also."

"Okay, now I want to see their stuff."

"What stuff, Mister Deng?"

"The gangsters' possessions."

"Mister Deng, the police searched their room earlier. They took away—"

Ma Meili held her breath as Fatty Deng jabbed the end of his pistol hard into Mister Li's forehead, fearing the pistol might go off by mistake.

"I won't ask you again, Mister Li," said Fatty Deng. "You know exactly what I am talking about. I want the bag those gangsters were carrying out and about on Friday night. It would not have been left in their room."

"Show him, Husband," screamed Bing Ting.

Mister Li still hesitated though and Ma Meili thought she would be witness to his death, Fatty Deng squeezing back on the trigger. But Mister Li suddenly decided he wanted to live, saying, "Okay! Okay!" and reached across his desk to pick up a bunch of keys.

Mister Li led them out of the little office. Ma Meili followed Mister Li and Fatty Deng up a flight of stairs to the first floor, while pushing before her the distraught Bing Ting. Mister Li stopped outside a door marked, 'PRIVATE – STAFF ONLY'.

"Open it!" commanded Fatty Deng.

Mister Li, sweat pouring from his head, rattled the key in the lock and pushed open the door to reveal a small storeroom. Fatty Deng elbowed him out of the way and switched on the light. Ma Meili could see shelves full of box-files – the hotel's business paperwork, she supposed – as well as a large safe in the corner that looked strong enough to survive an explosion. Apart from that there wasn't anything else to see. Ma Meili was disappointed. Until, that is, Fatty Deng, without any prompting from Mister Li, reached up to the top shelf and pulled down a number of the box-files to reveal a slim, long, black canvas bag hidden behind them. Fatty Deng took it down from the shelf and laid it on the storeroom floor. It was not just Ma Meili who gasped, but Mister Li and Bing Ting also, when Fatty Deng unzipped the bag to reveal a fully assembled sniper rifle minus its magazine. Fatty Deng soon found the magazine as well as a couple of small boxes of powerful 7.62x54mm ammunition in a separate section within the bag. Ma Meili was furious again, not just because Mister Li had allowed the bad soldiers to hide such a weapon in his storeroom, but also because the local police had been so stupid as to only search the bad soldiers' room.

"You'll be going away for a long time, Mister Li," said Fatty Deng, zipping the bag up again.

"No! Please, Mister Deng – I never knew what was in the bag!" squealed Mister Li.

"Yes, you did," said Fatty Deng.

"My husband truly did not know," chipped in Bing Ting. "We discussed the bag, I admit, after seeing Mister Wang and Mister Wang hurry out with it late on Friday night and then return it to the storeroom a few hours after. But we didn't dare look in it. My husband had promised Major-General Zi Hong he would not be overly curious."

"Well, you can give all your excuses to Prosecutor Xu," said Fatty Deng. "I am sick of the pair of you. You may have seen Prosecutor Xu recently on TV. I don't think either of you will ever see the light of day again."

"Mister Deng, you must show us mercy," pleaded Mister Li.

"Mercy," echoed his wife.

"How could I refuse a man like Major-General Zi Hong?" asked Mister Li. "I am wholly blameless."

"Blameless? You are a fucking idiot," said Fatty Deng. "And your wife is a fucking idiot for marrying you."

Ma Meili abhorred the use of bad language. But she had to admit, this one time, that Fatty Deng had hit the nail on the head. She waited down in the lobby with Mister Li and his wife, him wringing his hands and she crying into a handkerchief, while Fatty Deng went to fetch the car, taking the sniper rifle in its case with him. Ma Meili felt very good about the finding of the rifle – surely it was the weapon that had done for Primo Gong – and the uncovering of two more black-hearted conspirators, as Fatty Deng had so eloquently put it. In good humour, she took it upon herself to tell the young woman behind the desk in the lobby, who had gone very pale at the sudden reversal in her employers' fortunes, that she would be in charge of the Laughing Panda Hotel for the foreseeable future. Ma Meili thought this quite funny, laughing out loud when the young woman began to cry. And, to cap off a good morning, once Mister Li and his wife had both been handcuffed and pushed into the back of the Mercedes, and with Ma Meili herself safely in the passenger seat and with the engine running, Fatty Deng had banged his fist twice on the roof of the police car parked out the front of the hotel, startling the two sleeping officers inside, before jumping into the Mercedes and driving them all away at high speed. Ma Meili hadn't laughed so hard in years. She really liked Fatty Deng. Investigating murders with him was such good fun. Also, Fatty Deng's brain was not as damaged as she had thought. As they had been leaving Mister Li's office before searching the storeroom, she had watched him replace his pistol back in its holster underneath his colourful Hawaiian shirt. The pistol's safety had been on during the whole interrogation of Mister Li.

Fifty-Five

— · —

I t was Day Na who had forced the door to Ms. Lu's apartment. By then, Madame Ding, clutching onto her handbag as if her life depended on it, had become quite distressed. Not only had a couple of the other residents in the apartment block said they had not seen Ms. Lu since Friday, to Xu Ya the air smelt very bad outside her door. It did not augur well. But, before she could suggest putting Madame Ding back inside the Na brothers' car to avoid the ordeal that was likely to come, Philip Ye – as thoughtless as only a man could be – had ordered Day Na to force the lock on the door.

Day Na did not disappoint. A collective groan went up from the neighbours looking on as the lock broke and wood splintered. Xu Ya could not go in. The smell of death was too intense. The shades to the apartment were closed but she could see a slight figure hanging by a cord from a light fitting in the ceiling of the lounge, a stool lying nearby on its side. Madame Ding, for her part, was overcome with emotion. She buried her head into Xu Ya's shoulder and began to sob.

"It's the heat," said Day Na, about the smell. "Everything decomposes quicker in this weather."

Regardless, Philip Ye did enter and Xu Ya was proud of him for doing so. The brothers Na were itching to follow him but hung back, having no orders to do otherwise. Xu Ya waited as long as she could, as she watched Philip Ye stare up at the body and then move slowly from room to room, before shouting out her question, "Suicide?"

He did not reply. She was forced to wait. She took out her impatience on the neighbours, snapping at them, telling them to all go back inside their homes. The brothers Na laughed at her show of temper.

"Don't get angry, Prosecutor," said Day Na.

"Yes, there's no point," said Night Na.

"The boss answers only to the ghosts," said Day Na.

"Only to the ghosts," echoed Night Na.

Still encumbered by Madame Ding's sobbing form, Xu Ya contented herself with waving an accusatory finger at the twins. "Don't you start that little joke with me again. I am wise to you two tricksters. I am not some impressionable little schoolgirl to be frightened by your silly stories."

"But, Prosecutor!"

"It's the truth!"

Before she could respond to the brothers Na with an even harsher reprimand, Philip Ye suddenly emerged from the apartment, taking his phone from his ear. "What's going on?"

"Nothing, Boss," said the brothers Na, innocently.

"No, nothing," said Xu Ya, glaring at the twins.

"That's good to know," said Philip Ye. "I have just been in touch with Doctor Kong. She'll be on her way soon. It looks like suicide. The apartment is clean and orderly, no signs of a struggle, no defensive wounds that I can see on the body. And Ms. Lu, if that is who is hanging within, has left a note, citing loneliness after a failed love affair."

Madame Ding wasn't so overcome with emotion that she was unable to speak her mind. "That cannot be true! She told me there was no man in her life. She had never been romantically inclined or felt the need for children."

"I will not argue with you, Madame Ding," replied Philip Ye. "Ms. Lu has been dead since Friday night at least...which fits in with the other murders. And there is something about the note that doesn't sit well with me. The writing is very shaky, possibly coerced – not what you'd expect from a former military secretary. We must wait for Doctor Kong's opinion on the body before we draw any formal conclusions."

"What about her beloved cats?" asked Madame Ding.

"Nowhere to be seen," replied Philip Ye.

Madame Ding began to sob again but Xu Ya had caught the lie on Philip Ye's tongue. He would also not meet her eyes. The cats were dead, Xu Ya was sure of it, their throats cut or drowned in the bath. The murderer might have tortured the cats in front of Ms. Lu to get information from her if that was what was required, or even persuade her to slip a noose over her own head on the promise the cats would be let live. But, Xu Ya knew, from bitter experience, having had to oversee a couple of suicide cases when she was working for the Procuratorate in Chongqing, that it was just as likely, not wanting the animals to continue in this world without her, for a suicide to dispatch them first before she dispatched herself.

"There were no computers or printers in the apartment," continued Philip Ye. "Madame Lu seems to have preferred an old electric typewriter...possibly a hangover from when she had been in the army. There was no sign of any manuscript from Jin Huiliang...nothing to suggest she had been working on anything at all. Of course, such a manuscript might have been taken. But if the apartment has been searched then it has been professionally done."

Xu Ya felt Madame Ding stiffen. "What is it?" Xu Ya asked.

"I cannot say," replied Madame Ding.

"Why not?"

"I am ashamed, Prosecutor."

"Tell me."

Madame Ding kept her dripping eyes downcast, her mouth shut.

"Tell me!" demanded Xu Ya.

"I forgot to deliver the General's latest writings," said Madame Ding.

"What do you mean?" asked Philip Ye.

"The General had been feeling especially unwell this last week," explained Madame Ding, accepting a fresh tissue for her eyes and nose from Xu Ya's own supply. "He did not even go out Wednesday afternoon to see his army friends at the teahouse. That's what he told me anyway. On Thursday morning he asked a favour of me. He wanted me to deliver his latest writings to Ms. Lu. I was very happy to do so. I was looking forward to taking tea again with Ms. Lu...to listen to some more of her stories. Then my daughter rang me on the afternoon and we talked so much – it had been weeks since I had heard from her – that the General's writings went right out of my head. The next morning I was too frightened to tell the General. He just assumed I had delivered them like I promised. I was going to visit Ms. Lu on the Friday afternoon but with all the rain, and the expected flooding, and the possibility that the buses would not be running properly, I thought another day or so delay would not matter. Then I found the General dead and...well...I promised myself to deliver the papers on the afternoon, after I had told Ms. Lu the terrible news."

"You came to this apartment after you spoke to me?" asked Philip Ye, incredulous.

"I am so sorry, Superintendent. I didn't think it important. I didn't think you would care. I came here yesterday and knocked and knocked. That is when I assumed Ms. Lu must have gone to Anhui Province to visit her family. I didn't know her to be dead. If I had known then—"

Xu Ya made a grab for Madame Ding's handbag before Philip Ye could react. She put her hand inside and fished out a thick sheaf of handwritten papers.

"You've been carrying around these papers all this time," said Philip Ye, furious.

Madame Ding hung her head. "I didn't want the General to think that I had failed him."

"Control your temper, Superintendent," Xu Ya told Philip Ye, starting to read. "It's fortunate for us Madame Ding didn't get to deliver the papers or we might not have them now."

"Take Madame Ding back to the house for safekeeping," Philip Ye ordered the brothers Na. "I'll wait here with our little TV star for Doctor Kong to arrive."

"Yes, Boss," they intoned, together.

Xu Ya ignored Philip Ye's little dig at her, wanting to concentrate on what she was reading. But she had noticed Day Na surreptitiously pass him a pistol which he swiftly secreted in his raincoat pocket. She was mildly irritated that she herself was not offered a pistol, not that she would have known what to do with it.

It fascinated her that Philip Ye's lack of patience, despite all that deep-breathing he did, was on a par with her own. The brothers Na and Madame Ding had been gone only a few moments when, desperate to know what it was Jin Huiliang had been working on, he asked, "Well?"

"I'm not sure," she replied, honestly. "This manuscript is nothing to do with Jin Huiliang's specialism, the Song Dynasty – or anything to do with Primo Gong for that matter. Not what I've read so far anyway. These first pages are concerned with events in Chongqing during 1942, just after the United States had entered the Second World War and decided, as it would help their own purposes, to assist us in our war against the Japanese. It's a brief potted history of the creation of SACO – the Sino-American Cooperation Organisation – and the role of covert U.S. naval personnel in setting up meteorological stations all across China, some even behind enemy lines, and in the training of some of the Nationalist troops for guerrilla activity."

"The Second World War, are you sure?"

"Yes, odd, isn't it?" said Xu Ya, "especially as one of the other Historians – Lan Liu, if my memory serves me correctly – has as his specialism the resistance against the Japanese at this time, especially in the south of China. I cannot believe Jin Huiliang wouldn't have at least discussed this work him with."

"Ah, so a little suspicion is at last creeping into your thinking in regard to The Historians?"

Xu Ya felt the colour rise in her face. "Jin Huiliang's writing is not the easiest to decipher. I will read more later when—"

"*We* will read more later," Philip Ye corrected her.

"That's what I meant," she said, determined not to let this manuscript out of her hands. It was important. If Ms. Lu had been killed for it – which was a distinct possibility – then it was evidence, Procuratorate evidence!

They fell into an uneasy silence.

Thankfully the wait for Doctor Kong and her team of forensics specialists was not long. Xu Ya regretted very much not being able to utilise Doctor Kong back at the scene of Primo Gong's murder, which seemed so long ago now. They could only do so now as no one in Doctor Kong's team would ever connect the death of Ms. Lu to Primo Gong and thereby leak the news to the world that Primo Gong was dead.

Doctor Kong ignored Philip Ye completely. "Prosecutor, how nice to see you. What do we have here?"

"Apparent suicide, possible murder," replied Xu Ya. "A copy of your report direct to me only."

"Naturally," said Doctor Kong, before fixing her mask over her face and leading her white-suited team into the apartment.

"She doesn't like you," Xu Ya said to Philip Ye.

"I had noticed."

"I don't think she likes me either," Xu Ya whispered to him. "A month ago I invited both Doctor Kong and Maggie Loh to my apartment. I had met them at an official reception not long after I arrived in Chengdu."

"The Women in Law Enforcement reception at the Mayor's Office?"

His memory surprised her. "Yes, I thought we might get to know each other better...make friends."

"I understand."

"It didn't go so well."

"You argued?"

Xu Ya shrugged. "No, not at all. They ate my food...drank my wine...told me as they were leaving that they had had a great time. But this is the first I have spoken to either of them since. I tried to call them. I left messages but..."

"I wouldn't take it personally," he said. "Doctor Kong thinks we are all backward in Chengdu – morally and technologically – and, as for Maggie Loh...well, she is always busy being Maggie Loh."

"Then it's not me?"

"I would say not."

"Are you being truthful with me?" she asked, needing to know, wanting his honest opinion.

But, before he could reply, the brothers Na returned from delivering Madame Ding to the safety of the Ye family mansion.

"Where to next, Boss...Prosecutor?" they asked.

"I think it's time for lunch," said Philip Ye.

"I'm not hungry," replied Xu Ya, not sure she could eat for a week, and desperate for a shower, the smell of death emanating from Ms. Lu's apartment all about her.

"Ah, but you are expected, Prosecutor," said Philip Ye.

"Who is expecting me?" she asked.

"Yes, who is expecting her, Boss?" asked the Na brothers.

FIFTY-SIX

— · —

The brothers Na continued to shadow them as Xu Ya drove, Philip Ye directing her in silence, not even a grunt to accompany the hand signals he was giving her, no clue offered as to where she was going. His mood had worsened, she thought – if that were possible. He was morose now rather than melancholy and seemed to be struggling with some kind of inner conflict or dilemma. Was he concerned about the investigation? The examination of Ms. Lu's apartment could not have been easy, even for an experienced homicide detective. Or was it her company? Had Philip Ye tired of her as quickly as Doctor Kong and Maggie Loh had done?

To distract herself from Philip Ye's depression, and from her nervousness about where he was taking her, Xu Ya began to sing. Not traditional opera – she knew her voice, though better than Madame Ding's, was not good enough for that particular discipline – but a catchy tune she had heard on the radio a few days ago. Every now and then, when she could take her eyes off the road for a few moments, she would glance over at Philip Ye. Her singing appeared to make no impression on him, good or bad. What did it take, she wondered, to impress him?

They arrived at an apartment block to the west of the city centre. Philip Ye got out of the car without comment and she followed him, glancing upwards as she did so as a slight shower began to fall, with a promise of much more rain to come. The brothers Na pulled to a stop behind them and jumped out expectantly. But they were to be disappointed. Philip Ye pointed to a small restaurant across the road where they were to take lunch.

Inside the apartment block, she chastised him. "That was cruel."

"They were not invited."

"And I am?"

"Indeed."

He said nothing more. As they rode up in the lift to the sixth floor she wondered how and when he had made these arrangements and just who it was he wanted her to meet. He knocked on the door of apartment 603. After a short wait, the silence difficult between them, the door opened to reveal a woman of middle years, slightly overweight, but bearing a wide, joyous smile.

"Philip, it is you! And you have brought her as promised! Oh, Prosecutor, it is so good to meet you in person. I thought my husband was teasing me when he told me who was coming to lunch. Come in, Prosecutor, come in! You must call me Zizi – everybody does."

Zizi took Xu Ya by the hands and pulled her inside the apartment. Sitting at a table in the lounge, looking pale and sickly, dressed in pyjamas and an old robe, was a man Xu Ya recognised from newspaper photographs from years before. It was Superintendent Zuo, the detective Philip Ye shared an office with, the man whose body Philip Ye had shielded with his own some years ago during that famous shoot-out on the East Zhemin Road.

"How is Ma Meili?" growled Superintendent Zuo.

"She has a bullet-hole in that ugly old jacket of hers but otherwise she is fine," replied Philip Ye, slipping off his raincoat.

"That girl is Heaven-sent, Philip – you have to be kinder to her," said Superintendent Zuo.

"Yes, Philip," agreed Zizi, punching him hard on the shoulder. "You must be kinder. Not everyone is as quick on the uptake as you – or has had the benefit of your expensive education. We wouldn't want the prosecutor here to believe you to be a boorish and intolerant man, incapable of simple kindnesses to the less fortunate."

"I believe that to be true already," said Xu Ya.

Zizi laughed out loud. "Oh, I knew you would be fun, Prosecutor – and not at all frightened of these two miserable old detectives."

Xu Ya would have liked to have heard more of what was then said between Philip Ye and Superintendent Zuo, but Zizi dragged her into the kitchen.

"Tea, Prosecutor?"

"Yes, thank you, Madame—"

"Zizi!"

"Of course, Zizi."

"There...that's not so hard, is it? I know you have to be all formal at the Procuratorate, and when you are in court in front of those crusty old judges. But here we are all friends. And you should know what an honour this is for me. I did not miss a minute of the trial on TV. You were so glamorous...so clever...a real heroine standing up for the people, taking on the rich, the powerful, and the corrupt. I could not believe it when you laid out all the evidence against Commissioner Ho. I was so shocked. I always knew that some of my husband's fellow officers were not model citizens but...ah, he tells me so little. He tries to protect me, I think. He only trusts Philip. But what about you, Prosecutor, out and about with Philip on a Sunday! You'll be the envy of every woman in Chengdu. How are you settling in? Do you miss Chongqing? I heard you were married but that your husband died."

"It was not a love-match," said Xu Ya, unable, on the spur of the moment, to think of anything else to say.

"Ah, say no more, Prosecutor. We all make mistakes."

"Some mistakes are ruinous."

"Do not say such a thing, Prosecutor!"

"Why not? It's true. No decent man would ever take a chance on me now."

Zizi put down the teacups she had fetched from the back of the cupboard – her best – and took Xu Ya's hands in her own. "There is always hope. You have a chance of a new life here in Chengdu. And I know what you are thinking, that with an unhappy marriage behind you, and the years flying by, that you are no longer a catch. Well, let me tell you, I was never as glamorous as you even when I was young. I was twenty-two, a plain-looking nurse making not much money, with a young son to raise, given me by a man who vanished as soon as he learned I was pregnant. My parents had thrown me out. I was fortunate that a neighbour, Grandma Zheng, had taken me in, and was happy to look after my baby son when I was out at work. Grandma Zheng is no longer with us. Every evening before I go to sleep, I say a prayer for that good woman. But even with the help of Grandma Zheng, I could see no future for myself except to be a good nurse and the best mother for my son. Then, one day, I happened to be working in the Accident and Emergency Department and I saw a man sitting in the waiting room, a bad cut to his head, waiting to be seen by one of the doctors. I thought he looked quite handsome, very solid, secure in himself, more so than any other man I had seen. I asked the other nurses if anyone knew who he was. The senior nurse told me he was a detective, name of Zuo. He had got hurt making an arrest, capturing a man who had murdered two young girls up north and who had been hiding out in Chengdu. The senior nurse said Zuo was known to be very grumpy, a bit eccentric, maybe even a depressive. She told me to go treat him if I wanted as the doctors were running well behind schedule and as his cut looked worse than it was. His cut was indeed not so bad and he let me put in a few stitches for him. And we got to talking. My life changed in that moment. He did not care that I had had a son without even being married. He did not care that I was rather plain. That is not to say that life has always been easy. My husband is truly grumpy a lot of the time. It has not been easy for him in the PSB. He is an honest man – too honest for his own good. And I am always afraid for him. I was at the hospital when I heard the news about the shoot-out on the East Zhemin Road. I knew, though I cannot say how, that my husband was involved. I collapsed on the spot. The doctors had to put me on a bed, treat me like I was one of the patients. Then a voice in my ear – who said it to me, I will never know – said, 'Zizi, do not worry, Philip kept him safe.' In that moment, Prosecutor, all my fears went away. My husband had been hurt – he hasn't walked properly since – but he lived still, and I am grateful for it, and ever grateful for Philip, who can be as grumpy sometimes as my husband, but otherwise is the best man there is under Heaven. Ah, but you know that already, Prosecutor – and I am not just talking about how handsome he is. I heard all about how he raced three hundred miles, as fast as his car would go, to save you from those crazy cultists. So, after a bad day, you should think on that and not lose hope for the future. To a good man – a man like my husband, a man like Philip Ye – a woman's past, no matter the mistakes she has made, is meaningless."

"You are a romantic, Zizi."

"I confess, it is true, Prosecutor!"

"Philip Ye has not said one kind word to me...ever."

"Oh, don't let that bother you – he has never been the most effusive of men. It couldn't have been easy growing up in that big house with that father of his. And then his fiancée, that young Englishwoman, died on him. It troubles him still, I know. But that is *karma*. And a man needs a wife, so that is that. And, you should know that you are the first woman Philip has ever brought to see us."

"I am not looking for romance," said Xu Ya, desperate not to show anything of what she really felt.

"Is that so?" said Zizi, laughing.

Xu Ya was thankful the talk around the table, when they all sat down to eat, was more restrained, more sombre. It appeared Superintendent Zuo was getting over a bad illness, a stomach infection of some kind. He only picked at his food while Zizi fussed over him. Philip Ye did most of the talking, not about the investigation but about PSB internal politics instead.

"Maggie Loh is manoeuvring to absorb the little that remains of Homicide into Robbery," he was saying. "She wants to create a big new division with her sitting at the very top."

"She does have the ear of the Chief," said Superintendent Zuo, "and many supporters on the Political and Legal Committee, Secretary Wu included if all the rumours are true. They say he is angling for her to be the first female chief of police in Chengdu. What about Commissioner Wei? What does he have to say?"

Philip Ye shook his head. "I don't think he cares anymore. His eyes are on the afterlife. You should get to see him at the hospital as soon as you can. It will not be long now."

"It's so sad," said Zizi.

"Crazy Maggie Loh," muttered her husband, shaking his head. "Heaven help us."

There was much more of this talk, very little of which interested Xu Ya. She was happy to switch off, exchange the occasional smile with Zizi, and enjoy the good food. Zizi was an excellent cook. And a good woman too. Superintendent Zuo was lucky to have married her, not the other way around. But she did have a simple-minded view of the world and no understanding of Philip Ye at all. Never in a million years, with his perverse need for perfection, would he ever consider lowering himself to damaged goods – which, like it or not, is what she was.

"Prosecutor, are you listening?" asked Superintendent Zuo.

"Forgive me, what?"

"Philip is about to start questioning my wife. I need you to act as a judge in this matter."

Confused, Xu Ya was sensitive to how the atmosphere in the room had suddenly changed, how it tingled with electricity, how Zizi now could not meet anyone's eyes.

"Madame Wang Zhilan, silence is not an option for you," said Philip Ye.

"I understand," replied Zizi, softly.

"You had opportunity."

"By which you mean, Superintendent Ye, that I have to cook for my husband every day, spending hours in the kitchen working like a slave to prepare his food for him."

"And you had motive."

"By which you mean, Superintendent Ye, that my son is now safe at university, and it is time for me to get shot of my grumpy policeman husband and run away with a much younger man."

"And you have access to all manner of poisons at the hospital."

"By which you mean, Superintendent Ye, the worst poisons imaginable."

"So, do you confess, Zizi?"

"I do, I do – but surely the law must be lenient as I have become mentally deranged from being married to a policeman and I am so incompetent I couldn't even murder him properly."

Philip Ye suddenly turned toward Xu Ya, his intense, green eyes boring into her. "Well, Prosecutor, do I or do I not have a case?"

Xu Ya had thought this all a joke about Superintendent Zuo's recent illness, a bit of fun, some make-believe about Zizi attempting to poison him. But as Philip Ye looked into her, searching out the workings of her very soul, she saw that this was not about Zizi and her husband at all, but a sick game concocted by Philip Ye with the sole purpose of trapping her into revealing something about the terrible night last summer when her own husband had died. And, like a hunted animal, she could either fight or flee. She chose to do both. Like a crazy person she jumped to her feet, slapped Philip Ye hard across the face, grabbed her handbag and fled the apartment.

FIFTY-SEVEN

—·—

In her car, driving too fast and in her bare feet – she could not recall how she had lost her shoes – and feeling that the walls, figuratively speaking, were closing in about her, Xu Ya made two very important decisions: firstly, her working with Philip Ye, or the wider PSB for that matter, was over – whether Secretary Wu liked it or not; secondly, she was leaving Chengdu as soon as she could. No one could possibly know the whole truth about the night her husband died – not Philip Ye, not Sarangerel – but she was not going to hang around to give them the chance to find out. As the tyres of her car squealed when she turned down into Tranquil Mountain Pavilions' underground car park, she dialled the number she had memorised from the rather thin file held in the Procuratorate archives.

"Who is this?"

"Prosecutor Xu."

"My son, is he—?"

"He is fine, Mayor Ye. Your offer of a job...I need to know...were you serious...does it still stand?"

"It does."

"Then I accept. I want to leave Chengdu as soon as possible."

"Where do you want to go?"

"Wherever you need me most."

"New York, London, Singapore – take your pick."

"London."

"Then London it is, Ms. Xu. A formal offer in writing will be sent to you. And I will have a contract drawn up that I am sure will meet with your approval."

"I have one condition."

"Name it."

"You must order your son to leave me alone, to stop looking into my past."

"Ah."

"The past is the past."

"I quite agree, Ms. Xu."

"Will you speak to him?"

"I will."

The phone call was ended.

It was done.

She was safe, her future assured.

Philip Ye, Sarangerel, and everyone else who would get in her way or who meant her harm, could go to hell. Yes, it would be sad to leave both Investigator Deng and Mouse behind. And her parents would be upset that she would be living and working so far away even though she hardly figured in their busy lives. But she could not continue in Chengdu. Last year her father had promised her that her bad marriage was well and truly buried. This had proved not to be the case. Someone else was going to have to bring the Rule of Law to Chengdu. It was not going to be her.

Her decision irrevocably made, Xu Ya suddenly felt as light as a feather. She pushed any qualms she might have about selling her soul to serve the business interests of the family Ye to the back of her mind. Needs must – and in that she was no better, and certainly no worse, than most other people throughout the ages.

Back in the comfort and peace of her own apartment, she sang to cheer herself up and prepared a light snack. Unfortunately, she had been unable to sample all of Zizi's fine cooking and was hungry still. Or maybe it was just the excitement of soon jetting off to London that was affecting her stomach. Sitting down in her favourite easy chair, staring at her bare feet – what *had* happened to her shoes? – and before she threw herself into a more detailed reading of Jin Huiliang's latest work, she made one more phone call.

"Yes, Prosecutor?"

"Investigator Deng, we are no longer cooperating with the PSB. Please dump Constable Ma wherever you please – the nearest pig-farm would be most apt – and come immediately to my apartment."

She ended the call, giving him no chance to reply, making herself smile. This was the new Xu Ya. This was the international, jet-setting lawyer and fixer for the family Ye; not someone to be trifled with, not someone to be trifled with at all.

She had a new life now.

She was going to London.

And Philip Ye, with his stupid handsome face, and his stupid green eyes, and his stupid three-piece suits, and his really stupid gold pocket-watch, could go to hell.

And so what if she had just lost her favourite shoes? In London, on the salary Ye Zihao was sure to pay her, she could buy as many shoes as she wanted.

She sipped some of her tea, had a few bites of her little snack, and then steeled herself to concentrate on Jin Huiliang's writings. She had yet to be convinced how the little slice of history Jin Huiliang had recently been working on, even if it was not his usual chosen subject, had anything to do with a series of present-day murders. But, until she had read the sheaf of handwritten papers from beginning to end, she could not be sure.

She already knew much of the history of the creation of the Sino-American Cooperation Organisation (SACO) and the war of resistance against the Japanese. She had been born and raised in Chongqing, after all, where much of that history had happened. And, while studying comparative law at Harvard in the United States, she had taken the opportunity to do some research of her own on the American presence in China at that time, troubled by the omissions and most glaring half-truths taught her by her parents and tutors as a child. It pleased her, as she began to read Jin Huiliang's writings, that all of what he was saying agreed with what she had discovered for herself in the United States, that he had not been shy of writing not only a more coherent history but also a more just history to that which she had been exposed to as a child.

Could it be that that lack of bias had got him killed?

Surely not.

Modern China, though maintaining a certain narrow perspective on the past, *was no longer the China of the past.* And, more importantly, why would the history of the creation of SACO inspire anyone to do murder so many years on?

In 1941, after Pearl Harbor, after the Americans had at last been forced to enter the war against the Japanese, China had already been standing alone and fighting those hated invaders for four years, since 1937 – though there are some historians, with more than enough justification, who point to the real starting point of the war as 1931, the year the Japanese had first occupied Manchuria to the north. It had been in 1937, after using a contrived pretext – the Marco Polo Bridge[1] Incident – that the Japanese had swept south from Manchuria, intent on conquering all of China, intent on subjugating all the Chinese people, intent on robbing China of all its natural resources to fuel its militaristic and imperialistic expansion across the whole of the East, all their talk of the creation of a pan-Asian empire, and the throwing off the yoke of the hated white colonialists for the benefit of all, nothing but a fraud. First came the destruction of Shanghai and then the infamous 'Rape of Nanjing'. The Nationalist armies under Chiang Kai-Shek[2] were forced to retreat deep inland, finally settling on Chongqing as a defensible and temporary seat of government.

No one came to China's aid.

While the world was consumed with Adolf Hitler's antics in Europe no one gave a damn about the suffering of China.

Not until 1941.

Not until Pearl Harbor.

To fight the Japanese, the Americans had to reach across the Pacific. But, to fight effectively on, above, and below that vast ocean, the Americans needed to accurately predict the weather. And with the prevailing winds in this part of the world moving from west to east, it did not take the United States Navy long to realise that without having some idea of the weather brewing over China, they would be at a serious disadvantage in progressing the war toward the Japanese home islands.

So, in 1942, a deal was struck, and a close relationship formed between Commander Milton 'Mary' Miles, acting for the United States Navy, and the Nationalist spy chief Dai Li, acting with the

---

1. Also known as Lugou Bridge, situated about 9 miles southwest of Beijing on the Yongding River

2. Jiang Jieshi

authority of Chiang Kai-shek, to allow the U.S. Navy to use covert operatives and technicians to set up mobile meteorological stations all over China, from the jungles of Yunnan in the deep south to the deserts of Mongolia in the far north. In return, the U.S. Navy would supply training and matériel to select Nationalist forces for their guerrilla operations behind Japanese lines.

That was the plan.

And it had worked.

Not as effectively as Commander Miles and Dai Li and its other proponents had wanted – the politics of war, within China and within the United States, as well as inter-agency squabbles had not made life easy – but well enough for all concerned.

Unfortunately, even before the onslaught by the Japanese, another war – a civil war – had been raging for years in China between the Nationalists and the Communists, a war that had supposedly been relegated to the background so that all Chinese, regardless of political hue, could face the bestial Japanese with a single heart. The problem was, as both the Nationalists and Communists were well aware, the outcome of the civil war, regardless of whatever happened with the Japanese, would decide the fate of China for generations to come. It should therefore surprise no one, that while the Communists and Nationalists struggled against the Japanese, they continued their struggle against each other – even when showing a united face to the wider world.

The Nationalist spy chief Dai Li, it was said, hated the Communists more than he did the Japanese, and considered the war against the Japanese nothing more than a distraction from the real job at hand: the extermination of every Communist he could lay his hands on. Known at the time by many as China's 'Himmler' for his ruthlessness in hunting down Communist agents, he was considered beyond the pale by many Americans – especially by the young and idealistic foreign service officers stationed at the American Embassy in Chongqing.

But Commander Miles of the U.S. Navy came to believe a different truth about Dai Li, and he and Dai Li became good friends. Dai Li allowed Commander Miles, under the aegis of SACO, to set up a base of operations in the hills outside of Chongqing, in a place the Americans came to name as 'Happy Valley'. However, this small

American base happened to be just part of a greater military complex created by Dai Li, a concentration camp some said, where Dai Li imprisoned, tortured, and finally executed his prisoners with the full knowledge of his American partners.

And who could forget, when the war against the Japanese had been finally won, after the Americans had turned two Japanese cities to nothing more than radioactive dust, after the long-simmering civil war between the Nationalists and the Communists had once more broken out into a wholesale conflagration, after three more years of conflict when the Nationalist armies had been put to the sword and were on the run, that one hundred communist prisoners had been brutally and needlessly executed within that camp in the hills outside of Chongqing within hours of their expected liberation – a terrible outrage that could never, and should never, be forgotten.

As a teenager, Xu Ya had read – as had many of her generation – of this dreadful incident in the popular novel Red Crag. She had almost torn her hair out in rage and grief by the time she had come to the end of the book, having learned all about the sufferings of the Communist prisoners in the camp – red heroes and heroines all, all loyal to the cause, all prepared to give their lives so that a better, fairer, more prosperous socialist China could be built. The cruelty of their gaolers had appalled Xu Ya, as had the presence – never described but always implied – of the hated Americans directing affairs from the shadows.

Xu Ya had insisted her parents take her to the monument to those red martyrs erected on the very site of the camp in the hills outside of Chongqing. And, standing before that monument, she had cried many tears when reading the list of those men and women who had died for no reason, the civil war then almost done, the liberating Communist armies only a few miles away at the time. She had also made a promise to herself never to forget or to forgive the Americans for the hand they had played in that bloody episode.

Xu Ya was a good hater.

She had learned that about herself then.

She had hated the Americans then as much as she now hated Philip Ye for what he had done to her in Superintendent Zuo's apartment.

There would be no forgiveness.

There would be no rapprochement – ever.

Jin Huiliang's manuscript was a history of those times, but it was a history somewhat different to that she learned as a child. This came as no surprise to her. While studying in the United States she had been curious about what American historians had been writing about this particular period of Chinese history, what the hated enemy might have to say about their collusion in these terrible crimes. Needless to say, she stumbled upon more histories written in the United States about this period than she could have possibly imagined, many of them first-hand accounts written by former American military personnel caught up in the war in China against the Japanese, men and women who, as they fought and sacrificed and sometimes died fighting the Japanese, also fell in love with China and its people.

Not only had she read of the young U.S. Navy personnel who had volunteered for hazardous duty and who had fought alongside Chinese soldiers behind Japanese lines, the weapons trainers, the radiomen, the meteorologists – called aerologists in those days – who had bravely travelled by any means they could, often over the most challenging of terrain and always with the fear of discovery and attack by the Japanese, but also of the American pilots who had volunteered to fight for China even before Pearl Harbor, before the United States had formally declared war on Japan. These pilots, led by the indomitable General Claire Chennault, had flown under the banner of the 'American Volunteer Group', but who had come to be known, and to achieve worldwide fame, as the 'Flying Tigers'.

It had shaken Xu Ya to her very core to read of the bravery of those few American pilots, how they had flown so skilfully and bravely against the Japanese bombers and fighters raining death and destruction against the Chinese people, always so few against so many. In an action she thought should be as famous as any major battle of the war, an action that may have even turned the course of the war in China, the Flying Tigers had rained down bombs upon a Japanese army about to cross the Salween Gorge in Yunnan and from there strike north to the provincial capital Kunming and on to Chongqing. It was an action hardly known even in the West, but those few American pilots, ably supported by some Chinese bombers, had stopped that Japanese army in its tracks.

Sitting in the university library in the United States where she read the majority of these accounts, she had felt great shame, not only because of her previous lack of knowledge and naive historical perspective but also because, in spite of what she had now learned, the hatred she had deep down in her heart for Americans remained. It was like there were two different kinds of memory: factual memory and emotional memory, the latter much harder to replace than the former.

At least she knew now that history was not quite as she had been taught it. The monument she had cried in front of not quite telling the whole story, not the whole story at all. Even the chronology as Xu Ya had understood it was wrong.

The war of resistance against the Japanese had ended in 1945, all the Americans, including Commander Miles, gone from Happy Valley not long after. As for the Nationalist spy chief Dai Li, he had died in a plane crash in 1946, his plane falling out of the sky in a terrible storm. The executions of defenceless Communist prisoners had indeed taken place as described in the novel Red Crag, but in 1949 though, with not a single American in sight, SACO already become a distant memory.

Much of what she had learned in the United States was detailed in Jin Huiliang's writings. There was no surprise in this. Times had changed in China. The supreme efforts and sacrifices of the Nationalist armies against the Japanese were now recognised and, quite rightly, applauded, and the Flying Tigers almost venerated. In his writings, Jin Huiliang had focused mainly on the creation of SACO, the unusual and warm relationship that had developed between Dai Li and Commander Miles, and the successful coordination between the Chinese forces and the U.S. Navy against a common foe. There was little in the way of emotion in Jin Huiling's writings – he was, after all, a military man – but there was an astonishing clarity of thought and expression, as well as the offering of a number of contentious opinions, such as Dai Li never being quite as bad as portrayed – either then or now – and how he compared most favourably with the Communist spy chief of the time, Kang Sheng.

But what really fascinated Xu Ya, was the method Jin Huiliang had used to bring this history to life. He had included a number of personal narratives, notably that of a young naval rating, a radioman, named Alessandro Ambrogetti, who, being an adventurous sort, had volunteered for 'special services' and found himself on the other side of the world from his home town of San Diego, California. There was also the story of Gong Dawei, Professor of Meteorology, Sichuan University, Chengdu, who had been recruited by SACO as a technical translator and who then, much to his amazement, had found himself accompanying teams of operatives far behind Japanese lines. It was during one of these highly dangerous excursions that Gong Dawei, the intellectual, scientist, and scion of a noble Chinese family, and the young Alessandro Ambrogetti, working-class American and sec-ond-generation Italian immigrant with a natural flair for electronics, had developed a warm but unlikely friendship of their own.

And that was where Jin Huiliang's writings ended, in mid-1944, just as the story of Alessandro Ambrogetti and Gong Dawei was getting interesting.

Xu Ya cursed.

She felt robbed.

Where was the rest?

Jin Huiliang's writings – it could hardly be called a manuscript at this moment – had to be a work in progress.

Maybe it was time to do a little research of her own. It had to be no coincidence that Primo Gong and Gong Dawei shared the same surname, that 'Primo' was Italian for 'first-born', and that the name of Primo Gong's company was Ambrogetti Global Software. The bond formed between Gong Dawei and Alessandro Ambrogetti must have outlasted the war. She got up from her chair and went into her study, taking a seat at her desk and switching on her laptop. She hoped she would find something useful.

She checked her watch.

Where was Investigator Deng?

FIFTY-EIGHT

— · —

The slap from Prosecutor Xu had been bad enough but as soon as she had fled the apartment Zizi let fly with her hands as well, punching Philip Ye again and again on the arm.

"What is wrong with you?" she asked. "Go after her. Bring that beautiful lady back, you fool!"

Philip Ye did his best to ignore her. To Superintendent Zuo, he said, "Well, what do you think? Did she murder her husband?"

Superintendent Zuo shrugged. "She's hiding something."

Zizi suddenly stopped her furious assault on Philip Ye's arm. "Murder? What is this talk of murder? Cannot someone's husband die without the pair of you thinking the worst? Didn't you see Prosecutor Xu on TV? She is a heroine – scourge of the corrupt and the morally depraved. I doubt there is any better woman in all of China."

Superintendent Zuo shrugged again. Zizi was a good nurse, kind, caring, always sensitive to the feelings of others. But, in many ways, she was not worldly-wise. Superintendent Zuo had never bothered to explain to her the ugly truth of how the justice system sometimes worked, especially how in the case of important officials charged with serious crimes – Commissioner Ho, for example – the courtroom drama would have been choreographed and scripted long before the first cameras were turned on.

Philip Ye stood up from the table, sad to abandon his food. "I had better go."

"Yes, you go," said Zizi. "And don't come back until you have apologised to her."

Outside the apartment, in the quiet of the corridor, Philip Ye took a moment to breathe and collect his senses.

In for eight, hold for four, out for eight. *In breath, there is life; in breath, there is clarity; in breath, there is serenity.*

He was in shock. With Superintendent Zuo's illness and his mock accusation of intentional poisoning directed at his wife, he had seen the opportunity to put pressure on Prosecutor Xu, to see how she would react, to see if she would reveal some of the workings of her inner mind. However, the suddenness and violence of her reaction – her slap had really stung – had surprised him. He had never seen anything like it. There had been real vehemence behind her strike – real fear.

He had touched a raw nerve.

She indeed had something to hide.

Had she been as quick and violent on the night of her husband's death? Had he chanced to say the wrong thing and ended up with a kitchen knife between his ribs?

Maybe.

But what to do about it now?

Instead of waiting for the lift, he took the stairs. He only realised he had followed Prosecutor Xu's route of escape from the apartment building when he chanced upon her discarded shoes. He stopped to pick them up, marvelling at how small they were, how expensive too – at least a month's salary for Constable Ma, maybe a month's salary for him also. As he slowly descended the remainder of the stairs, he could sense her panic in the air, the confusion in her mind, enough to raise the hairs on the back of his neck. He had experienced similar sensations before, at crime scenes, where a woman had fought – and lost – a battle for her life. By the time he had reached the door to the outside of the building he had begun to feel ashamed of himself, remembering how Du Luli had fled Plum Tree Pagodas, never to be seen again. And the Na brothers, when he got out onto the street, only piled on the guilt.

"What have you done, Boss?" asked Day Na.

"What did you do to upset her so?" asked Night Na.

"It doesn't matter," he replied, pushing her shoes into Day Na's hands. "Go after her! She's probably heading home. Put a watch on Tranquil Mountain Pavilions and keep her out of trouble. I have to be elsewhere."

The brothers Na did not hang about. They jumped in their car and with a screech of tyres they were gone. It was only then that Philip Ye realised that Prosecutor Xu had had the sense to remember to grab her handbag before she had fled. Jin Huiliang's manuscript had been in that handbag, the best clue they had had to date. Philip Ye cursed his stupidity, his putting his need to decide Prosecutor Xu's guilt or innocence over the needs of the investigation into the murders of Primo Gong, Jin Huiliang, Du Luli, and almost certainly the murder – not suicide – of the typist Ms. Lu.

He had been originally intent on catching up with Fatty Deng and Constable Ma. But an idea struck him as he flagged down a passing taxi.

"Imperial Jade Hotel," he told the driver.

The driver nodded, and after moaning about the next rainstorm that was due any hour now, and after asking after his father's health, the driver began to talk at length about the trial of Commissioner Ho.

"To think that such a flower as Prosecutor Xu works at our Procuratorate...and to have such brains...it almost boggles the mind. Have you ever met her, Superintendent Ye?"

Philip Ye shook his head.

"In your younger days, I am sure you would have chased after that one," said the driver.

Younger days.

Philip Ye was thirty-six, closing on thirty-seven. Was he already an old man?

The driver dropped him outside the front of the hotel, refusing any payment as he did so. Regardless, Philip Ye pushed a 50 yuan note into his hand.

"There is no more generous family than the family Ye," said the driver, real tears in his eyes.

That's debatable, thought Philip Ye.

There were two old hands loitering outside the hotel entrance, smoking, trying to look inconspicuous. But, as soon as they saw him, they grinned, threw their cigarettes away, and came over to greet him.

"Mister Ye – do you remember us?"

"Yes, Mister Ye – it's us!"

It was Constables Zhi and Zan, both of whom had shown considerable aptitude for surveillance at the commencement of their PSB careers, and who now spent all their days shadowing Western journalists and businesspeople, tourists who had come under suspicion, and other persons of interest. They hadn't worn a police uniform in years.

"Of course, I remember you both," said Philip Ye, shaking their hands.

"We know she's a friend of your father's," said Constable Zhi.

"We hope we're not making him mad," said Constable Zan.

"It's not personal."

"It's just orders."

"My father knows you are also keeping her safe," said Philip Ye, to reassure them. "Have you got a car nearby?"

"Sure, Mister Ye – in case she runs off in a taxi," replied Constable Zhi.

"But she hasn't been out of her room – number 305 – all morning," said Constable Zan. "That hotel manager has promised to give us plenty of warning when she is planning to head out."

"I just need a little word with her," said Philip Ye. "Then we're going to my father's house. You two can drive us. My father is cooking lunch and both of you are invited."

Constables Zhi and Zan could not believe their luck. Their faces lit up with happiness. They headed off to retrieve their car as another heavy shower began to fall. There was a low rumble of thunder in the distance. Philip Ye hurried into the lobby of the hotel. He smiled at the girl on reception, who immediately picked up the phone to tell the manager just who had walked in the door, and then he took the stairs two at a time up to the third floor. Walking down the empty corridor he became nervous for no good reason. As he knocked on the door to room 305 he realised he had got used to Constable Ma's hulking but observant presence at his side, and the pistol she always kept on her hip.

The door opened. "Philip! What a nice surprise!" exclaimed Stacey Corrigan.

Not so well turned out as the night before, she looked just as attractive in jeans and with very little make-up.

"May I come in?" he asked.

"Of course, I was just completing my background notes on Ambrogetti Global Software. Have you any news for me on Primo Gong's whereabouts? Have the Procuratorate really got him?"

The room was nice, practical rather than plush. She offered him a glass of mineral water and a chair. He took the water but not the chair, preferring to stand. "I need deep background on Primo Gong," he said.

"Sure, Philip – whatever I can tell you. I don't know much. Back in San Diego the family Gong are a secretive lot."

"Have you ever heard of the Sino-American Cooperation Organisation?"

"Oh, heavens, Philip – you are heading back in time."

"Then you've heard of it?"

She sat down in the chair at the desk where her laptop was set up and waved away his praise. "I know a little of China at the time of the Second World War. My grandfather flew bombers – B29s, the big Superfortresses – out of India to attack Japan. They used forward staging airfields built around Chengdu. It seems almost impossible to believe it now. I wonder how many people in Chengdu remember those airfields and that American planes once took off from here heading towards Japan, sometimes never to return. My grandfather never spoke about the war. I only found this out after he had died. I discovered his old medals after the funeral and did a little research. As for SACO, I learned about the connection between Primo Gong and the Sino-American Cooperation Organisation from one of my contacts back in San Diego. Primo Gong's paternal grandfather – a

Professor Gong Dawei, a meteorologist based at a university here in Chengdu – was recruited by SACO late in 1942."

"To do what?"

"I'm not sure – probably something to do with helping set up the mobile meteorological stations across China. That was what SACO was all about: predicting the weather for the U.S. Pacific fleet as they advanced across the Pacific toward Japan. When Professor Gong was recruited by SACO he went to live for a time in Chongqing and there he became friends with a young U.S. Navy radioman, a real electronics whizz – a second generation Italian immigrant named Alessandro Ambrogetti."

"Hence the name Ambrogetti Global Software."

"Exactly – but there's a lot more you ought to know, one of those strange stories that seem to happen during wartime. The Professor and the young radioman soon became inseparable, so much so that Alessandro would be invited to the Professor's home where Li Ju, the Professor's wife – at least fifteen years younger than the Professor – would cook for them both. Would you believe Li Ju only died a few years ago? I would have loved to interview her. Anyway, when the war was over and SACO was closed down, Alessandro waved the Gong family goodbye, returned to San Diego and opened up a little electronics shop. This was a smart move. Before the war San Diego had been a sleepy backwater – but no longer. And Alessandro proved to be no mug when it came to business. Soon one shop had turned into two, and the two into four, and he was spreading out all over California – and in a couple of decades it became Ambrogetti Global Electronics, the corporate behemoth it remains to this very day."

Philip Ye was perplexed. "Stacey, you are losing me. Are you saying that the family Gong followed Alessandro Ambrogetti to the United States and got involved in his business?"

"Gosh no, Philip – it's stranger than that. After the war, Professor Gong Dawei returned to his teaching job at the university here in Chengdu. But he and young Alessandro Ambrogetti had become such good friends that they kept in touch. Anyway, Professor Gong and his wife Li Ju had a son. They named him Alessandro to honour their young American friend. Is that not something?"

"It is," agreed Philip Ye, solemnly.

"You probably know much more of what was to come in China than I do, the continuation of the civil war, the Communists against the Nationalists, the Communists finally winning in 1949, the remaining Nationalists fleeing to Taiwan."

"Did the family Gong flee as well?"

"No – they seemed content to stay in Chengdu."

Philip Ye thought on this. It had not been uncommon for Communist informers to inhabit the Nationalist ranks. It had also not been uncommon for university academics and students to be very sympathetic to the Communist cause. Professor Gong Dawei might have welcomed the Communist armies when they had liberated Chengdu. All through the war against the Japanese, and during his time in SACO, he might well have spied for the Communists.

"Go on," Philip Ye said.

"Then Professor Gong Dawei died," said Stacey Corrigan, simply.

"How?"

"From TB, early in 1950, soon after the Communists had taken Chengdu."

"Tuberculosis? Are you sure?"

"Yes, that information I picked up from an old magazine interview given by Primo Gong's father, Alessandro Gong, back when he had just taken over running Ambrogetti Global Electronics from his stepfather."

"Stepfather?"

"Sorry, Philip – I am getting ahead of myself again. Professor Gong Dawei dies early in 1950. The wife, Li Ju, must have written to Alessandro Ambrogetti to give him the sad news. Now, I am not sure what happened next. Either Li Ju leaves Chengdu with her young son in tow and heads off to the United States on her own. Or, the more romantic story is that Alessandro Ambrogetti shuts his business down for a few weeks, flies across the Pacific, sneaks across the border into the newly created People's Republic of China and rescues Li Ju and her son from under the noses of the People's Liberation Army. Is that possible? I don't know. I guess from his time in SACO Alessandro Ambrogetti might have become proficient with the language and with how to blend in with the people."

"It is certainly possible," admitted Philip Ye. "The liberation of Sichuan Province by the PLA was not as complete or as clinical as some histories state. Sporadic fighting occurred here for years after 1949, between the PLA and the remnants of the Nationalist armies. I expect the borders were more than porous."

"Whatever the truth, Li Ju and her son soon popped up in San Diego and, before anyone could say boo, Alessandro and Li Ju were married – much to his family's dismay. They thought Li Ju had got her oriental claws into him. I have to say, from old photographs I've seen of Li Ju, I cannot blame him. She was a very attractive lady – a powerful personality too."

"Any chance that Li Ju's son was really Alessandro Ambrogetti's?"

"No, Philip, Alessandro Gong – he never took his stepfather's name – is as Chinese as they come. He actually went on to marry a woman from the Chinese community already settled in San Diego, which is why Primo Gong looks as Chinese as he does. However, Li Ju and Alessandro Ambrogetti did go on to have a couple of daughters – both renowned beauties in their own right – who went on to marry into other monied families in the area. They were marriages arranged by Li Ju. She was very much the matriarch of the family – a real Dragon Lady – more so after Alessandro Ambrogetti died. I can't imagine what she would have thought of Primo tearing up his U.S. passport. By all accounts, her hatred for the Communists, for the Party, knew no bounds. It's interesting that Primo only moved to Chengdu after her death."

"But he was allowed to use the family name Ambrogetti, and the connection with Ambrogetti Global Electronics, when he set up his own company."

"There is that, Philip. I have to admit the financing of Ambrogetti Global Software – apart from the grants given by the local authorities here – was a bit obscure. Maybe the family split was never as serious as publicised at the time. Or maybe the family are expecting Ambrogetti Global Software to be folded back into Ambrogetti Global Electronics at some future date."

"Did Primo Gong really come here to discover his family's roots?"

"That's what he told people. He was also banking on China soon ruling the business world. Not a bad bet...not a bad bet at all. He said he was going to research his family tree – I guess he trusted nothing Li Ju had to say about the past – and was intent on writing a combination of an autobiography and business self-help book."

"He was writing a book?"

"That's what he told everyone when he first got to Chengdu. Don't forget, he had already had a successful career with Ambrogetti Global Electronics. He had a lot to say about management styles and entrepreneurship. Of course, he was full of bravado then. That was before his pretty Caucasian wife had deserted him, deciding Chengdu was not quite for her, and took the kids back to San Diego. I understand she was fulsomely welcomed back into the family fold. And this was also before the rumours of problems Ambrogetti Global Software might be having with their star client, the Chengdu Cymbidium Bank."

But Philip Ye was no longer listening. He was staring out of the window. There was a high-rise office block over the street opposite him. He would be an easy target for a sniper, as Primo Gong had been Friday night. Had Primo Gong known why he had been targeted when the bullet had struck his chest? Philip Ye thought so. Primo Gong had known far more than he should.

An autobiography.

Researching family roots.

And surely assisted in this work by Jin Huiliang, the two of them introduced by Du Luli.

It was all beginning to fall into place now. Primo Gong and Jin Huiliang had uncovered something from the distant past, something that had remained buried until now, something terrible, something that someone had preferred to stay forgotten, something needing to be buried again along with the bodies of Primo Gong, Jin Huiliang, Du Luli, and Ms. Lu.

"Are you okay, Philip?"

"Sure."

"So has the Procuratorate arrested Primo Gong?"

"No, he's dead," replied Philip Ye, without thinking.

"Dead!" Stacey Corrigan reached for her phone.

"No!" snapped Philip Ye. "His death must be kept secret for the time being. Stacey, you can have your scoop when I have finished my investigation. It won't be long now. I am getting close."

"Your investigation?"

"He was murdered."

Stacey Corrigan put her hands to her mouth.

"Now get your stuff together," said Philip Ye. "I want you in a safer place than this."

"Am I in danger too?"

"I doubt it, but I want to err on the side of caution. Also, my father would be furious if something did happen to you. He is very fond of you."

"Philip, the world needs to know that Primo Gong is dead...the staff at Ambrogetti Global Software, the shareholders, as well as his parents and family back in San Diego."

"They will – just not yet. Now get your stuff together. I still have a lot I need to understand this day."

FIFTY-NINE

—·—

Fatty Deng wanted Mister Li and his wife from the Laughing Panda Hotel under lock and key – and not just to prevent them running away. Somewhere in the city was Captain Si Yu of the 14th Group Army, maybe others as well, who might be thinking it was high time to tie up a few loose ends. Fatty Deng did not want to drop the couple off at a local police station – too many potential questions, and there was the risk that additional police were involved in the conspiracy apart from the security detail in the Black House. As for the Procuratorate, there would be problems there as well, too much paperwork to sign, too much waiting around for the couple to be processed through the custody suite, and too many potential eyes on what he and Prosecutor Xu were up to. It was still supposed to be, after all, a secret investigation. He also had the sniper rifle as well as the dead soldiers' PLA IDs which he had discovered in a side-compartment in the rifle bag as he was stashing it safely in the boot of the car: Master Sergeants Lin and Meng, also of the 14th Group Army – and he would guess, like Captain Si Yu, also of the Special Operations Brigade. He didn't want to book either the rifle or the IDs into evidence just yet, at least not until Prosecutor Xu had got her hands on them. Evidence had a tendency to go missing from police evidence stores. He had to assume the same was true for the Procuratorate. So, with the local police station and the Procuratorate out of the question for now, the only safe place he could think of to hide Mister Li and his wife, as well as the physical evidence, was the Ye family mansion. He drove straight there.

On the way he received a particularly terse phone call from Prosecutor Xu. She gave him no chance to speak of his discoveries, the progress he had made. She wasn't in a listening mood. She told him that the brief liaison with the PSB was now over and to get to her apartment as soon as he could.

"What has happened?" asked Constable Ma, once Prosecutor Xu had terminated the call.

"I think Prosecutor Xu and Mister Ye have fallen out."

"I am not surprised," said Constable Ma.

Frankly, neither was Fatty Deng. They were too similar, both too stubborn, both too proud.

"She is in love with him," continued Constable Ma. "But, because she is evil, he wants nothing to do with her."

"I don't think that is it," said Fatty Deng, laughing.

"It must be."

"She's not in love with Mister Ye. She's also not evil – just a little highly-strung."

"I see what I see."

"Sister, you are biased."

Fatty Deng could see Constable Ma was not to be dissuaded, and, by the smile on her face, actually approved of this turn of events. Fatty Deng was saddened, however. Despite the constant friction between Prosecutor Xu and Philip Ye, four investigators working together as a team was far better than two groups of two investigators working apart. Furthermore, both he and Prosecutor Xu needed Philip Ye's experience *and* his self-assurance. Despite Prosecutor Xu's natural aversion to the police, and her constant deprecation of police abilities, Fatty Deng also knew, when Philip Ye opened his mouth she would listen – if she was in her right mind, that is. He wondered what had gone wrong.

"Where are you taking us?" asked Mister Li, concerned, from the back seat.

"Shut up!" replied Fatty Deng.

Mister Li bowed his head. Bing Ting began to cry again. Fatty Deng didn't have the patience for either of them. The sooner he dropped them off and got them out of his hair the better.

As he swung the Mercedes through the gates leading to the Ye family mansion and rolled it slowly up the drive, he saw figures patrolling the grounds, keeping to the trees and the shadows. It made no sense. He could understand how the brothers Na might end up working for the family Ye. But how could a former mayor – disgraced and expelled from the Party – have instant access to a private army? Still, at least it made the Ye family mansion a safe place to stash Mister Li and his wife, and for Sun Mei and her father to stay, until the conspiracy was rolled up. He shuddered again at the thought of what might have happened to Sun Mei if Constable Ma had not come running and done what she had.

"Thanks again for this morning," he told Constable Ma, as he parked the car in front of the great house, sad to see the back of it, not looking forward to getting back into his old jalopy.

"No problem, Fatty – they were bad men," replied Constable Ma, with no hint of emotion.

Mister Li and his wife went rigid with shock when they realised just where Fatty Deng had taken them. Most in Chengdu thought of the Ye family mansion with awe, and desired to visit at least once in their lives. But there were always those persistent rumours, about some who had come to visit, many years ago, who had never been seen again.

As he pushed Mister Li and his wife toward the house, Fatty Deng's phone rang. Constable Ma took over from him and propelled the couple inside. Fatty Deng stayed outside in the lightly falling rain and answered the phone. He was shocked to hear Secretary Wu's voice.

"Investigator Deng, how are things proceeding?"

"Very well, sir," Fatty Deng replied. He related the work he and Constable Ma had done that morning, the story – or lies – told by Superintendent Si Ying in the dank warehouse basement, the evidence recovered from the Laughing Panda Hotel, the information provided by Mister Li.

"Do you believe this Mister Li?" asked Secretary Wu.

"I do, sir."

"Yet we cannot be absolutely certain that this Mister Li received his instructions directly from Major-General Zi Hong of the 14th Group Army. Someone could have impersonated him."

"That is true, sir – but, before she joined the PSB, Superintendent Si Ying was an aide to Major-General Zi Hong, maybe also intimately involved with him. I also think it likely that Commissioner Yang Da of PSB Building Security knows Major-General Zi Hong. A pattern seems to be emerging, sir."

"I see."

"Sir, may I humbly suggest – and I haven't yet consulted with Prosecutor Xu about this – that Commissioner Yang Da should be picked up as soon as possible."

"That seems sensible, Investigator Deng. Unfortunately, Commissioner Ji Dan of PSB Internal Discipline does not return from the conference he is attending until sometime tomorrow morning. I was hoping to wait until then. I do not want to upset the police unduly. But I don't think we have a choice, not if Commissioner Yang Da could be sitting on crucial information about this Major-General Zi Hong. It is my understanding that Commissioner Yang Da is presently at home, in the midst of a funeral service for his father. I expect his house will be crowded. His father was a rich, well-respected man. Use your private contractors again, Investigator Deng. Assure them they will be paid double. Gain access to the house. Take Commissioner Yang Da away as quietly as possible. Do not use Constable Ma. I don't want her short career tainted by any actions against a fellow police officer. Commissioner Yang Da is a popular man among the senior ranks. Superintendent Si Ying does not count. Tell Constable Ma to continue her interrogation. Explain to Constable Ma that I want Superintendent Si Ying broken. Do you understand, Investigator Deng?"

"Yes, sir."

"How are Philip and Ms. Xu getting along?"

Fatty Deng could not think of a good response and decided to remain silent.

"That well, eh?" said Secretary Wu.

"Sir, I am sure it will work itself out. Prosecutor Xu has ordered me to go to her apartment immediately. I will speak to her."

"No, Investigator Deng – pick up Commissioner Yang Da as instructed. I will speak to Ms. Xu myself. I will also instruct Chief Di to have a sharp word with Philip. We'll knock their heads together if we have to."

"Yes, sir."

Then Secretary Wu was gone. He had not sounded in the best of moods. Fatty Deng wondered what he would think when he learned that Prosecutor Xu was intent on giving up her job and leaving Chengdu for good. He would not be impressed, that was for sure.

But Fatty Deng had problems enough of his own.

He now had to gatecrash a funeral.

He had to lift Commissioner Yang Da, quietly, out from under the noses of his relatives.

How the fuck was he going to do that?

"Fatty, are you okay?"

Fatty Deng was startled out of his premonition of trouble to come. Philip Ye was standing before him. He had just arrived with an attractive, smiling *laowai* and two likely lads Fatty Deng hadn't seen for years.

"Hey, Fatty, how's it going?" asked Constable Zhi.

"Heard over the radios that you've had another close call again," said Constable Zan, laughing.

Philip Ye waved them away toward the house, wanting to speak to Fatty Deng alone. "How have you got on this morning?"

Fatty Deng saw no harm in telling him everything he had told Secretary Wu, as well about the new orders Secretary Wu had given him – including those for Constable Ma to continue the interrogation of Superintendent Si Ying alone. Fatty Deng could see Philip Ye was not amused. But Philip Ye had also been in the job long enough to know when not to argue or complain, especially in regard to a case as politically sensitive as this.

"It is a good move to pick up Commissioner Yang Da," said Fatty Deng, trying to convince himself that extricating Commissioner Yang Da during his father's funeral had to go better than the lifting of Superintendent Si Ying off the street that morning.

Philip Ye nodded, lost in thought. Then he said, "What do we know of this Major-General Zi Hong?"

"Not enough," admitted Fatty Deng. "I am hoping Commissioner Yang Da can fill in all the gaps for us. How did you get on with The Historians?"

"As expected," replied Philip Ye, declining to say anymore.

Fatty Deng strove hard not to let his frustration show. What was the harm in Philip Ye giving his own account of what he had been up to that morning and how he might have moved the investigation along? Were they not all in this together? Fatty Deng felt some sympathy for Constable Ma then. She was a good girl. She deserved a better, more considerate, more communicative boss.

"How are you and Prosecutor Xu getting along?" Fatty Deng asked.

"Badly," replied Philip Ye, breaking out into a smile. "She ran away from me."

"Ran away?"

"It's a long story, Fatty – and not for the telling today. Come inside out of the rain and grab some lunch before you head off to pick up Commissioner Yang Da. I'm sure he can wait a few minutes more. And I want you to show me that sniper's rifle you've recovered."

Fatty Deng offered him back the keys to the Mercedes.

Philip Ye shook his head. "No, keep it for the afternoon. I'll make other arrangements when I figure out what I am doing next. Just don't break it or get any bullet holes in it."

Fatty Deng laughed, pleased that Philip Ye was as generous as he was closed-mouthed, certain that all the shooting was over for the day. At least he hoped so.

SIXTY

A part from the monthly parties held for senior police officers – those still professing their loyalty to his father, that is – Philip Ye could not remember when the house had seemed so alive. His father was holding court in the kitchen, where he fulsomely welcomed Stacey Corrigan into the bosom of the house, as well as the over-joyed (and not a little overawed) Constables Zhi and Zan, and a frankly terrified Mister Li and his wife, whose status as prisoners few seemed to comprehend or, if they did, to care about. Philip Ye watched Fatty Deng help himself to some of the massive spread Ye Zihao had cooked and that was laid out on the kitchen table, then take a seat next to Constable Ma who was already eating. Constable Ma refused to glance up from her food. He assumed she was still smarting from his going off with Prosecutor Xu to meet with The Historians without her. And now she had orders of her own, given to her by Secretary Wu himself, bypassing all the usual chains of command, to continue with the interrogation of Superintendent Si Ying.

It was a stupid order. Interrogations, especially of a hard case like Superintendent Si Ying, were no simple matter. But Philip Ye let the issue drop from his mind. He had more important matters to consider. And at least Constable Ma would be out of his hair for the rest of the day.

Upstairs, as he made his way to his private rooms, he found the maid Madame Ding busy with a mop and bucket in one of the guest bathrooms.

"Madame Ding, that is not necessary," he told her.

"If I do not do it, who will?" she replied.

That the bathroom floor was already, in his opinion, clean enough to eat off, seemed not to have occurred to her. A team of trusted professional cleaners visited the house every week, working from top to bottom under the close direction of the brothers Na. But Philip Ye chose not to stop Madame Ding. With the death of Jin Huiliang, she had lost her main income. Come the next morning she would be down the labour exchange, her future uncertain. If working with a mop and bucket took her mind off her worries, then so be it.

Once in his private rooms, he closed the door behind him, stripped off his clothes, and stood in the shower for a long time, feeling unclean. He reviewed in his mind over and over what had happened in Superintendent Zuo's apartment, how Prosecutor Xu had slapped him and fled in such a flight of panic that she had left her shoes behind – just as Du Luli had done. Waves of guilt threatened to drown him. He tried to reassure himself that he had done what had needed to be done, what any proper detective would have done, to stress her, to shake her tree so to speak, and see what fell out.

But what had he seen?

That she had secrets?

Yes, but who in China did not?

Secrets did not make her a murderess.

As for the violence of the slap, her propensity for rash action, that did not necessarily mean she could thrust a kitchen knife, say, between a man's ribs. In a woman, he thought, it would take a certain blind rage to do that. In Superintendent Zuo's apartment it had been fear he had been witness to – real fear – not rage. Could it be then that whatever had happened to Prosecutor Xu's husband on the night of his death had been nothing to do with her temper, had been more complicated than a simple spat between husband and wife that had spiralled out of control?

He towelled himself dry, content to explore in his mind this new avenue of investigation, wondering if Prosecutor Xu's husband, Yu Jianguo – a notoriously corrupt judge – might have brought trouble to his own door, or whether Prosecutor Xu's parents, concerned for their daughter being stuck in an abusive marriage, might have arranged some sort of intervention which had led – intended or not – to Judge Yu Jianguo's death. Who could blame Prosecutor Xu for covering up for her parents? In the past, had he not been guilty of the same?

Buttoning up a fresh shirt, Philip Ye happened to glance out of the window and saw the girl Du Yue sheltering from the rain under an awning, looking out onto the lake. Next to her sat the young woman from the tobacconists, Sun Mei. The rain had begun to pour, the heavy black clouds threatening no respite for hours. Du Yue was still clutching her favoured book to her chest. But Sun Mei had her arm around the girl's shoulders and spoke to her intently. Philip Ye would have loved to have heard whatever it was Sun Mei was saying. He expected it was words of comfort that he himself had been unable to offer the girl. Try as he might, all he could see in Du Yue's future was bitterness and unhappiness – with Sarangerel forever lurking in the shadows, waiting to pounce. But Sun Mei was made differently to him. There was a warmth emanating from her which he could sense even from this distance, from inside the house. She was a soul born for the welfare and caring of others – the young especially. She was very pretty too. It was no wonder Fatty Deng had gone back to the Lucky Dragon Tobacco Emporium for her, risking his own life in the process. In Fatty Deng's shoes, he would have done the same.

He turned at the knock on his door. "Yes?"

His father entered, no longer the jovial host of the party. His brow was furrowed, his dark eyebrows knotted together.

"Father, I am sorry for this disturbance today."

"No, Philip, don't be – they are all interesting people. Did you know Brother Wang was formerly employed by the gangster Freddie Yun – maybe still is?"

"No, Father."

"Where are the brothers Na?"

"Watching over Prosecutor Xu."

"Good, that is good...very good, in fact," said Ye Zihao, taking his pipe from his mouth and carefully examining the bowl as if he expected to find something more than burnt tobacco there.

"Father, what is troubling you?"

"I want you to leave Prosecutor Xu alone."

"Meaning?"

"Once all this nonsense with Primo Gong is resolved she is quitting the Procuratorate. She is going to be representing our family interests around the world. Your uncles are most excited – thrilled even. They could not get enough of her on TV. They agree that it is quite a coup for me to steal her from under the nose of Lucy Fu."

"Are you seeking my approval?"

Ye Zihao became furious. "Why would I need your approval? It is obvious to me you would never approve of any offer I made to that woman. It was a simple business decision and I make no apologies for that. What I want you to do is leave her alone. You know what I am talking about. Your behaviour toward her has been nothing but loutish."

"I am a homicide detective."

"You are family first!"

"I need to know what happened to her husband."

"Philip, that is ancient history."

"Her husband only died last summer."

"You know what I mean!"

"Father, I do not."

"Listen, her husband was a judge and everyone knows that every judge in Chongqing has been bought and paid for. Who cares what happened to him?"

"I care."

"It is meaningless history, Philip!"

"Not to me!"

Ye Zihao stuck his pipe in his mouth, took a lighter from his pocket, and put the flame to the bowl. He filled the room with clouds of fragrant smoke. Philip Ye shook his head and continued to button up his shirt. He had a choice of tie to make, not so easy with his father glaring at him.

"Mouse told me that Sarangerel has written Prosecutor Xu a threatening note," said Ye Zihao, his tone a little more muted.

"That is true."

"Has Mouse asked you to intervene?"

"She has."

"And have you?"

"I am working on it."

"Good...that is good. And how does she look?"

"Sarangerel?"

"Yes."

"As intoxicating, as manipulative, and as dangerous as ever."

Ye Zihao sighed and nodded, made a show of studying his pipe again and then walked out of the room.

Suddenly Philip Ye felt incredibly sad. So, Prosecutor Xu had definitely decided to run. The little hawk, the shikra, had been so thoroughly spooked by all the attention on her past that she was going to fly less threatening skies.

So much for all her talk on the TV.

So much for her promise to the people of Chengdu, her commitment to forever uphold the Rule of Law.

Sarangerel had caught some whiff of scandal in the air – from which direction Philip Ye could not tell – and then there had been his own clumsy efforts, based not on any real knowledge, and the little hawk had chosen to disappear over the horizon.

Maybe it was for the best.

He had no doubt she would do good work for the family Ye – even if she had to sell what remained of her soul to do it.

But poor Fatty Deng.

What would become of him?

According to Mouse, Prosecutor Xu had not exactly gone out of her way to make friends at the Procuratorate. With her gone, there would be many prepared to take their vengeance out on a defenceless investigator. Philip Ye wondered if there was any way he could get Fatty Deng back into the police – his natural home. He would have to have a word with Chief Di.

It was by sheer coincidence then that Chief Di phoned.

"Yes, Chief?"

"Philip, where are you?"

"At home, sir – about to go out again."

"Progress?"

"Some, sir."

"Party Chief Li and Secretary Wu are breathing down my neck. For some reason I am being blamed...the whole of the PSB is being blamed...for rogue military personnel running amok in Chengdu. Commissioner Yang Da is to be detained."

"I have heard."

"He is a good man, Philip – a scholar. I cannot believe that—"

"Sir, let us see how things play out."

"How close are you, Philip?"

"Very close, I think."

"I am relieved...more relieved than I can say. There has been trouble at PSB HQ. Ms. Miao has been threatened over the phone. She has been helping your Constable Ma get the service records of former military personnel by utilising her special contacts at Chengdu Military Region headquarters. But her sources have suddenly gone to ground. Then someone phoned her – I don't know who – and told her if she kept poking her nose where it didn't belong she would end up with a bullet in her head. They're nothing but animals – fucking animals!"

"How is she?"

"Shaken, Philip...very shaken. Of course, I am not letting her go home. I have even armed myself. I'll shoot any fucker that looks at her the wrong way. I have put SWAT on standby across the city. I think Constable Ma's killing of those two bastards on Liberation Street has stirred up a real hornet's nest. They are frightened. They're closing ranks."

"I understand."

"Philip...we must speak of Prosecutor Xu."

"What of her?"

"I hear that you and she have fallen out."

"Ah."

"Philip, what are you thinking? She is the Shanghai Clique's star-performer. I don't care whether she has been slowing you down or just making a nuisance of herself as prosecutors tend to do. But it is important that the PSB and the Procuratorate will be seen...when all the reports are written...to have been working hand-in-hand on this case. So go make nice to Prosecutor Xu. Go buy her some flowers. Grovel if you must. And when you solve this case – as I am sure you will – just make sure she is out in front, getting all the glory. She is the TV star, the local celebrity – not you anymore."

"I understand, sir – I am to be a good soldier."

"Not funny, Philip."

"Forgive my poor choice of words."

"Go find whoever is terrorising my city and who has threatened Ms. Miao."

"I will, sir."

"How is your father?"

"Fine, sir."

"Give him my best."

"Of course, sir."

"Oh, and one other thing, Philip. I have just had a very odd phone call from Mayor Cang. He seems to think you have a young girl in your possession. He wants the girl dropped off at his offices today...a new plaything for the witch, or so I understand."

"The girl is a material witness, sir."

"I don't care what she is. Just take a statement from her and get rid of her. Mayor Cang is a complete fuckwit but I don't want him on my back today as well as everyone else."

Chief Di terminated the call and Philip Ye threw the phone down on his desk in disgust. He stared out of the window again. Sun Mei and Du Yue were now laughing. This was Sun Mei's doing for sure. That young woman had such a good, open heart.

He turned away.

Mayor Cang and Sarangerel could wait.

Du Yue was not going anywhere.

First, he had to make peace with Prosecutor Xu – indeed, grovel if he must. And no doubt he would need another shower when he returned.

SIXTY-ONE

—·—

B efore the rain had begun to fall more heavily, Sun Mei had sat with the girl Du Yue and watched the swallows swooping low across the lake, chasing each other so swiftly that Sun Mei often only caught a flash of deep blue. Whether the swallows were taking drinks or feeding on insects Sun Mei could not tell, but they tumbled and swirled much as her own thoughts did on this strangest of days. Then, when the rain began to fall in earnest, the swallows simply vanished – she did not know where. All that remained were the ducks and the geese at the water's edge on the far side of the lake, birds happier than most in this sort of weather. Sun Mei wondered how Mister Wu of Mister Wu's Cycle Sales and Repair Shop was faring, how the drains on Liberation Street were coping. She also worried about the Lucky Dragon Tobacco Emporium. In the rush to leave the scene, after the shooting that would forever remain in her mind, she had not only left the shop open but she had also left behind her phone. Too shy to ask Mayor Ye or anyone else in the great house to borrow a phone, all she could do was trust to the good natures of the people of Liberation Street, that someone would have locked the shop up for her, or would indeed be at this very moment manning the counter in her absence.

It had taken Sun Mei a while to reach Du Yue. Seeing her constantly clutch that book to her chest, intensely quiet, and walk around the house in a daze, Sun Mei had realised immediately that there was something deeply wrong. Sun Mei had seen far too many children like this the past few years, dumped in her classes by uncaring parents, growing up in troubled homes or coming from disturbed school classrooms, children too frightened to speak or acting out in ways that were not normal, or so detached from their emotions that all they could do was sit at their desks and stare into space. With the majority of these children Sun Mei had eventually succeeded. All that had been needed was patience, a secure and disciplined environment, and a lot of love and attention. Unfortunately, a few had been taken away before she had made any headway, the family secrets Sun Mei might have unearthed being too dangerous to bring out into the open, the parents soon sensing that Sun Mei was not the sort just to teach and look the other way. Her father had taught her to always seek out the best in people. But Sun Mei found it all too easy to judge those who refused, whatever the reason, to take the best care of their children. So much evil had emanated from one mother that Sun Mei had actually run out into the street after her and slapped her in front of all the passers-by for the bruises she had left on her child. Sun Mei had never seen her again or her sadly mistreated daughter. That had been a hard life-lesson. Sometimes there was only so much one could do.

But Du Yue had proved far easier than most. No sooner had Sun Mei put an arm around her shoulders, not even speaking to her or asking her what it was that was ailing her, the young girl had begun to sob and pour out her whole life-story, how she had never known her father, how she had been sent to school in England at a very young age, how though she had only found kindness there she had felt for the longest time to be an alien only for years later to now feel an alien whenever she returned to Chengdu, how painful the partings and meetings with her mother had been through the years, how her mother had refused to give up her lifestyle, of dressing up and going out every evening, how that lifestyle had finally got her murdered, how any hope of returning to school in England was now lost – where was the money to come from? – and how the career in mathematics she had aspired to had come to nothing before it had even begun.

"Ms. Sun, they cannot find my mother's body," sobbed Du Yue.

Murder.

Sun Mei had never encountered murder before. What could be said to comfort a child whose only parent had been murdered? "Who has said this, that your mother is murdered?"

"Philip Ye," replied Du Yue.

Ah, thought Sun Mei.

Body or no body, there was to be no arguing with Philip Ye. Seeing him up close for the first time today, and not just staring at her out of pictures in society magazines, Sun Mei had sensed what she could of his character. Much had been concealed from her eyes. But, if he said someone was dead, she would not doubt it.

Sun Mei could offer Du Yue no useful words of comfort. It would do no good to try to tell a girl of thirteen or fourteen that life seldom turned out as it should, that her own life had been blighted by tragedy, that all her own hopes for the future, for a good marriage and a teaching position at a good school with a view to eventually becoming an inspirational head teacher, a paragon of the community, had come to nothing. All Sun Mei could do was just hold her and let her cry, allow her to give expression to all her pain. That would be healing enough for the day. As for her future, that would be in the hands of others – social services in all probability – who would offer her up a future of sorts. Du Yue was gifted. Anyone could see that there was a remarkable intelligence behind the weeping eyes. She would survive and prosper. She also had youth on her side. And good looks too. For if Sun Mei was any judge of children at all, Du Yue was set to grow up to be a famous beauty. Wasn't it one of life's golden rules, that it was far better to be beautiful than not?

And, speaking of beauty, when Du Yue's tears had slowed and they had both marvelled at the rain hammering down upon the surface of the lake, the colour of the water turning from slate grey to onyx black under the pressure of the raindrops, Sun Mei had asked about the prosecutor from the TV, the woman who, having caught her staring at Investigator Deng as he was changing his bloodied shirt, had given her a sharp glance – a look of possession if there ever was one.

"Prosecutor Xu is so stylish, so fierce," said Du Yue, drying her eyes with a tissue given her by Sun Mei. "She shouted at Mayor Ye, told him to stop smoking his pipe...in his own house! I was so frightened I thought my heart would stop. But to her it was nothing."

"Is she and Investigator Deng—?"

"Oh no, Ms. Sun, there is only one man meant for her and it is not Investigator Deng. But I am not allowed to speak of that. As for Investigator Deng, now I like him too. I do not mean that I have actually spoken to him. But I feel I would trust him with my life. And I know Philip Ye likes and respects him. I think Philip Ye does not respect that many people. Surely it follows then that Investigator Deng must be a very special person."

Sun Mei absorbed this, hesitated, then asked, "Is Investigator Deng married?"

"He lives alone with his mother."

"A girlfriend then?"

"No, he has spent the last few months in hospital. Have you seen his scars, Ms. Sun? Evil cultists did that to him, stabbing him over and over again. They were so stupid. But, then again, how could they know that he is a hero reborn – The Man Who Can Never Be Killed?"

"A hero reborn?"

Du Yue put her hand over her mouth. "Oh, don't mind me. I'm just being stupid. I have such a vivid imagination."

Sun Mei chose not to press the child. After sitting with her arm around Du Yue's shoulders a little longer, Sun Mei left her alone then with her book, intent on getting the pair of them some lunch which they could eat together outside under the awning where the air was a little cooler and fresher. She also wanted to check up on her father. He had been getting on famously with Brother Wang – a man Sun Mei instinctively did not trust. She entered the house from the garden just in time to see Investigator Deng leaving from the front door, again in the company of the big policewoman. Sun Mei had not even known he had returned. She ran after them both, wanting to say a few words of gratitude to him and to her, but by the time she had reached the front door they were already in the black Mercedes and speeding away down the drive. Like a fool she stood out in the rain getting soaked, guessing that Investigator Deng had wanted to avoid speaking to her, that he probably had no intention of speaking to her ever again.

"He will return."

Sun Mei turned around and found herself looking up into Philip Ye's strange green eyes, and under the protection of his umbrella.

"Investigator Deng doesn't look well," she said, the first sensible words that came into her mind.

Philip Ye shrugged. "He came back to work too soon, I think – Prosecutor Xu unable to cope without him. But he is strong and determined, and we need his hunting skills."

"He is going hunting?"

"For those responsible for Du Yue's mother's murder."

"Ah," said Sun Mei, feeling stupid.

"What is troubling you, Ms. Sun?"

"I don't think Investigator Deng will ever speak to me again. He blames me, I am sure. Back at the shop...back on Liberation Street...when he told me to run, I could not. I was so frightened. I did not know what to do for the best. I could have got us all killed. It is all my fault. He must think me the most useless woman under Heaven."

"Ms. Sun, I expect he is avoiding you because he blames himself for bringing trouble to your door. Fatty Deng is a rare man of conscience in this city. So do not berate yourself. And never forget that he came back for you when most would not. Now, I would like to converse with you longer and thank you properly for all the kind attention you have been showing Du Yue, but unfortunately I have to go back to work – and do an unseemly amount of grovelling."

Then, with a smile, Philip Ye was off, walking down the drive, holding his umbrella above him. Sun Mei stood in the rain and watched him until he was out of sight, obscured by the tall trees, a somewhat lonely figure she thought, going off to do battle with the forces of evil all on his own. She did not know why he walked when there were a number of cars parked outside the house. Nor did she know why a man such as he would ever have to grovel to anyone.

SIXTY-TWO

— · —

It did not feel right to leave Constable Ma down in the dank basement with Superintendent Si Ying. It felt more like abandonment, something else for which Fatty Deng had to feel guilty about this day. But Fatty Deng understood that Secretary Wu had had a point. Constable Ma was not PSB Internal Security. It would do her reputation with the PSB no good at all if she was present during the arrest of a fellow officer – even that of a senior officer up to his neck in a murderous conspiracy.

"Just don't strangle her," was the only advice Fatty Deng could give Constable Ma in respect of Superintendent Si Ying.

"Okay, Fatty," Constable Ma replied, her expression as miserable, as lost, as he had ever seen it.

He would have preferred to leave a couple of the brothers Ming with her, to keep her company, to make sure she didn't do anything stupid. But he was frightened that things could cut up rough at the funeral when he tried to lift Commissioner Yang Da in front of all his relatives. Constable Ma was a big girl, he reassured himself. She would be fine.

There was no argument from the brothers Ming. They were up for further action. Fatty Deng had the distinct impression that they would go with him for free, just for the fun of it. But he explained to them that the Procuratorate would pay them cash, double that which had been paid for snatching Superintendent Si Ying off the street earlier that morning. Unfortunately, this time, he told them, he had no plan at all. All he had was an address where Commissioner Yang Da was supposed to be and information that Commissioner Yang Da's wealthy father had died recently and that the wake was at this very moment ongoing at the house – or at least that was how he had understood it from Secretary Wu. They were to infiltrate the wake, find Commissioner Yang Da, pick their moment, and spirit him away – so to speak – from under the noses of his family without any commotion. What could be easier than that? Plan or no plan, the brothers Ming – good boys that they were – were up for the adventure.

None of them were exactly dressed for the occasion. Fatty Deng was wearing his fresh Hawaiian shirt and the brothers Ming were fashionably dressed in t-shirts and ripped jeans. Not exactly sombre attire. But the afternoon was moving on and there wasn't time to go home and change. Fatty Deng hoped a few bouquets of flowers would get them through the door. Deciding it was best to use both vehicles, Philip Ye's Mercedes and the van the brothers Ming had found – luckily, they had not yet dumped it and set fire to it as he was sure they had planned to do – they stopped at a florist on the way. The florist had no white irises that Fatty Deng had initially thought to buy, so he settled for small bouquets of white chrysanthemums all round, hoping that they would do and that the Procuratorate would reimburse him the cost. As for gifts of money in little white envelopes, or paper money to burn, that wasn't going to happen. Fatty Deng felt sad that Commissioner Yang Da had lost his father, but he was going to the wake to arrest the man, not to console him on his loss.

"This is going to be fun," commented one of the brothers Ming, laughing at the bouquet in his hands.

I doubt it, thought Fatty Deng, his swollen face still aching, feeling weary to the bone, and wanting nothing more than for this day to be over so he could see the inside of his bed.

Commissioner Yang Da's family home turned out to be within a brand-new luxury gated community on the eastern edge of the city. Fatty Deng could not believe his eyes. When Secretary Wu had told him that Commissioner Yang Da's father had been wealthy, he had not been kidding. Private security guards manned the barrier blocking entrance to the estate, dressed in fancy uniforms with gold braiding underneath their transparent plastic raincoats. When Fatty Deng pulled up at the barrier and dropped the window, he said, as confidently as he could, "We're here for the Yang family funeral."

"I need to see if you are on the list," said the guard. "What's your name?"

"I'm not on the list," replied Fatty Deng, his heart sinking. He hadn't expected this little complication.

"Then you cannot enter."

"We're from out of town. We told the family we didn't think we would be able to make it," said Fatty Deng. "Then, at the last moment, we could."

"Sorry," said the guard. "I cannot let you in. And may I say the way you are all dressed is not exactly respectful to—"

Fatty Deng pushed his badge and ID in the guard's face. "I'm with the People's fucking Procuratorate! If you don't lift this fucking barrier right now you will be queuing up at the labour exchange tomorrow morning looking for another job!"

He may as well have stuck his pistol in the guard's face. The guard, his eyes rolling with fear, backed away and gestured to his comrades to raise the barrier immediately. Fatty Deng drove through, satisfied with the response but not without another attack of guilt. The guard had only been doing his job. For a short time, Fatty Deng had himself been a private security guard. It hadn't been fun. The people hated private security more than they did the police. He was sure Sun Mei would not have been impressed with his behaviour either. Though why that should matter to him he did not know. In his rear-view mirror he could see the brothers Ming in their van laughing their heads off.

Fatty Deng drove slowly around the estate, marvelling at all the incredible houses, at how the rich people lived. Soon enough he had no idea where he was. It was the brothers Ming who first spotted the target house.

"On the right, Fatty," his radio crackled.

Sure enough, there was a long line of cars parked outside a massive modern house. It was nowhere near as big as the Ye family mansion but Fatty Deng was certain it was big enough to get lost in. Wanting a quick getaway, he drove past the house and then turned the car around before parking up. The brothers Ming did the same, parking their van behind him.

Maids admitted them to the house, hardly lifting their eyes to them, not bothering to ask their names or comment on their poor attire, but happy to take the bouquets off them which was all to the good. The air in the house was thick with the pungent smoke of burning incense-sticks and from somewhere Fatty Deng could hear the wailing of women. The maids didn't think it necessary to point them in any particularly direction so they were left to their own devices. They began to wander freely from room to room, Fatty Deng in the lead, no sign of any family members. As they did so, Fatty Deng heard constant gasps of astonishment from the brothers Ming, the brothers probably seeing for the very first time the grandeur, the ostentation, that a lot of money could bring.

Finally, when they found the kitchen, they discovered a long table piled high with food and bottles of booze.

"Fuck me, is that you Fatty?"

So transfixed had Fatty Deng been by the food and drink on offer, especially the bottles of the most expensive Moutai he had ever seen, he hadn't noticed an old man pouring himself a drink at the far end of the table. It was Supervisor Song Bo, his old training instructor from Police College, now long retired.

Dismayed by this turned of events, for some reason not expecting anyone from the PSB, current or former, to be at the wake other than Commissioner Yang Da, Fatty Deng did his best to cover his shock and went up to Song Bo and shook his hand.

"I was only speaking to the wife about you a few weeks ago," said Song Bo, "when Commissioner Ho's trial was all over the TV. I told her, 'You remember my best pupil from years ago, Fatty Deng, the only one of that class of idiots to pay attention to me? And remember how those Shanghai Clique bastards then gave him the chop during the purge? Well, you wouldn't believe that he has fallen on his feet and is now working for Prosecutor Xu herself, the Flower of the Procuratorate.' How are you, Fatty? You seem to be recovering from the wounds those bastard cultists gave you. And where the fuck did you get that shirt?"

"I'm well, sir, and your wife?" asked Fatty Deng.

"Oh, she's fine – but not here, thank the Heavens. I can drink myself into a stupor without getting an earful."

"I didn't know you knew the family Yang, sir," said Fatty Deng. "I thought Commissioner Yang Da joined the PSB long after you retired."

"I did some work for the old man a couple of years back...trained up some of his security personnel to guard his factories around the city. It wasn't proper work but it paid well. I heard the son had left the army and joined the PSB...somehow bribed his way into a top job. Only met him for the first time today. He's in the garden with the rest of the family, in full uniform would you believe it. Seems a decent chap, though."

"In the garden?"

"Yes, it's amazing, Fatty. They have a marquee to cover the coffin and everyone is standing around with their umbrellas up waiting for the entertainment to start. Apart from the free booze, the entertainment is the only reason I'm here. Anyway, what about you? How did you know the old man? You can't be mates with Commissioner Yang Da? It's not like you to consort with senior officers."

"I did some private investigation work for the father two summers ago," lied Fatty Deng. "It's a shame our paths didn't cross back then."

Song Bo shook his head, sadly. "Ah, you should have looked me up, Fatty. We could have gone out for a drink...had a laugh about the old times. It would have been nice to know that you were getting by. I miss the old days. But now you're the big man and working for the best-looking prosecutor in China. How about that! Life's good, eh?"

"Life's good," agreed Fatty Deng.

"But what happened to your face?"

"You should see the other guy – he's dead."

Song Bo laughed, not taking Fatty Deng seriously. "And who are these four handsome young fellows you've brought with you?"

"Cousins of mine...on my mother's side...from out of town. I was showing them the sights of Chengdu when I thought I ought to pop in and pay my respects."

"And see the entertainment," laughed Song Bo. "Come, Fatty, let's get into the garden. It's about to start and we don't want to miss a thing."

Fatty Deng felt the need to pour himself a tall glass of something really strong but decided against it, wanting to keep a clear head, mystified about this entertainment Song Bo was so excited about. He followed him out into the garden, the brothers Ming right behind him, worried that the rain was almost now torrential. He need not have been concerned though. Maids quickly brought umbrellas for them all and he was soon standing with the mass of relatives – many of the women still wailing at the top of their voices – waiting for something to happen. Incredibly, the deceased was indeed laid out in a closed coffin with a small white marquee that protected it from the rain. Next to the coffin was a massive portrait of the deceased and sprays of flowers that put the poor bouquets Fatty Deng and the brothers Ming had brought to shame.

"What is the entertainment?" whispered one of the brothers Ming into his ear.

Fatty Deng shook his head, having no idea and not really caring. He had just spotted Commissioner Yang Da – it had to be him – a slim, handsome man maybe ten years older than Fatty Deng, in full dress uniform, sitting in the midst of the mass of relatives in a place of honour, on a seat that more resembled a throne, a maid holding a large umbrella over him.

"They're supposed to be incredible," said Song Bo, glancing back at Fatty Deng, more excited than an old man ought to be.

"Who?" asked Fatty Deng.

"The sisters Ping, of course," Song Bo replied.

Fatty Deng had no time to figure out what this meant. For the wailing of the women suddenly stopped and rock music blared out across the garden, from where Fatty Deng could not quite tell. And then from out behind the marquee danced four young women, each carrying an umbrella against the rain, and dressed in long, slinky black plastic raincoats. Slow on the uptake, Fatty Deng only realised what was going on when each of the young women dextrously undid the belt at their waists with their free hands, gyrating to the music as they did so, to reveal just black satin lingerie.

"They were the old man's last request," Song Bo shouted to Fatty Deng over the music. "He had seen them on a business trip in Hubei and supposedly, though he was already a sick man, couldn't get them out of his head."

Fatty Deng felt a severe headache coming on.

Strippers at a funeral.

Fuck, whatever next?

He had heard of the practice in parts of Taiwan and some of the rural areas of Hubei, the strippers employed to attract a bigger audience to a funeral. But he had never heard of the practice in

Chengdu. Moreover, the Party had made it clear that it took a very dim view of such proceedings. Not that anyone here seemed to care. Even the women were clapping along and, from what Fatty Deng could see, Commissioner Yang Da – at his father's funeral! – appeared to be having the best day ever.

Fatty Deng had to admit the sisters Ping were good dancers, though. And extremely good-looking. Not that Sun Mei would approve of them or their performance, he thought, gloomily.

"They're quadruplets," Song Bo shouted at him.

Fatty Deng could believe it. The sisters Ping were as impossible to tell apart as the brothers Ming. But his eyes were soon taken away from the dancing sisters to a dark figure that had suddenly appeared in the garden, bursting out from between some bushes, his face hidden by a tiger's mask. Fatty Deng assumed the man was also part of the day's entertainment until he saw the pistol in his hand.

Whether it was the beating he had received earlier in the day, or the blaring rock music, or the hypnotic effect of the dancing sisters Ping, Fatty Deng was far too slow to react. Too late he reached for his pistol concealed under his shirt.

But the masked man had miscalculated. Not only did he slip on the wet grass as he ran toward the group of mourners with his pistol pointed at Commissioner Yang Da, but he also collided with one of the sisters Ping as he let off his first shots, knocking himself off balance, sending his first shots high and wide.

By then Fatty Deng had his pistol out and was moving. As the mourners screamed and scattered, he barrelled toward his target, pistol up, pulling the trigger as fast as he could, his bullets going who knew where. He had never been the best shot. Something to do with hand-eye coordination, his firearms instructor had once said. But Fatty Deng had the advantage of surprise, the attention of the man in the tiger's mask on Commissioner Yang Da, and at least one of his bullets struck home, for the masked man appeared to slip again on the grass, but this time did nothing to save himself and then lay still, face down, his arms splayed out wide.

By the time Fatty Deng was standing over the body, he realised he had used a full clip in all his fear and excitement. He quickly slid another magazine into the butt of the pistol and knelt down next to the body, the pouring rain already dispersing the blood that was

seeping out onto the grass. Fatty Deng turned the body over and
pulled off the tiger's mask.

Captain Si Yu.

Or at least it had been.

Fatty Deng felt no remorse. He could find no feeling within him
at all for the fallen man. Which wasn't right, he knew – shock
maybe. But what Fatty Deng did feel was that someone had panicked
– Major-General Zi Hong or one or all of The Historians – and
had ordered the tidying up of loose ends, one of whom had to be
Commissioner Yang Da, making him even more valuable than he had
already thought. Fatty Deng quickly pocketed Captain Si Yu's pistol,
searched his trouser pockets, finding nothing – not the army ID he
had hoped for – and looked over to where Commissioner Yang Da
had been sitting, quite prepared to see him shot to death.

Commissioner Yang was no longer on his throne. He was being
bundled back into the house by the brothers Ming – such good boys!
– who also, it seemed, had taken charge of the terrified sisters Ping.
As for the other mourners and his old friend Song Bo, there was no
sign. They had all fled. He saw there was nothing else he could do in
the garden. The uniformed police would soon arrive. He left Captain
Si Yu's body where it lay. At least Brother Wang would be happy,
payback for his missing ear. Fatty Deng hoped Captain Si Yu was the
last of the rogue PLA element in the city, that all the violence was
done for the day.

Fatty Deng knew he was done.

He had just killed a man.

He would need some time to think about that.

He hurried after the brothers Ming.

The house was all chaos and confusion, mourners running this way
and that, the wailing of the women greater than ever. It was may-
hem. Confused, losing his bearings, Fatty Deng suddenly couldn't
remember how to get out of the house. Fortunately, one of the
brothers Ming returned to find him, and dragged him from room
to room, and then out through the front door and onto the street.
Some of the mourners were already in their cars and careering off
in all directions. Fatty Deng jumped into the Mercedes and found
Commissioner Yang Da in the front passenger seat next to him. On
the back seat sat two of the brothers Ming who had not only lifted a

bottle of the expensive Moutai each for themselves from the kitchen table but had also lifted two of the sisters Ping, who were clinging onto to the brothers as tightly as they could.

It was no time to argue. Drawing great breaths of calming air into his lungs, Fatty Deng started the engine and gunned the car down the street. Behind him he saw the van, the other two brothers Ming in the front, and the other two sisters Ping sitting behind them, holding onto each other.

This cannot be happening, thought Fatty Deng.

He reached into his breast pocket for his cigarettes. But his hand was shaking so much that Commissioner Yang Da had to lean over and extricate the cigarettes for him. Commissioner Yang Da lit two cigarettes, pushing one between Fatty Deng's lips and keeping the other for himself. Fatty Deng breathed the smoke into his lungs, feeling some blessed relief. He pushed the Mercedes even harder down the street but then realised he was approaching the security barrier far too fast. There was no time for the security guards to raise the barrier, no time to hit the brake. Fatty Deng could only watch in horror as the barrier exploded against the front of the Mercedes with the brothers Ming in the van behind, doing their best to keep up, swerving wildly to avoid the worst of the debris.

"You saved my life," said Commissioner Yang Da.

"True," replied Fatty Deng, cracking a window to let the cigarette smoke out. "But don't get too excited. You're under arrest."

SIXTY-THREE

— · —

Xu Ya was close to despair. Her research using her laptop had come up empty. All she had been able to find was the same information distilled from Primo Gong's many interviews these last few years that had been rehashed into many different editorial pieces, about how proud Primo Gong had been of his Chinese heritage, how proud he had been that his family had originally come from Chengdu, and how proud he was that he had now set up a new business in Chengdu and would soon contribute to the city's bright future. There was nothing else she could find. There was no mention of the war, of SACO, of the meteorologist Professor Gong Dawei. If there was a link, a family connection, she couldn't find it. And, to cap it all, she had just received a blistering phone call from Secretary Wu.

"Ms. Xu, I don't care what has caused you and Superintendent Ye to squabble," he had said, shouting down the phone. "Both of you need to grow up! I do not expect to have to knock your heads together. We need to know who is behind this criminal conspiracy – and quickly!"

Xu Ya couldn't remember the last time she had been spoken to in such a fashion. Ever since she had left university she had been – professionally speaking, that is – the golden girl, the one prosecutor, either here in Chengdu or back in Chongqing, who really knew what she was doing. She did not make mistakes. She corrected *other* people's mistakes.

She realised the stakes were high for Secretary Wu. Rogue PLA personnel could not be tolerated rampaging across the city and the roots of the conspiracy had to be uncovered quickly – especially if it had, as was likely, seriously infected Chengdu PSB. But Xu Ya felt she was deserving of a little more respect. She and Investigator Deng had made tremendous progress – and in just two days. Any other prosecutor would still have been searching for a non-existent intruder at Plum Tree Pagodas, having believed all of Lucy Fu's nonsense.

It had also infuriated Xu Ya that Investigator Deng was not now coming to meet with her. Secretary Wu had seen fit to undermine the chain of command and give him orders to detain Commissioner Yang Da of PSB Building Security. This behaviour, she thought, was beyond the pale. It was not unusual for a local political and legal committee to insert themselves into procuratorate investigations, especially politically sensitive investigations. But no committee member, either here in Chengdu or back in Chongqing, had ever tried it on with *her* before. However, with Secretary Wu, she had bit her tongue. She had reminded herself that soon, in a few days or so, she would be leaving Chengdu, never to return. Then Secretary Wu would receive a phone call from her. And he would get an earful about everything she considered wrong with the Procuratorate, the Courts, the PSB, and anything else she could think of that annoyed her about Chengdu.

The trouble was, with her still smarting from Secretary Wu's phone call and the lack of progress she had made researching the Gong family's past, she now found it difficult to imagine herself away in a foreign land, living in a luxury apartment, and with plenty of money to spend. All she saw before her was a black void. Either she was never going to make it out of Chengdu alive, or, if she did, she was destined for a life of misery.

She put her head in her hands.

She did not know what to do.

She did not know how to move the investigation forward.

She was sure that Jin Huiliang's manuscript, all his notes about SACO and Professor Gong Dawei was the key – but to what exactly? And what if Investigator Deng's interrogation of Commissioner Yang Da yielded nothing? Or, more to the point and much more painful to her, what if the investigation, pushed forward by Investigator Deng and Superintendent Ye, progressed quite satisfactorily without her?

It should not matter – but it did.

"Oh, Beloved Mister Qin, help me," she whispered out loud.

Strangely, she thought then she could hear Beloved Mister Qin's kind voice in the distance, words she could not quite catch, and then she picked up the phone and dialled without thinking.

"Yes?"

"Superintendent Ye, I cannot do this alone," she said, her voice not quite her own.

"Then open your door," he replied.

She ran and opened her door. Superintendent Ye was walking down the corridor toward her, the most ungainly she had ever seen him, juggling not only his phone but also her lost shoes, a plastic bag of food that must have come from The Silver Tree, as well as a bouquet of the most marvellous array of flowers.

She should have been furious with the day concierge, Mister Gan. Somehow, Superintendent Ye had again talked himself past the front desk. But she had not eaten as much of Zizi's lovely food as she might and she was still ravenous. Also, Superintendent Ye was carrying flowers.

Flowers!

No one had ever bought her flowers.

It didn't matter that Superintendent Ye must have also been given an ear-bashing by someone, maybe Secretary Wu as well, and been ordered to apologise to her. The flowers were gorgeous – a perfect arrangement. He had spent a lot of money on her – which was only good and right.

She grabbed the flowers from him, and then her shoes – she had thought she would never see them again – and found an empty vase. She put the flowers pride of place on the table in her lounge and stood staring at them.

"It was wrong of me...in Superintendent Zuo's apartment," said Philip Ye. "It was just a silly game I was playing with Zizi. Your husband's death was a tragedy. I did not mean to imply—"

"Apology accepted," she said, not really knowing what to make of his words or the face of innocence he was showing her.

Had she over-reacted?

Had she misinterpreted the game with Zizi?

Had the invitation from Sarangerel made her paranoid?

Had she made the mistake of thinking – as was often the case – that everything being said was about her?

She stared at him for a moment. He was dressed in a different suit, shirt, and tie than from only a couple of hours before, his blank expression, his sparkling green eyes, his incredibly handsome face, giving absolutely nothing away. The one side of his face was still slightly reddened from where she had struck him.

Good, she thought.

But she said, "I am sorry too."

He held up the plastic bag. "I have food. Mister Qu sends his regards."

"I hope you paid him."

"Mister Qu is family."

"Even so, it is only right."

She took the plastic bag from him, excited by the aromas arising from within. The next day she would write a thank you note to Mister Qu. She took the bag into the kitchen and spread the various cartons out on the little kitchen table, all the while keeping an eye on Philip Ye. He slipped off his raincoat and draped it over the back of one of her chairs. She saw him studying her apartment, judging it again, obviously unhappy with the general disorder, her failure to achieve domestic perfection.

He would be a nightmare to live with, she thought.

"We shall eat and talk in the kitchen," she said.

She offered him tea but he accepted instead a mineral water. She pushed food his way but he refused it. It struck her that she had never seen him eat, not properly that is.

"Frightened of messing up your suit?" she asked.

"Maybe," he replied, with a slight smile.

She made a motion with her chopsticks to fling a morsel of beef in his direction, startling him somewhat.

Interesting.

He didn't like being teased.

She laughed and put the beef in her mouth, luxuriating as it dissolved on her tongue.

"What did you learn from Jin Huiliang's manuscript?" he asked.

"Very little...it reads more like an extended set of research notes...lots about SACO, the U.S. Navy, and the odd relationship between a local meteorologist, Professor Gong Dawei, and a young

American named Alessandro Ambrogetti. The notes are incomplete, though, ending in mid-1944, well before the end of the war."

"Professor Gong was Primo Gong's paternal grandfather."

"How do you know that?"

"Stacey Corrigan told me."

Xu Ya couldn't believe her ears. "Are you going to tell me what else she told you or are you just going to sit there looking smug?"

He smiled. "Maybe."

She felt like slapping him again but kept her temper, her mood much improved by the food and how he had come to apologise to her rather than she being forced to go find him. Her patience paid off. Soon enough he began to speak again.

"You know that Stacey Corrigan was writing an article on the software industry in Chengdu and was going to use the success of Ambrogetti Global Software as the focus of her story?"

"I do," she replied, wishing he would get on with the story. The afternoon was moving on and Secretary Wu wanted results.

"After you mentioned that Jin Huiliang's notes appeared to be about SACO and the war against the Japanese, I thought that Stacey Corrigan might have access to sources about that period that we did not – sources back in the United States. This assumption proved correct. She knows a lot more than I realised."

Philip Ye then began to relate all he had learned from the journalist about the family Gong, about how Professor Gong and his family had stayed in touch with the young Alessandro Ambrogetti after the war, how Professor Gong had died – possibly of TB – early in 1950 not long after the liberation of Chengdu by the Communist forces, how Alessandro Ambrogetti had returned to China and helped Professor Gong's wife and young son escape, taking them back to San Diego with him, to eventually marry her and adopt the young son as his own. Alessandro Ambrogetti had gone on to build his great electronics empire. And then, a couple of years ago, Primo Gong decided to leave the family business after the death of his grandmother and build a company all of his own back in Chengdu. It was a curious, bitter-sweet story, so odd that she did not doubt that it was true.

"I'm not sure Professor Gong died of TB though," said Philip Ye.

"Why not?"

"I suspect it is one of those untruths that parents pass down to their children – a false history, if you like – to make the past more palatable. I have an alternative theory."

"Which is?"

"I find it odd that a man such as Professor Gong, so connected to the Nationalist struggle against the Japanese and so closely aligned to SACO and the Americans, would not have fled with many other important Nationalists to Taiwan."

She made the mental leap. "Ah, you think him a Communist spy?"

"Yes – or a sympathiser at least. There were many such among the intelligentsia who were looking forward to the expected Communist utopia. But this is pure supposition. What is not supposition, and what you might not know, is that Fei Shi's father, the famous General Fei Song, was at the head of the Communist forces that liberated Chengdu at the end of 1949."

"How do you know that?"

"Back at the tea shop when I heard General Fei Song's name, I thought it was vaguely familiar to me. I have books at home. So, I used them."

She felt the weight of his judgment again. "I have books."

"I see only law books, Prosecutor."

"For your information, *Superintendent*, I have many types of books. But I haven't yet had time to bring them from my parents' house. Do you want to speak to my mother to confirm what I say is true?"

"No, I believe you," said Philip Ye, with a shrug.

"Then you are a gullible fool."

"Pardon?"

"All I read is law books. I have no interest in anything else. Now get on with the story before I die of boredom."

She saw the spark of anger in his green eyes.

He really did not like being teased.

How very interesting.

She watched, curious, as he briefly closed his eyes and did that stupid deep-breathing thing of his. She felt like sticking her chopsticks up his nose. That would give him something to meditate on. But, when he opened his eyes again, he continued as if nothing had happened.

"It is my belief," he said, "that somehow Professor Gong fell foul of the new Communist authorities in Chengdu. As yet I do not know why. Maybe the martial law that was imposed initially was not to his liking, not quite the Communist utopia he was expecting. Somehow, I think, he crossed paths with General Fei Song and things did not go well for him. They were difficult and dangerous times. Whatever really happened to Professor Gong, I have come to the conclusion that Jin Huiliang, doing research for Primo Gong's planned autobiography, uncovered the truth. And this truth did not sit well with Primo Gong. I think he discovered his family's past in Chengdu was not what he had understood it to be, that his grandfather had not died of TB. And I think he finally understood the reason for his grandmother's long-standing hatred for the Party."

Xu Ya's mind leapt forward again. "Fei Shi said he is writing a biography of his father. And if Primo Gong was writing his autobiography and was willing to be open about a difficult episode from the distant past then—"

"Not only would a business autobiography outsell a military biography these days," interrupted Philip Ye, "but China is now a very different place to when General Fei Song found military glory. The people are not so sympathetic to the darker periods of our past. If Professor Gong did die back in 1950 because of, or at the hand of, General Fei Song, then that could blacken his name, and reduce his glittering military career to one simple crime – if it was such."

"It is all supposition upon supposition," said Xu Ya, her heart beginning to race. "But it does give us motive."

"It could be that the family Fei could not take the risk of Primo Gong publishing the truth about what had happened to Professor Gong. Not only did Primo Gong have to die but everyone else involved who knew the truth also had to die: Jin Huiliang, Du Luli, and the typist Ms. Lu. It is fortunate for the maid Madame Ding that no one realised she had been carrying Jin Huiliang's manuscript around for a few days, even though it has added nothing to what we know about what happened early in 1950."

"Jin Huiliang had researchers working for him," said Xu Ya.

"That is true."

"There may be more bodies we have yet to find here in Chengdu, or in Chongqing, or even in Beijing."

"That is also true," said Philip Ye, solemnly.

"But for the family Fei, for The Historians, to arrange the death of Jin Huiliang, a war hero, their leader, their mentor, their comrade, their friend...."

"I suspect Jin Huiliang was uncompromising when it came to historical truth."

"Even so, I cannot quite believe—"

"Prosecutor, it is just a theory."

"For the moment it is the best we have. But we will need more evidence before we can question the family Fei. Maybe Commissioner Yang Da will give the family up when Investigator Deng detains him. Or maybe he will tell an entirely different story. If only we had access to a draft of Primo Gong's autobiography, or at least his notes. We don't know how far he got in its writing. Lucy Fu had all his electronics destroyed. Let's detain her. We would have all the proof we need if it wasn't for her."

"That would be a waste of time," said Philip Ye.

"It would make me feel better."

"We would never get permission from Party Chief Li or Secretary Wu. She has too many friends – not only here but far away in Beijing. The Shanghai Clique would never cross her or her father. I also suspect that, though she was Primo Gong's friend, she knows very little about what he was working on and cares even less."

"Well, you would know her best," said Xu Ya, tartly.

"The past has never interested her."

"I don't know what you saw in her."

"I was under pressure from my father to marry at the time," said Philip Ye, defensively. "My father saw the benefits of merging the Ye and Fu business empires. It was an ill-conceived plan, I grant you. Lucy Fu soon bored of me and very quickly put my father in his place."

"Families," she said.

"Indeed," he agreed.

"So do you think Jin Huiliang made the mistake of telling all his old comrades, the other Historians, what he was working on – the side-project they now deny he had?"

"It is possible. He was an honourable man. He may have wanted his friend Fei Shi to know what was in the pipeline, to give him

warning. There may have been arguments. The maid Madame Ding
has told us Jin Huiliang's health had not been great these last few
months, that he had not been quite his usual self. However, I think
our more likely culprit is Primo Gong himself. Being more American
than Chinese, I wouldn't have put it past him, on learning the truth
of his grandfather's death, whatever that was, to have gone directly
to the Fei family house to confront them, maybe even threaten them
that soon everyone in China would know what had happened back
in 1950. Entrepreneur he might have been, but I don't think he
was a subtle man. Maybe it was then Fei Shi, to protect his father's
reputation, decided he had to take action, maybe call up a few friends
in the PLA."

"Major-General Zi Hong of the 14th Group Army?"

"Yes, Prosecutor – I would think so. I have no doubt that Major-General Zi Hong and The Historians are well-acquainted. It is
likely Major-General Zi Hong served under at least one of them and
believes himself indebted in some way, or at least as protective of
General Fei Song's good name as anyone. We just need proof. Is it
likely that Primo Gong kept the notes of the autobiography he was
working on in his office?"

"It's possible," Xu Ya admitted. "But his love-sick personal assistant did make a point of telling me how oddly he had been behaving
these last few months, how secretive he had been. She made no
mention of any autobiography. She did not have access to his personal
files."

"Did he have a literary agent?"

"I have found nothing to suggest so."

"Or a publisher ready to go?"

"No – not that I know of. There is so much we don't know, Superintendent. We haven't even established Primo Gong's movements
for the Friday evening. He should have been at his usual dinner at
the Old Chengdu Restaurant with the executives from the Chengdu
Cymbidium Bank. That was the entry in his diary. But he did not
attend."

"What did the entry say exactly?"

"It just said 'CCB bank dinner'," replied Xu Ya.

As soon as she spoke the words Philip Ye met her eyes and she and
he both realised the stupid mistake she had made. "Oh Heaven," she

said. "Primo Gong, Du Luli, and maybe even Lucy Fu had all been socialising at the bank itself, hadn't they?"

Philip Ye pulled his phone out of his pocket.

"Who are you calling?"

"Min Fong – CEO of the bank. He is an old friend of the family Ye."

Of course, he is, thought Xu Ya, shaking her head at the smug expression that had returned to Philip Ye's face.

SIXTY-FOUR

—— o ——

Fatty Deng had been apologetic but nevertheless he had left her behind to watch over Superintendent Si Ying. Ma Meili assumed she was being side-lined from all the action either because she was too junior or because she was just not trusted to work what was to come. Fatty Deng had tried to explain.

"Sister, detaining a police officer can be a messy business. And there's a funeral underway at Commissioner Yang Da's house so this could be messier than usual."

It was not much of an explanation. And what if more shooting needed to be done? Furthermore, the brothers Ming – who, though very friendly, were not police officers – were all going along.

SWAT would never have left her behind.

SWAT would have allowed her to be first through the door.

"Just ask Superintendent Si Ying a few more questions," said Fatty Deng, as he was leaving. What those questions should be he did not say.

Ma Meili did not need anyone to tell her that she knew next to nothing about interviewing suspects. Unlike Superintendent Ye, to whom even the worst offenders seemed to want to tell their life stories, whenever she sat down alone in front of an offender they tended to shut their eyes as well as their mouths and begin to shake with fear. A month ago, as she was getting an interview room ready back at PSB HQ, a suspect had actually confessed to her. Very pleased with herself, she had reported her success to Superintendent Ye who had been delayed getting to the interview room, only for him to take apart the suspect's story in a matter of moments and prove the suspect innocent. Why someone would confess to a crime they had not committed baffled Ma Meili still. There had been no explanation offered by Superintendent Ye. And for once Superintendent Zuo had been less than helpful.

"Constable Ma," he had said, "we are here only to get to the truth. What goes on in people's heads does not concern us."

But Ma Meili thought this not right.

Not right at all.

Even she knew there was a difference between the criminal who wanted to murder someone and the criminal who unfortunately had killed someone by accident. What went on in people's heads was very important. It was just that Superintendent Ye and, sadly, in this instance Superintendent Zuo, thought her incapable of understanding people. She knew she was slow. She knew people in Chengdu were much more complicated than the people back home in Pujiang County. But she was willing to try to understand people, she was willing to learn.

At least she knew for sure Superintendent Si Ying was guilty of something. Fatty Deng had agreed that Superintendent Si Ying was a lying cow. Nothing about her smelt right. But she was not the woman who had murdered Jin Huiliang. Though Ma Meili had thrown the question at her earlier in the day about the green crocodile-skin handbag, Ma Meili guessed she had been wasting her breath. Superintendent Si Ying had the look – as Ma Meili had herself – of someone who had had a rough upbringing, someone who had grown up in poverty on a farm. Nor did she smoke the expensive Good Cat brand of cigarettes that Jin Huiliang's murderess had smoked. The brand of cigarettes they had found on Superintendent Si Ying had been the much cheaper Golden Bridge. And yet she was guilty of something – but what?

Superintendent Si Ying was where they had left her, still hooded and tied to a chair in the basement of the disused warehouse. Ma Meili removed her hood and offered her a drink of water before taking a seat before her.

"May I smoke?" she asked.

"No," replied Ma Meili.

"Then may I ask how long you are going to keep me in this stinking dungeon?"

"Until we figure out what you have done."

"My baby needs me."

"You do not look like much of a mother."

This truth hit home more than any of Fatty Deng's earlier questions had done. Ma Meili saw the flush rise in Superintendent Si Ying's cheeks, the flash of anger in her hard eyes, the real potential for violence. Not that Ma Meili was worried. Even if Superintendent Si Ying was untied, even if she fought dirty as no doubt she would, Ma Meili was certain she could squash her like a bug.

"I am innocent of any crime," said Superintendent Si Ying.

"I doubt that," said Ma Meili.

"I have powerful and influential friends."

"Not here, you don't."

"I don't think you are very bright, Constable Ma. I don't think you understand what having influential friends really means. This is why you have been left alone with me. It is you who will be sacrificed when this stupid investigation of yours turns up nothing. You are just naive, Constable Ma. I can see that. It is not your fault that you are caught up in events you do not understand. When it is decided that a great mistake has been made, it is you who will be out of a job and not that fat procuratorate investigator with the stupid shirts. Let me go. Let's you and I go sort this mess out. You might even get a promotion for helping me."

"No."

"Why not? What harm could it do?"

"You are a bad person."

Superintendent Si Ying laughed. "Constable, all I have done, as far as I can tell, is abandon my post at the Black House on Liberation Street for a few hours. So what? I had my orders from Commissioner Yang Da and—"

"People have been murdered!" Ma Meili blurted out.

"People? Which people?"

Ma Meili realised she had said too much. There was an art to the conduct of interrogations – an art she knew very little about. Superintendent Ye would get whatever he wanted from suspects by asking the oddest of questions, nothing very direct, nothing very confrontational – and yet those suspects would talk and talk and talk. And she had noted earlier that Fatty Deng had been very selective in his questioning of Superintendent Si Ying, only asking her about the

Black House and nothing more. He had never mentioned murder. That had had to be intentional. Fatty Deng was very deliberate in all he did. And she knew for a fact that Fatty Deng had spent much of his time in hospital convalescing reading all the books Superintendent Ye had given him – and, unlike her, probably understanding them.

"Who has been murdered?" asked Superintendent Si Ying.

"It is not for you to know."

"Tell me!"

Not liking being shouted at by anyone, Ma Meili shouted back, "Jin Huiliang!"

"I don't know who that is."

"He was the hero of Lao Cai."

"Where's that?

Ma Meili felt stupid again. She did not know for sure. "Somewhere in Vietnam."

"What is that place to me?"

Caught off balance, frustrated by how easy it had been for Superintendent Si Ying to turn the tables on her, to be the one asking all the questions, Ma Meili could not help herself and said, "Primo Gong is dead as well."

"Who is that?"

"An important businessman."

"Constable Ma, I don't know these people and so—"

"The prostitute Du Luli is dead also...picked up from outside of Plum Tree Pagodas on Friday night...never to be seen again."

"Who?"

The breath caught in Ma Meili's mouth. Superintendent Zuo had said to her only a few weeks before that in most interrogations there came a moment, a change of expression, perhaps a shifting of the hands or of the legs under the table, when all would become clear. Ma Meili had given up all hope of ever experiencing that moment for herself, Superintendent Ye's management of interrogations too fluid, too easy, and – it had to be said – sometimes too sleep-inducing. But now Ma Meili understood what Superintendent Zuo had been speaking about. It was not the name Du Luli. That truly had meant nothing to Superintendent Si Ying. But the mention of a woman being picked up from outside of Plum Tree Pagodas had caused the first real flicker of fear behind Superintendent Si Ying's eyes – and all the doubts were swept out of Ma Meili's mind.

"I don't know that person," Superintendent Si Ying repeated.

Ma Meili decided it was time to finish her off. "Because of your crimes you will never see your baby again."

"No, I am innocent of—"

"Liar!"

"No, I am—"

"Some of your friends from the 14th Group Army are already dead." Ma Meili lifted her phone so Superintendent Si Ying could see the photograph Superintendent Ye insisted be taken outside the Lucky Dragon Tobacco Emporium of the two dead men lying on the ground. "I killed them myself."

Superintendent Si Ying refused to look. "I don't know them."

"Liar! They are army friends of your cousin, Captain Si Yu, who is now being hunted like a dog all over Chengdu. I will shoot him too if necessary. You, I don't have to shoot. A proper executioner will do that for me. Who knows what will happen to your ugly baby then. It will probably end up in some horrible orphanage and grow up as wicked as you."

"I did nothing!" screamed Superintendent Si Ying.

"Yes, you did."

"I don't know what he did with her. He told me he had let her go. I only drove. You must believe me! I knew the city...the roads leading out into the countryside. If she is dead then it is nothing to do with me."

"Liar."

"I can show you."

"You are not going anywhere."

"Please let me show you, Constable Ma," pleaded Superintendent Si Ying. "Let me prove to you all I have said is true."

SIXTY-FIVE

— • —

Fatty Deng had originally planned to take Commissioner Yang Da back to the same disused warehouse in which Superintendent Si Ying was being held and to meet up with Constable Ma again. But, after shooting dead Captain Si Yu, and after escaping the chaotic funeral scene, he was no longer thinking straight. Before he knew it, he was rolling up the drive to the Ye family mansion, having no real recollection of how he had got there or why he had been drawn back to the great house again. As he parked up in front of the house, and as the van containing the other two brothers Ming and other two sisters Ping parked up alongside him, he warned the brothers Ming and the sisters Ping behind him on the back seat to behave themselves in the house and to watch their manners. He hoped Ye Zihao would not be angry about the new arrivals, that for today it was a case of the more the merrier. The two Ming brothers behind him clapped him on the back and told him it had been the best day of their lives, and the sisters Ping lent over and smothered him in kisses, before joining up with their fellow brothers and sisters from the van and running through the rain and into the house. Commissioner Yang Da had the good sense to keep his mouth shut and stay put while Fatty Deng then put a call into Prosecutor Xu.

The call was a waste of time. She was on the way, she said, with Philip Ye, to visit with Min Feng, the CEO of the Chengdu Cymbidium Bank. She did not explain why. She spoke breathlessly, asking no questions of him, saying she didn't have time to talk, that she would catch up with him later.

At least she had buried her differences with Philip Ye. Which was something, thought Fatty Deng. But he would have liked to have had the opportunity to tell her that he had detained Commissioner Yang Da and – he could not quite believe it himself – that he had just killed a man.

Fatty Deng decided to conduct Commissioner Yang Da's interrogation in the car, out of earshot of everyone in the house. He took his packet of cigarettes out of his breast pocket but his hands were still shaking so much that Commissioner Yang Da again had to light both their cigarettes. Fatty Deng sat back for a few moments, listening to the rain upon the roof of the car, finding it relaxing. He wondered how his mother was faring out on the Great Yangzi, and how she would take the news that her son had just fired off a whole magazine of bullets from his pistol – all fifteen of them – in the middle of a strip show at a funeral, with one of those bullets taking Captain Si Yu in the chest, killing him instantly. Unlike Constable Ma, who was certain to find it hilarious that he had no clue as to where the other fourteen bullets had gone, Fatty Deng doubted his mother would be impressed. Nor would Sun Mei, he thought, grimly – not that she counted, of course.

"Are you tight with the family Ye?" asked Commissioner Yang Da.

"Not especially."

"I've never seen you at one of the police parties here."

"I've never been invited."

"Ah."

"I was police for ten years before the fucking Shanghai Clique purged me," said Fatty Deng with more bitterness than he had intended.

"But now you are Procuratorate?"

"Yes."

"And you work directly for Prosecutor Xu Ya?"

"Yes."

Commissioner Yang Da nervously ran the back of his hand over the sheen of sweat that covered his forehead. "Am I in a lot of trouble?"

"It depends what you've done."

"The strippers, the sisters Ping, that was—"

"I don't care about them."

"Ah."

"I only care about what happened Friday night."

Commissioner Yang Da appeared mystified. "What happened Friday night?"

Fatty Deng thought he saw genuine confusion in Commissioner Yang Da. During his time in the police, he had never had any time for senior officers, thinking them all cut from the same mould: all ambitious, all happy to walk on the heads of those beneath them to get to wherever they wanted to go, all content to spend their days in a cosy office rather than out hunting for criminals. But, in the short time he had spent with Commissioner Yang Da, Fatty Deng had taken a liking to the older man. Commissioner Yang Da was quiet, thoughtful, his uniform worn properly and well-kept, and he had understood the need to light Fatty Deng's cigarette for him without being asked. There was also the fact that he had been born into a family of wealth and yet had chosen to serve, firstly in the army and now in the police. Admittedly, PSB Building Security wasn't exactly frontline policing, but it was enough to differentiate Commissioner Yang Da from the average civilian.

"I want to know what happened Friday night," said Fatty Deng.

"Friday night," repeated Commissioner Yang Da, softly, shaking his head, coming up with nothing.

"You made a phone call."

"Did I?"

"To the Black House on Liberation Street."

Commissioner Yang Da rolled his eyes and let out a moan of despair. "Fuck...that phone call. I knew she was going to be the death of me one day. I haven't slept right since I took her on. One look at her and I knew she was going to be trouble."

"Superintendent Si Ying?"

"Yes."

"Tell me about the phone call."

Commissioner Yang looked away from Fatty Deng, out of the window, at the Ye family mansion. "I got a phone call myself...on the Wednesday...from someone I knew when I was serving in the army."

"Major-General Zi Hong."

Commissioner Yang did not hide his astonishment. "You know?"

"What did he want?"

"A favour – as always. It's like I haven't even retired from the army. It's always that way with Major-General Zi Hong. He remembers names, faces, and seems to keep a track of everyone who interests him...or might prove useful to him...even after they have left the army. But the favour seemed simple this time."

"There have been others?"

"Yes."

"What did he want you to do Friday evening?"

"Order Superintendent Si Ying and her team out of the Black House, just after eleven in the evening."

"Why?"

"He did not say."

"Did you ask?"

"No – I did not see the point."

"Commissioner, you're PSB now...not army!"

"Investigator Deng, you don't understand. I *was* army. I was a major on Major-General Zi Hong's intelligence staff. I owe him so much."

"Old PLA loyalties," said Fatty Deng, contemptuously.

"Yes – and he's also not the kind of man you refuse."

"What about your loyalty to the PSB?"

"Investigator Deng, you don't understand, I was already compromised." Commissioner Yang Da ran the back of his hand across his forehead again. "I did him a little favour about a year ago. I thought it a trifling thing at the time. But it's all I think about these days. Early last summer, at the start of the beautification campaign...you know, when we were ordered to recruit pretty girls to make the police seem more attractive to the people...Major-General Zi Hong phoned me up, out of the blue. I was honoured to speak to him again, so pleased that he still remembered me. I had been out of the army two years by then, you understand. He asked me to help out a fellow soldier, a senior NCO from his staff who was leaving the army...get her into Chengdu PSB. I didn't see the consequences of that favour. I thought being ex-army she would be an asset to the PSB. And, in Building Security, if she proved useless, how much harm could she do? But it didn't work out that easy. I didn't realise until afterwards that she was Major-General Zi Hong's mistress."

"So Superintendent Si Ying's baby isn't yours?"

Commissioner Yang Da was horrified. "Have you met her, Investigator Deng? Some might like their women straight off the farm, but I don't. I found out later from my old army contacts that Major-General Zi Hong had spotted her in the ranks, promoted her, and took her as a personal aide, got her pregnant and then, deciding a scandal wouldn't be good for his career, threw her out of the army. But he either had a soft spot for her or for the baby. He bought an apartment for her in Chengdu – close enough for him to visit from Chongqing and yet far enough away for no one to suspect anything. I expect, after the baby had arrived, and she had quickly decided full-time mothering was not for her, she called him and threatened to make a scene unless he got her a job in the police."

"So Major-General Zi Hong phoned you?"

"Yes," said Commissioner Yang. "And I have regretted agreeing to the favour he asked of me ever since. I made sure she didn't have to go to Police College and just assigned her to a security detail. It isn't exactly difficult work. But then she gets ideas above her station and tells me she wants to be promoted. I said no and then I get another call from Major-General Zi Hong. He told me that when she's unhappy, he's unhappy. That's when I realised I was up to my neck in it...that I would never be rid of her and Major-General Zi Hong. I promoted her to Superintendent third class and told her that any higher and she would have to appear before a formal promotion board which she would be bound to fail. Not the truth, as I expect you know, but she's so stupid she doesn't know any different. It was the best I could do to contain the situation."

"Let's return to Friday evening – where did you send her and her team?"

"There's a new police station being built in the middle of the Fuqing Residential District. I told her to go inspect the site, make sure all was as it should be."

"Did she go?"

"I assume so."

"You don't know for sure?"

"Investigator Deng, I didn't want to know what she was up to. I just went to bed. I wasn't even on duty. All I could guess is she and her team needed to be away from the Black House for a few hours. My phone call would provide her and her team cover. It would appear on the phone log if anyone looked."

"What do you suspect she was up to?"

"I don't know."

"Don't you care?"

Commissioner Yang Da grew angry. "Of course I care! I lay awake in bed for hours wondering what she and her team were up to, fearing the worst, that they might be breaking into apartments and robbing old people of their life-savings. I wouldn't put it past her or the others in her detail. They're all under her spell."

"Maybe she just left the door of the Black House open so someone could get in?"

Commissioner Yang Da went pale and stubbed his cigarette out. Fatty Deng offered him the packet. He took another, murmuring his thanks, also lighting another for Fatty Deng.

"Well?" asked Fatty Deng.

"I have never given the Black House door codes to anyone."

"And Superintendent Si Ying?"

"I don't know."

"Commissioner!"

"Honestly, I don't."

"But you have a suspicion, don't you?"

"Investigator Deng...you must understand...Major-General Zi Hong doesn't trust anyone. Lying in bed Friday night, I wondered if he wanted Superintendent Si Ying and her team out of the way so he could check up on me. Not only is she as thick as a brick, she has a big mouth. Better she was out of the way so someone could have a good root round, see if I had done as asked."

"Root around?"

"For the fucking file!" exclaimed Commissioner Yang Da, exasperated.

"What file?"

Commissioner Yang Da calmed down. "Isn't the file what this is all about?"

"I'm running a murder investigation."

"Murder! Who's dead?"

"Primo Gong."

"Who?" asked Commissioner Yang, plainly baffled.

"And Jin Huiliang."

Commissioner Yang blinked. "Who?"

"Jin Huiliang, the Hero of Lao Cai."

"Ah, of course, Lieutenant-General Jin Huiliang...yes, I remember...I heard him lecture years many ago, maybe just after I was posted to the 14th Group Army. But I didn't know that he was dead."

"Murdered, here in Chengdu, Friday night."

Commissioner Yang Da went pale. "You don't think that Superintendent Si Ying and her team—?"

"Commissioner, let me ask you this: who did you think was trying to kill you back at the funeral?"

"I thought it was one of the fucking caterers."

Fatty Deng couldn't believe his ears. "One of the caterers?"

"Investigator Deng, my father knew he was going to die. He made most of the arrangements himself, which included booking the sisters Ping and the catering staff. When I read the catering contract after he had died, I saw that we were being ripped off blind. I tore it up and brought in some other caterers. Then I found out from one of the Intelligence guys back at PSB HQ that my original caterers were somehow connected to the gangster Freddie Yun, some lowlife up in Wukuaishi. I thought Freddie Yun had sent someone to—"

"Commissioner, your prospective assassin was Captain Si Yu, Special Operations Brigade, 14th Group Army," said Fatty Deng. "He also happened to be Superintendent Si Ying's cousin. Tell me, why does Major-General Zi Hong want you dead?"

"He wants me dead?" said Commissioner Yang Da, incredulous. "Are you sure?"

"Yes."

"But I've done all he asked of me!"

"Tell me about the file?"

"The Black House file?"

"Yes."

Commissioner Yang Da took a deep breath. "Major-General Zi Hong phoned me about a month ago. He wanted another favour. I couldn't exactly refuse him now as one little whisper about the other favours I had done him and my career at the PSB would be over. He asked me to order the Black House security detail away for a few hours one evening, enter the Black House myself and find a file in the archive from the year 1950."

"Are you serious?"

"You wouldn't believe what is stored in that Black House. And I am not just talking about old PSB files. There is all sorts in there...ancient Party files...real secret stuff. Anyway, Major-General Zi Hong gave me a file number. He told me that it was a copy of an old military file that had somehow ended up in the old archive by mistake. He just wanted it destroyed."

"You destroyed a Black House file?"

"Ah, well—"

"Hold on! Hold on! Tell me first why Major-General Zi Hong didn't ask his mistress to do this?"

"Like I've already said, Superintendent Si Ying isn't the brightest star in the sky. She's also not the most patient. It took me hours to go through all those dusty files and find the right one. When I had got my hands on it, I phoned Major-General Zi Hong and told him not to worry, that I had removed and destroyed it."

"But you didn't, did you?"

Commissioner Yang Da shook his head. "Doing his mistress a favour by giving her a job is one thing, but destroying a file quite another. It's like wiping out a bit of history."

"What did you do with it?"

"I put it in the archive for 1977."

"1977?"

"Basically, I made it disappear."

"Did you read it?"

"Sure, I flicked through it. I wanted to know what it was that Major-General Zi Hong wanted removing from the historical record. But I was none the wiser. It was dated from the end of January 1950, just after the liberation of Chengdu by the PLA. The police force had yet to be reconstituted in the city under the new regime, so a woman, name of Li Ju, had been forced to bring a complaint of murder before a Revolutionary Military Tribunal."

"Who had been murdered?"

"Her husband...an academic from the university here in the city...a Professor Gong Dawei. She was obviously educated herself. The complaint had been made in her own handwriting. Believe it or not, her original complaint is held in the file. She alleged that a senior PLA officer, named Fei Song, had come to their house one night early in January with other soldiers, dragged her husband out of his bed, and murdered him in the street. It was convincing stuff...lots of detail. Anyway, reading forward through the notes of the tribunal, they interviewed this Li Ju, ridiculed her, accused her of lying, had her beaten and then, a month or so later, had her handed over to the newly formed police force for further punishment – which is how I assume the file ended up in the PSB's hands, stashed away in the Black House and forgotten."

"How did Major-General Zi Hong know about the file?" asked Fatty Deng.

"I have no idea. He's still alive, you know?"

"Who?"

"General Fei Song – revolutionary war hero and acclaimed liberator of Chengdu, veteran of the Korean War, and commander of the 14th Group Army when it was sent into Vietnam to punish our communist brothers back in 1979. He is long retired now, of course. But to the PLA he is a living legend. When I was in the army it is no exaggeration to say that his name was still revered. In fact, I believe he lives here in Chengdu now...with his son, Fei Shi...who, if my memory serves me well, fought in the war against Vietnam under the command of his father."

"I want that file," said Fatty Deng.

"Really?"

"It might help you with Prosecutor Xu."

"Will it help me keep my job?"

"No – but producing the file might help you keep your head."

"That's something, I suppose," said Commissioner Yang Da, disconsolate.

Fatty Deng was surprised by a knock on the car window. Standing out in the rain, shielded by a large umbrella, was Sun Mei, looking distinctly unhappy.

"That your girlfriend?" asked Commissioner Yang Da.

"No."

"Pity – she's very displeased with you but very pretty."

For any inobservant person taking in the goings on within the Ye family mansion, they would have been under the distinct impression that there was a fabulous party underway. There was wonderful food, alcoholic drinks on offer, and much laughter from the kitchen where the former mayor Ye Zihao held court. And this was especially so since the arrival of the irrepressible brothers Ming, who, on entering the kitchen had each bowed very low to Mayor Ye, pleasing him greatly, and the scantily-clad sisters Ping – strippers, apparently – who had, in turn, each kissed Mayor Ye, pleasing him more so. But, in other parts of the house, there were little isolated pockets of misery: Madame Ding, moving from room to room with her mop, bucket, dusters, and cleaning fluids who was mourning someone she called 'The General'; the girl Du Yue, now retired to her bedroom with her book, grieving over the loss of both her mother and her bright future; and finally Mister Li and his wife, proprietors of the Laughing Panda Hotel, who sat together in a room all on their own, clinging onto each other, alternatively weeping and shaking with fear, saying to anyone who inquired after their welfare that they were under 'arrest' and destined never to see each other again.

Sun Mei was not one for parties, not since the death of her mother. Yes, she found joy in the teaching of the children, but she had lost touch with all her old school-friends, could not remember the last time she had been anywhere just to have fun, and worried continually over the health of her father and the financial stability of the Lucky Dragon Tobacco Emporium. Life had become one long bitter struggle. But still she did not isolate herself in the Ye family mansion as the other sad people had done. She sat in the kitchen in the midst of the party, one eye out of the window on Investigator Deng as he sat in the car talking with someone she understood to be a Commissioner Yang Da – the name seemed to mean nothing to anybody – the other on the melodrama being acted out by the brothers Ming and the sisters Ping. They had wanted to recreate for Mayor Ye's enjoyment the events that had had happened only a short while ago, in Commissioner Yang Da's house during the funeral for his father. Sun Mei had not approved, thinking it all in very bad taste. But Mayor Ye had been all for it and soon everybody, except those who did not wish to socialise, had crowded into the kitchen to watch the drama unfold. Sun Mei had been furious with her father as both he and Brother Wang – who was still behaving strangely and talking nonsense under the influence of powerful pain-killing drugs – had ogled the sisters Ping as they had danced around the kitchen table to pretend music, opening their long raincoats at regular intervals to reveal far too much of themselves, the brothers Ming playing the gathered host of grieving relatives. Then one of the brothers Ming, who had vanished into another room, reappeared in the doorway of the kitchen, holding one hand in front on him shaped in such a way as to emulate a pistol and held his other hand over his face to give the impression of a masked man.

"Bang! Bang! Bang!" he shouted, shaking Sun Mei to her very soul, the violent events of the morning in Liberation Street still more than fresh in her memory.

The sisters Ping all issued little screams to show how afraid they had been, and ran this way and that about the kitchen, showing off even more flesh as they did so to the delight of all the men present. Then another of the brothers Ming, whose acting skills were more than considerable, lumbered forward pretending to be a heavy-set man, very tired and sad-looking, ground down by life, holding a pretend pistol out before him as well.

Sun Mei knew instantly who this was supposed to be, as did Mayor Ye who clapped enthusiastically.

"Bang! Bang! Bang!" shouted this brother Ming, who was meant to be Investigator Deng, as he gunned down the masked intruder to the funeral. That brother Ming playing his part well, had fallen to the floor of the kitchen, clutching his chest, not to move again – or at least not until one of the sisters Ping had pulled him up from the floor and kissed him passionately, calling him her hero, as then did each of the other sisters Ping to whichever of the brothers Ming they had decided to pair off with.

Sun Mei had to look away, not only from the lack of decorum shown by the sisters Ping, but also because she wanted again to stare out of the window through the falling rain and into the car where Investigator Deng and Commissioner Yang Da were still in deep conversation.

Investigator Deng had just killed a man.

And yet he looked no different to her, no worse or no better, uncaring even, just smoking a cigarette, and listening intently to whatever it was Commissioner Yang Da had to say.

This was not right.

To kill a man, even a bad man, was a terrible thing.

And then there was the arrest of Mister Li and his wife. That was not right either.

As the brothers Ming and the sisters Ping, to wide acclaim, began a re-enactment of the flight from Commissioner Yang Da's home – which seemed to involve the sisters Ping running even faster around the kitchen table and showing off even more of their bare flesh – Sun Mei found she could take no more and ran out of the kitchen. Before she knew it she had opened the front door and was staring out at Investigator Deng and Commissioner Yang Da as they continued to talk, unable to decide what to do.

"It's disgusting."

Sun Mei turned at the sound of Madame Ding's voice. Madame Ding had finally worked her way through much of the house and was now ready to swing her mop back and forth over the marble floor of the entrance hall.

"What's disgusting, Madame Ding?"

"Strippers at a funeral, Ms. Sun. Who has heard of such a thing? Do those naughty girls have no family? Do they not have fathers and mothers to be ashamed of them? What has become of China? It is like the whole world has gone to hell. I fear for the future, for our children, for our children's children."

"I don't think I will ever have children of my own," said Sun Mei, sadly.

Madame Ding snorted. "Well, you won't if you continue to hover in that doorway like a frightened rabbit. Make a decision, young lady!"

Sun Mei nodded, picked out an umbrella from a collection in the stand by the front door, ran outside, opened it against the rain, worried about her sallow-looking skin and the awful blandness of her eyes as well as the dark shadows underneath them – how could any modest young woman compete with the sisters Ping? – and hurried over to the black Mercedes. She knocked on the window before her courage failed her.

Investigator Deng, with some surprise, turned toward her. When she saw his face, how he seemed to have aged ten years since the first time she had seen him, she realised her mistake, how much her presumption about him feeling nothing about killing a man was wrong, how little she knew of him, how little she knew of anything or anyone beyond the people and shops of Liberation Street.

"What is it, Ms. Sun?" he asked, stepping out of the car.

She covered him with the big umbrella as best she could, her arms not quite long enough to cope with his height and not wanting to step too close to him. She had so many questions for him, so much she wanted to know, so much she wanted to understand, who he really was, what his friends were like, what he did during his time off from work, how close to death he had really come when he had been attacked by those evil cultists, how much the many stab wounds had hurt him, what his family was like, whether his parents were still alive, and what his ambitions were for the future – that is, if he had any. But she asked none of these questions, fearing not only that it was not the time and he would get angry with her, but also that a man like him, who worked for the famous and glamorous Prosecutor Xu of the Chengdu People's Procuratorate, would have nothing to say to a nobody who ran a tobacco shop.

"Well, Ms. Sun?"

Her mind suddenly blank, she heard herself say, "I wish to speak up for Mister Li and his wife of the Laughing Panda Hotel."

Investigator Deng appeared confused, as if he could not even remember who Mister Li and his wife were.

"It was wrong of you to push a pistol in Mister Li's face and threaten to shoot," she heard herself continue. "He told me what you did."

"Ms. Sun, this is not the time to—"

"No, Investigator Deng, this is the time. You know there will be no other time. Mister Li and his wife are good people. Mister Li comes into my shop all the time to buy cigarettes. There is no more courteous man in all of Chengdu. And, though he is always rushed off his feet looking after his many guests at the hotel, he always finds a couple of hours every week to visit with my father and talk about old times in the military. Though they did not serve together, they had similar experiences. You do not realise how much his visits mean to my father...and to me. Mister Li is kindness itself. He had no idea those two men staying at his hotel were up to no good. How could he? He is not a mind-reader. If he had to have a pistol pushed in his face...if he had to be arrested...then you may as well put a pistol in my face and arrest me. I sell cigarettes to many people. Some of them are bound to be criminals. So how is that different to what Mister Li has done? Mister Li has apologised to me for what the two men did and as far as I am concerned the matter is closed. Please forgive him, Investigator Deng. Please release Mister Li and his wife and spare them any further misery. My father says you are a hero. Well, if that were true, then—"

"Ms. Sun, this is not your concern."

"But—"

"Please go inside. This day is nearly done and soon it will be safe for you to return home."

"But—"

"Ms. Sun!"

She saw his eyes change before her. The sadness, the kindness she had always seen in his eyes did not disappear. But a steeliness she had not seen before appeared in him. But she could not let the matter of Mister Li and his wife drop, no matter how much her heart wanted her to, no matter how much she just wanted to throw her arms around Investigator Deng and comfort him – and be comforted in return. It was a matter of right and wrong. It was a matter of justice...of morality.

"Mister Li and his wife are good people," she insisted.

Furious now, he snapped at her, making her jump back a step or two, her umbrella moving with her, leaving him at the mercy of the pounding rain.

"Ms. Sun, you have no idea! Just because you are a good person, you think everyone who is nice to you must also be a good person. I know you have had a difficult life. I know that all your dreams have come to nothing, that you have not fulfilled your ambition to become a schoolteacher, and that your idiot boyfriend left you because he didn't want to marry a shopkeeper. I am very glad the people of Liberation Street understand the difficulties of your life and help you out. I am very glad everyone there looks out for one another. But I exist in a different world. My world, ever since I joined the police, is full of thieves, murderers, rapists, pimps, prostitutes, drug-dealers, and every callous con-artist who has ever walked the streets. This is my world. And I am happy in it. I understand it. It makes sense to me. I know the people of this world. And, because I know those people, I know what sort of person Mister Li is. He purports to be the nicest person under Heaven, whereas in reality he turns a blind eye to murder. I pushed a pistol in his face because I was tired, because the day was not moving quickly enough for me, because I was afraid that more good people like you were going to get hurt. Do you understand, Ms. Sun? Outside of Liberation Street nothing is quite what it seems. As for what will happen to Mister Li and his wife, I do not know and nor do I care. That is for Prosecutor Xu and the People's Courts to decide. So, my advice to you, Ms. Sun, is to forget about Mister Li and his wife. When it is safe for you to do so, go back to Liberation Street, live your life, take care of your father, teach the children, manage the Lucky Dragon Tobacco Emporium, and continue to be the good person that you are. Leave the rest of the world, and all the evil that's in it, to me. It is what I am good for...what I understand. Stay away from me in future and others like me. You would not let a child attend your classes with dirty hands. Well, my hands are always dirty. Get too close to me and that dirt will rub off on you. Do you see?"

He then dropped the car keys into her hands. "Return these to Mister Ye and apologise for me for the damage and the smell of smoke in the car. He will advise you when it's safe to leave. And don't speak to him about Mister Li. Mister Ye has far less patience than I do. Someone will be down from the Procuratorate before the day is out to pick them up and take them into custody. It won't be me. Goodbye, Ms. Sun, and if you are very fortunate – and I hope you are – you will not see me, or anyone like me, ever again."

Investigator Deng then walked away, taking a glum-looking Commissioner Yang Da with him. They both got into Investigator Deng's old car with its smashed front and rear windscreens and that Sun Mei guessed was, by now, full of rainwater. After a few false starts, the engine coughed into life, and soon they were gone, off down the drive, Investigator Deng not even affording her a single backward glance.

Back in the house, Sun Mei put the dripping umbrella back in its stand and closed the front door.

"Don't cry, my dear," said Madame Ding, leaning on her mop.

"I am not crying," protested Sun Mei, wiping her eyes.

"Life can be one long, bitter struggle."

"I know."

"He is not worth your tears."

"I know that also."

"But I did like his colourful shirts."

Sun Mei tried to smile through her pain. "I liked them too, Madame Ding."

Sixty-Six

— · —

Xu Ya kept Philip Ye waiting. Disinclined to turn up to a meeting with Min Feng, the CEO of the Chengdu Cymbidium Bank, in the light floral summer dress she had been wearing all day – and in looking as if she had been sleeping in it as well – she opted first to take a shower, and spend some time as she dried her hair thinking of what to wear. Mindful of the oppressive heat that the rainstorm now settled over Chengdu was doing so little to alleviate, she chose a long, but clingy, canary yellow dress – that quite coincidentally happened to coordinate with the yellow in Philip Ye's tie – and a pair of black high-heeled ankle-boots that had yet to have their first serious outing. As she admired herself in the mirror, more than pleased with her 'new look', she was amazed at how happy she was, despite all she had endured this weekend. Whether it was Mister Qu's wonderful food, or the glorious bunch of flowers bought her by Philip Ye, or even the brief apology Philip Ye had made – forcing her to conclude that he neither knew nor suspected anything about the night her husband had died – or the simple fact that in a matter of days she would be leaving Chengdu forever, Xu Ya felt like a teenager again, full of energy and excitement, much like the day she had left home for the very first time to take up her place at the University of Wuhan. There was trepidation, naturally, now as there had been then – the not-knowing quite what was to come. But, with the acceptance of Ye Zihao's incredible offer, were not all the bad days now behind her, the remaining days of her life nothing but one long adventure?

On returning to the lounge, she had prepared herself for Philip Ye to be angry with her, anxious not to be late for the hastily arranged meeting with Min Feng. She had been ready to laugh off his concerns.

A public prosecutor was never late, no matter the time, she had been prepared to tell him. However, instead of pacing angrily, he was sitting in her favourite chair, staring out of the window at the rain, lost in a world of his own, the atmosphere about him as dark and depressing as the world had become outside. It was as if her university days had never ended: she was staring at Melancholy Ye again.

He was mooning over his fiancée, she was sure. What kind of hold did that dead Englishwoman have over him? How had she trapped him so, that fifteen years after her death or more he still could not escape her charms?

Not wanting her own present good mood to be undermined by his misery, and thinking her 'new look' should brighten his day, she said, "Well?"

He turned slowly toward her, his eyes at first unfocused as he returned to this world, noting her presence for the first time.

"A compliment would be nice," she said, twirling on the spot, so that the dress would cling to her figure more so and show it off to the best effect.

"I am sure Min Feng will have a flower in that exact same shade," he said, mystifying Xu Ya, the reference to a flower confusing her. It was not the reaction she had been hoping for.

"We'll take my car again," she told him, fuming, grabbing up her car keys and handbag, and wishing – and not for the first time – that Philip Ye had never walked into her life.

He followed her in silence out of the apartment and down in the lift to the underground carpark. As far as she could tell, he seemed not only downcast but also to be struggling with some kind of inner dilemma. It was not what she needed right now, not when they were closing in on the conspiracy behind the killing of Primo Gong.

"For Heaven's sake!" she shouted at him, as they exited the lift. "Do your stupid breathing exercises. You are going to give me a headache. I cannot abide depressed people."

He kept his silence even as they both squeezed into her little sports car, his shoulder rubbing up against hers again, making her feel even more hemmed in by his downcast mood. She mouthed a curse on all impossible men, started the engine, switched the headlights on against the gloom, and laughed as she made the tyres squeal racing up and out of the car park and onto the street, the wipers set at double-speed against the rain. Luckily, she knew where she was going and didn't have to ask Philip Ye for directions, Min Feng's apartment complex not more than twenty minutes away. She laughed again when, in the rear-view mirror, she saw a black Mercedes tuck in behind her, the brothers Na waving at her and grinning like monkeys.

Min Feng lived in the penthouse apartment of The Whispering Bamboo Grove – an exclusive complex of fully-serviced apartments, for the residents much like permanently taking up rooms in a five-star hotel. Thankfully, according to the quick bit of research she had done on her phone as she had been drying her hair, the building was not owned by the family Fu. There was next to no chance of bumping into Lucy Fu and having to be polite, instead of smacking her across the mouth as she deserved. Once inside the lobby of the building, Xu Ya and the still silent, still morose Philip Ye were quickly approached by a most business-like young woman – a Ms. Lü – who introduced herself as their personal escort, there to take them up to the top floor to Min Feng's apartment, who passed them each a business card if either of them, or both together, wished to discuss the rates for the few remaining vacant apartments.

Philip Ye remained close-mouthed, so it was up to Xu Ya to engage with Ms. Lü in conversation as they went up in the lift, to ask her about the history of the building, all while Ms. Lü was smiling stupidly at Philip Ye and pushing her chest out as much as she could so as to impress him.

Xu Ya should have told her she was wasting her time. The only woman Philip Ye was interested in, had ever been truly interested in, was a ghost.

Ms. Lü waved them goodbye on the top floor and told them to call her anytime – by which she meant, in regard to Philip Ye, *anytime*, night or day. Ignoring her, Xu Ya knocked on the door. In no time at all it was opened by a teenage girl, no more than fifteen years of age, who rushed past Xu Ya and threw herself into Philip Ye's arms.

"Oh, Uncle! Uncle!" she cried. "It has been so long since you have come to visit."

Shocked out of his depressed state – maybe *she herself* should have tried this radical approach, thought Xu Ya – Philip Ye laughed and hugged the girl, kissing her on her forehead, showing her more affection than Xu Ya had ever seen him show anyone, telling her how much she had grown since he had last seen her, how pretty she had become, how proud her mother and father must be.

"You will come to my recital, won't you?" asked the girl, using both her hands to drag Philip Ye into the apartment. "It will be a small occasion, just a hundred or so people, next Saturday evening in the foyer of the bank. Father has arranged it. You know how he is, how much he wants the best for me. Will you come, Uncle? Will you come? I sent the formal invites out only yesterday. Yours might not have arrived just yet."

"Of course," said Philip Ye, before adding the proviso, "work permitting."

Xu Ya followed them into the apartment, feeling forgotten and invisible, not understanding what all the talk of a recital was about until she saw the Steinway Grand Piano taking up most of one corner of a very expansive lounge.

The girl, bubbling over with excitement and energy, barefoot Xu Ya noticed, and clothed only in a too-short pink shift that was as good as see-through and left nothing to the imagination about the girl's underwear and rapidly blossoming body, bounced over to the piano, took her seat and began to play. It was a classical piece, Western, Russian maybe – not that Xu Ya could name it or the composer.

"Min Yan is a prodigy," Philip Ye said to Xu Ya.

"Ah," replied Xu Ya.

"You should attend the recital, Prosecutor – it might broaden your horizons."

"My horizons are broad enough," replied Xu Ya, sharply, feeling rather useless and unattractive compared to the skimpily-clad prodigy, having no intention of attending.

Then, belatedly, she wondered if Philip Ye had been asking her out on a date. But, by the time she glanced up at him to see if she could comprehend exactly what he had intended, he had given his full attention back to Min Yan and her playing and the moment – if indeed it had been a moment – was missed.

Min Yan – she had to be Min Feng's daughter – suddenly stopped the movement of her hands across the piano keys and said, "He is in the conservatory...getting his fingers dirty again."

She then began to play again, her eyes closed this time, a different piece, very romantic, swaying in time to the music as she did so.

Having no musical aptitude whatsoever, except her perfectly tolerable singing-voice, Xu Ya could only wonder at the unfairness of life, the lottery by which gifts were handed out by Heaven to some and not to others, and followed Philip Ye who was already walking out of the lounge.

Philip Ye knew where he was going. It was quite apparent that he really did know the family well, that he had been to the apartment many times before – but maybe not that recently, as demonstrated by the approach made by Ms. Lü who had to be new in her post. Philip Ye led Xu Ya up a short flight of stairs. She was convinced he was going to take them out onto the roof. And he did in a sense, for the door they next came to opened out into an incredible glasshouse – much more than a simple conservatory – that was filled with the most breath-taking collection of flowering plants.

At last Xu Ya understood the reference he had made earlier to her dress as she spotted, only an arm's length away from her, an orchid, the shade of whose flower perfectly matched the yellow of her dress. Both the walls of the conservatory and the roof were made of glass, making it feel not only that she had stepped into some sort of primeval garden but that she was also lost in the rain clouds. The sensation all but took her breath away.

Down one of the aisles between the long tables of plants, she spotted a short, stocky man, smiling to himself as he re-potted a specimen, dressed casually in slippers, slacks, and a thin cardigan. Xu Ya would have thought him as nothing but a gardener if she had not recognised his picture from the quick bit of research she had done on her phone. He had a most unexpected hobby for a CEO of one of the most important banks in Chengdu.

Philip Ye led the way and this time Xu Ya was content to follow, happy to take in the wondrous collection of flowers on all sides of her, and to take the time to put her nose close to a few on the way, finding it strange that some gave off the most intense and intoxicating perfumes while others possessed no scent at all.

Philip Ye happily took Min Feng's extended hand. But when he introduced Min Feng to Xu Ya, and Xu Ya realised that the daughter Min Yan had not been joking about the grubby fingers, she had to steel herself to do the same. It did not seem like a test. Min Feng appeared a quite genial man, uncaring and maybe unaware of the state of his hands, as well as the dirt down his shirt and cardigan – not quite the ruthless and powerful financier Xu Ya had been expecting.

"How is your father?" asked Min Feng of Philip Ye, as he cleared a small table of plants and arranged some simple wooden seats for them to sit upon. A maid appeared – the first domestic Xu Ya had seen – as if from nowhere, carrying a tray of tea and a plate of biscuits. The maid laid the tray down and then hurried away.

"My father is well, sir," replied Philip Ye.

"Is he keeping busy?" asked Min Feng.

"I would imagine so," replied Philip Ye. "He is always on the phone or at his desk, planning and scheming at I do not know what, getting up to all kinds of mischief."

"I will call him soon, I promise," said Min Feng.

"He would appreciate that," said Philip Ye.

"And you, Prosecutor Xu, are you keeping busy?" asked Min Feng. "I watched you on TV. A most impressive debut. The people of Chengdu will not forget you in a hurry."

"Thank you," she replied, immediately taking to Min Feng.

"Now, what is it I can do for you, Prosecutor?" asked Min Feng. "Philip said over the phone that you had a rather delicate matter to discuss. It surely cannot be as urgent a matter as that of my friend, Primo Gong, who is being held in a rather unpleasant cell in the basement of the Procuratorate – that is, if all the rumours swilling around the business community are to be believed."

Xu Ya supposed she should not have been surprised, the genial collector of flowers being only one aspect of Min Feng's personality. But the speed with which the gentle aspect to his face had disappeared, the rapidity at which his eyes had hardened upon her, had shocked her.

"I cannot confirm the truth of those rumours," she replied, coldly.

"Prosecutor, do not play games with me," said Min Feng. "One phone call from me and—"

"Then make your phone call!" she dared him.

Min Feng glared at her and then turned toward Philip Ye. Xu Ya was astounded and disappointed that Philip Ye did not immediately leap to her defence, merely shrugging and relaxing back on his seat, his expression opaque, as impossible to read as usual.

"It saddens me, Philip, that you are part of this charade," said Min Feng. "There is no better man than Primo Gong, no more loyal patriot, no better friend to me or this city. I would like to know what this is about...who he has fallen afoul of to attract the attention of the Flower of the Procuratorate."

Min Feng said this last with evident distaste.

Xu Ya would not be ignored. "It is not for you to know what—"

"Primo Gong is dead," said Philip Ye, speaking over her. "He has been murdered."

At first Xu Ya thought that she was hearing things, that she was having some sort of psychotic breakdown, unable to believe that Philip Ye would not only betray her confidence but also act contrary to the strict instructions issued by Party Chief Li and Secretary Wu. But as Min Feng's mouth dropped open in shock, she realised she had not been imagining things and that any advantage she had had in the interrogation of future witnesses and suspects – for surely word would now leak out – was lost.

"How?" asked Min Feng.

"Late Friday night, in his apartment – an intruder, we think," replied Philip Ye.

"Robbery?" asked Min Feng.

"It is the likely motive," replied Philip Ye.

Why, after giving away the truth of Primo Gong's violent demise, Philip Ye had now chosen to tell only half the story and suggest an already disproven theory, Xu Ya could not guess. But she was not going to let the interview spin any further out of control or allow any more of Min Feng's questions to be answered.

"I am leading the investigation," she said to Min Feng, wagging her finger at him to get his full attention. "Not Superintendent Ye, do you understand. You are to forget all he has told you, and are not to mention Primo Gong to anyone. That order comes down directly from the Party. Is that clear?"

"Perfectly," replied Min Feng, seemingly unruffled.

"I have some questions for you," said Xu Ya. "We are looking to understand Primo Gong's movements on Friday evening. It is most important that we fill in all the gaps."

"He was at the bank with me," said Min Feng.

"For a meeting?" asked Xu Ya.

Min Feng shook his head. "It was a dinner...a celebratory banquet. As you no doubt are aware, it was Mayor Cang's birthday last Tuesday. He has been a great friend to me and to the bank these last few years. I thought to hold a private dinner for him, in his honour, not at a restaurant, but away from the people, away from all their phones and cameras. At the bank, in the banquet room, I thought Mayor Cang could really relax. My wife sent out all the invitations. You may not believe it, but Mayor Cang has hardly travelled out of China. He loves stories of foreign lands – the United States especially. What better then but for my wife to invite Primo Gong? Mayor Cang and Primo Gong have always got on famously. And we knew Primo Gong would be free as he usually dines on Friday evenings at the Old Chengdu Restaurant with my senior executives, to talk a little business and work through the problems of the week."

"Who else?" asked Xu Ya.

"Pardon?"

"Who else was invited to this banquet at the bank?"

"Why is that important, Prosecutor?" asked Min Feng.

"Please answer my question."

Min Feng glanced over at Philip Ye for support but, thankfully, this time, Philip Ye kept his mouth shut.

"Well?" insisted Xu Ya, deciding now that Min Feng, with his superb apartment, his collection of flowers, his ridiculously gifted, flirty, and precocious daughter, was not a man she could ever like.

"My wife was there, of course," said Min Feng.

"Did Primo Gong bring a date?"

"He did."

"Du Luli?"

Surprised, Min Feng raised his eyebrows and glanced again at Philip Ye before opening his mouth. "Yes, she was there."

"Had you met her before?"

"No."

Xu Ya thought him a liar, for she noted a slight stiffening of his body. She wondered, if Min Feng had not met with Primo Gong and Du Luli as a couple before, then whether he had known Du Luli from another place and another time, whether *his* business card was to be found stuck to one of the earlier pages in Du Luli's scrapbook. She made a mental note to get that scrapbook off Philip Ye, to make a record of all those business cards – if not for this case, for her own gratification. Who knew when such information might prove of use in the future?

"Who else?" she asked.

"A couple of friends of mine were in town this last week, so my wife invited them too."

"Their names?" asked Xu Ya, feeling like she was trying to squeeze blood out of a stone.

"Zhou Dong and Zhu Fu, financiers from Beijing, their wives also. I can forward their details to you. They have already returned to Beijing."

"Who else?" she asked.

"Your list is complete," said Min Feng.

"You have forgotten Lucy Fu," said Xu Ya.

If Min Feng was shocked by her assertion, this time he hid it well. There was no stiffening of the body, no subtle glance at Philip Ye this time to look for assistance with a difficult public prosecutor. "She was not present."

"You are sure?"

Min Feng shrugged. "She was invited, of course. But she chose to be elsewhere that evening, I don't know where. I assure you, there were no more people present."

"You forgot Sarangerel," said Philip Ye.

What passed then between the two men, the sharp, angry look Min Feng extended to Philip Ye, the complete lack of any reaction Min Feng received in return, almost took Xu Ya's breath away. It was a reminder of how much of a recent arrival in Chengdu she was, how little she understood of Chengdu politics, how Sarangerel seemed to be often at the centre of it all.

"I did not mention Sarangerel because it is well known that Mayor Cang goes nowhere without the witch," said Min Feng. "She was on good form Friday evening, dressed in next to nothing, doing her best to seduce all of the men with her eyes, making a fool out of Mayor Cang as usual. It is a great pity. On his own, Mayor Cang is a man of rare wit and intelligence. She has reduced him to nothing more than a willing slave. Philip, the day your father returned with that—"

"Tell me about Primo Gong's mental state?" asked Xu Ya.

"What about it?" asked Min Feng, impatiently.

"Was he happy? Sad? Distracted?"

"Prosecutor, what is it that you really wish to ask me?"

"I understand he has not been himself these last few months, that he was not providing the leadership at Ambrogetti Global Software quite as he should, that there were ongoing problems with the roll-out of the new software for your bank, that he had been spending more time than he should researching his family roots in Chengdu and writing a combination of a business motivational book and autobiography."

"You are very well-informed," said Min Feng.

"It is my job to be," replied Xu Ya.

"I fail to see what—"

"Tell me what I wish to know then I will leave you in peace."

Min Feng picked up his teacup and took a sip of his tea. She guessed he was playing for time, stalling so that he could get his words and thoughts in order. She noticed a hint of a smile cross Philip Ye's handsome face at Min Feng's discomfort, and, despite him opening his big mouth and revealing Primo Gong's murder, Xu Ya now felt both strengthened and cheered by his presence. Philip Ye was the most impossible, most annoying, most incomprehensible man. But Xu Ya sensed then, if need be – much as Investigator Deng would – he would step between her and any trouble that was heading her way, that if Min Feng had reached across the table in an attempt to strangle her – an extreme example, she knew – he would intervene. The realisation was such that for a brief moment she thought she might cry.

"Prosecutor, I consider myself severely chastened," said Min Feng. "I regret to say that, in the past, I have considered public prosecutors to be nothing more than bumbling civil servants – morons who could hardly investigate themselves out of a dung heap. After seeing you on TV, I should have known better. Your information is correct. But, and this is most important, the inference I think you make is not entirely so. There *are* problems with the roll-out of the software. We are running a couple of months behind on the project. But the project should not be considered to be in any real difficulty. The board at the bank is fully aware of the problem. At the banquet on Friday evening, Primo Gong had arranged with me to come brief the board this coming week on the plan he had devised to remedy the situation. I am distraught that my friend is no longer in a position to do this. He was my friend – a very dear friend. I admit our friendship had been challenged these last few months. He had known I did not approve of his relationship with Du Luli. I knew what she was, or at least what she had been. I also did not approve of all the work he had been doing on that stupid book of his. I told him China did not need another business self-help book, or to hear the sad story of how his family had left Chengdu just after the Revolution, or how they had made a fortune in the United States, or why he had decided to return. I told him to make a success out of Ambrogetti Global Software first, to repay the shareholders for all of the faith they had put in his company. But, I think, Du Luli was of the opposite mind. She encouraged Primo Gong in ways she should not have, probably thinking that if she did so he might love her more, draining him of his vital energies in much the same way as that the witch drains Mayor Cang of much that is good in him. And before you ask me, Prosecutor, I never once caught sight of the manuscript Primo Gong had been working on. I did not want to encourage him by asking to see it. I am not ashamed to say that Primo Gong and I had argued repeatedly these last few months. But this last week he called me and apologised, told me how foolish he had been, that he was now putting the book aside. The dinner on Friday evening was not just to celebrate Mayor Cang's birthday, but also to celebrate the renewal of my and Primo Gong's friendship. It is difficult for me to say how distressed I am that he is now gone, that a simple burglary could have ended his life when—"

The ringing of Xu Ya's phone saved her from any more of this emotional rubbish. It was Investigator Deng. She excused herself and stood up from the table, walking some way down an aisle between two long tables festooned with plants, away from the two men so she would not be overheard. Earlier, she had put off Investigator Deng making an immediate report on the arrest of Commissioner Yang Da, telling him she would catch up with him later. She had wanted to concentrate on the upcoming meeting with Min Feng. It had been a mistake. Min Feng had told her nothing of interest, nothing she hadn't already known – except perhaps the interesting presence of Mayor Cang and Sarangerel at the dinner, and that Lucy Fu had been elsewhere, not that that had any bearing on her investigation. Now it was time to hear what Investigator Deng had to say, in the hope that he had learned something useful that would propel her and the investigation in a more profitable direction.

"Yes, Investigator Deng?"

He told her he was inside the Black House.

That he had hold of a secret file.

A file that had recently been ordered destroyed.

He read to her, word for word, a complaint made by a woman, name of Li Ju, dated the 27th January 1950, to a Revolutionary Military Tribunal.

She almost screamed out loud in exultation at the detail provided her.

What a find Investigator Deng had made!

What a gem of a man he was!

What a smart decision she had made to recruit him!

When Investigator Deng had rung off, Xu Ya returned to Min Feng and Philip Ye, the pair of them sitting seemingly in an uncomfortable silence, and said, "Forgive me, but I must conclude our little discussion prematurely. There is somewhere else I have to be. It is time for me to make an arrest."

SIXTY-SEVEN

—·—

Constable Ma was on the move with Superintendent Si Ying but Fatty Deng did not know why or where. She had tried to explain over the phone but he was too tired to comprehend exactly what she was rattling on about, too tired to caution her never to turn her back on Superintendent Si Ying, too tired to care. His face hurt, his heart hurt, and he felt weary to the bone. His day was almost done.

He had driven Commissioner Yang Da in his old wreck of a car to Liberation Street and then parked up just around the corner from the Black House. Fatty Deng had asked Commissioner Yang Da to repeat his phone call of Friday night, and order the security detail inside to abandon their post and go inspect the site where the new police station was being built in the Fuqing Road Residential District. That would keep them away for hours. After watching the two men of the day shift leave the Black House and hurry off through the rain to the nearby car park to pick up their car, Commissioner Yang Da punched in the codes to the front door and let Fatty Deng inside.

Before this, the closest Fatty Deng had got to the inside of a Black House was when he had delivered the charming, Gauloises Blondes smoking lawyer, Mister Li, to the front door of this very building at the very beginning of his police career. And so, as he followed Commissioner Yang Da inside, he had not known quite what to expect, fearing the atmosphere would be one of terror, deprivation, and loneliness – the residue of the acute suffering of the inmates that had at one time been held within. He even feared that he might find Mister Li still imprisoned here, forgotten by all. But Mister Li was nowhere to be seen. And the atmosphere of the building, despite what it had once been used for, was just full of the unpleasant smell of old paper, mould, dust, and decay.

"It's like a museum," said Commissioner Yang Da. "A testament to the passing of time."

Cardboard boxes full of innumerable paper files were stacked everywhere: in corridors, blocking doorways, and floor to ceiling in rooms once used as interrogation suites or cells. It looked like no one had tidied up for a long time, with paper files spilling out of many of the boxes, at places spread all over the floor, others piled up on window ledges and ready to topple over at the slightest nudge. Fatty Deng followed Commissioner Yang Da's lead, trying not to step upon any of the files, wondering why no one had bothered to tidy them up. Commissioner Yang Da pointed out the security detail's office on the ground floor – the only place devoid of files – complete with a small kitchenette, comfy chairs, a small table at which to play cards or *majiang*, and a couple of grainy black and white CCTV screens mounted on the wall being fed images of Liberation Street from various angles, and from the disused entrance at the back of the Black House. Fatty Deng did not know how anyone could work here and stay sane.

As if reading his mind, Commissioner Yang Da said, without a trace of humour, "It takes a low-level of mental activity to be able to survive in here."

Commissioner Yang Da led him deeper into the building. Fatty Deng could discern no order to the unstable towers of cardboard boxes, the loose paper files left lying everywhere. But somehow Commissioner Yang Da could see what Fatty Deng could not. As he made his way down the corridor and then up a flight of narrow stairs, he shouted out the years to Fatty Deng – 1954, 1963, 1957, and so on – pointing to various stacks of boxes as he did so, but from where he got his information Fatty Deng could not tell. There were markings on some of the boxes, numerical codes and suchlike, but nothing that made sense to Fatty Deng. Commissioner Yang was also at pains to point out that many of the files were not actually PSB files, but stored on behalf of any number of government and Party agencies.

"Why?" asked Fatty Deng.

"I don't know," replied Commissioner Yang Da. "But it's possible that the contents of the majority of these files were considered interesting or useful to the PSB at the time. I have looked through a number of them and found little of interest – nothing that immediately screamed out to me as secret or embarrassing to someone high up in the Party if released. It is just history, years and years of history that nobody cares about, except maybe curious academics – not that such people would ever be allowed a peek in here. It's probably best if it all went up in smoke one day."

"I wouldn't feel good about that," said Fatty Deng.

"I did not take you for a historian," said Commissioner Yang Da.

"I'm not, but—"

"Are you thinking of the supposed burning of the books during the Qin Dynasty?"

Fatty Deng laughed, noting the wry smile on Commissioner Yang Da's face, finding him entertaining. "No – but in Police College I was taught that the filling out and the preserving of reports was everything, that unless something was properly written down, using the correct turn of phrase, signed off by my boss, and then archived in the right place, it hadn't actually happened. That lesson has stayed with me to this very day."

"You are a rare man, Investigator Deng," said Commissioner Yang Da, using his shoulder to push open a door off the main corridor on the first floor which got them access to a room measuring no more than two metres by three. "Most PSB reports that cross my desk are barely comprehensible – possibly intentionally so."

Commissioner Yang Da switched on the light and gestured to the paper chaos that lay within the small room. "Believe it or not, this room contains files pertaining to the first quarter of 1977. This is where I hid the file Major-General Zi Hong wanted me to destroy."

Fatty Deng was pessimistic about Commissioner Yang Da quickly laying his hand on the file he needed. But he needn't have worried. Commissioner Yang Da pushed his hand into a stack of loose files on top of three cardboard boxes and came out with one file with a cover of a slightly different shade of grey, the thin paper within curled and browned with age, the type-written print badly faded.

But the print was readable. As Fatty Deng flicked through the pages, he not only found the minutes of various meetings held by the Revolutionary Military Tribunal through the end of January 1950 and into the following February, but also the full transcript of the

interrogation of a woman named Li Ju, and – more important still –
the original of her handwritten complaint made to the Committee.

Fatty Deng read the complaint from start to finish as Commissioner Yang Da stood by patiently. It was incredible. Li Ju described
in detail an attack on her home in the middle of the night by a unit
of the PLA, not long having liberated Chengdu from the Nationalist
forces. The soldiers had broken down her door. They had threatened
to bash the brains in of her young son. They had dragged her husband
from his bed. They had beaten him up in the street, egged on by a
baying mob. And then, they had made her husband kneel, tied his
hands behind his back, and beheaded him.

'They said he was an American spy,' Li Ju had stated in her
complaint, the words strangely devoid of any emotion, almost as if
she had been an uninterested party – nothing more than an uncaring
witness.

She was in shock, thought Fatty Deng. He knew all about that.

"You say that the officer who wielded the sword, the man who
actually committed the murder of Li Ju's husband, this General Fei
Song, is still alive?"

"Yes," replied Commissioner Yang Da. "And living in Chengdu."

"Fuck me."

"I have my doubts that Li Ju's husband, Professor Gong Dawei,
was really an American spy," said Commissioner Yang Da. "They
were brutal, febrile times. And stupid accusations were flying around
with people using the chaos to settle old scores. And, though nothing
is explicitly stated in the file, it is likely that Professor Gong Dawei
was the exact opposite of what the PLA soldiers thought. I think
he was a spy for the Party against the Nationalists. I sensed severe
embarrassment in the minutes of the meeting of the Committee. And
though Li Ju was beaten for having the nerve to make a complaint
about such a revolutionary hero as General Fei Song, and even though
General Fei Song was not punished or even brought before the
Committee to explain himself, the fact – as noted toward the back of
the file – that he was quickly transferred to a command in Chongqing
says it all. If Professor Gong Dawei had been an American spy, or just
a university nobody, no one would have bothered."

"Fuck me," repeated Fatty Deng.

"I agree," said Commissioner Yang Da.

Fatty Deng wondered about the file he was holding in his hands. If Major-General Zi Hong had dispatched Captain Si Yu and his fellow soldiers from the 14th Group Army Special Operations Brigade to have Primo Gong assassinated, if he had called up Mister Li of the Laughing Panda Hotel asking him to provide a room to two of those soldiers and turn a blind eye to whatever it was that they were up to, then he was high up in the conspiracy – if not at its very head. It could be no coincidence that Major-General Zi Hong, a month ago, had wanted this file from 1950 destroyed. It surely had relevance to all that had happened – the murder of Primo Gong, the disappearance of Du Luli, the murder of Jin Huiliang – on Friday night. Furthermore, though the exchange of information between Prosecutor Xu and himself, and Superintendent Ye and Constable Ma, had been little more than a fucking disgrace, he was certain that one of the former soldiers, The Historians, that Prosecutor Xu and Superintendent Ye had gone to meet earlier that morning in the teahouse, had also been named Fei. If so, the file in his hand was surely treasure. Fatty Deng did not know what sort of treasure, or indeed how valuable a treasure it was, but it was treasure nevertheless.

"I want to see the top floor now," said Fatty Deng.

"What for?" asked Commissioner Yang Da.

"Just get me up there."

Commissioner Yang Da did as he was ordered and took Fatty Deng up more flights of narrow stairs. Soon enough, Fatty Deng had found the room he was looking for, as piled high with boxes and loose paper files as any other. The room looked nothing out of the ordinary, except that the window ledge was clear. A few flakes of rust from the iron window frame had fallen down onto the window ledge. Unlike the windows off the other rooms, these windows had been opened recently. Fatty Deng turned the window catch and pushed open the window. Hardly visible through the pouring rain, the late afternoon almost as dark as night as the rainstorm pummelled the city, Fatty Deng could just about make out Plum Tree Pagodas, with Primo Gong's window directly opposite him, the broken window now temporarily boarded up with wood.

"What are you staring at?" asked Commissioner Yang Da.

"Nothing," said Fatty Deng, too tired to explain.

There were no boot marks, no shell casings, no cigarette butts, but Fatty Deng was certain Captain Si Yu's sniper team had set up here, had bided their time waiting for Primo Gong to return from wherever he had been on Friday night, and who had taken their chance when Primo Gong had stood in front of the window of his apartment, firing off the round that had traversed the distance between the two buildings in a fraction of a second, punching through his heart and throwing him back on his bed, killing him instantly.

Fatty Deng looked down at the river of rainwater coursing down Liberation Street. It was not quite a flood – the drains were just about coping – but from up where he was the current seemed strong enough to knock someone off their feet. There was a light on in the Lucky Dragon Tobacco Emporium, someone other than Sun Mei – maybe Mister Wu, of Mister Wu's Cycle Sales and Repair Shop – manning the till. Fatty Deng felt despondent. He would never see Sun Mei again. It troubled him that they had argued before they had parted, that he had left her with no better memory of himself. But maybe that was for the best. She was better off having no further dealings with law enforcement. Sun Mei was a good person. He hoped she would maintain that goodness to the end of her life. Heaven knows, Chengdu was desperately short of good people. And, maybe she would one day find a good man not ashamed to marry a simple shopkeeper, and maybe she would get a few hours off a day from the Lucky Dragon Tobacco Emporium so she could return to college and get her teaching certificate, and maybe then she could achieve her ambition of teaching in a real school somewhere. Fatty Deng hoped so. And he hoped the gods were listening as he offered up a prayer so all her dreams might come true. It was the least he could do for her, after bringing so much trouble, so much danger, into her life.

"What next?" asked Commissioner Yang Da.

"I have to make a phone call," replied Fatty Deng.

He phoned Prosecutor Xu and read out to her the handwritten complaint made by the woman Li Ju back in the year 1950. His instincts were correct. The file was indeed treasure and Prosecutor Xu told him so. She ordered him not to let it out of his hands, or lose Commissioner Yang Da for that matter, and that she was now – based upon what he had read out to her – about to make an arrest.

She did not stop to explain why the file was so important, what the murder of a university professor back in 1950 by a PLA officer had to do with what had occurred this Friday night just gone. But Fatty Deng was too tired to care. His day was now definitely done.

"What happens to me?" asked Commissioner Yang Da, when Fatty Deng ended the call.

"You will be interrogated by Prosecutor Xu at the Procuratorate."

"That will not go well for me, will it?"

"I wouldn't have thought so," replied Fatty Deng.

"My family, my father's funeral...."

"I will inform them."

"Thank you, Investigator Deng."

"Call me Fatty – everyone else does," said Fatty Deng, offering the despondent policeman another cigarette.

"That wouldn't be right," said Commissioner Yang Da.

"It's what my friends call me."

"I am hardly your friend, Investigator Deng."

"I beg to differ. Earlier I saved your life. And this file you conveniently preserved has probably provided me the key to my case. Do you fancy a drink?"

"What?"

"Look...I'm dead on my feet. The cells at the Procuratorate can wait for you awhile. Let's sink a few beers, have a bite to eat, make a toast to your departed father. What do you say?"

"I would like that," said Commissioner Yang Da, his eyes filling with tears.

And so they did.

Sixty-Eight

— • —

From the outset Philip Ye had felt in his heart that the investigation had never been quite his, that he had been at best a passenger just along for the ride. He had been up in the air, returning from the United Kingdom, when all of the murders had occurred. And Constable Ma, easily manipulated by PSB Dispatch, had been pressured into straying from their assigned patch to attend a murder scene that should have been the responsibility of someone else. It was not that he had not been useful. He had provided some much-needed focus for all concerned. He had also helped Prosecutor Xu join the dots in regard to Primo Gong, Du Luli, and Jin Huiliang. But he suspected Prosecutor Xu would have got there eventually. Even his intuitive insight, while sitting with The Historians in the Cry of the Crane Teahouse, that the emotional Fei Shi was their man, would have occurred to Prosecutor Xu soon enough – once she had sat down and had time to reflect on all that had been said. And then there was Fatty Deng. His natural good sense and his nose for following the right trail would have helped Prosecutor Xu come to the right conclusions and keep her feet on the ground. As for the appearance of the ghost of Du Luli back at the airport, Philip Ye now understood it had nothing to do with the investigation at all. It had not been a cry from beyond the grave for justice. All Du Luli had done was speak of the future, thank him for what he had been about to do: keep her daughter safe from the unsavoury influence of Sarangerel – at least for now.

In fact, if truth be told, rather than the investigation, it had been Prosecutor Xu who had stayed at the forefront of his mind. He had wanted to watch her, consider her, understand just what it was that made her tick – and hopefully discover along the way whether this time last summer she had perhaps stuck a kitchen knife between her husband's ribs.

During her summing up of the evidence amassed against Commissioner Ho, Prosecutor Xu had paused, turned, and spoken directly into the TV cameras. It had been a speech like no other Philip Ye had ever heard. She had spoken of the Rule of Law, of its fundamental importance, about how, if China was to take its place at the head of all nations – surely its rightful place – then the upholding of the Rule of Law, and the enforcement of it, was paramount.

Philip Ye had watched the speech on the TV in his father's study. His father had been sitting on the sofa next to him, muttering to himself, seeing only the threat that Prosecutor Xu, the new darling of the people, posed to him. But, hearing the slight tremor in her voice – evidence of the powerful emotion she was struggling to contain? – and the intensity of her eyes, a jolt of electricity had coursed through Philip Ye's body, the like of which he had never before experienced. Something in her words, or the spirit behind those words, had touched his soul. No speech, no person living or dead, had ever affected him so.

"What an actress!" his father had exclaimed.

No, had thought Philip Ye, she had not been acting. He had seen more than enough liars in his time.

And yet, as the days had gone by, he had begun to doubt what he had seen and heard – all that had so powerfully resonated within him. He began to wonder if his father had not been right – doubts he had carried with him all the way to the United Kingdom and back.

This current investigation Prosecutor Xu was now working could not exactly be described as transparent – not a shining example of how a criminal investigation should be conducted according to the Rule of Law. There had been no announcement of Primo Gong's death, no proper examination of the body by Doctor Kong, and a veil of secrecy had been thrown over all that had transpired in Plum Tree Pagodas late Friday night. And all this because Party Chief Li and his Shanghai Clique cronies needed time to divest themselves of all their stock in Ambrogetti Global Software before word leaked out and the share price crashed. But Prosecutor Xu could be forgiven. She was following orders – as he would have had to do in her place. Like it or not, the Party was in charge. And as long as all the evidence was collected properly and correctly interpreted, as long as the innocent were allowed to go on their way and only the guilty charged, then the Rule of Law could cope. What he could not forgive, what he could never forgive, was if, in speaking about the Rule of Law with such passion, Prosecutor Xu had indeed been acting, that away from the cameras, out of the public eye, she was nothing but another spineless public prosecutor who talked a good game and who had murdered her husband just because, one summer evening last year, she had felt like it. If so, then her speech had been worse than an act: it had been a betrayal of all those men and women who had stood up for what was right through the thousands of years of Chinese civilisation, those people who had held fast to the Rule of Law through war, plague, famine, tyranny, and chaos.

He watched her now, standing in the grand lobby of The Whispering Bamboo Grove, as she spoke to Secretary Wu on the phone, informing him of the incredible discovery Fatty Deng had made at the Black House. She was doing her best – using all that passion and intensity – to convince him that it was time to swoop down on the Fei family home, as a brave little shikra would, and make a much-needed arrest.

"The family Fei has committed murder for no other reason than to protect their family name," she told Secretary Wu. "This is all this complicated and upsetting case has ever been about."

Philip Ye felt utterly deflated.

The little hawk had to have her kill.

Woe betide anyone who now got in her way.

He had tried.

He had done his best in the lift down to the lobby to tell her that any arrest was far too premature, that there was so much as yet unknown – the complicity, or not, of the other Historians, for example, or how deep the rot went into the PLA, or even into Chengdu PSB.

But she would not listen.

On exiting the lift, she had raised her voice to him, embarrassing him in front of the concierge and the other staff, saying, "Superintendent, either do your best to keep up with me or go home! I don't care which!"

She had then turned her back on him and made her phone call to Secretary Wu, the people then staring at him – including the overly attentive Ms. Lü – perhaps judging him as weak, as someone who had no choice but to cling to the coat tails of the brilliant and impassioned Prosecutor Xu.

He did his best to ignore all the eyes upon him.

He could not go home.

He had his orders from Chief Di.

He had to stick close.

He was required to keep the little shikra safe.

After all, she was the star of this show.

In the car, a few minutes later, Secretary Wu having extended to her all the freedom of action and authority she needed, she was again all smiles.

"Secretary Wu was worried for my safety," she said. "He wanted me to wait for reinforcements to be properly organised. I told him not to be so silly, that I would not come to any harm – after all I have a very melancholy policeman by my side. Oh, he did laugh."

Philip Ye thought not. Secretary Wu had never been the laughing kind. Philip Ye assumed Secretary Wu was as concerned as he was, and was really depending on him to make sure events turned out as well as could be expected, and to keep Prosecutor Xu out of harm's way.

As usual, she drove too fast. She talked non-stop as she drove, sliding the car around corners, ploughing through puddles of uncertain depth, carelessly drenching those pedestrians unfortunate enough to be out and about as she raced by. She spoke mainly nonsense. Hardly taking a breath, she gabbled on about how successful she was going to be representing the business interests of the family Ye, about the fine home she was going to have, about the friends of many cultures she would certainly make, and about the places around the world she had been longing to visit and now would definitely see.

Soon tiring of all this inane chatter, more than concerned about what they were soon to encounter at the Fei family home, and the lack of the planning and preparation that should have been done before any such raid was executed, Philip Ye said, furiously, "For Heaven's sake, stop talking!"

He had caught her in mid-sentence. She turned and glared at him, the car swerving dangerously across the road. But she caught the swerve just in time and returned her focus to what was in front of her, her breathing shallow and rapid, her faced flushed, her knuckles white upon the steering wheel.

"I don't like you," she said, a few moments later.

He ignored her.

"I didn't like you back at university."

He continued to ignore her.

"You are the one person I will not miss when I leave this stupid city for good."

He closed his eyes. He forced himself to settle into his preferred breathing pattern: in for eight, hold for four, out for eight. *In breath, there is life; in breath, there is clarity; in breath, there is serenity.* He extended his mind forward, seeking out the house that was their destination. He hoped to see what awaited them there. He hoped this little psychic trick of his – which sometimes worked and sometimes didn't – would give him some inkling of what to expect.

A large townhouse flashed into mind. He saw the front door hanging open, two young women – maids? – fleeing through the rain as if for their lives.

Then the image was gone and Philip Ye pondered its meaning. Had he seen the past, the present, or the future? Or had it been nothing but a product of an over-active imagination? He put his hand in his raincoat pocket and felt the reassuring presence of the pistol he had brought with him. He hoped not to use it. He was not that good a shot, not like Constable Ma. He wondered where she was, what she was up to, whether she had made any headway with Superintendent Si Ying. It saddened him that she was not here with him now, that he had not found a way to reach her, to instruct her better, that all he had done was throw books at her and chastise her and poison the relationship between them. She had deserved better from him, as everybody had been so keen to point out.

He opened his eyes.

Prosecutor Xu had been staring at him. She quickly returned her attention back to the road.

"Having regrets about working for me, Superintendent?"

He ignored her again.

She muttered something incomprehensible under her breath. This was probably for the best, her words almost certainly far from complimentary. It occurred to him then how little he knew of her, her background, her childhood, her education, her experiences working for the Procuratorate in Chongqing – no easy job that – and, most importantly of all, why she had married the man she had, and whether indeed, one fine evening last summer, she had chosen to end it violently.

The car skidded to a halt outside a large townhouse much like the image that had flashed in his mind, except a high wall surrounded the estate and enclosed a substantial garden to the rear. The iron gates that led into a short driveway, as well the front door, had been left ajar. There was no one to be seen.

"You can stay here if you like," said Prosecutor Xu, before quickly jumping out of the car.

He cursed her for the reckless and headstrong woman she was, and followed suit, hating the rain that instantly pummelled his face, pulling his pistol from his pocket, checking the safety was off, and indicating as best he could to the brothers Na as they pulled up to take station at the front of the house to guide in the reinforcements that were surely on their way. Secretary Wu may well have surrendered to Prosecutor Xu's will, but he was no fool. He would have ordered the mobilisation of every available law enforcement tactical unit in Chengdu.

By the time he returned his attention to the house, Prosecutor Xu was already through the front door. All she had with her was her handbag. She had no pistol, no baton, nothing. Philip Ye cursed her again, wondering what it was she was trying to prove. He ran after her. Once through the door, he immediately sensed the house was empty, except for Prosecutor Xu, who was nothing but a blur, flitting rapidly from room to room, exasperated that she could find no one to arrest. Philip Ye paid her no heed, almost choking on the atmosphere of the house, it being so thick with grief and regret – much as Bo Qi's house had been the day before.

"They have run," he told Prosecutor Xu when she suddenly appeared before him.

"It's your fault!" she shouted at him, exploding with frustration. "It was your stupid idea to waste our time with Min Feng."

Not quite history as he remembered it. Philip Ye tried to catch hold of her then, to grab her arm, to slow her down, but his fingers slipped on the wet sleeve of her dress and then she was gone, running up the stairs. He let her go, wanting first to have a quick look around the expansive lounge. Unlike Jin Huiliang's simple abode, the Fei family house was extensively decorated with all kinds of militaria and PLA memorabilia, not just paintings and photographs of soldiers mounted on the walls, but also glass cabinets displaying helmets and tunics from as far back as the 1920s, as well as various swords, daggers, pistols, muskets, and rifles – hopefully deactivated – dating from as early as the 18th Century. Philip Ye was glad to see none of the display cabinets appeared to have been opened, the weapons remaining undisturbed.

Satisfied there was nothing on the ground floor that required his attention, he followed Prosecutor Xu up the stairs. The house was bigger than it appeared from the outside, the stairs taking him up to a gallery that ran almost the full 360 degrees around the top floor, with eight doors leading off it to bedrooms and bathrooms, he supposed. There were more ancient swords mounted on the walls of the gallery, more glass display cabinets full of military history. Again, there was no sense of anyone lurking on the first floor. But, if anything, the atmosphere was even thicker with grief. Philip Ye put his hand to his mouth in a vain effort not to breathe in the polluted air.

He found Prosecutor Xu in one of the bedrooms. She was staring down at a very old man lying on a bed, connected up to a whirring machine that was feeding pure oxygen into his lungs. For a moment Philip Ye feared that his instincts, his intuitive understanding that the house was empty, had led him astray. The old man was definitely alive, his rheumy eyes wide open, his frail chest moving up and down. But Philip Ye quickly saw he had not been mistaken after all, for behind the old man's eyes there was no intelligence, no flicker of recognition that he and Prosecutor Xu were even there. It was nothing but a body kept alive by drugs and copious amounts of oxygen. Alzheimer's disease or some other form of dementia, Philip Ye wasn't sure what, but General Fei Song – it had to be him – was no longer cognisant of his surroundings. His state made a lie of what Bo Qi had said of him that very morning in the teahouse, that General Fei Song's remaining memories were like diamonds. There were no diamonds to be had here.

Prosecutor Xu took up her phone again, informing Secretary Wu that the birds had flown, that security at the airport had to be alerted, and that it was imperative that investigators from the Central Commission for Discipline Inspection be sent to detain Major-General Zi Hong at his barracks in Kunming.

Philip Ye left her to make her case, curiously feeling some sympathy for her that she had not had her moment of glory before handing in her resignation to take off for a new life abroad. He returned his pistol to his raincoat pocket and began to explore the other bedrooms, bothered by the lack of any physical disruption to the house that should have been evidence of a family making haste to flee. But then he came upon the master bedroom. A framed wedding photograph, of a young Fei Shi and the woman who had to be his new bride, lay broken on the floor, shards of glass everywhere. Someone, Philip Ye presumed, had thrown it against a wall. A chair had been toppled over and clothes were laid out on the bed in some disarray. But there were no suitcases to be seen, nothing that pointed toward the couple making a purposeful attempt to pack up their life and run. By the side of the bed Philip Ye found a green crocodile-skin handbag. He could not help but smile. Constable Ma would be so pleased when he told her. He bent down and used a pen from his pocket to open it slightly and look inside. He saw the packet of Good Cat cigarettes he had been expecting. It had been the wife – a woman whose name he did not even know – who had crept up on Jin Huiliang, plunged an ice-axe into the back of his skull, and calmly smoked an expensive cigarette while watching him die. It was almost too much to believe. The woman smiling out of the wedding photograph – admittedly it appeared as if it had been taken sometime in the mid-1980s – had looked anything other than a cold-blooded killer. But appearances were often deceptive, as he had to remind himself day after day.

Philip Ye made his way to the window to stare out at the rain, feeling sadder than he had in many, many years – incomprehensibly so. The afternoon was now almost as dark as night, the rain sheeting down. Distant flashes of lightning arced across the sky to the south. Through the rainwater coursing down the window, Philip Ye could see a well-appointed ornamental garden. There was a tidy square of cut lawn and a stone path running down its length. It led to a low arched bridge that spanned a mid-sized fish pond and then to the rear of the garden, to a small copse of trees – a simple apple orchard, he thought. But something was not quite right about the apple trees. A vague dark shape, nothing more than an indistinct blur, did not belong.

Leaving Prosecutor Xu to her phone call, Philip Ye returned back down stairs, found his way out to the garden, grimaced as he looked to the sky, wondering if what he was going to do was worth a soaking to the skin. He then thought to hell with it, that he was here to do a job, turned his collar up against the rain, and made his way down the garden path. He was careful with his footing as he crossed the narrow bridge over the fish pond, the water made cloudy from the pouring rain, not a colourful fish to be seen. He hurried onwards. When he reached the orchard, he could see small apples already appearing on branches of the trees. But it was not the apples that had attracted his attention from the bedroom. As he stared upward, raising his arm above his head to shield his face from the stinging rain, he saw a pale, lifeless figure hanging from the thickest branch of the tallest apple tree. Dressed in an old-fashioned PLA uniform, a long line of medals on display, Fei Shi hung from the tree, swaying slightly in the occasional gust of wind that crossed the garden, rainwater dripping from his downturned face and limp hands. How long he had taken to die, Philip Ye did not know. But the length of the rope was such that it was doubtful Fei Shi's neck had snapped in the fall. It had to have been an extended and excruciating asphyxiation.

"Who are you?"

Startled by the woman's voice, Philip Ye turned, and found himself looking down the long barrel of a shotgun. With his focus entirely on the body hanging up above him, and the incessant rain drowning out all but the loudest sounds, he had lost awareness of all about him. He swiftly decided against any precipitate movement such as reaching inside his pocket for his pistol, even a flinch on his part sure to bring him instantaneous death.

"Who are you?" asked the woman again, the threat, the impatience, in her voice unmistakeable.

"A friend," he said.

"I don't think so."

The woman squinted at him through the rain, her skirt and blouse soaked through, her feet muddied and bare, a much older, much more frightening version of the woman he had seen in the smashed wedding photograph.

"I am a friend of your husband," said Philip Ye.

"No, you're not!" the woman screeched. "I know all of his friends. They are so few and you are not one of them. But I think I know who you are. My husband, spineless fool that he was, was terrified of you. You are the *laowai* policeman, aren't you? When my husband returned at midday, you were all he could speak about. He had become a gibbering fool. He said we were doomed. He said a *laowai* policeman was coming for us, that all was lost...that my perfect plan had fallen into so many broken pieces. I have never seen a man so afraid, a man so undeserving of his father's name."

"What is your name?" asked Philip Ye, trying to control his fear, the knowledge he was only but a short finger-pull from death.

She ignored the question, indicating with a jutting movement of her head, that he should look upwards again. "Look at him, Mister Policeman. The question you should be asking is: how could I have ever married such a craven coward? I have no good answer for you. I just naturally assumed, as any woman would, that the son would be as the father had been. Was that not a reasonable assumption to make, Mister Policeman?"

"It was," he replied to her, searching for options but finding none, trying to buy himself time.

"I should have married the father not the son."

"I understand."

"My husband was nothing more than a baby, crying out during the night because of all he had supposedly seen during the war. I was disgusted with him. I would have divorced him...should have divorced him...but I could never have abandoned the true love of my life."

"General Fei Song," said Philip Ye.

"A true, revolutionary hero – a man, a real man, who never suffered a single bad dream in his life. I could not have left him. He needed me. He appreciated me. He trusted me to do all the things that needed to be done."

"I would like to meet him."

"I do not think so, Mister Policeman," she said, taking a step forward, the shotgun hardly an arm's length from his face now. "You are to die here in this garden with my husband. I will bury you both under these trees. You deserve nothing less for poking your big *laowai* nose into our private family business."

If he had not believed it before, he saw it in her eyes then, her intention indeed to kill him.

His thoughts came lightning quick: how stupid he had been in blundering toward his death, more concerned about Prosecutor Xu and her safety rather than his own; how his body – ripped apart by shotgun pellets – would be discovered by reinforcements that now must be surely close by; how those reinforcements would sit in the bars and the teahouses for months to come and debate just why he had not delayed entering the house until their arrival; how his father would rant and rave and, as always, assert his right to take a terrible revenge; how he had never given himself the time to get to the bottom of the mystery that was Prosecutor Xu; and finally if, on entering the afterlife, Isobel, or anyone else for that matter, would be waiting to greet him.

He thought not.

He sensed no ghosts about him.

He was very much alone.

A primal howl then rent the air and the shotgun roared. The rush of hot air to the side of his face and the shock knocked him backwards down into the mud, feeling no sensation, no pain at all, except a ringing in his ears. When he opened his eyes, hardly believing he was still alive, he saw Prosecutor Xu on top of Fei Shi's wife, screaming with rage, pulling at her hair, gouging at her eyes, and fighting for control of the shotgun. But the wife was stocky and strong, and the shotgun roared again, but still Prosecutor Xu clung on, refusing to give up on her prey.

Philip Ye came to his senses and struggled to his feet. Unable to use his pistol – the two battling women were almost as one – and recognising the shotgun, being of a modern semi-automatic type, was not out of shells, he threw himself into the fray, grabbing hold of the barrel of the gun and keeping it skywards and away from where it might do harm, and jabbing the middle finger of his free hand into the base of the wife's neck, seeking out the pressure-point where it would cause the utmost pain.

The shotgun came free in his hand as the wife fell to her knees, screaming in agony. Prosecutor Xu tumbled off her and onto the ground. Philip Ye, breathing hard, unable to quite fathom how and why he still lived, threw the shotgun to one side and rolled the now screeching wife onto her front, pushed her face into the mud, somehow found his handcuffs, and restrained her. When he glanced up, he saw Prosecutor Xu had got to her feet, her long hair in complete disarray as if she had been standing in the teeth of a gale, her face streaked with blood, her bright yellow dress stained with mud and torn as high as her thigh, her eyes like that of the little raptor he always imagined her to be, wild and overly bright.

"Are you okay?" he asked of her.

She nodded, unable to speak, offering him a weak smile instead. She swayed from side to side, either from shock or because she was missing the heel of one of her boots.

Then the brothers Na found them, pistols drawn, having come running at the sound of the first shotgun blast. They sized up the situation quickly, glared furiously at Philip Ye as if he had committed the most abominable sin, turned their backs on him, and then extended what care and attention they could to Prosecutor Xu.

Sixty-Nine

— ⋅ —

P hilip Ye couldn't remember a time when he had ever felt so relieved to hear the sound of Constable Ma's voice. He had been standing idle in the house, unsure as to what to do with himself, watching the brothers Na tend to the bloody but otherwise superficial cut to Prosecutor Xu's forehead. The wife of the late Fei Shi lay bound face down on the floor, raving, the words spewing forth from her mouth difficult to understand, a torrent of vitriol and invective. The reinforcements from the Procuratorate and PSB were yet to arrive. Philip Ye was beginning to wonder if they had been given the wrong address. And then Constable Ma phoned.

"Superintendent, I have found her," she said. "Please come."

He had reassured her that he would, immediately.

Taking the Na brothers' car keys – they could find their own way home – Philip Ye told them and Prosecutor Xu that there was somewhere else he needed to be. He did not bother to explain. He just wanted to get away from the oppressive atmosphere of the house and as far from Prosecutor Xu as he could manage.

There was much he needed to ponder. Prosecutor Xu was someone he hardly knew, a woman whose past and whose motivations he considered highly suspect, and whose relationship with him – such as it was – could be described as nothing other than difficult. And yet Prosecutor Xu had appeared out of nowhere and in the nick of time, and thrown herself bodily on top of an armed madwoman, risking everything to save his life.

It did not make sense.

Her speed of action, her decision-making, had to have been instinctive, arising from the very core of her being.

He did not understand it.

And, because he did not understand it, he was disturbed by what she had done – and not a little ashamed that he had been so stupid as to have put himself in such a position as to need saving in the first instance.

There was indeed much to ponder.

Out of the house, he jumped into the Na brothers' Mercedes, and without looking back took the best route he could think of to take him quickly out of the city and into the surrounding countryside. If anything, the storm had worsened, the sky as black as night, the rain bucketing down – an outward manifestation of his dark mood.

He did not enjoy being beholden to anyone. The principle of *guanxi* – of favours done in the expectation of favours to be received – had never sat well with him. It was no simple thing to be obligated to someone, especially if one served in law enforcement; it could be difficult to refuse a favour asked, even if the granting of that favour could lead to the crossing of a legal or moral line.

And what bigger obligation could there be than to owe someone one's life?

None he could think of.

Prosecutor Xu had tried to make light of the situation beneath the apple trees, saying, "Superintendent, now we are even."

By which he had understand her to mean that she had now repaid him for rescuing her from The Willow Woman cult three months earlier.

But there was no true equivalence. Three months earlier, he had had a great deal of help from his good friend Wolf; three months earlier, he had not placed his own life in any great peril.

It was not the same.

He now owed her.

And she knew it.

As did the brothers Na, who would never fail to keep reminding him of the fact.

And it did him no good to remind himself that in a few days she would be leaving Chengdu to take up his father's job offer in some foreign land. He could feel it in his bones. He was far from done with Prosecutor Xu. Somehow events – who knew what those events might be – would conspire to bring their paths together again. In saving his life, she may as well have thrown a noose around his neck and tied herself to him. The effect was the same. He and she were bound until the end of time, the obligation, the binding, tighter than had ever existed between him and his fiancée Isobel – a binding so permanent he might even take it with him to beyond the grave.

The roads deteriorated as he left the city behind him. Distrusting the car's satnav outside of the city, hoping he had properly understood the directions given him by Constable Ma, he drove as fast as he dared down country lanes, some no better than shallow lakes, others so narrow he was sometimes forced to pull over and stop to let vehicles pass him travelling the other way. In no time at all, disorientated by the poor visibility, the weather well and truly closing in, he became hopelessly lost.

Maddened by his failure, by the obligation now owed to Prosecutor Xu that was already eating away at his soul, he stopped the car and slammed both his hands upon the steering wheel in frustration.

"If she has murdered her husband, I will not help her conceal her crime!" he shouted out loud.

Feeling somewhat better, he took up his phone, was surprised he still had a signal, and dialled the number Constable Ma had asked him to memorise. The call was soon answered by the taxi driver who had brought Constable Ma out into this bewildering rural landscape, and who supposedly had an intimate knowledge of all the local roads, lanes, and dirt-tracks – a Mister Zhu.

Not only did Mister Zhu realise instantly where Philip Ye was from the poor description offered him of the last village Philip Ye had passed through, in no time at all he had Philip Ye moving in the right direction. When Philip Ye was getting close, Mister Zhu was out of his taxi and waving a torch around to bring him right where he needed to be. When a relieved Philip Ye got out of the car, Mister Zhu rushed over to shield him with an umbrella. Philip Ye gladly shook his hand.

"Superintendent, it is an honour," said Mister Zhu, over the noise of the torrential rain. "How is your father?"

"He is well, thank you," replied Philip Ye, looking about him, seeing nothing but the deserted and desolate road they were standing upon, a line of trees either side, the flooded fields beyond. "Where is she?"

Mister Zhu pointed toward the south, to where all the bad weather was coming from. Philip Ye peered out between the trees and across a flooded field. In a far corner he could just make out a single-storey building, nothing more than an abandoned ruin. He could not imagine how Constable Ma had got all the way out there. He glimpsed a brief flicker of torchlight from within the building.

"I told her not to go," said Mister Zhu. "But she wouldn't listen to me."

"What is that place?"

"An old temple, Superintendent. I've never had the need to visit it myself. It is rumoured to be over two hundred years old. Some of the locals say it is cursed. Maybe it is, maybe it isn't – but what is certain is that it is full of venomous snakes and spiders. Your constable was very brave to go wading out there. She is a most impressive woman."

"She is that," said Philip Ye, dismayed by what lay in front of him, not wanting to lose face in front of Mister Zhu.

Philip Ye had no boots or waterproof clothing of any kind with him. They were all in the boot of his own car which he had foolishly lent out to Fatty Deng. All the brothers Na had in the boot of their Mercedes was a variety of weaponry – nothing to help him in his present predicament. He glanced down at his shoes and suit trousers that were already wet and muddied by the violent encounter with the insane wife of the late Fei Shi. He cursed under his breath at what he now had to do.

"I have your constable's prisoner in the back of my taxi," said Mister Zhu.

Philip Ye was astonished. He had forgotten all about Superintendent Si Ying. He looked inside the taxi. Dull, expressionless eyes stared back at him.

"She has been no trouble," said Mister Zhu. "Your constable has bound her very tightly. She has not said a word to me. I offered her a drink of water which was refused. I think she is resigned to her fate – whatever that fate may be."

"Please look after her a while longer," said Philip Ye. "I must go and see what my constable has found."

"I suppose it would do no good for me to advise you to stay here on the road," said Mister Zhu.

"No," replied Philip Ye, wishing it could be otherwise.

He did take Mister Zhu's offered umbrella with him, though. He first steadied himself by taking hold of the trunk of a tree at the side of the road, careful not to trip over any of the protruding roots, and then tried to figure out how Constable Ma had made it down into the flooded field without mishap. He spied a muddy path down through the dense vegetation. There was no other way. He let go of the tree and slipped down the path, nearly losing his footing in the mud, his patent leather shoes doing little to steady him, and then landed in the field up to his shins in filthy water that stank of rotting vegetation and sewage. Mister Zhu's umbrella helped him steady his balance as he began to slosh his way through the water across the field, the mud underneath attempting to suck his shoes off with every step. He hoped he was following the path taken by Constable Ma, that there were no hidden trenches about to swallow him whole. Once underneath the polluted water he doubted he would ever surface again, or, if he did, if his health would ever be the same.

When he neared the temple ruin, he could see that most of its roof had fallen within. The crumbling walls were festooned with creepers, and, where the walls were bare, desecrated with a jumble of obscene graffiti. He wondered to whom the temple had originally been raised, to which god or important local personage. The characters that had been engraved above the entrance were now broken away, lost. He muttered an apology for the state of the temple, hoping, somewhere, his voice might be heard. He then called out and was gratified to hear a muted reply from within. As he waded closer to the entrance, he saw something dark and long slither away across the surface of the water. He remembered Mister Zhu's warning about venomous snakes and spiders. But he then caught the sweet, sickly odour of death from within the temple, thought nothing more about the dangerous local fauna, and joined Constable Ma inside.

She first played her torch upon him, fearing, he supposed, that it might not be him, and then returned the beam to the object of her attention. Against the back wall of the temple, afloat on the polluted water, surrounded by old soda cans and food wrappers – someone had been using the old temple, maybe local junkies shooting up – was a terribly bloated and discoloured corpse. It was impossible to make out whether it was that of a man or a woman.

"I have called Doctor Kong," said Constable Ma.

"That is good," replied Philip Ye, having never seen Constable Ma looking so lost, so forlorn. Her clothes were soaked through. He guessed she had been standing in the roofless temple for ages.

"Doctor Kong said she would be here within the hour...two at the very most. Mister Zhu told me he would wait to guide her here also."

"You think this is Du Luli?" he asked.

"Yes, Superintendent," replied Constable Ma. "I think it can be no other. They tortured her. They did terrible things to her before she died."

Philip Ye wasn't so sure. The lack of available light within the temple, the rain pouring in, and the poor state of the corpse – a result of the intense heat the last few days as well as the probable troubling of the body by foxes, rats, and other creatures – made the cause of death impossible for him to determine, let alone what she might have suffered prior to death. It was possible that even on a dry autopsy table back in morgue in Chengdu, Doctor Kong might have trouble coming to any definite conclusions.

"Let us come away from this awful place," said Philip Ye. "Let us wait for Doctor Kong and her team back at the road."

She shook her head. "Superintendent, I cannot leave Du Luli."

"She will not mind."

Constable Ma shook her head again and brushed the rainwater from her face. Philip Ye noticed she was shivering. It could not be from cold. The heat within the temple, despite the rain pouring in the through the large holes in the roof, was suffocating.

"How do we tell all this to the girl?" asked Constable Ma. "How do we tell this to Du Yue?"

"We will lie."

"I do not lie."

"Sometimes it is necessary."

"But how do I hide what I have seen from my face?"

"You will learn."

"Superintendent, I have never seen anything so heartless...anything so cruel. Superintendent Si Ying told me what happened. They were waiting in a car outside of Plum Tree Pagodas late on Friday night – she and her cousin, Captain Si Yu. She said she had no idea what she was doing there, why her cousin wanted her to be his driver. I think her a stinking liar. I think she knew that they were there in case the sniper missed Primo Gong, in case Primo Gong came running out of the building intent on making his escape. But they saw Du Luli come running out instead. They recognised her as Primo Gong's girlfriend. Maybe they were in radio contact with the snipers. They pretended to be real police. They offered to help her. They persuaded her to get into the car. Then they drove her all the way out here. I think Du Luli knew very quickly something was wrong. I think in the back of that car she fought for her life. Maybe Captain Si Yu beat her to silence her. Superintendent Si Ying told me the car was got rid of, so I think the evidence of what happened in the car is lost. Superintendent Si Ying knows the roads around here very well. I don't know how. She did not grow up around here. It could be – she wouldn't tell me if this was true – that she had been searching for days for a good place to dump a body. She told me she stopped the car when her cousin told her to, and that he then pushed Du Luli down into this field only to return a few minutes later saying that he had let her go. But Superintendent Si Ying is a stinking liar. I think she helped her cousin drag Du Luli all the way out here. I think Du Luli knew no help would come, that there was no one around for miles. I think Superintendent Si Ying held Du Luli down while her cousin tortured her and then cut her throat. I cannot speak about what I feel about this, Superintendent. I have never felt so bad in all of my life. I know Du Luli was a prostitute, something a mother should not be. But if I returned to the road this moment and got back into Mister Zhu's taxi, then I think I would beat Superintendent Si Ying to death with my bare hands. I do not think I can ever look upon her again. It is no real comfort to know that her cousin is now dead."

"Captain Si Yu is dead?"

Constable Ma's lips turned up into a grim smile. "Fatty did it. He phoned me not long ago...said he was now in a bar getting drunk...that a couple of hours ago at Commissioner Yang Da's family home he saw Captain Si Yu and shot him dead. I do not know the details. Fatty swore to me it was true. He asked me to teach him how to shoot properly. He used up all fifteen bullets in his pistol just to put Captain Si Yu down. I told him not to worry, that dead was dead no matter how many bullets were used, and that it was a very good thing he had done. I really like Fatty. He doesn't mess about or say stupid stuff. He just gets on with the job."

Unsure whether this was yet another none-too-subtle poke at him, Philip Ye said, "Come, let us leave this place. Du Luli is going nowhere and Doctor Kong will be here soon."

"No, Superintendent."

"I thought you had a SWAT party to attend this evening."

"You know about that?"

"Of course."

"Are you invited too, Superintendent?"

"No – homicide detectives tend to dampen the spirit of any party. Mostly, we are a dour lot."

"I am a homicide detective."

"Are you, Constable? Are you really?"

She brushed more rainwater from her face and stared at him, her big moon eyes larger than ever. "I was not sure. I have been so unhappy these last few months...until I waded across this field and found her. I was just looking at Du Luli, wondering how anyone could do such a thing, when I realised that if I did not do this job, if I did not remain in Homicide until the end of my days, then I would not be able to live with myself. What happens when you retire, Superintendent? What happens when Superintendent Zuo retires? If I'm not around, who will look for the bodies? If I do not bring the guilty to justice, then who will?"

He did not doubt that she meant every word. "SWAT will be disappointed."

"I am used to disappointing people. I have already disappointed you," she said, miserably.

"Perhaps, but we all approach this work differently. I am intolerant of any method except my own. I have also been an indifferent, if not poor, teacher. The fault has been mine, Constable – everybody says so."

"I will try to be a better student," she said.

"And I a better teacher."

"I cannot leave her."

"So it seems."

Philip Ye left Constable Ma to keep watch over the body of Du Luli and to await the arrival of Doctor Kong and her forensic team. He told himself she would be fine, that no venomous snakes or spiders would dare bite her, that Heaven itself protected those who had just discovered their true calling.

With some difficulty he made his way back across the flooded field, but would never have managed to climb back up the muddy bank to the road if not for a timely helping hand from Mister Zhu.

"How bad is it, Superintendent?"

"Very bad," replied Philip Ye, catching his breath.

"Superintendent, if you wish to return to Chengdu with your prisoner, it would be an honour for me to stay and watch over your constable. She said I might be needed to guide a certain Doctor Kong here."

"You would do that?"

"Yes, anything for the family Ye."

Philip Ye pulled his wallet from his jacket pocket and took out five 100-*yuan* notes. Mister Zhu shook his head emphatically but Philip Ye insisted. "You must be paid for your time and you have been more helpful than most."

Mister Zhu bowed, touched the notes to his forehead, and then stuffed them inside his trouser pocket. Philip Ye pulled an unresisting Superintendent Si Ying from the taxi and pushed her onto the back seat of the Mercedes, making sure that she was indeed properly bound, not wanting her to reach over and strangle him from behind as he was driving her back to the city. He shook Mister Zhu's hand, accepted a few much-needed directions again, and then headed back to Chengdu.

"Where are you taking me?" asked Superintendent Si Ying.

"The custody suite at the Procuratorate."

"But I am police."

"I would disagree."

"I did not hurt that woman."

"My constable thinks you a liar."

"My baby needs me."

"The woman you killed was a mother also."

SEVENTY

—◦—

E arly evening, not long after the wet and murky day had faded into night and the patter of rain on the windows had finally lessened, a change had come over the Ye family mansion. Sun Mei had been sitting by herself in a library she had found, wanting to be alone with her thoughts, unhappy with herself, with the way she had stupidly argued with Investigator Deng before they had parted, and unable to look the terrified Mister Li and his wife in the eye or enjoy herself with the others. But she felt the change in the air as if the house itself had let out a sigh. She left the library and found that people had already begun leaving, that a small fleet of taxis were parked outside of the house. Mister Li and his wife were already gone, taken away by some uniformed police, her father said.

No one could tell her what had changed out in the city, why they were now safe to go back to their normal humdrum lives. All her father could tell her was that Philip Ye had returned, the bottoms of his suit trousers and his shoes inexplicably covered in mud, and had inexplicably announced to Mayor Ye, "It is done."

It is done.

But what had been done?

And what had become of Investigator Deng?

And what would become of Mister Li and his wife?

And who would look after the Laughing Panda Hotel in their absence if they ended up in prison?

Sun Mei was too late to witness the departure of the irrepressible brothers Ming and the scandalous sisters Ping. But she was in time to witness the frankly ridiculous and emotional leave-taking between her father and Brother Wang in the TV room. Her father unable to stand, Brother Wang had been forced to get down on his knees and embrace him as a brother, tears streaming down his face, the powerful pain-killing – and possibly mind-altering – drugs apparently not yet out of his system.

"I promise I will soon visit the Lucky Dragon Tobacco Emporium," said Brother Wang. "When my ear grows back, I will visit you, Mister Sun."

Sun Mei thought both highly unlikely. She had learned that Brother Wang lived a fair distance away, in the north of the city, in Wukuaishi – as did Investigator Deng. Who would brave all those traffic jams just to purchase some cigarettes and sit around talking about nothing? As for Brother Wang's ear growing back, she considered this to be a particularly cruel jest perpetrated by the brothers Na when they had been bandaging Brother Wang's head earlier in the day – a jest, incredibly, not corrected by the doctor later summoned to attend him.

Leaving her father and Brother Wang still hugging each other, Sun Mei went in search of Madame Ding. She soon learned, to her great regret, that the 'Woman with the Mop' – as some in the house had come to call Madame Ding – had already gone, apparently without saying farewell to anyone. Sun Mei thought her a lonely soul, having to work in Chengdu while her children and husband were far away, and now needing to find a new job as her last employer had been murdered. Sun Mei had wanted to wish Madame Ding well, to say that she would pray for her.

Sun Mei went upstairs to find Du Yue instead. The girl was in the bedroom allotted to her, lying on the bed, staring at the ceiling, clutching her book to her chest.

"I am to leave now," Sun Mei told her.

Du Yue got up from the bed and embraced her. "They have found my mother, Teacher Sun."

"I am glad."

"I am not allowed to look upon her, though."

"I am sure that is for the best...you should remember her as she was."

"I am frightened for the future."

"I know...but try not to worry too much. Write to me or visit me if you wish. You know where to find me at the Lucky Dragon

Tobacco Emporium. If I can help in any way then I will. But I am sure things will work out for you. Remember to work hard at your studies whichever school you are sent to, to always respect your elders, and to never give up on your dreams."

"I will, Teacher Sun."

Sun Mei thought she might cry as Du Yue hugged her all the tighter. She kissed Du Yue on the forehead though the girl was so tall Sun Mei had to stand on tiptoes to do so, and then Sun Mei left her to continue grieving for her mother.

Back in the TV lounge, Sun Mei was faced with the problem of how to move her father. They had left Liberation Street in such a rush no one had thought to bring his wheelchair. But the problem soon resolved itself with the appearance of Philip Ye, dressed in yet another fine suit and wearing shoes that looked like they had never seen a speck of mud ever.

"Allow me," he said.

Her father protested, saying he was not worthy of being carried by the scion of such an illustrious family. But Philip Ye – ever the gentleman – told him he was speaking nonsense, and carried him out to the waiting taxi. Sun Mei just had time to run into the kitchen, to do what was polite, and thank their host in person. The kitchen was now empty except for Mayor Ye and the American woman with the wondrous auburn hair.

"Mayor Ye, my father and I were undeserving of your famous hospitality," she said, dropping down into a slight curtsey. "But we are eternally grateful to you for opening your fine house to us anyway."

"It was my pleasure, Ms. Sun. And I wish you and the Lucky Dragon Tobacco Emporium the best of fortune."

He said nothing more, and thinking there was nothing more to be said, Sun Mei returned the American woman's smile, curtsied again, and hurried from the kitchen. She wondered how Mayor Ye had come to know her name and why, even more curiously, he had bothered to remember it.

Outside, the air was as humid as ever but the rain had almost stopped. Not that the worst of the summer weather was over. According to her father, who had heard the long-range forecast, there were more storms to come. But the respite from the rain was very welcome, and Sun Mei stood for a moment, closed her eyes and breathed in the heady scents of the trees and the flowers of the Ye family gardens, believing she would never return. Then she told herself it was indeed time to leave, that she had to return to her normal life, that all that had transpired this weekend would soon pass into distant memory and eventually be lost. Her father was already in the back of the taxi, Philip Ye standing nearby, staring at the damage to the front of his car.

Sun Mei went up to him and said, "Superintendent, I am sure Investigator Deng didn't intend this damage."

"He has already apologised."

Her heart skipped a beat. "Then he is safe?"

"I suppose as safe as one can ever be in a sleazy bar somewhere in the city."

"Oh."

"Does that bother you, Ms. Sun?" Philip Ye asked, with a slight smile.

Sun Mei tried to hide from her face the fact that she had been worrying about Investigator Deng all this time, and was now angered to discover he was already in some smoke-filled bar, almost certainly filled with dreadful characters like Brother Wang and women even more sluttish than the sisters Ping.

"Superintendent, it was just that...well, we did not part on the best of terms...and I had wanted to apologise to him again for causing so much trouble...for nearly getting us all killed. As I will never see him again, would it be too much to ask...I know I do not have the right to ask...that you pass him a message for me?"

"What message?"

"That I am sorry about everything."

Philip Ye shook his head. "No, I will not pass on such a message. You have nothing to apologise for. You were unfortunate enough to get caught up in a war that had nothing to do with you. I am just glad you and your father remain unscathed. In wartime, that is the best anyone can hope for, don't you think?"

Frustrated, unable to communicate what was in her heart – or even make sense of it herself – Sun Mei climbed into the taxi next to her father. Philip Ye told them not to worry, the fare was already paid. He closed the door on them and the taxi rolled down the drive. Sun

Mei turned in her seat to look one last time back on the great house. She saw Philip Ye leaning down close to his car, continuing to inspect the damage.

Her father asked the taxi driver about Liberation Street. The driver told them, as far as he knew, there was nothing to worry about, that Liberation Street had been lucky and was still passable, and that the worst of the flooding had hit other parts of the city.

Nothing to worry about.

If only that were true, thought Sun Mei.

All she ever did was worry, about her father, about the children, about the Lucky Dragon Tobacco Emporium. And now she had someone else to worry about, Investigator Deng, even though she would never see him again. She would wonder in the days, months, and years to come what sort of secret investigation he was working on, how much danger he was in, and whether he would ever settle down – it would have to be with a very tough woman who understood the world he lived in – and have children of his own.

As the taxi drove on, down streets unfamiliar to Sun Mei, she caught a glimpse of a lonely figure standing at a bus stop, waiting for a bus that, because of the weather, might not come. It looked like Madame Ding. But then the taxi was past the woman, too quickly for Sun Mei to be sure. But, if it had been Madame Ding, Sun Mei felt desperately sad for her. And, for some inexplicable reason, she felt desperately sad for herself.

SEVENTY-ONE

— • —

The shock of what had happened to him under the apple trees in the garden of the Fei family home still resonated within him, causing him to doubt yet again the value of any psychic gifts he might possess. What was the use of being able to remotely explore the inside of a house if in fact the threat lay outside? So, he drove to the ultra-modernist construction of glass, concrete, and steel that was the home of Bo Qi without bothering to search ahead in his mind, too tired anyway to make the effort, deciding to trust only in the pistol he took with him. For whatever reason, basic intuition or maybe just hope, he expected no meaningful opposition. Still, he was surprised to see the lights of the house blazing out into the darkness, Bo Qi not fled, and even more so when Bo Qi's young and bespectacled private secretary not only buzzed him through the gates without argument but also opened the front door to him.

"Good evening, Superintendent, I am afraid you have had a wasted journey. Mister Bo is not well. He is not receiving guests at the moment."

"He will see me."

"But—"

"Your work is done for the day."

Rattled, the private secretary glanced back into the house as if looking for guidance or assistance, and then, when such assistance failed to appear, stepped away from the doorway to allow Philip Ye into the house and began to collect together the papers that were dispersed across the table in the large open-plan lounge. Philip Ye watched him as he stuffed his papers into a briefcase and threw a thin coat over his suit.

"Superintendent, there is no better man than—"

"Go home," said Philip Ye.

The private secretary lowered his head and walked out of the door. Philip Ye shut the door after him, wanting no surprises, no one else sneaking in after him.

He stood for a moment to soak up the atmosphere of the house, to take in once more the expensive antiques on show, the reproductions of ancient priceless artworks hanging from the walls. It did not feel like much of a home. It was more like a glass and concrete shell with a few items on show to sate a visitor's curiosity, objects to distract from the great human void within. He wondered if Bo Qi's wife actually lived here. There was no sign of a woman's touch – the house bleak, empty, and emotionally cold. Even the great distress and regret he had sensed before had faded away. History might be seen in the statues in glass cabinets and paintings that adorned the walls, but the history that really mattered, the history that was personal, was nowhere to be seen or felt.

Philip Ye wandered the large house, unsettled by all the large glass windows, by being easily visible from the outside and sometimes from almost every direction. Like Primo Gong, if a bullet was meant for him, he would never see it coming. But he finally found Bo Qi without incident, sitting in a comfy leather chair in a brightly lit study, seemingly defeated and downcast, a glass of spirits in his hands, an opened bottle of fine Rémy Martin XO cognac on a small table to his side.

"Have you come to arrest me, Superintendent?"

"That depends."

"Will you sit and join me while you consider my fate? Would you drink with me?"

Against his preferred practice of hardly ever letting alcohol pass his lips, especially when working, Philip Ye found himself a glass from the drinks cabinet and poured himself a small measure of the cognac. He then took a seat opposite Bo Qi, swilling the golden liquid around in the glass, warming it with the palm of his hand. Bo Qi, satisfied, offered him a grim smile.

"What should we drink to, Superintendent?"

Philip Ye pondered the question for a short while and then said, "The souls of all those who have recently passed."

Bo Qi nodded, the vivid white scar on his forehead gleaming under the bright ceiling lights of the study. He raised his glass and sipped some of the cognac, as did Philip Ye. The cognac came as a shock to Philip Ye's system. It had been some months since he had last drunk anything so strong. But, as it warmed his insides, not unpleasantly, and dulled his senses somewhat, he felt himself relax and became glad he had taken up Bo Qi's invitation.

"Where is the fragrant Prosecutor Xu this evening?" asked Bo Qi.

"At the Procuratorate, I presume."

"Are you not working this investigation together?"

Philip Ye could not stifle the bitter laugh that burst forth from him. "Prosecutor Xu and I do not make the best of work-partners. Let us just say that our interests differ somewhat. She has a prosecution file to create – as hastily, and as efficiently, as she can. She is also most determined to impress her political masters. I, on the other hand, do not feel the need to impress anyone. There will be no medals for me or promotion, no matter what kind of show I put on. But I have a psychological need to explore beyond the narrow confines of the evidence to be presented in court. Sometimes I have to understand the true origins of things."

"Then you are a historian too."

"I suppose."

"But should I not be telling my story in an interrogation room?"

"In an ideal world, a just world, yes – but from my experience of the hasty and often sloppy manner in which justice is administered in this city I believe the investigation has run its course. Our law courts prefer simplicity over complexity."

"Yes, I can see that."

"A set of facts that even a gibbering monkey could understand."

"I am in no mood for humour, Superintendent."

"Then please begin with what happened in 1950."

Bo Qi shook his head. "No, I have little knowledge of what really happened back then. My story, the story of The Historians, the only story that matters to me, begins in 1979."

"The war?"

"Yes, Deng Xiaoping's bloody little campaign."

"Surely you are not going to lecture me about true comradeship, about loyalty, about the unbreakable bonds forged in the cauldron of battle – things you might consider so much more important than the Rule of Law?"

"Superintendent, your cynicism is understandable – but misplaced. You wanted to know the origin of things. If you let me, I will tell you. And, as for the Rule of Law, I do not know what that is. As far as I could tell – and this is the only time that will ever matter to me – there was no law at all on the battlefield. You see, to understand the events of the past few days, I must take you back to 1979, when I and my fellow junior officers were told by our seniors that a war was in the offing. I need to properly convey to you the shock we all felt then, how our world – our understanding of how things were, are, and should be – was suddenly turned upside down. For three decades we Chinese had been fully supportive of our socialist comrades in Vietnam, first against the cruel French colonialists and then against the trigger-happy American imperialists. We supplied the Vietnamese with weapons, with ammunition, and with advisors. These advisors fought shoulder-to-shoulder with our Vietnamese comrades, shedding blood with them in the mountains, the jungles, and the paddy fields. The PLA was never in Vietnam in the greatest of numbers, but we were always enough for Vietnam to be certain that China was their most determined ally. However, by 1975, when the war in Vietnam was in its final throes and the Americans had run from Saigon with their tails between their legs, the world about us was no longer as it once had been. China was no longer friends with the Soviet Union, Vietnam's other great ally. And in Cambodia, as an unfortunate and unlooked for consequence of the long Vietnamese struggle, the genocidal Khmer Rouge had come to power. They were determined to return that tragic country to the 'Year Zero', about to impose upon the unlucky Cambodian people the most extreme form of Maoist doctrine the world had ever seen."

"We called the Khmer Rouge our friends."

"That we did, Superintendent – to what should remain our ever-lasting shame. But, as a rule, we Chinese have never cared that much about the morality of other nations. As for the Khmer Rouge, they were as insolent as they were murderous, involving themselves in numerous clashes with the People's Army of Vietnam along the border with Vietnam – a situation that worsened with every passing year. Soon the Vietnamese had had enough. And, it had to be said, the Vietnamese had always wished to exert political control over Cambodia – not that a socialist nation could ever act as a colonial or imperialist power."

Bo Qi laughed then, contemptuous of his own words. He drained his glass and poured himself another measure, offering more to Philip Ye, who, happy to nurse what he had already got, politely declined.

"So, in 1979," continued Bo Qi, "Vietnam invaded Cambodia with the stated intention of ridding the world of a cabal of murderous madmen. In reality, Vietnam wanted to punish a troublesome neighbour, and to take control of Cambodia for itself."

"China could not stand by and do nothing," said Philip Ye.

"No, for after all the Khmer Rouge were our friends. But, more so, China was frightened. Vietnam had been falling deeper and deeper into the Soviet Union's pocket. It looked like we were being surrounded, indeed suffocated, by a cordon of Soviet influence. It should also be said, that unlike many in the higher echelons of the PLA, and even in the Politburo itself, our paramount leader then, Deng Xiaoping, had never ever formed a close friendship with any Vietnamese. He considered the Vietnamese people not only arrogant but also ungrateful for all the assistance China had given them through the years. Being the arch-pragmatist and political realist that he was, Deng Xiaoping was not going to let any shared history, any sentiment, creep into his thinking. It was announced to all us junior officers that the Vietnamese, our socialist brothers-in-arms of three decades, were now our mortal enemy.

"I do not exaggerate, Superintendent, when I tell you that it seemed to us young soldiers that the world had suddenly turned upside down. The shock was that profound. Even now, when I think back to those times, I shiver."

Bo Qi paused then in the narration of his recollections. Comfortable with the silence, in no particular hurry, and curious about just how Bo Qi was going to use his recollections to rationalise his part in the crimes of the weekend, Philip Ye sipped at his cognac and waited. Lightning could still be seen out of the window, flickering occasionally in the far distance, the rainstorm long past now. A peaceful night ahead was promised for Chengdu. Or so it was said on the radio in his car on the drive over.

"You have to realise," began Bo Qi again, "that we were in no way ready for war. The PLA was then nothing but a joke. It is true that we had millions of men at our disposal. But, during the 1960s, during the madness of the Cultural Revolution, we had been so heavily politicised that not only was there no longer a proper rank structure but we still clung to Mao Zedong's precepts about how to fight a war. Now do not mistake me, Superintendent. Mao Zedong was a genius in regard to the proper conduct of a guerrilla campaign. But he understood nothing at all about large-scale conflicts between nations, about the importance of logistics, about combined arms, about the proper use of land, sea, and air power."

"Spare me a lecture on the proper strategies and tactics of fighting a war," said Philip Ye.

Taking no offence, Bo Qi said, "Yes, the details of our little war with Vietnam are not necessary for you to know. There are history books aplenty – some of them even factual – if you wish to learn more. Suffice to say we were told we would be confronting poorly trained local militia and village defence forces, the majority of the People's Army of Vietnam away fighting in Cambodia. This proved to be a fatal assessment. Soon enough, I found myself fighting over the most inhospitable terrain, always short of ammunition, always thirsty, always hungry, and locked in combat with some of the most experienced, most battle-hardened, soldiers in the world."

"Were all of The Historians there?"

"Yes – in various capacities. We all saw combat, if that's what you mean. Each of us saw things that will stay with us until the end of our days. Initially, we all thought we would be heroes, my friend Fei Shi certainly, for he was the son of the PLA legend that was General Fei Song. Great deeds were expected of him. But we were all soon to learn hard lessons about ourselves. And some of us were soon to discover the terrible truth about General Fei Song. He had been placed in charge of the 14th Group Army for the duration of the expected short campaign. After I was lightly wounded at the outset of the campaign, I found myself posted to headquarters as an aide. I had the privilege for a while of watching General Fei Song in action. I saw him then for what he really was, not the stuff of legend at all, and certainly no Red Hero. He was a terrible leader, a man who was uncaring and wasteful of the lives of those men under his command, a man who had so little comprehension of the realities of the battle unfolding before his eyes it was almost comical, and whose real skills lay in the art of self-promotion. Thankfully, wiser heads than his took notice, secret communiqués flew back and forth between the frontline and Beijing, and he was quietly relieved of command none too soon. However, he was allowed to retire with his glorious reputation intact – as befitting a true legend of the PLA. The PLA needs its heroes, even if their heroics have never been quite as advertised. But one true hero did emerge from the carnage on the road to Lao Cai."

"Jin Huiliang?"

"Yes," said Bo Qi, with a smile. "We had always thought him the most unlikely of us to succeed. During training he had always been so quiet, so wrapped up in his books. We thought him no more than a soft intellectual. But under fire he surprised us all. In battle he became a lion, the sort of leader we all hoped to be but found we were not – a man soldiers would follow anywhere, even through the gates of hell itself."

"Did you know him well at that time?"

"No, not well enough to call him a true friend. And even after the war, after we had all met up again in Chengdu and formed our happy band of writers, I am not sure whether there was any real human warmth between us. He was someone to be listened to and respected, that was for sure. But, as far as I am aware, he never opened his heart to any. In hindsight, I suspect the war had affected him as much as it did all of us...and not for the better. I think he had discovered his fighting spirit during the war, and an unbending will. But I also think he had become prideful of his great accomplishments, too certain of his own opinions, and intolerant of the views of others."

"And yet it was this strength of mind that brought all of you to Chengdu, to accept his leadership again, his help in coping with the trauma of battle."

Bo Qi glanced down at his empty glass. "I do not deny that, Superintendent. But to rub along with others, to live in harmony with one's fellow man, it is necessary at times to exhibit tact, to compromise, to respect another's point of view."

"Or else one might be murdered?"

Bo Qi looked askance at Philip Ye, sighed, and poured himself another cognac. "I should now mention Fei Shi's wife, Fei Qin. She was born Li Qin. I forget where. Fei Shi had been badly wounded during the war – in body and mind. He had been sent to the PLA hospital in Kunming for treatment and convalescence. I went to visit him there and I found Li Qin already sitting by his side. I thought she was a nurse. It was a while before I learned she was an intelligence officer – an expert on the politics, military tactics, history, and language of the Soviet Union."

"You think theirs was no chance meeting?"

"My belief is she knew who his father was. Imagining that the son would be as the father – a Red Hero – she had somehow tracked him down and dug her claws into him. It did not take me long to realise she had accepted without question all of General Fei Song's myth-making and wanted nothing more than to be linked to that famous family. Needless to say – and at that time I had no great advice to give – Fei Shi thought himself fortunate to have captured the heart of such a talented woman and married her in haste. Unusually, she took her new family's name as women tend to do in the West, rather than keep her own. I have never heard her once mention the family of her birth. I don't think her satisfaction lasted long, though. It probably didn't take her too much time to realise that the son was nothing like as she had imagined the father to be. Fei Shi was actually rather a gentle soul. I think she was sickened by the nightmares that plagued him every night. There are rumours that she beat him and cursed him, lamenting day after day that she had married such a spineless coward. There are also rumours about the son."

"They have a child?"

Bo Qi nodded. "He's a captain now, in the PLA garrison in Hong Kong. I have never met him. I suspect his choice of unit had something to do with his troubled upbringing, and the rumours swirling about the family that he was actually the unnatural product of his mother and General Fei Song. I don't know the truth, Super-intendent. And I do not wish to know. The boy should be left alone. He was never a part of all that has happened this weekend."

"Fei Qin had other affairs, didn't she?"

"I believe so."

"Major-General Zi Hong, now head of the 14th Group Army?"

"You are most perceptive, Superintendent. I was a fool to throw you out of this house yesterday. I should have realised then the game was up. But I was in shock because of the death of Jin Huiliang. And when you appeared again in the Cry of the Crane Teahouse my heart sank. We saw Prosecutor Xu could be easily diverted from her task, quick-witted though she might be. But your presence proved to me that you are like a hunting dog, content to run all the hours of the day and night to chase down your prey. I tried to explain to the others, those who did not know who you are, that all was about to be uncovered. I hoped Fei Shi might speak to his wife, and she would find some way, through her friendship with Major-General Zi Hong, to get you off our scent."

"You wanted me killed?"

"I don't know what I wanted. It was not personal. I have no particular animus toward you, no matter what I said to you yesterday morning in respect of your family. It was just war. But Fei Shi did not bother to speak to his wife. He sent me a final message, a goodbye, so you don't need to tell me what he has done. I guess all he wanted to do was enter the afterlife as quickly as he could and apologise to the shade of Jin Huiliang for what was never meant to happen."

"Are you telling me that Jin Huiliang wasn't supposed to die?"

"No, Superintendent – not in our darkest dreams did we foresee what was going to come to pass. We had been such a happy company, all content – as much as we could ever be with damaged minds – with our writing projects. Our gatherings at the teahouse were, for all of us, simply the best of times."

"Until Primo Gong arrived on the scene."

"Yes, Superintendent, the loud-mouth American – a man who thought himself Chinese and yet who acted anything but, and who treated us, and the shared history of us old soldiers, with nothing but contempt. Jin Huiliang had been quite open with us. A few months ago, he told us that he was working on a little side-project for a businessman whose family roots lay in Chengdu. We thought nothing of it at the time. We assumed Jin Huiliang was doing a little bit of paid work to supplement his pension. I have told you about the shock we junior officers felt back in 1979 when told that Vietnam was now our mortal enemy rather than our bosom friend. So, when Jin Huiliang finally revealed to us what his researches on behalf of Primo Gong had uncovered, that he was going to assist Primo Gong with the publication of a book, and reveal to the world just what General

Fei Song had done to Primo Gong's grandfather back in 1950, it was like history was repeating itself. We were all stunned, Superintendent – shaken to the core. None of us could understand why Jin Huiliang would do this, why he would betray us this way, particularly why he would betray Fei Shi who had always worshipped Jin Huiling as the elder brother he had never had. We could not understand why Jin Huiliang would threaten all that we had just to bring an obscure and meaningless bit of history to light.

"But Jin Huiliang would not be reasoned with. He told us he had no choice but to betray our comradeship, our collective loyalty to the family Fei – to the myth the PLA had woven about General Fei Song. He told us a wrong had to be righted, an unquiet ghost put to rest. It was pure madness. There is no law in war, we told him. There are millions upon millions of unhappy, wandering ghosts in China, what good does it do to placate just one? But he would not listen. He could not see that the legend of General Fei Song, nonsense though it might be, served the greater purpose of inspiring all those already in the PLA, and those who wish to enrol, to defend our country to the last drop of blood. A country needs its legends, does it not, Superintendent?

"But, as I have said, I now believe the war had damaged Jin Huiliang more than any of us had ever suspected. I believe now that historical truth, and the revealing of such, had become the one stabilising factor in his mind. Historical truth had become like a religion to him, the bedrock of his existence. He would accept no argument, tolerate no compromise. Truth is truth, he told us. We pleaded with him, Fei Shi especially so, for it was he who had the most to lose with the tarnishing of his family name. But it did no good. Jin Huiliang would not be diverted. He was determined to help Primo Gong publish the facts about the death of a grandfather he had never known."

"His health was not so good these last few months."

"Who?"

"Jin Huiling."

"Ah, I did not know that."

"I believe he understood the enormity of what he was doing – and it was tearing him apart."

Bo Qi stood, took up the bottle of cognac and poured them each a new measure. "He was never meant to die."

"Primo Gong only?"

"He was so rude, so foolish, so taken up with his own concerns...so very American. Did you know he visited the Fei family home? He turned up one evening, banging on the door, wanting to be let in, demanding a personal apology from General Fei Song. Even when he saw for himself – and Fei Shi did indeed show him – the present state of General Fei Song, that the old man's memory is gone, his awareness of this world diminishing by the day, the American could find no compassion, no forgiveness, within himself. I don't regret his murder, Superintendent. He had it coming. He could not think beyond himself and his own petty concerns."

"Did he encounter Fei Qin?"

"Oh yes, and from that moment on the American's life was forfeit. She had never been one to accept any slur to the name of the family Fei."

"Are you telling me that neither you, Fei Shi, or any of the other Historians had any part in the planning of what was to come?"

"I am, Superintendent."

"But you were prepared to turn a blind eye?"

"In regard to Primo Gong – yes."

"And you did not know what Fei Qin had in mind for Jin Huiliang?"

"No – and if we had we would have stopped her. She kept her husband in the dark as well. When Fei Qin had returned late Friday night from committing murder, and had boasted of it, Fei Shi had phoned me in such despair that I thought he might take his own life there and then. I calmed him as well as I could. Then I drove to Jin Huiliang's apartment to see for myself whether what she had boasted of was true. It was the middle of the night and no one saw me, and I left no trace of my presence."

"Jin Huiliang's journal was missing."

"That was probably Fei Qin. I took nothing from his apartment. I merely stood for a few moments, hung my head, and said my farewells."

"The ice-axe?"

"I do not know. Maybe Fei Qin was trying to send us all a message, that she could reach out and touch any of us no matter where we were, as Stalin had once reached out and touched Trotsky in Mexico City."

"To keep you all in line...to make sure none of you would ever betray the Fei family name?"

"It's possible – but it is also just as likely that she came across the ice-axe somewhere and decided, cold-blooded creature that she is, that it would make the perfect weapon, having no thoughts about Trotsky at all. Has she been captured alive?"

"She has."

"And is she talking, Superintendent?"

"Incoherently, when I last saw her, though I expect that will change. She seemed proud of what she had done. I believe she will take responsibility for it all."

"She has made no mention of me, the other Historians?"

"Not that I am aware of."

"I am astonished."

"Procurator Xu is on the trail of Major-General Zi Hong. He had dispatched a special operations team from Kunming at Fei Qin's urging, I suspect."

"I care not to hear the details, Superintendent."

"A sniper's bullet did for Primo Gong. His woman, Du Luli, was picked up on the street as she ran for her life, her body dumped in a remote abandoned temple. And Jin Huiliang's typist, Ms. Lu, was, I believe, tortured by having her beloved cats drowned in front of her for any knowledge she might have of Jin Huiliang's writings, and then strung up as an apparent suicide. I have rarely seen anything so cruel."

Bo Qi covered his eyes with his free hand. "Enough, Superintendent, I am tired of so much death."

"I suspect there are other bodies to be found too, those researchers Jin Huiliang paid to examine the military archives for him, both in Chengdu and in Kunming, all made to look like unfortunate accidents. Maybe these people are known to you, maybe they have done research work for you too."

Bo Qi said nothing. He reached for the bottle of cognac yet again. He offered it up but Philip Ye refused, having had quite enough, fearing that if he imbibed any more he would lose all his inhibitions and shoot Bo Qi on the spot.

"The special operations team, those operating in and about Chengdu, are now dead," said Philip Ye. "I expect Major-General Zi Hong soon to be taken into custody."

"And what about me?"

Philip Ye stood and placed his empty glass on the small table. "What about you?"

"Are you not going to take me in?"

"No."

"But I could have prevented all this."

"I do not doubt that. But it is not my decision to make. As I have already told you, this has never really been my investigation. As for the Procuratorate, I doubt if Prosecutor Xu will come calling. With Fei Shi dead and Fei Qin in custody, she will not trouble herself unduly with any possible loose ends. That being said, I do not envy you. You already carry the burden of one war; that of another – a war that could and should have been prevented – might prove the straw that breaks the camel's back."

"But you do understand, don't you?"

"Understand what?"

"All that I have been trying to tell you, about the shock we all felt when Jin Huiliang chose to help Primo Gong ruin the good name of the family Fei, the same shock we all felt when Deng Xiaoping said that Vietnam was no longer our friend. The world turned upside down for us. None of us could think straight."

"I have heard better excuses from children for their misde-meanours. Fei Shi had the right idea. No one might be coming for you, Mister Bo, but in your place I would do as he did and find myself the nearest apple tree."

Philip Ye left the house then, got into his car, and, without looking back, drove off, promising himself never to return. He had had his fill of The Historians, of their wars, of those who simply refused to do the right thing.

SEVENTY-TWO

—·—

Xu Ya was furious with Investigator Deng. She had assumed, after her last phone call with him, after he had detained Commissioner Yang Da and uncovered the old paper file that had finally made sense of the conspiracy they had been investigating, that he would have made his way to the Procuratorate to await her arrival. But he was nowhere to be seen. He was also not answering his phone. None of the skeleton staff on duty at the Procuratorate this Sunday evening claimed to have heard from him. After all that had happened during the weekend, she could not help but be worried sick. The last time she had seen him, back at the Ye family mansion earlier that morning, he had not looked well at all. She hoped nothing untoward had happened, that Commissioner Yang Da had not overpowered him before making an escape, or that yet another, hitherto unknown, member of the special operations kill team sent to Chengdu by Major-General Zi Hong had surfaced to do further harm. Not wanting to face the embarrassment of alerting the PSB that her investigator had gone missing, she told herself not to worry; Investigator Deng was a tough man, a born survivor, who would turn up soon enough.

So, determined not to waste any time, she began the interrogation of Fei Qin, dragging in some witless duty prosecutor from the Economic Crime Section to sit in so that all the usual protocols were observed. Fei Qin needed no prompting to make a full confession, not only boasting that she had been the one to plunge the ice-axe into the back of Jin Huiliang's skull – so engrossed in his writing that it had been easy for her to creep up on him – she also claimed that it had been she who had persuaded her close friend, Major-General Zi Hong of the 14th Group Army – her 'docile, little puppy' – to take care of everyone else who threatened to slander the good name of the family Fei.

Not knowing quite what to make of Fei Qin – to Xu Ya she did not seem to meet the standard of what it took to be declared criminally insane – Xu Ya asked question after question, trying to get to the bottom of how complicit, if at all, The Historians had been in the conspiracy. She got no straight answer. Fei Qin had no time for The Historians. She called them all spineless fools – her late husband especially – none of them fit to clean her father-in-law's boots. But she saved the majority of her vitriol for Jin Huiliang, whom she described as nothing less than a traitor. Xu Ya found Fei Qin's anger, her vehemence, difficult to stomach. Nevertheless, she was relieved that Fei Qin never once implicated The Historians. And, with no evidence to the contrary, she felt she could safely strike them from the investigation. She had liked them all immensely, and had never enjoyed the thought of perhaps having to order their arrest – especially after all they had endured during wartime.

Xu Ya then separately interviewed Mister Li and his wife, the proprietors of the Laughing Panda Hotel. The wife proved to be incoherent, unable to stop herself crying. Mister Li was slightly more helpful, able to detail the date and time he had received a phone call from Major-General Zi Hong, and that he believed himself to be more of a stupid man than a criminal, a man who had foolishly put past loyalties – to the PLA – above his duty to be a good citizen. He apologised to her, to the Procuratorate, and to the people of Chengdu. He then threw herself on her mercy.

Xu Ya had some sympathy for him. There were many in Chengdu, put in exactly the same position, who would have acted as Mister Li had. And yet the question remained: if Major-General Zi Hong had asked Mister Li to do more, to actively assist in committing murder, would he have done so?

She put the question to him.

Mister Li had blanched, stuttered, and explained that since leaving the PLA he had taken up the study of Buddhism. He now thought himself incapable of committing murder – in fact he tried never to kill any living thing – and just wanted a simple and profitable life as a hotel owner.

It had not been quite the straight answer she had been looking for. However, by then, she had become bored with Mister Li. What she was going to do with him, his wailing wife also, would have to await further consideration. They seemed more useful as witnesses than defendants. Though she did not rule out recommending to the court some form of punishment.

As she was wrapping up the interview with Mister Li, there was a knock on the door of the interrogation room. A flustered officer from the custody suite had come to find her as a matter of urgency.

"What is it?" she asked, standing in the corridor, after closing the door on Mister Li.

"Ah, Prosecutor, Superintendent Ye of the PSB has dropped off Superintendent Si Ying."

"Oh, good, I wish to speak to—"

"I am afraid Superintendent Ye did not linger."

"Did he—?"

"Yes, Prosecutor, he left a message. He said that the body of Du Luli is most likely found and will be recovered this evening by Doctor Kong for autopsy."

"That was all he said?"

"Yes, Prosecutor, but that is not why I have come to find you."

"It is not?"

"We have a problem in the custody suite. There is nothing in the regulations that instructs us on what we must do."

The custody officer seemed too frightened to offer up any further explanation. She followed him down the stairs, and there, at the front desk, where the criminals were booked in, she saw a sight that defied all rational explanation: Investigator Deng and Commissioner Yang Da, arm-in-arm, swaying from side to side, giggling like demented schoolboys, pleading to be put in the same cell together. They were such good friends, you see.

Xu Ya was lost for words. Braving the stench of alcohol that surrounded them, she quickly liberated the service pistol from Investigator Deng's holster, passed it to one of the custody officers for safe-keeping, and took for herself the priceless file from the Black House that Investigator Deng was somehow still carrying under his arm. Then, with a lot of shouting on her behalf, and with the help of four of the burliest of the custody officers, she managed to separate the inebriated pair and get Commissioner Yang Da into a cell on his own.

With Investigator Deng now draped all over her, she told the custody officers, "There will be no record of this incident. As you can see, Investigator Deng suffered a severe concussion from the beating he received this morning. He has also been having unfortunate reactions to the medication he has been taking as part of his convalescence."

The custody officers nodded and muttered that concussion was no joke and that medicines in China were hardly ever to be trusted. One of them kindly phoned for a taxi, while the others helped her walk Investigator Deng out of the Procuratorate using a rarely used exit so no one else would see anything untoward. She waited for the taxi with Investigator Deng after thanking the custody officers for their good sense and compassion and dismissing them.

The two of them stood quietly on the street for a while, her slight figure next to his much more substantial figure, arm in arm, as he had been with Commissioner Yang Da but Investigator Deng more thoughtful, more introspective now. She could not look at him. She was so mad at him. But she could not hate him for the embarrassment he had caused her. He had been through such a lot this weekend; indeed, he had been through such a lot these last few months. And, without him, she knew her investigation into the murder of Primo Gong would have been stillborn.

"Prosecutor, you have hurt your head," he said to her.

"I know," she said, pushing his hand away from the cut on her forehead.

"How?"

"It is not important," she replied, not wanting to speak about what had happened in the garden of the Fei family house.

"You are still beautiful."

"Thank you."

"What will happen to me?" he asked.

"For being drunk on duty?"

"No, when you leave to go abroad?"

The arrival of the taxi saved her from having to think up an answer. She had made no friends within the Procuratorate. The knives would be out for Investigator Deng as soon as she stepped on that flight for London. Telling herself he would survive, that she would do her utmost to extract a promise from Secretary Wu that he would be looked after, she pushed Investigator Deng into the taxi and then some cash into the taxi driver's hands telling him, in no uncertain terms, that if Investigator Deng did not arrive home safely, she would not only have his operating licence she would also shut down the entire taxi firm.

As the taxi drove away, Investigator Deng waved her goodbye, pushing his bruised and swollen face up against the window like a child forcibly separated from his parents. It was heart-wrenching. But what choice did she have other than to leave Chengdu? Sarangerel was breathing down her neck and Ye Zihao had offered her a job of a lifetime.

She took herself up to her office on the fourth floor, locked the door and cried for a short time. Then her phone rang. She blew her nose, dried her eyes and picked up the phone.

"Ms. Xu, how are you holding up?" asked Secretary Wu.

"Very well, sir."

"You are required to brief a full session of the Political and Legal Committee within the hour. Will you be ready?"

"Within the hour?"

"That is what I said. For your convenience, we will gather in the main conference room at the Procuratorate. Party Chief Li will be in attendance. There will be other interested parties there also: investigators from the PLA as well as from the Central Commission for Discipline Inspection. It is most important that you put on a good show, Ms. Xu."

"I will be ready, sir," she replied, her stomach churning.

"I expected nothing less."

Xu Ya touched up her make-up using a mirror from her handbag, glad that she had changed earlier, having had the good sense to always keep a spare trouser suit and pair of shoes in the office. The cut on her forehead looked as angry as it was sore, but at least it would show the Political and Legal Committee that this weekend had been more than just a figurative battle to get at the truth. She had also ruined a perfectly good summer dress as well as discovered that a significant part of her was far from sane. On glancing out of the bedroom window of the Fei family home, and seeing Fei Qin stalking an unaware Philip Ye with a shotgun, she had, without a rational thought in her head, flown down the stairs and out of the house, raced across the sodden garden and thrown herself bodily on top of Fei Qin.

Had it been worth it?

All Philip Ye had done afterward was stare at her as if she were some kind of alien. It had been too much for him to even offer her a simple thank you.

The brothers Na had put it best, saying, "Don't take it personally, Prosecutor; the family Ye are a miserable and ungrateful bunch."

Which begged the question as to why the brothers Na had given their lives over in service to the family Ye.

Getting herself together, putting all thoughts of Philip Ye aside and how she might have been killed wrestling with Fei Qin, Xu Ya got to the conference room early and arranged a marker board and a set of pens for her use during the meeting. Then she personally greeted each and every one of the Committee members and the others too, even the military investigators decked out in their dress uniforms, as well as, quite unexpectedly, Chief of Police Di and his cool and very aloof personal assistant, Ms. Miao. Once Party Chief Li and Secretary Wu had arrived, and Secretary Wu had whispered to her the rules of the game – there was to be no mention of Lucy Fu, Du Luli's professional relationship to the family Fu, the help afforded her by Philip Ye and Constable Ma, or Party Chief Li's earlier fiery and emotional conviction that Ye Zihao was behind the murder of Primo Gong, but she could, and should, be quite liberal with her criticism of the PSB – she was free to begin.

The lights were dimmed and, in the spotlight that remained only on her, she held up the ancient file that had been obtained from the Black House.

"The roots of this weekend's litany of criminality lie in the distant past," she announced, "in 1950 to be exact, when this file was created, within which is to be found a highly flawed response to a terrible injustice. A celebrated PLA officer was allowed to get away with the brutal murder of an innocent man, a Professor Gong Dawei, both a scientist and a patriot, and, almost certainly, a long-time agent of the Party."

As Xu Ya continued to speak, she used different coloured pens on the marker board to lay out who was who, who was related to whom, and where their loyalties lay. And she did not mince her words, understanding that she had been given particular licence this evening in regard to the PSB, when it came to pointing out that the shot that had killed Primo Gong had been fired from the Black House on Liberation Street, that serving members of the PSB had formed part of the murderous conspiracy, and that these police officers from the Building Security Section had been content to take their orders from a serving PLA general rather than honour their own chain of command, or indeed the oath of service they had made to the Constitution of the People's Republic of China and the people.

"An utter disgrace!" Xu Ya exclaimed, pointing at Chief of Police Di, the adrenalin of the moment getting the better of her.

Chief of Police Di sat still, like a statue. But, in the silence that followed her outburst, all eyes turned toward him and Xu Ya felt the mood of the room darken. Only Ms. Miao, sitting next to him, resolutely kept her eyes on the marker board.

Xu Ya then continued, explaining in detail how the conspiracy had been conceived to preserve history – or a version of such – and to protect the *undeserved* good name of a PLA legend: General Fei Song. She explained about the battle of the books, about how the famous businessman and personal friend of Party Chief Li, Primo Gong, had been researching his family history with the intention of including this research as an introduction to a proposed business motivational book, and how this book would, in these enthusiastically commercial times, surely sell in far greater numbers than the military biography planned by the son of General Fei Song – as well as being much more credible.

"The family Fei saw themselves backed into a corner," said Xu Ya. "Rather than allow true history to be revealed and the Fei family name to be blackened, they saw fit to act contrary to the Constitution, the Criminal Law, and the good of the people. That they sought help in their criminal endeavours and received it, not only from the serving officers of the PLA but also from elements of Chengdu PSB, almost beggars belief."

Xu Ya then pointed a finger at the uniformed military investigators. "Is Major-General Zi Hong in custody yet?"

Put on the spot, one of the investigators – a senior colonel – stood, bowed to everyone around the conference table, and said, "I am sorry to inform this Committee that Major-General Zi Hong has not yet been located."

"What an utter disgrace!" Xu Ya found herself exclaiming again, the senior colonel retaking his seat and hanging his head in shame.

When Xu Ya was done, when she had detailed on the marker board the names of the dead and those who were now in custody awaiting formal charges, a hand was raised by a member of the Political and Legal Committee – a man about whom Xu Ya knew nothing except that his name was Zhou.

"Prosecutor Xu, is there no truth then to the rumour that former mayor Ye Zihao is involved in this conspiracy?" asked Mister Zhou.

Xu Ya had to wonder whether this question was a plant, some kind of test for her – or perhaps a rare show of individuality on behalf of a Committee member. She had been fully prepared for difficult questions, however, including this one, and replied, "It is my con-sidered belief that Ye Zihao, though he remains under house-arrest, is quite capable of making mischief in Chengdu. But, in regards to this conspiracy, I have confronted him, questioned him, and found him to have played no part in it. I should make it clear – and forgive me for being so outspoken – that trouble-maker though Ye Zihao definitely is, I consider him a man of yesterday, a man of the past. I suggest you dismiss all consideration of him from your minds. He is not the future of Chengdu – we are! And we will stop at nothing to create a prosperous future for Chengdu – a future underpinned by the Rule of Law."

Party Chief Li so enjoyed this little speech that he jumped out of his seat, stood next to Xu Ya in the spotlight, and shouted out, "Ye Zihao *is* a man of the past! Never forget that!"

Then he pointed at Chief of Police Di and said, "You and I will have a lot to discuss first thing in the morning." Then he pointed at the military investigators, and those from the Central Commission for Discipline Inspection, and said, "Go find this evil Major-General Zi Hong. It took our Prosecutor Xu just two days, without any help from anyone, to sort this mess out in Chengdu. And yet, as far as I can see, you and your teams of investigators have yet to get off your lazy backsides and do anything useful."

As if on cue, the whole of the Political and Legal Committee rose as one in applause. They then got into line to shake Xu Ya's hand

and offer her their personal congratulations. Xu Ya basked in the adulation. She only wished Investigator Deng was there – sober or not – to see for himself the good they had done.

"Well done," said Chief of Police Di, when he reached her in the line, looking deathly pale, as if he had just died a thousand deaths.

"Congratulations," said his personal assistant Ms. Miao, both her hand and eyes like ice.

With the room emptied, and the doors secured, Party Chief Li shook Secretary Wu's hand, the happiest Xu Ya had ever seen him. "Did you see Chief Di squirm?" said Party Chief Li. "Did you see it?"

"I did, sir – I did," replied Secretary Wu.

"That tricky bastard will have to make concessions now."

"He will, sir – he will."

Party Chief Li then spoke to Xu Ya. "You must dine with me this evening, Ms. Xu. You must tell me all about your encounter with that degenerate Ye Zihao."

"Of course, sir – I will be honoured," replied Xu Ya, dreading the thought and, now that the adrenalin in her bloodstream had dispersed, wanting nothing more than to crawl into her bed.

"It is a pity Chief Prosecutor Gong is not here to witness this great victory for the Procuratorate," said Secretary Wu.

"More fool him," replied Party Chief Li, "for going on a holiday to Africa to shoot stupid animals. I don't know why we keep him in post."

"He has his uses," said Secretary Wu.

"Does he? I forget," said Party Chief Li.

SEVENTY-THREE

T he evening was getting late by the time Philip Ye arrived at the Sichuan Cancer Hospital. Commissioner Wei was fast asleep, the only sign he lived the shallow rise and fall of his emaciated chest and the flicker of his eyelids as he dreamed. Philip Ye shed his raincoat and took a seat at the end of the bed. There were only a few nurses walking the corridor outside, the lights now dimmed, the hospital – or at least this part of it – settling down for the night. Philip Ye closed his eyes, glad of the peace, and glad the long day had almost come to an end. He found himself almost instantly dragged into a vivid dream: he was arguing with his mother again, she trying to convince him it was time to marry, him shouting back at her, telling her that the life of a policeman, the things he had to see, the things he had to do, the secrets he had to keep, made him particularly unsuited to the institution of marriage. All the while the argument raged, the beloved shikra from his childhood – the bird he had lost almost as soon as it had entered into his life – circled above them. Then a familiar perfume touched his nostrils and the dream faded from view. He opened his eyes. Sarangerel had taken the other seat in the room.

"I have been watching you," she said.

"How long?"

"Five minutes, no more."

"Did I talk in my sleep?"

"A little, but in English – or at least I think so."

"I am surprised you never learned."

"I have been busy doing other things," she said, her smile teasing, provocative. She was dressed as she had been the evening before, in a raincoat belted at the waist, with presumably nothing underneath, so much copper-hued skin on show that little was left to the imagination. Philip Ye wondered why she had bothered. The joke had been unfunny yesterday; it was just as unfunny today.

He nodded toward the sleeping Commissioner Wei. "How long?"

"Can you not see, Philip?" she replied. "He does not dream as you and I dream. He already walks the afterlife. Soon he will choose not to return – two days, maybe three, no more than that."

If there was one thing Sarangerel was guaranteed *not* to lie about it was death. Philip Ye felt incredibly sad. He had expected this time to come but not so soon. He was going to miss Commissioner Wei's company, not to mention his guidance, his moral strength. Much as he liked Maggie Loh, if she got her way, if she managed to combine Robbery and Homicide under her sole command, he was not sure how happy he would be. Maggie Loh's management style was a bit too distrusting for his liking. She liked to look over the shoulders of all who worked for her. Commissioner Wei, on the other hand, had always expected results, but how you got them – provided no law was broken, or at least stretched too far – was left up to you.

"Where is the girl?" asked Sarangerel.

Philip Ye returned his gaze to the tall, Mongolian beauty. "You failed to tell me that you had attended a certain banquet at the Chengdu Cymbidium Bank on Friday evening."

"I attend banquets all the time," said Sarangerel, a chill brusqueness creeping into her voice.

"Not like this banquet."

"Chief Di has ordered you to give up the girl!" said Sarangerel angrily, struggling to keep her voice down so as not to bring any of the nurses running.

"I have been busy doing other things...like discovering that you lied to me. You told me you dreamed of Du Yue's mother, that you saw her as a corpse in some water-logged field."

"I did dream it."

"Why tell me about this supposed dream and forget to tell me that you had sat down at a table with Du Luli on Friday evening?"

"I am no murderess."

"Are you not?"

"Philip, just give me the girl. You know she is meant for me. The spirits all agree. Just one look at her face and you will see that we could be mother and daughter, or even sisters."

"Tell me about the banquet."

"Why?"

"Because I want to know."

Sarangerel shook her long mane of black hair in exasperation. "Very well, but nothing I say will profit you any. Mayor Cang received the invitation almost a week ago. We were due to be elsewhere but that snake Min Feng phoned and pleaded with him. Min Feng said that the loud-mouthed American was going to be there."

"Primo Gong?"

"Yes – for some reason Mayor Cang had taken a real liking to him. I do not know why. I had always found him dull and boorish, as only Americans can be. I was going to stay behind, feign illness, but then—"

"A communication from the spirit-world?"

"Don't mock me, Philip – they talk to you as much as they talk to me. However, this time there was no voice, no whisper in my ear, just an inner urge that I should attend. It was fate, you see. It had been arranged perhaps since the beginning of time that I should sit down and speak with Du Luli before she met her end."

"Who else was there?"

"Min Feng's awful wife, a couple of nobodies from the financial world – I paid them no attention at all."

"Lucy Fu?"

"No, your old girlfriend was at a special reception in Chongqing. FUBI International has just won an important construction contract awarded by the 14th Group Army, or so I am told – and against stiff competition. I wonder what Lucy Fu had to promise to win." Sarangeral smiled, looking for some reaction, but sighed when she found none and continued, "What is important is that I was seated next to Du Luli. I saw the mark of death upon her. I knew immediately her ending was no more than a few hours away."

"Had you met her before?"

"I had seen her around, accompanying other men, in years gone by. I had never had occasion to speak to her, but I could tell she was a fine actress, as well as being clever, discreet, and very, very careful. And

then, for some reason, she chose to fall in love with Primo Gong –
her one and only mistake. But maybe that was to be her fate all along.
For when she showed me the photograph of her daughter during the
banquet, I saw myself staring back at me. I was in shock. Never have
I experienced such a feeling before. Never has life so surprised me. I
understood then why I had felt the inner urge to attend the banquet.
I was to take the girl Du Yue as my own daughter, hone her talents –
make her greater than either of us. But soon I had tired of conversing
with a woman who was not long for this world. Mayor Cang took me
home. I went to my bed then and I did dream. I observed the passing
of Du Luli into the afterlife. I saw the girl, flying toward me aboard
an aircraft, soon to be mine. But then I made a mistake. I took my
time in tracking her down. By the time I had reached her apartment
you had already whisked her into the Ye family mansion. I cried bitter
tears, Philip. I knew you would use Du Yue to taunt me, torment me
– to punish me all over again for the hold I once had over your father.
So I have waited, and I have suffered, for a night and a day, and now
it is time to hand her over to me. You have been ordered to do it.
Mayor Cang has ordered Chief of Police Di who has ordered you, so
you must comply."

"I offer you a trade."

"No, Philip – she is meant for me!" hissed Sarangerel, fearful now,
jumping up from her chair, still trying to keep her voice down.

"A trade," Philip Ye insisted, also rising to his feet.

"You have nothing that I need," she said, moving closer to him, her
hand reaching out to touch his.

He avoided her touch as one would avoid the kiss of a serpent,
pulled a slim, white envelope from his suit pocket and placed the
envelope in her hand instead.

"What is this?" she asked.

"Freedom."

"I do not need freedom."

"I think you do. The future is an uncertain place – even for the
Witch-Queen of Chengdu. A queen only occupies the throne for a
limited time. Another will soon arise to challenge you, perhaps with
even less of a conscience than you. And when that time comes – as
surely it will – you will need a means of escape. In that envelope are
two slips of paper. On one slip is written the name of a fascinating

man who lives in the Tibetan Quarter. He has the skill to fabricate any document you might wish: passport, visa, whatever your heart's desire. On the other slip is written a number of a special account held with the Royal Bank of Canada, together with the security codes to grant you access to ten million dollars Canadian – enough for you to start a new life anywhere in the world. I am offering you freedom, Sarangerel – a freedom no other man would offer you."

"No, Philip!"

"Take the trade, Sarangerel."

"No, this is not fair—"

"I am offering you freedom in exchange for the girl...for who knows what tomorrow might bring. All of us need at least one escape route out of Chengdu."

Tears sprang from Sarangerel's eyes. "But, Philip—"

"When Du Yue is eighteen, if she wishes it, and if you still wish it, then I will allow you to meet with her. But until then you will not go near her. She is under my protection."

"Have you no heart?"

"I will not have you make her over in your image."

"Do you think me so bad?"

"Take the trade, Sarangerel."

Her tears dried as if on cue, and she stuffed the envelope in the pocket of her raincoat. Her face grew hard, her eyes harder still. "Your little hawk made a good speech at the Procuratorate an hour or so ago. She took all the credit for her success. She made no mention of you."

"Is that supposed to wound me?"

"We are to have dinner together tomorrow evening."

"Touch one hair of her head and—"

"She will be your downfall, Philip."

"Is that so?"

"She will learn what sort of man you are, how you aspire to be the perfect son, determined to protect his father no matter what he has done – even if it means obstructing or diverting an investigation, if it means breaking the law. I hear whispers, Philip – so many whispers. A certain holding company based out of Qingdao has spent the last two weeks slowly and quietly disposing of its shares in Ambrogetti Global Software. Curious, you might think, especially as the holding company is said – by those who know about such things – to have links to the bewildering and ever-shifting business empire of the family Ye. I have also heard that there is an unusual connection between your father and a retired PLA officer by the name of General Fei Song. Years ago, when your father was still mayor, he held a special little reception at the Ye family mansion for the family Fei and their close friends, to honour the taking up of residence in Chengdu of the legendary General Fei Song. Not that many would recall this little reception now or, if they did, think it important. I have also heard that maybe, just maybe, some weeks ago, a phone call was placed by the family Fei to the Ye family mansion. I do not know for certain what was discussed during that phone call. It could have just been a conversation between friends. Or perhaps advice was being sought, or perhaps permission, or perhaps just a promise not to intervene. Philip, I am telling you nothing that you do not already know, do not already suspect. But if a little shikra should hear of these things I wonder what she might then think, and whether, in the future, she would be so keen again to fly to your rescue."

"You do not frighten me, Sarangerel."

"You have stolen Du Yue from me, Philip. You have hurt me...cut me to the quick."

Were there real tears again in Sarangerel's eyes as she turned away from him and ran from the room? Philip Ye did not know. But he was glad of her leaving, even if he felt some sympathy for her despite the many wrongs she had done in her life – and the many wrongs she was sure to do in the future.

"Has the witch gone?" asked Commissioner Wei, his voice a barely audible croak.

"She has," replied Philip Ye, as he bent down to help Commissioner Wei rise up onto his pillows, and to take a sip of water. There would be no beer and cigarettes this evening.

"Pay her no heed, Philip."

"I won't."

"I have been dreaming."

"Is that so?"

"I was speaking to a man, a detective I knew back in the old days, back in Shanghai – long dead now. He was telling me that my new office is ready, that there is a stack of paperwork awaiting my attention and a couple of curious cases that require my expertise."

"I am glad, sir – very glad."

"The dream felt so real, Philip."

"I am sure."

Philip Ye watched as Commissioner Wei's eyes slowly closed again, his breathing became more rhythmic, and a faint smile played across his pale, thin lips. Philip Ye waited a few moments to make sure his dying friend remained comfortable. He then threw on his raincoat, bent down, and laid a slight kiss on Commissioner Wei's forehead, bade him a silent goodbye and walked down the deserted hospital corridor, following in Sarangerel's footsteps, the scent of her lingering perfume catching in his throat, making him cough.

SEVENTY-FOUR

— • —

I t was a little after three in the morning when she was woken by the murmuring of countless restless ghosts. She sat up in bed, wondering how anyone could get a good night's sleep in the Ye family mansion. Admittedly, she had not yet adjusted to the Chengdu time zone, but it seemed to her that she would never feel properly at peace here. She clambered out of bed, pulled on the white towelling dressing-gown she had been given, and stood at the window looking out over the extensive gardens. The sky had cleared. A brilliant full moon cast a ghostly silvery radiance over the trees and the lake and the freshly-cut lawns. It seemed to her that she had landed upon some alien world, never to return from whence she had come. The past had gone. She knew that. Her mother was now far away. And though this alien world was full of exciting possibilities – money would never now be a problem – she could not help but feel that she had crossed some fateful line, some invisible threshold, that her future life was to be anything but normal – no longer that of a simple academic struggling to extend the frontiers of mathematical knowledge.

She had already made one important discovery about the house which she was now required to call home. Only a very few of the restless ghosts actually walked the house and the grounds. In the main, the constant murmuring came from the city that surrounded the Ye family estate on all sides. Some of these ghosts had passed over to the afterlife quite recently, others centuries long past. But common to them all was the sad fact that they could not quite let the world of the living go, either bearing grudges toward the living, or still desperately seeking remedies for whatever injustices they believed themselves to have suffered while alive.

It troubled her that she had not heard this murmuring before, whenever she had stayed at her mother's apartment during the school holidays. The only conclusion she could reach was that there was something special about the Ye family mansion and grounds. Perhaps the fabric that separated the world of the living from the lands of the dead was somehow thinner or even non-existent here. It was as if the Ye family mansion stood atop some kind of portal, or that someone had worked long and hard performing the appropriate sacrifices, recited rambling screeds of incantations from ancient and prohibited books, had drawn complex ritualistic diagrams using the blood of chickens or worse on the ceilings, walls, and floors, and all just to reach through the veil to the lands of the dead.

Her vivid imagination amused her. She really did not know much about such practices. All she had ever learned of the occult had been from the most lurid horror films – not exactly reputable sources of historical truth. She wished to hear the views of her good friend Uncle Qin on the matter. But he was still not talking to her. She had a feeling he was sulking somewhere, but about what she did not know. He could not be critical of the choice she had made. He had made an unholy mess of his life. She refused to do the same. The past was past. Her mother was gone. What else was there to say?

Regardless, she picked up the book of Qin Jiushao's life, still finding comfort in its presence, and stepped in her bare feet out into the dimly lit landing outside. She was done grieving. She was done hiding away. It was time to explore. There was a powerful aroma of sweet tobacco smoke in the air. She was not the only person awake and walking about the great house. But, before going in search of *him*, she headed first for Philip Ye's private rooms, just a little way along the landing. It was not exactly spying, she told herself. She was merely exercising a young person's natural curiosity.

She gently pushed open the door that led to his private suite, looking in on a small sitting-room that was lit by a lamp left burning on a desk in a corner, seeing a couple of empty leather armchairs, a TV affixed to a wall, a large photograph of a young woman on the wall opposite – Isobel? – and a darkened doorway leading into what she had to assume was his bedroom. She listened and heard only the rhythmic breathing of a man sound asleep. The last time she had seen

Philip Ye, just before midnight, he had looked dead on his feet. He would not be waking again anytime soon.

She crept inside, glad of the soft pile carpet, and made her way over to the desk. She wanted to see what he had been working on, whether any of the papers he had left out had anything to do with the disappearance of her mother. On the left side of the desk lay a thick sheaf of papers that looked like a lengthy type-written police report. She picked up the report so she could more easily read the title.

AS EASY AS BREAKING BAMBOO!

She smiled to herself. It was not a police report at all. She wondered if Philip Ye, in his spare time, had been writing some kind of novel. However, as she flicked through the pages, she saw the written voice was not that of Philip Ye's, and that the subject was that of a military campaign that had taken place toward the end of the 11th Century. Quickly bored – ancient battles held no interest for her – she placed the manuscript back down on the desk and picked up a sole piece of paper that had been lying next to it, some handwritten notes upon it, made by a fountain pen, and in Philip Ye's hand. She would recognise his handwriting anywhere. When he had spoken to her just before midnight to reassure her that the investigation was done, that those responsible for her mother's disappearance and death were themselves either dead or locked up within the Procuratorate and under the care of Prosecutor Xu, he had referred at length to his police notebook. At the time she had seen it to be a diversionary tactic, him not wanting her to see directly into his eyes, she deciding that he had chosen to protect her by keeping some of the awful truth of her mother's passing a secret. Strangely, it had not been the heavily edited version of her mother's murder that had interested her, but Philip Ye's handwriting. It was not as neat as she would have expected, considering the fastidiousness of his dress; the inner demons that plagued him, she supposed, surfacing in the movements of the hand. She ran her eyes down this new page of notes of his desk, certain that Philip Ye had definitely been the author.

The Banquet – carefully choreographed to control his movements that evening – to give the shooters advance notice of his return to Plum Tree Pagodas?

Min Feng – complicit?

And what about Plum Tree Pagodas? Had he purposely been persuaded to accept an apartment so that his window directly faced the Black House? Was the following destruction of his phone, his laptop, and his tablet all part of the original plan? And, most callously, was a phone call made to Superintendent Si Ying or her cousin to advise them that there was a witness, a runner from the apartment, soon to appear out on the street?

And what about the contract awarded to FUBI International by the 14th Group Army?

Lucy Fu – complicit?

Is anything ever to be trusted that comes out of Sarangerel's mouth?

She read through the notes again and again but they meant nothing to her. She was forced to conclude that the notes pertained to a different case he was working on. Which was a great pity as she would have liked to have known more of her mother's passing, much more than Philip Ye had told her, much more than a simple description of where her body had been found – supposedly a peaceful old temple in the countryside – and how she had come to be there, having had the most unfortunate bad luck as to having got caught up in some kind of gang warfare that had nothing whatsoever to do with her.

Sad that she had learned nothing more, she let the paper fall back down on the desk. Then inspiration struck. She carefully pulled open a desk drawer and found Philip Ye's store of blank paper. She took out two pieces of paper, gently slid the drawer back into place so Philip Ye would not notice anything untoward, picked up his fountain pen, and drew on each paper a circle, within which she wrote all manner of meaningless mathematical notations. Replacing the fountain pen on the desk where she had found it, she walked out of the sitting-room and back onto the landing, quietly pulling the door to behind her. She made her way past the room that had been allocated to her, and on to part of the upper house she had not yet explored. But she knew where she was heading. The brothers Na were not the quietest about the great house.

The door to their private room she also found conveniently ajar. She peered inside. Again, she heard nothing but the sounds of men fast asleep. Usually, so she understood it, one of the brothers slept during the day, the other during the night, so at least one of them was at the beck and call of Mayor Ye at all times. But this last weekend they had hardly rested. So now both of them slept, on separate beds, quite exhausted from whatever it was they had been up to. Careful so as not to disturb them, she crept across the large bedroom, and laid a paper each at the foot of their beds, her drawings sure to be taken by the brothers as some kind of terrible charms, the very worst black sorcery – surely the work of a witch to be feared.

That would give them something to worry about, she thought, trying not to laugh out loud.

She left the brothers Na and walked the rest of this part of the house, finding much of interest, whole suites of rooms unoccupied, and one suite in particular that was so precise in its décor, so mathematical, and with a view of the driveway leading up to the house so any occupier could observe all of the comings and goings, that she decided it had to be hers. She would make her case in the morning.

Finally, having had enough of exploring, she quietly made her way down the stairs and found Mayor Ye sitting at the kitchen table, calmly smoking his pipe.

"So, young lady, what do you make of my house?"

"It is spectacular, Mayor Ye."

"You may call me Grandfather."

"Yes, Grandfather."

"Come, sit down at the table and spend some time with me. In a short while I will make us both a mug of hot chocolate. That might help us both sleep, I think."

She put her book on a nearby counter so as not to anger him, and then took a seat at the table opposite him – the most intense, the most formidable, the most unpredictable character she had ever encountered in her short life.

"When Philip came to me a few hours ago," he said, "and told me in no uncertain terms that he was intending to adopt you, I confess I did not know what to think. I asked him why. He raised his voice to me. Can you believe that, young lady? My own son actually raised his voice to me. He said, 'Father, adopting her is the least we can do!' I have no idea what he meant by this – my son has always been a mystery to me – but I could think of no good reason to refuse. To be honest, I have always indulged him. Of my children, he has always been my favourite. But I must tell you, young lady, that I sincerely doubt the quality of his parenting skills. He is usually lost in a world of his own, working all the hours under Heaven on those murder investigations of his. I suppose I will have to do most of the work for him. I have already spoken to his mother in England. She is a professor of chemistry at the University of Oxford, and there is not a more charming, funny, or intelligent woman alive. She has her quirks, I admit, like frittering away all her spare time on meaningless social causes. But she is very excited about you...about having a future mathematician in the family. She has assured me she will seek out the best tutors for you and smooth the path of your academic career. You may even stay with her in Oxford during your school holidays if that is what you wish. All I ask is that you return here immediately whenever you are summoned. Is that acceptable to you?"

"Yes, Grandfather."

"And I will speak to your school this coming week and arrange the funding for the next academic year. All your school reports will be sent directly to me. Is that also acceptable to you?"

"Yes, Grandfather."

"Good – now what name have you chosen for yourself?"

"Jenny Ye."

"Yes, it has a nice ring to it. It is always best to leave the past completely behind. I have no time for the past myself, unlike Philip who seems to enjoy delving into the shadows more than any grown man should. I do not expect you to completely forget your mother. It would be inhuman of me to ask that of you. But I insist you fully embrace the opportunity life has now presented you, that you embrace the family Ye as the only family you will ever need. Can you do that, do you think?"

"Yes, Grandfather."

"Excellent, now before I make that mug of hot chocolate for us both, let me tell you a little family story. It is about my father. I do not remember him. He died when I was but a baby. But I am told that there was never a more dashing or courageous man. He was a fighter pilot for the Nationalist Air Force in the 1930s flying against the Japanese. Russian pilots flew alongside him then, and he called them his comrades and friends. Then the Russians were summoned home – the politics of international relations as complicated as ever – only to be replaced soon after by volunteer American pilots, whom my father also called his comrades and friends. At the end of that war, the civil war broke out again between the Nationalists and the Communists. My father flew against the Communists. But, before the ending of that war, before the final victory of the Communists in 1949, my father swapped sides and flew against his old comrades and friends, the Nationalists. And then, in 1950, with the outbreak of the Korean War, my father found himself flying jets in defence of North Korea, together with the Russians again, but against the Americans this time. My father was lost in that war. He took off one day never to return. As a child, when I heard all these stories of him, I liked to think of him still alive somewhere, having made it safely to some foreign country, having had a bellyful of war. But, as I grew older, and saw how difficult it was for my mother to raise me and my two brothers on her own, I thought it right not to think of my father at all. I was done with him. Now, young lady, what wisdom do you take from this story?"

Jenny Ye saw quickly what was expected of her. "That the world is inconstant, that our friends may one day become our enemies, and that our enemies may one day become our friends. That no one outside of family is ever to be relied upon. That it is to family our first duty must lie. That it is to family our thoughts must always turn, no matter where in the world we might be."

"The family Ye."

"Yes, Grandfather – always the family Ye."

Ye Zihao took his pipe from his mouth, smiled, and pointed the stem of the pipe toward her. "I believe, Jenny Ye, that you and I are going to get along quite famously."

MONDAY

SEVENTY-FIVE

— . —

Ye Zihao sat at his desk and reflected on a weekend that had far exceeded his expectations. Nothing had quite gone to plan, starting with his son's early return from England and Constable Ma's surprising decision to take the lead on a murder investigation a few miles off their usual patch. But what unlooked for rewards had come from those turn of events! Not only had he had the opportunity to meet a bunch of fascinating people (all of whose names, occupations, and potential uses had been noted) but he had also had a thrilling confrontation with Prosecutor Xu – a confrontation that had ended with him stealing her away from under the noses of the family Fu. It was almost as great a victory as that yet to come. After the Shanghai Clique released their version of the demise of Primo Gong, *another* version would be released – in the more trustworthy international media – written by the well-respected and fabulously auburn-haired Stacey Corrigan. The Shanghai Clique's credibility would be soon be in tatters, Chengdu not quite the welcoming business environment as advertised. It was highly likely Party Chief Li would be summoned to Beijing to answer a few questions. With luck, he might not return.

"Boss?"

Ye Zihao looked up from his reverie to see Day Na standing in the doorway. Day Na was still deathly pale. Earlier that morning he and his twin brother had had quite a shock. Not only had they discovered that there had been a most delightful addition to the family, agreed to their chagrin while they had been asleep, but also that the young lady in question had left for them each a present on their beds during the night. Trying not to laugh, Ye Zihao had had to work hard to persuade the brothers Na not to quit. Allowances had to be made, he told them, as she had just lost her mother. He had told them that he was sure – unlike Sarangerel, whom she uncannily resembled – Jenny Ye was not capable of drawing real curses but he would have a sharp word later today so nothing like it would ever happen again.

"What is it?"

"Boss, Mister Qu has arrived. He says he doesn't have an appointment but he needs to speak to you on a matter of urgent family business."

Out of all those who had married into the family Ye through the years – including those married into his brothers' branches of the family – Ye Zihao considered Mister Qu by far the most sensible. Everything Mister Qu did was properly considered; everything that came out of his mouth needed saying.

"Please show him in," said Ye Zihao.

While waiting for Mister Qu to be shown to his study, Ye Zihao took up his pipe and filled the bowl with a tobacco Philip had just brought back from England, a tobacco he had not tried before, 221B Baker Street by Dunhill, a Virginia/Burley blend, the aroma on opening the tin mild and sweet. Ye Zihao expected it to be a good morning smoke. He had hardly put a match to the bowl when Mister Qu, briefcase in hand, appeared in the doorway.

"Thank you for receiving me, Mayor Ye," said Mister Qu, with a slight bow.

"Are you well?"

"I am, sir."

"And my daughter?"

"In excellent health, sir. And I am pleased to say that your grandsons are also in excellent health and that they continue to excel at their studies."

"Very good – please take a seat, Mister Qu."

"Thank you, sir," replied Mister Qu, sitting down and gently laying his briefcase on his knees.

"How is the restaurant?"

"The Silver Tree continues to be very profitable and my plans to open up another establishment are now quite advanced. I am hoping to brief you fully in a couple of weeks and to heed any advice you have to give."

"That is excellent, Mister Qu. But, if all is progressing well, then I am confused as to the point of your visit."

"Sir, I have heard the most disturbing news."

"What news?"

"That you have offered Prosecutor Xu a job overseas."

Ye Zihao was now even more confused. Mister Qu, as a matter of principle – he did not consider himself qualified – had never involved himself in the family Ye business empire, no matter how many times Ye Zihao had tried to persuade him otherwise. Mister Qu considered himself a lowly restauranteur and nothing more.

"Forgive me, sir."

"For what?"

"For over-stepping my position in this family. My wife does not know I am here and would be furious with me if she knew what was on my mind. However, my best girl Lin is in full agreement with me."

"Lin, your senior waitress?"

"Yes, sir."

"So, Mister Qu, what is your objection to Prosecutor Xu working for the family Ye?"

"Ah, none, sir – but if you would allow me to consult my notes then I could perhaps better explain."

Ye Zihao waited patiently as Mister Qu opened his briefcase and took out a piece of paper on which had been written a series of bullet points. Mister Qu began to read them to himself, his mouth opening and closing, silently forming all the words. Ye Zihao appreciated Mister Qu's detailed preparation and his determination to say things just so, if not his speed of delivery.

"Sir," said Mister Qu, finally, "I am led to understand that Philip has already left for work this morning?"

"He has."

"I am glad, for I would not wish him to overhear what I have to say. I am terribly concerned about him. He is thirty-six years old."

"Soon to be thirty-seven."

"Yes, sir – and he is still not married."

Ye Zihao struggled to contain his displeasure. Not this old chestnut again. "Mister Qu, I agree that Philip's refusal to consider matrimony is a concern. But what can I do? He has just returned home after arguing with his mother about this very subject. She is most upset.

And I have vowed never to involve myself in his personal life again, not after the debacle with that vixen Lucy Fu. Philip has yet to forgive me for promoting that ill-starred match. Worse still, he shows less interest in women by the day. Sad to say, he seems to prefer the company of murderers and their victims. I am quite at a loss, Mister Qu. It grieves me to say it, but I am."

"I understand, sir."

"So, I appreciate your concern, but—"

"Sir, I have a new candidate."

"Excuse me?"

"Sir, I do not mean to be presumptuous, but I believe I have found Philip – by which I really mean the family Ye – the ideal woman."

"You have?"

"Yes, sir."

"Who?"

"Prosecutor Xu."

Ye Zihao could not help but laugh out loud. "Mister Qu, don't you realise that the Shanghai Clique brought Prosecutor Xu to Chengdu to be my most dangerous enemy? That is why, when the opportunity unexpectedly presented itself to me, I offered her a job. I admit that I was as nervous as a cat until she accepted. But soon enough she will be far away, an asset to me rather than a threat. I am quite proud of myself."

"Sir, you have made a dreadful mistake," said Mister Qu, bluntly. "For once you were thinking of yourself rather than the greater good of the family Ye."

If these words had been uttered by anyone other than Mister Qu, Ye Zihao would have thrown them out of the house. As it was, Ye Zihao had to stand and turn his back on Mister Qu, and puff steadily on his pipe while staring out of the window upon the calming waters of the lake so as to put a check on his temper. When he felt more in control of himself, he retook his seat and asked Mister Qu to explain.

"Sir, you know how much affection I have for Philip. He has always been good to me. And he is a most excellent uncle to the boys. But you have said it yourself that he is a very odd fish, more interested in the dead than in the living. I do not know whether it is because he is half-English, or because the stars were not well-aligned at the moment of his birth, but I do not see him as your natural heir. And, forgive me for mentioning this, but you yourself have told me that your brothers' children are best described as useful idiots. The family Ye will not survive in all its glory with either them or Philip at the helm."

"Please continue," said Ye Zihao, placing his pipe down in the crystal ashtray, fearing what further home truths were going to come issuing forth from Mister Qu's mouth.

"Sir, I wish you to consider Prosecutor Xu for a moment. She has a most haughty and imperious manner. She is a beauty like no other – by which I mean a true, unaffected, natural beauty. She is the cleverest woman in all of Chengdu. She lives wholly in the moment and does not waste her days mulling over the past. She is brave beyond words, does not suffer fools, and in short, it seems to me, has more of the family Ye about her than Philip will ever have."

"Please continue, Mister Qu."

"Sir, on Saturday evening I witnessed a most shocking event. I have seen nothing like it. I was shaken to my bones. Prosecutor Xu tore into Philip like you would not believe. I have never seen anyone get under Philip's skin so quickly. She is quite fearless – more than a match for him. It was proof to me then, that if a match could be arranged, theirs would be no ordinary marriage. For a start, she would stop him mooning over Isobel. She would also make him give up his stupid job. A woman like that, a real lady, could not bear being married to a lowly police superintendent. I do understand what an asset she could be working in foreign lands for the family Ye, but imagine what good she could do working for the family here in Chengdu. The Shanghai Clique would be quaking in their boots. And if Prosecutor Xu and Philip had children – as they must – surely they would take after her rather than him. Imagine how ferocious she would be in the protection of those children, her cubs – a real tigress!"

Ye Zihao remembered how, in the safe room, Prosecutor Xu had taken his new granddaughter's hand, given her courage, and then had the temerity to tell him to put out his pipe. Who else had ever had the nerve to do that? Ferocious indeed! But there were serious issues that could not be denied.

"She has been married," said Ye Zihao.

"He is dead," countered Mister Qu.

"There is some mystery attached to his death."

Mister Qu quickly referred to his notes again. "With Lin's help, I have been conducting some research. I have found that her late husband was considered to be a corrupt judge and most likely a wastrel. I expect he treated Prosecutor Xu abominably. I do not think her a murderess, but if – and this is just speculation, sir – she was forced for some reason to act decisively to save her own skin, then that should be taken as a further recommendation for her being married into the family Ye."

"What does my daughter think of her?"

"My wife detests her."

"So, yet another recommendation...."

"My wife recognises the power Prosecutor Xu wields and fears it."

Ye Zihao put his hands over his eyes in deep regret. "But I have already offered her a job in London."

"Job offers can be rescinded."

"And Philip—"

"Does not know what is good for him. His feelings should not form part of our reasoning."

"But he will need to be convinced...as will Prosecutor Xu."

"If you are willing, sir, then you and I – with the help of my best girl Lin, who tells me she knows a thing or two about modern romance – should develop a strategy for a short but bloody campaign. We will knock their heads together if we have to. The future of the family Ye is at stake. And we must move quickly. Prosecutor Xu is such a beauty, and is so famous now, I am certain the wolves are already circling. I do not think we should relax for a moment – not until they are safely married."

"Do you have any doubts, Mister Qu?"

"None, sir – she is the one."

Ye Zihao stood again and once more turned his back on Mister Qu to stare out of the window. He had been a fool. As Mister Qu had rightly said, in attempting to send Prosecutor Xu abroad he had been thinking more of his own safety than the future of the family Ye. He closed his eyes and imagined her living under the roof of his house, tending to her litter of cubs, alert to anyone or anything that might threaten them. No one would get through the door without her say so. That in itself could lead to complications, but she would definitely straighten Philip out once and for all. The image was so clear, so convincing, so thrilling, he felt a great weight fall from his shoulders – the future of the family Ye suddenly assured.

He turned back toward Mister Qu. "I would wish to convene the first strategy meeting this coming week."

"Of course, sir."

"Your arrival today has been most timely."

"I am just doing my duty, sir."

Ye Zihao clapped his hands together.

Day Na came running. "Yes, Boss?"

"I understand from reviewing the household accounts that you have had a surveillance operation running these last few months."

Day Na feigned innocence. "A surveillance operation, Boss?"

Ye Zihao was having none of it. "Who are you using?"

Day Na sighed heavily. "Mister Wei."

"Is he any good?"

"The best in Chengdu."

"And what is he doing for you?"

"Just watching, reporting – looking out for threats."

"I am extremely disappointed in you and your brother."

"But, Boss, we—"

"You are not spending enough! Continue with Mister Wei but I want you to set up a quick intervention team. Prosecutor Xu is to be protected like family. Any man who attempts to get close to her is to be persuaded to walk away. There is also a nasty note-writing campaign against her at the Procuratorate. That is to stop now. Issue threats, break a few legs if you have to, but it must stop."

"Yes, Boss!" said Day Na, enthusiastically.

"Use the brothers Ming. I liked the look of those four young, enterprising men."

"We already have their contact details, Boss!"

"And put the sisters Ping on the payroll as well. Those charming girls are wasted as funeral strippers. Get them whatever training is required and put them in the field as quickly as you can. If anything happens to Prosecutor Xu then you and your brother will lose your heads."

Ye Zihao reached into his lower desk drawer and pulled out the bottle of 40-year-old Glenglassaugh scotch whiskey he had been keeping for a very special occasion. By the time he had broken open the seal, Day Na had vanished and returned with a grinning Night Na and four clean glasses. Ye Zihao poured a short measure for each of them.

"What are we drinking to?" asked Night Na, putting the glass up to his nose and sighing with pleasure despite the early hour.

Ye Zihao looked to Mister Qu.

"The family Ye," said Mister Qu, solemnly.

Ye Zihao and Day Na and Night Na and Mister Qu raised their glasses high in the air and shouted as one, "The family Ye!"

Seventy-Six

— ※ —

P hilip Ye got to the office early after a night of bad dreams. He
had the office to himself. Superintendent Zuo was still off sick
with his tender stomach and Constable Ma was yet to show.

It had been a quiet night in Chengdu, no new trade according to
Dispatch. A young family in the east of the city had driven into a
flooded sinkhole during the night. Fortunately, they had been rescued
by two deliverymen passing by, no lasting harm done. That was all.
The sun was now up, the sky a clear azure blue – it was set to be a
peaceful day.

Philip Ye phoned Stacey Corrigan. She was still in her hotel room,
not yet on her way to the airport.

"How much can you tell me?" she asked.

"Some," he replied.

He made no mention of Lucy Fu, the recovery of Du Luli, or of
any part his own father may or may not have played behind the scenes
of the weekend's drama. Instead, he told the story – as complete as he
knew it – of how, in conducting research for his book, Primo Gong
had stumbled on the truth behind his grandfather's death in 1950 –
a truth perhaps best left forgotten.

"It's odd to think that such an entrepreneur, such a forward-think-
ing man, should have died because of something that happened over
sixty years ago."

"But this is Chengdu, not San Diego – the people here learn very
young to leave the past where it is."

"If they know what's good for them," laughed Stacey Corrigan.

"Indeed – but it may be that Primo Gong had been prepared
to learn. Min Feng, of the CCB, told me he had persuaded Primo

Gong to drop all idea of the book. If true, then Primo Gong died for nothing."

"And the CCB contract?"

"Not as troubled as was rumoured by all accounts. But I am sure Ambrogetti Global Software's stock is set to plummet today when official news of Primo Gong's death is released, so who knows what will happen next. It could be that Min Feng and the CCB will pounce and take control of Ambrogetti Global Software just to guarantee they get the software they ordered, unless the family back in San Diego move in to prop things up. But that sort of financial speculation is more your line than mine."

"True – whatever happens it will be an interesting day. I have delayed my leaving Chengdu until Wednesday."

"Are you coming over for dinner again this evening?"

She laughed brightly. "Your father seems not to be accepting calls from me today. It could be our friendship has run its course."

"I'm sorry."

"Don't be, I'm a tough old reporter."

"Even so—"

"Your father is an unusual man."

Now it was Philip Ye's turn to laugh. "That is true."

"One thing troubles me, though, Philip – what about Li Ju?"

"What of her?"

"If she had hated the Communists and the Party so much, why did she lie? Why did she tell everyone her husband had died of TB rather than murdered in the street by General Fei Song? It doesn't make any sense. Primo Gong might have stayed in San Diego if he had known the truth, might never have come to Chengdu at all, and this whole tragedy could have been avoided."

"I have been pondering the same. All I can say is that, if she and her husband had been Communist agents, then she would have lived through the war years in great terror of being discovered. And in 1950, just after the liberation of Chengdu by the Communist forces, to then witness her husband being dragged out in the street and murdered by the very people she had been working for, who knows what that would have done to her mind. Better to escape Chengdu and say that her husband had died in his bed from a common illness, even better to believe it herself and bury the trauma deep."

"It's all so very sad."

"And a similar lie will be told today."

"Such as?"

"The Party will probably announce that Primo Gong has died suddenly in his bed from natural causes – the implication being that Chengdu is as safe for international businessmen as it ever was."

"And what should I write?"

"As little as your conscience will allow."

Stacey Corrigan laughed again. "By which you mean, not as much as your father would like."

"If I were you – and this is just a suggestion – why not write a personal piece about Chengdu and Primo Gong, about how your grandfather flew B29 Superfortresses from airfields around the city against Japan at the same time as Primo Gong's grandfather was helping the US Navy gather meteorological data, about how all those memories are fading away now, about how you understood Primo Gong's reasoning for coming to do business in the city and to rediscover his roots, how sad you are to hear about his death, how he will never now get to experience the brilliant future of Chengdu – the future he was helping to create. It would be a bit different to your usual pieces, but I am sure the Party would appreciate it even if my father doesn't."

"And what about Primo Gong's murder?"

"Is it really that important?"

"It was to you."

"I'm a homicide detective not a business journalist."

"Killing Primo Gong was also important to the family Fei."

"The family Fei were stupid."

"How so, Philip?"

"People have died these last few days over a family name, over an old man's fabled military career. If they had stopped to think they would have realised that nobody really cares about the legacy of General Fei Song except a few old soldiers. The Party certainly doesn't care about veterans. All the Party really cares about is the Party – its own history and its own image. Any furore created by Primo Gong's book – that is, if he had published it – would have quickly died down or been suppressed. Not that Fei Qin would have understood this. She is full of rage – murderous rage – for a life not as she wanted it, for a husband she detested, for a father-in-law she could not openly embrace."

"Isn't it rare for a woman to be so violent?"

"Rare – but not unheard of – and rarer still for a woman to have so much influence over others that they will kill at her command. Go tell your story, Stacey – a happy story, a story of Chengdu, a story of a colourful city with a colourful past, a story full of colourful characters, and with a colourful future ahead of it."

"But crime stories sell."

"This is more of a war story – a tragic war story."

"I will think about what you have said."

"Take care, Stacey."

"You too – and thank you. I'm basing myself in Singapore at present so if you're ever in town give me a call."

When Ma Meili reached the office, she found Superintendent Ye had already arrived. He was standing at the window looking out across the city while playing with his pocket-watch, opening and closing the case again and again. To her greeting he offered no reply. Nor did he even seem to notice her presence.

It was going to be one of *those* days.

She had wanted to tell him all about the recovery of Du Luli's body from the flooded ruin of a temple, about how kind and consoling Doctor Kong and her team had been, how Doctor Kong's initial impression had been strangulation by ligature. She had also wanted to tell him about how she had arrived late last evening at The Silver Tree to pick up her cat Yoyo, and how Ye Lan, his kind sister, had generously insisted she sit down to a proper meal – on the house! – before allowing her to go on her way. But since this was obviously going to be a day of limited conversation, or possibly none at all, she took herself off to the canteen to buy herself a bowl of fruit for breakfast. There she found Ms. Miao, sitting at a table all alone, deep in thought. On any other occasion Ma Meili would not have intruded on Ms. Miao's quiet time. But today Ma Meili had something to say and went over.

"Ms. Miao, please forgive my rudeness. I just wished to thank you for the help you gave me this weekend."

"Don't mention it, Constable – I was only too happy to assist your investigation. Sadly, I have discovered I have far fewer reliable contacts at Chengdu Military Region headquarters than I had originally thought. You may be interested to know that they are now in *crisis management mode* – whatever that may mean. I am hoping for a formal apology from them sometime in the next few days. Anyway, on a different matter entirely, I hope you haven't forgotten your English Language lessons are to begin this week."

Ma Meili's heart sank. "I remember, Ms. Miao."

"Good – now what is happening with you and SWAT?"

Ma Meili had no idea how Ms. Miao knew about her struggle to come to the right decision. "Last night I phoned Commissioner Zhu and turned down his invitation to join the team."

"I am glad, Constable – very glad. Your leaving would be a great loss to Homicide, no matter what Superintendent Ye might think."

"Thank you, Ms. Miao."

"Oh, and you must tell me if you ever cross paths with Prosecutor Xu again. You were right about there being not one good bone in her body. Last evening, during a briefing at the Procuratorate, she made no attempt to give you or Superintendent Ye any credit for bringing the family Fei's reign of terror on our streets to an end. It was an absolute disgrace. That woman also took the opportunity to make an unprecedented personal attack on Chief Di in front of the whole Political and Legal Committee. Not only did she make the PSB look rotten from the inside, but incompetent as well. I am still beside myself with rage. That woman is evil."

"Pure evil," agreed Ma Meili.

"But do not worry. We shall have our revenge. I have heard a few odd rumours coming out of Chongqing. I do not think our little TV star is as moral and squeaky-clean as she likes to make out. Did you know she had a husband?"

Ma Meili shook her head.

"He died last summer...quite suddenly...quite unexpectedly," whispered Ms. Miao.

Ma Meili put her hand to her mouth.

"Can you guess what I suspect?" asked Ms. Miao.

Ma Meili nodded, her blood suddenly running cold.

"Good – but keep this between us, Constable Ma. Speak not a word of it to Superintendent Ye. Men are not to be trusted around beautiful women. You and I will act when the time is right. Prosecutor Xu has to learn that you do not mess with the police. That is the Golden Rule. Now run along, work hard, and keep your head down. And come to me with any information that comes your way about that woman. I have created a special file for her this very morning."

After buying her bowl of fruit, Ma Meili returned to the Homicide Office. Superintendent Ye was still standing at the window playing with his stupid watch. She had never seen him so unhappy. What had got into him today?

With no orders forthcoming, Ma Meili didn't know what to do with herself. She had no files of her own to work on. All she had were the text books given her by Superintendent Ye and they were just as uninviting today as they had been a few months ago. She ate her bowl of fruit while staring at the phone, hoping it would ring and Dispatch would have another new case for them to work. It wasn't right to wish for a murder but that was how she felt.

"How many days have you worked straight?"

For a moment Ma Meili thought she was hearing things. She looked up at Superintendent Ye. He had put his pocket-watch away and was now staring right at her.

"Fifteen days, Superintendent."

"Go home."

"But—"

"That's an order, Constable. I will see you again on Wednesday."

Did he want her to take a much-needed rest?

Or did he merely want her out of the office?

She could not tell.

She gathered all her stuff together, put on her summer jacket – some light showers were forecast for the afternoon – threw her bag over her shoulder, said goodbye to Superintendent Ye, who was staring out of the window again and chose not respond, and walked out of the office.

At first, she thought she would just catch the bus home, do some shopping at the local supermarket for some much-needed supplies, and then cuddle up next to Yoyo and watch TV for the rest of the day. But, instead, she caught a bus in a different direction, a bus that dropped her off near to the Xiaojia River Residential District, not far from Jin Huiliang's apartment. Only a short walk from the bus stop was Madame Song's shop, Magical Wilderness Adventures. Ma Meili stared for a long time at the poster in the window, of the climber standing on a mountaintop knee-deep in pure white snow with the crystal-clear sky above him, and thought back to how she had spent her afternoon and evening the day before, up to her knees in a fetid flooded field, staring down at a bloated dead body, soaked to the skin from the torrential rain. It would be nice to stand above the clouds, to breathe air so pure it hurt one's lungs. She went inside.

Madame Song was pleased to see her. "Constable, did you catch your murderer?"

"Oh yes, the woman with the crocodile-skin handbag has been arrested. She will probably die for her crimes."

There were gasps from the silly shop girls. Ma Meili gave them a hard stare. If they had remembered Fei Qin's name then the investigation might have been wrapped up a lot sooner.

"I ruined my boots yesterday," said Ma Meili to Madame Song. "I would like to try on some new ones."

"Certainly," said Madame Song. "I will assist you myself. Have you had any thoughts about my offer of a modelling contract? You would be so perfect, Constable Ma. It is good money and I will give you thirty percent discount on your new boots."

"I will do it," said Ma Meili, liking the idea of earning a little extra cash. And, having come to the conclusion after standing for so many hours looking down at poor Du Luli that life was far too short to procrastinate, Ma Meili added, "I would also like any contact details you might have for the Chengdu Mountaineering Society. Like that man on the poster in your window, I want to climb to the top of the world."

SEVENTY-SEVEN

— · —

It was mid-morning when Fatty Deng was woken by someone banging on the apartment door. For a brief moment, not having escaped fully from intricate and confusing dreams replete with exotic dancing girls, shootings, and ever-rising floodwaters, he thought his mother must have returned home early from her excursion up the Yangzi. Only when he had sat up in bed did he remember that his mother would always first use her key, and that it was more likely Prosecutor Xu had come in person to personally dismiss him from the Procuratorate for carrying a loaded pistol while up to his eyeballs in drink. His head pounding from what he had done to himself the evening before, and not a little dizzy and shaky on his feet, he struggled out of bed, wrapped his old threadbare robe about himself, and went to answer the door.

It was not Prosecutor Xu. It was a heavily perspiring deliveryman who had struggled up the stairs with a large cardboard box for him. Fatty Deng had no memory of recently ordering anything. In fact, after all the alcohol he had consumed the previous evening, he had hardly any memory left at all.

"Are you Mister Deng?" asked the deliveryman.

"I suppose," said Fatty Deng.

"What happened to your face?"

"I got beaten up. What the fuck do you think?"

"You should go to the police."

"What are you, some kind of fucking comedian?"

"No, I—"

Fatty Deng snatched the box from the man and slammed the door in his face. He laid the box down on the table in the lounge and then went straight into the bathroom to stare into the mirror. A monster stared back at him. His eyes were puffy and red, his face so swollen it looked like he was having some kind of extreme allergic reaction. The bruised skin ranged in hue from bright yellow to deep purple. Those special operators had done a real job on him outside the Lucky Dragon Tobacco Emporium. His mother would have one of her famous nervous collapses when she got home. It would be better for him, for everybody, if he went back into his bedroom, locked the door, and didn't emerge for a month.

Since that was not an option, he went instead into the kitchen, poured himself a glass of cold mineral water to slake the terrible thirst that had built up through the night, and knocked back a couple of painkillers to offset the pounding between his temples. He drank long and deep from the water, pulling back the blinds of the kitchen window as he did so. The glare from the bright sunlight stung his eyes. There was not a cloud in the sky. It was going to be another very hot day.

Out on the street he could see his car parked up in its usual spot. This did not make sense. His best recollection was that a taxi had brought him home. He had no memory of what he had done with his car. And someone had also arranged for his front and rear windscreens to be fixed.

This had to be Prosecutor Xu's doing. She must have taken his car keys from him at the same time she had relieved him of his pistol and detailed someone from the Procuratorate to go find his car, get it fixed, hopefully mop out all the rainwater from within it, and deliver it home for him. It would be just like her. One moment she could be raging at him, the next she could be the kindest, most thoughtful person under Heaven.

He was going to miss her. She was the best boss he had ever had. It broke his heart imagining her getting on that flight to London and never coming back.

He took his glass of water into the lounge and stared for a while at the box on the table, not certain he wanted to know what was inside. He was afraid his mother had wasted a pile of cash on holiday by buying some tat aimed directly at the tourist market and posting it home.

There was only one way to find out.

Using his bare hands, he broke the seal on the box and prised it open. On top of the packing straw was a note. It read:

FOR A JOB WELL DONE

He had no idea what this meant. He rummaged in the packing straw and came up with a bottle of 25-year-old Macallan whiskey and a whole carton of luxury Huanghelou 1916 gold-tipped cigarettes. He was stunned. With the state his head was in, he found it impossible to calculate the value of what he had been sent, how many months of his Procuratorate salary it represented.

However, he was given little time to reflect on Secretary Wu's thoughtfulness and generosity when someone began banging on his apartment door again.

Cursing, wishing he could be left alone to nurse his hangover as well as his many aches and pains, he quickly buried the whiskey and cigarettes deep into the packing straw, closed up the box, and went to open the door.

"Oh, Investigator Deng, it has all gone wrong!" exclaimed Prosecutor Xu, in some apparent emotional distress, her tears making a mess of her mascara.

In the kitchen, ashamed of the state of his robe as well as the state he had got himself into the previous evening, Fatty Deng put some water on to boil for tea as Prosecutor Xu threw herself down into the nearest chair in the lounge and dabbed at her eyes with a tissue. When he returned to the lounge with a tray of tea, he saw she had returned his pistol, having placed it down on the table next to the box from Secretary Wu. This was a tremendous relief. If she had been about to charge him with gross misconduct, and relieve him of his post, she would not have brought the pistol with her.

"Investigator Deng, I have been played for a fool," she said.

He passed her a cup of tea. "How so?"

"They are laughing at me."

"Who is laughing at you?"

"Oh, the family Ye!"

Fatty Deng took a seat, as confused as he could be. "Prosecutor, what are you talking about?"

"The job offer, of course."

A faint hope kindled inside Fatty Deng. "The job offer from the family Fu?"

"No, you dummy – I could never work for Lucy Fu. I'm talking about the job offer from Ye Zihao. I am sure I told you about it. I *must* have told you about it. Anyway, Ye Zihao asked me to represent the family Ye's business interests abroad. It was an offer I couldn't refuse. But he has just phoned me and told me he had made a terrible mistake. There was no position for me to fill at the moment. He then had the nerve to invite me to dinner next weekend. I was so angry I put the phone down on him. I couldn't believe I had trusted him. I have always known what sort of man he was. But I was so desperate to escape Chengdu that I had convinced myself the job offer was real. I hope he burns in hell. He is nothing but an evil bastard!"

Fatty Deng laughed out loud, never before having heard her swear. He was overjoyed she was now not going anywhere, that his job at the Procuratorate was safe for the time being.

"Don't look so happy!" she scolded him.

"But I am happy, Prosecutor."

She dabbed at her eyes again, brushed away the hair that was falling wild and loose across her face, and asked, "Have you heard from him?"

"Heard from who?"

"Superintendent Ye."

"No, Prosecutor."

"I saved his life yesterday."

"You did?"

"Yes, and he could not bring himself to say one word of thanks to me. Like father, like son – he is an evil bastard too!"

Fatty Deng laughed again, liking this new, profane Prosecutor Xu. "You shouldn't take it personally. Mister Ye has never been an easy man to understand."

"But it is personal!"

"I mean it is not worth getting upset about."

"You don't understand."

"What don't I understand?"

"He should like me. And he should protect me in return. Police are supposed to protect people, aren't they? Now I have to have dinner with Sarangerel this evening with no one to watch over me."

Fatty Deng thought he was hearing things. "You have been invited to dinner with Sarangerel?"

"Oh, it's a long story. No matter what happens, think kindly of me, Investigator Deng. I have made such a mess of my life. From the moment I laid eyes on Philip Ye on that first day at university nothing has gone right for me. My bad marriage was nothing but a reaction to him never once looking in my direction – not once! Because of him, because of that whole degenerate family, I am doomed. And it is no less than I deserve. There has always been a hole within me. Inside, where there should only be morality, where there should only be the intention to bring the Rule of Law to the people, there is a black hole of pain and loneliness and longing. It has been there, I think, from the time of my birth. It has always been my weakness. Now it has been my downfall."

"Prosecutor, I will go to dinner with Sarangerel with you."

"No," she said, standing up, "I must face my fate alone. I will find my courage. You have to stay home and get better. You must recover your health. I don't want to see you at the Procuratorate for at least another two weeks. And you must consult that psychiatrist I told you about. He will help you with your nerves and your hypervigilance."

"But, the witch—"

"No, I must be brave for once in my life and face her on my own. And I don't believe in witches, or ghosts, or demons, or any of that nonsense. You must stay home and get better. But I appreciate the offer, Investigator Deng – I really do. You are the best of men, the best of friends."

"I will do as you wish," he assured her, also standing, still feeling shaky on his legs, embarrassed by her praise.

"Good, now I suppose, before I go, I should tell you what is happening with our investigation. It is not good. It is all being taken out of my hands. On the plus side Major-General Zi Hong was picked up by military investigators in the middle of the night trying to sneak across the border into Myanmar. I have been told he will stand trial in Kunming alongside Fei Qin and Superintendent Si Ying. No one is able to tell me what the charges will be. I tried to argue the point that all their crimes – the ones we know about, at least – were committed in Chengdu. But I may as well have been speaking to a brick wall. As to how Primo Gong died, that is to remain a state secret. I have had a long conversation with Commissioner Ji Dan of PSB Internal Security. He seems to be the only person with any sense at PSB HQ. Thank goodness he is back from his conference. He has assured me that he will detain and deal with – he did not say how – the remainder of Superintendent Si Ying's Black House security detail. As to your drinking buddy Commissioner Yang Da, he is to be allowed to quietly resign from the PSB. I have been told – and Commissioner Ji Dan is furious about this – that another high-profile trial of a senior police officer in Chengdu this summer will only serve to undermine further the little faith the people already have in the police. It makes me wonder why we bothered getting out of bed this weekend."

"What about Mister Li and his wife – the owners of the Laughing Panda Hotel?"

She put her hand to her forehead. "Goodness, I had completely forgotten about them. They have been in the cells all night. What do you suggest?"

"Kick them loose."

"Really?"

"Prosecutor, they manage a hotel. All kinds of people, including many foreigners, stay there throughout the year. I am sure in exchange for their freedom they would be happy to give us a call in the future if they notice anything strange."

"You wish them to be informers?"

"It is how things are done, Prosecutor."

"Fine, fine...on your head be it. Now I must dash. I have so much to do today."

She then surprised him by throwing herself at him and hugging him before vanishing out of the door. She had not touched a drop of her tea. From the window, he watched her race away in her little sports car, paying no attention to the give way sign as she did so. He had to laugh. She would never change.

He took the pistol she had returned and the box sent him by Secretary Wu into his bedroom. He put the pistol to one side. It needed cleaning and oiling. He also needed to give the big girl a call. She had promised she would take him down the PSB range and teach him how to shoot properly.

He opened the cardboard box again, ignored the whiskey – it would be a few days before he could face alcohol again – and tore open the cigarette carton. He broke the seal on a packet and lit one of the outrageously expensive cigarettes. He sucked the smoke into his lungs, and sighed with pleasure.

He lay back on his bed and closed his eyes. He was glad about Commissioner Yang Da being allowed to quietly resign from the police. He was not a bad man. He had just got stuck in a web of loyalty from which he could not escape. And he had done the right thing by not destroying the all-important file from the Black House. He had also been the ideal drinking-partner, easy-going and full of humorous stories. But Fatty Deng had realised very quickly that he was not a natural policeman. Commissioner Yang Da liked the uniform and the air of authority it gave him, but he had no inner drive to do anything with that authority, no need to do real good out in the world, to keep the peace, to bring some justice to the lives of the common people. Now that his father was dead, and he had no job, Commissioner Yang Da would have no choice but to take over the management of his family's business. This was all to the good. In a couple of weeks Fatty Deng would give him a call, see how he was getting on, maybe go out for drinks with him again. There was no harm in cultivating what could prove to be – in the long run – a very useful friendship. Corruption was endemic in the high-powered business circles Commissioner Yang Da would be moving in. If he was to become a better investigator for the Procuratorate, Fatty Deng had to understand the workings of the business world – Primo Gong's world – and become confident enough to walk into a high-tech company, say, as Prosecutor Xu had done, and ask all the right questions.

His thoughts returned to Prosecutor Xu and her dinner with Sarangerel. He felt he should have done more to persuade her to let him tag along, even if the dinner was probably more about Sarangerel's fears than Prosecutor Xu's. Like most everybody else in Chengdu, Sarangerel must have seen Prosecutor Xu on TV and taken note of Prosecutor Xu's resulting fame. As there could only ever be one queen bee in a hive, Sarangerel presumably wanted to take a closer look at the opposition – nothing more.

And yet....

Fatty Deng reached for his phone and dialled.

"How are you, Fatty?"

"Fine, Mister Ye – but I have a favour to ask."

"Which is?"

"Prosecutor Xu is to have dinner this evening with Sarangerel and—"

"Protection will be in place."

"Thank you, Mister Ye."

"Take care of yourself, Fatty – and keep in touch."

Fatty Deng put the phone to one side and closed his eyes. Now Prosecutor Xu was safe his thoughts turned to Sun Mei and the Lucky Dragon Tobacco Emporium. He regretted the way it had ended with her. He regretted not finding at least one kind word to say to her before he had driven off and left her standing outside the Ye family mansion in the rain. He should have treated her better.

But Sun Mei was of a different world to him. She belonged in his world no more than he belonged in hers. There was no denying that important truth.

He stubbed out his cigarette and settled down to get a few more hours of sleep. By late afternoon his mother would be home and life would return to normal again. In a week or so, he would have forgotten all about Sun Mei. Of that he was certain. For, to think otherwise, was to assume he could, or should, have done things differently – that the different worlds they occupied were not so far apart after all.

SEVENTY-EIGHT

It being Monday morning, the Labour Exchange was full to over-flowing. Some men had just come in, looking for cleaning staff, promising to pay a good daily rate, but Madame Ding had paid them no attention. She could tell what they were, little more than slave-bosses. Madame Ding knew she would never work again for a man such as the General. He had been a war hero and a gentleman – a gem among so much gravel. But she would never put herself in the power of those slave-bosses, no matter how desperate she was, unlike the handful of women, their faces pictures of misery, who got up off their seats and went with them.

She had spoken to her husband the previous evening by phone. He had told her she could not afford to be fussy, that the few hours work she did at the local school in the evening was not going to pay the bills, let alone enable her to put something away for the future. She had told him she wanted to work for a nice household if she could, to be a maid to a professional couple, to cook, clean, and look after their children. He had told her not to hope for too much but to take the first decent offer she got. He also asked her to consider moving across the country to be with him in Shenzhen. But, much as she missed him, she did not fancy that. She had come to like Chengdu, despite the recent proliferation of murder.

She had got up early and queued in the rising heat outside of the Labour Exchange with a host of others looking for work. Then, when inside, she sat and waited and waited for a suitable vacancy to materialise. "To expect a miracle to strike once is bad enough," her husband had said, "but to expect a miracle to strike twice is madness." He was right, of course. Getting that job working for the General had been the miracle of her life. How could she, a very ordinary woman of no education, of no special abilities, and no more deserving than anyone else, expect a second miracle? But, during the night, after telling her husband that she was always thinking of him and their children, and that it wouldn't be long before they would all be together for the national holidays of the first week in October, she had had the most vivid dream. She had been mopping the floor of a palatial home full of light – she did not know where – when, who should come walking by but the General.

"Madame Ding, thank you for your years of service to me," he said. "Do not worry. You are to be taken care of. She will be along shortly."

If that dream was not a good omen, what was?

Madame Ding had no idea who *she* could be. Madame Ding hoped she would be a lovely young wife with a child on the way. But, as she sat at the labour exchange, hour after hour, the hope the dream had given her soon began to fade. Her husband had been right. Miracles do not strike twice. Soon enough it was midday and, as many people began to leave, their hopes dashed at finding work that day, Madame Ding wondered if she should not do the same, and get up early the following day to try again.

And then the second miracle did strike, not that it was quite the miracle that Madame Ding had been hoping for.

The door to the labour exchange opened and in *she* walked, her hand to her nose as if she didn't like the smell of so many hot, sweating people in one small area, the security guards converging on her quickly, recognising her from the TV, bowing and scraping, hoping to be of some service to her, to be remembered by her.

Oh no, thought Madame Ding.

Madame Ding tried to make herself as small in her seat as she could, hung her head so her face could be seen, and hoped to hide behind the bag she carried on her lap. But it did no good. Prosecutor Xu had eyes like a hawk. She came right over, her high heels clicking across the floor, the security guards glaring at anyone who might impede her progress.

"Madame Ding, I thought I might find you here."

"Ah, yes, Prosecutor, I am looking to work for a nice family who—"

"You will work for me. This morning when I awoke I assumed I was soon to be leaving for London. Now it is not so. I am to stay in Chengdu. You and I will have to make the best of it. I need a maid and you need a job – so come along!"

If the spirit of the General thought that this was some kind of joke then Madame Ding assured him, silently, that she, for one, was not laughing. Prosecutor Xu was very famous and clever and beautiful, but anyone with eyes in their head could see she was not an orderly person, not like the General, not someone easy to get along with. Madame Ding gave one last lingering look around the Labour Exchange, hoping some nice family might suddenly appear. And, when that faint hope failed to materialise, she followed Prosecutor Xu out onto the street, the doors held open for them by the genuflecting security guards, and soon found herself crammed into the passenger seat of a little sports car.

It got worse.

Prosecutor Xu started dabbing at her eyes.

Madame Ding sighed. "What is wrong, Prosecutor?"

"Oh, this day is turning into a nightmare, Madame Ding. Firstly, I lost an opportunity of a lifetime in London. And then my friend Mouse, my one true female friend, came back from a stupid camping trip in the mountains—"

"In all the bad weather?"

"Exactly, Madame Ding – you and I are of one mind. Anyway, she came back and told me she is to be married, that Captain Wang, her boyfriend – who is an officer in the People's Armed Police, which, I can tell you, is no recommendation at all – has proposed to her and she has accepted. I couldn't believe my ears. And then she told me the wedding is to take place in only a couple of months and the ceremony and reception is to be held at the Ye family mansion. She wants me to be her Maid of Honour."

Madame Ding put her hand to her mouth.

"I agree, Madame Ding – I was as shocked as you are now. I was not even aware that Mouse knew the family Ye. I tried to persuade her not to rush into this marriage, not to make the same mistake I had made. But it was like I was talking to myself. And can you guess what else Mouse told me?"

Madame Ding shook her head.

"That Philip Ye is to adopt the girl Du Yue!"

Madame Ding was relieved. The tall, strange girl needed a new family now her mother was gone. "Is that not a good thing, Prosecutor?"

"How can it be? What does Philip Ye know about being a father? He didn't even call me to ask my opinion or request my help with all the legal paperwork. Do I look invisible to you, Madame Ding? Do I look invisible?"

Madame Ding shook her head again, terrified.

"It has been a day of betrayals. I don't even have a criminal conspiracy to prosecute. I don't know how this day could get any worse. I wish I hadn't saved his life."

"Whose life did you save, Prosecutor?"

"Philip Ye's – not that I got a single word of thanks for my trouble. He only gave me flowers when he wanted to get back into my good graces. But I have shown him. I threw all of his stupid flowers out of the window this morning."

"My goodness!" exclaimed Madame Ding.

Prosecutor Xu started the engine, the tyres of the little car squealing as it darted out into the traffic. Madame Ding held onto her bag for dear life.

"All I expect from you is absolute loyalty, Madame Ding," she said, "and to clean and shop and do some cooking for me. You are to give up your other job at the school. You will be paid well enough. I cannot have you being distracted by other work. And you must not speak of anything you see in my apartment. I will often bring home confidential papers. I just want my apartment to look presentable, you understand...in case he comes by again."

"Who comes by, Prosecutor?"

"Who do you think? I just want the apartment to be presentable, not be such a mess...not to reflect badly on me. I have so little time you see, and he is so judgmental. I am not naturally a messy person. I just have so many other things to worry about. You do see the problem, don't you, Madame Ding? I'm thinking of moving anyway so he won't know where I live. I am sick of being beholden to the family Fu. But where would I get another such fine apartment and at such a preferential rate? Maybe you can advise me, Madame Ding. It wouldn't hurt for me to rough it a bit. But, then again, I work so hard, don't I deserve to live in some comfort? Is that too much to ask?"

Madame Ding, nodded, thinking her new boss was completely crazy. She said a silent prayer to the spirit of the General, wishing him safe travels in the afterlife, and hoping, in return, he would send her some strength – as much as he could spare. She was going to need it.

SEVENTY-NINE

—·—

F or all their crimes, for all their madness, Xu Ya understood the family Fei. As for them, the past for Xu Ya was a living thing, dangerous, always threatening, at any moment able to snuff out the light of the future. Regardless of her father's promises, the night her husband died would haunt her forever. It could not be escaped. It could not be run from. Fate had made sure of that. The opportunity to flee to London had proved to be nothing more than a mirage. There was therefore no point in attempting to delay her dinner with Sarangerel. She might as well get the dreaded encounter over with.

This did not mean, however, that planning for the future needed to stop. Having processed the problem at the back of her mind all weekend, the only conclusion Xu Ya could reach – if Sarangerel had indeed stumbled over some terrible facts – was that Sarangerel wished from her some kind of favour in exchange for keeping her silence. And though Xu Ya would agree, as so many in her situation would, it would not be the end of the world. Bound then to Sarangerel to do her bidding forever, this did not mean in every other area of her life she could not do good. She would not be the first legal official to be so compromised. Chongqing, for instance, was plagued by such compromised men and women. But the justice system there trundled on, a giant ponderous machine, corrupt to its very core, but still able, many times a day, to deliver some form of justice, some semblance of the Rule of Law, to the people.

After showing Madame Ding around her apartment and delivering her back to her home – the salary and the basic rules of her engagement having been easily agreed – Xu Ya decided to take the afternoon off work and prepare herself mentally for what was to come. Chief Prosecutor Gong had returned from his holiday in Africa. She did not want to waste any time listening to him drone on about his many adventures and about how many animals he had crept up upon while they were sleeping with the help of local guides and shot. She had never had any great thoughts about conservation or the morality of hunting, but she could not help wishing that at least one of those poor animals had turned on Chief Prosecutor Gong and eaten him.

At home, she took a long, luxurious bath, resisting the temptation to slide beneath the water and drown herself. But that didn't mean she did not cry a little – more out of frustration with how her life had turned out rather than anything else.

Then, wrapping a large towel around herself, she had stared in the mirror at the cut on her forehead, wondering how best to conceal it for the dinner that evening, not wanting to be seen as some common girl willing to take on all-comers in wrestling matches. The cut would take a good few weeks to completely disappear, and then it might leave a scar. And she knew just who to blame. Experiencing yet another of those thoughtless episodes that had seemed to dog her whole life, she ran out of the bathroom and into her study, picked up her phone and dialled.

"Prosecutor Xu, what can I do for you?" said Philip Ye, his voice distant, suspicious.

"It seems I am not going away anymore."

"I have heard."

"How is it that a family such as yours can live in such a beautiful house, enjoy all the trappings of wealth, influence, and power, and yet do nothing but give hurt?"

There was silence on the line for a moment, and then Philip Ye replied, "I am adopting Du Yue."

Xu Ya quickly replied, "If I had been her, I would have opted to put myself in the care of Social Services. At least then—"

"Be careful of Sarangerel."

"How did you know I was—?"

"Goodbye, Prosecutor."

He put the phone down on her. Not the outcome she had intended. She, as with Ye Zihao earlier that day, had been determined to put the phone down on him; after, that is, he had thanked her from the bottom of his heart for saving his life.

Puzzling, as she was drying her hair, about how he had heard of her dinner engagement with Sarangerel, the phone rang. She ran to answer it, thinking Philip Ye had called back to apologise for his rudeness. But it was Secretary Wu, at last bringing her some good news. The Political and Legal Committee had just voted to support – in principle – her idea to eventually install a public prosecutor in every police station in Chengdu to monitor first-hand what the police were up to and to give them immediate legal guidance to keep them on the straight and narrow – and this vote having taken place before she had completed her pilot proposal! But she could guess what had happened. Secretary Wu, wily old fox that he was, had seen his opportunity and taken it. After the stinging criticism she had been allowed to direct at the PSB during the investigation briefing she had given at the Procuratorate last evening, Chief of Police Di had been put on the back foot. Chief Di would have attended the Committee meeting, along with the icy Ms. Miao. Prior to the taking of the vote, Chief Di would have seen no option but to acquiesce to the implementation of her plan – or at least the proposed pilot program. He would have meekly raised his hand. Xu Ya had to wonder whether her instructions at the investigation briefing not to spare the PSB's blushes had been intended by Secretary Wu to achieve this very outcome. If so, she did not mind being so used – especially if the effect was to bring the police in Chengdu finally to heel.

"Send me your finished proposal as soon as you can, Ms. Xu."

"I will, sir."

"Have you selected a police station for the pilot?"

She did not hesitate. "Wukuaishi, sir."

"Your reasoning?"

"Only that I hold a grudge. I have not forgotten the incompetence of that station in regard to The Willow Woman investigation."

Secretary Wu, in an unusually good mood, laughed. He told her he hoped to speak with her again in a few days.

Her hair dry, she wasted a few hours watching TV and dozing in her chair. Then, when it was time to get ready, she poured herself a glass of red wine, picked out a midnight blue evening dress from her wardrobe – with earrings, rings, and a necklace to match – and worked on herself until the cut on her forehead was nothing but an unfortunate blemish and no one would turn away from her in fright. If she was going to her doom – she felt much like an imperial princess about to be handed over to some barbarian despot to maintain an uneasy border peace – she might as well look the part.

On her way out of Tranquil Mountain Pavilions, she ignored the salutation offered her by the concierge Mister Gan – Mister Ni had yet to arrive for the nightshift – and climbed into what she thought was the taxi she had booked earlier. It did not take her long to realise her mistake, the taxi company logo quite different to the company she had phoned.

"Forgive me, it seems I have got into a car meant for someone else," she said, opening the door to get out.

"No, no, Prosecutor, this is your car," said the driver, a handsome young man, turning around in his seat. "Mister Pan, whose company you called, trusts his most important clients to me and my three brothers. We know Chengdu better than any. He passed her a card. "You can call us direct, if you like. Mister Pan will not mind. As a VIP taxi service, we are ready to take you anywhere you wish, at any time, day or night."

Xu Ya glanced at the card and slipped it into her purse. For some reason, she felt in very safe hands. "Do you know The Golden Persimmon restaurant?"

"Prosecutor, you will be there in no time at all," replied the young man.

"I am having dinner with Sarangerel," she added, inexplicably.

"I will be happy to wait outside for you for when you are ready to go home."

"That is very kind of you."

"It is all part of our prestige service."

The Golden Persimmon restaurant was situated on the top floor of a brand-new business and shopping complex, not far from the Tianfu Software Park where Ambrogetti Global Software was located – the stock of which had been plummeting all afternoon since the news had been released of Primo Gong's death (from natural causes!). When the maître d' escorted her to the table, she was pleased to note that the restaurant was quiet, the tables placed quite far apart, in the background only the soft sounds of Western classical piano music.

Whatever her moral flaws, it could not be argued that Sarangerel did not have good taste.

Sarangerel was already seated at a table placed next to a large plate-glass window. She was staring out of the window at the night-time city skyline. Xu Ya had done her research and had viewed every photograph of Sarangerel she could find. In almost every picture, the witch had opted for less is more in the clothes department. But this evening, surprisingly, Sarangerel wore a very conservative forest-green silk dress. She had made no attempt whatsoever to put her considerable feminine assets on show. To Xu Ya, she also appeared subdued, more fascinated by the lights of the city than in what was going on about her at the restaurant. The maître d' seated Xu Ya and then, suitably nervous, scuttled off.

"Excuse my tardiness," said Xu Ya.

"I was early," said Sarangerel, tearing herself away from the sights outside, casting large dark and knowing eyes upon Xu Ya, smiling as she did so.

Xu Ya realised immediately that she was seated across the table from no ordinary woman. There was something untamed, something animal, about Sarangerel. The heavy perfume that hung in the air about her evoked in Xu Ya memories of childhood holidays in the countryside, when her parents had taken her out of Chongqing and into the wilderness, into the mountains and the forests, and onto the grasslands and deserts in the north of China that went on and on as far as the eye could see. There was no Rule of Law in those wild places – except that of the law of nature, where only the strongest and fittest survived. And, as Xu Ya was swallowed up by Sarangerel's dark eyes, made darker still by mascara and black eyeliner judiciously applied, Xu Ya quickly intuited that the Rule of Law had no meaning either for Sarangerel – and could not help but be shocked by this realisation.

"Thank you for the invitation," said Xu Ya.

"I was not sure you would come."

Xu Ya tried to be strong. "Why would I refuse?"

"Why would you indeed?"

"This is a lovely restaurant."

"I thought you might enjoy a change from the clamour of The Silver Tree."

"Have you been there?"

Sarangerel smiled again, her eyes – a wolf's eyes – continued to pull Xu Ya deeper and deeper in. "No, I would not be welcome. The family Ye and I are not on the best of terms. Years ago, when I was younger, not as able to defend myself as I am now, I was forced into a blood-oath, made to promise never to frequent any establishment owned by that family."

"And have you kept that promise?"

"I have."

"You do not look the type to be frightened off by anyone."

"Frightened, no – but cautious, yes. Back in Mongolia, my home-land, it is traditional to keep large guard dogs, Bankhars, to protect our livestock and our lives. The family Ye has its own guard dog, always on watch – the most vicious dog of all."

"Philip Ye."

Before Xu Ya could react, Sarangerel reached across the table and took her hand – her grip hot, strong, and unyielding. Xu Ya had never felt such unbridled power surge into her from another person before.

"I knew we would think alike, you and I – both of us women of destiny."

"But your note—"

"Ah, I meant nothing by my words; a little tease, that is all, to get your attention. I have no interest in your dead husband. Any woman who acts decisively when she tires of a man has my undying respect."

Xu Ya kept her face like a mask, not knowing whether to be horrified or relieved. But she could do nothing to extract her hand from Sarangerel's tight grasp.

"I need a favour, though, to seal our friendship," said Sarangerel.

Here it comes, thought Xu Ya.

"Don't be concerned, Prosecutor. It is not a favour exactly, more something you should know...something a woman full of curiosity might find worthwhile investigating."

"I'm listening."

"The Ye family mansion."

"What of it?"

"You have visited?"

"I have."

"What do you think?"

"It is a home dreams are made of."

"It is haunted."

"I don't believe in ghosts."

Sarangerel let go of Xu Ya's hand then and laughed out loud. The wine waiter, who had been approaching, turned around and walked the other way.

"Prosecutor, I thought you dealt in facts, in evidence. That house is haunted. Did you not sense it? I lived there once and saw for myself that this is true. At the time of its construction a number of Ye Zihao's business associates – men he had had disagreements with – disappeared."

"What are you saying?"

"You know what I am saying. Take your time. Go correlate the time of the laying of the foundations of that accursed house with that of the disappearances of a number of notable businesspeople in Chengdu. It will not take you long to see what I am saying is true. Restless ghosts walk that house. Stay one night in that house and you will hear their cries for justice. You have the talent, I can tell. You also have an extraordinary gift. You have visions. You can move back and forth in time – almost at will. Ah, if you could only learn to control and direct such talent. I am glad we have finally met. You are much so more than I expected...."

Xu Ya began to feel ill. "What else...what else do you see in me?"

"I see Philip Ye."

Xu Ya's heart skipped a beat. "What about him?"

Sarangerel once more took her hand, once more swallowed her up with those wolf eyes. "Philip Ye is not what you think. He pretends to be good – and yet there is no goodness in him; he is police – and yet he will stop at nothing to cover up for his father's crimes. He is also a thief. He has stolen from me."

"Stolen from you?"

"Twice, Prosecutor: once, long ago, he stole my future; and then, only yesterday, he stole a gift to me from Heaven, a gift that was rightfully mine."

"What gift?"

"Do you know what he is?"

"I don't understand the—"

"He is a spirit-medium."

Xu Ya wanted to laugh but could not. She wanted to get up from the table and leave, but could not. It felt like someone had just poured ice-water down her spine. Her head began to spin. She remembered all the times she had thought the brothers Na had been joking with her.

"Ah, so you already know," said Sarangerel.

"I don't—"

"Prosecutor, you are no fool, I am sure you have always suspected there is something not quite right about Philip Ye. He has never let go of his dead fiancée. He has used every source of arcane lore he can find, every black ritual he could unearth, to upturn the natural order of things – all so he could force her ghost to return to him, to live with him. Whether he has succeeded or not, I cannot say. Indeed, I do not wish to know. But I will tell you now, that to interact with Philip Ye in any way is to put yourself in the gravest peril. I know what is said about me. I know the people call me the Witch-Queen of Chengdu. I do have special gifts, I assure you. And I am not shy about using them in a world run by men. But never...I repeat never...have I tried to upend the natural order of things. I am a shamaness, a daughter and granddaughter of shamanesses, dedicated to maintaining the balance of nature by listening to the advice of our ancestors – to only take what is needed, to conserve all that we have. Philip Ye is the opposite of what I am. He has made of himself an abomination. Get too close to him, Prosecutor, and he will take your soul – the threat to your person is that great. If you are thinking I exaggerate, go back to the Procuratorate and examine closely all of Philip Ye's homicide files. It will not take you long to see that something is not right. Despite his lowly rank, his clearance rate far exceeds every other policeman in Chengdu history. Trust me, he receives help from ghosts, those he has enslaved by his use of the black arts. I am sure you have already noticed in all your dealings with him how he has recovered certain evidence, or unearthed certain witnesses, without proper explanation. You will discover this time and time again in all of his case notes. Go look for yourself and you will see what I have told you is true. But take care then, Prosecutor. Get too close to Philip Ye and he will realise that you have learned his abhorrent secret. And then he will use all of his dark charms and spells to entrap you – to make of you his pet, the little shikra he loved and lost all those years ago. For this is something else you must learn, Prosecutor. His fiancée discovered it far too late. Everything Philip Ye touches, sooner or later, withers and dies."

Xu Ya woke naked in her bed, having no memory of how she had got there. Sarangerel's perfume lingered about her. Fearful that she had lost her mind and for some reason invited Sarangerel home with her, Xu Ya clambered with some difficulty out of bed, struggling to keep her balance, her bedroom nothing but a whirl. She saw her evening dress and underclothes had been left in a simple pile upon the bedroom floor. She reached for her robe, put it about her, feeling she was about to retch. She managed to move slowly from room to room and, to her great relief, saw nothing to make her believe Sarangerel had ever been in her apartment. Then, when she had settled slowly into a seat in the lounge and put her head in her hands, wishing the spinning of the room about her would stop, small snatches of memory began to return: of too much wine being drunk; of the finest food being brought to her and she hardly touching it; of Sarangerel's captivating wolf eyes staring into her, unsettling her, confusing her; and of Sarangerel talking and talking and talking – that strange Mongolian accent lulling her into an almost hypnogogic state.

Xu Ya had no idea what time the meal had finished. But she was certain now she had staggered out of that restaurant in a daze, arm-in-arm with Sarangerel, heading she did not know where. Then the young taxi driver had come to her rescue, somehow separating her from the witch – had Sarangerel been momentarily distracted by some sort of commotion out on the street? – and bundling her into the taxi so he could bring her safely home.

She hoped she had not been foolish enough to agree to another dinner with Sarangerel in the near future. She did not think her nerves could cope with another such encounter just at the moment. There was also a lot of thinking and work to be done before she met with the witch again – and research that could not be trusted to Mouse. She had to go into the archive of the Procuratorate alone and discover all she could of the building of the Ye family mansion and who in the business world, if anyone, might have vanished at that time. She also had to review all of Philip Ye's case files one by one to confirm what she had indeed already suspected, that something was not quite right about the conduct and timeline of those investigations, that Philip Ye had a habit of establishing connections and patterns that defied all reason.

And then, when all that was done, she had to discover what, under Heaven, was a shikra.

EPILOGUE

The flood that had been so feared had not come to Liberation Street. The street had been awash for a time but, unlike some more unfortunate parts of the city, the drains had managed to cope. Instead, as Philip Ye had said, a war had passed up and down the street, a war that no one on the street understood – least of all Sun Mei. But all the talk this day was not about the war. It was about the incredible visit that Mister Wu, of Mister Wu's Cycle Sales and Repair Shop, had received from a whole host of managers, administrators, and engineers from the Municipal Urban Planning and Management Bureau, the Municipal Environmental Protection Bureau, and even the Sichuan Provincial Headquarters for Flood Protection and Drought Control. They had all come, so they told Mister Wu, to study the poor performance of the drains of Liberation Street and to come up with a viable solution. The visit was so momentous, so unexpected, that Mister Wu had again called an extraordinary meeting of the Liberation Street Traders Association – to be convened after lunch in the Lucky Dragon Tobacco Emporium – so it could be discussed.

This was a pity.

Sun Mei had lost all interest in drains.

She wanted to talk about the war. She wanted to know why two men had been shot dead outside her shop. She wanted to know why

Investigator Deng had come into her life only to disappear again, leaving nothing behind but regret. And she wanted to know how a war could flow up and down the street and yet miraculously leave everyone who lived and worked there unscathed.

All the fears she had suffered, all her premonitions of the fat man soon to bring her doom, to change her life forever, had all come to nothing in spite of the war. This morning, the beginning of a new working week, everything was the same as it had always been: her father, the shop, and – thank Heaven for them – the children who were due to attend her class that evening. All she had to show for the trials of the weekend were a large bruise on her upper arm – the origin of which she could not fathom – and the terrible memory that refused to fade of her last encounter with Investigator Deng, him angry at her, shouting at her, insisting that she understand that the world in which he lived – in which he thrived – was not hers.

In the night she had woken and, like a little girl, had burst into tears. She had not been dreaming as such. It was more like she had been overcome in her sleep by the terrible feeling that all the days that remained of her life would be identical, that she would follow the same schedule from the moment she rose from her bed until the time she once again laid her head on her pillow. It was hard to put a finger on it, to identify what exactly she could have done differently this last weekend. But, as she cried herself back to sleep, she came to the conclusion that an opportunity of some sort had passed her by – a chance to create an entirely different future for herself.

After she had risen at dawn, and after she had made her father breakfast and watched the news on TV with him, she had gone out into the backyard, marvelled at the sun rising in a cloudless sky, and stared up at Plum Tree Pagodas. There were men already at work, repairing the broken window on the fifth floor. Soon, she realised, it would be as if nothing had ever happened, as if no rifle shots had ever been fired – the past erased, totally forgotten.

Perhaps that was for the best.

However, she couldn't help but remain curious. She could not help but want to know what had happened in that apartment on the fifth floor, why three rifle shots had been fired over the roof of the Lucky Dragon Tobacco Emporium, for whom those shots had been intended, and whether that person had died as a result.

She supposed someone must have died. Why else had Philip Ye been involved? He worked, as everyone in Chengdu knew, for PSB Homicide.

And it was not that Sun Mei needed to see grisly crime scene photographs. But she would have liked to have known the name of the person who had died, whether they had been a good person or bad, some details of the life they had lived, and how the things they had done in their life – for surely it had to be so – had brought them to such a violent end.

The news on the TV had been no help at all. Not even the shoot-out in front of her shop had deserved a mention. The talk on the TV had been all about the oppressive heat and the prospect of more storms to come. Later in the morning, when she went to check on her father, she found him watching a discussion program on the continuing tensions in the South China Sea. There had been a local newsflash, he told her, concerning the death from a heart attack of a supposedly famous businessman named Primo Gong. But that was all.

"Had you heard of him?" she asked of her father.

"No," he replied. "And Brother Wang has just phoned. He wanted me to know that he is doing just fine. He will be well enough to visit soon."

"I don't approve of him," said Sun Mei.

But her father was not listening. He had already turned his attention back to the TV.

Sun Mei returned to serving the many customers of the morning, most of them wanting to stop and have a chat, to get her opinion on the failed armed robbery of her shop and the presence of Philip Ye on Liberation Street the day before. Most were not concerned about what he might have been investigating. In the main they wanted to know what she thought of him, whether he was still as handsome as he had been as a young man, and whether – as if she would know – there was any sign of him finally settling down and getting married.

"It is a pity he didn't pick you, Sun Mei!" her few female customers would exclaim. But they were really talking about themselves, wishing they had been present on Liberation Street at the time of the shoot-out, wishing they could have pressed their case to Philip Ye in person.

It was difficult for Sun Mei to explain that she herself felt no such attraction to Philip Ye. It was not that he was not handsome – he was! It was not that he was not wealthy – he was! But, as a woman of no special consequence, of no special standing in the world – she was, after all, but a mere shopkeeper – she knew she had nothing to offer him. To stand next to such a man would be, for her, like standing next to the sun. She would melt. She would disappear. She would become as nothing.

"Sun Mei, have you no ambition?" these women would ask her, when she tried to explain how she felt.

"No, I am happy just being me," she would reply.

This was not quite a lie. She just could not imagine being married to a man such as Philip Ye, living in a great house (with a very odd atmosphere), and having Ye Zihao as a father-in-law. These did not seem to her to be the ingredients for a happy life. She would spend every day shaking in fear.

Her morning was brightened by a phone call from Du Yue, who was now Jenny Ye, and who was so happy that she was being adopted by the family Ye. She was to return to school in England at summer's end.

"I am glad for you," said Sun Mei.

"Teacher Sun, may I write to you?"

How could Sun Mei refuse? Jenny Ye was such a lovely girl, if a little other-worldly, and it would be a treat to receive letters all the way from England. Moreover, Sun Mei was certain Jenny Ye would go on to do great things – especially now with the limitless resources of the family Ye behind her. It would also be nice to learn from her all about the teaching methods used in England, about the culture there, about something other than the narrow concerns of the people of Liberation Street.

Further good news was to come.

Out of the blue, just before lunch, Mister Li of the Laughing Panda Hotel walked into the shop and asked for the week's usual cigarette order as if nothing had happened to him. He explained that the hotel was open for business as usual and that his detention at the Procuratorate – it could not really be described as an arrest – had turned out to be one big mistake.

"I was so afraid for you," said Sun Mei.

"They had confused me with someone else," said Mister Li.

Though she was overjoyed to see him, to Sun Mei his words did not quite ring true. He avoided her gaze a little too often as she put his order together and, when she did catch his eyes, he seemed to her like a haunted man. She was also now of the confirmed belief that Investigator Deng was not the kind of man to confuse Mister Li with anyone else. Not that she mentioned this to Mister Li. It was just a pity she did not know a little more, that she couldn't speak to Investigator Deng one last time, and find out the real reason he had put a pistol to Mister Li's face. Whatever the truth, she thought she might be a little more circumspect in the future about what she said to Mister Li, and might not encourage him so much to come around and spend time with her father.

Sun Mei ate her lunch standing behind the shop counter looking out of the window. The group of managers, administrators, and engineers were still walking up and down the street inspecting the drains and making copious notes, with Mister Wu always in hot pursuit, always willing to offer suggestions. The scene was quite comical.

Unfortunately, too soon for Sun Mei's liking, the local government employees departed and it was time to convene the extraordinary meeting of the Liberation Street Traders Association. With as many shopkeepers as could attend crammed into the Lucky Dragon Tobacco Emporium, and a couple of interested customers too, Mister Wu explained to all what had been going on. He had three important points to make, all to be noted carefully by Mister Han of the Bright Diamond Mini-Supermarket in the minutes: firstly, Liberation Street had been bumped up to the top of the list of those parts of the city needing immediate improvement; secondly, a provisional budget had already been approved; and thirdly, as soon as a detailed plan for the improvements to be made to Liberation Street had been drawn up – with a particular focus on the street's drainage – it would be made available to Mister Wu for consideration and comment before any public works were commenced.

"Is this not the best news?" said Mister Wu. "My words with Philip Ye were not wasted. One of the engineers told me that his boss had received a phone call late last night – a call he could not ignore. He would not say who it was from, but we can all guess, can't we?"

Sun Mei's father, seizing his opportunity, then launched into a lengthy monologue about their time at the Ye family mansion, describing at some length the opulent rooms of the house, the fabulous art treasures kept within, and the magnificent grounds that went on forever. He also, much to Mister Wu's frustration, spoke as if he were now a personal friend of Ye Zihao, how the former mayor had told him the most amazing stories of Chengdu of old, and all while cooking up the most amazing food. "It was by far the best day of my life," her father said.

When her father had finished, Mister Wu did his best to turn the meeting back to the original point of discussion, stating that he had learned that the coming improvements to the drains on Liberation Street was to form part of a much wider plan to make of Chengdu a 'sponge city', so as better to manage the floods and droughts of the future.

"Isn't it all marvellous!" said Mister Wu.

About to launch into much more detail about what making Chengdu a 'sponge city' actually involved, Mister Wu was silenced by the arrival of a police truck outside of the Black House across the street. A troop of uniformed police jumped out of the back of the truck, gained access to the Black House, and started taking from the building stacks of cardboard boxes and piles of paper files and loading them into the truck at some speed. It was incredible to watch. As soon as that police truck was full, it quickly sped away, only to be replaced with another.

"What is going on?" asked Mister Wu, the same question on everyone else's lips.

It was not long before a whole convoy of police trucks had arrived on Liberation Street. Sun Mei lost count of the number of police officers involved in the emptying out of the Black House. She could hardly believe her eyes. Could it really be true that the building that had blighted all their lives as far back as most could remember was about to be closed?

Like all the others, Sun Mei was so taken up by the sight of all the paper files being removed from the Black House, that she hadn't noticed the approach of a very senior police officer, who suddenly burst into the shop, pointed a finger at all of them, and demanded to know, in no uncertain terms, what the 'unauthorised' gathering of people was all about.

Mister Wu was so stunned he was lost for words. No one else could think of anything useful to say either. It was left to Sun Mei, whose shop it was, to speak up, somehow finding some courage within herself she did not know she had. Could it be that a little of Investigator Deng's inner strength had rubbed off on her?

"Sir," she said, "this is a meeting of the Liberation Street Traders Association. Yesterday, an armed robbery at my shop was foiled by the miraculous intervention of the PSB. We are discussing the drafting of a letter of sincere gratitude to be sent to Chief of Police Di. Without the PSB keeping us safe day and night, I do not know what any of us would do."

The officer, severely embarrassed, mumbled that the police could not do their work without the fulsome support of the people, that they could continue with their meeting as long as they did not get too boisterous in their deliberations. He then left the shop to supervise the emptying out of the Black House. Everyone in the Lucky Dragon Tobacco Emporium clapped, directing their applause at a now blushing Sun Mei.

"Sun Mei, you are a marvel," said Mister Wu. "When I am dead, you shall become Chair of our Association."

There was general murmur of agreement about this. But Sun Mei caught both her father's and Mister Han's eye, neither looking very impressed, this being the first time that anyone had learned that Mister Wu's elevation to Chair appeared to be a lifetime appointment. Not that it was the time or the place to get into that particular debate.

After the meeting had broken up, Sun Mei continued to watch from behind the counter the emptying out of the Black House. She wondered where all the files were being taken, what secret information they might contain. One of her customers suggested they were reports of all the UFO sightings made over Chengdu for the last fifty years. Another tried to convince her that they were lists of American agents who had been caught trying to infiltrate the city. And yet another, an old man shaking with rage, told her that the files were the old city records, that they were being taken away to be burnt on the orders of the Shanghai Clique – that the Shanghai Clique were determined to eradicate the city's proud history!

Sun Mei did not know what to believe. She wished she could speak to Investigator Deng. He would know. He would tell her the right thoughts to think.

She made dinner for her father.

She prepared the backroom for the children that evening: the desks properly arranged, a pencil and some paper on each desk, the first set of maths problems chalked up on the blackboard.

The children began to trickle in just after seven. She welcomed each with a hug and assured their parents that after the excitement of the day before everything was now as it should be. Little Xiulan, who was still sick, her throat still sore, was thoughtlessly dropped off by her parents. Sun Mei decided not to turn Little Xiulan away. She would be better off at the shop than at her home. Not wanting her in such proximity to the other children though, Sun Mei took the girl through to her father's room, so she could curl up and watch TV while her father kept an eye on her.

In the midst of her teaching, Sun Mei suddenly panicked, realising it was almost eight. She had forgotten to prepare the free cigarettes for the police on the nightshift at the Black House. She ran back into the shop, knocking packets of cigarettes from the shelves in her fear as she struggled to remember the Monday evening order. She then waited and waited but by a quarter past eight still no one had come. Looking across the street she saw that the last of the police trucks had gone. No lights burned from within the Black House.

Tears welled up in her eyes.

Could it be true?

Could it really be true?

Could the Black House be shut?

Could the days of having to give her stock away be over?

At ten, the majority of the parents had come to take their children home, some of them to be carried, asleep in their parents' arms. Sun Mei waited outside the shop in the warm night air with Little Xiulan, holding the girl's hand, looking up and down the street for her parents. The child had enjoyed herself immensely with Sun Mei's father.

"Why can't he use his legs?" asked Little Xiulan.

"He had an accident long ago."

"It is sad."

"It is," agreed Sun Mei, the child far too young to understand how that one accident had set in motion a series of sad events that had left Sun Mei where she was today: unmarried, without children of her own, and not, as she should be, teaching proper lessons as a very respectable schoolteacher in a very fine school.

Tired of waiting for Little Xiulan's idiotic parents, she waved at Mister Wu who was just shutting up his shop to come over and man her counter for a short while, and then picked up Little Xiulan and carried her home. Sun Mei found Little Xiulan's parents watching TV. They had lost track of time, they said. At least they had not been drinking. And at least – for Sun Mei did check – they had been giving Sun Mei her medication and incredibly at the right times.

When she returned to the shop, she thanked Mister Wu for his help.

"Is the little girl okay?" he asked.

"She will be," replied Sun Mei. "Though I can't take my eyes off her parents for a moment. They are quite useless."

"We are lucky, don't you think?"

"How so, Mister Wu?"

"That on Liberation Street we all look out for one another. So many bad things happen in other parts of the city, in other parts of the world. And yet we, in spite of our problems, just keep our heads down, help each other out, and get along."

"I suppose," said Sun Mei.

"You look tired."

"I am."

"You look sad also."

"I think I am missing my mother today."

Mister Wu nodded, understanding, and bade her good evening. She went to check on her father. He was fine. He didn't need any more tea but could she fetch him a cold beer from the fridge?

Back behind the counter, she prepared a few standing orders for the following morning. The cigarettes she had gift-wrapped for the police she returned to the shelves. She glanced out of the window. The street was more or less deserted now, the Black House devoid of all life. She wondered what would happen to it, whether it would be demolished or converted into office space or apartments. She was not sure she would care either way. Liberation Street would find a way to stay the same. People like Mister Wu would see to that. As for herself, all she could see in her future was one sad day merging into another. Soon enough she would be the middle-aged Sun Mei, and then the elderly Sun Mei – known to all only as the kindly old woman who had taught all the local children for free and who owned the best cigarette shop in the city.

Perhaps that was enough.

Perhaps that would be a fitting epitaph.

For who could say that one person's life was better or more valuable than another's?

As for happiness, was that not surely a fleeting thing, not worth worrying about, not worth much contemplation. To be of service to the people, wasn't that all that mattered?

Her phone rang.

It was Mister Wu.

"Sun Mei, do not be alarmed."

"I am not alarmed," she replied, her heart racing, her mouth dry.

"You must quickly lock your door and turn off the lights."

"You are frightening me, Mister Wu."

"He has returned."

"Who has returned, Mister Wu?"

"The fat man, of course! As I speak, he is walking toward your shop, wearing one of those stupid colourful shirts of his. He is also carrying a big bunch of flowers. Run and lock the door before it is too late!"

Sun Mei dropped the phone, forgetting instantly all the good advice she had just been given. She ran to the bathroom, quickly freshened her face with a cold flannel, anguished over how sickly and tired she looked, pawed at the shadows that seemed to have taken up permanent residence under her eyes, regretted she didn't have the time to put on even a dab of make-up – just a little would have helped – and was back behind the counter and pretending nothing was amiss when he pushed open the door.

THE END